A master storyteller, [...]
eighteen novels (wh[...]
copies), over 200 [...]
major motion pictures and six Broadway plays, ranking him as one of the world's most prolific writers. His first book, *The Naked Face*, was acclaimed by the *New York Times* as 'the best first mystery novel of the year' and subsequently each of his highly popular books have hit No. 1 on the *New York Times* bestseller list. His latest bestseller, *Are You Afraid of the Dark?*, cements Sheldon's reputation as the master of the unexpected.

For more about Sidney Sheldon, visit his website at www.sidneysheldon.com.

For automatic updates on Sidney Sheldon visit HarperCollins.co.uk/sidneysheldon and register for AuthorTracker.

By the same author

The Naked Face
The Other Side of Midnight
A Stranger in the Mirror
Bloodline
Rage of Angels
Master of the Game
If Tomorrow Comes
Windmills of the Gods
The Sands of Time
Memories of Midnight
The Doomsday Conspiracy
The Stars Shine Down
Nothing Lasts Forever
Morning, Noon and Night
The Best Laid Plans
Tell Me Your Dreams
The Sky is Falling
Are You Afraid of the Dark?

SIDNEY SHELDON

The Other Side of Midnight

The Sands of Time

HARPER

HarperCollins*Publishers*
77–85 Fulham Palace Road,
Hammersmith, London W6 8JB

www.harpercollins.co.uk

This omnibus edition 2008
1

A catalogue record for this book is available from the British Library

ISBN 978-0-00-783998-8

Typeset in Sabon by Palimpsest Book Production Limited,
Polmont, Stirlingshire
Printed and bound in Great Britain by Clays Ltd, St Ives plc

The Other Side of Midnight

To Jorja
who pleasures me in a thousand ways

ACKNOWLEDGMENTS

I wish to express my gratitude to those who generously helped me colour the mosaic of this novel with the tiles of their knowledge, expertise and memories.

In a few instances where I felt it would enhance the narrative, I have taken literary licence; but any factual errors are my responsibility alone.

My grateful thanks go to the following:

In London:

Ms V. Shrubsall, Air Historical Branch, British Ministry of Defence, for invaluable information on the Eagle Squadron, the group of American pilots who flew with the RAF before the United States entered World War II.

Earl Boebert, for additional material on the Eagle Squadron.

In Paris:

André Weil-Curiel, former Vice-Mayor of Paris, for helpful suggestions and recollections of Paris under the German occupation.

Madame Chevaulet, Head Archivist for the Comédie Française, for allowing me access to her files on the history of the French theatre.

Claude Baigneres, journalist for *El Figaro*, for his assistance in helping me track down sources of firsthand information about the French occupation.

In Athens:

Mrs Aspa Lambrou, who magically opened all doors and was unfailingly and generously helpful.

Jean Pierre de Vitry D'Avaucourt, personal pilot to Aristotle Onassis, for his technical advice and suggestions.

Costas Efstathiades, distinguished attorney, for his assistance on Greek criminal law procedures.

In Los Angeles:

Raoul Aglion, Conseiller Economique of the Banque Nationale de Paris, for sharing his knowledge of French history and French customs.

Except for the mention of various historical world leaders, all characters in this book are fictional.

PROLOGUE

Athens: 1947

Through the dusty windshield of his car Chief of Police Georgios Skouri watched the office buildings and hotels of down-town Athens collapse in a slow dance of disintegration, one after the other like rows of giant pins in some cosmic bowling alley.

'Twenty minutes,' the uniformed policeman at the wheel promised. 'No traffic.'

Skouri nodded absently and stared at the buildings. It was an illusion that never ceased to fascinate him. The shimmering heat from the pitiless August sun enveloped the buildings in undulating waves that made them seem to be cascading down to the streets in a graceful waterfall of steel and glass.

It was ten minutes past noon, and the streets were almost deserted, but even the few pedestrians abroad were too lethargic to give more than a passing curious glance at the three police cars racing east towards Hellenikon, the airport that lay twenty miles from the centre of Athens. Chief Skouri was riding in the first car. Under ordinary circumstances, he would have stayed in his comfortable, cool office while his subordinates went out to work in the blazing noon heat, but these circumstances were far from ordinary and Skouri had a twofold reason for being here personally. First, in the course of this day planes would be arriving carrying VIPs from various parts of the globe, and it was necessary to see that they were welcomed properly and whisked through Customs with a minimum of bother. Second, and more important the airport would be crowded with foreign newspaper reporters and newsreel cameramen. Chief Skouri was not a fool, and it had occurred to him as he had shaved that morning that it would do no harm to his career if he were shown in newsreels as he took the eminent visitors into his charge. It was an extraordinary stroke of fate that had decreed that a worldwide event as sensational as this one had occurred in his domain, and he would be stupid not to take advantage of it. He had discussed it in great detail with the two people in the world closest to him: his wife and his mistress. Anna, a middle-aged, ugly, bitter woman of peasant stock, had ordered him to keep away from the airport and stay in the background so that he could not be blamed if anything went wrong. Melina, his sweet, beautiful young angel, had advised him to greet the dignitaries. She agreed with him that an event like this could catapult him into instant fame. If Skouri handled this well, at the very least he would get a raise in salary and – God willing – might even be made Commissioner of Police when the present Commissioner retired. For the hundredth time Skouri reflected on the irony that Melina was his wife and Anna was his mistress, and he wondered again where he had gone wrong.

Now Skouri turned his thoughts to what lay ahead. He must make certain that everything went perfectly at the airport. He was bringing with him a dozen of his best men. His main problem, he knew, would be controlling the press. He had been astonished by the number of important newspaper and magazine reporters that had poured into Athens from all over the world. Skouri himself had been interviewed six times – each time in a different language. His answers had been translated into German, English, Japanese, French, Italian and Russian. He had just begun to enjoy his new celebrity when the Commissioner had called to inform him that he felt it was unwise for the Chief of Police to comment publicly on a murder trial that had not yet taken place. Skouri was sure that the Commissioner's real motivation was jealousy, but he had prudently decided not to press the issue and had refused all further interviews. However, the Commissioner certainly could not complain if he, Skouri, happened to be at the airport at the centre of activity while the newsreel cameras were photographing the arriving celebrities.

As the car sped down Sygrou Avenue and swung

left at the sea towards Phaleron, Skouri felt a tightening in his stomach. They were now only five minutes from the airport. He mentally checked over the list of celebrities who would be arriving in Athens before nightfall.

Armand Gautier was suffering from airsickness. He had a deep-seated fear of flying that stemmed from an excessive love of himself and his life and that, combined with the turbulence usually found off the coast of Greece in summer, had made him violently nauseous. He was a tall, ascetically thin man with scholarly features, a high forehead and a perpetually sardonic mouth. At twenty-two Gautier had helped create *La Nouvelle Vague* in France's struggling movie industry and in the years that followed had gone on to even bigger triumphs in the theatre. Now acknowledged as one of the world's greatest directors, Gautier lived his role to the hilt. Until the last twenty minutes it had been a most pleasant flight. The stewardesses recognizing him had catered to his needs and had let him know they were available for other activities. Several passengers had come up to him during the flight to say how much they admired his films and plays, but he was most interested in the pretty English University student who was attending St Anne's at Oxford. She was writing a thesis on the theatre for her master's and had chosen Armand Gautier as her subject. Their conversation had gone well until the girl had brought up the name of Noelle Page.

'You used to be her director, didn't you?' she said. 'I hope I can get into her trial. It's going to be a circus.'

Gautier found himself gripping the sides of his seat, and the strength of his reaction surprised him. Even after all these years the memory of Noelle evoked a pain in him that was as sharp as ever. No one had ever touched him as she had, and no one ever would again. Since Gautier had read of Noelle's arrest three months earlier, he had been able to think of nothing else. He had cabled her and written her, offering to do whatever he could to help, but he had never received a reply. He had had no intention of attending her trial, but he knew he could not stay away. He told himself that it was because he wanted to see whether she had changed since they had lived together. And yet he admitted to himself there was another reason. The theatrical part of him had to be there to view the drama, to watch Noelle's face as the judge told her whether she was to live or die.

The metallic voice of the pilot came over the intercom to announce that they would be landing in Athens in three minutes, and the excitement of the anticipation of seeing Noelle again made Armand Gautier forget his airsickness.

Dr Israel Katz was flying to Athens from Capetown, where he was the resident neurosurgeon and chief of staff at Groote Schuur, the large new hospital that had just been built. Israel Katz was recognized as one of the leading neurosurgeons in the world. Medical journals were filled with his innovations. His patients included a prime minister, a president and a king.

He leaned back in the seat of the BOAC plane, a man of medium height, with a strong, intelligent face, deep-set brown eyes and long, slender, restless hands. Dr Katz was tired, and because of that he began to feel the familiar pain in a right leg that was no longer there, a leg amputated six years earlier by a giant with an axe.

It had been a long day. He had done predawn surgery, visited half a dozen patients and then walked out of a Board of Directors' meeting at the hospital in order to fly to Athens for the trial. His wife, Esther, had tried to dissuade him.

'There is nothing you can do for her now, Israel.'

Perhaps she was right, but Noelle Page had once risked her life to save his and he owed her something. He thought of Noelle now, and he felt the same indescribable feeling that he had felt whenever he had been with her. It was as though the mere memory of her could dissipate the years that separated them. It was romantic fantasy, of course. Nothing could ever bring those years back. Dr Israel Katz felt the plane shudder as the wheels were lowered and it started its descent. He looked out the window and spread out below him was Cairo, where he would transfer to a TAE plane to Athens, and Noelle. Was she guilty of murder? As the plane headed for the runway he thought about the other terrible murder she had committed in Paris.

Philippe Sorel stood at the railing of his yacht watching the harbour of Piraeus moving closer. He had enjoyed the sea voyage because it was one of the rare opportunities he had to escape from his fans. Sorel was one of the few sure box-office attractions in the world, and yet the odds against his ever rising to stardom had been tremendous. He was not a handsome man. On the contrary. He had the face of a boxer who had lost his last dozen matches, his nose had been broken several times, his hair was thin and he walked with a slight limp. None of these things mattered, for Philippe Sorel had sex appeal. He was an educated, soft-spoken man, and the combination of his innate gentleness and truck-driver's face and body drove the women frantic and made men look up to him as a hero. Now as his yacht approached the harbour, Sorel wondered again what he was doing here. He had postponed a movie that he had wanted to make in order to attend Noelle's trial. He was only too well aware of what an easy target he would be for the press as he sat in the courtroom every day, completely unprotected by his press agents and managers. The reporters were certain to misunderstand his attendance and think that it was a bid to reap publicity from the murder trial of his former mistress. Any way he looked at it, it was going to be an agonizing experience, but Sorel had to see Noelle again, had to find out if there was some way in which he could help her. As the yacht began to slide into the white-stoned breakwater of the harbour, he thought about the Noelle he had known, lived with and loved, and he came to a conclusion: Noelle was perfectly capable of murder.

As Philippe Sorel's yacht was approaching the coast of Greece, the Special Assistant to the President of the United States was in a Pan American Clipper, one hundred air miles northwest of the Hellenikon Airport. William Fraser was in his fifties, a handsome grey-haired man with a craggy face and an authoritative manner. He was staring at a brief in his hand, but he had not turned a page or stirred for more than an hour. Fraser had taken a leave of absence to make this journey, even though it had come at a most inconvenient time, in the midst of a congressional crisis. He knew how painful the next few weeks were going to be for him, and yet he felt that he had no choice. This was a journey of vengeance, and the thought filled Fraser with a cold satisfaction. Deliberately Fraser forced his thoughts away from the trial that would begin tomorrow and looked out the window of the plane. Far below he could see an excursion boat bobbing its way towards Greece, its coast looming in the distance.

Auguste Lanchon had been seasick and terrified for three days. He was seasick because the excursion boat which he had boarded in Marseille had been caught in the tail end of a mistral, and he was terrified because he was afraid that his wife would find out what he was doing. Auguste Lanchon was in his sixties, a fat, bald-headed man with small stumpy legs and a pockmarked face with porcine eyes and thin lips that constantly had a cheap cigar clamped between them. Lanchon owned a dress shop in Marseille and he could not afford – or at least that is what he constantly told his wife – to take a vacation like rich people. Of course, he reminded himself, this was not truly a vacation. He had to see his darling Noelle once again. In the years since she had left him, Lanchon had followed her career avidly in the gossip columns, in newspapers and magazines. When she had starred in her first play, he had taken the train all the way to Paris to see her, but Noelle's stupid secretary had kept them apart. Later he had watched Noelle's movies, seeing them again and again and remembering how she had once made love to him. Yes, this trip would be expensive, but Auguste Lanchon knew that it would be worth every sou of it. His precious Noelle would remember the good times they used to have together, and she would turn to him for protection. He would bribe a judge or some other official – if it did not cost too much – and Noelle would be freed, and he would set her up in a little apartment in Marseille where she would always be available to him when he wanted her.

If only his wife did not find out what he was doing.

In the city of Athens Frederick Stavros was working in his tiny law office on the second floor of an old run-down building in the poor Monastiraki section of the city. Stavros was an intense young man, eager and ambitious, struggling to make a living from his chosen profession. Because he could not afford an assistant, he was forced to do all the tedious background legal research himself. Ordinarily he hated this part of his work, but this time he did not mind because he knew that if he won this case his services would be in such demand that he would never have to worry again for the rest of his life. He and Elena could be married and begin to raise a family. He would move into a suite of luxurious offices, hire law clerks and join a fashionable club like the Athenee Lesky, where one met affluent potential clients. The metamorphosis had already begun. Every time Frederick Stavros walked out into the streets of Athens, he was recognized and stopped by someone who had seen his picture in the newspaper. In a few short weeks he had jumped from anonymity to the attorney who was defending Larry Douglas. In the privacy of his soul Stavros admitted to himself that he had the wrong client. He would have preferred to be defending the glamorous Noelle Page instead of a nonentity like Larry Douglas, but he himself was a nonentity. It was enough that he, Frederick

Stavros, was a major participant in the most sensational murder case of the century. If the accused were acquitted, there would be enough glory for everyone. There was only one thing that plagued Stavros, and he thought about it constantly. Both defendants were charged with the same crime, but another attorney was defending Noelle Page. If Noelle Page was found innocent, and Larry Douglas was convicted . . . Stavros shuddered and tried not to think about it. The reporters kept asking him whether he thought the defendants were guilty. He smiled to himself at their naïveté. What did it matter whether they were guilty or innocent? They were entitled to the best legal defence that money could buy. In his case he admitted that the definition was stretched a bit. But in the case of Noelle Page's lawyer . . . ah, that was something else again. Napoleon Chotas had undertaken her defence, and there was no more brilliant criminal lawyer in the world. Chotas had never lost an important case. As he thought about that, Frederick Stavros smiled to himself. He would not have admitted it to anyone, but he was planning to ride to victory on Napoleon Chotas' talent.

While Frederick Stavros was toiling in his dingy law office, Napoleon Chotas was attending a black-tie dinner party at a luxurious home in the fashionable Kolonaki section of Athens. Chotas was a thin, emaciated-looking man with the large, sad eyes of a bloodhound in a corrugated face. He concealed a brilliant, incisive brain behind a mild, vaguely baffled manner. Now toying with his dessert, Chotas sat, preoccupied, thinking about the trial that would begin tomorrow. Most of the conversation that evening had centred around the forthcoming trial. The discussion had been a general one, for the guests were too discreet to ask him direct questions. But towards the end of the evening as the ouzo and brandy flowed more freely, the hostess asked, 'Tell us, do you think they are guilty?'

Chotas replied innocently, 'How could they be? One of them is my client.' He drew appreciative laughter.

'What is Noelle Page really like?'

Chotas hesitated. 'She's a most unusual woman,' he replied carefully. 'She's beautiful and talented –' To his surprise he found that he was suddenly reluctant to discuss her. Besides, there was no way one could capture Noelle with words. Until a few months ago he had only been dimly aware of her as a glamorous figure flitting through the gossip columns and adorning the covers of movie magazines. He had never laid eyes on her, and if he had thought of her at all, it had been with the kind of indifferent contempt he felt towards all actresses. All body and no brain. But, God, how wrong he had been! Since meeting Noelle he had fallen hopelessly in love with her. Because of Noelle Page he had broken his cardinal rule: Never become emotionally involved with a client. Chotas remembered vividly the afternoon he had been approached to undertake her defence. He had been in the midst of packing for a trip that he and his wife were going to make to New York where their daughter had just had her first baby. Nothing, he had believed, could have stopped him from making that journey. But it had only taken two words. In his mind's eye he saw his butler walk into the bedroom, hand him the telephone and say, 'Constantin Demiris.'

The island was inaccessible except by helicopter and yacht, and both the airfield and the private harbour were patrolled twenty-four hours a day by armed guards with trained German shepherds. The island was Constantin Demiris' private domain, and no one intruded without an invitation. Over the years its visitors had included kings and queens, presidents and ex-presidents, movie stars, opera singers and famous writers and painters. They had all come away awed. Constantin Demiris was the third wealthiest, and one of the most powerful men in the world, and he had taste and style and knew how to spend his money to create beauty.

Demiris sat in his richly panelled library now, relaxed in a deep armchair, smoking one of the flat-shaped Egyptian cigarettes especially blended for him, thinking about the trial that would begin in the morning. The press had been trying to get to him for months, but he had simply made himself unavailable. It was enough that his mistress was going to be tried for murder, enough that his name would be dragged into the case, even indirectly. He refused to add to the furore by granting any interviews. He wondered what Noelle was feeling now, at this moment, in her cell in the Nikodemous Street Prison. Was she asleep? Awake? Filled with panic at the ordeal that lay before her? He thought of his last conversation with Napoleon Chotas. He trusted Chotas and knew that the lawyer would not fail him. Demiris had impressed upon the attorney that it did not matter to him whether Noelle was innocent or guilty. Chotas was to see to it that he earned every penny of the stupendous fee that Constantin Demiris was paying him to defend her. No, he had no reason to worry. The trial would go well. Because Constantin Demiris was a man who never forgot anything, he remembered that Catherine Douglas' favourite flowers were Triantafylias, the beautiful roses of Greece. He reached forwards and picked up a note pad from his desk. He made a notation. *Triantafylias. Catherine Douglas.*

It was the least he could do for her.

BOOK ONE

ONE

Catherine

Chicago: 1919–1939

Every large city has a distinctive image, a personality that gives it its own special cachet. Chicago in the 1920's was a restless, dynamic giant, crude and without manners, one booted foot still in the ruthless era of the tycoons who helped give birth to it: William B. Ogden and John Wentworth, Cyrus McCormick and George M. Pullman. It was a kingdom that belonged to the Philip Armours and Gustavus Swifts and Marshall Fields. It was the domain of cool professional gangsters like Hymie Weiss and Scarface Al Capone.

One of Catherine Alexander's earliest memories was of her father taking her into a bar with a sawdust-covered floor and swinging her up to the dizzyingly high stool. He ordered an enormous glass of beer for himself and a Green River for her. She was five years old, and she remembered how proud her father was as strangers crowded around to admire her. All the men ordered drinks and her father paid for them. She recalled how she had kept pressing her body against his arm to make sure he was still there. He had only returned to town the night before, and Catherine knew that he would soon leave again. He was a travelling salesman, and he had explained to her that his work took him to distant cities and he had to be away from her and her mother for months at a time so that he could bring back nice presents. Catherine had desperately tried to make a deal with him. If he would stay with her, she would give up the presents. Her father had laughed and said what a precocious child she was and then had left town, and it was six months before she saw him again. During those early years her mother whom she saw every day seemed a vague, shapeless personality, while her father, whom she saw only on brief occasions, was vivid and wonderfully clear. Catherine thought of him as a handsome, laughing man, full of sparkling humour and warm, generous gestures. The occasions when he came home were like holidays, full of treats and presents and surprises.

When Catherine was seven, her father was fired from his job, and their life took on a new pattern. They left Chicago and moved to Gary, Indiana, where he went to work as a salesman in a jewellery store. Catherine was enrolled in her first school. She had a wary, arms-length relationship with the other children and was terrified of her teachers, who misinterpreted her lonely standoffishness as conceit. Her father came home to dinner every night, and for the first time in her life Catherine felt that they were a real family, like other families. On Sunday the three of them would go to Miller Beach and rent horses and ride for an hour or two along the sand dunes. Catherine enjoyed living in Gary, but six months after they moved there, her father lost his job again and they moved to Harvey, a suburb of Chicago. School was already in session, and Catherine was the new girl, shut out from the friendships that had already been formed. She became known as a loner. The children, secure in the safety of their own groups, would come up to the gangly newcomer and ridicule her cruelly.

During the next few years Catherine donned an armour of indifference, which she wore as a shield against the attacks of the other children. When the armour was pierced, she struck back with a trenchant, caustic wit. Her intention was to alienate her tormentors so that they would leave her alone, but it had an unexpectedly different affect. She worked on the school paper, and in her first review about a musical that her classmates had staged, she wrote, 'Tommy Belden had a trumpet solo in the second act, but he blew it.' The line was widely quoted, and – surprise of surprises – Tommy Belden came up to her in the hall the next day and told Catherine that he thought it was funny.

In English the students were assigned *Captain*

Horatio Hornblower to read. Catherine hated it. Her book report consisted of one sentence: 'His barque was worse than his bight,' and her teacher, who was a weekend sailor, gave her an 'A.' Her classmates began to quote her remarks and in a short time she was known as the school wit.

That year Catherine turned fourteen and her body was beginning to show the promise of a ripening woman. She would examine herself in the mirror for hours on end, brooding about how to change the disaster she saw reflected. Inside she was Myrna Loy, driving men mad with her beauty, but her mirror – which was her bitter enemy – showed hopelessly tangled black hair that was impossible to manage, solemn grey eyes, a mouth that seemed to grow wider by the hour and a nose that was slightly turned up. Maybe she wasn't really *ugly*, she told herself cautiously, but on the other hand no one was going to knock down doors to sign her up as a movie star. Sucking in her cheeks and squinting her eyes sexily she tried to visualize herself as a model. It was depressing. She struck another pose. Eyes open wide, expression eager, a big friendly smile. No use. She wasn't the All-American type either. She wasn't anything. Her body was going to be all right, she dourly supposed, but nothing special. And that, of course, was what she wanted more than anything in the world: to be something special, to be Somebody, to be Remembered, and never, never, never, never, to die.

The summer she was fifteen, Catherine came across *Science and Health* by Mary Baker Eddy and for the next two weeks she spent an hour a day before her mirror, willing her reflection to become beautiful. At the end of that time the only change she could detect was a new patch of acne on her chin and a pimple on her forehead. She gave up sweets, Mary Baker Eddy and looking in the mirror.

Catherine and her family had moved back to Chicago and settled in a small, dreary apartment on the north side, in Rogers Park, where the rent was cheap. The country was moving deeper into an economic depression. Catherine's father was working less and drinking more, and he and her mother were constantly yelling at each other in a never-ending series of recriminations that drove Catherine out of the house. She would go down to the beach half a dozen blocks away and walk along the shore, letting the brisk wind give wings to her thin body. She spent long hours staring at the restless grey lake, filled with some desperate longing to which she could not put a name. She wanted something so much that at times it would engulf her in a sudden wave of unbearable pain.

Catherine had discovered Thomas Wolfe, and his books were like a mirror image of the bittersweet nostalgia that filled her, but it was a nostalgia for a future that had not happened yet, as though somewhere, sometime, she had lived a wonderful life and was restless to live it again. She had begun to have her periods, and while she was physically changing into a woman, she knew that her needs, her longings, this aching-wanting was not physical and had nothing to do with sex. It was a fierce and urgent longing to be recognized, to lift herself above the billions of people who teemed the earth, so everyone would know who she was, so when she walked by, they would say, 'There goes Catherine Alexander, the great –' The great *what*? There was the problem. She did not know what she wanted, only that she ached desperately for it. On Saturday afternoons whenever she had enough money, she would go to the State and Lake Theatre or to the McVickers or the Chicago, and see movies. She would completely lose herself in the wonderful, sophisticated world of Cary Grant and Jean Arthur, laugh with Wallace Beery and Marie Dressler and agonize over Bette Davis' romantic disasters. She felt closer to Irene Dunne than to her mother.

Catherine was in her senior year at Senn High School and her archenemy, the mirror, had finally become her friend. The girl in the mirror had a lively, interesting face. Her hair was raven black and her skin a soft, creamy white. Her features were regular and fine, with a generous, sensitive mouth and intelligent grey eyes. She had a good figure with firm, well-developed breasts, gently curving hips and shapely legs. There was an air of aloofness about her image, a hauteur that Catherine did not feel, as though her reflection possessed a characteristic that she did not. She supposed that it was part of the protective armour she had worn since her early school days.

The Depression had clutched the nation in a tighter and tighter vice, and Catherine's father was incessantly involved in big deals that never seemed to materialize. He was constantly spinning dreams, inventing things that were going to bring in millions of dollars. He devised a set of jacks that fitted above the wheels of an automobile and could be lowered by the touch of a button on the dashboard. None of the automobile manufacturers was interested. He worked out a continuously rotating electric sign to carry advertisements inside stores. There was a brief flurry of optimistic meetings and then the idea faded away.

He borrowed money from his younger brother, Ralph, in Omaha to outfit a shoe-repair truck to travel around the neighbourhood. He spent hours discussing the scheme with Catherine and her mother. 'It can't fail,' he explained. 'Imagine having the shoemaker coming to your door! No one's ever done it before. I have one Shoe-mobile out now, right? If it only makes twenty dollars a day, that's a hundred and twenty dollars a week. Two trucks will bring in two hundred and forty a week. Within a year I'll have twenty trucks. That's two thousand four hundred dollars a week. A hundred and twenty-five thousand a year. And that's only the beginning. . . .' Two months later the shoemaker and the truck disappeared, and that was the end of another dream.

Catherine had hoped to be able to go to Northwestern University. She was the top scholar in her class, but even on a scholarship college would be difficult to manage, and the day was coming, Catherine knew, when she would have to quit school and go to work full time. She would get a job as a secretary, but she was determined that she would never surrender the dream that was going to give such rich, wonderful meaning to her life; and the fact that she did not know what either the dream or the meaning was made it all the more unbearably sad and futile. She told herself that she was probably going through adolescence. Whatever it was, it was hell. *Kids are too young to have to go through adolescence*, she thought bitterly.

There were two boys who thought they were in love with Catherine. One was Tony Korman who was going to join his father's law firm one day and who was a foot shorter than Catherine. He had pasty skin and myopic watery eyes that adored her. The other was Dean McDermott, who was fat and shy and wanted to be a dentist. Then of course, there was Ron Peterson, but he was in a category by himself. Ron was Senn High's football star, and everybody said he was a cinch to go to college on an athletic scholarship. He was tall and broad-shouldered, had the looks of a matinee idol and was easily the most popular boy in school.

The only thing that kept Catherine from instantly getting engaged to Ron was the fact that he was not aware she was alive. Every time she passed him in the school corridor, her heart would begin to pound wildly. She would think up something clever and provocative to say so he would ask her for a date. But when she approached him, her tongue would stiffen, and they would pass each other in silence. Like the *Queen Mary* and a garbage scow, Catherine thought hopelessly.

The financial problem was becoming acute. The rent was three months overdue, and the only reason they had not been evicted was that the landlady was captivated by Catherine's father and his grandiose plans and inventions. Listening to him, Catherine was filled with a poignant sadness. He was still his cheerful, optimistic self, but she could see behind the frayed facade. The marvellous, careless charm that had always given a patina of gaiety to everything he did had eroded. He reminded Catherine of a small boy in a middle-aged man's body spinning tales of the glorious future to hide the shabby failures of the past. More than once she had seen him give a dinner party for a dozen people at Henrici's and then cheerfully take one of his guests aside and borrow enough to cover the cheque plus a lavish tip, of course. Always lavish, for he had his reputation to maintain. But in spite of all these things and in spite of the fact that Catherine knew that he had been a casual and indifferent father to her, she loved this man. She loved his enthusiasm and smiling energy in a world of frowning, sullen people. This was his gift, and he had always been generous with it.

In the end, Catherine thought, he was better off with his wonderful dreams that would never materialize, than her mother who was afraid to dream.

In April Catherine's mother died of a heart attack. It was Catherine's first confrontation with death. Friends and neighbours filled the little apartment, offering their condolences, with the false, whispered pieties that tragedy invokes.

Death had diminished Catherine's mother to a tiny shrivelled figure without juices or vitality, or perhaps life had done that to her, Catherine thought. She tried to recall memories that she and her mother had shared, laughter that they had had together, moments when their hearts had touched; but it was Catherine's father who kept leaping into her mind, smiling and eager and gay. It was as though her mother's life was a pale shadow that retreated before the sunlight of memory. Catherine stared at the waxen figure of her mother in her casket, dressed in a simple black dress with a white collar, and thought what a wasted life it had been. What had it all been for? The feelings Catherine had had years ago came over her again, the determination to be somebody, leave a mark on the world, so she would not end up in an anonymous grave with the world neither knowing nor caring that Catherine Alexander had ever lived and died and been returned to the earth.

Catherine's Uncle Ralph and his wife, Pauline, flew in from Omaha for the funeral. Ralph was ten years younger than Catherine's father and totally unlike his brother. He was in the vitamin mail-order business and very successful. He was a large, square man, square shoulders, square jaw, square chin, and, Catherine was sure, a square mind. His wife was a bird of a woman, all flutter and twitter. They were decent enough people, and Catherine knew that her uncle had loaned a great deal of money to his brother, but Catherine felt that she had nothing in common with them. Like Catherine's mother, they were people without dreams.

After the funeral, Uncle Ralph said that he wanted to talk to Catherine and her father. They sat in the tiny living room of the apartment, Pauline flitting about with trays of coffee and cookies.

'I know things have been pretty rough for you financially,' Uncle Ralph said to his brother. 'You're too much of a dreamer, always were. But you're my brother. I can't let you sink. Pauline and I talked it over. I want you to come to work for me.'

'In Omaha?'

'You'll make a good, steady living and you and Catherine can live with us. We have a big house.'

Catherine's heart sank. Omaha! It was the end of all her dreams.

'Let me think it over,' her father was saying.

'We'll be catching the six o'clock train,' Uncle Ralph replied. 'Let me know before we leave.'

When Catherine and her father were alone, he groaned, 'Omaha! I'll bet the place doesn't even have a decent barber shop.'

But Catherine knew that the act he was putting

on was for her benefit. Decent barber shop or no, he had no choice. Life had finally trapped him. She wondered what it would do to his spirit to have to settle down to a steady, dull job with regular hours. He would be like a captured wild bird beating his wings against his cage, dying of captivity. As for herself, she would have to forget about going to Northwestern University. She had applied for a scholarship but had heard nothing. That afternoon her father telephoned his brother to say that he would take the job.

The next morning Catherine went to see the principal to tell him that she was going to transfer to a school in Omaha. He was standing behind his desk and before she could speak, he said, 'Congratulations, Catherine, you've just won a full scholarship to Northwestern University.'

Catherine and her father discussed it thoroughly that night, and in the end it was decided that he would move to Omaha and Catherine would go to Northwestern and live in one of the dormitories on the campus. And so, ten days later, Catherine took her father down to the La Salle Street station to see him off. She was filled with a deep sense of loneliness at his departure, a sadness at saying goodbye to the person she loved the most; and yet at the same time she was eager for the train to leave, filled with a delicious excitement at the thought that she would be free, living her own life for the first time. She stood on the platform watching the face of her father pressing against the train window for a last look; a shabbily handsome man who still truly believed that one day he would own the world.

On the way back from the station Catherine remembered something and laughed aloud. To take him to Omaha, to a desperately needed job, her father had booked a Drawing Room.

Matriculation day at Northwestern was filled with an almost unbearable excitement. For Catherine it held a special significance that she could not put into words: It was the key that would unlock the door to all the dreams and nameless ambitions that had burned so fiercely within her for so long. She looked around the huge assembly hall where hundreds of students were lined up to register, and she thought: *Someday you'll all know who I am. You'll say, 'I went to school with Catherine Alexander.'* She signed up for the maximum number of allowed courses and was assigned to a dormitory. That same morning she found a job working afternoons as a cashier at the Roost, a popular sandwich and malt shop across from the campus. Her salary was fifteen dollars a week, and while it would not afford her any luxuries, it would take care of her school books and basic necessities.

By the middle of her sophomore year Catherine decided that she was probably the only virgin on the entire campus. During the years she was growing up, she had overheard random snatches of conversations as her elders discussed sex. It sounded wonderful, and her strongest fear was that it would be gone by the time she was old enough to enjoy it. Now it looked as though she had been right. At least as far as *she* was concerned. Sex seemed to be the single topic of conversation at school. It was discussed in the dormitories, in classrooms, in the washrooms and at the Roost. Catherine was shocked by the frankness of the conversations.

'Jerry is unbelievable. He's like King Kong.'

'Are you talking about his cock or his brain?'

'He doesn't need a brain, honey. I came six times last night.'

'Have you ever gone out with Ernie Robbins? He's small, but he's mighty.'

'Alex asked me for a date tonight. What's the dope?'

'The dope is Alex. Save yourself the trouble. He took me out to the beach last week. He pulled down my pants and started to grope me, and I started to grope him, but I couldn't find it.' Laughter.

Catherine thought the conversations were vulgar and disgusting and she tried not to miss a word. It was an exercise in masochism. As the girls described their sexual exploits, Catherine visualized herself in bed with a boy, having him make wild and frantic love to her. She would feel a physical ache in her groin and press her fists hard against her thighs, trying to hurt herself, to take her mind off the other pain. *My God*, she thought, *I'm going to die a virgin. The only nineteen-year-old virgin at Northwestern. Northwestern, hell, maybe even the United States! The Virgin Catherine. The Church will make me a*

Saint and they'll light candles to me once a year. What's the matter with me? she thought. *I'll tell you,* she answered herself. *Nobody's asked you and it takes two to play. I mean, if you want to do it right, it takes two to play.*

The name that most frequently cropped up in the girls' sexual conversations was Ron Peterson. He had enrolled at Northwestern on an athletic scholarship and was as popular here as he had been at Senn High School. He had been elected freshman class president. Catherine saw him in her Latin class the day the term began. He was even better looking than he had been in high school, his body had filled out, and his face had taken on a rugged devil-may-care maturity. After class, he walked towards her, and her heart began to pound.

Catherine Alexander!

Hello, Ron.

Are you in this class?

Yes.

What a break for me.

Why?

Why? Because I don't know anything about Latin and you're a genius. We're going to make beautiful music. Are you doing anything tonight?

Nothing special. Do you want to study together?

Let's go to the beach where we can be alone. We can study any time.

He was staring at her.

'Hey! . . . er –?' trying to think of her name.

She swallowed, trying desperately to remember, herself. 'Catherine,' she said quickly. 'Catherine Alexander.'

'Yeah. How about this place! It's terrific, isn't it?'

She tried to put eagerness in her voice to please him, agree with him, woo him. 'Oh yes,' she gushed, 'it's the most –'

He was looking at a stunning blond girl waiting at the door for him. 'See you,' he said, and moved away to join the girl.

And that was the end of the Cinderella and Prince Charming story, she thought. They lived happily ever after, he in his harem and she in a windswept cave in Tibet.

From time to time Catherine would see Ron walking along the campus, always with a different girl and sometimes two or three. *My God, doesn't he ever get tired?* she wondered. She still had visions that one day he would come to her for help in Latin, but he never spoke to her again.

At night lying in her lonely bed, Catherine would think about all the other girls making love to their boyfriends, and the boy who would always come to her was Ron Peterson. In her mind he would undress her and then she would slowly undress him, the way they always did it in romantic novels, taking off his shirt and gently running her fingers over his chest, then undoing his trousers and pulling down his shorts. He would pick her up and carry her towards the bed. At that point Catherine's comic sense would get the better of her and he would sprain his back and fall to the floor, moaning and groaning with pain. *Idiot*, she told herself, *you can't even do it right in your fantasies*. Maybe she should enter a nunnery. She wondered if nuns had sexual fantasies and if it was a sin for them to masturbate. She wondered if priests ever had sexual intercourse.

She was sitting in a cool, tree-shaded courtyard in a lovely old abbey outside Rome, trailing her fingers in the sun-warmed water of an ancient fish pond. The gate opened, and a tall priest entered the courtyard. He wore a wide-brimmed hat and a long black cassock and he looked exactly like Ron Peterson.

Ah, scusi, signorina, he murmured, *I did not know I had a visitor*.

Catherine quickly sprang to her feet. *I shouldn't be here*, she apologized. *It was just so beautiful I had to sit here and drink it in*.

You are most welcome. He moved towards her, his eyes dark and blazing. *Mia cara . . . I lied to you*.

Lied to me?

Yes. His eyes were boring into hers. *I knew you were here because I followed you*.

She felt a thrill go through her. *But – but you are a priest*.

Bella signorina, I am a man first and a priest afterwards. He lurched forwards to take her in his arms, and he stumbled on the hem of his cassock and fell into the fish pond.

Shit!

* * *

Ron Peterson came into the Roost every day after school and would take a seat at the booth in the far corner. The booth would quickly fill up with his friends and become the centre of boisterous conversation. Catherine stood behind the counter near the cash register and when Ron entered, he would give her a pleasant, absent nod and move on. He never addressed her by name. *He's forgotten it*, Catherine mused.

But each day when he walked in, she gave him a big smile and waited for him to say hello, ask her for a date, a glass of water, her virginity, anything. She might as well have been a piece of furniture. Examining the girls in the room with complete objectivity she decided she was prettier than all but one girl, the fantastic looking Jean-Anne, the Southern blonde with whom Ron was most often seen, and she was certainly brighter than all of them put together. What in God's name then was wrong with her? Why was it that not one single boy asked her for a date? She learned the answer the next day.

She was hurrying south along the campus headed for the Roost when she saw Jean-Anne and a brunette whom she did not know, walking across the green lawn towards her.

'Well, it's Miss Big Brain,' Jean-Anne said.

And Miss Big Boobs, Catherine thought enviously. Aloud she said, 'That was a murderous Lit quiz, wasn't it?'

'Don't be condescending,' Jean-Anne said coldly.

'You know enough to teach the Lit course. And that's not all you could teach us, is it, honey?'

Something in her tone made Catherine's face begin to redden.

'I – I don't understand.'

'Leave her alone,' the brunette said.

'Why should I?' Jean-Anne asked. 'Who the hell does she think she is?' She turned to Catherine. 'Do you want to know what everyone says about you?'

God, no. 'Yes.'

'You're a lesbo.'

Catherine stared at her, unbelievingly. 'I'm a *what*?'

'A lesbian, baby. You're not fooling anybody with that holier-than-thou act.'

'Th – that's ridiculous,' Catherine stammered.

'Did you really think you could fool people?' Jean-Anne asked. 'You're doing everything but carrying a sign.'

'But I – I never –'

'The boys get it up for you, but you never let them put it in.'

'Really –' Catherine blurted.

'Fuck off,' Jean-Anne said. 'You're not our type.'

They walked away, leaving her standing there, numbly staring after them.

That night, Catherine lay in bed, unable to sleep.

How old are you, Miss Alexander?

Nineteen.

Have you ever had sexual intercourse with a man?

Never.

Do you like men?

Doesn't everyone?

Have you ever wanted to make love to a woman?

Catherine thought about it long and hard. She had had crushes on other girls, on women teachers but that had been part of growing up. Now she thought about making love to a woman, their bodies intertwining, her lips on another woman's lips, her body being caressed by soft, feminine hands. She shuddered. *No!* Aloud, she said, 'I'm normal.' But if she was normal, why was she lying here like this? Why wasn't she out somewhere getting laid like everyone else in the world? Perhaps she was frigid. She might need some kind of operation. A lobotomy, probably.

When the Eastern sky began to lighten outside the dormitory window, Catherine's eyes were still open, but she had made a decision. She was going to lose her virginity. And the lucky man was going to be every maiden's bedside companion, Ron Peterson.

TWO

Noelle

Marseille–Paris: 1919–1939

She was born a Royal Princess.

Her earliest memories were of a white bassinet covered with a lace canopy, decorated with pink ribbons and filled with soft stuffed animals and beautiful dolls and golden rattles. She quickly learned that if she opened her mouth and let out a cry, someone would hurry to hold and comfort her. When she was six months old her father would take her out in the garden in her perambulator and let her touch the flowers and he would say, 'They're lovely, Princess, but you're more beautiful than any of them.'

At home she enjoyed it when her father lifted her up in his strong arms and carried her to a window where she could look out and see the roofs of the high buildings, and he would say, 'That's your Kingdom out there, Princess.' He would point to the tall masts of ships bobbing at anchor in the bay. 'Do you see those big ships? One day they'll all be yours to command.'

Visitors would come to the castle to see her, but only a few special ones were permitted to hold her. The others would stare down at her as she lay in her crib and would exclaim over her unbelievably delicate features, and her lovely blond hair, her soft honey-coloured skin, and her father would proudly say, 'A stranger could tell she is a Princess!' And he would lean over her crib and whisper, 'Someday a beautiful Prince will come and sweep you off your feet.' And he would gently tuck the warm pink blanket around her and she would drift off to a contented sleep. Her whole world was a roseate dream of ships, tall masts and castles, and it was not until she was five years old that she understood that she was the daughter of a Marseille fishmonger, and that the castles she saw from the window of her tiny attic room were the warehouses around the stinking fish market where her father worked, and that her navy was the fleet of old fishing ships that set out from Marseille every morning before dawn and returned in the early afternoon to vomit their smelly cargo into the waterfront docks.

This was the kingdom of Noelle Page.

The friends of Noelle's father used to warn him about what he was doing. 'You mustn't put fancy ideas in her head, Jacques. She'll think she's better than everybody else.' And their prophecies came true.

On the surface Marseille is a city of violence, the kind of primitive violence spawned in any waterfront town crowded with hungering sailors with money to spend and clever predators to relieve them of it. But unlike the rest of the French, the people of Marseille have a sense of solidarity that comes from a common struggle for survival, for the lifeblood of the town comes from the sea, and the fishermen of Marseille belong to the family of fishermen all over the world. They share alike in the storms and the calm days, the sudden disasters and the bountiful harvests.

So it was that Jacques Page's neighbours rejoiced at his good fortune in having such an incredible daughter. They too recognized the miracle of how, out of the dung of the dirty, ribald city, a true Princess had been spawned.

Noelle's parents could not get over the wonder of their daughter's exquisite beauty. Noelle's mother was a heavyset, coarse-featured peasant woman with sagging breasts and thick thighs and hips. Noelle's father was squat, with broad shoulders and the small suspicious eyes of a Breton. His hair was the colour of the wet sand along the beaches of Normandy. In the beginning it had seemed to him that nature had made a mistake, that this exquisite blond fairy creature could not really belong to him and his wife, and that as Noelle grew older she would turn into an ordinary, plain-looking girl like all the other daughters of his friends. But the miracle continued to grow and flourish, and Noelle became more beautiful each day.

Noelle's mother was less surprised than her husband by the appearance of a golden-haired beauty in the family. Nine months before Noelle had been born, Noelle's mother had met a strapping Norwegian sailor just off a freighter. He was a giant Viking god with blond hair and a warm, seductive grin. While Jacques was at work, the sailor had spent a busy quarter of an hour in her bed in their tiny apartment.

Noelle's mother had been filled with fear when she saw how blond and beautiful her baby was. She walked around in dread, waiting for the moment that her husband would point an accusing finger at her and demand to know the identity of the real father. But, incredibly, some ego-hunger in him made him accept the child as his own.

'She must be a throwback to some Scandinavian blood in my family,' he would boast to his friends, 'but you can see that she has my features.'

His wife would listen, nodding agreement, and think what fools men were.

Noelle loved being with her father. She adored his clumsy playfulness and the strange, interesting smells that clung to him, and at the same time she was terrified by the fierceness of him. She would watch wide-eyed as he yelled at her mother and slapped her hard across the face, his neck corded with anger. Her mother would scream out in pain, but there was something beyond pain in her cries, something animal and sexual and Noelle would feel pangs of jealousy and wish she were in her mother's place.

But her father was always gentle with Noelle. He liked to take her down to the docks and show her off to the rough, crude men with whom he worked. She was known up and down the docks as The Princess and she was proud of this, as much for her father's sake as for her own.

She wanted to please her father, and because he loved to eat, Noelle began cooking for him, preparing his favourite dishes, gradually displacing her mother in the kitchen.

At seventeen the promise of Noelle's early beauty had been more than fulfilled. She had matured into an exquisite woman. She had fine, delicate features, eyes a vivid violet colour and soft ash-blond hair. Her skin was fresh and golden as though she had been dipped in honey. Her figure was stunning, with generous, firm, young breasts, a small waist, rounded hips and long shapely legs, with delicate ankles. Her voice was distinctive, soft and mellifluous. There was a strong, smouldering sensuality about Noelle, but that was not her magic. Her magic lay in the fact that beneath the sensuality seemed to lie an untouched island of innocence, and the combination was irresistible. She could not walk down the streets without receiving propositions from passersby. They were not the casual offers that the prostitutes of Marseille received as their daily currency, for even the most obtuse men perceived something special in Noelle, something that they had never seen before and perhaps would never see again, and each was willing to pay as much as he could afford to try to make it a part of himself, however briefly.

Noelle's father was conscious of her beauty, too. In fact, Jacques Page thought of little else. He was aware of the interest that Noelle aroused in men. Even though neither he nor his wife ever discussed sex with Noelle, he was certain she still had her virginity, a woman's little capital. His shrewd peasant mind gave long and serious thought to how he could best capitalize on the windfall that nature had unexpectedly bestowed upon him. His mission was to see that his daughter's beauty paid off as handsomely as possible for Noelle and for him. After all, he had sired her, fed her, clothed her, educated her – she owed him everything. And now it was time for him to be repaid. If he could set her up as some rich man's mistress, it would be good for her, and he would be able to live the life of ease to which he was entitled. Each day it was getting more and more difficult for an honest man to make a living. The shadow of war had begun to spread across Europe. The Nazis had marched into Austria in a lightning coup that had left Europe stunned. A few months later the Nazis had taken over the Sudeten area and then marched into Slovakia. In spite of Hitler's assurances that he was not interested in further conquest, the feeling persisted that there was going to be a major conflict.

The impact of events was felt sharply in France. There were shortages in the stores and markets, as the government began to gear for a massive defence effort. Soon, Jacques feared, they would even stop the fishing and then where would he be? No, the answer to his problem was in finding a suitable lover for his daughter. The trouble was that he knew no wealthy men. All his friends were piss-poor like himself, and he had no intention of letting any man near her who could not pay his price.

The answer to Jacques Page's dilemma was inadvertently supplied by Noelle herself. In recent months Noelle had become increasingly restless. She did well in her classes, but school had begun to bore her. She told her father that she wanted to get a job. He studied her silently, shrewdly weighing the possibilities.

'What kind of job?' he asked.

'I don't know,' Noelle replied. 'I might be able to work as a model, papa.'

It was as simple as that.

Every afternoon for the next week Jacques Page went home after work, carefully bathed to get the smell of fish out of his hands and hair, dressed in his good suit and went down to the Canebière, the main street that led from the old harbour of the city to the richer districts. He walked up and down the street exploring all the dress salons, a clumsy peasant in a world of silk and lace, but he neither knew nor cared that he was out of place. He had but one objective and he found it when he reached the Bon Marché. It was the finest dress shop in Marseille, but that was not why he chose it. He chose it because it was owned by Monsieur Auguste Lanchon. Lanchon was in his fifties, an ugly bald-headed man with small stumpy legs and a greedy, twitching mouth. His wife, a tiny woman with the profile of a finely honed hatchet, worked in the fitting room, loudly supervising the tailors. Jacques Page took one look at Monsieur Lanchon and his wife and knew that he had found the solution to his problem.

Lanchon watched with distaste as the shabbily dressed stranger entered the door of his shop. Lanchon said rudely, 'Yes? What can I do for you?'

Jacques Page winked, poked a thick finger in Lanchon's chest and smirked, 'It is what I can do for *you*, Monsieur. I am going to let my daughter work for you.'

Auguste Lanchon stared at the lout standing before him, an expression of incredulity on his face.

'You are going to *let* –'

'She will be here tomorrow, nine o'clock.'

'I do not –'

Jacques Page had left. A few minutes later, Auguste Lanchon had completely dismissed the incident from his mind. At nine o'clock the next morning, Lanchon looked up and saw Jacques Page entering the shop. He was about to tell his manager to throw the man out, when behind him he saw Noelle. They were walking towards him, the father and his unbelievably beautiful daughter, and the old man was grinning. 'Here she is, ready to go to work.'

Auguste Lanchon stared at the girl and licked his lips.

'Good morning, Monsieur,' Noelle smiled. 'My father told me that you had a job for me.'

Auguste Lanchon nodded his head, unable to trust his voice.

'Yes, I – I think we could arrange something,' he managed to stammer. He studied her face and figure and could not believe what he saw. He could already imagine what that naked young body would feel like under him.

Jacques Page was saying, 'Well, I will leave you two to get acquainted,' and he gave Lanchon a hearty whack on the shoulder and a wink that had a dozen different significances, none of them leaving any doubt in Lanchon's mind about his intentions.

For the first few weeks Noelle felt that she had been transported to another world. The women who came to the shop were dressed in beautiful clothes and had lovely manners, and the men who accompanied them were a far cry from the crude, boisterous fishermen with whom she had grown up. It seemed to Noelle that for the first time in her life the stench of fish was out of her nostrils. She had never really been aware of it before, because it had always been a part of her. But now everything was suddenly changed. And she owed it all to her father. She was proud of the way he got along with Monsieur Lanchon. Her father would come to the shop two or three times a week and he and Monsieur Lanchon would slip out for a cognac or a beer and when they returned there would be an air of camaraderie between them. In the beginning Noelle had disliked Monsieur Lanchon, but his behaviour towards her was always circumspect. Noelle heard from one of the girls that Lanchon's wife had once caught him in the stockroom with a model and had picked up a pair of shears and had barely missed castrating him. Noelle was aware that Lanchon's eyes followed her everywhere she went, but he was always scrupulously polite. 'Probably,' she thought, with satisfaction, 'he is afraid of my father.'

At home the atmosphere suddenly seemed much brighter. Noelle's father no longer struck her mother and the constant bickering had stopped. There were steaks and roasts to eat, and after dinner Noelle's father would take out a new pipe and fill it with a rich smelling tobacco from a leather pouch. He bought himself a new Sunday suit. The international situation was worsening and Noelle would listen to discussions between her father and his friends. They all seemed to be alarmed by the imminent threat to their livelihood, but Jacques Page appeared singularly unconcerned.

On September 1, 1939, Hitler's troops invaded Poland and two days later Great Britain and France declared war against Germany.

Mobilization was begun and overnight the

streets were filled with uniforms. There was an air of resignation about what was happening, a *dèjá vu* feeling of watching an old movie that one had seen before; but there was no fear. Other countries might have reason to tremble before the might of the German armies but France was invincible. It had the Maginot Line, an impenetrable fortress that could protect France against invasion for a thousand years. A curfew was imposed and rationing was started, but none of those things bothered Jacques Page. He seemed to have changed, to have calmed. The only time Noelle saw him fly into a fury was one night when she was in the darkened kitchen kissing a boy whom she dated occasionally. The lights suddenly went on and Jacques Page stood in the doorway trembling with rage.

'Get out,' he screamed at the terrified boy. 'And keep your hands off my daughter, you filthy pig!'

The boy fled in panic. Noelle tried to explain to her father that they had been doing nothing wrong, but he was too furious to listen.

'I will not have you throw yourself away,' he roared. 'He is a nobody, he is not good enough for my Princess.'

Noelle lay awake that night marvelling at how much her father loved her and vowing that she would never do anything to distress him again.

One evening just before closing time a customer came into the shop and Lanchon asked Noelle to model some dresses. By the time Noelle finished, everyone had left the shop except Lanchon and his wife, who was working on the books in the office. Noelle went into the empty dressing room to change. She was in her bra and pants when Lanchon walked into the room. He stared at her and his lips began to twitch. Noelle reached for her dress, but before she could put it on Lanchon swiftly moved towards her and shoved his hand between her legs. Noelle was filled with revulsion, her skin beginning to crawl. She tried to pull away, but Lanchon's grip was strong and he was hurting her.

'You are beautiful,' he whispered. 'Beautiful. I will see that you have a good time.'

At that moment Lanchon's wife called out to him and he reluctantly let go of Noelle and scurried out of the room.

On the way home Noelle debated whether to tell her father what had happened. He would probably kill Lanchon. She detested him and could not bear to be near him, and yet she wanted the job. Besides, her father might be disappointed if she quit. She decided that for the moment she would say nothing and would find a way to handle it herself.

The following Friday Madame Lanchon received a call that her mother was ill in Vichy. Lanchon drove his wife to the railroad station and then raced back to the shop. He called Noelle into his office and told her he was going to take her away for the weekend. Noelle stared at him, thinking at first that it was some kind of joke.

'We will go to Vienne,' he babbled. 'There is one of the great restaurants of the world there, Le Pyramide. It is expensive, but it doesn't matter, I can be very generous to those who are good to me. How soon can you be ready?'

She stared at him. 'Never' was all she could bring herself to say. 'Never.' And she turned and fled into the front of the shop. Monsieur Lanchon looked after her for a moment, his face mottled with fury, then snatched up the telephone on his desk. An hour later Noelle's father walked into the shop. He made straight for Noelle and her face lit up with relief. He had sensed that something was wrong and had come to rescue her. Lanchon was standing at the door to his office. Noelle's father took her arm and hurried her into Lanchon's office. He swung around to face her.

'I'm so glad you came, Papa,' Noelle said. 'I –'

'Monsieur Lanchon tells me that he made you a splendid offer and you refused him.'

She stared at him, bewildered. 'Offer? He asked me to go away with him for the weekend.'

'And you said no?'

Before Noelle could answer, her father drew his hand back and slapped her hard across the cheek. She stood there in stunned disbelief, her ears ringing, and through a filmy haze heard her father saying, 'Stupid! stupid! It's time you started thinking of someone besides yourself, you selfish little bitch!' And he hit her again.

Thirty minutes later as her father stood at the

kerb watching them drive off, Noelle and Monsieur Lanchon left for Vienne.

The hotel room consisted of a large double bed, cheap furniture and a washstand and basin in one corner. Monsieur Lanchon was not a man to throw away his money. He gave the bellboy a small tip and the moment the bellboy left, Lanchon turned towards Noelle and began to tear off her clothes. He cupped her breasts in his hot, moist hands and squeezed them hard.

'My God, you are beautiful,' he panted. He pulled down her skirt and pants and pushed her onto the bed. Noelle lay there unmoving, uncaring, as though she were suffering from some kind of shock. She had not uttered one word driving down in the car. Lanchon hoped that she was not ill. He could never explain it to the police or, God forbid, his wife. He hastily took off his clothes, throwing them on the floor and then moved onto the bed beside Noelle. Her body was even more splendid than he had anticipated.

'You father tells me you have never been fucked.' He grinned. 'Well, I am going to show you what a man feels like.' He rolled his plump belly on top of her and thrust his organ between her legs. He began to push harder and harder, forcing himself into her. Noelle felt nothing. In her mind she was listening to her father yelling. *You should be grateful to have a kind gentleman like Monsieur Lanchon wanting to take care of you. All you have to do is be nice to him. You will do it for me. And for yourself.* The whole scene had been a nightmare. She was sure that her father had somehow misunderstood, but when she started to explain, he had struck her again and begun screaming, 'You will do as you are told. Other girls would be grateful for your chance.' *Her chance.* She looked up at Lanchon, the squat ugly body, the panting animal face with its piggish eyes. This was the Prince to whom her father had sold her, her beloved father who cherished her and could not bear to let her waste herself on anyone unworthy. And she remembered the steaks that had suddenly appeared on the table and her father's new pipes and his new suit and she wanted to vomit.

It seemed to Noelle that in the next few hours she died and was born again. She had died a Princess, and she was reborn a slut. Slowly she had become aware of her surroundings and of what was happening to her. She was filled with a hatred such as she had not known could exist. She would never forgive her father for his betrayal. Oddly enough she did not hate Lanchon, for she understood him. He was a man with the one weakness common to all men. From now on, Noelle decided, that weakness was going to be her strength. She would learn to use it. Her father had been right all along. She *was* a Princess and the world did belong to her. And now she knew how to get it. It was so simple. Men ruled the world because they had the strength, the money and the power;

therefore it was necessary to rule men, or at least one man. But in order to do that one had to be prepared. She had a great deal to learn. And this was the beginning.

She turned her attention to Monsieur Lanchon. She lay under him, feeling, experiencing how the male organ fit and what it could do to a woman.

In his frenzy at having this beautiful creature under his fat, bucking body, Lanchon did not even notice that Noelle simply lay there, but he would not have cared. Just feasting his eyes on her was enough to rouse him to heights of passion he had not felt in years. He was accustomed to the accordioned, middle-aged body of his wife and the tired merchandise of the whores of Marseille, and to find this fresh, young girl under him was like a miracle come into his life.

But the miracle was just beginning for Lanchon. After he had spent himself making love to Noelle for the second time, she spoke and said, 'Lie still.' She began to experiment on him with her tongue and her mouth and her hands, trying new things, finding the soft, sensitive areas of his body and working on them until Lanchon cried aloud with pleasure. It was like pressing a series of buttons. When Noelle did *this*, he moaned and when she did *this*, he writhed in ecstasy. It was so easy. This was her school, this was her education. This was the beginning of power.

They spent three days there and never once went to Le Pyramide, and during those days and nights, Lanchon taught her the little that he knew about sex, and Noelle discovered a great deal more.

When they drove back to Marseille, Lanchon was the happiest man in all France. In the past he had had quick affairs with shopgirls in a *cabinet particuliers*, a restaurant that had a private dining room with a couch; he had haggled with prostitutes, been niggardly with presents for his mistresses, and notoriously penurious with his wife and children. Now he found himself saying magnanimously, 'I'm going to set you up in an apartment, Noelle. Can you cook?'

'Yes,' Noelle replied.

'Good. I will come for lunch every day and we will make love. And two or three nights a week, I will come for dinner.' He put his hand on her knee and patted it. 'How does that sound?'

'It sounds wonderful,' Noelle said.

'I will even give you an allowance. Not a large one,' he added quickly, 'but enough so you can go out and buy pretty things from time to time. All I ask is that you see no one but me. You belong to me now.'

'As you wish, Auguste,' she said.

Lanchon sighed contentedly, and when he spoke, his voice was soft. 'I've never felt this way about anyone before. And do you know why?'

'No, Auguste.'

'Because you make me feel young. You and I are going to have a wonderful life together.'

They reached Marseille late that evening, driving in silence, Lanchon with his dreams, Noelle with hers.

'I will see you in the shop tomorrow at nine o'clock,' Lanchon said. He thought it over. 'If you are tired in the morning, sleep a little longer. Come in at nine-thirty.'

'Thank you, Auguste.'

He pulled out a fistful of francs and held them out.

'Here. Tomorrow afternoon you will look for an apartment. This will be a deposit to hold it until I can see it.'

She stared at the francs in his hand.

'Is something wrong?' Lanchon asked.

'I want us to have a really beautiful place,' Noelle said, 'where we can enjoy being together.'

'I'm not a rich man,' he protested.

Noelle smiled understandingly and put her hand on his thigh. Lanchon stared at her a long moment and then nodded.

'You're right,' he said. He reached into his wallet and began peeling off francs, watching her face as he did so.

When she seemed satisfied, he stopped, flushed with his own generosity. After all what did it matter? Lanchon was a shrewd businessman, and he knew that this would insure that Noelle would never leave him.

Noelle watched him as he drove happily away, then she went upstairs, packed her things and removed her savings from her hiding place. At ten o'clock that night, she was on a train to Paris.

When the train pulled into Paris early the next morning, the PLM Station was crowded with those travellers who had eagerly just arrived, and those who were just as eagerly fleeing the city. The din in the station was deafening as people shouted cheerful greetings and tearful farewells, rudely pushing and shoving, but Noelle did not mind. The moment she stepped off the train, before she had even had a chance to see the city, she knew that she was home. It was Marseille that seemed like a strange town and Paris the city to which she belonged. It was an odd, heady sensation, and Noelle revelled in it, drinking in the noises, the crowds, the excitement. It all belonged to her. All she had to do now was claim it. She picked up her suitcase and started towards the exit.

Outside in the bright sunlight with the traffic insanely whizzing around, Noelle hesitated, suddenly realizing that she had nowhere to go. Half a dozen taxis were lined up in front of the station. She got into the first one.

'Where to?'

She hesitated. 'Could you recommend a nice inexpensive hotel?'

The driver swung around to stare at her appraisingly. 'You're new in town?'

'Yes.'

He nodded. 'You'll be needing a job, I suppose.'

'Yes.'

'You're in luck,' he said. 'Have you ever done any modelling?'

Noelle's heart leaped. 'As a matter of fact, I have,' she said.

'My sister works for one of the big fashion houses,' the driver confided. 'Just this morning she mentioned that one of the girls quit. Would you like to see if the vacancy is still open?'

'That would be wonderful,' Noelle replied.

'If I take you there, it will cost you ten francs.'

She frowned.

'It will be worth it,' he promised.

'All right.' She leaned back in the seat. The driver put the taxi in gear and joined the maniacal traffic heading towards the centre of town. The driver chattered as they drove, but Noelle did not hear a word he said. She was drinking in the sights of her city. She supposed that because of the blackout, Paris was more subdued than usual, but to Noelle it seemed a city of pure magic. It had an elegance, a style, even an aroma all its own. They passed Notre Dame and crossed the Pont Neuf to the Right Bank and swung towards Marshall Foch Boulevard. In the distance Noelle could see the Eiffel Tower, dominating the city. Through the rearview mirror, the driver saw the expression on her face.

'Nice, huh?'

'It's beautiful,' Noelle answered quietly. She still could not believe she was here. It was a Kingdom fit for a Princess . . . for her.

The taxi pulled up in front of a dark, grey stone building on the rue de Provence.

'We're here,' the driver announced. 'That's two francs on the metre and ten francs for me.'

'How do I know the job will still be open?' Noelle asked.

The driver shrugged. 'I told you, the girl just left this morning. If you don't want to go in, I'll take you back to the station.'

'No,' Noelle said quickly. She opened her purse, took out twelve francs and handed them to the driver. He stared at the money, then looked at her. Embarrassed, she reached into her purse and handed him another franc.

He nodded, unsmiling, and watched her lift her suitcase out of the taxi.

As he started to drive away, Noelle asked, 'What's your sister's name?'

'Jeanette.'

Noelle stood on the kerb watching the taxi disappear, then turned to look at the building. There was no identifying sign in front, but she supposed that a fashionable dress house did not need a sign. Everyone would know where to find it. She picked up her suitcase, went up to the door and rang the bell. A few moments later the door was opened by a maid wearing a black apron. She looked at Noelle blankly.

'Yes?'

'Excuse me,' Noelle said. 'I understand that there is an opening for a model.'

The woman stared at her and blinked.

'Who sent you?'

'Jeanette's brother.'

'Come in.' She opened the door wider and Noelle stepped into a reception hall done in the style of the 1800's. There was a large Baccarat chandelier hanging from the ceiling, several more scattered around the hall, and through an open door, Noelle could see a sitting room filled with antique furniture and a staircase leading upstairs. On a beautiful inlaid table were copies of *Figaro* and *L'Echo de Paris*. 'Wait here. I'll find out if Madame Delys has time to see you now.'

'Thank you,' Noelle said. She set her suitcase down and walked over to a large mirror on the wall. Her clothes were wrinkled from the train ride, and she suddenly regretted her impulsiveness in coming here before freshening up. It was important to make a good impression. Still, as she examined herself, she knew that she looked beautiful. She knew this without conceit, accepting her beauty as an asset, to be used like any other asset. Noelle turned as she saw a girl in the mirror coming down the stairs. The girl had a good figure and a pretty face, and was dressed in a long brown skirt and a high-necked blouse. Obviously the quality of models here was high. She gave Noelle a brief smile and went into the drawing room. A moment later Madame Delys entered the room. She was in her forties and was short and dumpy with cold, calculating eyes. She was dressed in a gown that Noelle estimated must have cost at least two thousand francs.

'Regina tells me that you are looking for a job,' she said.

'Yes, ma'am,' Noelle replied.

'Where are you from?'

'Marseille.'

Madame Delys snorted. 'The playpen of drunken sailors.'

Noelle's face fell.

Madame Delys patted her on the shoulder. 'It does not matter, my dear. How old are you?'

'Eighteen.'

Madame Delys nodded. 'That is good. I think my customers will like you. Do you have any family in Paris?'

'No.'

'Excellent. Are you prepared to start work right away?'

'Oh, yes,' Noelle assured her eagerly.

From upstairs came the sound of laughter and a moment later a red-headed girl walked down the stairs on the arm of a fat, middle-aged man. The girl was wearing only a thin negligee.

'Finished already?' Madame Delys asked.

'I've worn Angela out,' the man grinned. He saw Noelle. 'Who's this little beauty?'

'This is Yvette, our new girl,' Madame Delys said. And without hesitation added, 'She's from Antibes, the daughter of a Prince.'

'I've never screwed a Princess,' the man exclaimed. 'How much?'

'Fifty francs.'

'You must be joking. Thirty.'

'Forty. And believe me, you'll get your money's worth.'

'It's a deal.'

They turned to Noelle. She had vanished.

Noelle walked the streets of Paris, hour after hour. She strolled along the Champs-Élysées, down one side and up the other, wandering through the Lido Arcade and stopping at every shop to gaze at the incredible cornucopia of jewellery and dresses and leather goods and perfumes, and she wondered what Paris was like when there were *no* shortages. The wares displayed in the windows were dazzling, and while one part of her felt like a country bumpkin, another part of her knew that one day these things would belong to her. She walked through the Bois and down the rue du Faubourg-St.-Honoré and along the avenue Victor-Hugo, until she began to feel tired and hungry. She had left her purse and suitcase at Madame Delys', but she had no intention of going back there. She would send for her things.

Noelle was neither shocked nor upset by what had happened. It was simply that she knew the difference between a courtesan and a whore. Whores did not change the course of history: courtesans did. Meanwhile she was without a cent. She had to find a way to survive until she could find a job the next day. Dusk was beginning to brush the sky, and the merchants and hotel doormen were busy putting up blackout curtains against possible air attacks. To solve her immediate problem, Noelle needed to find someone to buy her a good hot dinner. She asked directions from a gendarme and then headed for the Crillon Hotel. Outside, forbidding iron shutters covered the windows, but inside, the lobby was a masterpiece of subdued elegance, soft and understated. Noelle walked in confidently as if she belonged there and took a seat in a chair facing the elevator. She had never done this before, and she was a bit nervous. But she remembered how easy it had been to handle Auguste Lanchon. Men were really very uncomplicated. There was only one lesson a girl had to remember: A man was soft when he was hard and hard when he was soft. So it was only necessary to keep him hard until he gave you what you wanted. Now, looking around the lobby, Noelle decided that it would be a simple matter to catch the eye of an unattached male on his way, perhaps, to a lonely dinner.

'Pardon, mademoiselle.'

Noelle turned her head to look up at a large man in a dark suit. She had never seen a detective in her life, but there was no doubt whatever in her mind.

'Is Mademoiselle waiting for someone?'

'Yes,' Noelle replied, trying to keep her voice steady. 'I'm waiting for a friend.'

She was suddenly acutely aware of her wrinkled dress, and the fact that she carried no purse.

'Is your friend a guest of this hotel?'

She felt a surge of panic rising in her. 'He – er – not exactly.'

He studied Noelle a moment, then said in a hardened tone. 'May I see your identification?'

'I – I don't have it with me,' she stammered. 'I lost it.'

The detective said, 'Perhaps Mademoiselle will come with me.' He put a firm hand on her arm, and she rose to her feet.

And at that moment someone took her other arm and said, 'Sorry I'm late, cheri, but you know how those damned cocktail parties are. You have to blast your way out. Been waiting long?'

Noelle swung around in astonishment to look at the speaker. He was a tall man, his body lean and hard-looking, and he wore a strange, unfamiliar uniform. He had blue-black hair with a widow's peak and eyes the colour of a dark, stormy sea, with long, thick lashes. His features had the look of an old Florentine coin. It was an irregular face, the two profiles not quite matching, as though the minter's hand had slipped for an instant. It was a face that was extraordinarily alive and mobile so that you felt it was ready to smile, to laugh, to frown. The only thing that saved it from being femininely beautiful was a strong, masculine chin with a deep cleft in it.

He gestured towards the detective. 'Is this man bothering you?' His voice was deep, and he spoke French with a very slight accent.

'N-no,' Noelle said, in a bewildered voice.

'I beg your pardon, sir,' the hotel detective was saying. 'I misunderstood. We have been having a problem here lately with . . .' He turned to Noelle. 'Please accept my apologies, Mademoiselle.'

The stranger turned to Noelle. 'Well now, I don't know. What do you think?'

Noelle swallowed and nodded quickly.

The man turned to the detective. 'Mademoiselle's being generous. Just watch yourself in the future.' He took Noelle's arm and they headed for the door.

When they reached the street, Noelle said, 'I – I don't know how to thank you, Monsieur.'

'I've always hated policemen.' The stranger grinned. 'Do you want me to get you a taxi?'

Noelle stared at him, the panic beginning to rise in her again, as she remembered her situation. 'No.'

'Right. Good night.' He walked over to the stand and started to get into a taxi, turned around and saw that she was standing there, rooted, staring after him. In the doorway of the hotel was the detective watching. The stranger hesitated, then walked back to Noelle. 'You'd better get out of here,' he advised. 'Our friend's still interested in you.'

'I have nowhere to go,' she replied.

He nodded and reached into his pocket.

'I don't want your money,' she said quickly.

He looked at her in surprise. 'What *do* you want?' he asked.

'To have dinner with you.'

He smiled and said, 'Sorry. I have a date, and I'm late already.'

'Then go ahead,' she said. 'I'll be fine.'

He shoved the bills back into his pocket. 'Suit yourself, honey,' he said. '*Au 'voir.*' He turned and began walking towards the taxi again. Noelle looked after him, wondering what was wrong with her. She knew she had behaved stupidly, but she also knew that she could not have done anything else. From the first moment she had looked at him she had experienced a reaction that she had never felt before, a wave of emotion so strong that she could almost reach out and touch it. She did not even know his name, and would probably never see him again. Noelle glanced towards the hotel and saw the detective moving purposefully towards her. It was her own fault. This time she would not be able to talk her way out of it. She felt a hand on her shoulder, and as she turned to see who it was, the stranger took her arm and propelled her towards the taxi, quickly opened the door and climbed in beside her. He gave the driver an address. The taxi pulled away, leaving the detective at the kerb, staring after them. 'What about your date?' Noelle asked.

'It's a party,' he shrugged. 'One more won't make any difference. I'm Larry Douglas. What's your name?'

'Noelle Page.'

'Where are you from, Noelle?'

She turned and looked into his brilliant dark eyes

and said, 'Antibes. I am the daughter of a Prince.'

He laughed, showing even, white teeth.

'Good for you, Princess,' he said.

'Are you English?'

'American.'

She looked at his uniform. 'America is not at war.'

'I'm in the British RAF,' he explained. 'They've just formed a group of American flyers. It's called the Eagle Squadron.'

'But why should you fight for England?'

'Because England's fighting for us,' he said. 'Only we don't know it yet.'

Noelle shook her head. 'I don't believe that. Hitler is a Boche clown.'

'Maybe. But he's a clown who knows what the Germans want: to rule the world.'

Noelle listened, fascinated, as Larry discussed Hitler's military strategy, the sudden withdrawal from the League of Nations, the mutual defence pact with Japan and Italy, not because of what he was saying but because she enjoyed watching his face as he talked. His dark eyes sparkled with enthusiasm as he spoke, blazing with an overpowering, irresistible vitality.

Noelle had never met anyone like him. He was – that rarity of rarities – a spendthrift with himself. He was open and warm and alive, sharing himself, enjoying life, making sure that everyone around him enjoyed it. He was like a magnet pulling into his orbit everyone who approached.

They arrived at the party, which was being given in a small flat on the rue Chemin Vert. The apartment was filled with a group of laughing, shouting people, most of them young. Larry introduced Noelle to the hostess, a predatory, sexy-looking redhead, and then was swallowed by the crowd. Noelle caught glimpses of him during the evening, surrounded by eager young girls, each trying to capture his attention. And yet there was no ego about him, Noelle thought. It was as though he were totally unaware of how attractive he was. Someone found a drink for Noelle and someone else offered to bring her a plate of food from the buffet, but she was suddenly not hungry. She wanted to be with the American, wanted him away from the girls who crowded around him. Men were coming up to her and trying to start conversations, but Noelle's mind was elsewhere. From the moment they had walked in, the American had completely ignored her, had acted as though she did not exist. *Why not?* Noelle thought. Why should he bother with her when he could have any girl at the party? Two men were trying to engage her in conversation, but she could not concentrate. The room had suddenly become unbearably hot. She looked around for a means of escape.

A voice said in her ear, 'Let's go,' and a few moments later she and the American were out on the street, in the cool night air. The city was dark and quiet against the invisible Germans in the sky, and the cars glided through the streets like silent fish in a black sea.

They could not find a taxi, so they walked, had dinner in a little bistro on the place des Victoires and Noelle found that she was starved. She studied the American sitting across from her, and she wondered what it was that had happened to her. It was as though he had touched some wellspring deep within her that she had never even known existed. She had never felt happiness like this before. They talked about everything. She told him about her background, and he told her that he came from South Boston and was Boston Irish. His mother had been born in Kerry County.

'Where did you learn to speak French so well?' Noelle asked.

'I used to spend my summers at Cap D'Antibes when I was a kid. My old man was a stock-market tycoon until the bears got him.'

'Bears?'

So Larry had to explain to her about the arcane ways of the stock market in America. Noelle did not care what he talked about, so long as he kept talking.

'Where are you living?'

'Nowhere.' She told him about the taxi driver and Madame Delys and the fat man believing she was a Princess and offering to pay forty francs for her, and Larry laughed aloud.

'Do you remember where the house is?'

'Yes.'

'Come on, Princess.'

When they arrived at the house on the rue de

Provence, the door was opened by the same uniformed maid. Her eyes lit up as she saw the handsome young American, then darkened when she saw who was with him.

'We want to see Madame Delys,' Larry said. He and Noelle walked into the reception hall. There were several girls in the drawing room beyond. The maid left and a few minutes later Madame Delys entered. 'Good evening, Monsieur,' she said to Larry. She turned to Noelle, 'Ah, I hope you have changed your mind.'

'She hasn't,' said Larry, pleasantly. 'You have something that belongs to the Princess.'

Madame Delys looked at him questioningly.

'Her suitcase and purse.'

Madame Delys hesitated a moment, then left the room. A few minutes later the maid returned, carrying Noelle's purse and suitcase.

'*Merci*,' Larry said. He turned to Noelle. 'Let's go, Princess.'

That night Noelle moved in with Larry, to a small, clean hotel on the rue Lafayette. There was no discussion about it, it was inevitable for both of them. When they made love that night, it was more exciting than anything Noelle had ever known, a wild primitive explosion that shook them both. She lay in Larry's arms all night, holding him close, happier than she had ever dreamed possible.

The next morning they awoke, made love, and went out to explore the city. Larry was a wonderful guide, and he made Paris seem a lovely toy for Noelle's amusement. They had lunch in the Tuileries, spent the afternoon at Mal Maison and spent hours wandering around the place des Vosges at the end of Notre Dame, the oldest section of Paris, built by Louis XIII. He showed her places that were off the beaten track of the tourists, the place Maubert with its colourful street market and the quai de la Mégisserie with its cages of brightly hued birds and squeaky animals. He took her through the Marché de Buci and they listened to the din of the hawkers, pitching the merits of their bins of fresh tomatoes, their seaweed-bedded oysters, their neatly labelled cheeses. They went to the Du Pont, on Montparnasse. They had dinner on the Bateau Mouche and finished up by having onion soup at four in the morning at Les Halles with the butchers and truck drivers. Before they were through Larry had collected a large group of friends, and Noelle realized that it was because he had the gift of laughter. He had taught her to laugh and she had not known that laughter was within her. It was like a gift from a god. She was grateful to Larry and very much in love with him. It was dawn when they returned to their hotel room. Noelle was exhausted, but Larry was filled with energy, a restless dynamo. Noelle lay in bed watching him as he stood at the window looking at the sun rise over the rooftops of Paris.

'I love Paris,' he said. 'It's like a temple to the best things that men have ever done. It's a city of beauty and food and love.' He turned to her and grinned, 'Not necessarily in that order.'

Noelle watched as he took off his clothes and climbed into bed beside her. She held him, loving the feel of him, the male smell of him. She thought of her father and how he had betrayed her. She had been wrong to judge all men by him and Auguste Lanchon. She knew now that there were men like Larry Douglas. And she also knew that there could never be anyone else for her.

'Do you know who the two greatest men who ever lived were, Princess?' he was asking.

'You,' she said.

'Wilbur and Orville Wright. They gave man his real freedom. Have you ever flown?' She shook her head. 'We had a summer place in Montauk – that's at the end of Long Island – and when I was a kid I used to watch the gulls wheel through the air over the beach, riding the current, and I would have given my soul to be up there with them. I knew I wanted to be a flyer before I could walk. A friend of the family took me up in an old biplane when I was nine, and I took my first flying lesson when I was fourteen. That's when I'm really alive, when I'm in the air.'

And later:

'There's going to be a world war. Germany wants to own it all.'

'It won't get France, Larry. No one can cross the Maginot Line.'

He snorted: 'I've crossed it a hundred times.'

She looked at him puzzled. 'In the air, Princess. This is going to be an air war . . . my war.'

And later, casually:

'Why don't we get married?'

It was the happiest moment of Noelle's life.

Sunday was a relaxed, lazy day. They had breakfast at a little outdoor café in Montmartre, went back to the room and spent almost the entire day in bed. Noelle could not believe anyone could be so ecstatic. It was pure magic when they made love, but she was just as content to lie there and listen to Larry talk and watch him as he moved restlessly about the room. Just being near him was enough for her. It was odd, she thought, how things worked out. She had grown up being called Princess by her father, and now, even though it had happened as a joke, Larry was calling her Princess. When she was with Larry, she *was* something. He had restored her faith in men. He was her world, and Noelle knew that she would never need anything more, and it seemed incredible to her that she could be so lucky, that he felt the same way about her.

'I wasn't going to get married until this war was over,' he told her. 'But to hell with that. Plans are made to be changed, right, Princess?'

She nodded, filled with a happiness that threatened to burst inside her.

'Let's get married by some *maire* in the country,' Larry said. 'Unless you want a big wedding?'

Noelle shook her head. 'The country sounds wonderful.'

He nodded. 'Deal. I have to report back to my Squadron tonight. I'll meet you here next Friday. How does that sound?'

'I – I don't know if I can stand being away from you that long.' Noelle's voice was shaky.

Larry took her in his arms and held her. 'Love me?' he asked.

'More than my life,' Noelle replied simply.

Two hours later Larry was on his way back to England. He did not let her drive to the airport with him. 'I don't like good-byes,' he said. He gave her a large fistful of franc notes. 'Buy yourself a wedding gown, Princess. I'll see you in it next week.' And he was gone.

Noelle spent the next week in a state of euphoria, going back to the places she and Larry had been, spending hours dreaming about their life together. The days seemed to drag by, the minutes stubbornly refusing to move, until Noelle thought she would go out of her mind.

She went to a dozen shops looking for her wedding dress, and finally she found exactly what she wanted, at Madeleine Vionett. It was a beautiful white organza with a high-necked bodice, long sleeves with a row of six pearl buttons, and three crinoline petticoats. It cost much more than Noelle had anticipated, but she did not hesitate. She used all the money that Larry had given her and nearly all her own savings. Her whole being was centred on Larry. She thought about ways to please him, she searched through her mind for memories that might amuse him, anecdotes that would entertain him. She felt like a schoolgirl.

And so it was that Noelle waited for Friday to come, in an agony of impatience, and when it finally arrived she was up at dawn and spent two hours bathing and dressing, changing clothes and changing again, trying to guess which dress would please Larry most. She put on her wedding gown, but quickly took it off again, afraid that it might bring bad luck. She was in a frenzy of excitement.

At ten o'clock Noelle stood in front of the pier glass in the bedroom, and she knew that she had never looked as beautiful. There was no ego in her appraisal; she was simply pleased for Larry, glad that she could bring him this gift. By noon he had not appeared, and Noelle wished that he had told her what time he expected to arrive. She kept phoning the desk for messages every ten minutes and kept picking up the phone to make sure it was working. By six o'clock that evening, there was still no word from him. By midnight he had not called, and Noelle sat huddled in a chair, staring at the phone, willing it to ring. She fell asleep, and when she woke, it was dawn, Saturday. She was still in the chair, stiff and cold. The dress she had so carefully chosen was wrinkled, and there was a run in her stocking.

Noelle changed clothes and stayed in the room all that day, stationing herself in front of the open window, telling herself that if she stayed there, Larry would appear; if she left, something terrible would happen to him. As Saturday morning lengthened into afternoon, she began to be filled with the conviction that there had been an accident. Larry's plane had crashed, and he was lying in a field or in a hospital, wounded or dead. Noelle's mind was filled with ghastly visions. She sat up all night Saturday, sick with worry, afraid to leave the room and not knowing how to reach Larry.

When Noelle had not heard from him by Sunday noon, she could stand it no longer. She had to telephone him. But how? With a war on it was difficult to place an overseas call and she was not even certain where Larry was. She knew only that he flew with the RAF in some American squadron. She picked up the telephone and spoke to the switchboard operator.

'It is impossible,' the operator said flatly.

Noelle explained the situation, and whether it was her words or the frantic despair in her voice she never knew, but two hours later she was talking to the War Ministry in London. They could not help her, but they transferred her to the Air Ministry at Whitehall who put her through to Combat Operations, where she was disconnected before she could get any information. It was four more hours before Noelle was reconnected, and by then she was on the verge of hysteria. Air Operations could give her no information and suggested she try the War Ministry.

'I've talked to them!' Noelle screamed into the phone. She began to sob, and the male English voice at the other end of the phone said in embarrassment, 'Please, miss, it can't be that bad. Hold on a moment.'

Noelle held the receiver in her hand, knowing that it was hopeless, certain that Larry was dead and that she would never know how or where he died. And she was about to replace the receiver when the voice spoke in her ear again and said cheerfully, 'What you want, miss, is the Eagle Squadron. They're the Yanks, based in Yorkshire. It's a bit irregular, but I'm going to put you through to Church Fenton, their airfield. Their chaps will be able to help you.' And the line went dead.

It was eleven o'clock that night before Noelle could get the call through again. A disembodied voice said, 'Church Fenton Air Base,' and the connection was so bad that Noelle could barely hear him. It was as though he were speaking from the bottom of the sea. He was obviously having difficulty hearing her. 'Speak up, please,' he said. By now, Noelle's nerves were so frayed that she could hardly control her voice.

'I'm calling' – she did not even know his rank. Lieutenant? Captain? Major? 'I'm calling Larry Douglas. This is his fiancée.'

'I can't hear you, miss. Can you speak louder, please?'

On the edge of panic Noelle screamed out the words again, sure that the man at the other end of the phone was trying to conceal from her that Larry was dead. For a miraculous instant the line cleared, and she heard the voice saying as though he were in the next room, 'Lieutenant Larry Douglas?'

'Yes,' she said, holding on tightly to her emotions.

'Just a moment, please.'

Noelle waited for what seemed an eternity and then the voice came back on the line and said, 'Lieutenant Douglas is on weekend leave. If it's urgent, he can be reached at the Hotel Savoy ballroom in London, General Davis' party.' And the line went dead.

When the maid came in to clean the room the next morning, she found Noelle on the floor, semiconscious. The maid stared at her a moment, tempted to mind her own business and leave. Why did these things always have to happen in *her* rooms? She went over and touched Noelle's forehead. It was burning hot. Grumbling, the maid waddled down the hall and asked the porter to send up the manager. One hour later an ambulance pulled up outside the hotel and two young interns carrying a stretcher were directed to Noelle's room. Noelle was unconscious. The young intern in charge raised her eyelid, put a stethoscope to her chest and listened to the rales as she breathed. 'Pneumonia,' he said to his companion. 'Let's get her out of here.'

They lifted Noelle onto the stretcher and five minutes later the ambulance was racing towards the hospital. She was rushed into an oxygen tent, and it was four days before she was fully conscious. She dragged herself reluctantly up from the murky green depths of oblivion, subconsciously knowing something terrible had happened and fighting not to remember what it was. As the awful thing floated closer and closer to the surface of her mind, and she struggled to keep it from herself, it suddenly came to her clear and whole. Larry Douglas. Noelle began to weep, racked with sobs until she finally drifted off into a half-sleep. She felt a hand gently holding hers, and she knew that Larry had come back to her, that everything was all right. Noelle opened her eyes and stared at a stranger in a white uniform, taking her pulse. 'Well! Welcome back,' he announced cheerfully.

'Where am I?' Noelle asked.

'L'Hotel-Dieu, the City Hospital.'

'What am I doing here?'

'Getting well. You've had double pneumonia. I'm Israel Katz.' He was young, with a strong, intelligent face and deepset brown eyes.

'Are you my doctor?'

'Intern,' he said. 'I brought you in.' He smiled at her. 'I'm glad you made it. We weren't sure.'

'How long have I been here?'

'Four days.'

'Would you do me a favour?' she asked weakly.

'If I can.'

'Call the Hotel Lafayette. Ask them –' she hesitated. 'Ask them if there are any messages for me.'

'Well, I'm awfully busy –'

Noelle squeezed his hand fiercely. 'Please. It's important. My fiancé is trying to get in touch with me.'

He grinned. 'I don't blame him. All right. I'll take care of it,' he promised. 'Now you get some sleep.'

'Not until I hear from you,' she said.

He left, and Noelle lay there waiting. Of course Larry had been trying to get in touch with her. There had been some terrible misunderstanding. He would explain it all to her and everything would be all right again.

It was two hours before Israel Katz returned. He walked up to her bed and set down a suitcase. 'I brought your clothes. I went to the hotel myself,' he said.

She looked up at him, and he could see her face tense.

'I'm sorry,' he said, embarrassed. 'No messages.'

Noelle stared at him for a long time, then turned her face to the wall, dry-eyed.

Noelle was released from the hospital two days later. Israel Katz came to say good-bye to her. 'Do you have any place to go?' he asked. 'Or a job?'

She shook her head.

'What work do you do?'

'I'm a model.'

'I might be able to help you.'

She remembered the taxi driver and Madame Delys. 'I don't need any help,' she said.

Israel Katz wrote a name on a piece of paper. 'If you change your mind, go there. It's a small fashion house. An aunt of mine owns it. I'll talk to her about you. Do you have any money?'

She did not answer.

'Here.' He pulled a few francs out of his pocket and handed them to her. 'I'm sorry I don't have more. Interns aren't very well paid.'

'Thank you,' Noelle said.

She sat at a small street café sipping a coffee and deciding how to pick up the pieces of her life. She knew that she had to survive, for she had a reason to live now. She was filled with a deep and burning hatred that was so all-consuming that it left no room for anything else. She was an avenging Phoenix rising from the ashes of the emotions that Larry Douglas had murdered in her. She would not rest until she had destroyed him. She did not know how, or when, but she knew that one day she would make it happen.

Now she needed a job and a place to sleep. Noelle opened her purse and took out the piece of paper that the young intern had given her. She studied it a moment and made up her mind. That afternoon she went to see Israel Katz's aunt and was given a job modeling in a small, second-rate fashion house on the rue Boursault.

Israel Katz's aunt turned out to be a middle-aged, grey-haired woman with the face of a harpy and the soul of an angel. She mothered all her girls and they adored her. Her name was Madame Rose.

She gave Noelle an advance on her salary and found her a tiny apartment near the salon. The first thing Noelle did when she unpacked was to hang up her wedding dress. She put it in the front of the closet so that it was the first thing she saw in the morning and the last thing she saw when she undressed at night.

Noelle knew that she was pregnant before there were any visible signs of it, before any tests had been made, before she missed her period. She could sense the new life that had formed in her womb, and at night she lay in bed staring at the ceiling thinking about it, her eyes glowing with wild animal pleasure.

On her first day off Noelle phoned Israel Katz and made a date to meet him for lunch.

'I'm pregnant,' she told him.

'How do you know? Have you had any tests?'

'I don't need any tests.'

He shook his head. 'Noelle, a lot of women think they are going to have babies when they are not. How many periods have you missed?'

She pushed the question aside, impatiently. 'I want your help.'

He stared at her. 'To get rid of the baby? Have you discussed this with the father?'

'He's not here.'

'You know abortions are illegal. I could get into terrible trouble.'

Noelle studied him a moment. 'What's your price?'

His face tightened angrily. 'Do you think everything has a price, Noelle?'

'Of course,' she said simply. 'Anything can be bought and sold.'

'Does that include you?'

'Yes, but I'm very expensive. Will you help me?'

There was a long hesitation. 'All right. I'll want to make some tests first.'

'Very well.'

The following week Israel Katz arranged for Noelle to go to the laboratory at the hospital. When the test results were returned two days later, he telephoned her at work. 'You were right,' he said. 'You're pregnant.'

'I know.'

'I've arranged for you to have a curettage at the hospital. I've told them that your husband was killed in an accident and that you are unable to have the baby. We'll do the operation next Saturday.'

'No,' she said.

'Is Saturday a bad day for you?'

'I'm not ready for the abortion yet, Israel. I just wanted to know that I could count on you to help me.'

Madame Rose noticed the change in Noelle, not merely a physical change, but something that went much deeper, a radiance, an inner glow that seemed to fill her. Noelle walked around with a constant smile, as though hugging some wonderful secret.

'You have found a lover,' Madame Rose said. 'It shows in your eyes.'

Noelle nodded. 'Yes, Madame.'

'He is good for you. Hold onto him.'

'I will,' Noelle promised. 'As long as I can.'

Three weeks later Israel Katz telephoned her. 'I haven't heard from you,' he said. 'I was wondering if you had forgotten?'

'No,' Noelle said. 'I think of it all the time.'

'How do you feel?'

'Wonderful.'

'I've been looking at the calendar. I think that we had better go to work.'

'I'm not ready yet,' Noelle said.

Three weeks passed before Israel Katz telephoned her again.

'How about having dinner with me?' he asked.

'All right.'

They arranged to meet at a cheap café on the rue de Chat Qui Peche. Noelle had started to suggest a better restaurant when she remembered what Israel had said about interns not having much money.

He was waiting for her when she arrived. They chatted aimlessly through dinner and it was not until the coffee arrived that Israel discussed what was on his mind.

'Do you still want to have the abortion?' he asked.

Noelle looked at him in surprise. 'Of course.'

'Then you must have it right away. You're more than two months pregnant.'

She shook her head. 'No, not yet, Israel.'

'Is this your first pregnancy?'

'Yes.'

'Then let me tell you something, Noelle. Up until three months, an abortion is usually an easy matter. The embryo has not been fully formed and all you need is a simple curettage, but after three months' – he hesitated – 'it's another kind of operation, and it becomes dangerous. The longer you wait, the more dangerous it becomes. I want you to have the operation now.'

Noelle leaned forwards. 'What's the baby like?'

'Now?' He shrugged. 'Just a lot of cells. Of course, all the nuclei are there to form a complete human being.'

'And after three months?'

'The embryo starts to become a person.'

'Can it feel things?'

'It responds to blows and loud noises.'

She sat there, her eyes locked onto his. 'Can it feel pain?'

'I suppose so. But it is protected with an amniotic sac.' He suddenly felt an uneasy stirring. 'It would be pretty hard for anything to hurt it.'

Noelle lowered her eyes and sat staring at the table, silent and thoughtful.

Israel Katz studied her a moment and then said shyly, 'Noelle, if you want to keep this baby and are afraid to because it will have no father . . . well, I would be willing to marry you and give the baby a name.'

She looked up in surprise. 'I have already told you. I don't want this baby. I want to have an abortion.'

'Then, for Christ's sake, have it!' Israel shouted. He lowered his voice as he realized that other patrons were staring at him. 'If you wait much longer, there isn't a doctor in France who will do it. Don't you understand? If you wait too long, you could die!'

'I understand,' Noelle said quietly. 'If I were going to have this baby, what kind of diet would you put me on?'

He ran his fingers through his hair, bewildered. 'Lots of milk and fruit, lean meat.'

That night on her way home Noelle stopped at the corner market near her apartment and bought two quarts of milk and a large box of fresh fruit.

Ten days later Noelle went into Madame Rose's office and told her that she was pregnant and asked for a leave of absence.

'For how long?' Madame Rose asked, eyeing Noelle's figure.

'Six or seven weeks.'

Madame Rose sighed. 'Are you sure what you are doing is the best thing?'

'I'm sure,' Noelle replied.

'Is there anything I can do?'

'Nothing.'

'Very well. Come back to me as soon as you can. I will ask the cashier to give you an advance on your salary.'

'Thank you, Madame.'

For the next four weeks Noelle never left her apartment, except to buy groceries. She felt no hunger and ate very little for herself, but she drank enormous quantities of milk for the baby and crammed her body with fruit. She was not alone in the apartment. The baby was with her and she talked to him constantly. She knew it was a boy just as she had known she was pregnant. She had named him Larry.

'I want you to grow to be big and strong,' she said as she drank her milk. 'I want you to be healthy . . . healthy and strong when you die.' She lay in bed every day plotting her vengeance against Larry and his son. What was in her body was not a part of her. It belonged to him and she was going to kill it. It was the only thing of his that he had left her, and she was going to destroy it just as he had tried to destroy her.

How little Israel Katz had understood her! She was not interested in a formless embryo that knew nothing. She wanted Larry's spawn to feel what was going to happen to him, to suffer, as she had suffered. The wedding dress was hanging near her bed now, always in sight, a talisman of evil, a reminder of his betrayal. *First, Larry's son, then Larry.*

The phone rang often, but Noelle lay in bed, lost in her dreams until it stopped. She was sure that it was Israel Katz trying to reach her.

One evening there was a pounding on the door. Noelle lay in bed, ignoring it, but finally when the pounding continued, she dragged herself up and opened the door.

Israel Katz was standing there, his face filled with concern. 'My God, Noelle, I've been calling you for days.'

He looked at her bulging stomach. 'I thought you might have had it done somewhere else.'

She shook her head. 'No. You're going to do it.'

Israel stared at her. 'Haven't you understood anything I told you? It's too late! No one's going to do it.'

He saw the empty bottles of milk and the fresh fruit on the table, then looked back at her. 'You *do* want the baby,' he said. 'Why won't you admit it?'

'Tell me, Israel, what's he like now?'

'Who?'

'The baby. Does he have eyes and ears? Does he have fingers and toes? Can he feel pain?'

'For Christ's sake, Noelle, stop it. You talk as if . . . as if . . .'

'What?'

'Nothing.' He shook his head in despair. 'I don't understand you.'

She smiled softly. 'No. You don't.'

He stood there a moment, making up his mind.

'All right, I'm putting my ass in a sling for you, but if you're really determined to have an abortion, let's get it over with. I have a doctor friend who owes me a favour. He'll . . .'

'No.'

He stared at her.

'Larry's not ready yet,' she said.

* * *

Three weeks later at four o'clock in the morning, Israel Katz was awakened by a furious concierge pounding on his door. 'Telephone, Monsieur Night Owl!' he yelled. 'And tell your caller that it is the middle of the night, when respectable people are asleep!'

Israel stumbled out of bed and sleepily made his way down the hall to the telephone, wondering what crisis had arisen. He picked up the receiver.

'Israel?'

He did not recognize the voice at the other end of the phone.

'Yes?'

'Now . . .' It was a whisper, disembodied and anonymous.

'Who is this?'

'Now. Come now, Israel . . .'

There was an eeriness to the voice, an unearthly quality that sent a chill down his spine. 'Noelle?'

'Now . . .'

'For Christ's sake,' he exploded. 'I won't do it. It's too late. You'll die, and I'm not going to be responsible. Get yourself to a hospital.'

There was a click in his ear, and he stood there holding the phone. He slammed the receiver and went back to his room, his mind churning. He knew that he could not do any good now, no one could. She was five and a half months pregnant. He had warned her time and time again, but she had refused to listen. Well, it was her responsibility. He wanted to have no part of it.

He began to dress as fast as he could, his bowels cold with fear.

When Israel Katz walked into her apartment, Noelle was lying on the floor in a pool of blood, hemorrhaging. Her face was dead white, but it showed no sign of the agony that must have been racking her body. She was wearing what appeared to be a wedding dress. Israel knelt at her side. 'What happened?' he asked. 'How did –?' He stopped, as his eyes fell on a bloody, twisted wire coat hanger near her feet.

'Jesus Christ!' He was filled with a rage and at the same time a terrible frustrating feeling of helplessness. The blood was pouring out faster now, there was not a moment to lose.

'I'll call an ambulance,' and he started to rise.

Noelle reached up and grabbed his arm with surprising strength, and pulled him back down to her.

'Larry's baby is dead,' she said, and her face was lit with a beautiful smile.

A team of six doctors worked for five hours trying to save Noelle's life. The diagnosis was septic poisoning, perforated womb, blood poisoning and shock. All the doctors agreed that there was little chance that she could live. By six o'clock that night Noelle was out of danger and two days later, she was sitting up in bed able to talk. Israel came to see her.

'All the doctors say that it is a miracle you're alive, Noelle.'

She shook her head. It was simply not her time to die. She had taken her first vengeance on Larry, but it was only the beginning. There was more to come. Much more. But first she had to find him. It would take time. But she would do it.

THREE

Catherine

Chicago: 1939–1940

The growing winds of war that were blowing across Europe were reduced to no more than gentle, warning zephyrs when they reached the shores of the United States.

On the Northwestern campus, a few more boys joined the ROTC, there were student rallies urging President Roosevelt to declare war on Germany and a few seniors enlisted in the Armed Forces. In general, however, the sea of complacency remained the same, and the underground swell that was soon to sweep over the country was barely perceptible.

As she walked to her cashier's job at the Roost that October afternoon, Catherine Alexander wondered whether the war would change her life, if it came. She knew one change that she had to make, and she was determined to do it as soon as possible. She desperately wanted to know what it was like to have a man hold her in his arms and make love to her, and she knew that she wanted it partly because of her physical needs, but also because she felt she was missing out on an important and wonderful experience. My God, what if she got run over by a car and they did a post mortem on her and discovered she was a virgin! No, she had to do something about it. Now.

Catherine glanced around the Roost carefully, but she did not see the face she was looking for. When Ron Peterson came in an hour later with Jean-Anne, Catherine felt her body tingle and her heart begin to pound. She turned away as they walked past her, and out of the corner of her eye she saw the two make their way to Ron's booth and sit down. Large banners were strung around the room, 'TRY OUR DOUBLE HAMBURGER SPECIAL' . . . 'TRY OUR LOVER'S DELIGHT' . . . 'TRY OUR TRIPLE MALT.'

Catherine took a deep breath and walked over to the booth. Ron Peterson was studying the menu, trying to make up his mind. 'I don't know what I want,' he was saying.

'How hungry are you?' Jean-Anne asked.

'I'm starved.'

'Then try this.' They both looked up in surprise. It was Catherine standing over the booth. She handed Ron Peterson a folded note, turned around and walked back to the cash register.

Ron opened the note, looked at it and burst into laughter. Jean-Anne watched him coolly.

'Is it a private joke or can anyone get in on it?'

'Private,' Ron grinned. He slipped the note into his pocket.

Ron and Jean-Anne left shortly afterwards. Ron didn't say anything as he paid his cheque, but he gave Catherine a long, speculative look, smiled and walked out with Jean-Anne on his arm. Catherine looked after them, feeling like an idiot. She didn't even know how to make a successful pass at a boy.

When her shift was up, Catherine got into her coat, said good night to the girl coming in to relieve her and went outside. It was a warm autumn evening with a cooling breeze skipping in off the lake. The sky looked like purple velvet with soft, far-flung stars just out of reach. It was a perfect evening to – what? Catherine made a list in her mind.

I can go home and wash my hair.

I can go to the library and study for the Latin exam tomorrow.

I can go to a movie.

I can hide in the bushes and rape the first sailor who comes along.

I can go get myself committed.

Committed, she decided.

As she started to move along the campus towards the library, a figure stepped out from behind a lamp post.

'Hi, Cathy. Where you headed?'

It was Ron Peterson, smiling down at her, and Catherine's heart started to pound until it began to burst out of her chest. She watched as it took off on its own, beating its way through the air. She became aware that Ron was staring at her. No wonder. How many girls did he know who could do that heart trick? She desperately wanted to comb her hair and fix her makeup and check the seams of her stockings, but she tried to let none of her nervousness show. Rule one: Keep calm.

'Blug,' she mumbled.

'Where are you headed?'

Should she give him her list? God, no! He'd think she was insane. This was her big chance and she must not do a single thing to destroy it. She looked up at him, her eyes as warm and inviting as Carole Lombard's in *Nothing Sacred*.

'I didn't have any special plans,' she said invitingly.

Ron was studying her, still not sure of her, some primeval instinct making him cautious. 'Would you *like* to do something special?' he asked.

This was it. The Proposition. The point of no return. 'Name it,' she said, 'and I'm yours.' And cringed inwardly. It sounded so corny. No one said, 'Name it and I'm yours' except in bad Fannie Hurst novels. He was going to turn on his heel and walk away in disgust.

But he didn't. Incredibly, he smiled, took her arm and said, 'Let's go.'

Catherine walked along with him, stunned. It had been as simple as that. She was on her way to getting laid. She began to tremble inside. If he found out she was a virgin, she would be finished.

And what was she going to talk about when she was in bed with him? Did people talk when they were actually doing it, or did they wait until it was over? She didn't want to be rude, but she had no idea what the rules were.

'Have you had dinner?' Ron was asking.

'Dinner?' She stared up at him, trying to think. Should she have had dinner? If she said yes, then he could take her right to bed and she could get it over with. 'No,' she said quickly, 'I haven't.' *Now why did I say that? I've ruined everything.* But Ron did not seem upset.

'Good. Do you like Chinese food?'

'It's my favourite.' She hated it, but the gods certainly weren't going to count a little yellow lie on the biggest night of her life.

'There's a good Chinese joint over on Estes. Lum Fong's. Do you know it?'

No, but she would never forget it as long as she lived.

What did you do the night you lost your cherry?

Oh, I went to Lum Fong's first and had some Chinese food with Ron Peterson.

Was it good?

Sure. But you know Chinese food. An hour later, I was sexy again.

They had reached his car, a maroon Reo convertible. Ron held the door open for Catherine, and she sat in the seat where all the other girls she envied had once sat. Ron was charming, handsome, a top athlete. And a sex maniac. It would make a good title for a movie. *The Sex Maniac and the Virgin.* Maybe she should have held out for a nicer restaurant like Henrici's in the Loop and then Ron would have thought, *This is the kind of girl I want to take home to Mother.*

'A penny for your thoughts,' he said.

Oh, great! All right, so he wasn't the most brilliant conversationalist in the world. But that wasn't why she was here, was it? She looked up at him sweetly. 'I was just thinking about you.' She snuggled against him.

He grinned. 'You really had me fooled, Cathy.'

'I did?'

'I always thought you were pretty standoffish – I mean, not interested in men.'

The word you're fumbling for is lesbian, Catherine thought, but aloud she said, 'I just like to pick my time and place.'

'I'm glad you picked me.'

'So am I.' And she was. She really was. She could be certain that Ron was a good lover. He had been factory-tested and approved by every horny coed within a radius of a hundred and fifty miles. It would have been humiliating to have had her first sexual experience with someone as ignorant as she was. With Ron she was getting a master. After tonight she would not be calling herself Saint Catherine any longer. Instead she would probably be known as 'Catherine the Great.' And this time she would know what the 'Great' stood for. She would be fantastic in bed. The trick was not to panic. All the wonderful things she had read about in the little green books she used to keep hidden from her mother and father were about to happen to her. Her body was going to be an organ filled with exquisite music. Oh, she knew it would hurt the first time; it always did. But she would not let Ron know. She would move her behind around a lot because men hated for a woman to just lie there, motionless. And when Ron penetrated her, she would bite her lip to conceal the pain and cover it up with a sexy cry.

'What?'

She turned to Ron, appalled, and realized she had cried aloud. 'I – I didn't say anything.'

'You gave a kind of funny cry.'

'Did I?' She forced a little laugh.

'You're a million miles away.'

She analysed the line and decided it was bad. She must be more like Jean-Anne. Catherine put her hand on his arm and moved closer. 'I'm right here,' she said.

She tried to make her voice throaty, like Jean Arthur in *Calamity Jane*.

Ron looked down at her, confused, but the only thing he could read in her face was an eager warmth.

Lum Fong's was a dreary-looking, run-of-the-mill Chinese restaurant located under the Elevated. All through dinner they could hear the rumble of the trains as they ran overhead rattling the dishes. The restaurant looked like a thousand other anonymous Chinese restaurants all over America, but

Catherine carefully absorbed the details of the booth they were seated in, committing to memory the cheap, spotted wallpaper, the chipped china teapot, the soy-sauce stains on the table.

A little Chinese waiter came up to the table and asked if they wanted a drink. Catherine had tasted whiskey a few times in her life and hated it, but this was New Year's Eve, the Fourth of July, the End of her Maidenhood. It was fitting to celebrate.

'I'll have an old-fashioned with a cherry in it.' *Cherry*! *Oh, God*! It was a dead giveaway.

'Scotch and soda,' Ron said.

The waiter bowed himself away from the table. Catherine wondered if it were true that Oriental women were built slantwise.

'I don't know why we never became friends before,' Ron was saying. 'Everyone says you're the brightest girl in the whole goddamned university.'

'You know how people exaggerate.'

'And you're damned pretty.'

'Thank you.' She tried to make her voice sound like Katherine Hepburn in *Alice Adams* and looked meaningfully into his eyes. She was no longer Catherine Alexander. She was a sex machine. She was about to join Mae West, Marlene Dietrich, Cleopatra. They were all going to be sisters under the foreskin.

The waiter brought the drink and she finished it in one quick nervous gulp. Ron watched her in surprise.

'Easy,' he warned. 'That's pretty potent stuff.'

'I can handle it,' Catherine assured him, confidently.

'Another round,' he told the waiter. Ron reached across the table and caressed her hand. 'It's funny. Everybody at school had you wrong.'

'Wrong. No one at school's had me.'

He stared at her. *Careful, don't be clever*. Men preferred to bed girls who had excessively large mammary glands and gluteus maximus muscles and exceedingly small cerebrums.

'I've had a – thing for you for a long time,' she said, hurriedly.

'You sure kept it a secret.' Ron pulled out the note she had written and smoothed it out. 'Try our Cashier,' he read aloud, and laughed. 'So far I like it better than the Banana Split.' He ran his hands up and down Catherine's arm and his touch sent tiny ripples down her spine, just like the books said it would. Perhaps after tonight she would write a manual on sex to instruct all the poor, dumb virgins who didn't know what life was all about. After the second drink Catherine was beginning to feel sorry for them.

'It's a pity.'

'What's a pity?'

She had spoken aloud again. She decided to be bold. 'I was feeling sorry for all the virgins in the world,' she said.

Ron grinned at Catherine. 'I'll drink to that.' He lifted his glass. She looked at him sitting across from her obviously enjoying her company. She had nothing to worry about. Everything was going beautifully. He asked if she would like another drink, but Catherine declined. She did not intend to be in an alcoholic stupor when she was deflowered. *Deflowered? Did people still use words like deflowered?* Anyway, she wanted to remember every moment, every sensation. *Oh, my God! She wasn't wearing anything! Would he? Surely a man as experienced as Ron Peterson would have something to put on, some protection so she wouldn't get pregnant. What if he was expecting the same thing? What if he was thinking that a girl as experienced as Catherine Alexander would surely have some protection? Could she come right out and ask him? She decided that she would rather die first, right at the table. They could carry her body away and give her a ceremonial Chinese burial.*

Ron ordered the dollar seventy-five six-course dinner, and Catherine pretended to eat it, but it might as well have been Chinese cardboard. She was beginning to get so tense she couldn't taste anything. Her tongue was suddenly dry and the roof of her mouth felt strangely numb. *What if she had just had a stroke*? If she had sex right after a stroke, it would probably kill her. Perhaps she should warn Ron. It would hurt his reputation if they found a dead girl in his bed. Or maybe it would enhance it.

'What's the matter?' Ron asked. 'You look pale.'

'I feel great,' Catherine said, recklessly. 'I'm just excited about being with you.'

Ron looked at her approvingly, his brown eyes taking in every detail of her face and moving down to her breasts and lingering there. 'I feel the same way,' he replied.

The waiter had taken the dishes away, and Ron had paid the cheque. He looked at her, but Catherine couldn't move.

'Do you want anything else?' Ron asked.

Do I? Oh, yes! I want to be on a slow boat to China. I want to be in a cannibal's kettle being boiled for dinner. I want my mother!

Ron was watching her, waiting, Catherine took a deep breath. 'I – I can't think of anything.'

'Good.' He drew the syllable out, long and lastingly so that it seemed to put a bed on the table between them. 'Let's go.' He stood up and Catherine followed. The euphoric feeling from the drinks had completely vanished and her legs began to tremble.

They were outside in the warm night air when a sudden thought hit Catherine and filled her with relief. *He's not going to take me to bed tonight. Men never do that with a girl on the first date. He's going to ask me out to dinner again and next time we'll go to Henrici's and we'll get to know each other better. Really know each other. And we'll probably fall in love – madly – and he'll take me to meet his parents and then everything will be all right . . . and I won't feel this stupid panic.*

'Do you have any preference in motels?' Ron asked.

Catherine stared up at him, speechless. Gone were the dreams of a genteel musicale evening with his mother and father. The bastard was planning to take her to bed in a motel! Well, that was what she wanted, wasn't it? Wasn't that the reason she had written that insane note?

Ron's hand was on Catherine's shoulder now, sliding down her arm. She felt a warm sensation in her groin. She swallowed and said, 'If you've seen one motel, you've seen them all.'

Ron looked at her strangely. But all he said was, 'OK. Let's go.'

They got into his car and started driving west. Catherine's body had turned into a block of ice, but her mind was racing at a feverish pitch. The last time she had stayed in a motel was when she was eight and was driving across country with her mother and father. Now she was going to one to go to bed with a man who was a total stranger. What did she know about him anyway? Only that he was handsome, popular and knew an easy lay when he saw one.

Ron reached over and took her hand. 'Your hands are cold,' he said.

'Cold hands, hot legs.' *Oh, Christ*, she thought. *There I go again*. For some reason, the lyrics of 'Ah, Sweet Mystery of Life' started to go through Catherine's head. Well she was about to solve it. She was on her way to finding out what everything was all about. The books, the sexy advertisements, the thinly veiled love lyrics – 'Rock Me in the Cradle of Love,' 'Do It Again,' 'Birds Do It.' *OK*, she thought. *Now Catherine is going to do it.*

Ron turned south onto Clark Street.

Ahead on both sides of the street were huge blinking red eyes, neon signs that were alive in the night, screaming out their offers of cheap and temporary havens for impatient young lovers. 'EASY REST MOTEL.' 'OVERNIGHT MOTEL,' 'COME INN,' (*Now that had to be Freudian!*) 'TRAVELLER'S REST.' The paucity of imagination was staggering, but on the other hand the owners of these places were probably too busy bustling fornicating young couples in and out of bed to worry about being literary.

'This is about the best of them,' Ron said, pointing to a sign ahead.

'PARADISE INN – VACANCY.'

It was a symbol. There was a vacancy in Paradise, and she, Catherine Alexander, was going to fill it.

Ron swung the car into the courtyard next to a small white-washed office with a sign that read: RING BELL AND ENTER. The courtyard consisted of about two dozen numbered wooden bungalows.

'How does this look?' Ron asked.

Like Dante's Inferno. Like the Colosseum in Rome when the Christians were about to be thrown to the lions. Like the Temple of Delphi when a Vestal Virgin was about to get hers.

Catherine felt that excited feeling in her groin again. 'Terrific,' she said. 'Just terrific.'

Ron smiled knowingly. 'I'll be right back.' He put his hand on Catherine's knee, sliding it up towards her thigh, gave her a quick, impersonal kiss and swung out of the car and went into the office. She sat there, looking after him, trying to make her mind blank.

She heard the wail of a siren in the distance. *Oh, my God*, she thought wildly, *it's a raid! They're always raiding these places!*

The door to the manager's office opened and Ron came out. He was carrying a key and apparently was deaf to the siren which was coming closer and closer. He walked over to Catherine's side of the car and opened the door.

'All set,' he said. The siren was a screaming banshee moving in on them. Could the police arrest them for merely being in the courtyard?

'Come on,' Ron said.

'Don't you hear that?'

'Hear what?'

The siren passed them and went ululating down the street away from them, receding into the distance. Damn! 'The birds,' she said weakly.

There was a look of impatience on Ron's face.

'If there's anything wrong –' he said.

'No, no,' Catherine cut in quickly. 'I'm coming.' She got out of the car and they moved towards one of the bungalows. 'I hope you got my lucky number,' she said brightly.

'What did you say?'

Catherine looked up at him and suddenly realized no words had come out. Her mouth was completely dry. 'Nothing,' she croaked.

They reached the door and it said number thirteen. It was exactly what she deserved. It was a sign from heaven that she was going to get pregnant, that God was out to punish Saint Catherine.

Ron unlocked the door and held it open for her. He flicked on the light switch and Catherine stepped inside. She could not believe it. The room seemed to consist of one enormous bed. The only other furniture was an uncomfortable-looking easy chair in a corner, a small dressing table with a mirror over it, and next to the bed, a battered radio with a slot for feeding it quarters. No one would ever walk in here and mistake this room for anything but what it was: a place where a boy brought a girl to screw her. You couldn't say, Well, here we are in the ski lodge, or the war games room, or the bridal suite at the Ambassador. No. What this was was a cheap love nest. Catherine turned to see what Ron was doing and he was throwing the bolt on the door. *Good. If the Vice Squad wanted them, they'd have to break down the door first.* She could see herself being carried out in the nude by two policemen while a photographer snapped her picture for the front page of the *Chicago Daily News*.

Ron moved up to Catherine and put his arms around her. 'Are you nervous?' he asked.

She looked up at him and forced a laugh that would have made Margaret Sullavan proud. 'Nervous? Ron, don't be silly.'

He was still studying her, unsure. 'You've done this before, haven't you, Cathy?'

'I don't keep a scorecard.'

'I've had a strange feeling about you all evening.'

Here it comes. He was going to throw her out on her virgin ass and tell her to get lost in a cold shower. Well, she wasn't going to let that happen. Not tonight. 'What kind of feeling?'

'I don't know.' Ron's voice was perplexed. 'One minute you're kind of sexy and, you know, *with* it, and the next minute your mind is way off somewhere and you're as frigid as ice. It's like you're two people. Which one is the real Catherine Alexander?'

Frigid as ice, she automatically said to herself. Aloud she said, 'I'll show you.' She put her arms around him and kissed him on the lips and she could smell egg foo young.

He kissed her harder and pulled her close to him. He ran his hands over her breasts, caressing them, pushing his tongue into her mouth. Catherine felt a hot moisture deep down inside her and she could feel her pants dampen. *Here I go*, she thought. *It's really going to happen! It's really going to happen!* She clung to him harder, filled with a growing, almost unbearable excitement.

'Let's get undressed,' Ron said hoarsely. He stepped back from her and started to take off his jacket.

'No,' she said. 'Let me.' There was a new confidence in her voice. If this was the night of nights, she was going to do it right. She was going to remember everything she had ever read or heard. Ron wasn't going back to school to snicker to the girls about how he had made love to a dumb little virgin. Catherine might not have Jean-Anne's bust measurement, but she had a brain ten times as useful, and she was going to put it to work to make Ron so happy in bed he wouldn't be able to stand it. She took off his jacket and laid it on the bed, then reached for his tie.

'Hold it,' Ron said. 'I want to see you undress.'

Catherine stared at him, swallowed, slowly reached for her zipper and got out of her dress. She was standing in her bra, slip, pants, shoes and stockings.

'Go on.'

She hesitated a moment, then reached down and stepped out of her slip. *Lions, 2 – Christians, 0*, she thought.

'Hey, great! Keep going.'

Catherine slowly sat down on the bed and carefully removed her shoes and stockings, trying to make it look as sexy as she could. Suddenly she felt Ron behind her, undoing her bra. She let it fall to the bed. He lifted Catherine to her feet and started sliding her pants down. She took a deep breath and closed her eyes, wishing that she were in another place with another man, a human being who loved her, whom she loved, who would father splendid children to bear his name, who would fight for her and kill for her and for whom she would be an adoring helpmate. *A whore in his bed, a great cook in his kitchen, a charming hostess in his living room* . . . a man who would kill a son of a bitch like Ron Peterson for daring to bring her to this tacky, degrading room. Her pants fell to the floor. Catherine opened her eyes.

Ron was staring at her, his face filled with admiration. 'My God, Cathy, you're beautiful,' he said. 'You're really beautiful.' He bent down and kissed her breast. She caught a glimpse in the dressing-table mirror. It looked like a French farce, sordid and dirty. Everything inside her except the hot pain in her groin told her that this was dreary and ugly and wrong, but there was no way to stop it now. Ron was whipping off his tie and unbuttoning his shirt, his face flushed. He undid his belt and stripped down to his shorts, then sat down on the bed and started to take off his shoes and socks. 'I mean it, Catherine,' he said, his voice tight with emotion. 'You're the most beautiful goddamn thing I've ever laid eyes on.'

His words only increased Catherine's panic. Ron stood up, a broad, anticipatory grin on his face, and let his shorts drop to the floor. His male organ was standing out stiffly, like an enormous, inflated salami with hair around it. It was the largest, most incredible thing Catherine had ever seen in her life.

'How do you like that?' he said, looking down at it proudly.

Without thinking, Catherine said, 'Sliced on rye. Hold the mustard and lettuce.'

And she stood there, watching it go down.

In Catherine's sophomore year there was a change in the atmosphere of the campus.

For the first time there was a growing concern about what was happening in Europe and an increasing feeling that America was going to get involved. Hitler's dream of the thousand-year rule of the Third Reich was on its way to becoming a reality. The Nazis had occupied Denmark and invaded Norway.

Over the past six months the talk on campuses across the country had shifted from sex and clothes and proms to the ROTC and the draught and lend-lease. More and more college boys were appearing in army and navy uniforms.

One day Susie Roberts, a classmate from Senn, stopped Catherine in the corridor. 'I want to say good-bye, Cathy. I'm leaving.'

'Where are you going?'

'The Klondike.'

'The *Klondike*?'

'Washington, D.C. All the girls are striking gold there. They say for every girl there are at least a hundred men. I like those odds.' She looked at Catherine. 'What do you want to stick around this place for? School's a drag. There's a whole big world waiting out there.'

'I can't leave just now,' Catherine said. She was

not sure why: She had no real ties in Chicago. She corresponded regularly with her father in Omaha and talked to him on the telephone once or twice a month and each time he sounded as though he were in prison.

Catherine was on her own now. The more she thought about Washington, the more exciting it seemed. That evening she phoned her father and told him she wanted to quit school and go to work in Washington. He asked her if she would like to come to Omaha, but Catherine could sense the reluctance in his voice. He did not want her to be trapped, as he had been.

The next morning Catherine went to the dean of women and informed her she was quitting school. Catherine sent a telegram to Susie Roberts and the next day she was on a train to Washington, D.C.

FOUR

Noelle

Paris: 1940

On Saturday, June 14, 1940, the German Fifth Army marched into a stunned Paris. The Maginot Line had turned out to be the biggest fiasco in the history of warfare and France lay defenceless before one of the most powerful military machines the world had ever known.

The day had begun with a strange grey pall that lay over the city, a terrifying cloud of unknown origin. For the last forty-eight hours sounds of intermittent gunfire had broken the unnatural, frightened silence of Paris. The roar of the cannons was outside the city, but the echoes reverberated into the heart of Paris. There had been a flood of rumours carried like a tidal wave over the radio, in newspapers and by word of mouth. The Boche were invading the French coast . . . London had been destroyed . . . Hitler had reached an accord with the British government . . . The

Germans were going to wipe out Paris with a deadly new bomb. At first each rumour had been taken as gospel, creating its own panic, but constant crises finally exert a soporific affect, as though the mind and body, unable to absorb any further terror, retreat into a protective shell of apathy. Now the rumour mills had ground to a complete halt, newspaper presses had stopped printing and radio stations had stopped broadcasting. Human instinct had taken over from the machines, and the Parisians sensed that this was a day of decision. The grey cloud was an omen.

And then the German locusts began to swarm in.

Suddenly Paris was a city filled with foreign uniforms and alien people, speaking a strange, guttural tongue, speeding down the wide, tree-lined avenues in large Mercedes limousines flying Nazi flags or pushing their way along the sidewalks that now belonged to them. They were truly the *über Mensch*, and it was their destiny to conquer and rule the world.

Within two weeks an amazing transformation had taken place. Signs in German appeared everywhere. Statues of French heroes had been knocked down and the swastika flew from all state buildings. German efforts to eradicate everything Gallic reached ridiculous proportions. The markings on hot and cold water taps were changed from *chaud* and *froid* to *heiss* and *kalt*. The place de Broglie in Strasbourg became Adolf Hitler Platz. Statues of Lafayette, Ney and Kleber were dynamited by squadrons of Nazis. Inscriptions on the monuments for the dead were replaced by 'GEFALLEN FUR DEUTSCHLAND.'

The German occupation troops were enjoying themselves. While French food was too rich and covered with too many sauces, it was still a pleasant change from war rations. The soldiers neither knew nor cared that Paris was the city of Baudelaire, Dumas and Molière. To them Paris was a garish, eager, overpainted whore with her skirts pulled up over her hips and they raped her, each in his own way. The Storm-troopers forced young French girls to go to bed with them, sometimes at the point of a bayonet, while their leaders like Goering and Himmler raped the Louvre and the rich private estates they greedily confiscated from the newly created enemies of the Reich.

If French corruption and opportunism rose to the surface in the time of France's crisis, so did the heroism. One of the underground's secret weapons was the *Pompiers*, the fire department, which in France is under the jurisdiction of the army. The Germans had confiscated dozens of buildings for the use of the army, the Gestapo and various ministries, and the location of these buildings was of course no secret. At an underground resistance headquarters in St Remy resistance leaders pored over large maps detailing the location of each building. Experts were then assigned their targets, and the following day a speeding car or an innocent-looking bicyclist would pass by one of the buildings and fling a homemade bomb through the window. Up to that point the damage was slight. The ingenuity of the plan lay in what followed next.

The Germans would call in the *Pompiers* to put out the fire. Now it is instinctive in all countries that when there is a conflagration the firemen are in complete charge: And so it was in Paris. The *Pompiers* raced into the building while the Germans stood meekly aside and watched them destroy everything in sight with high-pressure hoses, axes and – when the opportunity presented itself – their own incendiary bombs. In this way the underground managed to destroy priceless German records locked away in the fortresses of the Wehrmacht and the Gestapo. It took almost six months for the German high command to figure out what was happening, and by that time irreparable damage had been done. The Gestapo could prove nothing, but every member of the *Pompiers* was rounded up and sent to the Russian front to fight.

There was a shortage of everything from food to soap. There was no gasoline, no meat, no dairy products. The Germans had confiscated everything. Stores that carried luxury goods stayed open, but their only customers were the soldiers who paid in occupation marks which were identical with the regular marks except that they lacked the white strip at the edge and the printed promise to pay was not signed.

'Who will redeem these?' the French shopkeepers moaned.

And the Germans grinned, 'The Bank of England.'

Not all Frenchmen suffered, however. For those with money and connections there was always the Black Markct.

Noelle Page's life was changed very little by the occupation. She was working as a model at Chanel's on rue Canbon in a hundred-and-fifty-year-old greystone building that looked ordinary on the outside, but was very smartly decorated within. The war, like all wars, had created overnight millionaires, and there was no shortage of customers. The propositions that came to Noelle were more numerous than ever; the only difference was that most of them were now in German. When she was not working, she would sit for hours at small outdoor cafés on the Champs-Élysées, or on the Left Bank near the Pont Neuf. There were hundreds of men in German uniforms, many of them with young French girls. The French civilian men were either too old or lame, and Noelle supposed that the younger ones had been sent to camps or conscripted for military duty. She could tell the Germans at a glance, even when they were not in uniform. They had a look of arrogance stamped on their faces, the look that conquerors have had since the days of Alexander and Hadrian. Noelle did not hate them, nor did she like them. They simply did not touch her.

She was filled with a busy inner life, carefully planning out each move. She knew exactly what her goal was, and she knew that nothing could stop her. As soon as she was able to afford it, she engaged a private detective who had handled a divorce for a model with whom she worked. The detective's name was Christian Barbet, and he operated out of a small, shabby office on the rue St Lazare. The sign on the door read:

ENQUÊTES

PRIVÉES ET COMMERCIALES

RECHERCHES
RENSEIGNEMENTS
CONFIDENTIELS
FILATURES
PREUVES

The sign was almost larger than the office. Barbet was short and bald with yellow, broken teeth, narrow squinting eyes and nicotine-stained fingers.

'What can I do for you?' he asked Noelle.

'I want information about someone in England.'

He blinked suspiciously. 'What kind of information?'

'Anything. Whether he's married, who he sees. Anything at all. I want to start a scrapbook on him.'

Barbet gingerly scratched his crotch and stared at her.

'Is he an Englishman?'

'An American. He's a pilot with the Eagle Squadron of the RAF.'

Barbet rubbed the top of his bald head, uneasily. 'I don't know,' he grumbled. 'We're at war. If they caught me trying to get information out of England about a flyer –'

His voice trailed off and he shrugged expressively. 'The Germans shoot first and ask questions afterwards.'

'I don't want any military information,' Noelle assured him. She opened her purse and took out a wad of franc notes. Barbet studied them hungrily.

'I have connections in England,' he said cautiously, 'but it will be expensive.'

And so it began. It was three months before the little detective telephoned Noelle. She went to his office, and her first words were: 'Is he alive?' and when Barbet nodded, her body sagged with relief and Barbet thought, *It must be wonderful to have someone love you that much.*

'Your boyfriend has been transferred,' Barbet told her.

'Where?'

He looked down at a pad on his desk. 'He was attached to the 609th Squadron of the RAF. He's been transferred to the 121st Squadron at Martlesham East, in East Anglia. He's flying Hurri –'

'I don't care about that.'

'You're paying for it,' he said. 'You might as

well get your money's worth.' He looked down at his notes again. 'He's flying Hurricanes. Before that he was flying American Buffaloes.'

He turned over a page and added, 'It becomes a little personal here.'

'Go on,' Noelle said.

Barbet shrugged. 'There's a list of girls he is sleeping with. I didn't know whether you wanted –'

'I told you – everything.'

There was a strange note in her voice that baffled him. There was something not quite normal here, something that did not ring true. Christian Barbet was a third-rate investigator handling third-rate clients, but because of that he had developed a feral instinct for truth, a nose for smelling out facts. The beautiful girl standing in his office disturbed him. At first Barbet had thought she might be trying to involve him in some kind of espionage. Then he decided that she was a deserted wife seeking evidence against her husband. He had been wrong about that, he admitted, and now he was at a loss to figure out what his client wanted or why. He handed Noelle the list of Larry Douglas' girl friends and watched her face as she read it. She might have been reading a laundry list.

She finished and looked up. Christian Barbet was totally unprepared for her next words. 'I'm very pleased,' Noelle said.

He looked at her and blinked rapidly.

'Please call me when you have something more to report.'

Long after Noelie Page had gone, Barbet sat in his office staring out the window, trying to puzzle out what his client was really after.

The theatres of Paris were beginning to boom again. The Germans attended to celebrate the glory of their victories and to show off the beautiful Frenchwomen they wore on their arms like trophies. The French attended to forget for a few hours that they were an unhappy, defeated people.

Noelle had attended the theatre in Marseille a few times, but she had seen sleazy amateur plays acted out by fourth-rate performers for indifferent audiences. The theatre in Paris was something else again. It was alive and sparkling and filled with the wit and grace of Molière, Racine and Colette. The incomparable Sacha Guitry had opened his theatre and Noelle went to see him perform. She attended a revival of Büchner's *La Morte de Danton* and a play called *Asmodée* by a promising new young writer named François Mauriac. She went to the Comédie Française to see Pirandello's *Chacun La Verité* and Rostand's *Cyrano de Bergerac*. Noelle always went alone, oblivious of the admiring stares of those around her, completely lost in the drama taking place on the stage. Something in the magic that went on behind the footlights struck a responsive chord in her. She was playing a part just like the actors on stage, pretending to be something that she wasn't, hiding behind a mask.

One play in particular, *Huis Clos* by Jean Paul

Sartre, affected her deeply. It starred Philippe Sorel, one of the idols of Europe. Sorel was ugly, short and beefy, with a broken nose and the face of a boxer. But the moment he spoke, a magic took place. He was transformed into a sensitive handsome man. *It's like the story of the Prince and the Frog*, Noelle thought, watching him perform. *Only he is both*. She went back to watch him again and again, sitting in the front row studying his performance, trying to learn the secret of his magnetism.

One evening during intermission an usher handed Noelle a note. It read, 'I have seen you in the audience night after night. Please come backstage this evening and let me meet you. P.S.' Noelle read it over, savouring it. Not because she gave a damn about Philippe Sorel, but because she knew that this was the beginning she had been looking for.

She went backstage after the performance. An old man at the stage door ushered her into Sorel's dressing room. He was seated before a makeup mirror, wearing only shorts, wiping off his makeup. He studied Noelle in the mirror. 'It's unbelievable,' he said finally. 'You're even more beautiful up close.'

'Thank you, Monsieur Sorel.'

'Where are you from?'

'Marseille.'

Sorel swung around to look at her more closely. His eyes moved to her feet and slowly worked their way up to the top of her head, missing nothing. Noelle stood there under his scrutiny, not moving. 'Looking for a job?' he asked.

'No.'

'I never pay for it,' Sorel said. 'All you'll get from me is a pass to my play. If you want money, fuck a banker.'

Noelle stood there quietly watching him. Finally Sorel said, 'What *are* you looking for?'

'I think I'm looking for you.'

They had supper and afterwards went back to Sorel's apartment in the beautiful rue Maurice-Barres, overlooking the corner where it became the Bois de Boulogne. Philippe Sorel was a skilful lover, surprisingly considerate and unselfish. Sorel had expected nothing from Noelle but her beauty, and he was astonished by her versatility in bed.

'Christ!' he said. 'You're fantastic. Where did you learn all that?'

Noelle thought about it a moment. It was really not a question of learning. It was a matter of feeling. To her a man's body was an instrument to be played on, to explore to its innermost depths, finding the responsive chords and building upon them, using her own body to help create exquisite harmonies.

'I was born with it,' she said simply.

Her fingertips began to lightly play around his lips, quick little butterfly touches, and then moved down to his chest and stomach. She saw him starting to grow hard and erect again. She arose and went into the bathroom and returned a moment later and slid his hard penis into her mouth. Her mouth was hot, filled with warm water.

'Oh, Christ,' he said.

They spent the entire night making love, and in the morning. Sorel invited Noelle to move in with him.

Noelle lived with Philippe Sorel for six months. She was neither happy nor unhappy. She knew that her being there made Sorel ecstatically happy, but this did not matter in the slightest to Noelle. She regarded herself as simply a student, determined to learn something new every day. He was a school that she was attending, a small part in her large plan. To Noelle there was nothing personal in their relationship, for she gave nothing of herself. She had made that mistake twice, and she would never make it again. There was room for only one man in Noelle's thoughts and that was Larry Douglas. Noelle would pass the place des Victoires or a park or restaurant where Larry had taken her, and she would feel the hatred well up within her, choking her, so it became difficult to breathe, and there was something else mixed in with the hatred, something Noelle could not put a name to.

Two months after moving in with Sorel, Noelle received a call from Christian Barbet.

'I have another report for you,' the little detective said.

'Is he all right?' Noelle asked quickly.

Again Barbet was filled with that sense of uneasiness. 'Yes,' he said.

Noelle's voice was filled with relief. 'I'll be right down.'

The report was divided into two parts. The first dealt with Larry Douglas' military career. He had shot down five German planes and was the first American to become an Ace in the war. He had been promoted to Captain. The second part of the report interested her more. He had become very popular in London's wartime social life and had become engaged to the daughter of a British Admiral. There followed a list of girls that Larry was sleeping with, ranging from show girls to the wife of an under-secretary in the Ministry.

'Do you want me to keep on with this?' Barbet asked.

'Of course,' Noelle replied. She took an envelope from her purse and handed it to Barbet. 'Call me when you have anything further.'

And she was gone.

Barbet sighed and looked up at the ceiling. '*Folle*,' he said thoughtfully. '*Folle*.'

If Philippe Sorel had had any inkling of what was going on in Noelle's mind, he would have been astonished. Noelle seemed totally devoted to him. She did everything for him: cooked wonderful meals, shopped, supervised the cleaning of his apartment and made love whenever the mood stirred him. And asked for nothing. Sorel congratulated himself on having found the perfect mistress. He took her everywhere, and she met all his friends. They were enchanted with her and thought Sorel a very lucky man.

One night as they were having supper after the show, Noelle said to him, 'I want to be an actress, Philippe.'

He shook his head. 'God knows you're beautiful enough, Noelle, but I've been up to my ass in actresses all my life. You're different, and I want to keep you that way. I don't want to share you with anyone.' He patted her hand. 'Don't I give you everything you need?'

'Yes, Philippe,' Noelle replied.

When they returned to the apartment that night, Sorel wanted to make love. When they finished, he was drained. Noelle had never been as exciting, and Sorel congratulated himself that all she needed was the firm guidance of a man.

The following Sunday was Noelle's birthday, and Philippe Sorel gave a dinner party for her at Maxim's. He had taken over the large private dining room upstairs, decorated with plush red velvet and deep dark wood panelling. Noelle had helped write the guest list, and there was one name she included without mentioning it to Philippe. There were forty people at the party. They toasted Noelle's birthday and gave her lavish gifts. When dinner was over, Sorel rose to his feet. He had drunk a good deal of brandy and champagne and he was a little unsteady, his words a bit slurred.

'My friends,' he said, 'we've all drunk to the most beautiful girl in the world and we've given her lovely birthday presents, but I have a present for her that's going to be a *big* surprise.' Sorel looked down at

Noelle and beamed, then turned to the crowd. 'Noelle and I are going to be married.'

There was an approving cheer and the guests raced up to clap Sorel on the back and wish luck to the bride-to-be. Noelle sat there smiling up at the guests, murmuring her thank-yous. One of the guests had not risen. He was seated at a table at the far end of the room, smoking a cigarette in a long holder and viewing the scene sardonically. Noelle was aware that he had been watching her during dinner. He was a tall, very thin man, with an intense, brooding face. He seemed amused by everything that was happening around him, more an observer at the party than a guest.

Noelle caught his eye and smiled.

Armand Gautier was one of the top directors in France. He was in charge of the French Repertory Theatre, and his productions had been acclaimed all over the world. Having Gautier direct a play or a motion picture was an almost certain guarantee of its success. He had the reputation of being particularly good with actresses and had created half a dozen important stars.

Sorel was at Noelle's side, talking to her. 'Were you surprised, my darling?' he asked.

'Yes, Philippe,' she said.

'I want us to be married right away. We'll have the wedding at my villa.'

Over his shoulder Noelle could see Armand Gautier watching her, smiling that enigmatic smile. Some friends came and took Philippe away and when Noelle turned, Gautier was standing there.

'Congratulations,' he said. There was a mocking note in his voice. 'You hooked a big fish.'

'Did I?'

'Philippe Sorel is a great catch.'

'For someone perhaps,' Noelle said indifferently.

Gautier looked at her in surprise. 'Are you trying to tell me you're not interested?'

'I'm not trying to tell you anything.'

'Good luck.' He turned to go.

'Monsieur Gautier . . .'

He stopped.

'Could I see you tonight?' Noelle asked quietly. 'I would like to talk to you alone.'

Armand Gautier looked at her for a moment, then shrugged. 'If you wish.'

'I will come to your place. Will that be satisfactory?'

'Yes, of course. The address is –'

'I know the address. Twelve o'clock?'

'Twelve o'clock.'

Armand Gautier lived in a fashionable old apartment building on rue Marbeuf. A doorman escorted Noelle into the lobby and an elevator boy took her to the fourth floor and indicated Gautier's apartment. Noelle rang the bell. A few moments later the door was opened by Gautier. He wore a flowered dressing gown.

'Come in,' he said.

Noelle walked into the apartment. Her eye was

untrained, but she sensed that it was done in beautiful taste and that the objets d'art were valuable.

'Sorry I'm not dressed,' Gautier apologized. 'I've been on the telephone.'

Noelle's eyes locked onto his. 'It will not be necessary for you to be dressed.' She moved over to the couch and sat down.

Gautier smiled. 'That was the feeling I had, Miss Page. But I'm curious about something. Why me? You're engaged to a man who is famous and wealthy. I am sure that if you are looking for some extracurricular activities, you could find men more attractive than I, and certainly richer and younger. What is it you want from me?'

'I want you to teach me to act,' Noelle said.

Armand Gautier looked at her a moment, then sighed. 'You disappoint me. I expected something more original.'

'Your business is working with actors.'

'With actors, not amateurs. Have you ever acted?'

'No. But you will teach me.' She took off her hat and her gloves. 'Where is your bedroom?' she asked.

Gautier hesitated. His life was full of beautiful women wanting to be in the theatre, or wanting a bigger part, or the lead in a new play, or a larger dressing room. They were all a pain. He knew that he would be a fool to get involved with one more. And yet there was no need to get involved. Here was a beautiful girl throwing herself at him. It would be a simple matter to take her to bed and then send her away. 'In there,' he said, indicating a door.

He watched Noelle as she walked towards the bedroom. He wondered what Philippe Sorel would think if he knew that his bride-to-be was spending the night here. Women. Whores, all of them. Gautier poured himself a brandy and made several phone calls. When he finally went into the bedrom, Noelle was in his bed, naked, waiting for him. Gautier had to admit that she was an exquisite work of nature. Her face was breath-taking, and her body was flawless. Her skin was the colour of honey, except for the triangle of soft golden hair between her legs. Gautier had learned from experience that beautiful girls were almost invariably narcissistic, so preoccupied with their own egocentricities that they were lousy lays. They felt their contribution to lovemaking was simply conferring their presence in a man's bed, so that the man ended up making love to an unmoving lump of clay and was expected to be grateful for the experience. Ah, well, perhaps he could teach this one something.

As Noelle watched him, Gautier undressed, leaving his clothes carelessly strewn on the floor, and moved towards the bed. 'I'm not going to tell you you are beautiful,' he said. 'You've heard it too many times already.'

'Beauty is wasted,' Noelle shrugged, 'unless it is used to give pleasure.'

Gautier looked at her in quick surprise, then smiled. 'I agree. Let's use yours.' He sat down beside her.

Like most Frenchmen, Armand Gautier prided

himself on being a skilled lover. He was amused by the stories he had heard of Germans and Americans whose idea of making love consisted of jumping on top of a girl, having an instant orgasm, and then putting on their hat and departing. The Americans even had a phrase for it. 'Wham, bam, thank you ma'am.' When Armand Gautier was emotionally involved with a woman, he used many devices to heighten the enjoyment of lovemaking. There was always a perfect dinner, the right wines. He arranged the setting artistically so that it was pleasing to the senses, the room was delicately scented and soft music was playing. He aroused his women with tender sentiments of love and later the coarse language of the gutter. And Gautier was adept at the manual foreplay that preceded sex.

In Noelle's case he dispensed with all of these. For a one-night stand there was no need for perfume or music or empty endearments. She was here simply to get laid. She was indeed a silly fool if she thought that she could trade what every woman in the world carried between her legs for the great and unique genius that Armand Gautier possessed in his head.

He started to climb on top of her. Noelle stopped him.

'Wait,' she whispered.

As he watched, puzzled, she reached for two small tubes that she had placed on the bedside table. She squeezed the contents of one into her hand and began to rub it onto his penis.

'What is this all about?' he asked.

She smiled. 'You'll see.' She kissed him on the lips, her tongue darting into his mouth in quick bird-like movements. She pulled away and her tongue started moving towards his belly, her hair trailing across his body like light, silky fingers. He felt his organ begin to rise. She moved her tongue down his legs to his feet and began to suck gently on his toes. His organ was stiff and hard now and she mounted him as he lay there. As he felt himself penetrating her, the warmth of her vagina acted on the cream she had put on his penis and the sensation became unbearably exciting. As she rode him, moving up and down, her left hand was caressing his testicles and they began to grow hot. There was menthol in the cream on his penis and the sensation of the cold while inside her warmth, and the heat of his testicles, drove him into an absolute frenzy.

They made love all night long and each time Noelle made love to him differently. It was the most incredibly sensuous experience he had ever had.

In the morning Armand Gautier said, 'If I can get up enough energy to move, I'll get dressed and take you out to breakfast.'

'Lie there,' Noelle said. She walked over to a closet, selected one of his robes and put it on. 'You rest. I'll be back.'

Thirty-five minutes later Noelle returned with a breakfast tray. On it were freshly squeezed orange juice, a delicious sausage-and-chive omelet, heated, buttered croissants and jam and a pot of black coffee. It tasted extraordinarily good.

'Aren't you having anything?' Gautier asked.

Noelle shook her head. 'No.' She was seated in an easy chair watching him as he ate. She looked even more beautiful wearing his dressing gown open at the top, revealing the curves of her delicious breasts. Her hair was tousled and carefree.

Armand Gautier had radically revised his earlier estimate of Noelle. She was not any man's quick lay; she was an absolute treasure. However, he had met many treasures in his career in the theatre, and he was not about to spend his time and talent as a director on a starry-eyed amateur who wanted to break into the theatre, no matter how beautiful she might be, or how skilled in bed. Gautier was a dedicated man who took his art seriously. He had refused to compromise it in the past, and he was not about to start now.

The evening before, he had planned to spend the night with Noelle and send her packing in the morning. Now as he ate his breakfast and studied her, he was trying to figure out a way to hold onto Noelle as a mistress until he got bored with her, without encouraging her as an actress. He knew that he had to hold out some bait. He felt his way cautiously. 'Are you planning to marry Philippe Sorel?' he asked.

'Of course not,' Noelle replied. 'That is not what I want.'

Now it was coming. 'What do you want?' Gautier asked.

'I told you,' Noelle said quietly. 'I want to be an actress.'

Gautier bit into another croissant, stalling for time. 'Of course,' he said. Then he added, 'There are many fine dramatic coaches I could send you to, Noelle, who would . . .'

'No,' she said. Noelle was watching him pleasantly, warmly, as though eager to accede to anything he suggested. And yet Gautier had a feeling that inside her was a core of steel. There were many ways she could have said 'no.' With anger, reproach, disappointment, sulking, but she had said it with softness. And absolute finality. This was going to be more difficult than he had anticipated. For a moment Armand Gautier was tempted to tell her, as he told dozens of girls every week, to go away, that he had no time to waste on her. But he thought of the incredible sensations he had experienced during the night and he knew he would be a fool to let her go so soon. She was surely worth a slight, a very slight, compromise.

'Very well,' Gautier said. 'I will give you a play to study. When you have memorized it, you will read it to me and we will see how much talent you have. Then we can decide what to do with you.'

'Thank you, Armand,' she said. There was no triumph in her words, nor even any pleasure that he could detect. Just a simple acknowledgment of the inevitable. For the first time Gautier felt a small twinge of doubt. But that of course was ridiculous. He was a master at handling women.

While Noelle was getting dressed, Armand Gautier went into his book-lined study and scanned the familiar-looking worn volumes on the shelves. Finally, with a wry smile, he selected Euripides' *Andromache*. It was one of the most difficult classics to act. He went back into the bedroom and handed the play to Noelle.

'Here you are, my dear,' he said. 'When you have memorized the part, we shall go over it together.'

'Thank you, Armand. You will not be sorry.'

The more he thought about it, the more pleased Gautier was with his ploy. It would take Noelle a week or two to memorize the part, or what was even more likely, she would come to him and confess that she was unable to memorize it. He would sympathize with her, explain how difficult the art of acting was, and they could assume a relationship untainted by her ambition. Gautier made a date to have dinner with Noelle that evening, and she left.

When Noelle returned to the apartment she shared with Philippe Sorel, she found him waiting for her. He was very drunk.

'You bitch,' he yelled. 'Where have you been all night?'

It would not matter what she said. Sorel knew that he was going to listen to her apologies, beat her up, then take her to bed and forgive her.

But instead of apologizing Noelle merely said,

'With another man, Philippe. I've come to pick up my things.'

And as Sorel watched her in stunned disbelief, Noelle walked into the bedroom and began to pack.

'For Christ's sake, Noelle,' he pleaded. 'Don't do this! We love each other. We're going to get married.' He talked to her for the next half hour, arguing, threatening, cajoling, and by that time Noelle had finished packing and had left the apartment and Sorel had no idea why he had lost her, for he did not know that he had never possessed her.

Armand Gautier was in the middle of directing a new play that was to open in two weeks and he spent all day at the theatre in rehearsals. As a rule when Gautier was in production, he thought of nothing else. Part of his genius was the intense concentration he was able to bring to his work. Nothing existed for him but the four walls of the theatre and the actors he was working with. This day however was different. Gautier found his mind constantly wandering to Noelle and the incredible night they had had together. The actors would go through a scene and then stop and wait for his comments, and Gautier would suddenly realize that he had been paying no attention. Furious with himself he tried to focus his attention on what he was doing, but thoughts of Noelle's naked body and the amazing things it had done to him would keep coming back. In the middle of one dramatic scene he found that he was walking around the stage with an erection, and he had to excuse himself.

Because Gautier had an analytical mind he tried to figure out what it was about this girl that had affected him like this. Noelle was beautiful, but he had slept with some of the most beautiful women in the world. She was consummately skilled at love-making but so were other women to whom he had made love. She seemed intelligent but not brilliant; her personality was pleasant but not complex. There was something else, something the director could not quite put his finger on. And then he remembered her soft 'no' and he felt that it was a clue. There was some force in her that was irresistible, that would obtain anything she wanted. There was something in her that was untouched. And like other men before him Armand Gautier felt that though Noelle had affected him more deeply than he cared to admit to himself, he had not touched her at all, and this was a challenge that his masculinity could not refuse.

Gautier spent the day in a confused state of mind. He looked forward to the evening with tremendous anticipation, not so much because he wanted to make love to Noelle but because he wanted to prove to himself that he had been building something out of nothing. He wanted Noelle to be a disappointment to him so that he could dismiss her from his life.

As they made love that night, Armand Gautier made himself consciously aware of the tricks and devices and artifices Noelle used so he would realize that it was all mechanical, without emotion. But he was mistaken. She gave herself to him fully and completely, caring only about bringing him pleasure such as he had never known before and revelling in his enjoyment. When morning came Gautier was more firmly bewitched by her than ever.

Noelle prepared breakfast for him again, this time delicate crêpes with bacon and jam, and hot coffee, and it was magnificent.

'All right,' Gautier told himself. 'You have found a young girl who is beautiful to look at, who can make love and cook. Bravo! But is that enough for an intelligent man? When you are through making love and eating, you must talk. What can she talk to you about?' The answer was that it didn't really matter.

There had been no more mention of the play and Gautier was hoping that Noelle had either forgotten about it or had been unable to cope with memorizing the lines. When she left in the morning, she promised to have dinner with him that evening.

'Can you get away from Philippe?' Gautier asked.

'I've left him,' Noelle said simply. She gave Gautier her new address.

He stared at her for a moment. 'I see.'

But he did not. Not in the least.

They spent the night together again. When they were not making love, they talked. Or rather Gautier talked. Noelle seemed so interested in him that he found himself talking about things he had not discussed in years, personal things that he had never revealed to anyone before. No mention was made of the play he had given her to read, and Gautier congratulated himself on having solved his problem so neatly.

The following night when they had had dinner and were ready to retire, Gautier started towards the bedroom.

'Not yet,' Noelle said.

He turned in surprise.

'You said you would listen to me do the play.'

'Well, of – of course,' Gautier stammered, 'whenever you're ready.'

'I am ready.'

He shook his head. 'I don't want you to read it, cherie,' he said. 'I want to hear it when you have memorized it so that I can really judge you as an actress.'

'I have memorized it,' Noelle replied.

He stared at her in disbelief. It was impossible that she could have learned the entire part in only three days.

'Are you ready to hear me?' she asked.

Armand Gautier had no choice. 'Of course,' he said. He gestured towards the centre of the room. 'That will be your stage. The audience will be here.' He sat down on a large comfortable settee.

Noelle began to do the play. Gautier could feel the goose-flesh begin to crawl, his own personal stigmata, the thing that happened to him when he encountered real talent. Not that Noelle was expert. Far from it. Her inexperience shone through every move and gesture. But she had something much more than mere skill: She had a rare honesty, a natural talent that gave every line a fresh meaning and colour.

When Noelle finished the soliloquy, Gautier said warmly, 'I think that one day you will become an important actress, Noelle. I really mean that. I am going to send you to Georges Faber, who is the best dramatic coach in all of France. Working with him, you will –'

'No.'

He looked at her in surprise. It was that same soft 'no' again. Positive and final.

'"No" what?' Gautier asked in some confusion. 'Faber does not take on anyone but the biggest actors. He will only take you because I tell him to.'

'I am going to work with you,' Noelle said.

Gautier could feel the anger mounting in him. 'I don't coach anyone,' he snapped. 'I am not a teacher. I direct professional actors. When you are a professional actor, then I will direct you.' He was fighting to check the anger in his voice. 'Do you understand?'

Noelle nodded. 'Yes, I understand, Armand.'

'Very well then.'

Mollified, he took Noelle in his arms and received a warm kiss from her. He knew now that he had worried unnecessarily. She was like any other woman, she needed to be dominated. He would have no further problem with her.

Their lovemaking that night surpassed anything that had gone before, possibly, Gautier thought, because of the added excitement of the slight quarrel they had had.

During the night he said to her, 'You really can bc a wonderful actress, Noelle. I'm going to be very proud of you.'

'Thank you, Armand,' she whispered.

Noelle fixed breakfast in the morning, and Gautier left for the theatre. When he telephoned Noelle during the day, she did not answer, and when he arrived home that night she was not there. Gautier waited for her to return, and when she did not appear he lay awake all night wondering if she could have been in an accident. He tried to phone Noelle at her apartment, but there was no answer. He sent a telegram that went undelivered, and when he stopped at her apartment after rehearsal, no one answered his ring.

During the week that followed, Gautier was frantic. Rehearsals were turning into a shambles. He was screaming at all the actors and upsetting them so badly that his stage manager suggested they stop for the day and Gautier agreed. After the actors had left, he sat on the stage alone, trying to understand what had happened to him. He told himself that Noelle was just another woman, a cheap ambitious blonde with the heart of a shop-girl who wanted to be a star. He denigrated her in every way he could think of, but in the end he knew it was no use. He had to have her. That night he wandered the streets of Paris, getting drunk in small bars where he was unknown. He tried to think of ways to reach Noelle but to no avail. There was no one he could even talk to about her, except Philippe Sorel, and that, of course, was out of the question.

A week after Noelle had disappeared, Armand Gautier arrived home at four o'clock in the morning, drunk, opened the door and walked into the living room. All the lights were on. Noelle was curled up in an easy chair dressed in one of his robes, reading a book. She looked up as he entered, and smiled.

'Hello, Armand.'

Gautier stared at her, his heart lifting, a feeling of infinite relief and happiness flooding through him. He said, 'We'll begin working tomorrow.'

FIVE

Catherine

Washington: 1940

Washington, D.C., was the most exciting city that Catherine Alexander had ever seen. She had always thought of Chicago as the heartland, but Washington was a revelation. Here was the real core of America, the pulsating centre of power. At first, Catherine had been bewildered by the variety of uniforms that filled the streets: Army, Navy Air Corps, Marines. For the first time Catherine began to feel the grim possibility of war as something real.

In Washington the physical presence of war was everywhere. This was the city where war, if it came, would begin. Here it would be declared and mobilized and masterminded. This was the city that held in its hand the fate of the world. And she, Catherine Alexander, was going to be a part of it.

She had moved in with Susie Roberts, who was living in a bright and cheery fourth floor walk-up apartment with a fair-sized living room, two small adjoining bedrooms, a tiny bathroom and a kitchenette built for a midget. Susie had seemed glad to see her. Her first words were:

'Hurry and unpack and get your best dress steamed out. You have a dinner date tonight.'

Catherine blinked. 'What took you so long?'

'Cathy, in Washington, it's the *girls* who have the little black books. This town is so full of lonely men, it's pitiful.'

They had dinner that first evening at the Willard Hotel. Susie's date was a congressman from Indiana and Catherine's date was a lobbyist from Oregon, and both men were in town without their wives. After dinner they went dancing at the Washington Country Club. Catherine had hoped that the lobbyist might be able to give her a job. Instead she got the offer of a car and her own apartment, which she declined with thanks.

Susie brought the congressman back to the apartment, and Catherine went to bed. A short time later she heard them go into Susie's bedroom, and the bedsprings began to creak. Catherine pulled a pillow over her head to drown out the sound, but it was impossible. She visualized Susie in bed with her date making wild, passionate love. In the morning when Catherine got up for breakfast, Susie was already up, looking bright and cheerful, ready to go to work. Catherine searched for telltale wrinkles and other signs of dissipation on Susie, but there were none. On the contrary she looked radiant, her skin absolutely flawless. *My God*, Catherine thought, *she's a female Dorian Grey. One day she's going to come in looking great, and I'll look a hundred and ten years old.*

A few days later at breakfast Susie said, 'Hey, I heard about a job opening that might interest you. One of the girls at the party last night said she's quitting to go back to Texas. God knows why anyone who ever got away from Texas would want to go back there. I remember I was in Amarillo a few years ago and . . .'

'Where does she work?' Catherine interrupted.

'Who?'

'The girl,' Catherine said patiently.

'Oh. She works for Bill Fraser. He's in charge of public relations for the State Department. *Newsweek* did a cover story on him last month. It's supposed to be a cushy job. I just heard about it last night, so if you get over there now, you should beat all the other girls to it.'

'Thanks,' Catherine said gratefully. 'William Fraser, here I come.'

Twenty minutes later Catherine was on her way to the State Department. When she arrived, the guard told her where Fraser's office was and she took the elevator upstairs. *Public Relations. It sounded exactly like the sort of job she was looking for.*

Catherine stopped in the corridor outside the office and took out her hand mirror to check her makeup. She would do. It was not yet nine-thirty so she should have the field to herself. She opened the door and walked in.

The outer office was packed with girls standing, sitting, leaning against the wall, all seemingly talking at once. The frantic receptionist behind the beleaguered desk was vainly trying to bring order into the scene. 'Mr Fraser's busy right now,' she kept repeating. 'I don't know when he can see you.'

'Is he interviewing secretaries or isn't he?' one of the girls demanded.

'Yes, but . . .' She looked around desperately at the mob. 'My God! This is ridiculous!'

The corridor door opened and three more girls pushed their way in, shoving Catherine to one side.

'Is the job filled yet?' one of them asked.

'Maybe he'd like a harem,' another girl suggested. 'Then we can all stay.'

The door to the inner office opened, and a man came out. He was just a little under six feet, and had the almost-slim body of a nonathlete who keeps in shape at the athletic club three mornings a week. He had curly blond hair greying at the temples, bright blue eyes and a strong, rather forbidding jaw line. 'What in hell's going on here, Sally?' His voice was deep and authoritative.

'These girls heard about the vacancy, Mr Fraser.'

'Jesus! I didn't hear about it myself until an hour ago.' His eyes swept over the room. 'It's like jungle drums.' As his eyes moved towards Catherine, she stood up straight and gave him her warmest I'll-be-a-great-secretary smile, but his eyes passed right over her and went back to the receptionist. 'I need a copy of *Life*,' he told her. 'An issue that came out three or four weeks ago. It has a picture of Stalin on the cover.'

'I'll order it, Mr Fraser,' the receptionist said.

'I need it now.' He started back towards his office.

'I'll call the Time-Life Bureau,' the receptionist said, 'and see if they can dig up a copy.'

Fraser stopped at the door. 'Sally, I have Senator Borah on the line. I want to read him a paragraph from that issue. You have two minutes to find a copy for me.' He went into his office and closed the door.

The girls in the room looked at one another and shrugged. Catherine stood there, thinking hard. She turned and pushed her way out of the office.

'Good. That's one down,' one of the girls said.

The receptionist picked up the telephone and dialled information. 'The number for the Time-Life Bureau,' she said. The room grew silent as the girls watched her. 'Thank you.' She replaced the receiver, then picked it up and dialled again. 'Hello. This is Mr William Fraser's office in the State Department. Mr Fraser needs a back issue of *Life* immediately. It's the one with Stalin on the cover . . . You don't keep any back issues there? Who could I talk to? . . . I see. Thank you.' She hung up.

'Tough luck, honey,' one of the girls said.

Another added: 'They sure come up with some

beauties, don't they? If he wants to come over to my place tonight, I'll read to him.' There was a laugh.

The intercom buzzed. She flipped down the key.

'Your two minutes are up,' Fraser's voice said. 'Where's the magazine?'

The receptionist drew a deep breath. 'I just talked to the Time-Life Bureau, Mr Fraser, and they said it would be impossible to get . . .'

The door opened and Catherine hurried in. In her hand was a copy of *Life* with a picture of Stalin on the cover. She pushed her way through to the desk and placed the magazine in the receptionist's hand. The receptionist stared at it incredulously. 'I . . . I have a copy of it here, Mr Fraser. I'll bring it right in.' She rose, gave Catherine a grateful smile and hurried into the inner office. The other girls turned to stare at Catherine with suddenly hostile eyes.

Five minutes later the door to Fraser's office opened, and Fraser and the receptionist appeared. The receptionist pointed to Catherine. 'That's the girl.'

William Fraser turned to regard Catherine speculatively. 'Would you come in, please?'

'Yes, sir.' Catherine followed Fraser into his office, feeling the eyes of the other girls stabbing into her back. Fraser closed the door.

His office was the typical, bureaucratic Washington office, but he had decorated it in style, stamping it with his personal taste in furniture and art.

'Sit down, Miss . . .'

'Alexander, Catherine Alexander.'

'Sally tells me that you came up with the *Life* magazine.'

'Yes, sir.'

'I assume you didn't just happen to have a three-week-old issue in your purse.'

'No, sir.'

'How did you find it so quickly?'

'I went down to the barber shop. Barber shops and dentists' offices always have old issues lying around.'

'I see.' Fraser smiled, and his craggy face seemed less formidable. 'I don't think that would have occurred to me,' he said. 'Are you that bright about everything?'

Catherine thought about Ron Peterson. 'No, sir,' she replied.

'Are you looking for a job as a secretary?'

'Not really.' Catherine saw his look of surprise. 'I'll take it,' she added hastily. 'What I'd really like to be is your assistant.'

'Why don't we start you out as a secretary today?' Fraser said dryly. 'Tomorrow you can be my assistant.'

She looked at him hopefully. 'You mean I have the job?'

'On trial.' He flicked down the intercom key and leaned towards the box. 'Sally, would you please thank the young ladies. Tell them the position is filled.'

'Right, Mr Fraser.'

He flicked the button up. 'Will thirty dollars a week be satisfactory?'

'Oh yes, sir. Thank you, Mr Fraser.'

'You can start tomorrow morning, nine o'clock. Have Sally give you a personnel form to fill out.'

When Catherine left the office, she walked over to the *Washington Post*. The policeman at the desk in the lobby stopped her.

'I'm William Fraser's personal secretary,' she said loftily, 'over at the State Department. I need some information from your morgue.'

'What kind of information?'

'On William Fraser.'

He studied her a moment and said, 'That's the weirdest request I've had all week. Has your boss been bothering you, or something?'

'No,' she said disarmingly. 'I'm planning to write an exposé on him.'

Five minutes later, a clerk was showing her into the morgue. He pulled out the file on William Fraser, and Catherine began to read.

One hour later Catherine was one of the world's foremost authorities on William Fraser. He was forty-five years old, had been graduated from Princeton summa cum laude, had started an advertising agency, Fraser Associates, which had become one of the most successful agencies in the business, and had taken a leave of absence a year ago at the request of the President, to work for the government. He had been married to Lydia Campion, a wealthy socialite. They had been divorced for four years. There were no children. Fraser was a millionaire and had a home in Georgetown and a summer place at Bar Harbour, Maine. His hobbies were tennis, boating and polo. Several of the news stories referred to him as 'one of America's most eligible bachelors.'

When Catherine arrived home and told Susie her good news, Susie insisted that they go out to celebrate. Two rich Annapolis cadets were in town.

Catherine's date turned out to be a pleasant enough boy, but all evening she kept mentally comparing him to William Fraser, and compared to Fraser the boy seemed callow and dull. Catherine wondered whether she was going to fall in love with her new boss. She had not felt any girlish tingly feeling when she had been with him, but there was something else, a liking for him as a person and a feeling of respect. She decided that the tingly feeling probably existed only in French sex novels.

The cadets took the girls to a small Italian restaurant on the outskirts of Washington where they had an excellent dinner, then went to see *Arsenic and Old Lace*, which Catherine enjoyed tremendously. At the end of the evening the boys brought them home, and Susie invited them in for a nightcap. When it appeared to Catherine that they were starting to settle down for the night, she excused herself and said she had to go to bed.

Her date protested. 'We haven't even gotten started yet,' he said. 'Look at them.'

Susie and her escort were on the couch, locked in a passionate embrace.

Catherine's escort clutched her arm. 'There could be a war soon,' he said earnestly. Before Catherine could stop him, he took her hand and placed it against the hardness between his legs. 'You wouldn't send a man into battle in this condition, would you?'

Catherine withdrew her hand, fighting not to be angry. 'I've given it a lot of thought,' she said evenly, 'and I've decided to sleep only with the walking wounded.' She turned and went into her bedroom, locking the door behind her. She found it difficult to go to sleep. She lay in bed thinking about William Fraser, her new job and the male hardness of the boy from Annapolis. An hour after she had gone to bed, she heard Susie's bedsprings creaking wildly. From then on sleep was impossible.

At eight-thirty the next morning Catherine arrived at her new office. The door was unlocked, and the light in the reception office was on. From the inner office she heard the sound of a man's voice and she walked inside.

William Fraser was at his desk, dictating into a machine. He looked up as Catherine entered and snapped off the machine. 'You're early,' he said.

'I wanted to look around and get my bearings before I began work.'

'Sit down.' There was something in his tone that puzzled her. He seemed angry. Catherine took a seat. 'I don't like snoops, Miss Alexander.'

Catherine felt her face redden. 'I – I don't understand.'

'Washington's a small town. It's not even a town. It's a goddamn village. There's nothing that goes on here that everybody doesn't know about in five minutes.'

'I still don't –'

'The publisher of the *Post* phoned me two minutes after you arrived there to ask why my secretary was doing research on me.'

Catherine sat there stunned, not knowing what to say.

'Did you find out all the gossip you wanted to know?'

She felt her embarrassment swiftly changing to anger. 'I wasn't snooping,' Catherine said. She rose to her feet. 'The only reason I wanted information on you was so that I would know what kind of man I was working for.' Her voice was trembling with indignation. 'I think a good secretary should adapt to her employer, and I wanted to know what to adapt to.'

Fraser sat there, his expression hostile.

Catherine stared at him, hating him, on the verge of tears. 'You don't have to worry about it anymore, Mr Fraser. I quit.' She turned and started towards the door.

'Sit down,' Fraser said, his voice like a whiplash. Catherine turned, in shock. 'I can't stand goddamn prima donnas.'

She glared at him. 'I'm not a . . .'

'OK. I'm sorry. Now, will you sit down. Please?' He picked up a pipe from his desk and lit it.

Catherine stood there not knowing what to do, filled with humiliation. 'I don't think it's going to work,' she began. 'I . . .'

Fraser drew on the pipe and flicked out the match. 'Of course it'll work, Catherine,' he said reasonably. 'You can't quit now. Look at all the trouble I'd have breaking in a new girl.'

Catherine looked at him and saw the glint of amusement in his bright blue eyes. He smiled, and reluctantly her lips curved into a small smile. She sank into a chair.

'That's better. Did anyone ever tell you you're too sensitive?'

'I suppose so. I'm sorry.'

Fraser leaned back in his chair. 'Or maybe I'm the one who's oversensitive. It's a pain in the ass being called "one of America's most eligible bachelors."'

Catherine wished he would not use words like that. *But what bothered her most?* she wondered. *Ass or bachelor?*

Maybe Fraser was right. Perhaps her interest in him was not as impersonal as she thought. Perhaps subconsciously . . .

'. . . a target for every goddamned idiotic unmarried female in the world,' Fraser was saying. 'You wouldn't believe it if I told you how aggressive women can be.'

Wouldn't she? Try our cashier. Catherine blushed as she thought of it.

'It's enough to turn a man into a fairy.' Fraser sighed. 'Since this seems to be National Research Week, tell me about you. Any boyfriends?'

'No,' she said. 'That is, no one special,' she added quickly.

He looked at her quizzically. 'Where do you live?'

'I share an apartment with a girl who was a classmate at college.'

'Northwestern.'

She looked at him in surprise, then realized he must have seen the personnel form she had filled out.

'Yes, sir.'

'I'm going to tell you something about me that you didn't find in the newspaper morgue. I'm a tough sonofabitch to work for. You'll find me fair, but I'm a perfectionist. We're hard to live with. Do you think you can manage?'

'I'll try,' Catherine said.

'Good. Sally will fill you in on the routine around here. The most important thing you have to remember is that I'm a chain coffee drinker. I like it black and hot.'

'I'll remember.' She got to her feet and started towards the door.

'And, Catherine?'

'Yes, Mr Fraser?'

'When you go home tonight, practise saying some profanity in front of the mirror. If you're going to keep wincing every time I say a four-letter word, it's going to drive me up the wall.'

He was doing it to her again, making her feel like a child. 'Yes, Mr Fraser,' she said coldly. She stormed out of the office, almost slamming the door behind her.

The meeting had not gone anything like Catherine had expected. She no longer liked William Fraser. She thought he was a smug, dominating, arrogant boor. No wonder his wife had divorced him. Well she was here and she would start, but she made up her mind that she would begin looking for another job, a job working for a human being instead of a despot.

When Catherine walked out of the door, Fraser leaned back in his chair, a smile touching his lips. Were girls still that achingly young, that earnest and dedicated? In her anger with her eyes blazing and her lips trembling Catherine had seemed so defenceless that Fraser had wanted to take her in his arms and protect her. Against himself, he admitted ruefully. There was a kind of old-fashioned shining quality about her that he'd almost forgotten existed in girls. She was lovely and she was bright, and she had a mind of her own. She was going to become the best goddamn secretary that he had ever had. And deep down Fraser had a feeling that she was going to become more than that. How much more, he was not sure yet. He had been burned so often that an automatic warning system took over the moment his emotions were touched by any female. Those moments had come very seldom. His pipe had gone out. He lit it again, and the smile was still on his face. A little later when Fraser called her in for dictation, Catherine was courteous but cool. She waited for Fraser to say something personal so she could show him how aloof she was, but he was distant and businesslike. He had, Catherine thought, obviously wiped the incident of this morning from his mind. How insensitive could a man be?

In spite of herself Catherine found the new job fascinating. The telephone rang constantly, and the names of the callers filled her with excitement. During the first week the Vice-President of the United States called twice, half a dozen senators, the Secretary of State and a famous actress who was in town publicizing her latest picture. The week was climaxed by a telephone call from President Roosevelt, and Catherine was so nervous she dropped the phone and disconnected his secretary.

In addition to the telephone calls Fraser had a constant round of appointments at the office, his country club or at one of the better-known restaurants. After the first few weeks Fraser allowed Catherine to set up his appointments for him and make the reservations. She began to know who Fraser wanted to see and who he wanted to avoid. Her work was so absorbing that by the end of the month she had totally forgotten about looking for another job.

Catherine's relationship with Fraser was still on a very impersonal level, but she knew him well enough now to realize that his aloofness was not unfriendliness. It was a dignity, a wall of reserve that served as a shield against the world. Catherine had a feeling that Fraser was really very lonely. His job called for him to be gregarious, but she sensed that by nature he was a solitary man. She also sensed that William Fraser was out of her league. *For that matter so is most of male America*, she decided.

She double-dated with Susie every now and then but found most of her escorts were married sexual athletes, and she preferred to go to a movie or the theatre alone. She saw Gertrude Lawrence and a new comedian named Danny Kaye in *Lady in the Dark*, and *Life with Father*, and *Alice in Arms*, with a young actor named Kirk Douglas. She loved *Kitty Foyle* with Ginger Rogers because it reminded her of herself. One night at a performance of *Hamlet* she saw Fraser sitting in a box with an exquisite girl in an expensive white evening gown that Catherine had seen in *Vogue*. She had no idea who the girl was. Fraser made his own personal dates, and she never knew where he was going or with whom. He looked across the theatre and saw her. The next morning he made no reference to it until he had finished the morning's dictation.

'How did you like *Hamlet*?' he asked.

'The play's going to make it, but I didn't care much for the performances.'

'I liked the actors,' he said. 'I thought the girl who played Ophelia was particularly good.'

Catherine nodded and started to leave.

'Didn't you like Ophelia?' Fraser persisted.

'If you want my honest opinion,' Catherine said carefully, 'I didn't think she was able to keep her head above water.' She turned and walked out.

When Catherine arrived at the apartment that night, Susie was waiting for her. 'You had a visitor,' Susie said.

'Who?'

'An FBI man. They're investigating you.'

My God, thought Catherine. *They found out I'm a virgin, and there's probably some kind of law against it in Washington.* Aloud she said, 'Why would the FBI be investigating me?'

'Because you're working for the government now.'

'Oh.'

'How's your Mr Fraser?'

'My Mr Fraser's just fine,' Catherine said.

'How do you think he'd like me?'

Catherine studied her tall, willowy brunette roommate. 'For breakfast.'

As the weeks went by Catherine became acquainted with the other secretaries working in nearby offices. Several of the girls were having affairs with their bosses, and it did not seem to matter to them whether the men were married or single. They envied Catherine's working for William Fraser.

'What's Golden Boy really like?' one of them asked Catherine one day at lunch. 'Has he made a pass at you yet?'

'Oh, he doesn't bother with that,' Catherine said earnestly. 'I just come in at nine o'clock every morning, we roll around on the couch until one o'clock, then we break for lunch.'

'Seriously, how do you find him?'

'Resistible,' Catherine lied. Her feelings towards William Fraser had mellowed considerably since their first quarrel. He had told her the truth when he said he was a perfectionist. Whenever she made a mistake, she was reprimanded for it, but she had found him to be fair and understanding. She had watched him take time out from his own problems to help other people, people who could do nothing for him, and he always arranged it so that he never took credit for it. Yes, she liked William Fraser very much indeed, but that was no one's business but her own.

Once when they had had a great deal of work to catch up on, Fraser had asked Catherine to have dinner with him at his home so that they could work late. Talmadge, Fraser's chauffeur, was waiting with the limousine in front of the building. Several secretaries coming out of the building watched with knowing eyes as Fraser ushered Catherine into the back seat of the car and slid in next to her. The limousine glided smoothly into the late afternoon traffic.

'I'm going to ruin your reputation,' Catherine said.

Fraser laughed. 'I'll give you some advice. If you ever want to have an affair with a public figure, do it out in the open.'

'What about catching cold?'

He grinned. 'I meant, take your paramour – if they still use that word – out to public places, well-known restaurants, theatres.'

'Shakespearean plays?' Catherine asked innocently.

Fraser ignored it. 'People are always looking for devious motives. They'll say to themselves, "Uh-huh, he's taking so-and-so out in public. I wonder who he's seeing secretly." People never believe the obvious.'

'It's an interesting theory.'

'Edgar Allen Poe wrote a story based on deceiving people with the obvious,' Fraser said. 'I don't recall the name of it.'

'It was Arthur Conan Doyle. "The Purloined Letter."' The moment Catherine said it, she wished she hadn't. Men did not like smart girls. But then what did it matter? She was not his girl, she was his secretary.

They rode the rest of the way in silence.

Fraser's home in Georgetown was something out of a picture book. It was a four-storey Georgian house that must have been over two hundred years old. The door was opened by a butler in a white jacket. Fraser said, 'Frank, this is Miss Alexander.'

'Hello, Frank. We've talked on the phone,' Catherine said.

'Yes, ma'am. It's nice to meet you, Miss Alexander.'

Catherine looked at the reception hall. It had a

beautiful old staircase leading to the second floor, its oak wood burnished to a sheen. The floor was marble, and overhead was a dazzling chandelier.

Fraser studied her face. 'Like it?' he asked.

'*Like* it? Oh, yes!'

He smiled, and Catherine wondered if she had sounded too enthusiastic, like a girl who was attracted by wealth, like one of those aggressive females who were always chasing him. 'It's . . . it's pleasant,' she added lamely.

Fraser was looking at her mockingly, and Catherine had the terrible feeling that he could read her thoughts. 'Come into the study.'

Catherine followed him into a large book-lined room done in dark paneling. It had an aura of another age, the graciousness of an easier, friendlier way of life.

Fraser was studying her. 'Well?' he asked gravely.

Catherine was not going to be caught again. 'It's smaller than the Library of Congress,' she said, defensively.

He laughed aloud. 'You're right.'

Frank came into the room carrying a silver ice bucket. He set it on top of the bar in the corner. 'What time would you like dinner, Mr Fraser?'

'Seven-thirty.'

'I'll tell the cook.' Frank left the room.

'What may I fix you to drink?'

'Nothing, thank you.'

He looked over at her. 'Don't you drink, Catherine?'

'Not when I'm working,' she said. 'I get my *p*'s and *o*'s mixed up.'

'You mean *p*'s and *q*'s, don't you?'

'*P*'s and *o*'s. They're next to each other on the typewriter.'

'I didn't know.'

'You're not supposed to. That's why you pay me a king's ransom every week.'

'What do I pay you?' Fraser asked.

'Thirty dollars and dinner in the most beautiful house in Washington.'

'You're sure you won't change your mind about that drink?'

'No, thank you,' Catherine said.

Fraser mixed a martini for himself, and Catherine wandered around the room looking at the books. There were all the traditional classic titles and, in addition, a whole section of books in Italian and another section in Arabic.

Fraser walked over to her side. 'You don't really speak Italian and Arabic, do you?' Catherine asked.

'Yes. I lived in the Middle East for a few years and learned Arabic.'

'And the Italian?'

'I went with an Italian actress for a while.'

Her face flushed. 'I'm sorry. I didn't mean to pry.'

Fraser looked at her, his eyes filled with amusement, and Catherine felt like a schoolgirl. She was not sure whether she hated William Fraser or loved him. Of one thing she was sure. He was the nicest man she had ever known.

Dinner was superb. All the dishes were French with divine sauces. The dessert was Cherries Jubilee. No wonder Fraser worked out at the club three mornings a week.

'How is it?' Fraser asked her.

'It's not like the food in the commissary,' she said and smiled.

Fraser laughed. 'I must eat in the commissary one day.'

'I wouldn't if I were you.'

He looked at her. 'Food that bad?'

'It's not the food. It's the girls. They'd mob you.'

'What makes you think so?'

'They talk about you all the time.'

'You mean they ask questions about me?'

'I'll say,' she grinned.

'I imagine when they're through, they must feel frustrated by the lack of information.'

She shook her head. 'Wrong. I make up all kinds of stories about you.'

Fraser was leaning back in his chair, relaxing over a brandy. 'What kind of stories?'

'Are you sure you want to hear?'

'Positive.'

'Well, I tell them that you're an ogre and that you scream at me all day long.'

He grinned. 'Not *all* day long.'

'I tell them that you're a nut about hunting and that you carry a loaded rifle around the office while you dictate and I'm constantly afraid that it'll go off and kill me.'

'That must hold their interest.'

'They're having a fine time trying to figure out the real you.'

'Have you figured out the real me?' Fraser's tone had become serious.

She looked into his bright blue eyes for a moment, then turned away. 'I think so,' she said.

'Who am I?'

Catherine felt a sudden tension within her. The bantering was over and a new note had crept into the conversation. An exciting note, a disturbing note. She did not answer.

Fraser looked at her for a moment, then smiled. 'I'm a dull subject. More dessert?'

'No, thank you. I won't eat again for a week.'

'Let's go to work.'

They worked until midnight. Fraser saw Catherine to the door, and Talmadge was waiting outside to drive her back to the apartment.

She thought about Fraser all the way home. His strength, his humour, his compassion. Someone had once said that a man had to be very strong before he could allow himself to be gentle. William Fraser was very strong. This evening had been one of the nicest evenings of Catherine's life and it worried her. She was afraid that she might turn into one of those jealous secretaries who sits around the office all day hating every girl who telephones her boss. Well, she was not going to allow that to happen. Every eligible female in Washington was throwing herself at Fraser's head. She was not going to join the crowd.

When Catherine returned to the apartment, Susie was waiting up for her. She pounced on Catherine the moment she came in.

'Give!' Susie demanded. 'What happened?'

'Nothing happened,' Catherine replied. 'We had dinner.'

Susie stared at her incredulously. 'Didn't he even make a pass at you?'

'No, of course not.'

Susie sighed. 'I should have known it. He was afraid to.'

'What do you mean by that?'

'What I mean by that, sweetie, is that you come off like the Virgin Mary. He was probably afraid if he laid a finger on you, you'd scream "rape" and faint dead away.'

Catherine felt her cheeks redden. 'I'm not interested in him that way,' she said stiffly. 'And I don't come off like the Virgin Mary.' *I come off like the Virgin Catherine. Dear old Saint Catherine*. All she had done was to move her holy headquarters to Washington. Nothing else had changed. She was still doing business at the same old church.

During the next six months Fraser was away a good deal. He made trips to Chicago and San Francisco and to Europe. There was always enough work to keep Catherine busy, and yet the office seemed lonely and empty with Fraser gone.

There was a constant stream of interesting visitors, most of them men, and Catherine found herself barraged with invitations. She had her choice of lunches, dinners, trips to Europe and bed. She accepted none of the invitations, partly because she was not interested in any of the men but mostly because she felt that Fraser would not approve of her mixing business with pleasure. If Fraser was aware of the constant opportunities she declined, he said nothing. The day after she had had dinner with him at his home he had given her a ten-dollar-a-week raise.

It seemed to Catherine that there was a change in the tempo of the city. People were moving faster, becoming more tense. The headlines screamed of a constant series of invasions and crises in Europe. The fall of France had affected Americans more deeply than the other swift-moving events in Europe, for they felt a sense of personal violation, a loss of liberty in a country that was one of the cradles of Liberty.

Norway had fallen, England was fighting for its life in the battle of Britain and a pact had been signed between Germany, Italy and Japan. There was a growing feeling of inevitability that America was going to get into the war. Catherine asked Fraser about it one day.

'I think it's just a question of time before we get involved,' he said thoughtfully. 'If England can't stop Hitler, we're going to have to.'

'But Senator Borah says . . .'

'The symbol of the America Firsters should be an ostrich,' Fraser commented angrily.

'What will you do if there's a war?'

'Be a hero,' he said.

Catherine visualized him handsome in an officer's uniform going off to war, and she hated the idea. It seemed stupid to her that in this enlightened age people should still think they could solve their differences by murdering one another.

'Don't worry, Catherine,' Fraser said. 'Nothing will happen for a while. And when it does happen, we'll be ready for it.'

'What about England?' she asked. 'If Hitler decides to invade, will it be able to stand up against him? He has so many tanks and planes and they have nothing.'

'They will have,' Fraser assured her. 'Very soon.'

He had changed the subject, and they had gone back to work.

One week later the headlines were filled with the news of Roosevelt's new concept of lend-lease. So Fraser had known about it and had tried to reassure her without revealing any information.

The weeks went by swiftly. Catherine accepted an occasional date, but each time she found herself comparing her escort to William Fraser, and she wondered why she bothered going with anyone. She was aware that she had backed herself into a bad emotional corner, but she did not know how to get out of it. She told herself that she was merely infatuated with Fraser and would get over it, but meanwhile her feelings kept her from enjoying the company of other men because they all fell so far short of him.

Late one evening as Catherine was working, Fraser came back to the office unexpectedly after attending a play. She looked up, startled, as he walked in.

'What in hell are we running here?' he growled. 'A slave ship?'

'I wanted to finish this report,' she said, 'so you could take it with you to San Francisco tomorrow.'

'You could have mailed it to me,' he replied. He sat down in a chair opposite Catherine and studied her. 'Don't you have better things to do with your evenings than get out dull reports?' he asked.

'I happened to be free this evening.'

Fraser leaned back in the chair, folded his fingers together and dropped them under his chin, staring at her. 'Do you remember what you said the first day you walked into this office?'

'I said a lot of silly things.'

'You said you didn't want to be a secretary. You wanted to be my assistant.'

She smiled. 'I didn't know any better.'

'You do now.'

She looked up at him. 'I don't understand.'

'It's very simple, Catherine,' he said quietly. 'For the past three months, you've really been my assistant. Now I'm going to make it official.'

She stared at him, unbelievingly. 'Are you sure that you . . . ?'

'I didn't give you the title or a salary raise sooner because I didn't want it to scare you. But now you know you can do it.'

'I don't know what to say,' Catherine stammered. 'I – you won't be sorry, Mr Fraser.'

'I'm sorry already. My assistants always call me Bill.'

'Bill.'

Later that night as Catherine lay in bed, she remembered how he had looked at her and how it had made her feel, and it was a long time before she was able to go to sleep.

Catherine had written to her father several times asking him when he was coming to Washington to visit her. She was eager to show him around the city and introduce him to her friends and to Bill Fraser. She had received no reply to her last two letters. Worried, she telephoned her uncle's house in Omaha. Her uncle answered the phone.

'Cathy! I – I was just about to call you.'

Catherine's heart sank.

'How's father?'

There was a brief pause.

'He's had a stroke. I wanted to call you sooner but your father asked me to wait until he was better.'

Catherine gripped the receiver.

'Is he better?'

'I'm afraid not, Cathy,' her uncle's voice said. 'He's paralysed.'

'I'm on my way,' Catherine said.

She went in to Bill Fraser and told him the news.

'I'm sorry,' Fraser said. 'What can I do to help?'

'I don't know. I want to go to him right away, Bill.'

'Of course.' And he picked up a telephone and began to make calls. His chauffeur drove Catherine to her apartment, where she threw some clothes into a suitcase, and then took her to the airport, where Fraser had arranged a plane reservation for her.

When the plane landed at the Omaha airport, Catherine's aunt and uncle were there to meet her, and one look at their faces told her that she was too late. They drove in silence to the funeral parlour and as Catherine entered the building she was filled with an ineffable sense of loss, of loneliness. A part of her had died and could never be recovered. She was ushered into the small chapel. Her father's body was lying in a simple coffin wearing his best suit. Time had shrunk him, as though the constant abrasion of living had worn him down and made him smaller. Her uncle had handed Catherine her father's personal affects, the accumulations and treasures of a lifetime, and they consisted of fifty dollars in cash, some old snapshots, a few receipted bills, a wristwatch, a tarnished silver penknife and a collection of her letters to him, neatly tied with a piece of string and dog-eared from constant reading. It was a pitiful legacy for any man to have left, and Catherine's heart broke for her father. His dreams were so big and his successes so small. She remembered how alive and vital he had been when she was a little girl and the excitement when he came home from the road with his pockets full of money and his arms full of presents. She remembered his wonderful inventions that never quite worked. It wasn't much to remember, but it was all there was left of him. There were suddenly so many things Catherine wanted to say to him, so much she wanted to do for him; and it would always be too late.

They buried her father in the small graveyard next to the church. Catherine had planned on spending the night with her aunt and uncle and taking the train back the next day, but suddenly she could not bear to stay a moment longer, and she called the airport and made a reservation on the next plane to Washington. Bill Fraser was at the airport to meet her, and it seemed the most natural thing in the world for him to be there, waiting for her, taking care of her when she needed him.

He took Catherine to an old country inn in Virginia for dinner, and he listened while she talked about her father. In the middle of telling a funny story about him, Catherine began to cry, but strangely she felt no embarrassment in front of Bill Fraser.

He suggested that Catherine take some time off, but she wanted to keep busy, wanted to keep her mind filled with anything but the death of her father. She slipped into the habit of having dinner with Fraser once or twice a week, and Catherine felt closer to him than ever before.

It happened without any planning or forethought. They had been working late at the office. Catherine was checking some papers and sensed Bill Fraser standing in back of her. His fingers touched her neck, slowly and caressingly.

'Catherine . . .'

She turned to look up at him and an instant later she was in his arms. It was as though they had kissed a thousand times before, as though this was her past as well as her future, where she had always belonged.

It's this simple, Catherine thought. *It's always been this simple, but I didn't know it.*

'Get your coat, darling,' Bill Fraser said. 'We're going home.'

In the car driving to Georgetown they sat close together, Fraser's arm around Catherine, gentle and protective. She had never known such happiness. She was sure she was in love with him, and it did not matter if he was not in love with her. He was fond of her, and she would settle for that. When she thought of what she had been willing to settle for before – Ron Peterson – she shuddered.

'Anything wrong?' Fraser asked.

Catherine thought of the motel room with the dirty cracked mirror. She looked at the strong intelligent face of the man with his arm around her. 'Not now,' she said gratefully. She swallowed. 'I have to tell you something. I'm a virgin.'

Fraser smiled and shook his head in wonder. 'It's incredible,' he said. 'How did I wind up with the only virgin in the city of Washington?'

'I tried to correct it,' Catherine said earnestly, 'but it just didn't work out.'

'I'm glad it didn't,' Fraser said.

'You mean you don't mind?'

He was smiling at her again, a teasing grin that lit up his face. 'Do you know your problem?' he asked.

'I'll say!'

'You've been worrying too much about it.'

'I'll say!'

'The trick is to relax.'

She shook her head gently.

'No, darling. The trick is to be in love.'

Half an hour later the car pulled up in front of his house. Fraser led Catherine inside to the library.

'Would you like a drink?'

She looked at him. 'Let's go upstairs.'

He took her in his arms and kissed her hard. She held him fiercely, wanting to draw him into her. *If anything goes wrong tonight*, Catherine thought, *I'll kill myself. I really will kill myself.*

'Come on,' he said. He took Catherine's hand.

Bill Fraser's bedroom was a large masculine-looking room with a Spanish highboy against one wall. At the far end of the room was an alcove with a fireplace and in front of it, a breakfast table. Against one wall was a large double bed. To the left was a dressing room and off that, a bathroom.

'Are you sure you wouldn't care for that drink?' Fraser asked.

'I don't need it.'

He took her in his arms again and kissed her. She felt the male hardness of him, and a delicious warmth coursed through her body.

'I'll be back,' he said.

Catherine watched him disappear into the dressing room. This was the nicest, most wonderful man she had ever known. She stood there thinking about him, then suddenly realized why he had left the room. He wanted to give her a chance to undress alone, so that she would not be embarrassed. Quickly Catherine began taking off her clothes. She stood there a minute later nude and looked down at her body and thought, *Goodbye, Saint Catherine*. She went over to the bed, pulled back the spread and crawled between the sheets.

Fraser walked in, wearing a cranberry moiré silk dressing gown. He came over to the bed and stared at her. Her black hair was fanned out against the white pillow, framing her beautiful face. It was all the more stirring because he knew that it was totally unplanned.

He slipped the robe off and moved into the bed beside her. She suddenly remembered.

'I'm not wearing anything,' Catherine said. 'Do you think I'll get pregnant?'

'Let's hope so.'

She looked at him, puzzled, and opened her mouth to ask him what he meant, but he put his lips on hers and his hands began to move down her body, gently exploring, and she forgot everything except what was happening to her, her whole consciousness concentrated on one part of her body, feeling him try to enter her, hard and pulsing, forcing, an instant of sharp, unexpected pain, then sliding in, moving faster and faster, an alien body in her body, plunging deep inside her, moving with a rhythm that grew more and more frantic, and he said, 'Are you ready?' She was not sure what she was supposed to be ready for, but she said, 'Yes,' and suddenly he cried, 'Oh, Cathy!' and made one last sporadic thrust and lay still on top of her.

And it was all over, and he was saying, 'Was it wonderful for you?' and she said, 'Yes, it was wonderful,' and he said, 'It gets better as it goes along,' and she was filled with joy that she was able to bring him this happiness, and she tried not to worry about what a disappointment it had been. Perhaps it was like olives. You had to acquire a taste for it. She lay in his arms, letting the sound of his voice wash over her, comforting her, and she thought *This is what is important, being together as two human beings, loving and sharing each other*. She had read too many lurid novels, heard too many promising love songs. She had been expecting too much. Or perhaps – and if this were true, she must face it – she was frigid. As though reading her thoughts, Fraser pulled her closer and said, 'Don't worry if you're disappointed, darling. The first time is always traumatic.'

When Catherine did not answer, Fraser raised

himself up on an elbow and looked at her, concerned, and said, 'How do you feel?'

'Fine,' she said quickly. She smiled. 'You're the best lover I ever had.'

She kissed him and held him close, feeling warm and safe until finally the hard knot inside her began to dissolve, and a feeling of relaxation filled her, and she was content.

'Would you like a brandy?' he asked.

'No, thanks.'

'I think I'll fix myself one. It isn't every night a man beds a virgin.'

'Did you mind that?' she asked.

He looked at her with that strange, knowing look, started to say something and changed his mind. 'No,' he said. There was a note in his voice that she did not understand.

'Was I –?' she swallowed. 'You know – all right?'

'You were lovely,' he said.

'Truth?'

'Truth.'

'Do you know why I almost didn't go to bed with you?' she asked.

'Why?'

'I was afraid that you wouldn't want to see me again.'

He laughed aloud. 'That's an old wives' tale fostered by nervous mothers who want to keep their daughters pure. Sex doesn't drive people apart, Catherine. It brings them closer together.' And it was true. She had never felt so close to anyone.

Outwardly she might look the same, but Catherine knew that she had changed.

The young girl who had come to this house earlier in the evening had vanished forever and in her place was a woman. William Fraser's woman. She had finally found the mysterious Holy Grail that she had been searching for. The quest was over.

Now even the FBI would be satisfied.

SIX

Noelle

Paris: 1941

To some the Paris of 1941 was a cornucopia of riches and opportunity; to others it was a living hell. Gestapo had become a word of dread, and tales of their activities became a chief – if whispered – topic of conversation. The offences against the French Jews, which had begun as almost a prankish breaking of a few shop windows, had been organized by the efficient Gestapo into a system of confiscation, segregation and extermination.

On May 29, a new ordinance had been issued. '. . . a six-pointed star with the dimensions of the palm of a hand and a black edge. It is to be made of yellow cloth and bear in black lettering the inscription JUDEN. It must be worn from the age of six visibly on the left side of the chest solidly sewn to the clothing.'

Not all Frenchmen were willing to be stepped

on by the German boot. The Maquis, the French underground resistance, fought cleverly and hard and when caught were put to death in ingenious ways.

A young Countess whose family owned a chateau outside Chartres was forced to quarter the officers of the local German Command in her downstairs rooms for six months, during which time she had five wanted members of the Maquis hidden on the upper floors of the chateau.

The two groups never met, but in three months the Countess' hair had turned completely white.

The Germans lived as befit the status of conquerors, but for the average Frenchman there was a shortage of everything except cold and misery. Cooking gas was rationed, and there was no heat. Parisians survived the winters by buying sawdust by the ton, storing it in one-half of their apartments and keeping the other half warm by means of special sawdust-burning stoves.

Everything was ersatz, from cigarettes and coffee to leather. The French joked that it did not matter what you ate; the taste was all the same. The French women – traditionally the most smartly dressed women in the world – wore shabby coats of sheepskin instead of wool and platform shoes of wood, so that the sound of women walking the streets of Paris resembled the clip-clop of horses' hooves.

Even baptisms were affected, for there was a shortage of sugar almonds, the traditional sweet for the baptismal ceremony, and candy shops displayed invitations to come in and register for sugar almonds. There were a few Renault taxis on the street, but the most popular form of transportation was the two-seater cabs with tandem bikes.

The theatre, as always in times of prolonged crisis, flourished. People found escape from the crushing realities of everyday life in the movie houses and on the stages.

Overnight, Noelle Page had become a star. Jealous associates in the theatre said that it was due solely to the power and talent of Armand Gautier, and while it was true that Gautier had launched her career, it is axiomatic among those who work in the theatre that no one can make a star except the public, that faceless, fickle, adoring, mercurial arbiter of a performer's destiny. The public adored Noelle.

As for Armand Gautier, he bitterly regretted the part he had played in starting Noelle's career. Her need of him was now gone; all that held her to him was a whim, and he lived in constant dread of the day she would leave him. Gautier had worked in the theatre most of his life, but he had never met anyone like Noelle. She was an insatiable sponge, learning everything he had to teach her and demanding more. It had been fantastic to watch the metamorphosis in her as she went from the halting, external beginnings of grasping a part to the self-assured inner mastery of the character. Gautier had known from the very beginning that Noelle was going to be a star – there was never any question about it – but what astonished him as he learned to know her better was that stardom was not her goal. The truth was that Noelle was not even interested in acting.

At first, Gautier simply could not believe it. Being a star was the top of the ladder, the *sine qua non*. But to Noelle acting was simply a stepping stone, and Gautier had not the faintest clue as to what her real goal was. She was a mystery, an enigma, and the deeper Gautier probed, the more the riddle grew, like the Chinese boxes that opened and revealed further boxes inside. Gautier prided himself on understanding people, particularly women, and the fact that he knew absolutely nothing about the woman he lived with and loved drove him frantic. He asked Noelle to marry him, and she said, 'Yes, Armand,' and he knew that she meant nothing by it, that it meant no more to her than her engagement to Philippe Sorel or God alone knew how many other men in her past life. He realized that the marriage would never take place. When Noelle was ready, she would move on.

Gautier was sure that every man who met her tried to persuade her to go to bed with him. He also knew from his envious friends that none of them had succeeded.

'You lucky son of a bitch,' one of his friends had said. 'You must be hung like *un taureau*. I offered her a yacht, her own chateau and a staff of servants in Cap d'Antibes, and she laughed at me.'

Another friend, a banker, told him, 'I have finally found the first thing money cannot buy.'

'Noelle?'

The banker nodded. 'That's right. I told her to name her price. She was not interested. What is it you have for her, my friend?'

Armand Gautier wished he knew.

Gautier remembered when he had found the first play for her. He had read no more than a dozen pages when he knew it was exactly what he was looking for. It was a tour de force, a drama about a woman whose husband had gone to war. A soldier appeared at her home one day telling her that he was a comrade of her husband with whom he had served on the Russian Front. As the play developed, the woman fell in love with the soldier, unaware that he was a psychopathic killer and that her life was in danger. It was a great acting role for the wife, and Gautier agreed to direct it immediately, on condition that Noelle Page play the lead. The backers were reluctant to star an unknown but agreed to have her audition for them. Gautier hurried home to bring the news to Noelle. She had come to him because she wanted to be a star and now he was going to give her her wish. He told himself this would bring them closer together, would make her really love him. They would get married and he would possess her, always.

But when Gautier had told her the news, Noelle

had merely looked up at him and said, 'That is wonderful, Armand, thank you.' In exactly the same tone of voice in which she might have thanked him for telling her the correct time or lighting her cigarette.

Gautier watched her for a long moment, knowing that in some strange way Noelle was sick, that some emotion in her had either died, or had never been alive and that no one would ever possess her. He knew this and yet he could not really believe it, because what he saw was a beautiful, affectionate girl who happily catered to his every whim and asked for nothing in return. Because he loved her, Gautier put his doubts aside, and they went to work on the play.

Noelle was brilliant at the audition and got the part without question, as Gautier had known she would. When the play opened in Paris two months later, Noelle became, overnight, the biggest star in France. The critics had been prepared to attack the play and Noelle because they were aware that Gautier had put his mistress, an inexperienced actress, in the lead, and it was a situation too delicious for them to pass up. But she had completely captivated them. They searched for new superlatives to describe her performance and her beauty. The play was a complete sellout.

Every night after the performance, Noelle's dressing room was filled with visitors. She saw everyone: shoe clerks, soldiers, millionaires, shop girls, treating them all with the same patient courtesy. Gautier would watch in amazement. *It is almost as though she were a Princess receiving her subjects, he thought.*

Over a period of a year Noelle received three letters from Marseille. She tore them up, unopened, and finally they stopped coming.

In the spring, Noelle starred in a motion picture that Armand Gautier directed, and when it was released, her fame spread. Gautier marvelled at Noelle's patience in giving interviews and being photographed. Most stars hated it and did it either to help increase their box office value or for reasons of ego. In Noelle's case, she was indifferent to both motivations. She would change the subject when Gautier questioned her about why she was willing to pass up a chance to rest in the South of France in order to stay in a cold, rainy Paris to do tiresome poses for *Le Matin, La Petite Parisienne* or *L'Illustration*. It was just as well, for Gautier would have been stunned if he had known her real reason. Noelle's motivation was very simple.

Everything she did was for Larry Douglas.

When Noelle posed for photographs, she visualized her former lover picking up a magazine and recognizing her picture. When she played a scene in a movie, she saw Larry Douglas sitting in a theatre one night in some far-off country, watching her. Her work was a reminder to him, a message from the past, a signal that would one day bring him back to her; and that was all Noelle wanted, for him to come back to her, so that she could destroy him.

Thanks to Christian Barbet, Noelle had an ever-growing scrapbook on Larry Douglas. The little detective had moved from his shabby offices to a large, luxurious suite on the rue Richer, near the Folies-Bergère. The first time Noelle had gone to see him in his new offices, Barbet had grinned at her surprised expression and said, 'I got it cheap. These offices were occupied by a Jew.'

'You said you had some news for me,' Noelle said curtly.

The smirk left Barbet's face, 'Ah yes.' He did have news. It was difficult getting information from England under the very nose of the Nazis, but Barbet had found ways. He bribed sailors on neutral ships to smuggle in letters from an agency in London. But that was only one of his sources. He appealed to the patriotism of the French underground, the humanity of the International Red Cross and the cupidity of black marketeers with overseas connections. To each of them he told a different story, and the flow of information kept coming in.

He picked up a report on his desk. 'Your friend was shot down over the English Channel,' he said without preamble. Out of the corner of his eye he watched Noelle's face, waiting for her aloof facade to crumble, taking enjoyment in the pain he was inflicting. But Noelle's expression never changed. She looked at him and said confidently, 'He was rescued.' Barbet stared at her and swallowed and answered reluctantly, 'Well, yes. He was picked up by a British Rescue boat.' And wondered how the devil she could have known.

Everything about this woman baffled him, and he hated her as a client and was tempted to drop her, but Barbet knew that that would have been stupid.

He had attempted once to make a pass at her, hinting that his services would be less expensive, but Noelle had rebuffed him in a manner that made him feel like a clumsy lout, and he would never forgive her for that. One day, Barbet promised himself quietly, one day this tight-assed bitch would pay.

Now, as Noelle stood in his office, a look of distaste on her beautiful face, Barbet hurriedly went on with the report, eager to get rid of her.

'His squadron has moved to Kirton, in Lincolnshire. They're flying Hurricanes and –' Noelle was interested in something else.

'His engagement to the Admiral's daughter,' she said, 'it's off, isn't it?'

Barbet looked up in surprise and mumbled, 'Yes. She found out about some of his other women.' It was almost as though Noelle had already seen the report. She had not, of course, but it did not matter. The bond of hatred that tied Noelle to Larry Douglas was so strong it seemed that nothing important could ever happen to him without her knowing it. Noelle took the report and left. When she returned home she read it over slowly, then carefully filed it among the other reports and locked it up where it could not be found.

One Friday night after a performance, Noelle was

in her dressing room at the theatre creaming off her makeup when there was a knock at the door, and Marius, the elderly, crippled stage doorman, entered.

'Pardon, Miss Page, a gentleman asked me to bring these to you.'

Noelle glanced up in the mirror and saw that he was carrying an enormous bouquet of red roses in an exquisite vase.

'Set it down there, Marius,' Noelle said, and she watched as he carefully placed the vase of roses on a table.

It was late November and no one in Paris had seen roses for more than three months. There must have been four dozen of them, ruby red, long-stemmed, wet with dew. Curious, Noelle walked over and picked up the card. It read: 'To the lovely Fräulein Page. Would you have supper with me? General Hans Scheider.'

The vase that the flowers rested in was delft, intricately patterned and very expensive. General Scheider had gone to a great deal of trouble.

'He would like an answer,' the stage doorman said.

'Tell him I never eat supper and take these home to your wife.'

He stared at her in surprise. 'But the General . . .'

'That is all.'

Marius nodded his head, picked up the vase and hurried out. Noelle knew that he would rush to spread the story of how she had defied a German general. It had happened before with other German officials, and the French people regarded her as some kind of heroine. It was ridiculous. The truth of the matter was that Noelle had nothing against the Nazis, she was merely indifferent to them. They were not a part of her life or her plans, and she simply tolerated them, awaiting the day when they would return home. She knew that if she became involved with any Germans it would hurt her. Not now, perhaps, but it was not the present Noelle was concerned about; it was the future. She thought that the idea of the Third Reich ruling for one thousand years was *merde*. Any student of history knew that eventually all conquerors were conquered. In the meantime she would do nothing that would allow her fellow Frenchmen to turn on her when the Germans were finally ousted. She was totally untouched by the Nazi occupation and when the subject came up – as it constantly did – Noelle avoided any discussion about it.

Fascinated by her attitude, Armand Gautier often tried to draw her out on the subject.

'Don't you care that the Nazis have conquered France?' he would ask her.

'Would it matter if I cared?'

'That's not the point. If everyone felt as you do, we would be damned.'

'We are damned anyway, are we not?'

'Not if we believe in free will. Do you think our life is ordained from the time we are born?'

'To some degree. We are given bodies, our

birthplace and our station in life, but that does not mean that we cannot change. We can become anything we want to be.'

'My point exactly. That is why we must fight the Nazis.'

She looked at him. 'Because God is on our side?'

'Yes,' he replied.

'If there is a God,' Noelle answered reasonably, 'and He created them, then He must be on their side, also.'

In October, the first anniversary of Noelle's play, the backers gave a party for the cast at Tour d'Argent. There was a mixture of actors, bankers and influential businessmen. The guests were mostly French, but there were a dozen Germans at the party, a few of them in uniform, all of them except one with French girls. The exception was a German officer in his forties, with a long, lean intelligent face, deep green eyes and a trim, athletic body. A narrow scar ran from his cheekbone to his chin. Noelle was aware that he had been watching her all evening although he had not come near her.

'Who is that man?' she casually asked one of the hosts.

He glanced over at the officer who was sitting alone at a table sipping champagne, then turned to Noelle in surprise. 'It is strange you should ask. I thought he was a friend of yours. That is General Hans Scheider. He is on the General Staff.' Noelle remembered the roses and the card. 'Why did you think he was a friend of mine?' she asked.

The man appeared flustered. 'I naturally assumed . . . I mean, every play and motion picture produced in France must be approved by the Germans. When the censor tried to stop your new movie from being made, the General personally stepped in and gave his approval.'

At that moment Armand Gautier brought someone to meet Noelle and the conversation changed.

Noelle paid no further attention to General Scheider.

The next evening when she arrived at her dressing room, there was one rose in a small vase with a little card that said: 'Perhaps we should start smaller. May I see you? Hans Scheider.'

Noelle tore up the note and threw the flower into the wastebasket.

After that night Noelle became aware that at almost every party she and Armand Gautier attended, General Scheider was there. He always remained in the background watching her. It happened too often to be a coincidence. Noelle realized that he must be going to a great deal of trouble to keep track of her movements and to get himself invitations to places where she would be.

She wondered why he was so interested, but it was an idle speculation and it did not really bother her. Occasionally Noelle would amuse herself by accepting an invitation and not showing up, then checking with the hostess the next day to see if

General Scheider had been there. The answer was always 'Yes.'

Despite the swift and lethal punishment meted out by the Nazis to anyone who opposed them, sabotage continued to flourish in Paris. In addition to the Maquis there were dozens of small groups of freedom-loving French who risked their lives to fight the enemy with whatever weapons were at hand. They murdered German soldiers when they could catch them off guard, blew up supply trucks and mined bridges and trains. Their activities were denounced in the controlled daily press as deeds of infamy, but to the loyal French the deeds of infamy were glorious exploits. The name of one man kept cropping up in the newspapers – he was nicknamed *Le Cafard*, the cockroach, because he seemed to scurry around everywhere, and the Gestapo was unable to catch him. No one knew who he was. Some believed that he was an Englishman living in Paris; another theory held that he was an agent of General De Gaulle, the leader of the Free French Forces; and some even said that he was a disaffected German. Whoever he was, drawings of cockroaches were beginning to spring up all over Paris, on buildings, sidewalks, and even inside German Army headquarters. The Gestapo was concentrating its efforts on catching him. Of one fact there was no doubt. *Le Cafard* had become an instant folk hero.

On a rainy afternoon in December, Noelle attended the opening of an art exhibition of a young artist whom she and Armand knew. The exhibit was held in a gallery on the rue du Faubourg-St-Honoré. The room was crowded. Many celebrities were in attendance and photographers were everywhere. As Noelle walked around, moving from painting to painting, she felt someone touch her arm. She turned and found herself looking into the face of Madame Rose. It took Noelle a moment to recognize her. The familiar, ugly face was the same, and yet it seemed twenty years older, as though through some alchemy in time she had become her own mother. She wore a big black cape, and somewhere at the back of Noelle's consciousness was the fleeting thought that she was not wearing the prescribed yellow JUDEN star.

Noelle started to speak, but the older woman stopped her by squeezing her arm.

'Could you meet me?' she asked in a barely audible voice. 'Les Deux Magots.'

Before Noelle could reply, Madame Rose melted into the crowd, and Noelle was surrounded by photographers. As she posed and smiled for them, Noelle was remembering Madame Rose and her nephew, Israel Katz. They had both been kind to her in a time of need. Israel had saved her life twice. Noelle wondered what Madame Rose wanted. Money, probably.

Twenty minutes later Noelle slipped away and took a taxi to the place St Germain des Prés. It had been raining on and off all day, and now the rain had started to turn into a cold, driving sleet.

As her taxi pulled up in front of Les Deux Magots and Noelle stepped out into the biting cold, a man in a raincoat and wide-brimmed hat appeared at her side out of nowhere. It took Noelle a moment to recognize him. Like his aunt, he looked older, but the change went deeper than that. There was an authority, a strength that had not been there before. Israel Katz was thinner than when she had last seen him, and his eyes were hollowed, as though he had not slept in days. Noelle noticed that he was not wearing the yellow six-pointed Jewish star.

'Let's get out of the rain,' Israel Katz said.

He took Noelle's arm and led her inside. There were half a dozen customers in the café, all French. Israel led Noelle to a table in a back corner.

'Would you like something to drink?' he asked.

'No, thank you.'

He took off his rain-soaked hat, and Noelle studied his face. She knew instantly that he had not called her here to ask for money. He was watching her.

'You're still beautiful, Noelle,' he said quietly. 'I've seen all of your movies and plays. You're a great actress.'

'Why didn't you ever come backstage?'

Israel hesitated, then grinned shyly. 'I didn't want to embarrass you.'

Noelle stared at him a moment before she realized what he meant. To her, 'Juden' was just a word that appeared in newspapers from time to time, and it meant nothing in her life; but what must it be like to *live* that word, to be a Jew in a country sworn to wipe you out, exterminate you, particularly when it was your own motherland.

'I choose my own friends,' Noelle replied. 'No one tells me whom to see.'

Israel smiled wryly. 'Don't waste your courage,' he advised. 'Use it where it can help.'

'Tell me about you,' she said.

He shrugged. 'I live a very unglamorous life. I became a surgeon. I studied under Dr Angibouste. Have you heard of him?'

'No.'

'He's a great heart surgeon. He made me his protégé. Then the Nazis took away my licence to practise medicine.' He held up his beautifully sculptured hands and examined them as though they belonged to someone else. 'So I became a carpenter.'

She looked at him for a long moment. 'Is that all?' she asked.

Israel studied her in surprise. 'Of course,' he said. 'Why?'

Noelle dismissed the thought at the back of her mind.

'Nothing. Why did you want to see me?'

He leaned closer to her and lowered his voice. 'I need a favour. A friend –'

At that moment, the door opened and four German soldiers in grey-green uniforms walked into the bistro, led by a corporal. The corporal called out in a loud voice: '*Achtung*! We wish to see your identity papers.'

Israel Katz stiffened, and it was as though a mask fell into place. Noelle saw his right hand slide into the pocket of his overcoat. His eyes flickered towards the narrow passageway that led to an exit in the rear, but one of the soldiers was already moving towards it, blocking it. Israel said in a low urgent voice, 'Get away from me. Walk out the front door. Now.'

'Why?' Noelle demanded.

The Germans were examining the identification papers of some customers at a table near the entrance.

'Don't ask questions,' he commanded. 'Just go.'

Noelle hesitated a moment, then rose to her feet and started towards the door. The soldiers were moving on to the next table. Israel had pushed his chair back to give himself more freedom. The movement attracted the attention of two of the soldiers. They walked over to him.

'Identity papers.'

Somehow Noelle knew that it was Israel the soldiers were looking for and that he was going to try to escape and they would kill him. He had no chance.

She turned and called out to him. 'François! We are going to be late for the theatre. Pay the cheque and let's go.'

The soldiers looked at her in surprise. Noelle started back towards the table.

Corporal Schultz moved to face her. He was a

blond, apple-cheeked boy in his early twenties. 'Are you with this man, Fräulein?' he asked.

'Of course I am! Haven't you anything better to do than pester honest French citizens?' Noelle demanded, angrily.

'I am sorry, my good Fräulein, but . . .'

'I am not your good Fräulein!' Noelle snapped. 'I am Noelle Page. I am starring at the Variétés Theatre, and this man is my costar. Tonight, when I am having supper with my dear friend, General Hans Scheider, I shall inform him of your behaviour this afternoon and he will be furious with you.'

Noelle saw the look of recognition come into the corporal's eyes, but whether it was a recognition of her name or General Scheider's, she could not be sure.

'I – I am sorry, Fräulein,' he stammered. 'Of course I recognize you.' He turned to Israel Katz, who sat there silently, his hand in his coat pocket. 'I do not recognize this gentleman.'

'You would if you barbarians ever went to the theatre,' said Noelle with stinging contempt. 'Are we under arrest or may we leave?'

The young corporal was aware of everyone's eyes on him. He had to make an instant decision. 'Of course the Fräulein and her friend are not under arrest,' he said. 'I apologize if I have inconvenienced you. I –'

Israel Katz looked up at the soldier and said coolly, 'It's raining outside, Corporal. I wonder if one of your men could find us a taxi.'

'Of course. At once.'

Israel got into the taxi with Noelle, and the German corporal stood in the rain watching as they drove away. When the taxi stopped for a traffic light three blocks away, Israel opened the door, squeezed Noelle's hand once and disappeared without a word into the night.

At seven o'clock that evening when Noelle walked into her theatre dressing room, there were two men waiting for her. One of them was the young German corporal from the bistro that afternoon. The other was in mufti. He was an albino, completely hairless, with pink eyes, and he somehow reminded Noelle of an unformed baby. He was in his thirties, with a moon face. His voice was high-pitched and almost laughably feminine, but there was an ineffable quality, a deadliness about him that was chilling. 'Miss Noelle Page?'

'Yes.'

'I am Colonel Kurt Mueller, Gestapo. I believe you have met Corporal Schultz.'

Noelle turned to the corporal, indifferently, 'No, I don't believe I have.'

'At the *kaffehause* this afternoon,' the corporal said helpfully.

Noelle turned to Mueller. 'I meet so many people.'

The colonel nodded. 'It must be difficult to remember everyone when you have so many friends, Fräulein.'

She nodded. 'Exactly.'

'For example, this friend you were with this afternoon.' He paused, watching Noelle's eyes. 'You told Corporal Schultz that he is starring in the show with you?'

Noelle looked at the Gestapo man in surprise. 'The corporal must have misunderstood me.'

'Nein, Fräulein,' the corporal replied indignantly. 'You said . . .'

The colonel turned to give him a freezing look, and the corporal's mouth snapped closed in mid-sentence.

'Perhaps,' said Kurt Mueller amiably. 'This kind of thing can happen so easily when one is trying to communicate in a foreign language.'

'That is true,' said Noelle quickly.

Out of the corner of her eye she saw the corporal's face redden with anger, but he kept his mouth shut.

'I'm sorry to have troubled you over nothing,' Kurt Mueller said.

Noelle felt her shoulders relax and she suddenly realized how tense she had been.

'That's perfectly all right,' she said. 'Perhaps I can give you tickets for the play.'

'I have seen it,' the Gestapo man said, 'and Corporal Schultz has already bought his ticket. But thank you.'

He started towards the door, then paused. 'When you called Corporal Schultz a barbarian, he decided to buy a ticket this evening to see your performance. When he looked at the actors' photographs in the lobby, he did not see the picture of your friend from the *kaffehause*. That is when he called me.'

Noelle's heart began to beat faster.

'Just for the record, Mademoiselle. If he was not your costar, who was he?'

'A – a friend.'

'His name?' The high-pitched voice was still soft, but it had become dangerous.

'What difference does it make?' Noelle asked.

'Your friend answers the description of a criminal we are looking for. He was reported seen in the vicinity of the place St Germain des Prés this afternoon.'

Noelle stood watching him, her mind racing.

'What is the name of your friend?' Colonel Mueller's voice was insistent.

'I – I don't know.'

'Ah, then he was a stranger?'

'Yes.'

He stared at her, his cold pink eyes drilling into hers. 'You were sitting with him. You stopped the soldiers from looking at his papers. Why?'

'I felt sorry for him,' Noelle said. 'He came up to me . . .'

'Where?'

Noelle thought quickly. Someone could have seen them going into the bistro together. 'Outside the café. He told me that the soldiers were looking for him because he had stolen some groceries for his wife and children. It seemed such a minor crime that I . . .' She looked up at Mueller appealingly, 'I helped him.'

Mueller studied her a moment and nodded his head admiringly. 'I can understand why you are such a big star.' The smile died from his face, and when he spoke again his voice was even softer. 'Let me give you some advice, Mademoiselle Page. We wish to be on good terms with you French. We want you to be our friends as well as our allies. But anyone who helps our enemy becomes our enemy. We will catch your friend, Mademoiselle, and when we do, we will question him, and I promise you he will talk.'

'I have nothing to be afraid of,' Noelle said.

'You are wrong.' She could barely hear him. 'You have me to be afraid of.' Colonel Mueller nodded to the corporal and started towards the door again. He turned once more. 'If you hear from your friend, you will report it to me at once. If you fail to do so . . .' He smiled at her. And the two men were gone.

Noelle sank into a chair, drained. She was aware that she had not been convincing, but she had been caught completely off guard. She had been so sure that the incident had been forgotten. She remembered now some of the stories she had heard about the Gestapo, and a small chill went through her. Supposing they caught Israel Katz and he did talk. He could tell them that they were old friends, that Noelle had lied about not knowing him. But surely that could not be important. Unless . . . the name she had thought of in the restaurant popped into her mind again. *Le Cafard.*

Half an hour later when Noelle went on stage, she managed to put everything out of her mind but the character she was playing. It was an appreciative audience and as she took her curtain calls, she received a tremendous ovation. She could still hear the applause as she walked back to her dressing room and opened the door. Seated in a chair was General Hans Scheider. He rose to his feet as Noelle entered and said politely, 'I was informed that we have a supper date this evening.'

They had supper at Le Fruit Perdu along the Seine, about twenty miles outside of Paris. They had been driven there by the General's chauffeur in a shiny, black limousine. The rain had stopped, and the night was cool and pleasant. The General had made no reference to the day's incident until they had finished eating. Noelle's first impulse had been not to go with him, but she decided that it was necessary to learn how much the Germans really knew and how much trouble she might be in.

'I received a call from Gestapo headquarters this afternoon,' General Scheider was saying. 'They informed me that you had told a Corporal Schultz that you were having supper with me this evening.' Noelle watched him, saying nothing. He went on. 'I decided that it would be most unpleasant for you if I said "No," and most pleasant for me if I said "Yes."' He smiled. 'So here we are.'

'This is all so ridiculous,' Noelle protested. 'Helping a poor man who stole some groc –'

'Don't!' The General's voice was sharp. Noelle looked at him in surprise. 'Don't make the mistake of believing that all Germans are fools. And do not underestimate the Gestapo.'

Noelle said, 'They have nothing to do with me, General.'

He toyed with the stem of his wine glass. 'Colonel Mueller suspects you of having helped a man he wants very badly. If that is true, you are in a great deal of trouble. Colonel Mueller neither forgives nor forgets.' He looked at Noelle. 'On the other hand,' he said carefully, 'if you should not see your friend again, this whole thing could simply blow over. Would you like a cognac?'

'Please,' Noelle said.

He ordered two Napoleon brandies. 'How long have you been living with Armand Gautier?'

'I am sure you know the answer to that,' Noelle replied.

General Scheider smiled. 'As a matter of fact, I do. What I really wanted to ask you is why you refused to have dinner with me before. Was it because of Gautier?'

Noelle shook her head. 'No.'

'I see,' he said stiffly. There was a note in his voice that surprised her.

'Paris is full of women,' Noelle said. 'I am sure you could have your pick.'

'You don't know me,' the General said quietly,

'or you wouldn't have said that.' He sounded embarrassed. 'I have a wife and child in Berlin. I love them very much, but I have been away from them for more than a year now, and I have no idea when I will see them again.'

'Who forced you to come to Paris?' Noelle asked cruelly.

'I was not making a bid for sympathy. I just wanted to explain myself a little. I am not a promiscuous man. The first time I saw you on the stage,' he said, 'something happened to me. I felt I wanted to know you very much. I would like us to be good friends.'

There was a quiet dignity about the way he spoke.

'I can promise nothing,' Noelle said.

He nodded. 'I understand.'

But of course he did not. Because Noelle intended never to see him again. General Scheider tactfully changed the conversation and they talked of acting and the theatre, and Noelle found him surprisingly knowledgeable. He had an eclectic mind and a deep intelligence. Casually he ranged from topic to topic, pointing out the mutual interests that the two of them shared. It was a skillful performance and Noelle was amused. He had gone to a great deal of trouble to learn about her background. He looked every inch the German General in his olive-green uniform, strong and authoritative, but there was a gentleness that bespoke another kind of man altogether, an intellectual quality that belonged to the scholar rather than the soldier. And yet there was the scar running across his face.

'How did you get your scar?' Noelle asked.

He ran his finger along the deep incision. 'I was in a duel many years ago,' he shrugged. 'In German, we call this *wild-fleisch* – it means "proud skin."'

They discussed the Nazi philosophy.

'We are not monsters,' General Scheider stated. 'And we have no wish to rule the world. But neither do we intend to sit still and be punished any longer for a war we lost more than twenty years ago. The Treaty of Versailles is a bondage that the German people have finally broken out of.'

They spoke of the occupation of Paris. 'It was not the fault of your French soldiers that it was so easy for us,' General Scheider said. 'A good deal of the responsibility must fall on the shoulders of Napoleon the Third.'

'You're joking.' Noelle replied.

'I am perfectly serious,' he assured her. 'In the days of Napoleon, the mobs were constantly using the tangled, twisted streets of Paris for barricades and ambushes against his soldiers. In order to stop them, he commissioned Baron Eugene Georges Haussmann to straighten out the streets and fill the city with nice, wide boulevards.' He smiled. 'The boulevards down which our troops marched. I am afraid history will not be kind to planner Haussmann.'

After dinner, driving back to Paris, he asked, 'Are you in love with Armand Gautier?'

His tone was casual, but Noelle had the feeling that her answer was important to him.

'No,' she said slowly.

He nodded, satisfied. 'I did not think so. I believe I could make you very happy.'

'As happy as you make your wife?'

General Scheider stiffened for a moment as though he had been struck and then turned to look at Noelle.

'I can be a good friend,' he said quietly. 'Let us hope that you and I are never enemies.'

When Noelle returned to the apartment, it was almost 3:00 A.M., and Armand Gautier was waiting for her in a state of agitation.

'Where the hell have you been?' he demanded, as she walked in the door.

'I had an engagement.' Noelle's eyes moved past him into the room. It looked as though a cyclone had struck. Desk drawers were open and the contents strewn around the room. The closets had been ransacked, a lamp had been overturned and a small table lay on its side, one leg broken.

'What happened?' Noelle asked.

'The Gestapo was here! My God, Noelle, what have you been up to?'

'Nothing.'

'Then why would they do this?'

Noelle began to move around the room, straightening the furniture, thinking hard. Gautier grabbed her shoulders and turned her around. 'I want to know what's happening.'

She took a deep breath. 'All right.'

She told him of the meeting with Israel Katz, leaving out his name and the conversation later with Colonel Mueller. 'I don't know that my friend is *Le Cafard*, but it is possible.'

Gautier sank into a chair, stunned. 'My God!' he exclaimed. 'I don't care *who* he is! I don't want you to have anything more to do with him. We could both be destroyed because of this. I hate the Germans as much as you do . . .' He stopped, not sure whether Noelle hated the Germans or not. He began again, 'Cherie, as long as the Germans are making the rules, we must live under them, Neither of us can afford to get involved with the Gestapo. This Jew – what did you say his name was?'

'I didn't say.'

He looked at her a moment. 'Was he your lover?'

'No, Armand.'

'Does he mean anything to you?'

'No.'

'Well, then.' Gautier sounded relieved. 'I don't think we have anything to worry about. They can't blame you if you had one accidental meeting with him. If you don't see him again, they'll forget the whole thing.'

'Of course they will,' Noelle said.

On the way to the theatre the next evening, Noelle was followed by two Gestapo men.

From that day on Noelle was followed everywhere she went. It first began as a feeling, a premonition that she was being stared at. Noelle would turn and see in a crowd a young Teutonic-looking man in civilian clothes who seemed to be paying no attention to her. Later, the feeling would return, and this time it would be another young Teutonic-looking man. It was always someone different and though they were in plain clothes, they wore a uniform that was distinctively theirs: an attitude of contempt, superiority and cruelty, and the emanations were unmistakable.

Noelle said nothing to Gautier about what was happening for she saw no point in alarming him any further. The incident with the Gestapo in the apartment had made him very nervous. He could talk of nothing but what the Germans could do to both his and Noelle's career if they wished to, and Noelle was aware that he was right. One had only to look at the daily newspapers to know that the Nazis showed no mercy to their enemies. There had been several telephone messages from General Scheider, but Noelle had ignored them. If she did not want the Nazis as an enemy, neither did she want them as a friend. She decided that she would remain like Switzerland: neutral. The Israel Katzes of the world would have to take care of themselves. Noelle was mildly curious about what he had wanted from her, but she had no intention of getting involved.

Two weeks after Noelle had seen Israel Katz, the newspapers carried a front-page story that the Gestapo had caught a group of saboteurs headed by

Le Cafard. Noelle read all the stories carefully, but nothing was mentioned about whether *Le Cafard* himself had been captured. She remembered Israel Katz' face when the Germans had started to close in on him, and she knew that he would never let them take him alive. *Of course*, Noelle told herself, *it could be my fantasy. He is probably a harmless carpenter, as he said*. But if he was harmless, why was the Gestapo so interested in him? Was he *Le Cafard*? And had he been captured, or had he escaped? Noelle walked over to the window of her apartment that faced on the Avenue Martigny. Two black rain-coated figures stood under a streetlamp, waiting. For what? Noelle began to feel the sense of alarm that Gautier felt, but with it came a feeling of anger. She remembered Colonel Mueller's words: *You have me to be afraid of*. It was a challenge. Noelle had the feeling she was going to hear from Israel Katz again.

The message came the next morning from – of all the unlikely people – her concierge. He was a small, rheumy-eyed man in his seventies, with a wizened, leathery face and no lower teeth, so that it was difficult to understand him when he spoke. When Noelle rang for the elevator he was waiting inside. They rode down together, and as they neared the lobby, he mumbled, 'The birthday cake you ordered is ready at the bakery at rue de Passy.'

Noelle stared at him a moment, not sure whether she had heard him correctly, then said, 'I didn't order any cake.'

'Rue de Passy,' he repeated stubbornly.

And Noelle suddenly understood. Even then, she would have done nothing about it if she had not seen the two Gestapo agents waiting for her across the street. To be followed around like a criminal! The two men were in conversation. They had not seen her yet. Angrily Noelle turned to the concierge and said, 'Where is the service entrance?'

'This way, Mam'selle.'

Noelle followed him through a back corridor, down a flight of stairs to the basement and out to an alley. Three minutes later she was in a taxi, on her way to meet Israel Katz.

The bakery was an ordinary-looking shop in a run-down, middle-class neighbourhood. The lettering on the window read *B O U L A N G E R I E*, and the letters were flaked and chipped. Noelle opened the door and stepped inside. She was greeted by a small dumpling of a woman in a spotless white apron.

'Yes, Mademoiselle?'

Noelle hesitated. There was still time to leave, still time to turn back and not get involved in something dangerous that was none of her business.

The woman was waiting.

'You – you have a birthday cake for me,' Noelle said, feeling foolish at the game-playing, as though somehow the gravity of what was happening was demeaned by the childish artifices that were employed.

The woman nodded. 'It is ready, Miss Page.' She

put a *CLOSED* sign on the door, locked it and said, 'This way.'

He was lying on a cot in the small back room of the bakery, his face a mask of pain, bathed in perspiration. The sheet twisted around him was soaked in blood, and there was a large tourniquet around his left knee.

'Israel.'

He moved to face the door, and the sheet fell away, revealing a sodden pulp of mashed bone and flesh where his knee had been.

'What happened?' Noelle asked.

He tried to smile but did not quite make it. His voice was hoarse and strained with pain. 'They stepped on *Le Cafard*, but we're not easy to kill.'

So she had been correct. 'I read about it,' Noelle said. 'Are you going to be all right?'

Israel took a deep painful breath and nodded. His words came in laboured gasps.

'The Gestapo is turning Paris upside down looking for me. My only chance is to get out of the city. . . . If I can get to Le Havre, I have friends who will help me get on a boat out of the country.'

'Can't you get a friend to drive you out of Paris?' Noelle asked. 'You could hide in the back of a truck –'

Israel shook his head weakly. 'Road blocks. Not a mouse can get out of Paris.'

Not even *un Cafard*, Noelle thought. 'Can you travel with that leg?' she asked, stalling for time, trying to come to a decision.

His lips tightened in the rictus of a smile.

'I'm not going to travel with this leg,' Israel said.

Noelle looked at him, not understanding, and at that moment the door opened and a large, heavy-shouldered, bearded man entered. In his hand he carried an axe. He walked up to the bed and pulled back the sheet, and Noelle felt the blood drain from her face. She thought of General Scheider and the hairless albino from the Gestapo and what they would do to her if they caught her.

'I will help you,' Noelle said.

SEVEN

Catherine

Washington–Hollywood: 1941

It seemed to Catherine Alexander that her life had entered a new phase, as though somehow she had climbed to some higher emotional level, a heady and exhilarating peak. When Bill Fraser was in town, they had dinner together every night and went to concerts or the theatre or the opera. He found a small, charming apartment for her near Arlington. He wanted to pay her rent, but Catherine insisted on paying it herself. He bought her clothes and jewellery. She had resisted at first, embarrassed by some deeply ingrained Protestant ethic, but it had given Fraser such obvious pleasure that finally Catherine had stopped arguing about it.

Whether you like it or not, she thought, *you're a mistress*. It had always been a loaded word for her, filled with connotations of cheap, slinky women in back-street apartments, living out lives of emotional frustration. But now that it was happening to her, Catherine found that it was not really like that at all. It just meant that she was sleeping with the man she loved. It did not feel dirty or sordid, it felt perfectly natural. *It's interesting*, she thought, *how the things that other people do seem so horrible, and yet when you're doing them they seem so right. When you are reading about the sexual experiences of someone else, it's* True Confessions, *but when it's you it's the* Ladies' Home Journal.

Fraser was a thoughtful and understanding companion, and it was as though they had been together always. Catherine could predict his reactions to almost any situation and knew his every mood. Contrary to what Fraser had said, sex with him did not become more exciting, but Catherine told herself that sex was only a small part of a relationship. She was not a schoolgirl who needed constant titillation, she was a mature woman. *Give or take a little*, she thought, wryly.

Fraser's advertising agency was being run in his absence by Wallace Turner, a senior account executive. William Fraser tried to have as little to do with the business as possible, so he could devote himself to his job in Washington, but whenever a major problem arose at the agency and they needed his advice, Fraser got in the habit of discussing it with Catherine, using her as a sounding board. He found that she had a natural flair for the business. Catherine often came up with ideas for campaigns that proved very affective.

'If I weren't so selfish, Catherine,' Fraser said

one night at dinner, 'I'd put you in the agency and turn you loose on some of our accounts.' He covered her hand with his. 'I'd miss you too much,' he added. 'I want you here with me.'

'I want to be here, Bill. I'm very happy with things the way they are.' And it was true. She had thought that if she were ever in a situation like this, she would want desperately to get married, but somehow there seemed no urgency about it. In every important way they were already married.

One afternoon as Catherine was finishing some work, Fraser walked into her office.

'How would you like to take a drive out to the country tonight?' he asked.

'Love it. Where are we going?'

'To Virginia. We're having dinner with my parents.'

Catherine looked up at him in surprise. 'Do they know about us?' she asked.

'Not everything,' he grinned. 'Just that I have a fantastic young assistant and I'm bringing her to dinner.'

If she felt a pang of disappointment, she did not let it show on her face. 'Fine,' she said. 'I'll stop by the apartment and change.'

'I'll pick you up at seven o'clock.'

'Date.'

The Frasers' house, set in the beautiful rolling hills of Virginia, was a large Colonial farmhouse with sixty acres of vivid green grass and farmland surrounding it. The house dated back to seventeen hundred.

'I've never seen anything like it,' Catherine marvelled.

'It's one of the best breeding farms in America,' Fraser informed her.

The car drove past a corral filled with beautiful horses, past the neatly kept paddocks and the caretaker's cottage.

'It's like another world,' Catherine exclaimed. 'I envy your growing up here.'

'Do you think you'd like living on a farm?'

'This isn't exactly a farm,' she said dryly. 'It's more like owning your own country.'

They had arrived in front of the house.

Fraser turned to her. 'My mother and father are a little formal,' he warned, 'but there's nothing for you to worry about. Just be yourself. Nervous?'

'No,' Catherine said. 'Panicky.' And as she said it, she realized with a sense of astonishment that she was lying. In the classic tradition of all girls about to meet the parents of the man they loved, she should have been petrified. But she felt nothing except curiosity. There was no time to wonder about that now. They were getting out of the car and a butler in full livery was opening the door, greeting them with a welcoming smile.

Colonel Fraser and his lady could have been living out of the pages of an ante-bellum story book. The first thing that struck Catherine was how old and fragile-looking they were. Colonel

Fraser was a pale carbon of what had once been a handsome, vital man. He reminded Catherine very strongly of someone, and with a shock, she realized who it was: an old, worn-out version of his son. The colonel had sparse white hair and walked with a painful stoop. His eyes were pale blue and his once-powerful hands were gnarled with arthritis. His wife had the look of an aristocrat and still retained traces of a girlish beauty. She was gracious and warm to Catherine.

In spite of what Fraser had told her, Catherine had the feeling that she was there for their inspection. The colonel and his wife spent the evening questioning her. They were very discreet but thorough. Catherine told them about her parents and her childhood, and when she talked about moving from school to school, she made it sound like adventurous fun, rather than the agony it had been. As she talked she could see Bill Fraser proudly beaming at her. Dinner was superb. They dined by candlelight in a large, old-fashioned dining room with a real marble fireplace and liveried servants. *Old silver, old money and old wine.* She looked at Bill Fraser and a wave of warm gratitude went through her. She had the feeling that this kind of life could be hers if she wanted it. She knew that Fraser loved her, and she loved him. And yet there was something missing: a sense of excitement. *Possibly*, she thought, *I'm expecting too much. I've probably been warped* by *Gary Cooper, Humphrey Bogart and Spencer Tracy! Love isn't a knight in shining armour. It's a gentleman farmer in a grey tweed suit. Damn all those movies and books*! As she looked at the colonel, she could see Fraser twenty years hence, looking exactly the same as his father. She was very quiet during the rest of the evening.

On the way home Fraser asked, 'Did you enjoy the evening?'

'Very much. I liked your parents.'

'They liked you, too.'

'I'm glad.' And she was. Except for the vaguely disquieting thought in the back of her mind that somehow she should have been more nervous about meeting them.

The following evening, while Catherine and Fraser were having dinner at the Jockey Club, Fraser told her that he had to go to London for a week. 'While I'm gone,' he said, 'I have an interesting job for you. They've asked our office to supervise an Army Air Corps recruiting film they're shooting at MGM studios in Hollywood. I'd like you to handle the picture while I'm gone.'

Catherine stared at him incredulously. 'Me? I can't even load a Brownie. What do I know about making a training film?'

'About as much as anyone else,' Fraser grinned. 'It's all pretty new, but you don't have to worry. They'll have a producer and everything. The Army plans to use actors in the film.'

'Why?'

'I guess they feel that soldiers won't be convincing enough to play soldiers.'

'That sounds like the Army.'

'I had a long talk with General Mathews this afternoon. He must have used the word "glamour" a hundred times. That's what they want to sell. They're starting a big recruitment drive aimed at the elite young manhood of America. This is one of the opening guns.'

'What do I have to do?' Catherine asked.

'Just see that everything runs smoothly. You'll have final approval. You have a reservation to Los Angeles on a nine A.M. plane tomorrow.'

Catherine nodded. 'All right.'

'Will you miss me?'

'You know I will,' she replied.

'I'll bring you a present.'

'I don't want any presents. Just come back safely.' She hesitated. 'The situation's getting worse, isn't it, Bill?'

He nodded. 'Yes,' he said. 'I think we're going to be at war soon.'

'How horrible.'

'It's going to be even more horrible if we *don't* get into it,' he said quietly. 'England got out of Dunkirk by a miracle. If Hitler decides to cross the Channel now, I don't think the British can stop him.' They finished their coffee in silence, and he paid the cheque.

'Would you like to come to the house and spend the night?' Fraser asked.

'Not tonight,' Catherine said. 'You have to get up early, and so do I.'

'All right.'

After he had dropped her off at her apartment and she was getting ready for bed, Catherine asked herself why she had not gone home with Bill on the eve of his departure.

She had no answer.

Catherine had grown up in Hollywood even though she had never been there. She had spent hundreds of hours in darkened theatres, lost in the magic dreams manufactured by the film capital of the world, and she would always be grateful for the joy of those happy hours.

When Catherine's plane landed at the Burbank airport, she was filled with excitement. A limousine was waiting to drive her to her hotel. As they drove down the sunny, broad streets, the first thing Catherine noticed was the palm trees. She had read about them and had seen pictures of them, but the reality was overwhelming. They were everywhere, stretching tall against the sky, the lower part of their graceful trunks bare and the upper part beautiful and verdant. In the centre of each tree was a ragged circle of fronds, like a dirty petticoat, Catherine thought, hanging unevenly below a green tutu.

They drove by a huge building that looked like a factory. A large sign over the entrance said 'Warner Bros.' and under it, 'Combining Good Pictures with Good Citizenship.' As the car went past the gate, Catherine thought of James Cagney in *Yankee*

Doodle Dandy, and Bette Davis in *Dark Victory* and smiled happily.

They passed the Hollywood Bowl, which looked enormous from the outside, turned off Highland Avenue and went west on Hollywood Boulevard. They passed the Egyptian Theatre and two blocks to the west, Grauman's Chinese, and Catherine's spirits soared. It was like seeing two old friends. The driver swung down Sunset Boulevard and headed for the Beverly Hills Hotel. 'You'll enjoy this hotel, miss. It's one of the best in the world.'

It was certainly one of the most beautiful that Catherine had ever seen. It was just north of Sunset, in a semicircle of sheltering palm trees surrounded by large gardens. A graceful driveway curved up to the front door of the hotel, painted a delicate pink. An eager young assistant manager escorted Catherine to her room, which turned out to be a lavish bungalow on the grounds behind the main building of the hotel. There was a bouquet of flowers on the table with the compliments of the management and a larger, more beautiful bouquet with a card that read: 'Wish I were there or you were here. Love, Bill.' The assistant manager had handed Catherine three telephone messages. They were all from Allan Benjamin, whom she had been told was the producer of the training film. As Catherine was reading Bill's card, the phonc rang. She ran to it, picked up the receiver and said eagerly, 'Bill?' But it turned out to be Allan Benjamin.

'Welcome to California, Miss Alexander,' his

voice shrilled through the receiver. 'Corporal Allan Benjamin, producer of this little clambake.'

A corporal. She would have thought that they would have put a captain or a colonel in charge.

'We start shooting tomorrow. Did they tell you that we're using actors instead of soldiers?'

'I heard,' Catherine replied.

'We start shooting at nine in the morning. If you could get here by about eight, I'd like to have you take a look at them. You know what the Army Air Corps wants.'

'Right,' said Catherine briskly. She had not the faintest idea what the Army Air Corps wanted, but she supposed that if one used common sense and picked out types that looked like they might be pilots, that would be sufficient.

'I'll have a car there for you at seven thirty A. M.,' the voice was saying. 'It'll only take you half an hour to get to Metro. It's in Culver City. I'll meet you on Stage Thirteen.'

It was almost four o'clock in the morning before Catherine fell asleep, and it seemed the moment her eyes closed, the phone was ringing and the operator was telling her that a limousine was waiting for her.

Thirty minutes later Catherine was on her way to Metro-Goldwyn-Mayer.

It was the largest motion picture studio in the world. There was a main lot consisting of thirty-two sound stages, the enormous Thalberg Administration Building which housed Louis B. Mayer, twenty-five executives, and some of the most famous directors, producers and writers in show business. Lot two contained the large standing outdoor sets which were constantly re-dressed for various movies. Within a space of three minutes, you could drive past the Swiss Alps, a western town, a tenement block in Manhattan and a beach in Hawaii. Lot three on the far side of Washington Boulevard housed millions of dollars' worth of props and flat sets and was used to shoot outdoor spectacles.

All this was explained to Catherine by her guide, a young girl who was assigned to take her to Stage 13. 'It's a city in itself,' she was saying proudly. 'We produce our own electricity, make enough food in the commissary to feed six thousand people a day and build all our own sets right on the back lot. We're completely self-sufficient. We don't need anybody.'

'Except an audience.'

As they walked along the street, they passed a castle that consisted of a facade with two by four's propping it up. Across from it was a lake, and down the block was the lobby of a San Francisco theatre. No theatre, just the lobby.

Catherine laughed aloud, and the girl stared at her.

'Is there anything wrong?' she asked.

'No,' Catherine said. 'Everything is wonderful.'

Dozens of extras walked along the street, cowboys and Indians chatting amiably together as they walked towards the sound stages. A man appeared unexpectedly from around a corner and as Catherine stepped back to avoid him, she saw that he was a knight in armour. Behind him walked a group of girls in bathing suits. Catherine decided that she was going to like her brief fling in show business. She wished her father could have seen this. He would have enjoyed it so much.

'Here we are,' the guide said. They were in front of a huge, grey building. A sign on the side of it said 'STAGE 13.'

'I'll leave you here. Will you be all right?'

'Fine,' Catherine said. 'Thank you.'

The guide nodded and left. Catherine turned back to the sound stage. A sign over the door read: 'DO NOT ENTER WHEN RED LIGHT IS ON.' The light was off, so Catherine pulled the handle of the door and opened it. Or tried to. The door was unexpectedly heavy, and it took all her strength to get it open.

When she stepped inside, Catherine found herself confronted by a second door as heavy and massive as the first. It was like entering a decompression chamber.

Inside the cavernous sound stage, dozens of people were racing around, each one busy on some mysterious errand. A group of men were in Air Corps uniforms, and Catherine realized that they were the actors who would appear in the film. At a far corner of the sound stage was an office set complete with desk, chairs and a large military map hanging on the wall. Technicians were lighting the set.

'Excuse me,' she said to a man passing by. 'Is Mister Allan Benjamin here?'

'The little corporal?' He pointed. 'Over there.'

Catherine turned and saw a slight, frail-looking man in an ill-fitting uniform with corporal's stripes. He was screaming at a man wearing a general's stars.

'Fuck what the casting director said,' he yelled. 'I'm up to my ass in generals. I need non-coms.' He raised his hands in despair. 'Everybody wants to be a chief, nobody wants to be an Indian.'

'Excuse me,' said Catherine, 'I'm Catherine Alexander.'

'Thank God!' the little man said. He turned to the others, bitterness in his voice. 'The fun and games are over, you smart-asses. Washington's here.'

Catherine blinked. Before she could speak, the little corporal said, 'I don't know what I'm doing here. I had a thirty-five-hundred-dollar-a-year job in Dearborn editing a furniture trade magazine, and I was draughted into the Signal Corps and sent to write training films. What do I know about producing or directing? This is the most disorganized mess I've ever seen.' He belched and touched his stomach. 'I'm getting an ulcer,' he moaned, 'and I'm not even in show business. Excuse me.'

He turned and hurried towards the exit, leaving Catherine standing there. She looked around, helplessly. Everyone seemed to be staring at her, waiting for her to do something.

A lean, grey-haired man in a sweater moved

towards her, an amused smile on his face. 'Need any help?' he asked quietly.

'I need a miracle,' Catherine said frankly. 'I'm in charge of this, and I don't know what I'm supposed to be doing.'

He grinned at her. 'Welcome to Hollywood. I'm Tom O'Brien, the A.D.'

She looked at him, quizzically.

'The assistant director. Your friend, the corporal, was supposed to direct it, but I have a feeling he won't be back.' There was a calm assurance about the man which Catherine liked.

'How long have you worked at Metro-Goldwyn-Mayer?' she asked.

'Twenty-five years.'

'Do you think you could direct this?'

She saw the corner of his lips twist. 'I could try,' he said gravely. 'I've done six pictures with Willie Wyler.' His eyes grew serious. 'The situation isn't as bad as it looks,' he said. 'All it needs is a little organization. The script's written, and the set's ready.'

'That's a beginning,' Catherine said. She looked around the sound stage at the uniforms. Most of them were badly fitted, and the men wearing them looked ill at ease.

'They look like recruiting ads for the Navy,' Catherine commented.

O'Brien laughed appreciatively.

'Where did these uniforms come from?'

'Western Costume. Our Wardrobe Department

ran out. We're shooting three war pictures.'

Catherine studied the men critically. 'There are only half a dozen that are really bad,' she decided. 'Let's send them back and see if we can't do better.'

O'Brien nodded approvingly. 'Right.'

Catherine and O'Brien walked over to the group of extras. The din of conversation on the enormous stage was deafening.

'Let's hold it down, boys,' O'Brien yelled. 'This is Miss Alexander. She's going to be in charge here.'

There were a few appreciative whistles and cat calls.

'Thanks,' Catherine smiled. 'Most of you look fine, but a few of you are going to have to go back to Western Costume and get different uniforms. Let's line up, so we can take a good look at you.'

'I'd like to take a good look at *you*. What are you doing for dinner tonight?' one of the men called.

'I'm having it with my husband,' Catherine said, 'right after his match.'

O'Brien formed the men into a ragged line. Catherine heard laughter and voices nearby and turned in annoyance. One of the extras was standing next to a piece of scenery, talking to three girls who were hanging on his every word and giggling hysterically at everything he said. Catherine watched a moment, then walked over to the man and said, 'Excuse me. Would you mind joining the rest of us?'

The man turned slowly. 'Are you talking to me?' he asked lazily.

'Yes,' Catherine said. 'We'd like to go to work.' She walked away.

He whispered something to the girls which drew a loud laugh, then slowly moved after Catherine. He was a tall man, his body lean and hard-looking, and he was very handsome, with blue-black hair and stormy dark eyes. His voice, when he spoke, was deep and filled with insolent amusement. 'What can I do for you?' he asked Catherine.

'Do you want to work?' Catherine replied.

'I do, I do,' he assured her.

Catherine had once read an article about extras. They were a strange breed of people, spending their anonymous lives on sound stages, lending background atmosphere to crowd scenes in which stars appeared. They were faceless, voiceless people, inherently too ambitionless to seek any kind of meaningful employment. The man in front of her was a perfect example. Because he was outrageously handsome, someone from his hometown had probably told him that he could be a star, and he had come to Hollywood, learned that talent was necessary as well as good looks and had settled for being an extra. The easy way out.

'We're going to have to change some of the uniforms,' Catherine said patiently.

'Is there anything wrong with mine?' he asked.

Catherine took a closer look at his uniform. She

had to admit that it fitted perfectly, emphasizing his broad shoulders but not exaggerating them, tapering in at his lean waist. She looked at his tunic. On his shoulders were the bars of a captain. Across his breast he had pinned on a splash of brightly coloured ribbons.

'Are they impressive enough, Boss?' he asked.

'Who told you you were going to play a captain?'

He looked at her, seriously, 'It was my idea. Don't you think I'd make a good captain?'

Catherine shook her head. 'No. I don't.'

He pursed his lips thoughtfully. 'First lieutenant?'

'No.'

'How about second lieutenant?'

'I don't really feel you're officer material.'

His dark eyes were regarding her quizzically. 'Oh? Anything else wrong?' he asked.

'Yes,' she said. 'The medals. You must be terribly brave.'

He laughed. 'I thought I'd give this damned film a little colour.'

'There's only one thing you forgot,' Catherine said crisply. 'We're not at war yet. You'd have had to win those at a carnival.'

The man grinned at her. 'You're right,' he admitted sheepishly. 'I didn't think of that. I'll take some of them off.'

'Take them all off,' Catherine said.

He gave her that slow, insolent grin again. 'Right, Boss.'

She almost snapped, 'Stop calling me boss,' but

thought, *the hell with him*, and turned on her heel to talk to O'Brien.

Catherine sent eight of the men back to change their uniforms and spent the next hour discussing the scene with O'Brien. The little corporal had come back briefly and then had disappeared. It was just as well, Catherine thought. All he did was complain and make everyone nervous. O'Brien finished shooting the first scene before lunch, and Catherine felt it had not gone too badly. Only one incident had marred her morning. Catherine had given the infuriating extra several lines to read in order to humiliate him. She had wanted to show him up on the set, to pay him back for his impertinence. He had read his lines perfectly, carrying off the scene with aplomb. When he had finished, he had turned to her and said, 'Was that all right, Boss?'

When the company broke for lunch, Catherine walked over to the enormous studio commissary and sat at a small table in the corner. At a large table next to her was a group of soldiers in uniform. Catherine was facing the door, when she saw the extra walk in, the three girls hanging on him, each one pushing to get closer to him. Catherine felt the blood rush to her face. She decided it was merely a chemical reaction. There were some people you hated on sight, just as there were others you liked on sight. Something about his overbearing arrogance rubbed her the wrong way. He would have made a perfect gigolo and that was probably exactly what he was.

He seated the girls at a table, looked up and saw Catherine, then leaned over and said something to the girls. They all looked at her and then there was a burst of laughter. Damn him! She watched as he moved towards her table. He stared down at her, that slow, knowing smile on his face. 'Mind if I join you a moment?' he asked.

'I –' but he was already seated, studying her, his eyes probing and amused.

'What is it you want?' Catherine asked stiffly.

His grin widened. 'Do you really want to know?'

Her lips tightened with anger. 'Listen –'

'I wanted to ask you,' he said quickly, 'how I did this morning.' He leaned forwards earnestly. 'Was I convincing?'

'You may be convincing to them,' Catherine said, nodding towards the girls, 'but if you want my opinion, I think you're a phony.'

'Have I done something to offend you?'

'Everything you do offends me,' she said evenly. 'I don't happen to like your type.'

'What is my type?'

'You're a fake. You enjoy wearing that uniform and strutting around the girls, but have you thought about enlisting?'

He stared at her incredulously. 'And get shot at?' he asked. 'That's for suckers.' He leaned forwards and grinned. 'This is a lot more fun.'

Catherine's lips were quivering with anger. 'Aren't you eligible for the draught?'

'I suppose technically I'm eligible, but a friend

of mine knows a guy in Washington and' – he lowered his voice – 'I don't think they'll ever get me.'

'I think you're contemptible,' Catherine exploded.

'Why?'

'If you don't know why, I could never explain it to you.'

'Why don't you try? At dinner tonight. Your place. Do you cook?'

Catherine rose to her feet, her cheeks flushed with anger. 'Don't bother coming back to the set,' she said. 'I'll tell Mr O'Brien to send you your cheque for this morning's work.'

She turned to go, then remembered and asked, 'What's your name?'

'Douglas,' he said. 'Larry Douglas.'

Fraser telephoned Catherine from London the next night to find out how things had gone. She reported to him the day's happenings but made no mention of the incident with Larry Douglas. When Fraser returned to Washington, she would tell him about it, and they would laugh over it together.

Early the next morning as Catherine was getting dressed to go to the studio, the doorbell rang. She opened the bungalow door and a delivery boy stood there holding a large bouquet of roses.

'Catherine Alexander?' he asked.

'Yes.'

'Sign here please.'

She signed the form that he handed her.

'They're lovely,' she said, taking the flowers.

'That'll be fifteen dollars.'

'I beg your pardon?'

'Fifteen dollars. They're C.O.D.'

'I don't under –' her lips tightened. Catherine reached for the card attached to the flowers and pulled it out of the envelope. The card read: 'I would have paid for these myself, but I'm not working. Love, Larry.'

She stared at the card unbelievingly.

'Well, do you want 'em or not?' asked the delivery boy.

'Not,' she snapped. She thrust the flowers back in his arms.

He looked at her, puzzled. 'He said you'd laugh. That it was kind of a private joke.'

'I'm not laughing,' Catherine said. She slammed the door furiously.

All that day, the incident kept rankling her. She had met egotistical men but never anyone with the outrageous conceit of Mr Larry Douglas. She was sure that he had had an endless succession of victories with empty-headed blondes and bosomy brunettes who couldn't wait to fling themselves into his bed. But for him to put her in that category made Catherine feel cheap and humiliated. The mere thought of him made her flesh crawl. She determined to put him out of her mind.

At seven o'clock that evening Catherine started to leave the stage. An assistant came up to her, an envelope in his hand.

'Did you charge this, Miss Alexander?' he asked. It was a charge slip from central casting and it read:

One uniform (captain)
Six service ribbons (assorted)
Six medals (assorted)
Actor's Name: Lawrence Douglas . . . (Personal Charge to Catherine Alexander-MGM).

Catherine looked up, her face flushed.

'No!' she said.

He stared. 'What shall I tell them?'

'Tell them I'll pay for his medals if they're awarded posthumously.'

The picture finished shooting three days later. Catherine looked at the rough-cut the following day and approved it. The film would not win any awards, but it was simple and affective. Tom O'Brien had done a good job.

On Saturday morning Catherine boarded a plane for Washington. She had never been so glad to leave a city. Monday morning she was back in her office trying to catch up on the work that had piled up during her absence.

Just before lunch, her secretary, Annie, buzzed her. 'A Mr Larry Douglas is on the phone from Hollywood, California, collect. Do you want to take the call?'

'No,' she snapped. 'Tell him that I – never mind, I'll tell him myself.' She took a deep breath and pressed the phone button. 'Mr Douglas?'

'Good morning.' His voice had the consistency of hot fudge. 'I had a hard time tracking you down. Don't you like roses?'

'Mr Douglas –' Catherine began. Her voice quavered with fury. She took a deep breath and said, 'Mr Douglas, I love roses. I don't like you. I don't like anything about you. Is that clear?'

'You don't know anything about me.'

'I know more than I want to know. I think you're cowardly and despicable, and I don't want you ever to call me again.' Trembling, she slammed down the receiver, her eyes filled with tears of anger. How dare he! She would be so glad when Bill returned.

Three days later Catherine received a ten by twelve photograph of Lawrence Douglas in the mail. It was inscribed, 'To the boss, with love from Larry.'

Annie stared at it in awe, and said, 'My God! Is he real?'

'Fake,' retorted Catherine. 'The only real thing is the paper it's printed on.' She savagely tore the picture to shreds.

Annie watched, dismayed. 'What a waste. I've never seen one like that in the flesh.'

'In Hollywood,' Catherine said grimly, 'they have sets that are all front – no foundation. You've just seen one.'

During the next two weeks, Larry Douglas phoned at least a dozen times. Catherine instructed Annie to tell him not to call again and not to bother telling her about his calls. One morning while Annie was taking dictation, she looked up and said apologetically, 'I know you told me not to bother you with Mr Douglas' calls, but he called again, and he sounded so desperate and well . . . kind of lost.'

'He *is* lost,' Catherine said coldly, 'and if you're smart, you won't try to find him.'

'He sure sounds charming.'

'He invented treacle.'

'He asked a lot of questions about you.' She saw Catherine's look. 'But, of course,' she added hastily, 'I didn't tell him anything.'

'That was very bright of you, Annie.'

Catherine began to dictate again, but her mind was not on it. She supposed the world was full of Larry Douglases. It made her appreciate William Fraser all the more.

Bill Fraser returned the following Sunday morning, and Catherine went to the airport to meet him. She watched as he finished with Customs and came towards the exit where she was standing. His face lit up when he saw her.

'Cathy,' he said. 'What a lovely surprise. I didn't expect you to meet me.'

'I couldn't wait,' she smiled and gave him a warm hug that made him look at her quizzically.

'You've missed me,' he said.

'More than you know.'

'How was Hollywood?' he asked. 'Did it go well?'

She hesitated. 'Fine. They're very pleased with the picture.'

'So I hear.'

'Bill, next time you go away,' she said, 'take me with you.'

He looked at her, pleased and touched.

'It's a deal,' Fraser said. 'I missed you. I've been doing a lot of thinking about you.'

'Have you?'

'Do you love me?'

'Very much, Mr Fraser.'

'I love you, too,' he said. 'Why don't we go out tonight and celebrate?'

She smiled. 'Wonderful.'

'We'll have dinner at the Jefferson Club.'

She dropped Fraser at his house.

'I have a few thousand calls to make,' he said. 'Could you meet me at the club? Eight o'clock.'

'Fine,' she said.

Catherine went back to her apartment and did some washing and ironing. Each time she passed the telephone, she half-expected it to ring, but it remained silent. She thought of Larry Douglas trying to pump Annie for information about her and she found that she was gritting her teeth. Maybe she would speak to Fraser about turning Douglas' name in to his draught board. *No, I won't bother*, she thought. *They'd probably turn him down. He'd be tried and found wanton*. She washed her hair, took a long luxurious bath and was drying herself when the phone rang. She tensed, went over to it and picked it up. 'Yes?' she said coldly.

It was Fraser. 'Hi,' he said. 'Anything wrong?'

'Of course not, Bill,' she said quickly. 'I – I was just in the bath.'

'I'm sorry.' His voice took on a teasing tone. 'I mean I'm sorry I'm not there with you.'

'So am I,' she replied.

'I called to tell you I miss you. Don't be late.'

Catherine smiled. 'I won't.'

She hung up, slowly, thinking about Bill. For the first time she felt that he was ready to propose. He was going to ask her to become Mrs William Fraser. She said the name aloud. 'Mrs William Fraser.' It had a nice dignified sound to it. *My God*, she thought. *I'm becoming blasé. Six months ago, I would have been jumping out of my skin, and now all I can say is it has a nice dignified sound to it.* Had she really changed that much? It was not a comforting thought. She looked at the clock and hurriedly began to dress.

The Jefferson Club was on 'F' Street, a discreet brick building set back from the street and surrounded by a wrought-iron fence. It was one of the most exclusive clubs in a city full of exclusive clubs. The easiest way to become a member was to have a father who belonged. If one lacked that foresight, then it was necessary to be recommended by three members. Membership proposals were brought up once a year and one blackball was sufficient to keep a person out of the Jefferson Club for the rest of his life, since it was a firm rule that no candidate could ever be proposed twice.

William Fraser's father had been a founding member of the club, and Fraser and Catherine had dinner there at least once a week. The chef had been with the French branch of the Rothschilds for twenty years, the cuisine was superb, and the wine cellar ranked as the third best in America. The club had been decorated by one of the world's leading decorators and careful attention had been paid to the colours and the lighting, so the women were bathed in candlelight glow that enhanced their beauty. On any given night, diners would brush elbows with the Vice-President, members of the Cabinet or Supreme Court, senators and the powerful industrialists who controlled worldwide empires.

Fraser was in the foyer waiting for Catherine when she arrived.

'Am I late?' she asked.

'It wouldn't matter if you were,' Fraser said, looking at her with open admiration. 'Do you know you're fantastically beautiful?'

'Of course,' she replied. 'Everybody knows I'm the fantastically beautiful Catherine Alexander.'

'I mean it, Cathy.' His tone was so serious that she was embarrassed.

'Thank you, Bill,' she said awkwardly. 'And stop staring at me like that.'

'I can't help it,' he said. He took her arm.

Louis, the maître d', led them to a corner booth. 'There you are, Miss Alexander, Mr Fraser, enjoy your dinner.'

Catherine liked being known by name by the maître d' of the Jefferson Club. She knew that it was childish and naïve of her, but it gave her a feeling of being somebody, of belonging. Now she sat back, relaxed and contented, surveying the room.

'Will you have a drink?' Fraser asked.

'No, thank you,' Catherine said.

He shook his head. 'I've got to teach you some bad habits.'

'You already have,' Catherine murmured.

He grinned at her and ordered a scotch and soda.

She studied him, thinking what a dear, sweet man he was. She was sure that she could make him very happy. And she would be happy married to him. *Very happy*, she told herself fiercely. Ask anybody. Ask *Time* magazine. She hated herself for the way her mind was working. What in God's name was wrong with her? 'Bill,' she began – and froze.

Larry Douglas was walking towards them, a smile of recognition on his lips as he saw Catherine. He was wearing his Army Air Corps uniform from Central Casting. She watched unbelievingly as he came over to their table, grinning happily. 'Hello there,' he said. But he was not speaking to Catherine. He was speaking to Bill, who was getting up and shaking his hand.

'It's great to see you, Larry.'

'It's good to see you, Bill.'

Catherine stared at the two of them, her mind paralysed, refusing to function.

Fraser was saying, 'Cathy, this is Captain Lawrence Douglas. Larry, this is Miss Alexander – Catherine.'

Larry Douglas was looking down at her, his dark eyes mocking her. 'I can't tell you what a pleasure this is, Miss Alexander,' he said solemnly.

Catherine opened her mouth to speak, but she suddenly realized there was nothing that she could say. Fraser was watching her, waiting for her to speak. All she could manage was a nod. She did not trust her voice.

'Will you join us, Larry?' Fraser asked.

Larry looked at Catherine and said modestly, 'If you're sure I'm not intruding –'

'Certainly not. Sit down.'

Larry took a seat next to Catherine.

'What would you like to drink?' Fraser asked.

'Scotch and soda,' Larry replied.

'I'll have the same,' Catherine said recklessly. 'Make it a double.'

Fraser looked at her in surprise. 'I can't believe it.'

'You said you wanted to teach me some bad habits,' Catherine said. 'I think I'd like to start now.'

When Fraser had ordered the drinks, he turned to Larry and said, 'I've been hearing about some of your exploits from General Terry – both in the air and on the ground.'

Catherine was staring at Larry, her mind spinning, trying to adjust. 'Those medals . . .' she said.

He was looking at her innocently.

'Yes?'

She swallowed. 'Er – where did you get them?'

'I won them in a carnival,' he said gravely.

'Some carnival,' Fraser laughed. 'Larry's been flying with the RAF. He was the leader of the American Squadron over there. They talked him into heading up a fighter base in Washington to get some of our boys ready for combat.'

Catherine turned to stare at Larry. He was smiling at her benevolently, his eyes dancing. Like the rerun of an old movie, Catherine remembered every word of their first meeting. She had ordered him to take off his captain's bars and his medals, and he had cheerfully obliged. She had been smug, overbearing – and she had called him a coward! She wanted to crawl under the table.

'I wish you had let me know you were coming into town,' Fraser was saying. 'I would have trotted out a fatted calf for you. We should have had a big party to celebrate your return.'

'I like this better,' Larry said. He looked over at Catherine, and she turned away, unable to meet his eyes. 'As a matter of fact,' Larry continued innocently, 'I looked for you when I was in Hollywood, Bill. I heard you were producing an Air Corps training film.'

He stopped to light a cigarette and carefully blew out the match. 'I went over to the set, but you weren't there.'

'I had to fly to London,' Fraser replied. 'Catherine was there. I'm surprised you didn't run into each other.'

Catherine looked up at Larry, and he was watching her, his eyes amused. Now was the time to mention what had happened. She would tell Fraser, and they would all laugh it off as an amusing anecdote. But somehow the words stuck in her throat.

Larry gave her a moment, then said, 'It was a pretty crowded set. I guess we missed each other.'

She hated him for helping her out, for making them fellow conspirators against Fraser.

When the drinks arrived, Catherine downed hers quickly and asked for another. This was going to be the most terrible evening of her life. She could not wait to get out of there, to get away from Larry Douglas.

Fraser asked him about his war experiences, and Larry made them sound easy and amusing. He obviously didn't take anything seriously. He was a lightweight. And yet in all fairness, Catherine reluctantly admitted to herself that a lightweight did not volunteer for the RAF and become a hero fighting against the Luftwaffe. Irrationally, she hated him even more because he was a hero. Her attitude didn't make sense to her, and she brooded about it over her third double scotch. What difference did it make whether he was a hero or a bum? And then she realized that as long as he was a bum, he fitted neatly into a pigeonhole that she could deal with. Through the haze of the liquor she sat back and listened to the two men talk. There was an eager enthusiasm about Larry when he spoke, a vitality that was so palpable it reached across and touched her. He seemed to her now like the most alive man she had ever met. Catherine had a feeling that he held nothing back from life, that he gave himself to everything wholeheartedly and that he mocked those who were afraid to give. Who were afraid, period. Like herself.

She hardly touched her food, and she had no idea what she was eating. She met Larry's eyes, and it was as though he were already her lover, as if they had already been together, belonged together, and she knew it was insane. He was like a cyclone, a force of nature, and any woman who got sucked up in the vortex was going to be destroyed.

Larry was smiling at her. 'I'm afraid we've been excluding Miss Alexander from the conversation,' he said politely. 'I'm sure she's more interesting than the both of us put together.

'You're wrong,' Catherine said thickly. 'I live a very dull life. I work with Bill.' The moment she said it she heard how it sounded and turned red. 'I didn't mean it like that,' she said. 'I meant –'

'I know what you meant,' Larry said helpfully.

And she hated him. He turned to Bill. 'Where did you find her?'

'I got lucky,' Fraser said warmly. 'Very lucky. You're still not married?'

Larry shrugged. 'Who'd have me?'

You bastard, Catherine thought. She looked around the room. Half a dozen women were staring at Larry, some covertly, some openly. He was like a sexual magnet. 'How were the English girls?' Catherine asked recklessly.

'They were fine,' he said, politely. 'Of course, I didn't have much time for that sort of thing. I was busy flying.'

Like hell you didn't, Catherine thought. *I'll bet there wasn't a virgin left standing within a hundred miles of you*. Aloud, she said, 'I feel sorry for those poor girls. Look at all they missed.' Her tone was more biting than she had intended.

Fraser was looking at her, puzzled by her rudeness. 'Cathy,' he said.

'Let's have another drink,' Larry cut in quickly.

'I think perhaps Catherine's had enough,' Fraser replied.

'Thash not so,' Catherine began, and to her horror she realized she was slurring her words. 'I think I want to go home,' she said.

'All right' – Fraser turned to Larry – 'Catherine doesn't drink as a rule,' he said apologetically.

'I imagine she's excited about seeing you again,' Larry said.

Catherine wanted to pick up a glass of water

and throw it at him. She had hated him less when he was a bum. Now she hated him more. And she did not know why.

The next morning Catherine woke up with a hangover that she was convinced would make medical history. She had at least three heads on her shoulders, all of them pounding to the beat of different drummers. Lying still in bed was agony but trying to move was worse. As she lay there fighting nausea, the whole evening flooded back in her memory, and the pain increased. Unreasonably she blamed Larry Douglas for her hangover, for if it had not been for him, she would not have had anything to drink. Painfully Catherine turned her head and looked at the clock beside her bed. She had overslept. She debated whether to stay in bed or call a pulmotor squad. Carefully she pulled herself out of her deathbed and dragged herself into the bathroom. She stumbled into the shower, turned the water on cold and let the icy jets stream against her body. She screamed out loud as the water hit her, but when she came out of the shower, she was feeling better. *Not good*, she thought carefully. *Just better*.

Forty-five minutes later she was at her desk. Her secretary, Annie, came in full of excitement. 'Guess what,' she said.

'Not this morning,' Catherine whispered. 'Just be a good girl and speak softly.'

'Look!' Annie thrust the morning paper at her. 'It's *him*.'

On the front page was a picture of Larry Douglas in uniform, grinning at her insolently. The caption read: 'AMERICAN RAF HERO RETURNS TO WASHINGTON TO HEAD UP NEW FIGHTER UNIT.' A two-column story followed.

'Isn't that exciting?' Annie cried.

'Terribly,' Catherine said. She slammed the paper into the wastebasket. 'Can we get on with our work?'

Annie looked at her, surprised. 'I'm sorry,' she said. 'I – I thought since he was a friend of yours, you'd be interested.'

'He's not a friend,' Catherine corrected her. 'He's more of an enemy.' She saw the look on Annie's face. 'Could we just forget about Mr Douglas?'

'Certainly,' Annie said in a puzzled voice. 'I told him I thought you'd be pleased.'

Catherine stared at her. 'When?'

'When he called this morning. He's called three times.'

Catherine steeled herself to make her voice casual. 'Why didn't you tell me?'

'You asked me not to tell you when he called.' She was watching Catherine, her face filled with confusion.

'Did he leave a number?'

'No.'

'Good.' Catherine thought of his face, of those large, dark teasing eyes. 'Good,' she said again, more firmly. She finished dictating some letters and when Annie had left the room, Catherine went over to the wastebasket and retrieved the newspaper. She read the story about Larry word for word. He was an ace with eight German planes to his credit. He had been shot down twice over the Channel. She buzzed Annie. 'If Mr Douglas calls again, I'll talk to him.'

There was only a fractional pause. 'Yes, Miss Alexander.'

After all, there was no point in being rude to the man. Catherine would simply apologize for her behaviour at the studio and ask him to stop calling her. She was going to marry William Fraser.

She waited for another call from him all afternoon. He had not called by six o'clock. *Why should he*? Catherine asked herself. *He's out laying six other girls. You're lucky. Being involved with him would be like going to a butcher shop. You take your number and wait your turn.*

On the way out she said to Annie, 'If Mr Douglas calls tomorrow, tell him I'm not in.'

Annie did not even blink. 'Yes, Miss Alexander. Good night.'

'Good night.'

Catherine rode down in the elevator, lost in thought. She was sure that Bill Fraser wanted to marry her. The best thing to do would be to tell him that she wanted to get married right away. She would tell him tonight. They would go away for a honeymoon. By the time they got back, Larry Douglas would have left town. Or something.

The elevator door opened at the lobby, and

Larry Douglas was standing there, leaning against the wall. He had taken off his medals and ribbons and was wearing the bars of a second lieutenant. He smiled and walked up to her.

'Is this better?' he asked brightly.

Catherine stared at him, her heart pounding. 'Isn't – isn't wearing the wrong insignia against regulations?'

'I don't know,' he said earnestly. 'I thought you were in charge of all that.'

He stood there looking down at her, and she said in a small voice, 'Don't do this to me. I want you to leave me alone. I belong to Bill.'

'Where's your wedding ring?'

Catherine brushed past him and started towards the street door. When she reached it, he was there ahead of her, holding it open for her.

Outside he took her arm. She felt a shock go through her whole body. There was an electricity that came from him that burned her. 'Cathy –' he began.

'For God's sake,' she said desperately. 'What do you want from me?'

'Everything,' he said quietly. 'I want you.'

'Well, you can't have me,' she wailed. 'Go torture somebody else.' She turned to walk away, and he pulled her back.

'What is that supposed to mean?'

'I don't know,' Catherine said, her eyes filling with tears. 'I don't know what I'm saying. I – I have a hangover. I want to die.'

He grinned sympathetically. 'I have a marvellous cure for hangovers.' He guided her into the garage of the building.

'Where are we going?' she asked in a panic.

'We're getting my car.'

Catherine looked up at him, searching his face for a sign of triumph, but all she saw was his strong, incredibly handsome face filled with warmth and compassion.

The attendant brought up a tan sports convertible with the top down. Larry helped Catherine into the car and slid in behind the wheel. She sat there looking straight ahead, knowing that she was throwing her whole life away and totally unable to stop herself. It was as though all this were happening to someone else. She wanted to tell the silly, lost girl in the car to flee.

'Your place or mine?' Larry asked gently.

She shook her head. 'It doesn't matter,' she said hopelessly.

'We'll go to my place.'

So he was not totally insensitive. Or else he was afraid to compete with the shadow of William Fraser.

She watched him as he deftly tooled the car through the early evening traffic. No, he was not afraid of anything. That was part of his goddamn attraction.

She tried to tell herself that she was free to say no to him, free to walk away. How could she love William Fraser and feel this way about Larry?

‘If it helps any,’ Larry said quietly, ‘I’m as nervous as you are.’

Catherine looked over at him. ‘Thanks,’ she said. He was lying, of course. He probably said that to all his victims as he took them up to his bed to seduce them. But at least he wasn’t gloating about it. What bothered her most was that she was betraying Bill Fraser. He was too dear a man to hurt, and this was going to hurt him very much. Catherine knew that and knew that what she was doing was wrong and senseless, but it was as though she had no will of her own anymore.

They had reached a pleasant residential area with large, shady trees lining the street. Larry pulled the car up in front of an apartment building. ‘We’re home,’ he said quietly.

Catherine knew that this was her final chance to say no, to tell him to keep away from her. She watched silently as Larry came around and opened the door. She got out of the car and walked into his apartment building.

Larry’s apartment had been decorated for a man. It had strong solid colours, and masculine-looking furniture.

As they walked in, Larry took off Catherine’s coat and she shivered.

‘Are you cold?’ he asked.

‘No.’

‘Would you like a drink?’

‘No.’

Gently he took her in his arms, and they kissed.

It was as though her body were being set aflame. Without a word Larry led her into the bedroom. There was a growing urgency as they both silently undressed. She lay on the bed naked, and he moved beside her.

'Larry –' but his lips were on hers, and his hands began to move down her body, gently exploring, and she forgot everything except the pleasure that was happening to her, and her hands began to grope for him. And she felt him hot and hard and pulsating and his fingers were inside her, opening her up gently and lovingly and he was on top of her and in her, and there was an exquisite joy that she had never dreamed possible and then they were together, moving faster and faster in a fantastic rhythm that rocked the room and the world and the universe until there was an explosion that became a delirious ecstasy an unbelievable shattering journey an arriving and departure an ending and a beginning and Catherine lay there spent and numb holding him tightly never wanting to let him go never wanting this feeling to stop. Nothing she had ever read or heard could have prepared her for this. It was unbelievable that another person's body could bring such joy. She lay there at peace: a woman. And she knew that if she never saw him again, she would be grateful to him for the rest of her life.

'Cathy?'

She turned to look at him, slowly and lazily. 'Yes?' Even her voice seemed deeper to her, more mature.

'Could you get your nails out of my back?'

She suddenly realized that she had been digging into his flesh. 'Oh, I'm sorry!' she exclaimed. She started to examine his back, but he caught her hands and pulled her close to him.

'It doesn't matter. Are you happy?'

'Happy?' Her lip trembled and to her horror she began to cry. Great sobs that wrenched her body. He held her in his arms, stroking her soothingly, letting the storm spend itself.

'I'm sorry,' she said. 'I don't know what made me do that.'

'Disappointment?'

Catherine looked at him quickly to protest, then saw that he was teasing her. He took her into his arms and made love to her again. It was even more incredible than before. Afterwards they lay in bed and he talked, but she didn't listen. All she wanted to hear was the sound of his voice, and it didn't matter to her what he said. She knew there would never be anyone for her but this man. And she knew that this man could never belong to any one woman and that she would probably never see him again, that she was just another conquest to him. She was aware that his voice had stopped and that he was watching her.

'You haven't heard a word I said.'

'Sorry,' she said. 'I was daydreaming.'

'I should be hurt,' he said reproachfully. 'You're only interested in me for my body.'

She ran her hands over his lean tanned chest

and stomach. 'I'm no expert,' she said, 'but I think this one will do nicely.' She smiled. 'It *did* nicely.' She wanted to ask him whether he had enjoyed her, but she was afraid to.

'You're beautiful, Cathy.'

She thrilled to his saying it and at the same time resented it. Anything he said to her he had said a thousand times to other women. She wondered how he was going to say goodbye. *Call me sometime?* Or, *I'll call you sometime?* Perhaps he would even want to see her again once or twice before he went on to someone else. Well, she had no one to blame but herself. She had known what she was getting into. *I walked into this with my eyes and my legs wide open. No matter what happens, I must never blame him.*

He slid his arms around her and held her close.

'Do you know you're a very special girl, Cathy?'

Do you know you're a very special girl – Alice, Susan, Margaret, Peggy, Lana.

'I felt it from the first time I saw you. I've never felt this way about anyone before.'

– Janet, Evelyn, Ruth, Georgia, ad infinitum. She buried her head in his chest, not trusting herself to speak, and held him tightly, silently saying good-bye.

'I'm hungry.' Larry said. 'Do you know what I feel like?'

Catherine smiled. 'Yes, I certainly do.'

Larry grinned down at her. 'You know something?' he asked. 'You're a sex maniac.'

She looked up. 'Thank you.'

He led her into the shower and turned it on. He took a shower cap from a hook on the wall and put it on Catherine's head, tucking in her hair. 'Come on,' he said, and pulled her into the piercing jet water. He took a bar of soap and began to wash her body, starting with her neck and working down to her arms and slowly circling her breasts and moving down to her stomach and her thighs. She began to feel an excitement in her groin and she took the soap from him and began to wash him, lathering his chest and stomach and moving down between his legs. His organ began to grow hard in her hand.

He spread her legs and put his male hardness inside her and Catherine was transported again, drowning in a torrent of water that beat against her body, while inside she was filled with the same unbearable joy, until she screamed aloud in sheer happiness.

Afterwards they dressed, got into his car and drove to Maryland, where they found a little restaurant that was still open and they had lobster and champagne.

At five o'clock in the morning, Catherine dialled William Fraser's number at home and stood there listening to the long rings eighty miles away until finally Fraser's sleepy voice came on the phone, and said, 'Hello. . . .'

'Hello, Bill. It's Catherine.'

'Catherine! I've been trying to call you all

evening. Where are you? Are you all right?'

'I'm fine. I'm in Maryland with Larry Douglas. We just got married.'

EIGHT

Noelle

Paris: 1941

Christian Barbet was an unhappy man. The bald little detective sat at his desk, a cigarette between his stained, broken teeth and gloomily contemplated the folder in front of him. The information it contained was going to cost him a client. He had been charging Noelle Page outrageous fees for his services, but it was not only the loss of the income that saddened him: He would miss the client herself. He hated Noelle Page and yet she was the most exciting woman he had ever met. Barbet built lurid fantasies around Noelle in which she always ended up in his power. Now the assignment was about to come to an end, and he would never see her again. He had kept her waiting in the reception office while he tried to figure out a way to handle things so that he could squeeze some additional money out of her to prolong the case. But he reluctantly concluded that there was no way. Barbet sighed, snuffed out his cigarette, walked over to the door and opened it. Noelle was sitting on the black imitation leather couch, and as he studied her, his heart caught in his throat for a moment. It was unfair for any woman to be so beautiful. 'Good afternoon, Mademoiselle,' he said. 'Come in.'

She entered his office moving with the grace of a model. It was good for Barbet to have a name client like Noelle Page, and he was not above dropping her name frequently. It attracted other clients, and Christian Barbet was not a man to lose any sleep over ethics. 'Please sit down,' he said, indicating a chair. 'Can I get you a brandy, an aperitif?'

Part of his fantasy was getting Noelle drunk so that she would beg him to seduce her.

'No,' she replied. 'I came for your report.'

The bitch could have had a last drink with him! 'Yes,' Barbet said. 'As a matter of fact I have several pieces of news.' He reached over to the desk and pretended to study the dossier, which he had already memorized.

'First,' he informed her, 'your friend was promoted to Captain and transferred to the one hundred thirty-third squadron, where he was put in command. The field is at Coltisall, Duxtford, in Cambridgeshire. They flew' – he spoke slowly and deliberately, knowing that she was not interested in the technical part – 'Hurricanes and Spitfire II's and then switched to Mark V's. They then flew –'

'Never mind,' Noelle interrupted impatiently. 'Where is he now?'

Barbet had been waiting for the question. 'In the United States.' He saw the reaction before she could control it, and he took savage satisfaction in it. 'In Washington, D.C.,' he continued.

'On leave?'

Barbet shook his head. 'No. He's been discharged from the RAF. He's a Captain in the United States Army Air Corps.'

He watched Noelle digesting the information, her expression giving no clue to what she was feeling. But Barbet was not finished with her yet. He picked up a newspaper clipping between his stained sausage fingers and handed it to her.

'I think this will interest you,' he said.

He saw Noelle stiffen, and it was almost as though she knew what she was going to see. The clipping was from the New York *Daily News*. The caption read 'War Ace Weds' and above it was a photograph of Larry Douglas and his bride. Noelle looked at it for a long moment, then held out her hand for the rest of the file. Christian Barbet shrugged, and slid all the papers into a manila envelope and handed it to her. As he opened his mouth to make his farewell speech, Noelle Page said, 'If you don't have a correspondent in Washington, get one. I shall expect weekly reports.' And she was gone, leaving Christian Barbet staring after her in a state of complete confusion.

When she returned to her apartment, Noelle

went into the bedroom, locked the door and took the newspaper clippings out of the envelope. She laid them out on the bed before her and studied them. The photograph of Larry was exactly as she remembered him. If anything the image in her mind was clearer than the image in the newspaper, for Larry was more alive in her mind than he was in reality.

There was not a day that went by that Noelle did not relive the past with him. It was as though they had costarred in a play together long ago, and she was able to recapture scenes at will, playing some on certain days and saving others for other days, so that each memory was always alive and fresh.

Noelle turned her attention to Larry's bride. What she saw was a pretty, young, intelligent face with a smile on its lips.

The face of the enemy. A face that would have to be destroyed as Larry was going to be destroyed.

Noelle remained locked up with the photograph the whole afternoon.

Hours later when Armand Gautier pounded on her bedroom door, Noelle told him to go away. He waited outside in the drawing room, apprehensive about what her mood would be, but when Noelle finally emerged, she seemed unusually bright and gay, as though she had had a piece of good news. She offered no explanation to Gautier, and he knew her well enough not to ask for one.

After the theatre that evening she made love to

him with a wild passion that reminded him of their early days together. Later Gautier lay in bed trying to understand the beautiful girl who rested beside him but he did not have a clue.

During the night Noelle Page had a dream about Colonel Mueller. The hairless albino Gestapo officer was torturing her with a branding iron, making burning swastikas in her flesh. He kept asking her questions, but his voice was so soft that Noelle could not hear him, and he kept pressing the hot metal into her, and suddenly it was Larry on the table, screaming with pain. Noelle awoke in a cold sweat, her heart pounding, and turned on the bedside lamp. She lit a cigarette with trembling fingers and tried to calm her nerves. She thought about Israel Katz. His leg had been amputated with an axe, and though she had not seen him since that afternoon at the bakery, she had received word from the concierge that he was alive but weak. It was becoming more and more difficult to hide him, and he was helpless on his own. The search for him had intensified. If he was going to be transported out of Paris, it would have to be done quickly. Noelle had really done nothing for which the Gestapo could arrest her: yet. Was the dream a premonition, a warning not to help Israel Katz? She lay in bed remembering. He had aided her when she had the abortion. He had helped her kill Larry's baby. He had given her money and helped her find a job. Dozens of men had done more important things for her than he had, yet

Noelle felt no debt to them. Each of them, including her father, had wanted something from her, and she had paid in full for everything she had ever received. Israel Katz had never asked her for anything. She had to help him.

Noelle did not underestimate the problem. Colonel Mueller was already suspicious of her. She remembered her dream and shuddered. She must see to it that Mueller was never able to prove anything against her. Israel Katz had to be smuggled out of Paris, but how? Noelle was sure that all exits were closely watched. They would be watching the roads and the river. The Nazis might be *cochons*, but they were efficient *cochons*. It was a challenge and it could be a deadly one, but she was determined to try it. The problem was that there was no one she could turn to for help. The Nazis had reduced Armand Gautier to a quivering gelatin. No, she would have to do this alone. She thought of Colonel Mueller and General Scheider, and she wondered if a clash ever came, which one would emerge victorious.

The evening following Noelle's dream she and Armand Gautier attended a supper party. The host was Leslie Rocas, a wealthy patron of the arts. It was an eclectic collection of guests – bankers, artists, political leaders and a gathering of beautiful women whom Noelle felt were there mainly for the benefit of the Germans who were present. Gautier had noticed Noelle's preoccupation, but when he asked her what was wrong, she told him that everything was fine.

Fifteen minutes before supper was announced, a new arrival lumbered through the door and the moment that Noelle saw him she knew that her problem was going to be solved. She walked over to the hostess and said, 'Darling, be an angel and put me next to Albert Heller.'

Albert Heller was France's leading playwright. He was a large, shambling bear of a man in his sixties with a shock of white hair and broad, sloped shoulders. He was unusually tall for a Frenchman, but he would have stood out in a crowd in any case, for he had a remarkably ugly face and piercing green eyes that missed nothing. Heller had a vividly inventive imagination and had written more than a score of hit plays and motion pictures. He had been after Noelle to star in a new play of his and had sent her a copy of the manuscript. Now as she sat next to him at dinner, Noelle said, 'I just finished reading your new play, Albert. I adored it.'

His face lit up. 'Will you do it?'

Noelle put a hand on his. 'I wish I could, darling. Armand has committed me to another play.'

He frowned, then sighed resignedly. '*Merde*! Ah, well, one day we will work together.'

'I would enjoy that,' Noelle said. 'I love the way you write. It fascinates me the way writers create plots. I don't know how you do it.'

He shrugged. 'The same way you act. It is our trade, the way we make our living.'

'No,' she replied. 'The ability to use your imagination in that way is a miracle to me.' She gave an embarrassed laugh. 'I know. I've been trying to write.'

'Oh?' he said politely.

'Yes, but I'm stuck.' Noelle took a deep breath and then looked around the table. All the other guests were engrossed in their own conversations. She leaned towards Albert Heller and lowered her voice. 'I have a situation where my heroine is trying to smuggle her lover out of Paris. The Nazis are searching for him.'

'Ah.' The big man sat there, toying with a salad fork, drumming it against a plate. Then he said, 'Easy. Have him put on a German uniform and walk right through them.'

Noelle sighed and said, 'There is a complication. He's been wounded. He can't walk. He lost a leg.'

The drumming suddenly stopped. There was a long pause, then Heller said, 'A barge on the Seine?'

'Watched.'

'And all transportation out of Paris is being searched?'

'Yes.'

'Then you must have the Nazis do the work for you.'

'How?'

'Your heroine,' he said, without looking at Noelle, 'is she attractive?'

'Yes.'

'Supposing,' he said, 'your heroine befriended a German officer. Someone of high rank. Is that possible?' Noelle turned to look at him, but he avoided her eyes.

'Yes.'

'All right, then. Have her make a rendezvous with the officer. They drive off to spend a weekend somewhere outside Paris. Friends could arrange for your hero to be hidden in the trunk of the car. The officer must be important enough so that his car would not be searched.'

'If the trunk is locked,' Noelle asked, 'would he not smother?'

Albert Heller took a sip of wine, quietly lost in thought. Finally he said, 'Not necessarily.' He spoke to Noelle for five minutes, keeping his voice low, and when he had finished, he said, 'Good luck.' And he still did not look at her.

Early the next morning Noelle telephoned General Scheider. An operator answered the switchboard, and a few moments later Noelle was put through to an aide and finally to the General's secretary.

'Who is calling General Scheider, please?'

'Noelle Page,' she said, for the third time.

'I am sorry, but the General is in conference. He cannot be disturbed.'

She hesitated. 'Could I call him back later?'

'He will be in conference all day. I suggest you write the General a letter stating your business.'

Noelle sat there a moment contemplating the idea and an ironic smile touched her lips.

'Never mind,' she said. 'Just tell him I called.'

One hour later her phone rang, and it was General Hans Scheider. 'Forgive me,' he apologized. 'That idiot didn't give me your message until just now. I would have left word for them to put you through, but it never occurred to me that you would telephone.'

'I'm the one who should apologize,' Noelle said. 'I know how busy you are.'

'Please. What can I do for you?'

Noelle hesitated, choosing her words. 'Do you remember what you said about us at dinner?'

There was a short pause, then 'Yes.'

'I've been thinking about you a great deal, Hans. I would like very much to see you.'

'Will you have supper with me tonight?' There was a sudden eagerness in his voice.

'Not in Paris,' Noelle replied. 'If we're going to be together, I would like us to be away from here.'

'Where?' General Scheider asked.

'I want it to be some place special. Do you know Etratat?'

'No.'

'It's a lovely little village about a hundred and fifty kilometres from Paris, near Le Havre. There's a quiet old inn there.'

'It sounds wonderful, Noelle. It's not easy for me to get away right now,' he added apologetically. 'I am in the middle of –'

'I understand,' Noelle interrupted icily, 'perhaps some other time.'

'Wait!' There was a long pause. 'When could you get away?'

'Saturday night after the show.'

'I will make arrangements,' he said. 'We can fly down –'

'Why don't we drive?' Noelle asked. 'It's so pleasant.'

'Whatever you like. I'll pick you up at the theatre.'

Noelle thought quickly. 'I have to come home and change first. Pick me up at my apartment, would you?'

'As you wish, my *liebchen*. Until Saturday night.'

Fifteen minutes later Noelle was speaking to the concierge. He listened as she talked, shaking his head in vigourous protest.

'No, no, no! I will tell our friend, Mademoiselle, but he will not do it. He would be a fool to! You might as well ask him to go down and apply for a job at Gestapo headquarters.'

'It can't fail,' Noelle assured him. 'The best brain in France figured it out.'

When she walked out of the entrance of her apartment building that afternoon, she saw a man lounging against the wall pretending to be engrossed in a newspaper. As Noelle stepped into the crisp, winter air, the man straightened up and began to follow her at a discreet distance. Noelle strolled the streets slowly and leisurely, stopping to look into all the shop windows.

Five minutes after Noelle left the building, the concierge came out, glanced around to make sure he was not observed, then hailed a taxi and gave the address of a sporting goods shop in Montmartre.

Two hours later the concierge reported to Noelle. 'He will be delivered to you Saturday night.'

Saturday night when Noelle finished her performance, Colonel Kurt Mueller of the Gestapo was waiting for her backstage. A *frisson* of apprehension went through Noelle. The escape plan had been worked out to a split-second timing, and there was no room for any delays.

'I saw your performance from out front, Fräulein Page,' Colonel Mueller said. 'You improve each time.'

The sound of his soft, high-pitched voice brought her dream back vividly.

'Thank you, Colonel. If you'll excuse me, I have to change.'

Noelle started towards her dressing room, and he fell into step beside her.

'I will go with you,' Colonel Mueller said.

She walked into her dressing room, the hairless albino Colonel close behind her. He made himself comfortable in an armchair. Noelle hesitated a moment and then began to undress as he watched indifferently. She knew that he was a homosexual, which deprived her of a valuable weapon – her sexuality.

'A little sparrow whispered something in my

ear,' Colonel Mueller said. 'He is going to try to escape tonight.'

Noelle's heart skipped a beat, but her face showed nothing. She began removing her makeup, fighting for time as she asked, 'Who is going to try to escape tonight?'

'Your friend, Israel Katz.'

Noelle swung around, and the movement made her suddenly conscious of the fact that she had removed her brassiere. 'I don't know any –' She caught the quick triumphant gleam in his pink eyes and saw the trap just in time. 'Wait,' she said. 'Are you talking about a young intern?'

'Ah, so you *do* remember him!'

'Barely. He treated me for pneumonia some time ago.'

'And a self-induced abortion,' Colonel Mueller said in that soft, high-pitched voice. The fear flooded back into her. The Gestapo would not have gone to this much trouble if they were not sure that she was involved. She was a fool to have gotten herself into this; but even as Noelle thought it, she knew that it was too late to back out. The wheels had already been set in motion and in a few hours Israel Katz would be either free . . . or dead. And she?

Colonel Mueller was saying, 'You said that the last time you saw Katz was at the café a few weeks ago.'

Noelle shook her head. 'I said no such thing, Colonel.'

Colonel Mueller looked steadily into her eyes, then let his gaze drop insolently to her naked breasts and down her belly to her sheer pants. Then he looked up into Noelle's eyes again and sighed. 'I love beautiful things,' he said softly. 'It would be a shame to see beauty like yours destroyed. And all for a man who means nothing to you. How is your friend planning to get away, Fräulein?'

There was a quietness in his voice that sent shivers down her spine. She became Annette, the innocent, helpless character in her play.

'I really don't know what you're talking about, Colonel. I'd like to help you, but I don't know how.'

Colonel Mueller looked at Noelle a long time, then stiffly rose to his feet. 'I will teach you how, Fräulein,' he promised softly, 'and I will enjoy it.'

He turned at the door to deliver a parting shot. 'By the way, I have advised General Scheider not to go away with you for the weekend.'

Noelle felt her heart plummet. It was too late to reach Israel Katz. 'Do Colonels always interfere in the private lives of Generals?'

'In this case, no,' Colonel Mueller said regretfully. 'General Scheider intends to keep his rendezvous.' He turned and walked out.

Noelle stared after him, her heart racing. She looked at the gold clock on the dressing table and quickly began to dress.

* * *

At eleven forty-five the concierge telephoned Noelle to announce that General Scheider was on his way up to her apartment. His voice was trembling.

'Is his chauffeur in the car?' Noelle asked.

'No, Mademoiselle,' the concierge replied carefully. 'He's on his way up with the General.'

'Thank you.'

Noelle replaced the receiver and hurried into the bedroom to check her luggage once more. There must be no mistake. The front doorbell rang, and Noelle went into the living room and opened the door.

General Scheider stood in the corridor, his chauffeur, a young captain, behind him. General Scheider was out of uniform and looked very distinguished in a flawlessly cut charcoal-grey suit and a soft blue shirt and black tie. 'Good evening,' he said formally. He stepped inside, then nodded to his chauffeur.

'My bags are in the bedroom,' Noelle said. She indicated the door.

'Thank you, Fräulein.' The captain walked into the bedroom. General Scheider came over to Noelle and took her hands. 'Do you know what I have been thinking about all day?' he asked. 'I was thinking you might not be here, that you might change your mind. Every time the phone rang, I was afraid.'

'I keep my promises,' Noelle said. She watched as the captain came out of the bedroom carrying her makeup case and overnight bag. 'Is there anything else?' he asked.

'No,' Noelle said. 'That's all.'

The captain carried the suitcases out of the apartment.

'Ready?' General Scheider asked.

'Let's have a drink before we go,' Noelle replied quickly. She walked over to a bottle of champagne on the bar, resting in a bucket of ice.

'Let me.' He moved over to the ice bucket and opened the champagne.

'What shall we drink to?' he asked.

'Etratat.'

He studied her a moment and then said, 'Etratat.'

They touched glasses in a toast and drank. As Noelle set her glass down, she surreptitiously glanced at her wristwatch. General Scheider was talking to her, but Noelle only half-heard the words. Her mind was visualizing what was happening downstairs. She must be very careful. If she moved too quickly or too slowly, it would be fatal. For everyone.

'What are you thinking about?' General Scheider asked.

Noelle turned quickly. 'Nothing.'

'You were not listening.'

'I'm sorry. I suppose I was thinking about us.' She turned to him and gave him a quick smile.

'You puzzle me,' he said.

'Aren't all women a puzzle?'

'Not like you. I would never believe that you

are capricious and yet' – he made a gesture – 'first you will not see me at all and now we are suddenly spending a weekend in the country.'

'Are you sorry, Hans?'

'Of course not. But still I ask myself – why the country?'

'I told you.'

'As yes,' General Scheider said. 'It is romantic. That is something else that puzzles me. I believe you are a realist, not a romanticist.'

'What are you trying to say?' Noelle asked.

'Nothing,' the General replied easily. 'I am just thinking aloud. I enjoy solving problems, Noelle. In time I will solve you.'

She shrugged. 'Once you have the solution, the problem might not be interesting.'

'We shall see.' He set his glass down. 'Shall we go?'

Noelle picked up the empty champagne glasses. 'I'll just put these in the sink,' she said.

General Scheider watched as she walked into the kitchen. Noelle was one of the most beautiful and desirable women he had ever seen, and he meant to possess her. That did not mean, however, that he was either stupid or blind. She wanted something from him. He intended to find out what it was. Colonel Mueller had alerted him that she was in all probability giving aid to a dangerous enemy of the Reich, and Colonel Mueller made very few mistakes. If he was correct, Noelle Page was probably counting on General Scheider to protect her in some way. If so she knew nothing at all about the German military mind and still less about him. He would turn her over to the Gestapo without a qualm, but first he would have his pleasure. He was looking forward to the weekend.

Noelle came out of the kitchen. There was a worried expression on her face. 'How many bags did your chauffeur take down?' she asked.

'Two,' he replied. 'An overnight bag and a makeup case.'

She made a face. 'Oh dear, I'm sorry, Hans. He forgot the other case. Do you mind?'

He watched as Noelle walked over to the telephone, picked it up and spoke into it. 'Would you please ask the General's driver to come up again?' she said. 'There's another bag to go down.' She replaced the receiver. 'I know we're only going to be there for the weekend,' she smiled, 'but I want to please you.'

'If you want to please me,' General Scheider said, 'you will not need a lot of clothes.' He glanced at a picture of Armand Gautier on the piano. 'Does Herr Gautier know that you are going away with me?' he asked.

'Yes,' Noelle lied. Armand was in Nice meeting with a producer about a motion picture, and she had seen no reason to alarm him by telling him of her plans. The doorbell rang, and Noelle walked over to the door and opened it. The captain stood there. 'I understand there is another bag?' he asked.

'Yes,' Noelle apologized. 'It's in the bedroom.'

The captain nodded and went into the bedroom.

'When must you return to Paris?' General Scheider asked her.

Noelle turned and looked at him. 'I'd like to stay as long as I can. We'll come back late Monday afternoon. That will give us two days.'

The captain came out of the bedroom. 'Excuse me, Fräulein. What does the suitcase look like?'

'It is a large round blue case,' Noelle said. She turned to the General. 'It has a new gown in it that I haven't worn yet. I saved it for you.'

She was babbling now, trying to cover up her nervousness.

The captain had gone back into the bedroom. A few moments later, he came out again. 'I am sorry,' he said. 'I cannot find it.'

'Let me,' Noelle said. She went into the bedroom and began to search the closets. 'That idiot of a maid must have hidden it away somewhere,' she said. The three of them looked through every closet in the apartment. It was the General who finally found the bag in the hall closet. He lifted it and said, 'It seems to be empty.'

Noelle quickly opened the bag and looked inside. There was nothing in it. 'Oh, that fool,' she said. 'She must have crammed that beautiful new dress in the suitcase with my other clothes. I hope she hasn't ruined it.' She sighed in exasperation. 'Do you have that much trouble with maids in Germany?'

'I think it is the same everywhere,' General Scheider replied. He was watching Noelle closely. She was acting strangely, talking too much. She noticed his look.

'You make me feel like a schoolgirl.' Noelle said. 'I can't remember when I've been so nervous.'

General Scheider smiled. So that was it. Or was she playing some kind of game with him? If she was, he would soon find it out. He glanced at his watch. 'If we do not leave now, we will get there very late.'

'I'm ready,' Noelle said.

She prayed the others were.

When they reached the lobby, the concierge was standing there, his face chalk white. Noelle wondered if something had gone wrong. She looked at him for some signal, a sign, but before he could respond, the General had taken Noelle's arm and was leading her out the door.

General Scheider's limousine was parked directly in front of the door. The trunk of the car was closed. The street was deserted. The chauffeur sprang to open the rear door of the car. Noelle turned to look inside the lobby to see the concierge but the General moved in front of her and blocked her view. Deliberately? Noelle glanced at the closed trunk but it told her nothing. It would be hours before she knew whether her plan had succeeded, and the suspense was going to be unbearable.

'Are you all right?' General Scheider was staring at her. She felt that something had gone terribly wrong. She had to find an excuse to go back into the lobby, to be alone with the concierge for a few seconds. She forced a smile to her lips.

'I just remembered,' Noelle said. 'A friend is going to call me. I must leave a message –'

General Scheider gripped her arm.

'Too late,' he smiled. 'From this moment on you must think only of me.' And he guided her into the car. A moment later they were on their way.

Five minutes after General Scheider's limousine drove away from the apartment building, a black Mercedes screeched to a stop in front of the building and Colonel Mueller and two other Gestapo men spilled out of the car. Colonel Mueller looked hurriedly up and down the street. 'They've gone,' he said. The men sprinted into the lobby of Noelle's apartment building and rang the concierge's doorbell. The door opened and the concierge stood in the doorway, a startled expression on his face. 'What –?' Colonel Mueller shoved him inside his small apartment.

'Fräulein Page!' he snapped. 'Where is she?'

The concierge stared at him, panicky.

'She – she left,' he said.

'I know that, you stupid fool! I asked you where she went!'

The concierge shook his head helplessly. 'I have no idea, Monsieur. I only know she left with an army officer.'

'Didn't she tell you where she could be reached?'

'N – No, Monsieur. Mademoiselle Page does not confide in me.'

Colonel Mueller glared at the old man a moment and then turned on his heel.

'They can't have gotten far,' he said to his men. 'Contact all the roadblocks as fast as you can. Tell them that when General Scheider's car arrives I want them to hold it and call me at once!'

Because of the hour military traffic was light, which meant that there was virtually no traffic at all. General Scheider's car swung onto the West Road that led out of Paris, passing Versailles. They drove through Mantes, Vernon, and Gaillon and in twenty-five minutes they were approaching the major arterial intersection that branched out into Vichy, Le Havre and the Côte d'Azur.

It seemed to Noelle that a miracle had happened. They were going to get out of Paris without being stopped. She should have known that even the Germans with all their efficiency would not be able to check every single road out of the city. And even as she thought it, out of the darkness ahead of them loomed a roadblock. Flashing red lights blinked from the centre of the road, and in back of the lights a German Army lorry blocked the highway. On the side of the road were half a dozen German soldiers and two French police cars. A German Army lieutenant waved down the limousine and, as it came to a stop, he walked over to the driver.

'Get out and show your identification!'

General Scheider opened the rear window, leaned his head out and said, raspingly: 'General Scheider. What the hell's going on here?'

The lieutenant snapped to attention.

'Excuse me, General. I did not know it was your car.'

The General's eyes flicked over the roadblock. 'What's this all about?'

'We have orders to inspect every vehicle leaving Paris, Herr General. Every exit from the city is blocked.'

The General turned to Noelle. 'The damned Gestapo. I'm sorry, *liebchen*.'

Noelle could feel the colour drain from her face, and she was grateful for the darkness of the car. When she spoke, her voice was steady.

'It's not important,' she said.

She thought of the cargo in the trunk. If her plan had worked, Israel Katz was in there, and in a moment he would be caught. And so would she.

The German lieutenant turned to the chauffeur.

'Open the luggage compartment, please.'

'There's nothing in there but luggage,' the captain protested. 'I put it in myself.'

'I'm sorry, Captain. My orders are clear. Every vehicle out of Paris is to be inspected. Open it.'

Muttering under his breath, the driver opened his door and started to get out. Noelle's mind was racing furiously. She had to find a way to stop them, without arousing their suspicions. The driver was out of the car. Time had run out. Noelle stole a quick look at General Scheider's face. His eyes were narrowed and his lips were tight with anger. She turned to him and said guilelessly, 'Shall we get out, Hans? Will they be searching us?' She could feel his body tense with fury.

'Wait!' The General's voice was like the crack of a whip. 'Get back in the car,' he order his driver. He turned to the lieutenant and his voice was filled with rage. 'You tell whoever gave you your orders that they do not apply to generals of the German Army. I do not take orders from lieutenants. Get that roadblock out of my way.'

The hapless lieutenant stared at the General's furious face, clicked his heels to attention and said, 'Yes, General Scheider.' He signaled the driver of the truck blocking the road and the truck lumbered off to the side.

'Drive on,' General Scheider commanded.

And the car sped away into the night.

Slowly Noelle let her body relax into the seat, feeling the tension draining out of her. The crisis was past. She wished that she knew whether Israel Katz was in the trunk of the car. And if he was alive.

General Scheider turned to Noelle and she could feel the anger that was still seething in him.

'I apologize,' he said, wearily. 'This is a strange war. Sometimes it is necessary to remind the Gestapo that wars are run by armies.'

Noelle smiled up at him and put her arm through his. 'And armies are run by generals.'

'Exactly,' he agreed. 'Armies are run by generals. I am going to have to teach Colonel Mueller a lesson.'

Ten minutes after General Scheider's car had left the roadblock, a phone call came in from Gestapo Headquarters, alerting them to be on the lookout for the car.

'It has already passed through,' the lieutenant reported, a feeling of foreboding flooding through him. A moment later he was speaking with Colonel Mueller.

'How long ago?' the Gestapo officer asked softly.

'Ten minutes.'

'Did you search his car?'

The lieutenant felt his bowels turn to water. 'No, sir. The General would not permit –'

'*Scheiss*! Which way was he headed?'

The lieutenant swallowed. When he spoke again, it was in the hopeless voice of a man who knew that his future was finished.

'I am not certain,' he replied. 'This is a large crossroad here. He could have been going inland to Rouen or to the sea, to Le Havre.'

'I want you to present yourself to Gestapo Headquarters at nine A.M. tomorrow. My office.'

'Yes, sir,' the lieutenant responded.

Savagely Colonel Mueller rang off. He turned to the two men at his side and said, 'Le Havre. Get my car. We're going cockroach-hunting!'

* * *

The road to Le Havre winds along the Seine, through the beautiful Seine Valley with its rich hills and fertile farms. It was a clear, starlit night and the farmhouses in the distance were pools of light, like oases in the darkness.

In the comfortable back seat of the limousine Noelle and General Scheider talked. He told her about his wife and his children and how difficult marriage was for an army officer. Noelle listened sympathetically and told him how difficult a romantic life was for an actress. Each was aware that the conversation was a game, both of them keeping the talk on a superficial level that would give away no insights. Noelle did not for a moment underestimate the intelligence of the man sitting beside her, and she fully understood how dangerous was the adventure in which she was engaged. She knew that General Scheider was too clever to believe that she had suddenly found him irresistible, that he must suspect that she was after something. What Noelle was counting on was that she would be able to outmanoeuvre him in the game they were playing. The General touched only briefly on the war, but he said something that she remembered long afterwards.

'The British are a strange race,' he said. 'In peacetime, they are impossible to manage, but in a crisis they are magnificent. The only time a British sailor is truly happy is when his ship is sinking.'

They reached Le Havre in the small hours of the morning on their way to the village of Etratat.

'May we stop for a bite to eat?' Noelle asked. 'I'm starved.'

General Scheider nodded. 'Of course, if you wish.' He raised his voice. 'Look for an all-night restaurant.'

'I'm sure there's one by the pier,' Noelle suggested. The captain obediently swung the car towards the waterfront. He stopped the car at the water's edge, where several cargo ships were tied to the pier. A block away a sign said, 'Bistro.'

The captain opened the door and Noelle got out, followed by General Scheider.

'It's probably open all night for the dock workers,' Noelle said. She heard the sound of a motor and turned around. A cargo-loading fork-lift had driven up and stopped near the limousine. Two men wearing coveralls and long, visored caps that concealed their faces got out of the machine. One of the men looked hard at Noelle, then took out a tool kit and began to tighten the forklift. Noelle felt the muscles in her stomach constrict. She took General Scheider's arm and they started towards the restaurant. Noelle looked back at the chauffeur sitting behind the wheel.

'Wouldn't he like some coffee?' Noelle asked.

'He will stay with the car,' the General said.

Noelle stared at him. The chauffeur must *not* stay with the car or everything would be ruined. Yet Noelle dared not insist.

They walked on towards the café over the rough, uneven cobblestones. Suddenly, as she took a step, her ankle turned and Noelle fell, letting out a sharp cry of pain. General Scheider reached out and vainly tried to grab her before her body hit the cobblestones.

'Are you all right?' he asked.

The chauffeur, seeing what had happened, moved from behind the wheel of the car and started hurrying towards them.

'I'm so sorry,' Noelle said. 'I – I turned my ankle. It feels like it's broken.'

General Scheider ran his hand expertly over her ankle. 'There is no swelling. It is probably just a sprain. Can you stand on it?'

'I – I don't know,' Noelle said.

The chauffeur reached her side and the two men lifted her to her feet. Noelle took a step and the ankle gave way under her.

'I'm sorry,' she moaned. 'If I could just sit down.'

'Help me get her in there,' General Scheider said, indicating the café.

With the two men supporting her on either side, they walked into the restaurant. As she walked through the door, Noelle risked a quick look back at the car. The two dock workers were at the trunk of the limousine.

'Are you sure you wouldn't rather go straight on to Etratat?' the General was asking.

'No, believe me, I'll be fine,' Noelle replied.

The proprietor led them to a corner table, and the two men eased Noelle into a chair.

'Are you in much pain?' General Scheider asked.

'A bit,' Noelle replied. She put her hand on his. 'Don't worry. I won't let this spoil anything for you, Hans.'

At the moment Noelle and General Hans Scheider were sitting in the café, Colonel Mueller and two of his men were speeding into the city limits of Le Havre. The local captain of police had been roused from his sleep and was waiting for the Gestapo men in front of the police station. 'A gendarme has located the General's car,' he said. 'It is parked down by the waterfront.'

A gleam of satisfaction came into Colonel Mueller's face. 'Take me there,' he commanded.

Five minutes later, the Gestapo automobile with Colonel Mueller, his two men and the police captain raced up beside General Scheider's automobile on the pier. The men got out and surrounded the car. At that moment General Scheider, Noelle and the chauffeur were starting to leave the bistro. The chauffeur was the first to notice the men at the car. He started hurrying towards them.

'What's happening?' Noelle asked, and even as she spoke she recognized the figure of Colonel Mueller in the distance and felt a cold chill go through her.

'I don't know,' General Scheider said. He started towards the limousine with long strides, Noelle limping after him.

'What are you doing here?' General Scheider asked Colonel Mueller as he reached the car.

'I am sorry to disturb your holiday,' Colonel Mueller replied curtly. 'I would like to inspect the trunk of your car, General.'

'There is nothing but luggage in there.'

Noelle reached the group. She noticed that the forklift had gone. The General and the Gestapo men were glaring at each other.

'I must insist, General. I have reason to believe that a wanted enemy of the Third Reich is hiding in there and that your guest is his accomplice.'

General Scheider stared at him for a long moment, then turned to study Noelle.

'I don't know what he's talking about,' she said firmly.

The General's eyes travelled down to her ankle, then he made a decision and turned to his chauffeur. 'Open it.'

'Yes, General.'

All eyes were riveted on the trunk as the chauffeur reached for the handle and turned it. Noelle felt suddenly faint. Slowly the lid opened.

The trunk was empty.

'Someone has stolen our luggage!' exclaimed the chauffeur.

Colonel Mueller's face was mottled with fury. 'He got away!'

'Who got away?' demanded the General.

'*Le Cafard*,' raged Colonel Mueller. 'A Jew named Israel Katz. He was smuggled out of Paris in the trunk of this car.'

'That's impossible,' General Scheider retorted.

'That trunk was tightly closed. He would have suffocated.'

Colonel Mueller studied the trunk a moment, then turned to one of his men. 'Get inside.'

'Yes, Colonel.'

Obediently the man crawled into the trunk. Colonel Mueller slammed the lid tightly shut and looked at his watch. For the next four minutes, they stood there in silence, each engrossed in his own thoughts. Finally after what seemed an eternity to Noelle, Colonel Mueller opened the lid of the trunk. The man inside was unconscious. General Scheider turned to Colonel Mueller, a contemptuous expression on his face. 'If anyone was riding in that trunk,' the General declared, 'they removed his corpse. Is there anything else I can do for you, Colonel?'

The Gestapo officer shook his head, seething with rage and frustration. General Scheider turned to his chauffeur. 'Let's go.' He helped Noelle into the car, and they drove towards Etratat, leaving the knot of men fading away into the distance.

Colonel Kurt Mueller instituted an immediate search of the waterfront, but it was not until late the following afternoon that an empty oxygen tank was found in a barrel in a corner of an unused warehouse. An African freighter had set sail for Capetown out of Le Havre the night before but it was now somewhere on the high seas. The missing luggage turned up a few days later in the lost-and-found department of the Gare du Nord in Paris.

As for Noelle and General Scheider, they spent the weekend in Etratat and returned to Paris late Monday afternoon in time for Noelle to do her evening performance.

NINE

Catherine

Washington: 1941–1944

Catherine had quit her job with William Fraser the morning after she had married Larry. Fraser asked her to have lunch with him the day she returned to Washington. He looked drawn and haggard and suddenly older. Catherine had felt a pang of compassion for him, but that was all. She was sitting opposite a tall, nice-looking stranger for whom she felt affection, but it was impossible now to imagine that she had ever contemplated marrying him. Fraser gave her a wan smile.

'So you're a married lady,' he said.

'The most married lady in the world.'

'It must have happened rather suddenly. I – I wish I'd had a chance to compete.'

'*I* didn't even have a chance,' Catherine said honestly. 'It just – happened.'

'Larry's quite a fellow.'

'Yes.'

'Catherine' – Fraser hesitated – 'you don't really know much about Larry, do you?'

Catherine felt her back stiffening.

'I know I love him, Bill,' she said evenly, 'and I know that he loves me. That's a pretty good beginning, isn't it?'

He sat there frowning, silent, debating with himself. 'Catherine –'

'Yes?'

'Be careful.'

'Of what?' she asked.

Fraser spoke slowly, feeling his way carefully over a minefield of words. 'Larry's – different.'

'How?' she asked, refusing to help him.

'I mean, he's not like most men.' He saw the look on her face. 'Oh, hell,' he said. 'Don't pay any attention to me.' He managed a faint grin. 'You've probably read the biography Aesop did on me. The fox and the sour grapes.'

Catherine took his hand affectionately. 'I'll never forget you, Bill. I hope we can remain friends.'

'I hope so too,' Fraser said. 'Are you sure you won't stay on at the office?'

'Larry wants me to quit. He's old-fashioned. He believes that husbands should support their wives.'

'If you ever change your mind,' Fraser said, 'let me know.' The rest of the luncheon was concerned with office affairs and a discussion of who would take Catherine's place. She knew she would miss Bill Fraser very much. She supposed that the first man to seduce a girl would always hold a special place in that girl's life, but Bill had meant something to her beyond that. He was a dear man and a good friend. Catherine was disturbed by his attitude towards Larry. It was as though Bill had started to warn her about something and then stopped because he was afraid of spoiling her happiness. Or was it as he had said, just a case of sour grapes? Bill Fraser was not a small man or a jealous man. He would surely want her to be happy. And yet Catherine was sure he had tried to tell her something. Somewhere in the back of her mind was a vague foreboding. But an hour later when she met Larry and he smiled at her, everything went out of her head but the ecstasy of being married to this incredible, joyful, human being.

Larry was more fun to be with than anyone Catherine had ever known. Each day was an adventure, a holiday. They drove out to the country every weekend and stayed at small inns and explored county fairs. They went to Lake Placid and rode the huge toboggan slide and to Montauk where they went boating and fishing. Catherine was terrified of the water because she had never learned to swim, but Larry told her not to worry about it, and with him she felt safe.

Larry was loving and attentive and appeared to be remarkably unaware of the attraction he held for other women. Catherine seemed to be all that he wanted. On their honeymoon Larry had come across a little silver bird in an antique shop and

Catherine had liked it so much that he had found a crystal bird for her and it had become the start of a collection. On a Saturday night they drove to Maryland to celebrate their third-month anniversary and had dinner at the same little restaurant.

The next day, Sunday, December 7, Pearl Harbour was attacked by the Japanese.

America's declaration of war against Japan came the following day at 1:32 P.M., less than twenty-four hours after the Japanese attack. On Monday while Larry was at Andrews Air Base, Catherine, unable to bear being alone in the apartment, took a taxi to the Capitol Building to see what was happening. Knots of people pressed around a dozen portable radio sets scattered through the crowd that lined the sidewalks of the Capitol Plaza. Catherine watched as the Presidential caravan raced up the drive and stopped at the south entrance to the Capitol. She was close enough to see the limousine door open and President Roosevelt disembark, assisted by two aides. Dozens of policemen stood at every corner, alert for trouble. The mood of the crowd seemed to Catherine to be mainly outrage, like a lynch mob eager to get into action.

Five minutes after President Roosevelt entered the Capitol, his voice came over the radio, as he addressed the Joint Session of Congress. His voice was strong and firm, filled with angry determination.

'America will remember this onslaught . . .

Righteous might will win . . . We will gain the inevitable triumph, so help us, God.'

Fifteen minutes after Roosevelt had entered the Capitol, House Joint Resolution 254 was passed, declaring war on Japan. It was passed unanimously except for Representative Jeannette Rankin of Montana, who voted against the declaration of war, so the final vote was 388 to 1. President Roosevelt's speech had taken exactly ten minutes – the shortest war message ever delivered to an American Congress.

The crowd outside cheered, a full-throated roar of approval, anger and a promise of vengeance. America was finally on the move.

Catherine studied the men and women standing near her. The faces of the men were filled with the same look of exhilaration that she had seen on Larry's face the day before, as though they all belonged to the same secret club whose members felt that war was an exciting sport. Even the women seemed caught up by the spontaneous enthusiasm that swept through the crowd. But Catherine wondered how they would feel when their men were gone and the women stood alone waiting for news of their husbands and sons. Slowly Catherine turned and walked back towards the apartment. On the corner she saw soldiers with fixed bayonets.

Soon, she thought, the whole country would be in uniform.

It happened even faster than Catherine had anticipated. Almost overnight Washington was transformed into a world of a citizen army in khaki.

The air was filled with an electric, contagious excitement. It was as though peace were a lethargy, a miasma that filled mankind with a sense of ennui, and it was only war that could stimulate man to the full exhilaration of life.

Larry was spending sixteen to eighteen hours at the Air Base, and he often remained there overnight. He told Catherine that the situation at Pearl Harbour and Hickam Field was much worse than the people had been led to believe. The sneak attack had been devastatingly successful. For all practical purposes America's Navy and a good part of its Air Corps had been destroyed.

'Are you saying that we could lose this war?' Catherine asked, shocked.

Larry looked at her thoughtfully. 'It depends on how fast we can get ready,' he replied. 'Everyone thinks of the Japanese as funny little men with weak eyes. That's horseshit. They're tough, and they're not afraid to die. We're soft.'

In the months that followed it seemed that nothing could stop the Japanese. The daily headlines screamed out their successes: They were attacking Wake . . . softening up the Philippine Islands for invasion . . . landing in Guam . . . in Borneo . . . in Hong Kong. General MacArthur declared Manila an open city, and the trapped American troops in the Philippines surrendered.

One day in April, Larry telephoned Catherine

from the Base and asked her to meet him downtown for dinner at the Willard Hotel to celebrate.

'Celebrate what?' Catherine asked.

'I'll tell you tonight,' Larry replied. There was a note of high excitement in his voice.

When Catherine hung up, she was filled with a dread premonition. She tried to think of all the possible reasons that Larry would have to celebrate, but it always came back to the same thing and she did not think she would have the strength to face it.

At five o'clock that afternoon Catherine was fully dressed, sitting on her bed staring into the dressing-room mirror.

I must be wrong, she thought. *Maybe he's been promoted. That's what we're celebrating. Or he's had some good news about the war*. Catherine told herself this but she did not believe it. She studied herself in the mirror, trying to be objective. While she would not give Ingrid Bergman any sleepless nights, she was, she decided dispassionately, attractive. Her figure was good, full of provocative curves. *You're intelligent, cheerful, courteous, kind and a sex pot*, she told herself. *Why would any normal red-blooded male be dying to leave you so that he could go off to war and try to get himself killed?*

At seven o'clock Catherine walked into the dining room of the Willard Hotel. Larry had not arrived yet, and the maître d' escorted her to a table. She said no she would not have a drink, then nervously changed her mind and ordered a martini.

When the waiter brought it and Catherine started to pick it up, she found that her hands were shaking. She looked up and saw Larry moving towards her. He threaded his way between the tables, acknowledging greetings along the way. He carried with him that incredible vitality, that aura that made every eye turn in his direction. Catherine watched him, remembering the day he had come to her table at the MGM commissary in Hollywood. She realized how little she had known him then, and she wondered how well she knew him now. He reached the table and gave her a quick kiss on the cheek.

'Sorry I'm late, Cathy,' he apologized. 'The Base has been a madhouse all day.' He sat down, greeted the captain by name and ordered a martini. If he noticed that Catherine was drinking, he made no comment.

Catherine's mind was screaming out: *Tell me your surprise. Tell me what we're celebrating*. But she said nothing. There was an old Hungarian proverb: 'Only a fool rushes bad news.' She took another sip of her martini. Well maybe it wasn't an old Hungarian proverb. Maybe it was a new Catherine Douglas proverb designed to be worn over thin skins for protection. Maybe the martini was making her a little drunk. If her premonition was right, before this night was over she was going to get very drunk. But looking at Larry now, his face filled with love, Catherine knew that she had to be wrong. Larry could not bear to leave her any more than she could bear to leave him. She had been building up a nightmare out of whole cloth. From the happy expression on his face she knew that he had some really good news to tell her.

Larry was leaning towards her, smiling his boyish smile, taking her hand in his.

'You'll never guess what's happened, Cathy. I'm going overseas.'

It was as though a filmy curtain descended, giving everything an unreal, hazy look. Larry was sitting next to her, his lips moving, but his face was going in and out of focus and Catherine could not hear any words. She looked over his shoulder and the walls of the restaurant were moving together and receding. She watched, fascinated.

'Catherine!' Larry was shaking her arm and slowly her eyes focused on him and everything came back to normal. 'Are you all right?'

Catherine nodded, swallowed and said, shakily, 'Great. Good news always does that to me.'

'You understand that I have to do this, don't you?'

'Yes, I understand.' *The truth is, I wouldn't understand if I lived to be a million years old, my darling. But if I told you that, you'd hate me, wouldn't you? Who needs a nagging wife? Heroes' wives should send their men off smiling.*

Larry was watching, concerned. 'You're crying.'

'I am not,' Catherine said indignantly and found to her horror that she was. 'I – I just have to get used to the idea.'

'They're giving me my own squadron,' Larry said.

'Are they really?' Catherine tried to pump pride into her voice. His own squadron. When he was a small boy, he probably had had his own set of trains to play with. And now that he was a tall boy, they had given him his own squadron to play with. And these were real toys, guaranteed to get shot down and bleed and die. 'I'd like another drink,' she said.

'Of course.'

'When – when will you have to leave?'

'Not until next month.'

He made it sound as though he were eager to get away. It was terrifying, feeling the whole fabric of her marriage being torn apart. On the band-stand a singer was crooning, 'A trip to the moon on gossamer wings . . .' *Gossamer*, she thought. *That's what my marriage is made of: gossamer.* That Cole Porter knew everything.

'We'll have plenty of time before I leave,' Larry was saying.

Plenty of time for what? Catherine wondered bitterly. *Plenty of time to raise a family, to take our children skiing in Vermont, to grow old together?*

'What would you like to do tonight?' Larry asked.

I'd like to go down to the County Hospital and have one of your toes removed. Or have one of your ear drums pierced. Aloud, Catherine said, 'Let's go home and make love.' And there was a fierce, desperate urgency in her.

The next four weeks melted away. The clocks raced forwards in a Kafka-ish nightmare that turned days into hours and hours into minutes, and then incredibly it was Larry's last day. Catherine drove him to the airport. He was talkative and happy and gay and she was sombre and quiet and miserable. The last few minutes became a kaleidoscope of reporting in . . . a hurried good-bye kiss . . . Larry entering the plane that was to take him away from her . . . and a last farewell wave. Catherine stood on the field watching his plane dwindle to a small speck in the sky and finally disappear. She stood there for an hour, and finally when it got dark she turned and drove back into town to her empty apartment.

In the first year following the attack on Pearl Harbour, ten great sea and air battles were fought against the Japanese. The Allies won only three, but two of them were decisive: Midway and the Battle of Guadalcanal.

Catherine read word for word the newspaper reports of every battle and then asked William Fraser to get her further details. She wrote to Larry daily, but it was eight weeks before she received his first letter. It was optimistic and full of excitement. The letter had been heavily censored so Catherine had no idea where he had been or what he was doing. Whatever it was she had a feeling that he seemed to be enjoying it, and in the long lonely hours of the night Catherine lay in bed puzzling over that, trying to figure out what it was in Larry that made him respond to the challenge of war and death. It was not that he had a death wish, for

Catherine had never known anyone more alive and vital; but perhaps that was simply the other side of the coin, that what made the life-sense so keen was constantly honing it against death.

She had lunch with William Fraser. Catherine knew that he had tried to enlist and had been told by the White House that he could do more good by staying at his post. He had been bitterly disappointed. He had never mentioned it to Catherine, however. Now as Fraser sat across from Catherine at the luncheon table, he asked:

'Have you heard from Larry?'

'I got a letter last week.'

'What did he say?'

'Well, according to the letter, the war is a kind of football game. We lost the first scrimmage, but now they've sent the first team in, and we're gaining ground.'

He nodded. 'That's Larry.'

'But that's not the war,' Catherine said quietly. 'It's not a football game, Bill. Millions of people are going to be killed before this is over.'

'If you're in it, Catherine,' he said gently, 'I imagine it's easier to think of it as a football game.'

Catherine had decided that she wanted to go to work. The Army had created a branch for women called the WACs, and Catherine had thought of joining but had felt she might be more useful doing something more than driving cars and answering telephones. Although from what she had heard, the WACs were pretty colourful. There was so much pregnancy among them that there was a rumour that when volunteers went in for their physical examination, the doctors pressed their stomachs with a tiny rubber stamp. The girls tried to read the words but were unable to do so. Finally one of them hit upon the idea of getting a magnifying glass. The words read: 'When you can read this with the naked eye, report to me.'

Now as she sat lunching with Bill Fraser, she said, 'I want to work. I want to do something to help.'

He studied her a moment, then nodded. 'I may know just the thing for you, Catherine. The Government's trying to sell War Bonds. I think you could help coordinate it.'

Two weeks later Catherine went to work organizing the sale of War Bonds by celebrities. It had sounded ridiculously easy in concept, but the execution of it was something else again. She found the stars to be like children, eager and excited about helping the war effort, but difficult to pin down about specific dates. Their schedules had to be constantly juggled. Often it was not their fault, because pictures were delayed or schedules ran over. Catherine found herself commuting from Washington to Hollywood and New York. She got used to leaving on an hour's notice, packing enough clothes to last the length of each trip. She met dozens of celebrities.

'Did you really meet Cary Grant?' her secretary asked her when she returned from a trip to Hollywood.

'We had lunch together.'

'Is he as charming as they say?'

'If he could package it,' Catherine declared, 'he'd be the richest man in the world.'

It happened so gradually that Catherine was almost unaware of it. It had been six months earlier, when Bill Fraser told her about a problem that Wallace Turner was having with one of the advertising accounts that Catherine used to handle. Catherine had laid out a new campaign using a humorous approach, and the client had been very pleased. A few weeks later Bill had asked Catherine to help on another account, and before she realized it she was spending more than half her time with the advertising agency. She was in charge of half a dozen accounts, all of them doing well. Fraser had given her a large salary and a percentage. At noon on the day before Christmas Fraser came into her office. The rest of the staff had gone home, and Catherine was finishing up some last minute work.

'Having fun?' he asked.

'It's a living,' she smiled and added warmly, 'and a generous one. Thanks, Bill.'

'Don't thank me. You've earned every penny of it – and then some. It's the "then some" I want to talk to you about. I'm offering you a partnership.'

She looked at him in surprise. 'A partnership?'

'Half the new accounts we got in the last six months are because of you.' He sat there looking at her thoughtfully, saying nothing more. And she understood how much it meant to him.

'You have a partner,' she said.

His face lit up. 'I can't tell you how pleased I am.' Awkwardly, he held out his hand. She shook her head, walked past his outstretched arm, hugged him and gave him a kiss on the cheek.

'Now that we're partners,' she teased, 'I can kiss you.' She felt him suddenly hold her tighter.

'Cathy,' he said, 'I . . .'

Catherine put her finger to his lips. 'Don't say anything, Bill. Let's leave it the way it is.'

'You know I'm in love with you.'

'And I love you,' she said warmly. *Semantics*, she thought. The difference between 'I love you' and 'I'm in love with you' was a bridgeless chasm.

Fraser smiled. 'I won't bother you, I promise. I respect the way you feel about Larry.'

'Thank you, Bill.' She hesitated. 'I don't know whether this helps any, but if there ever were anyone else, it would be you.'

'That's a great help,' he grinned. 'It's going to keep me awake all night.'

TEN

Noelle

Paris: 1944

During the past year Armand Gautier had ceased broaching the subject of marriage. In the beginning he had felt himself in a superior position to Noelle. Now, however, the situation was almost reversed. When they gave newspaper interviews, it was Noelle to whom the questions were directed, and wherever they went together, Noelle was the attraction, he was the afterthought.

Noelle was the perfect mistress. She continued to make Gautier comfortable, act as his hostess and in effect make him one of the most envied men in France; but in truth he never had a moment's peace, for he knew that he did not possess Noelle, nor ever could, that there would come a day when she would walk out of his life as capriciously as she had wandered into it and when he remembered what had happened to him the one time that Noelle had left him, Gautier felt sick to his stomach.

Against every instinct of his intellect, his experience and his knowledge of women he was wildly, madly in love with Noelle. She was the single most important fact of his life. He would lie awake nights devising elaborate surprises to make her happy and when they succeeded, he was rewarded with a smile or a kiss or an unsolicited night of lovemaking. Whenever she looked at another man, Gautier was filled with jealousy, but he knew better than to speak of it to Noelle. Once after a party when she had spent the entire evening talking to a renowned doctor, Gautier had been furious with her. Noelle had listened to his tirade and then had answered quietly, 'If my speaking to other men bothers you, Armand, I will move my things out tonight.'

He had never brought up the subject again.

At the beginning of February, Noelle began her salon. It had started as a simple Sunday brunch with a few of their friends from the theatre, but as word about it got around, it quickly expanded and began to include politicians, scientists, writers – anyone whom the group thought might be interesting or amusing. Noelle was the mistress of the salon and one of the chief attractions. Everyone found himself eager to talk to her, for Noelle asked incisive questions and remembered the answers. She learned about politics from politicians and about finance from bankers. A leading art expert taught her about art, and she soon knew all the great French artists who were living in France. She learned about wine from the chief vintner of Baron Rothschild and about architecture from Corbusier. Noelle had the best tutors in the world and they in turn had a beautiful and fascinating student. She had a quick probing mind and was an intelligent listener.

Armand Gautier had the feeling that he was watching a Princess consorting with her ministers, and had he only been aware of it, it was the closest he would ever come to understanding Noelle's character.

As the months went by Gautier began to feel a little more secure. It seemed to him that Noelle had met everyone who might matter to her and she had shown no interest in any of them.

She had not yet met Constantin Demiris.

Constantin Demiris was the ruler of an empire larger and more powerful than most countries. He had no title or official position, but he regularly bought and sold prime ministers, cardinals, ambassadors and kings. Demiris was one of the two or three wealthiest men in the world and his power was legendary. He owned the largest fleet of cargo ships afloat, an airline, newspapers, banks, steel mills, gold mines – his tentacles were everywhere, inextricably woven throughout the woof and warp of the economic fabric of dozens of countries.

He had one of the most important art collections in the world, a fleet of private planes and a dozen apartments and villas scattered around the globe.

Constantin Demiris was above medium height, with a barrel chest and broad shoulders. His features were swarthy, and he had a broad Greek nose and olive black eyes that blazed with intelligence. He was not interested in clothes, yet he was always on the list of best-dressed men and it was rumoured that he owned over five hundred suits. He had his clothes made wherever he happened to be. His suits were tailored by Hawes and Curtis in London, his shirts by Brioni in Rome, shoes by Daliet Grande in Paris and ties from a dozen countries.

Demiris had about him a presence that was magnetic. When he walked into a room, people who did not know who he was would turn to stare. Newspapers and magazines all over the world had written an incessant spate of stories about Constantin Demiris and his activities, both business and social.

The Press found him highly quotable. When asked by a reporter if friends had helped him achieve his success, he had replied, 'To be successful, you need friends. To be *very* successful, you need enemies.'

When he was asked how many employees he had, Demiris had said, 'None. Only acolytes. When this much power and money is involved, business turns into a religion and offices become temples.'

He had been reared in the Greek Orthodox Church, but he said of organized religion: 'A thousand times more crimes have been committed in the name of love than in the name of hate.'

The world knew that he was married to the daughter of an old Greek banking family, that his wife was an attractive, gracious lady and that when Demiris entertained on his yacht or on his private island, his wife seldom went with him. Instead, he would be accompanied by a beautiful actress or ballerina or whoever else struck his current fancy. His romantic escapades were as legendary and as colourful as his financial adventures. He had bedded dozens of motion picture stars, the wives of his best friends, a fifteen-year-old novelist, freshly bereaved widows, and it was even rumoured that he had once been propositioned by a group of nuns who needed a new convent.

Half a dozen books had been written about Demiris, but none of them had ever touched on the essence of the man or managed to reveal the wellspring of his success. One of the most public figures in the world, Constantin Demiris was a very private person, and he manipulated his public image as a facade that concealed his real self. He had dozens of intimate friends in every walk of life and yet no one really knew him. The facts were a matter of public record. He had started life in Piraeus as the son of a stevedore, in a family of fourteen brothers and sisters where there was never enough food on the table and if anyone wanted anything extra, he had to fight for it. There was something in Demiris that constantly demanded more, and he fought for it.

Even as a small boy Demiris' mind automatically

converted everything into mathematics. He knew the number of steps on the Parthenon, how many minutes it took to walk to school, the number of boats in the harbour on a given day. Time was a number divided into segments, and Demiris learned not to waste it. The result was that without any real effort, he was able to accomplish a tremendous amount. His sense of organization was instinctive, a talent that operated automatically in even the smallest things he did. Everything became a game of matching his wits against those around him.

While Demiris was aware that he was cleverer than most men, he had no excess vanity. When a beautiful woman wanted to go to bed with him, he did not for an instant flatter himself that it was because of his looks or personality, but he never permitted that to bother him. The world was a marketplace, and people were either buyers or sellers. Some women, he knew, were attracted by his money, some by his power and a few – a rare few – by his mind and imagination.

Nearly every person he met wanted something from him: a donation to a charity, financing for a business project or simply the power that his friendship could bestow. Demiris enjoyed the challenge of figuring out exactly what it was that people were really after, for it was seldom what it appeared to be. His analytical mind was sceptical of surface truth, and as a consequence he believed nothing he heard and trusted no one.

The reporters who chronicled his life were permitted to see only his geniality and charm, the sophisticated urbane man of the world. They never suspected that beneath the surface, Demiris was a killer, a gutter-fighter whose instinct was to go for the jugular vein.

To the ancient Greeks the word *thekaeossini*, justice, was often synonymous with *ekthekissis*, vengeance, and Demiris was obsessed with both. He remembered every slight he had ever suffered, and those who were unlucky enough to incur his enmity were paid back a hundredfold. They were never even aware of it, for Demiris' mathematical mind made a game of exacting retribution, patiently working out elaborate traps, spinning complex webs that finally caught and destroyed its victims.

When Demiris was sixteen years old, he had gone into his first business enterprise with an older man named Spyros Nicholas. Demiris had conceived the idea of opening a small stand on the docks to serve hot food to the stevedores on the night shift. He had scraped together half the money for the enterprise, but when it had become successful Nicholas had forced him out of the business and had taken it over himself. Demiris had accepted his fate without protest and had gone ahead to other enterprises.

Over the next twenty years Spyros Nicholas had gone into the meat-packing business and had become rich and successful. He had married, had three children and was one of the most prominent men in Greece. During those years, Demiris patiently sat back and let Nicholas build his little empire. When he decided that Nicholas was as successful and as happy as he was ever going to be, Demiris struck.

Because his business was booming, Nicholas was contemplating buying farms to raise his own meat and opening a chain of retail stores. An enormous amount of money was required. Constantin Demiris owned the bank with which Nicholas did business, and the bank encouraged Nicholas to borrow money for expansion at interest rates that Nicholas could not resist. Nicholas plunged heavily, and in the midst of the expansion his notes were suddenly called in by the bank. When the bewildered man protested that he could not make the payments, the bank immediately began foreclosure proceedings. The newspapers owned by Demiris prominently played up the story on the front pages, and other creditors began foreclosing on Nicholas. He went to other banks and lending institutions, but for reasons he could not fathom, they refused to come to his assistance. The day after he was forced into bankruptcy Nicholas committed suicide.

Demiris' sense of *thekaeossini* was a two-edged sword. Just as he never forgave an injury, neither did he ever forget a favour. A landlady who had fed and clothed the young man when he was too poor to pay her suddenly found herself the owner of an apartment building, without any idea who her benefactor was. A young girl who had taken the penniless young Demiris in to live with her had been given a villa and a lifetime pension anonymously. The people who had had dealings with the ambitious young Greek lad forty years earlier had no idea how the casual relationship with him would affect their lives. The dynamic young Demiris had needed help from bankers and lawyers, ship captains and unions, politicians and financiers. Some had encouraged and helped him, others had snubbed and cheated him. In his head and in his heart the proud Greek had kept an indelible record of every transaction. His wife Melina had once accused him of playing God.

'Every man plays God,' Demiris had told her. 'Some of us are better equipped for the role than others.'

'But it is wrong to destroy the lives of men, Costa.'

'It is not wrong. It is justice.'

'Vengeance.'

'Sometimes it is the same. Most men get away with the evil they do. I am in a position to make them pay for it. That is justice.'

He enjoyed the hours he spent devising traps for his adversaries. He would study his victims carefully, analyzing their personalities, assessing their strengths and their weaknesses.

When Demiris had had three small freighters and needed a loan to expand his fleet, he had gone to a Swiss banker in Basel. The banker had not only turned him down but had telephoned other banker friends of his to advise them not to give the young Greek any money. Demiris had finally managed to borrow the money in Turkey.

Demiris had bided his time. He decided that the banker's Achilles' heel lay in his greed. Demiris was in negotiation with Ibn Saud of Arabia to take over leases on a newly discovered oil development there. The leases would be worth several hundred million dollars to Demiris' company.

He instructed one of his agents to leak the news to the Swiss banker about the deal that was about to take place. The banker was offered a 25-percent participation in the new company if he put up five million dollars in cash to buy shares of the stock. When the deal went through, the five million dollars would be worth more than fifty million. The banker quickly checked the deal and confirmed its authenticity. Not having that kind of money available personally, he quietly borrowed it from the bank without notifying anyone, for he had no wish to share his windfall. The transaction was to take place the following week, at which time he would be able to replace the money he had taken.

When Demiris had the banker's cheque in his hand, he announced to the newspapers that the arrangement with Arabia had been cancelled. The stock plummeted. There was no way for the banker to cover his losses, and his embezzlement was discovered. Demiris picked up the banker's shares of stock at a few cents on the dollar and then went ahead with the oil deal. The stock soared. The banker was convicted of embezzlement and given a prison sentence of twenty years.

There were a few players in Demiris' game with whom he had not yet evened the score, but he was in no hurry. He enjoyed the anticipation, the planning and the execution. It was like a chess game, and Demiris was a chess master. These days he made no enemies, for no man could afford to be his enemy, so his quarry was limited to those who had crossed his path in the past.

This, then, was the man who appeared one afternoon at Noelle Page's Sunday salon. He was spending a few hours in Paris on his way to Cairo, and a young sculptress he was seeing suggested that they stop in at the salon. From the moment Demiris saw Noelle, he knew that he wanted her.

Aside from royalty itself which was unavailable to the daughter of a Marseille fishmonger, Constantin Demiris was probably the closest thing there was to a king. Three days after she had met him Noelle quit her play without notice, packed her clothes and joined Constantin Demiris in Greece.

Because of the prominence of their respective positions it was inevitable that the relationship between Noelle Page and Constantin Demiris become an international *cause célèbre*. Photographers and reporters were constantly trying to interview Demiris' wife, but if her composure was ruffled, she never betrayed it. Melina Demiris' only comment to the press was that her husband had many good friends around the world and that she saw nothing wrong with that. Privately she told her outraged parents that Costa had had affairs before and that this would soon wear itself out like all the others. Her husband would leave on extended business trips, and she would see newspaper photographs of him with Noelle in Constantinople or Tokyo or Rome. Melina Demiris was a proud woman, but she was determined to endure the humiliation because she truly loved her husband. She accepted the fact, though she could never fathom the reason, that some men needed more than one woman and that even a man in love with his wife could sleep with another woman. She would have died before she let another man touch her. She never reproached Constantin, because she knew that it would serve no purpose except to alienate him. They had on balance a good marriage. She was aware that she was not a passionate woman, but she let her husband use her in bed whenever he wished, and she tried to give him what pleasure she could. If she had known of the ways that Noelle made love to her husband, she would have been shocked, and if she had known how much her husband enjoyed it, she would have been miserable.

Noelle's chief attraction for Demiris, for whom women no longer held any surprises, was that she was a constant surprise. To him who had a passion for puzzles, she was an enigma, defying solution.

He had never met anyone like her. She accepted the beautiful things he gave her, but she was just as happy when he gave her nothing. He bought her a lavish villa at Portofino overlooking the exquisite blue, horseshoe bay, but he knew that it would have made no difference if it had been a tiny apartment in the old Plaka section of Athens.

Demiris had met many women in his life who had tried to use their sex to manipulate him in one way or another. Noelle never asked anything of him. Some women had come to him to bask in his reflected glory, but in Noelle's case *she* was the one who attracted the newspapermen and photographers. She was a star in her own right. For a while Demiris toyed with the idea that perhaps she was in love with him for himself, but he was too honest to maintain the delusion.

In the beginning it was a challenge to try to reach the deep core inside Noelle, to subjugate it and make it his. At first Demiris had tried to do it sexually, but for the first time in his life, he had met a woman who was more than a match for him. Her sensual appetites exceeded his. Anything he could do, she could do better and more often and with more skill, until finally he learned to relax in bed and enjoy her as he had never enjoyed another woman in his life. She was a phenomenon, constantly revealing new facets for him to enjoy. Noelle could cook as well as any of the chefs to whom he paid a king's ransom and knew as much about art as the curators he kept on yearly retainers to seek out paintings and sculpture for him. He enjoyed listening to them discussing art with Noelle and their amazement at the depth of her knowledge.

Demiris had recently purchased a Rembrandt, and Noelle happened to be at his summer island when the painting arrived. There was a young curator there who had found the painting for him.

'It's one of the Master's greatest,' the curator had said as he unveiled it.

It was an exquisite painting of a mother and daughter. Noelle was seated in a chair, sipping an ouzo, quietly watching.

'It's a beauty,' Demiris agreed. He turned to Noelle. 'How do you like it?'

'It's lovely,' she said. She turned to the curator. 'Where did you find it?'

'I traced it to a private dealer in Brussels,' he replied proudly, 'and persuaded him to sell it to me.'

'How much did you pay for it?' Noelle asked.

'Two hundred and fifty thousand pounds.'

'It's a bargain,' Demiris declared.

Noelle picked up a cigarette, and the young man rushed to light it for her. 'Thank you,' she said. She looked at Demiris. 'It would have been more of a bargain, Costa, if he had bought it from the man who owned it.'

'I don't understand,' Demiris said.

The curator was looking at her oddly.

'If this is genuine,' Noelle explained, 'then it came from the estate of the Duke of Toledo in

Spain.' She turned to the curator. 'Is that not so?' she asked.

His face had turned white. 'I – I have no idea,' he stammered. 'The dealer didn't tell me.'

'Oh, come now,' Noelle chided him. 'You mean you bought a painting for this amount of money without establishing its provenance? That's difficult to believe. The estate priced the painting at one hundred and seventy-five thousand pounds. Someone's been cheated out of seventy-five thousand pounds.'

And it had proven to be true. The curator and the art dealer were convicted of collusion and sent to prison. Demiris returned the painting. In thinking it over later he decided that he was less impressed by Noelle's knowledge than by her honesty. If she had wished to, she could simply have called the curator aside, threatened to blackmail him and split the money with him. Instead she had challenged him openly in front of Demiris with no ulterior motive. He had bought her a very expensive emerald necklace in appreciation, and she had accepted it with the same casual appreciation with which she would have accepted a cigarette lighter. Demiris insisted on taking Noelle with him everywhere. He trusted no one in business and therefore was forced to make all his decisions by himself. He found it helpful to discuss business deals with Noelle. She was amazingly knowledgeable about business, and the mere fact of being able to talk with someone sometimes made it easier for Demiris to make a decision. In time Noelle knew more about his business affairs than anyone with the possible exception of his lawyers and accountants. In the past Demiris had always had several mistresses at a time, but now Noelle gave him everything he needed, and one by one he dropped them. They accepted the *congé* without bitterness, for Demiris was a generous man.

He owned a yacht that was a hundred and thirty-five feet long, with four G.M. diesels. It carried a seaplane, a crew of twenty-four, two speed boats and had a freshwater swimming pool. There were twelve beautifully appointed guest suites and a large apartment for himself, crammed with paintings and antiques.

When Demiris entertained on his yacht, it was Noelle who was his hostess. When Demiris flew or sailed to his private island, it was Noelle he took with him while Melina remained at home. He was careful never to bring his wife and Noelle together, but he knew of course that his wife was aware of her.

Noelle was treated like royalty wherever she went. But then it was only her due. The little girl who had looked out at her fleet of ships through the dirty apartment window in Marseille had moved on to the largest fleet in the world. Noelle was not impressed by Demiris' wealth or his reputation: She was impressed by his intelligence and strength. He had the mind and will of a giant and he made other men seem pusillanimous in comparison. She sensed the implacable cruelty in him, but somehow this made him even more exciting, for it was in her also.

Noelle constantly received offers to star in plays and in motion pictures, but she was indifferent. She was playing the lead in her own life story, and it was more fascinating than anything any scriptwriter could concoct. She dined with kings and prime ministers and ambassadors, and they all catered to her because they knew that she had the ear of Demiris. They would drop subtle hints about what their needs were and they promised her the world if she would help them.

But Noelle already had the world. She would lie in bed with Demiris and tell him what each man had asked for, and out of this information Demiris would gauge their needs and their strengths and their weaknesses. Then he would put on appropriate pressures, and from this more money would pour into his already overflowing coffers.

Demiris' private island was one of his great joys. He had purchased an island that was raw land and had transformed it into a paradise. It had a spectacular hilltop villa in which he lived, a dozen charming guest cottages, a hunting preserve, an artificial freshwater lake, a zoo, a harbour where his yacht could anchor and a landing field for his planes. The island was staffed by eighty servants, and armed guards kept out intruders. Noelle liked the solitude of the island, and she enjoyed it most when there were no other guests there. Constantin Demiris was flattered, assuming that it was because Noelle preferred to be alone with him. He would have been astonished if he had known how preoccupied she was with a man of whose existence he was not even aware.

Larry Douglas was half a world away from Noelle, fighting secret battles on secret islands, and yet she knew more about him than his wife, with whom he corresponded fairly regularly. Noelle travelled to Paris to see Christian Barbet at least once a month and the bald, myopic little detective always had an up-to-date report ready for her.

The first time Noelle had returned to France to see Barbet and had tried to leave, there had been trouble about her exit visa. She had been kept waiting in a Customs office for five hours and had finally been allowed to place a call to Constantin Demiris. Ten minutes after she had spoken to Demiris, a German officer had rushed in to offer the profuse apologies of his government. Noelle had been issued a special visa, and she had never been stopped again.

The little detective looked forward to Noelle's visits. He was charging her a fortune, but his trained nose smelled even bigger money. He was very pleased with her new liaison with Constantin Demiris. He had a feeling that in one way or another it was going to be of great financial benefit to him. First he had to make sure that Demiris knew nothing of his mistress' interest in Larry Douglas, then he had to find out how much the information would be worth to Demiris. Or to Noelle Page for him to keep quiet. He was on the verge of an enormous coup, but he had to play his cards carefully. The information Barbet was able to gather on Larry was surprisingly substantial, for Barbet could afford to pay his sources well.

While Larry's wife was reading a letter postmarked from an anonymous APO, Christian Barbet was reporting to Noelle, 'He's flying with the Fourteenth Fighter Group, Forty-eighth Fighter Squadron.'

Catherine's letter read '. . . all I can tell you is that I'm somewhere in the Pacific, baby . . .'

And Christian Barbet was telling Noelle, 'They're on Tarawa. Guam's next.'

'. . . I really miss you, Cathy. Things are picking up here. I can't give you any details, but we finally have planes that are better than the Jap Zeros . . .'

'Your friend is flying P-Thirty-eights, P-Forties and P-Fifty-ones.'

'. . . I'm glad you've been keeping busy in Washington. Just stay true to me, baby. Everything's fine here. I'll have a little news for you when I see you . . .'

'Your friend has been awarded the D.F.C. and has been promoted to Lieutenant-Colonel.'

While Catherine thought about her husband and prayed for him to come home safely, Noelle followed

Larry's every move and she too prayed for Larry's safe return. The war would be over soon and Larry Douglas would be coming home. To both of them.

ELEVEN

Catherine

Washington: 1945–1946

On the morning of May 7, 1945, at Rheims, France, Germany surrendered unconditionally to the Allies. The thousand-year reign of the Third Reich had come to an end. Those insiders who knew of the crippling devastation at Pearl Harbour, those who had watched Dunkirk narrowly miss going into history as England's Waterloo, those who had commanded the RAF and knew how helpless London's defences would have been against an all-out attack by the Luftwaffe: All these people were aware of the series of miracles that had brought victory to the Allies – and knew by what a narrow margin it had missed going the other way. The powers of evil had almost emerged triumphant, and the idea was so preposterous, so contrary to the Christian ethic of Right triumphing and Evil succumbing, that they turned away from it in horror, thanking God and burying their blunders from the eyes of posterity in mountains of files marked *TOP SECRET*.

The attention of the free world turned now to the Far East. The Japanese, those short, nearsighted comic figures, were bloodily defending every inch of land they held, and it looked as though it was going to be a long and costly war.

And then on August 6, an atomic bomb was dropped on Hiroshima. The destruction was beyond belief. In a few short minutes, most of the population of a major city lay dead, victims of a pestilence greater than the combined wars and plagues of all the Middle Ages.

On August 9, three days later, a second atomic bomb was dropped, this time on Nagasaki. The results were even more devastating. Civilization had finally reached its finest hour; it was able to achieve genocide that could be calculated at the rate of *x* number of millions of persons per second. It was too much for the Japanese, and on September 2, 1945, on the battleship *Missouri*, General Douglas MacArthur received the unconditional surrender of the Japanese Government. World War II was ended.

For one long moment when the news was flashed, the world held its breath and then let out a grateful heartfelt cheer. Cities and hamlets around the globe were filled with hysterical parades of people celebrating the end of the war to end all wars to end all wars to end all wars . . .

The following day, through some magic that he would never explain to Catherine, Bill Fraser was able to get a telephone call through to Larry Douglas on an island somewhere in the South Pacific. It was to be a surprise for Catherine. Fraser asked her to wait in her office for him so that they could go to lunch together. At 2:30 in the afternoon, she buzzed Bill on the intercom system.

'When are you going to feed me?' she demanded. 'It'll be time for dinner soon.'

'Sit tight,' Fraser replied. 'I'll be with you in a minute.'

Five minutes later, he buzzed her and said, 'There's a call for you on line one.'

Catherine picked up the phone. 'Hello?' She heard a crackling and a swell of sound like the waves of a distant ocean. 'Hello,' she repeated.

A male voice said, 'Mrs Larry Douglas?'

'Yes,' Catherine said, puzzled. 'Who's this?'

'Just a moment, please.'

Through the receiver, she heard a high-pitched whine. Another crackling sound and then a voice saying 'Cathy?'

She sat there, her heart pounding, unable to speak. 'Larry? Larry?'

'Yes, baby.'

'Oh, Larry!' She began to cry and unexpectedly her whole body was trembling.

'How are you, honey?'

She dug her fingernails into her arm, trying to hurt herself enough so that she could stop the hysteria that had suddenly swept over her. 'I'm f – fine,' she said. 'W – where are you?'

'If I tell you, we'll be cut off,' he said. 'I'm somewhere in the Pacific.'

'That's close enough!' She began to get control of her voice. 'Are you all right, darling?'

'I'm fine.'

'When will you be coming home?'

'Any second,' he promised.

Catherine's eyes flooded with tears again. 'OK, let's sy – synchronize our watches.'

'Are you crying?'

'Of course I'm crying, you idiot! I'm just glad you can't see the mascara running down my face. Oh Larry . . . Larry . . .'

'I've missed you, baby,' he said.

Catherine thought of the long, lonely nights that had stretched into weeks and months and years without him, without his arms around her, without his strong, wonderful body next to her, without his comfort and protection and love. And she said, 'I've missed you, too.'

A man's voice came on the line. 'I'm sorry, Colonel, but we're going to have to disconnect.'

Colonel!

'You didn't tell me you were promoted.'

'I was afraid it would go to your head.'

'Oh, darling, I –'

The roar of the ocean grew louder, and suddenly there was a silence and the line was dead. Catherine sat at her desk staring at the telephone. And then she buried her head in her arms and began to cry.

Ten minutes later, Fraser's voice came over the

intercom. 'I'm ready for lunch when you are, Cathy,' he said.

'I'm ready for anything now,' she said joyfully. 'Give me five minutes.' She smiled warmly as she thought of what Fraser had done and how much trouble it must have cost him. He was the dearest man she had ever known. Next to Larry, of course.

Catherine had visualized Larry's arrival so often that the arrival itself was almost an anticlimax. Bill Fraser had explained to her that Larry was probably coming home in an Air Transport Command plane or a MATS plane and they didn't run at fixed times like commercial scheduled airlines. You conned a ride on the first flight you could get on – and it didn't matter too much where the plane was headed – just so it was flying in the right general direction.

Catherine stayed home all day waiting for Larry. She tried to read, but she was too nervous. She sat and listened to the news and thought about Larry returning home to her, this time forever. By midnight, he had still not arrived. She decided he probably would not be home until the next day. At two in the morning, when Catherine could keep her eyes open no longer, she went to bed.

She was awakened by a hand on her arm and she opened her eyes and he was standing over her, her Larry was standing there, looking down at her, a grin on his lean, tanned face, and in a flash Catherine was in his arms and all the worry and loneliness and pain of the past four years were washed away in a cleansing flood of joy that seemed to fill every fibre of her being. She hugged him until she was afraid that she was going to break his bones. She wanted to stay like this forever, never letting him go.

'Easy, honey,' Larry said finally. He pulled away from her, a smile on his face. 'It's going to look funny in the newspapers. "Flyer comes home safely from the war and gets hugged to death by his wife."'

Catherine turned on the lights, every one of them, flooding the room so that she could see him, study him, devour him. His face had a new maturity. There were lines around his eyes and mouth that had not been there before. The overall affect was to make him handsomer than ever.

'I wanted to meet you,' Catherine babbled, 'but I didn't know where. I called the Air Corps and they couldn't give me any information at all, so I just waited here and . . .'

Larry moved towards her and shut her up with a kiss. His kiss was hard and demanding. Catherine had expected to feel the same physical eagerness for him and she was surprised to find that this was not so. She loved him very much and yet she would have been content to just sit with him and talk, instead of making love as he so urgently wanted to do. She had sublimated her sexual feelings for so long that they were deeply buried, and it would take time before they could be aroused and brought to the surface again.

But Larry was giving her no time. He was throwing

off his clothes and saying, 'God, Cathy, you don't know how I've dreamed about this moment. I was going crazy out there. And look at you. You're even more beautiful than I remembered.'

He ripped off his shorts and was standing there naked. And somehow it was a stranger pushing her down on the bed, and she wished that Larry would give her time to get used to his being home, to get used to his nakedness again. But he was getting on top of her without any preliminaries, forcing himself into her and she knew that she was not ready for him. He was tearing into her, hurting her and she bit her hand to keep from crying out as he lay on top of her, making love like a wild animal.

Her husband was home.

For the next month with Fraser's blessing Catherine stayed away from the office and she and Larry spent almost every moment together. She cooked for him all of his favourite dishes, and they listened to records and talked and talked, trying to fill in the gaps of the lost years between them. At night they went to parties or to the theatre and when they returned home, they made love. Her body was ready for him now and she found him as exciting a lover as always. Almost.

She did not want to admit it even to herself, but there was something indefinably changed about Larry. He was more demanding, less giving. There was still foreplay before they made love, but he did it mechanically, as though it were a duty to be disposed of before he went on to the sexual attack. And it was an attack, a savage and fierce taking, as though his body were seeking vengeance for something, meting out punishment. Each time they finished making love, Catherine felt bruised and battered, as though she had taken a beating. Perhaps, she defended him, it's just because he's been so long without a woman.

As the days passed, his lovemaking remained the same and it was that fact that finally led Catherine to look for other changes in Larry. She tried to study him dispassionately, tried to forget that this was the husband whom she adored. She saw a tall, well-built, black-haired man with deep dark eyes and a devastatingly beautiful face. Or perhaps 'beautiful' no longer applied. The lines around his mouth had added a harshness to his features. Looking at this stranger, Catherine would have thought, *Here is a man who could be selfish and ruthless and cold*. And yet she told herself that she was being ridiculous. This was her Larry, loving and kind and thoughtful.

She proudly introduced him to all her friends and the people she worked with, but they seemed to bore him. At parties he would wander off into a corner and spend the evening drinking. It seemed to Catherine that he made no effort to be sociable. 'Why should I?' he snapped at her one evening when she tried to discuss it with him. 'Where the fuck were all those fat cats when I was up there getting my ass shot at?'

A few times Catherine broached the subject of

what Larry was going to do with his future. She had thought that he would want to remain in the Air Corps, but almost the first thing Larry did when he returned home was to resign his commission.

'The Service is for suckers. There's nowhere to go but down,' he had said.

It was almost like a parody of the first conversation Catherine had had with him in Hollywood. Only then, he had been joking.

Catherine had to discuss the problem with someone and she finally decided to talk to Bill Fraser. She told him what was troubling her, leaving out the more personal things.

'If it's any consolation to you,' Fraser said sympathetically, 'there are millions of women all over the world going through what you're going through now. It's really very simple, Catherine. You're married to a stranger.'

Catherine looked at him, saying nothing.

Fraser stopped to fill his pipe and light it. 'You can't really expect to pick up where you left off when Larry went away four years ago, can you? That place in time doesn't exist any more. You've moved past it, and so has Larry. Part of what makes a marriage work is that a husband and wife have common experiences. They grow together and their marriage grows. You're going to have to find a common meeting ground again.'

'I feel disloyal even discussing it, Bill.'

Fraser smiled. 'I knew you first,' he reminded her. 'Remember?'

'I remember.'

'I'm sure that Larry's feeling his way, too,' Fraser continued. 'He's been living with a thousand men for four years and now he has to get used to living with a girl.'

She smiled. 'You're right about everything you said. I suppose I just had to hear someone say it.'

'Everyone's full of helpful advice about how to handle the wounded,' Fraser remarked, 'but there are some wounds that don't show. Sometimes they go deep.' He saw the look on Catherine's face. 'I don't mean anything serious,' he added quickly. 'I'm just talking about the horrors that any combat soldier sees. Unless a man is a complete fool, it's bound to have an enormous effect on his outlook. You see what I mean?'

Catherine nodded. 'Yes.' The question was: What effect had it had?

When Catherine finally went back to work, the men at the agency were overjoyed to see her. For the first three days she did almost nothing but go over campaigns and layouts for new accounts and catch up on old accounts. She worked from early in the morning until late in the evening, trying to make up for the time she had lost, badgering copywriters and sketch artists and reassuring nervous clients. She was very good at her job and she loved it.

Larry would be waiting for Catherine when she returned to the apartment at night. In the beginning she had asked what he did while she was gone, but his answers were always vague and she finally stopped asking him. He had put up a wall, and she did not know how to breach it. He took offence at almost everything Catherine said, and there were constant quarrels over nothing. Occasionally they would dine with Fraser and she went out of her way to make those evenings pleasant and gay so that Fraser would not think there was anything wrong.

But Catherine had to face the fact that something was very wrong. She felt that it was partly her failure. She still loved Larry. She loved the look of him and the feel of him and the memory of him, but she knew that if he went on this way, it would destroy them both.

She was having lunch with William Fraser.

'How's Larry?' he asked.

The automatic Pavlovian response of 'fine' started to come to her lips and she stopped. 'He needs a job,' Catherine said bluntly.

Fraser leaned back and nodded. 'Is he getting restless about not working?'

She hesitated, not wanting to lie. 'He doesn't want to do just anything,' she said carefully. 'It would have to be the right thing.'

Fraser studied her, trying to assess the meaning that lay behind her words.

'How would he like to be a pilot?'

'He doesn't want to go back into the Service again.'

'I was thinking about one of the airlines. I have a friend who runs Pan Am. They'd be lucky to get someone with Larry's experience.'

Catherine sat there thinking about it, trying to put herself in Larry's mind. He loved flying more than anything in the world. It would be a good job, doing what he loved to do. 'It – it sounds wonderful,' she said cautiously. 'Do you really think you could get it for him, Bill?'

'I'll give it a try,' he said. 'Why don't you sound Larry out first and see how he feels about it?'

'I will.' Catherine took his hand in hers gratefully. 'Thanks so much.'

'For what?' Fraser asked lightly.

'For always being there when I need you.'

He put his hand over hers. 'It goes with the territory.'

When Catherine told Larry about Bill Fraser's suggestion that night, he said, 'That's the best idea I've heard since I came home,' and two days later, he had an appointment to see Carl Eastman at Pan Am headquarters in Manhattan. Catherine pressed Larry's suit for him, selected a shirt and tie and shined his shoes until she could see her image in them. 'I'll call you as soon as I can and let you know how it went.' He kissed her, smiled that quick boyish grin of his and left.

In many ways Larry *was* like a small boy, Catherine thought. He could be petulant and quick-tempered and surly, but he was also loving and generous.

'My luck,' sighed Catherine. 'I have to be the only perfect person in the whole universe.'

She had a busy schedule ahead of her, but she was unable to think of anything but Larry and his meeting. It was more than just a job. She had a feeling that her whole marriage hinged on what was going to happen.

It was going to be the longest day of her life.

Pan American headquarters was in a modern building at Fifth Avenue and Fifty-third Street. Carl Eastman's office was large and comfortably furnished, and he obviously held a position of importance.

'Come in and sit down,' he greeted Larry as Larry entered the office.

Eastman was about thirty-five, a trim, lantern-jawed man with piercing hazel eyes that missed nothing. He motioned Larry to a couch, then sat on a chair across from him.

'Coffee?'

'No thanks,' Larry said.

'I understand you'd like to work for us.'

'If there's an opening.'

'There's an opening,' Eastman said, 'only a thousand stick jockeys have applied for it.' He shook his head ruefully. 'It's incredible. The Air Corps trains thousands of bright young men to fly the most complicated pieces of machinery ever made. Then when they do their job and do it damn well, the Air Corps tells 'em to get lost. They have nothing for them.' He sighed. 'You wouldn't believe the people who come in here all day long. Top pilots, aces like yourself. There's only one job open for every thousand applicants – and all the other airlines are in exactly the same position.'

A feeling of disappointment swept over Larry. 'Why did you see me?' he asked stiffly.

'Two reasons. Number One, because the man upstairs told me to.'

Larry felt an anger rising in him.

'I don't need –'

Eastman leaned forwards. 'Number Two, you have a damn good flying record.'

'Thanks,' Larry said, tightly.

Eastman studied him. 'You'd have to go through a training programme here, you know. It would be like going back to school.'

Larry hesitated, not certain where the conversation was leading.

'That sounds all right,' he said, cautiously.

'You'll have to take your training in New York out of LaGuardia.'

Larry nodded, waiting.

'There are four weeks of ground school and then a month of flight training.'

'You flying DC-Fours?' asked Larry.

'Right. When you finish your training, we'll put you on as a navigator. Your training base pay will be three fifty a month.'

He had the job! The son-of-a-bitch had needled him about all the thousands of pilots who were after it. But he had the job! What had he been worried about? No one in the whole damned Air Corps had a better record than he did.

Larry grinned. 'I don't mind starting as a navigator, Eastman, but I'm a pilot. When does *that* happen?'

Eastman sighed. 'The airlines are unionized. The only way anyone moves up is through seniority. There are a lot of men ahead of you. Do you want to give it a try?'

Larry nodded. 'What have I got to lose?'

'Right,' Eastman said. 'I'll arrange all the formalities. You'll have to take a physical, of course. Any problems there?'

Larry grinned. 'The Japanese didn't find anything wrong with me.'

'How soon can you go to work?'

'Is this afternoon too early?'

'Let's make it Monday.' Eastman scribbled a name on a card and handed it to Larry. 'Here. They'll be expecting you at nine o'clock Monday morning.'

When Larry phoned Catherine to tell her the news, there was an excitement in his voice that Catherine had not heard for a long time. She knew then that everything was going to be all right.

TWELVE

Noelle

Athens: 1946

Constantin Demiris owned a fleet of airplanes for his personal use, but his pride was a converted Hawker Siddeley that transported sixteen passengers in luxurious comfort, had a speed of three hundred miles per hour and carried a crew of four. It was a flying palace. The interior had been decorated by Frederick Sawrin and Chagall had done the murals on the walls. Instead of airplane seats, easy chairs and comfortable couches were sprinkled throughout the cabin. The aft compartment had been converted into a luxurious bedroom. Forwards behind the cockpit was a modern kitchen. Whenever Demiris or Noelle flew on the plane, there was a chef aboard.

Demiris had chosen as his personal pilots a Greek flyer named Paul Metaxas and an English ex-RAF fighter pilot named Ian Whitestone. Metaxas was a stocky, amiable man with a perpetual smile on his face and a hearty, contagious laugh. He had been a mechanic, had taught himself how to fly and had served with the RAF in the Battle of Britain, where he had met Ian Whitestone. Whitestone was tall, red-haired and painfully thin, with the diffident manner of a schoolmaster on his first day of the term at a second-rate school for incorrigible boys. In the air Whitestone was something else again. He had the rare, natural skill of a born pilot, a feel that can never be taught or learned. Whitestone and Metaxas had flown together for three years against the Luftwaffe and each had a high regard for the other.

Noelle made frequent trips in the large plane, sometimes on business with Demiris, sometimes for pleasure. She had gotten to know the pilots but had paid no particular attention to them.

And then one day she overheard them reminiscing about an experience they had had in the RAF.

From that moment on Noelle either spent some part of each flight in the cockpit talking to the two men or invited one of them to join her back in the cabin. She encouraged them to talk about their war experiences and, without ever asking a direct question, eventually learned that Whitestone had been a liaison officer in Larry Douglas' squadron before Douglas had left the RAF and that Metaxas had joined the squadron too late to meet Larry. Noelle began to concentrate on the

English pilot. Encouraged and flattered by the interest of his boss' mistress, Whitestone talked freely about his past life and his future ambitions. He told Noelle he had always been interested in electronics. His brother-in-law in Australia had opened a small electronics firm and wanted Whitestone to go in with him, but Whitestone lacked the capital.

'The way I live,' he said to Noelle, grinning, 'I'll never make it.'

Noelle continued to visit Paris once a month to see Christian Barbet. Barbet had established a liaison with a private detective agency in Washington, and there was a constant stream of reports on Larry Douglas. Cautiously testing Noelle, the little detective had offered to send the reports to her in Athens, but she told him that she preferred picking them up in person. Barbet had nodded his head slyly and said in a conspiratorial tone, 'I understand, Miss Page.' So she did *not* want Constantin Demiris to know about her interest in Larry Douglas. The possibilities for blackmail staggered Barbet's mind.

'You have been most helpful, Monsieur Barbet,' Noelle said, 'and most discreet.'

He smiled unctuously. 'Thank you, Miss Page. My business depends on discretion.'

'Exactly,' Noelle replied, 'I know you are discreet because Constantin Demiris has never mentioned your name to me. The day he does, I will ask him to destroy you.' Her tone was pleasant and conversational, but the affect was like a bombshell.

Monsieur Barbet stared at Noelle for a long, shocked moment, licking his lips. He scratched his crotch nervously and stammered, 'I – I assure you, Mademoiselle, that I would n – never . . .'

'I'm sure you won't,' Noelle said and departed.

On the commercial plane taking her back to Greece, Noelle read the confidential report in the sealed manila envelope.

ACME SECURITY AGENCY
1402 'D' Street
Washington, D.C.

Reference: #2-179-210 February 2, 1946

Dear Monsieur Barbet:

One of our operatives spoke to a contact in the personnel office at Pan Am: Subject is regarded as a skilled combat pilot, but they question whether he is disciplined enough to work out satisfactorily within a large, structured organization.

Subject's personal life-style follows the same pattern as in our previous reports. We have followed him to the apartments of various women whom he had picked up, where he remained for periods of from one hour to as long as five hours, and we presume that he is having a series of casual sexual relations with these women. (Names and addresses are on file if you wish them.)

In view of the Subject's new employment, it is possible that this pattern may change. We will follow up on this per your request.

Please find our bill enclosed.

Very truly yours,

R. Ruttenberg,
Managing Supervisor

Noelle returned the report to the folder and leaned back in her seat and closed her eyes. She visualized Larry, restless and tormented, married to a woman he did not love, caught in a trap baited with his own weaknesses.

His new job with the airline might slow Noelle's plan down a bit, but she had patience. In time she would bring Larry to her. Meanwhile there were certain steps she could take to move things along.

Ian Whitestone was delighted to be invited to lunch with Noelle Page. In the beginning he had flattered himself that she was attracted to him, but all of their encounters had been on a pleasant but formal basis that let him know that he was an employee, and she was an untouchable. He had often puzzled over what Noelle wanted of him, for Whitestone was an intelligent man, and he had the odd feeling that their random conversations meant something more to her than they meant to him.

On this particular day Whitestone and Noelle

drove to a small seaside town near Cape Sunion, where they were having lunch. Noelle was dressed in a white summer frock and sandals, with her soft blond hair blowing free, and she had never looked more beautiful. Ian Whitestone was engaged to a model in London and while she was pretty, she could not compare to Noelle. Whitestone had never met anyone who could, and he would have envied Constantin Demiris except that Noelle always seemed more desirable to him in retrospect. When Whitestone was actually with her, he found himself slightly intimidated. Now Noelle had turned the conversation to his plans for the future, and he wondered, not for the first time, whether she was probing on Demiris' orders to find out whether he was loyal to his employer.

'I love my job,' the pilot assured Noelle earnestly. 'I'd like to keep it until I'm too old to see where I'm flying.'

Noelle studied him a moment, aware of his suspicions. 'I'm disappointed,' she said ruefully. 'I was hoping that you had more ambition than that.'

Whitestone stared at her. 'I don't understand.'

'Didn't you tell me that you'd like to have your own electronics company one day?'

He recalled mentioning it to her casually, and it surprised him that she had remembered.

'That was just a pipe dream,' he replied. 'It would take a lot of money.'

'A man with your ability,' Noelle said, 'shouldn't be stopped by a lack of money.'

Whitestone sat there uneasily, not knowing what Noelle Page expected him to say. He did like his job. He was making more money than he had ever made in his life, the hours were good and the work was interesting. On the other hand he was at the beck and call of an eccentric billionaire who expected him to be available at any hour of the day or night. It had raised hell with his personal life, and his fiancée was not happy about what he was doing, good salary or no.

'I've been talking to a friend of mine about you,' Noelle said. 'He likes to invest in new companies.'

Her voice had controlled enthusiasm, as though she were excited about what she was saying and yet was being careful not to push him too hard. Whitestone raised his eyes and met hers.

'He's very interested in you,' she said.

Whitestone swallowed. 'I – I don't know what to say, Miss Page.'

'I don't expect you to say anything now,' Noelle assured him. 'I just want you to think about it.'

He sat there a moment, thinking about it. 'Does Mr Demiris know about this?' he asked finally.

Noelle smiled conspiratorially. 'I'm afraid Mr Demiris would never approve. He doesn't like to lose employees, especially good ones. However –' she paused fractionally, 'I think someone like you is entitled to get everything out of life that he can. Unless of course,' she added, 'you want to go on working for someone else the rest of your life.'

'I don't,' Whitestone said quickly and suddenly

realized that he had committed himself. He studied Noelle's face to see if there was any suggestion that this could be some kind of a trap, but all he saw was a sympathetic understanding. 'Any man worth his salt would like to have his own business,' he said defensively.

'Of course,' Noelle agreed. 'Give it some thought, and we'll talk about it again.' And then she added warningly, 'It will be just between us.'

'Fair enough,' Whitestone said, 'and thank you. If it works out, it will really be exciting.'

Noelle nodded. 'I have a feeling that it's going to work out.'

THIRTEEN

Catherine

Washington–Paris: 1946

At nine o'clock on Monday morning Larry Douglas reported to the chief pilot, Captain Hal Sakowitz, at the Pan American office at LaGuardia Airport in New York. As Larry walked in the door, Sakowitz picked up the transcript of Larry's service record that he had been studying and shoved it into a desk drawer.

Captain Sakowitz was a compact, rugged-looking man with a seamed, weather-beaten face and the largest hands that Larry had ever seen. Sakowitz was one of the real veterans of aviation. He had started out in the days of travelling air circuses, had flown single-engine airmail planes for the Government and had been an airline pilot for twenty years and Pan American's chief pilot for the past five years.

'Glad to have you with us, Douglas,' he said.

'Glad to be here,' Larry replied.

'Eager to get into a plane again?'

'Who needs a plane?' grinned Larry. 'Just point me into the wind, and I'll take off.'

Sakowitz indicated a chair. 'Sit down. I like to get acquainted with you boys who come in here to take over my job.'

Larry laughed. 'You noticed.'

'Oh, I don't blame any of you. You're all hot-shot pilots, you have great combat records, you come in here and think "if that schmuck Sakowitz can be Chief Pilot, they oughta make me Chairman of the Board." None of you guys plan to stay navigators very long. It's just a stepping stone to pilot. Well, that's fine. That's the way it should be.'

'I'm glad you feel that way,' Larry said.

'But there's one thing you have to know out front. We all belong to a union, Douglas, and promotions are strictly by seniority.'

'I understand.'

'The only thing you might *not* understand is that these are damn good jobs and there are more people coming in than there are leaving. That slows up the rate of promotion.'

'I'll take my chances,' Larry replied.

Sakowitz's secretary brought in coffee and Danish pastries and the two men spent the next hour talking and getting acquainted. Sakowitz's manner was friendly and affable, and many of his questions were seemingly irrelevant and trivial, but when Larry left to go to his first class, Sakowitz knew a great deal about Larry Douglas. A few minutes after Larry had departed, Carl Eastman came into the office.

'How did it go?' Eastman asked.

'OK.'

Eastman gave him a hard look. 'What do you think, Sak?'

'We'll try him.'

'I asked you what you thought.'

Sakowitz shrugged. 'OK. I'll tell you. My hunch is he's a goddamn good pilot. He has to be, with his war record. Put him in a plane with a bunch of enemy fighters shooting at him, and I don't think you'll find anyone better.' He hesitated.

'Go on,' Eastman said.

'The thing is, there aren't a hell of a lot of enemy fighters around Manhattan. I've known guys like Douglas. For some reason I've never figured out, their lives are geared for danger. They do crazy things like climbing impossible mountains or diving to the bottom of the ocean, or whatever the hell else danger they can find. When a war breaks out, they rise to the top like cream in a cup of scalding coffee.' He swerved his chair around and looked out the window. Eastman stood there, saying nothing, waiting.

'I have a hunch about Douglas, Carl. There's something wrong with him. Maybe if he were captain of one of our ships, flying it himself, he could make it. But I don't think he's psychologically geared to take orders from an engineer, a first officer and a pilot, especially when he thinks he could outfly them all.' He swung back to face Eastman. 'And the funny part is, he probably could.'

'You're making me nervous,' Eastman said.

'Me, too,' Sakowitz confessed. 'I don't think he's –' He stopped, searching for the right word, 'stable. Talking to him, you get a feeling he has a stick of dynamite up his ass, ready to explode.'

'What do you want to do?'

'We're doing it. He'll go to school and we'll keep a close eye on him.'

'Maybe he'll wash out,' Eastman said.

'You don't know that breed of cat. He'll come out number one man in his class.'

Sakowitz's prediction was accurate.

The training course consisted of four weeks of ground school followed by an additional month of flight training. Since the trainees were already experienced pilots with many years of flying behind them, the course was devised to serve two purposes: the first was to run through such subjects as navigation, radio, communication, map reading and instrument flying to refresh the memories of the men and pinpoint their potential weaknesses, and the second was to familiarize them with the new equipment they would be using.

The instrument flying was done in a Link Trainer, a small mock-up of an airplane cockpit that rested on a movable base, enabling the pilot in the cockpit to put the plane through any manoeuvre, including stalls, loops, spins and rolls. A black hood was put over the top of the cockpit so that the pilot was flying blind, using only the instruments in front of him. The instructor outside the Trainer fed orders to the pilot, giving him directions for takeoffs and landings in the face of strong wind velocity, storms, mountain ranges and every other simulated hazard conceivable. Most inexperienced pilots went into the Link Trainer with a feeling of confidence, but they soon learned that the little Trainers were much more difficult to operate than they appeared to be. It was an eerie sensation to be alone in the tiny cockpit, all senses cut off from the outside world.

Larry was a gifted pupil. He was attentive in class and absorbed everything he was taught. He did all his homework and did it well and carefully. He showed no sign of impatience, restlessness or boredom. On the contrary, he was the most eager pupil in the course and certainly the most outstanding. The only area that was new to Larry was the equipment, the DC-4. The Douglas planes were long, sleek aircraft with some equipment that had not been in existence when the war began. Larry spent hours going over every inch of the plane, studying the way it had been put together and the way it functioned. Evenings he pored over the dozens of service manuals of the plane.

Late one night after all the other trainees had left the hangar Sakowitz had come upon Larry in one of the DC-4s, lying on his back under the cockpit, examining the wiring.

'I tell you, the son-of-a-bitch is gunning for my job,' Sakowitz told Carl Eastman the next morning.

'The way he's going, he may get it,' Eastman grinned.

At the end of the eight weeks there was a little graduation ceremony. Catherine proudly flew to New York to be there when they presented Larry with his navigator's wings.

He tried to make light of it. 'Cathy, it's just a stupid little piece of cloth they give you so you'll remember what your job is when you get into the cockpit.'

'Oh, no, you don't,' she said. 'I talked to Captain Sakowitz and he told me how good you are.'

'What does a dumb Polack know?' Larry said. 'Let's go celebrate.'

That night Catherine and Larry and four of Larry's classmates and their wives went to the Twenty-one Club on East Fifty-second Street for dinner. The foyer was crowded, and the maître d' told them that without reservations there were no tables available.

'To hell with this place,' Larry said. 'Let's go next door to Toots Shor's.'

'Wait a minute,' Catherine said. She went over to the captain and asked to see Jerry Berns.

A few moments later a short, thin man with inquisitive grey eyes bustled up.

'I'm Jerry Berns,' he said. 'May I help you?'

'My husband and I are with some friends,' Catherine explained. 'There are ten of us.'

He started to shake his head. 'Unless you have a reservation . . .'

'I'm William Fraser's partner,' Catherine said.

Jerry Berns looked at Catherine reproachfully. 'Why didn't you tell me? Can you give me fifteen minutes?'

'Thank you,' Catherine said gratefully.

She went back to where the group was standing.

'Surprise!' Catherine said. 'We have a table.'

'How did you manage that?' Larry asked.

'It was easy,' Catherine said. 'I mentioned Bill Fraser's name.' She saw the look that came into Larry's eyes. 'He comes in here often,' Catherine went on quickly. 'And he told me if I ever came in and needed a table, to mention his name.'

Larry turned to the others. 'Let's get the hell out of here. This is for the birds.'

The group started towards the door. Larry turned to Catherine. 'Coming?'

'Of course,' Catherine said hesitantly, 'I just wanted to tell them that we're not . . .'

'Fuck 'em,' said Larry loudly. 'Are you coming or aren't you?'

People were turning to stare. Catherine felt her face redden.

'Yes,' she said. She turned and followed Larry out the door.

They went to an Italian restaurant on Sixth Avenue and had a bad dinner. Outwardly Catherine acted as though nothing had happened, but inwardly she was fuming. She was furious with

Larry for his childish behaviour and for humiliating her in public.

When they got home, she walked into the bedroom without saying a word, undressed, turned out the light and got into bed. She heard Larry in the living room, mixing a drink.

Ten minutes later he came into the bedroom and turned on the light and walked over to the bed. 'You planning to become a martyr?' he asked.

She sat up, furious. 'Don't try to put me on the defensive,' she said. 'Your behaviour tonight was inexcusable. What got into you?'

'The same guy that got into you.'

She stared at him. 'What?'

'I'm talking about Mr Perfection. Bill Fraser.'

She looked at him, not understanding. 'Bill's never, done anything but help us.'

'You bet your ass,' he said. 'You owe him your business. I owe him my job. Now we can't even sit down in a restaurant without Fraser's permission. Well, I'm sick of having him shoved down my throat every day.' It was Larry's tone that shook Catherine even more than what he was saying. It was so filled with frustration and impotence that she realized for the first time how tormented he must be. And why not? He had come back from four years of fighting to find his wife in partnership with her former lover. And to make it worse, he himself had not even been able to get a job without the help of Fraser.

As she looked at Larry, Catherine knew that this

was a turning point in their marriage. If she stayed with him, he would have to come first. Before her job, before everything. For the first time Catherine felt that she really understood Larry.

As though reading her mind Larry said contritely, 'I'm sorry I acted like a shit-heel this evening. But when we couldn't get a table until you mentioned Fraser's magic name, I – I'd suddenly had it up to *here*.'

'I'm sorry, Larry,' Catherine said, 'I'll never do that to you again.'

And they were in each other's arms, and Larry said, 'Please don't ever leave me, Cathy,' and Catherine thought of how close she had come to it, and she held him tighter and said, 'I won't leave you, darling, ever.'

Larry's first assignment as a navigator was on Flight 147 from Washington to Paris. He stayed over in Paris for forty-eight hours after each flight, then returned home for three days before he flew out again.

One morning Larry called Catherine at her office, his voice excited. 'Hey, I've got a great restaurant for us. Can you get away for lunch?'

Catherine looked at the pile of layouts that had to be finished and approved before noon. 'Sure,' she said, recklessly.

'I'll pick you up in fifteen minutes.'

'You're not leaving me!' Lucia, her assistant, wailed. 'Stuyvesant will have kittens if we don't get this campaign to him today.'

'It will have to wait,' Catherine said. 'I'm going to have lunch with my husband.'

Lucia shrugged. 'I don't blame you. If you ever get tired of him, will you let me know?'

Catherine grinned. 'You'll be too old.'

Larry picked Catherine up in front of the office, and she got into the car.

'Did I screw up your day for you?' he asked mischievously.

'Of course not.'

He laughed. 'All those executive types are going to have a stroke.'

Larry headed the car towards the airport.

'How far is the restaurant?' Catherine asked. She had five appointments in the afternoon; beginning at two o'clock.

'Not far . . . Do you have a busy afternoon?'

'No,' she lied. 'Nothing special.'

'Good.'

When they reached the airport turnoff, Larry swung the car into the entrance.

'Is the restaurant at the airport?'

'At the other end,' Larry replied. He parked the car, took Catherine's arm and led her inside to the Pan-Am gate. The attractive girl behind the desk greeted Larry by name.

'This is my wife,' Larry said proudly. 'This is Amy Winston.'

They exchanged hellos.

'Come on.' Larry took Catherine's arm and they moved towards the departure ramp.

'Larry –' Catherine began. 'Where . . . ?'

'Hey, you're the nosiest girl I've ever taken to lunch.'

They had reached Gate 37. Two men behind the ticket counter were processing the tickets of emplaning passengers. A sign on the information board read: 'Flight 147 to Paris – Departing 1:00 P.M.'

Larry walked up to one of the men behind the desk. 'Here she is, Tony.' He handed the man a plane ticket. 'Cathy, this is Tony Lombardi. This is Catherine.'

'I've sure heard a lot about you,' the man grinned. 'Your ticket's all in order.' He handed the ticket to Catherine.

Catherine stared at it, dazed. 'What's this for?'

'I lied to you,' Larry smiled. 'I'm not taking you to lunch. I'm taking you to Paris. Maxim's.'

Catherine's voice broke. 'M – Maxim's? In Paris? *Now?*'

'That's right.'

'I can't,' Catherine wailed. 'I can't go to Paris now.'

'Sure you can,' he grinned. 'I've got your passport in my pocket.'

'Larry,' she said, 'you're mad! I have no clothes. I have a million appointments. I –'

'I'll buy you some clothes in Paris. Cancel your appointments. Fraser can get along without you for a few days.'

Catherine stared at him, not knowing what to

say. She remembered the resolutions she had made to herself. Larry was her husband. He had to come first. Catherine realized that it wasn't just taking her to Paris that was important to Larry. He was showing off for her, asking her to fly in the plane he was navigating. And she had almost spoiled it. She put her hand in his and smiled up at him.

'What are we waiting for?' Catherine asked. 'I'm starved!'

Paris was a whirlwind of fun. Larry had arranged to take a full week off, and it seemed to Catherine that every hour of the day and night was crammed with things to do. They stayed at a charming little hotel on the Left Bank.

Their first morning in Paris Larry took Catherine to a salon on the Champs Élysées where he tried to buy out the entire store for her. She bought only the things she needed and was shocked at how expensive everything was.

'You know your problem?' Larry said. 'You worry too much about money. You're on your honeymoon.'

'Yes, sir,' she said. But she refused to buy an evening dress that she did not need. When she tried to ask Larry where all the money was coming from, he did not want to discuss it, but she finally insisted on knowing.

'I got an advance on my salary,' Larry told her. 'What's the big deal?'

And Catherine had not the heart to tell him. He was like a child about money, generous and carefree, and that was part of his charm.

Just as it had been part of her father's charm.

Larry took her on the visitor's tour of Paris: to the Louvre, the Tuileries and Les Invalides to see Napoleon's Tomb. He took her to a colourful little restaurant near the Sorbonne. They went to Les Halles, the storied marketplace of Paris, and watched the fresh fruit and meat and vegetables brought in from the farms of France, and spent their last Sunday afternoon at Versailles, and then had dinner in the breathtaking garden at the Coq Hardi outside of Paris. It was a perfect second honeymoon.

Hal Sakowitz sat in his office looking over the weekly personnel reports. In front of him was the report on Larry Douglas. Sakowitz was leaning back in his chair, studying it, pulling thoughtfully at his lower lip. Finally he leaned forwards and pressed an intercom switch. 'Send him in,' he said.

A moment later, Larry walked in, wearing his Pan-Am uniform and carrying his flight bag. He flashed Sakowitz a smile. 'Morning, Chief,' he said.

'Sit down.'

Larry slouched into a chair opposite the desk and lit a cigarette.

Sakowitz said, 'I have a report here that last Monday in Paris you checked in for your flight briefing forty-five minutes late.'

Larry's expression changed. 'I was caught in a parade on the Champs Élysées. The plane took off on time. I didn't know we were running a boy's camp here.'

'We're running an airline,' Sakowitz said, quietly. 'And we're running it by the book.'

'OK,' Larry said angrily. 'I'll keep away from the Champs Élysées. Anything else?'

'Yes. Captain Swift thinks you'd had a drink or two before takeoff on the last couple of flights.'

'He's a goddamned liar!' Larry snapped.

'Why would he lie?'

'Because he's afraid I'll take his job away.' There was a sharp anger in Larry's voice. 'The son-of-a-bitch is a timid old maid who should have been retired ten years ago.'

'You've flown with four different captains,' Sakowitz said. 'Which ones did you like?'

'None of them,' retorted Larry. He saw the trap too late. Quickly, he added, 'I mean – they're all right. I have nothing against them.'

'They don't like flying with you either,' Sakowitz said evenly. 'You make them nervous.'

'What the hell does that mean?'

'It means that if ever there's an emergency, you want to be damn sure about the man in the seat next to you. They're not sure about you.'

'For Christ's sake!' Larry exploded. 'I lived through four years of emergencies over Germany and in the South Pacific, risking my fucking neck every day, while they were back here sitting on their fat asses, collecting big salaries, and they don't have confidence in *me*? You must be joking!'

'No one says you're not great in a fighter plane,' Sakowitz replied quietly. 'But we're flying passengers. It's a different ball game.'

Larry sat there clenching his fists, trying to control his anger. 'OK,' he said sullenly. 'I get the message. If you're through, I have a flight leaving in a few minutes.'

'Someone else is taking it over,' Sakowitz said. 'You're fired.'

Larry stared at him unbelievingly. 'I'm *what*?'

'In a way, I suppose it's my fault, Douglas. I shouldn't have hired you in the first place.'

Larry got to his feet, his eyes blazing with fury. 'Then why the hell did you?' he demanded.

'Because your wife had a friend named Bill Fraser . . .' Sakowitz began.

Larry moved across the desk, his fist crashing into Sakowitz's face. The blow propelled Sakowitz against the wall. He used the momentum to bounce up. He hit Larry twice, then stepped back, fighting for control. 'Get out of here,' he said. 'Now!'

Larry stared at him, his face twisted with hatred. 'You son-of-a-bitch,' he said. 'I wouldn't come near this airline again if you begged me!' He turned and stormed out of the office.

Sakowitz stood there looking after him. His secretary came hurrying in. She saw the overturned chair and Sakowitz's bloody lip.

'Are you all right?' she asked.

'Terrific,' he said. 'Ask Mr Eastman if he can see me.'

Ten minutes later Sakowitz had finished relating the incident to Carl Eastman.

'What do you think's wrong with Douglas?' Eastman asked.

'Honestly? I think he's a psycho.'

Eastman regarded him with his piercing hazel eyes. 'That's pretty strong, Sak. He wasn't drunk when he was flying. No one could even prove that he'd had a drink on the ground. And anyone can be late once in a while.'

'If that's all it was, I wouldn't have fired him, Carl. Douglas has a low boiling point. To tell you the truth I was trying to provoke him today, and it wasn't hard. If he had stood up under the pressure, I might have taken a chance and kept him on. You know what worries me?'

'What?'

Sakowitz said, 'A few days ago I ran into an old buddy who flew with Douglas in the RAF. He told me a crazy story. It seems that when Douglas was in the Eagle Squadron he fell for a little English girl who was engaged to a boy named Clark in Douglas' Squadron. Douglas did everything he could to move in, but the girl wasn't having any. A week before she and Clark were to get married, the Squadron went up to cover some B-Seventeens in a raid over Dieppe. Douglas was flying at the rear of the Squadron. The fortresses dropped their bombs and everyone headed for home. Coming back over the Channel, they were hit by some Messerschmidts, and Clark was shot down.' He stopped, lost in some reverie of his own. Eastman waited for him to go on and finally Sakowitz looked up at him. 'According to my friend there were no Messerschmidts anywhere near Clark when he got it.'

Eastman stared at him unbelievingly. 'Jesus! Are you saying that Larry Douglas . . . ?'

'I'm not saying anything. I'm just telling you an interesting story I heard.' He put his handkerchief to his lip again. The bleeding had stopped. 'It's hard to tell what's happening in the middle of a dogfight. Maybe Clark just ran out of gas. One thing is certain. He sure as hell ran out of luck.'

'What happened to his girl?'

'Douglas moved in with her until he came back to the States, then he dumped her.' He looked at Eastman thoughtfully. 'I'll tell you one thing, for sure. I feel sorry for Douglas' wife.'

Catherine was in the conference room having a staff meeting when the door opened and Larry walked in.

His eye was bruised and swollen, his cheek was cut. She hurried over to him. 'Larry, what happened?'

'I quit my job,' he mumbled.

Catherine took him into her office, away from the curious gazes of the others, and put a cold cloth to his eye and his cheek. 'Tell me about it,' she said, holding in her anger at what they had done to him.

'They've been riding me for a long time, Cathy. I think they were jealous because I was in the war and they weren't. Anyway, today was the topper. Sakowitz called me in and told me the only reason they hired me in the first place was because you were Bill Fraser's sweetheart.'

Catherine looked at him, speechless.

'I hit him,' Larry said. 'I couldn't help it.'

'Oh, darling!' Catherine said. 'I'm so sorry.'

'Sakowitz is sorrier,' Larry replied. 'I really clobbered him. Job or no job, I wasn't going to let anyone talk about you that way.'

She held him close to her, reassuringly. 'Don't worry. You can go to work for any airline in the country.'

Catherine proved to be a poor prophet. Larry applied to all the airlines and several of them gave him interviews but nothing came of any of them. Bill Fraser had lunch with Catherine and she told him what had happened. Fraser said nothing, but he was very thoughtful all through lunch. Several times she felt he was on the verge of telling her something, but each time he stopped. Finally he said, 'I know a lot of people, Cathy. Would you like me to see what I can do for Larry somewhere else?'

'Thanks,' Catherine said gratefully. 'But I don't think so. We'll work it out ourselves.'

Fraser regarded her a moment, then nodded.

'Let me know if you change your mind.'

'I will,' she said appreciatively. 'It seems I'm always coming to you with my problems.'

ACME SECURITY AGENCY
1402 'D' Street
Washington, D.C.

Reference #2-179-210 April 1, 1946

Dear Monsieur Barbet:

Thank you for your letter of March 15, 1946, and your bank draught.

Since my last report, Subject has secured employment as a pilot with The Flying Wheels Transport Company, a small independent freight company operating out of Long Island. A Dun and Bradstreet cheque shows that they are capitalized under $750,000. Their equipment consists of a converted B-26 and a converted DC-3. They have bank loans in excess of $400,000. The Vice-President of the Banque de Paris in New York where they have their major account assures me that the company has an excellent growth potential and future. The bank is considering loaning them sufficient money to buy additional airplanes based on their current income of $80,000 per year with projected increases of 30% per year, over the next five years.

If you wish further details on the financial aspects of the company, please let me know.

Subject began work on March 19, 1946. The personnel manager (who is also one of the owners) informed my operative that he felt very fortunate to have Subject flying for him. More details to follow.

Sincerely,

R. Ruttenberg
Managing Supervisor

Banque de Paris
New York City, New York

Philippe Chardon
President of the Board

Chèr Nelle,

Tu es vraiment mauvaise! Je ne sais pas ce que cet homme t'a fait, mais quoique ce soit, il a payé. Il a été mis à la porte aux Flying Wheels cie, et mon ami me dit qu'il en a piqué une crise.

Je pense être à Athenes, et je compte te voir. Mes amitiés à Costa – et ne tien fais pas la petite faveur que je t'ai faite restera notre secret.

Affectuesement à toi,
Philippe

ACME SECURITY AGENCY
1402 'D' Street
Washington, D.C.

Reference #2-179-210 May 22, 1946

Dear Monseiur Barbet:

This is a follow-up to my report of May 1, 1946.

On May 14, 1946, Subject was fired by The Flying

Wheels Transport Company. I have tried to make discreet inquiries as to the reason, but each time have run up against a brick wall. No one there will discuss it, I can only assume that the Subject did something to disgrace himself, and they don't want to talk about it.

Subject is looking for another flying job, but apparently has no immediate prospects.

I will continue to try to get more information about why he was discharged.

Sincerely,

R. Ruttenberg
Managing Supervisor

C A B L E G R A M May 29, 1946

Christian Barbet
Cable Chrisbar
Paris, France

CABLE ACKNOWLEDGED STOP WILL IMMEDIATELY DROP INVESTIGATION OF REASON FOR SUBJECT BEING FIRED STOP WILL CONTINUE EVERYTHING ELSE AS BEFORE

REGARDS,

R. RUTTENBERG
ACME SECURITY AGENCY

ACME SECURITY AGENCY
1402 'D' Street
Washington, D.C.

Reference #2-179-210 June 16, 1946

Dear Monsieur Barbet:

Thank you for your letter of June 10th and your bank draught.

On June 15th, Subject obtained employment as a co-pilot with Global Airways, a regional feeder airline operating between Washington, Boston and Philadelphia.

Global Airways is a small new airline with a fleet of three converted war planes, and as far as I have been able to ascertain, they are under-capitalized and in debt. A Vice-President of the firm informed me that they have been promised a loan from the Dallas First National Bank within the next sixty days which will give them enough capital to consolidate their bills and to expand.

Subject is held in high esteem and appears to have a good future there.

Please let me know whether you require any further information about Global Airways.

Sincerely,

R. Ruttenberg,
Managing Supervisor

ACME SECURITY AGENCY
1402 'D' Street
Washington, D.C.

Reference #2-179-210 July 20, 1946

Dear Monsieur Barbet:

Global Airways has unexpectedly filed for bankruptcy and is going out of operation. As far as I can learn, this move was forced by the refusal of the Dallas First National Bank to grant the loan that was promised. Subject is now unemployed again and back to earlier patterns of behaviour, as outlined in previous reports.

I will not pursue any investigation into the reason for the bank's refusal of the loan or Global Airways' financial difficulties unless you specifically advise me to do so.

Sincerely,

R. Ruttenberg
Managing Supervisor

Noelle kept all the reports and the clippings in a special leather bag to which she had the only key. The bag was kept inside a locked suitcase and stored at the back of her bedroom closet, not because she thought Demiris would pry into her things, but because she knew how much he loved intrigue. This was Noelle's personal vendetta, and she wanted to be sure that Demiris remained unaware of it.

Constantin Demiris was going to play a part in her plan of vengeance, but he would never know about it. Noelle took a last look at the memorandum and locked it away, satisfied.

She was ready to begin.

It started with a phone call.

Catherine and Larry were having an uneasy silence-filled dinner at home. Larry had been home very little lately, and when he was home he was surly and rude. Catherine understood his unhappiness.

'It's as though some demon is on my back,' he had told her when Global Airways had gone bankrupt. And it was true. He had had an incredible run of bad luck. Catherine tried to reassure Larry, to keep reminding him of what a wonderful pilot he was and how lucky anyone would be to have him. But it was like living with a wounded lion. Catherine never knew when he would lash out at her, and because she was afraid of letting him down, she tried to understand his wild rages and overlook them. The phone rang as she was serving dessert. She picked up the receiver.

'Hello.'

There was an Englishman's voice on the other end of the line and it said, 'Is Larry Douglas in, please? Ian Whitestone here.'

'Just a moment.' She held the receiver out to Larry. 'It's for you. Ian Whitestone.'

He frowned, puzzled. 'Who?' Then his face cleared. 'For Christ's sake!' He walked over and took the receiver from Catherine. 'Ian?' He gave a short laugh. 'My God, it's been almost seven years. How the hell did you ever track me down?'

Catherine watched Larry nodding and smiling as he listened. At the end of what seemed like five minutes, he said, 'Well, that sounds interesting, old buddy. Sure I can. Where?' He listened. 'Right. Half an hour. I'll see you then.' Thoughtfully, he replaced the receiver.

'Is he a friend of yours?' Catherine asked.

Larry turned to face her. 'No, not really. That's what's so funny. He's a guy I flew with in the RAF. We never really got along all that well. But he says he has a proposition for me.'

'What kind of proposition?' Catherine asked.

Larry shrugged. 'I'll let you know when I get home.'

It was almost three o'clock in the morning when Larry returned to the apartment. Catherine was sitting up in bed, reading. Larry appeared at the bedroom door.

'Hi.'

Something had happened to him. He radiated an excitement that Catherine had not seen in him for a long time. He walked over to the bed.

'How did your meeting go?'

'I think it went great,' Larry said, carefully. 'In fact it went so great I still can't believe it. I think I may have a job.'

'Working for Ian Whitestone?'

'No. Ian's a pilot – like me. I told you we flew together.'

'Yes.'

'Well – after the war, a Greek buddy of his got him a job as a private pilot for Demiris.'

'The shipping tycoon?'

'Shipping, oil, gold – Demiris owns half the world. Whitestone had a beautiful setup over there.'

'What happened?'

Larry looked at her and grinned. 'Whitestone's quit his job. He's going to Australia. Someone's setting him up in his own business over there.'

'I still don't understand,' said Catherine. 'What does all this have to do with you?'

'Whitestone spoke to Demiris about my taking his place. He just quit, and Demiris hasn't had a chance to look around for a replacement. Whitestone thinks I'm a cinch for the job.' He hesitated. 'You don't know what this could mean, Cathy.'

Catherine thought of the other times, the other jobs, and she remembered her father and his empty dreams, and she kept her voice noncommittal, not wishing to encourage any false hopes in Larry, and yet not wanting to dampen his enthusiasm.

'Didn't you say you and Whitestone weren't particularly good friends?'

He hesitated. 'Yeah.' A small frown creased his forehead. The truth of the matter was that he and Ian Whitestone had never liked each other at all. The telephone call tonight had been a big surprise. At the meeting, Whitestone had seemed oddly ill at ease. When he had explained the situation and Larry had said, 'I'm surprised that you thought of me,' there had been an awkward pause, and then Whitestone had said, 'Demiris wants a great pilot, and that's what you are.' It was almost as though Whitestone were pressing the job on him and that Larry would be doing him a favour. He had appeared very relieved when Larry said he was interested and then seemed anxious to leave. All in all it had been a strange meeting.

'This could be the chance of a lifetime,' Larry told Cathy. 'Demiris was paying Whitestone fifteen thousand drachmas a month. That's five hundred dollars and he lived like a king over there.'

'But wouldn't that mean you'd be living in Greece?'

'*We'd* be living in Greece,' Larry corrected her. 'With that kind of money, we could save enough to be independent in a year. I've got to take a shot at it.'

Catherine was hesitant, choosing her words carefully. 'Larry, it's so far away and you don't even know Constantin Demiris. There must be a flying job here that . . .'

'No!' His tone was savage. 'Nobody gives a shit here how good a pilot you are. All they care about is how long you've paid your goddam union dues. Over there, I'd be independent. It's the kind of thing I've been dreaming of, Cathy. Demiris has a fleet of planes you wouldn't believe, and I'll be flying again, baby. The only one I'd have to please would be Demiris, and Whitestone says he'll love me.'

She thought again of Larry's job at Pan Am and the hopes he had had for it and his failures with the small airlines. *My God*, she thought. *What am I getting myself into*? It would mean giving up the business she had built, going to live in a strange place with strangers, with a husband who was almost a stranger.

He was watching her. 'Are you with me?'

She looked up at his eager face. This was her husband and if she wanted to keep her marriage, she would have to live where he lived. And how lovely it would be if it did work out. He would be the old Larry again. The charming, amusing, wonderful man she had married. She had to give it a chance.

'Of course I'm with you,' Catherine said. 'Why don't you fly over and see Demiris? If the job works out, then I'll come over and join you.'

He smiled, that charming, boyish grin. 'I knew I could count on you, baby.' He put his arms around her and held her close. 'You'd better take off that nightgown,' Larry said, 'or I'm going to poke holes in it.'

But as Catherine slowly took it off, she was thinking about how she was going to tell Bill Fraser.

Early the next morning Larry flew to Athens to meet Constantin Demiris.

During the next few days Catherine heard nothing from her husband. As the week dragged by, she found herself hoping that things had not worked out in Greece and that Larry would be coming home.

Even if he got the position with Demiris, there was no way of telling how long it would last. Surely he could find a job in the United States.

Six days after Larry had left, Catherine received an overseas phone call.

'Catherine?'

'Hello, darling.'

'Get packed. You're talking to Constantin Demiris' new personal pilot.'

Ten days later, Catherine was on her way to Greece.

BOOK TWO

FOURTEEN

Noelle and Catherine

Athens: 1946

Men mould some cities, some cities mould men. Athens is an anvil that has withstood the hammer of centuries. It has been captured and despoiled by the Saracens, the Anglos, the Turks, but each time it patiently survived. Athens lies towards the southern end of the great central plain of Attica, which slopes gently towards the Saronic Gulf on the southwest and is overlooked on the east by the majestic Mount Hymettus. Underneath the shiny patina of the city one still found a village filled with ancient ghosts and steeped in rich tradition of timeless glories, where its citizens lived as much in their past as in the present, a city of constant surprise, full of discovery, and in the end unknowable.

Larry was at the Hellenikon Airport to meet Catherine's plane. She saw him hurrying towards the ramp, his face eager and excited as he ran towards her. He looked tanner and leaner than when she had last seen him, and he seemed to be free of strain.

'I've missed you, Cathy,' he said as he scooped her up in his arms.

'I've missed you too.' And as she said it, she realized how much she meant it. She kept forgetting the strong physical impact that Larry had on her until they met after an absence and each time it hit her anew.

'How did Bill Fraser take the news?' Larry asked as he helped her through Customs.

'He was very good about it.'

'He had no choice, had he?' Larry said, sardonically.

Catherine remembered her meeting with Bill Fraser. He had looked at her, shocked. 'You're going to go off to Greece to *live*? Why, for God's sakes?'

'It's in the fine print of my marriage contract,' she had replied lightly.

'I mean, why can't Larry get a job here, Catherine?'

'I don't know why, Bill. Something always seems to go wrong. But he has a job in Greece and he seems to feel that it's going to work out.'

After his first impulsive protest Fraser had been wonderful. He had made everything easy for her and insisted that she keep her interest in the firm. 'You're not going to stay away forever,' he kept saying.

Catherine was thinking of his words now as she watched Larry arrange for a porter to carry her luggage to a limousine.

He spoke to the porter in Greek and Catherine marvelled at Larry's facility for language.

'Wait'll you meet Constantin Demiris,' Larry said. 'He's like a goddamn king. All the moguls in Europe seem to spend their time figuring out what they can do to please him.'

'I'm glad you like him.'

'And he likes me.'

She had never heard him sound so happy and enthusiastic. It was a good omen.

On the way to the hotel Larry described his first meeting with Demiris. Larry had been met at the airport by a liveried chauffeur. Larry had asked to take a look at Demiris' fleet of planes, and the chauffeur had driven him to an enormous hangar at the far end of the field. There were three planes, and Larry inspected each one with a critical eye. The Hawker Siddeley was a beauty, and he longed to get behind the wheel and fly it. The next ship was a six-place Piper in topnotch condition. He estimated that it could easily do three hundred miles per hour. The third plane was a two-seater converted L-5, with a Lycoming engine, a wonderful plane for shorter flights. It was an impressive private fleet. When Larry had finished his inspection, he rejoined the watching chauffeur.

'They'll do,' Larry said. 'Let's go.'

The chauffeur had driven him to a villa in

Varkiza, the exclusive suburb twenty-five kilometres from Athens.

'You wouldn't believe Demiris' place,' Larry told Catherine.

'What did it look like?' Catherine asked, eagerly.

'It's impossible to describe. It's about ten acres with electric gates, guards, watchdogs, the whole bit. The outside of the villa is a palace, and the inside is a museum. It has an indoor swimming pool, a full stage and a projection room. You'll see it one day.'

'Was he nice?' Catherine asked.

'You bet he was,' Larry smiled. 'I got the red-carpet treatment. I guess my reputation preceded me.'

In fact Larry had sat in a small anteroom for three hours waiting to see Constantin Demiris. In ordinary circumstances Larry would have been furious at the slight, but he knew how much depended on this meeting and he was too nervous to be angry. He had told Catherine how important this job was to him. But he had not told her how desperately he needed it. His one superb skill was flying and without it he felt lost. It was as though his life had sunk to some unexplored emotional depth and the pressures on him were too great to be borne. *Everything* depended on this job.

At the end of three hours a butler had come in and announced that Mr Demiris was ready to see him. He had led Larry through a large reception hall that looked like it belonged at Versailles. The walls were delicate shades of gold, green and blue, and Beauvais tapestries hung on the walls, framed by panels of rosewood. A magnificent oval Savonnerie rug was on the floor, and above it an enormous chandelier of crystal De Roche and bronze Doré.

At the entry to the library were a pair of green onyx columns with capitals of gold bronze. The library itself was exquisite, designed by a master artisan, and the walls were carved, panelled fruitwoods. In the centre of one wall stood a white marble mantelpiece with gold gilt ornamentations. On it rested two beautiful bronze Chénets of Philippe Caffieri.

From mantel top to ceiling rose a heavily carved trumeau mirror with a painting by Jean Honoré Fragonard. Through an open French window Larry caught a glimpse of an enormous patio overlooking a private park filled with statues and fountains.

At the far end of the library was a great Bureau Plat desk and behind it a magnificent tall back chair covered in Aubusson tapestry. In front of the desk were two bergères with Gobelin upholstery.

Demiris was standing near the desk, studying a large Mercator map on the wall, dotted with dozens of coloured pins. He turned as Larry entered and held out his hand.

'Constantin Demiris,' he said, with the faintest trace of an accent. Larry had seen photographs of him in news magazines throughout the years, but nothing had prepared him for the vital force of the man.

'I know,' Larry said, shaking his hand. 'I'm Larry Douglas.'

Demiris saw Larry's eyes go to the map on the wall. 'My empire,' he said. 'Sit down.'

Larry took a chair opposite the desk.

'I understand that you and Ian Whitestone flew together in the RAF?'

'Yes.'

Demiris leaned back in his chair and studied Larry. 'Ian thinks very highly of you.'

Larry smiled. 'I think highly of him. He's a hell of a pilot.'

'That's what he said about you, except he used the word "great."'

Larry felt again that sense of surprise he had had when Whitestone had first spelled out the offer. He had obviously given Demiris a big buildup about him, far out of proportion to the relationship that he and Whitestone had had. 'I'm good,' Larry said. 'That's my business.'

Demiris nodded. 'I like men who are good at their business. Did you know that most of the people in the world are not?'

'I hadn't given it much thought one way or the other,' Larry confessed.

'I have.' He gave Larry a wintry smile. 'That's *my* business – people. The great majority of people hate what they're doing, Mr Douglas. Instead of devising ways to get into something they like, they remain trapped all their lives, like brainless insects. It's rare to find a man who loves his work. Almost invariably when you find such a man, he is a success.'

'I suppose that's true,' Larry said modestly.

'You are *not* a success.'

Larry looked up at Demiris, suddenly wary. 'That depends on what you mean by success, Mr Demiris,' he said carefully.

'What I mean is,' Demiris said bluntly, 'you did brilliantly in the war, but you are not doing very well in the peace.'

Larry felt the muscles of his jaw begin to tighten. He felt that he was being baited, and he tried to hold back his anger. His mind raced frantically, trying to figure out what he could say to salvage this job he needed so desperately. Demiris was watching him, his olive black eyes quietly studying him, missing nothing.

'What happened to your job with Pan American, Mr Douglas?'

Larry found a grin he didn't feel. 'I didn't like the idea of sitting around for fifteen years waiting to become a copilot.'

'So you hit the man you worked for.'

Larry showed his surprise. 'Who told you that?'

'Oh, come, Mr Douglas,' Demiris said impatiently, 'if you went to work for me, I would be putting my life in your hands every time I flew with you. My life happens to be worth a great deal to me. Did you really think I would hire you without knowing *everything* about you?'

'I suppose not,' Larry said.

'You were fired from two flying jobs after you

were fired from Pan Am,' Demiris went on. 'That's a poor record.'

'It had nothing to do with my ability,' Larry retorted, anger beginning to rise in him again. 'Business was slow with one company, and the other couldn't get a bank loan and went bankrupt. I'm a damned good pilot.'

Demiris studied him a moment, then smiled. 'I know you are,' he said. 'You don't respond well to discipline, do you?'

'I don't like being given orders by idiots who know less than I do.'

'I trust I will not fall into that category,' Demiris said dryly.

'Not unless you're planning to tell me how to fly your planes, Mr Demiris.'

'No, that would be your job. It would also be your job to see that I got where I was going efficiently, comfortably and safely.'

Larry nodded. 'I'd do my best, Mr Demiris.'

'I believe that,' Demiris said. 'You've been out to look at my planes.'

Larry tried to keep the surprise out of his face. 'Yes, sir.'

'How did you like them?'

Larry could not conceal his enthusiasm. 'They're beauties.'

Demiris responded to the look on Larry's face. 'Have you ever flown a Hawker Siddeley?'

Larry hesitated a moment, tempted to lie. 'No, sir.'

Demiris nodded. 'Think you could learn?'

Larry grinned. 'If you've got someone who can spare ten minutes.'

Demiris leaned forwards in his chair and pressed his long, slender fingers together. 'I could choose a pilot who is familiar with all my planes.'

'But you won't,' Larry said, 'because you'll keep getting new planes, and you want someone who can adapt to anything you buy.'

Demiris nodded his head. 'You are correct,' he said. 'What I am looking for is a pilot – a pure pilot – a man who is at his happiest when he is flying.'

That was the moment when Larry knew the job was his.

Larry was never aware of how close he had come to not being hired. A great deal of Constantin Demiris' success was due to a highly developed instinct for trouble, and it had served him often enough so that he seldom disregarded it. When Ian Whitestone had come to inform him that he was quitting, a silent alarm went off in Demiris' mind. It was partly because of Whitestone's manner. He was acting unnaturally and seemed uneasy. It wasn't a question of money, he assured Demiris. He had a chance to go into business for himself with his brother-in-law in Sydney and he had to try it. Then he had recommended another pilot.

'He's an American, but we flew together in the RAF. He's not just good, he's great, Mr Demiris. I don't know a better flyer.'

Demiris quietly listened as Ian Whitestone went on extolling the virtues of his friend, trying to find the false note that jarred him. He finally recognized it. Whitestone was overselling, but possibly that was because of his embarrassment at quitting his job so abruptly.

Because Demiris was a man who left not even the smallest detail to chance, he made several phone calls to various countries after Whitestone left. Before the afternoon was over Demiris had ascertained that someone had indeed put up money to finance Whitestone in a small electronics business in Australia, with his brother-in-law. He had spoken to a friend in the British Air Ministry and two hours later had been given a verbal report on Larry Douglas. 'He was a bit erratic on the ground,' his friend had said, 'but he was a superb flyer.' Demiris had then made telephone calls to Washington and New York and had been quickly brought up-to-date on Larry Douglas' current status.

Everything on the surface appeared to be just as it ought to be. And yet Constantin Demiris still felt that vague sense of unease, a presentiment of trouble. He had discussed the matter with Noelle, suggesting that perhaps he might offer Ian Whitestone more money to stay on. Noelle had listened attentively and then said, 'No. Let him go, Costa. And if he recommends this American flyer so highly, then I would certainly try him.'

And that finally had decided him.

* * *

From the moment Noelle knew that Larry Douglas was on his way to Athens she was able to think of nothing else. She thought of all the years it had taken, the careful, patient laying of plans, the slow, inexorable tightening of the web, and she was sure that Constantin Demiris would have been proud of her if he had known. It was ironic, Noelle reflected. If she had never met Larry, she could have been happy with Demiris. They complemented each other perfectly. They both loved power and knew how to use it. They were above ordinary people. They were gods, meant to rule. In the end they could never lose, because they had a deep, almost mystic patience. They could wait forever. And now, for Noelle, the waiting was over.

Noelle spent the day in the garden lying in a hammock, going over her plan; and by the time the sun began to sink towards the western sky, she was satisfied. In a way, she thought, it was a pity that so much of the last six years had been filled with her plans for vengeance. It had motivated almost every waking moment, given her life a vitality and drive and excitement, and now in a few short weeks the quest would have come to an end.

At that moment, lying under the dying Grecian sun with the late afternoon breezes beginning to cool the quiet green garden, Noelle had no idea that it was just beginning.

* * *

The night before Larry was to arrive, Noelle was unable to sleep. She lay awake all night, remembering Paris and the man who had given her the gift of laughter and taken it away from her again . . . feeling Larry's baby in her womb, possessing her body as its father had possessed her mind. She remembered that afternoon in the dreary Paris flat and the agony of the pointed metal coat-hanger ripping into her flesh deeper and deeper until it tore into the baby with the sweet, unbearable pain driving her into a frenzy of hysteria and the endless river of blood pouring from her. She remembered all these things and relived them again . . . the pain, the agony and the hatred . . .

At five A.M., Noelle was up and dressed, sitting in her room looking out at the huge fireball rising over the Aegean. It reminded her of another morning in Paris when she had arisen early and dressed and waited for Larry – only this time he would be here. Because she had seen to it that he had to be. As Noelle needed him before, so Larry needed her now, even though he was still unaware of it.

Demiris sent a message up to Noelle's suite that he would like her to have breakfast with him, but she was too excited, and she was afraid that her mood might arouse his curiosity. She had long ago learned that Demiris had the sensitivity of a cat: He missed nothing. Again, Noelle reminded herself that she must be careful. She wanted to take care of Larry herself in her own way. She had thought long and hard about the fact that she was using Constantin Demiris as an unwitting tool. If he ever found out, he would not like it.

Noelle had a demitasse of thick Greek coffee and half a freshly baked roll. She had no appetite. Her mind was feverishly dwelling on the meeting that would take place in a few short hours. She had taken unusual care with her makeup and the selection of a dress, and she knew that she looked beautiful.

Shortly after eleven o'clock, Noelle heard the limousine pull up in front of the house. She took a deep breath to control her nervousness, then slowly walked over to the window. Larry Douglas was getting out of the car. Noelle watched as he moved towards the front door and it was as though the march of years had rolled away, and the two of them were back in Paris. Larry was a little more mature, and the fighting and the living had added new lines to his face, but they only served to make him handsomer than he had been. Looking at him through the window ten yards away Noelle could still feel the animal magnetism, still feel the old desire and it welled up in her, mixing with the hatred until she was filled with a sense of exhilaration that was almost like a climax. She took one last quick look at herself in the mirror and then went downstairs to meet the man she was about to destroy.

As she walked down the stairs, Noelle wondered what Larry's reaction would be when he saw her. Had he bragged to his friends and perhaps even his wife that Noelle Page had once been in love with him? She wondered, as she had wondered a hundred times before, whether he ever relived the magic of those days and nights they had together in Paris and whether he regretted what he had done to her. How it must have eaten at his soul that Noelle had become internationally famous and that his own life consisted of a series of small failures! Noelle wanted to see some of that in Larry's eyes now when they came face to face for the first time in almost seven years.

Noelle had reached the reception hall when the front door opened and the butler ushered him in. Larry was staring at the enormous foyer in awe when he turned and saw Noelle. He looked at her for a long moment, his face lighting up in appreciation at the sight of a beautiful woman. 'Hello,' he said, politely. 'I'm Larry Douglas. I have an appointment to see Mr Demiris.'

And there was no sign of recognition on his face.

None at all.

Driving through the streets of Athens towards their hotel, Catherine was dazed by the succession of ruins and monuments that appeared all around them.

Ahead she saw the breathtaking spectacle of the whitemarbled Parthenon rising high atop the Acropolis. Hotels and office buildings were everywhere, yet in an odd way it seemed to Catherine that the newer buildings appeared temporary and impermanent while the Parthenon loomed immortal and timeless in the chiselled clarity of the air.

'Impressive, isn't it?' Larry grinned. 'The whole city is like that. One big beautiful ruin.'

They passed a large park in the centre of the city with dancing fountains in the middle. Hundreds of tables with green and orange poles lined the park, and the air above them was carpeted with blue awnings.

'That's Constipation Square,' Larry said.

'What?'

'Its real name is Constitution Square. People sit at those tables all day drinking Greek coffee and watching the world go by.'

On almost every block there were outdoor cafés, and on the corners men were selling freshly caught sponges. Everywhere flowers were sold by vendors, and their booths were a rage of violently coloured blossoms.

'The city is so white,' Catherine said. 'It's dazzling.'

The hotel suite was large and charming, overlooking Syntagma Square, the large square in the centre of the city. In the room were beautiful flowers and an enormous bowl of fresh fruit.

'I love it, darling,' Catherine said, going around the suite.

The bellboy had put her suitcases down and Larry tipped him. '*Parapolee*,' the boy said.

'*Parakalo*,' Larry replied.

The bellboy left, closing the door behind him.

Larry walked over and put his arms around Catherine. 'Welcome to Greece.' He kissed her hungrily, and she felt the hardness of his body pressing into the softness of hers and she knew how much he had missed her and she was glad. He led her into the bedroom.

On the dressing table was a small package. 'Open it,' Larry told her.

Her fingers tore the wrapping apart and in a small box inside was a tiny bird carved in jade. As busy as he was, Larry had remembered, and Catherine was touched. Somehow the bird was a talisman, an omen that everything was going to be all right, that the problems of the past were finished.

As they made love, Catherine said a little prayer of gratitude, thankful to be in the arms of the husband whom she loved so much, in one of the most exciting cities in the world, starting out on a new life. This was the old Larry, and all their problems had only made their marriage stronger.

Nothing could hurt them now.

The next morning Larry arranged for a real-estate agent to show Catherine some apartments. The agent turned out to be a short, dark, heavily moustached man named Dimitropolous who spoke in a rapid tongue that he sincerely believed was perfect English but which consisted of Greek words interlaced with an occasional undecipherable English phrase.

By throwing herself on his mercy – a trick that Catherine was to use often in the months to come

– she persuaded him to speak very slowly so that she was able to sift out some of the English words and try to make a wild stab at what he was trying to say.

The fourth place he showed her was a bright and sunny four-room apartment in what she later learned was the Kolonaki section, the fashionable suburb of Athens, lined with beautiful residential buildings and smart shops.

When Larry returned to the hotel that evening, Catherine told him about the apartment, and two days later they moved in.

Larry was away during the day but he tried to be home to have dinner with Catherine. Dinner in Athens was any time between nine and twelve o'clock. Between two and five in the afternoon, everyone had a siesta, and the shops opened again until late evening. Catherine found herself completely absorbed in the city. On her third night in Athens Larry brought home a friend, Count George Pappas, an attractive Greek about forty-five, tall and slim with dark hair with a touch of grey at the temples. There was a curious old-fashioned dignity about him that Catherine liked. He took them to dinner at a small taverna in the Plaka, the ancient section of the city. The Plaka comprised a few steep acres carelessly flung together in the heart of downtown Athens, with twisting alleys and crumbling, worn-down staircases that led to tiny houses built under Turkish rule when Athens was a mere village.

The Plaka was a place of whitewashed, rambling structures, fresh fruit and flower stalls, the marvellous aroma of coffee roasting in the open, howling cats and vociferous street fights. The affect was enchanting. In any other city, Catherine thought, a section like this would be the slums. Here, it's a monument.

The taverna that Count Pappas took them to was outdoors on top of a roof overlooking the city; the waiters were dressed in colourful costumes.

'What would you like to eat?' the Count asked Catherine.

She studied the alien menu helplessly. 'Would you mind ordering for me? I'm afraid I might order the proprietor.'

Count Pappas ordered a sumptuous banquet, choosing a variety of dishes so Catherine would get a chance to taste everything. They had *dolmades*, meatballs wrapped in vine leaves; *moussaka*, a succulent meat and eggplant pie; *stiffado*, stewed hare with onions – Catherine wasn't told what it was until she had eaten half of it, and she was unable to eat another bite of it – and *taramosalata*, the Greek salad of caviar with olive oil and lemon. The Count ordered a bottle of retsina.

'This is our national wine,' he explained. He watched Catherine with amusement as she tasted it. It had a piney, resonated taste, and Catherine struggled gamely to down it.

'Whatever I had,' she gasped, 'I think this just cured it.'

As they ate, three musicians began to play Bozoukia music. It was lively and gay and infectious and, as the group watched, customers began to get to their feet and move out onto the dance floor to dance to the music. What amazed Catherine was that the dancers were all male, and they were magnificent. She was enjoying herself tremendously.

They did not leave the café until after three A.M. The Count drove them back to their new apartment. 'Have you done any sightseeing yet?' he asked Catherine.

'Not really,' she confessed. 'I'm waiting for Larry to get some time off.'

The Count turned to Larry. 'Perhaps I could show Catherine some of the sights until you are able to join us.'

'That would be great,' Larry said. 'If you're sure it wouldn't be too much trouble.'

'It would be my pleasure,' the Count replied. He turned to Catherine. 'Would you mind having me as your guide?'

She looked at him and thought of Dimitropolous, the little real-estate man who spoke fluent gibberish.

'I'd love it,' she replied sincerely.

The next few weeks were fascinating. Catherine would spend mornings fixing up the apartment, and in the afternoon, if Larry was away, the Count would pick her up and take her sightseeing.

They drove out to Olympia. 'This is the site of the first Olympic Games,' the Count told her. 'They were held here every year for a thousand years in spite of wars, plagues and famines.'

Catherine stood looking in awe at the ruins of the great arena, thinking of the grandeur of the contests that had been held there through the centuries, the triumphs, the defeats.

'Talk about the playing fields of Eton,' Catherine said. '*This* is where the spirit of sportsmanship really started, isn't it?'

The Count laughed. 'I'm afraid not,' he said. 'The truth is a little embarrassing.'

Catherine looked up, interested. 'Why?'

'The first chariot race ever held here was fixed.'

'Fixed?'

'I'm afraid so,' Count Pappas confessed. 'You see, there was a rich prince named Pelops who was feuding with a rival. They decided to hold a chariot race here to see who was the better man. The night before the race Pelops tampered with the wheel of his rival's chariot. When the race began, the whole countryside was here to cheer on their favourite. At the first turn the wheel of the rival's chariot flew off, and his chariot overturned. Pelop's rival was entangled in the reins and dragged to his death. Pelops drove on to victory.'

'That's terrible,' Catherine said. 'What did they do to him?'

'That's really the disgraceful part of the story,' the Count replied. 'By now the whole populace was aware of what Pelops had done. It made him such a big hero that a huge pediment was raised in his honour at Olympia's Temple of Zeus. It is still there.' He smiled wryly. 'I'm afraid that our villain prospered and lived happily ever after. As a matter of fact,' he added, 'the whole region south of Corinth is called the Peloponnesus after him.'

'Who said crime doesn't pay?' marvelled Catherine.

Whenever Larry was free, he and Catherine would explore the city together. They found wonderful shops where they would spend hours haggling over prices, and out-of-the-way little restaurants that they made their own. Larry was a gay and charming companion, and Catherine was grateful that she had given up her job in the States to be with her husband.

Larry Douglas had never been happier in his life. The job with Demiris was the dream of a lifetime.

The money was good, but Larry was not interested in that. He was interested only in the magnificent machines he flew. It took him exactly one hour to learn to fly the Hawker Siddeley and five more flights to master it. Most of the time Larry flew with Paul Metaxas, Demiris' happy-go-lucky little Greek copilot. Metaxas had been surprised by the sudden departure of Ian Whitestone, and he had been apprehensive about Whitestone's replacement. He had heard stories about Larry Douglas, and he was not sure he liked what he heard. Douglas, however, seemed genuinely enthusiastic about his new job and the first time Metaxas flew with him, he knew that Douglas was a superb pilot.

Little by little Metaxas relaxed his guard and the two men became friends.

Whenever he was not flying, Larry spent time learning every idiosyncrasy of Demiris' fleet of planes. Before he was through, he was able to fly them all better than anyone had ever flown them before.

The variety in his job fascinated Larry. He would fly members of Demiris' staff on business trips to Brindisi and Corfu and Rome, or pick up guests and fly them to Demiris' island for a party or to his chalet in Switzerland for skiing. He became used to flying people whose photographs he was constantly seeing on the front pages of newspapers and magazines, and he would regale Catherine with stories about them. He flew the president of a Balkan country, a British prime minister, an Arabian oil chieftain and his entire harem. He flew opera singers and a ballet company and the cast of a Broadway play that was staging a single performance in London for Demiris' birthday. He piloted Justices of the Supreme Court, a congressman and a former President of the United States. During the flights Larry spent most of the time in the cockpit, but from time to time he would wander back to the cabin to make sure the passengers were comfortable. Sometimes he would hear bits of discussion between tycoons about impending mergers or stock deals. Larry could have made a fortune from the information he gleaned but he was simply not interested. What concerned him was the airplane he flew, powerful and alive and in his control.

It was two months before Larry piloted Demiris himself.

They were in the Piper and Larry was flying his employer from Athens to Dubrovnik. It was a cloudy day and there was a report of wind storms and squalls along the route. Larry had carefully plotted out the least stormy course, but the air was so full of turbulence that it was impossible to avoid it.

An hour out of Athens he flashed on the 'seat belt' sign and said to Metaxas, 'Hold on, Paul. This may cost us both our jobs.'

To Larry's surprise Demiris appeared in the cockpit. 'May I join you?' he said.

'Help yourself,' Larry said. 'It's going to be rough.'

Metaxas gave up his seat to Demiris and Demiris strapped himself in. Larry would have preferred to have the copilot sitting next to him, ready to act if anything went wrong, but it was Demiris' airplane.

The storm lasted almost two hours. Larry circled the large mountains of clouds that puffed up ahead of them, lovely white and deadly.

'Beautiful,' Demiris commented.

'They're killers,' Larry said. 'Cumulus. The reason they're so nice and fluffy is that there's wind inside of them puffing them up. The inside of that cloud can tear a plane apart in ten seconds. You can rise and fall thirty thousand feet in less than a minute with no control of your plane.'

'I'm sure you won't let that happen,' Demiris said calmly.

The winds caught at the plane and tried to fling it across the sky, but Larry fought to keep it under control. He forgot that Demiris was there, focusing his entire attention on the craft he was flying, using every skill he had ever learned. Finally they were out of the storm. Larry turned, drained, and found that Demiris had left the cockpit. Metaxas was in the seat.

'That was a lousy first trip for him, Paul,' Larry said. 'I may be in trouble.'

He was taxiing down the small, mountain-ringed tabletop airport at Dubrovnik when Demiris appeared in the doorway of the cockpit.

'You were right,' Demiris said to Larry. 'You're very good at what you do. I'm pleased.'

And Demiris was gone.

One morning as Larry was getting ready to leave on a flight to Morocco, Count Pappas telephoned to suggest that he take Catherine driving through the countryside. Larry insisted that she go.

'Aren't you jealous?' she asked.

'Of the Count?' Larry laughed.

And Catherine suddenly understood. During the time she and the Count had spent together, he had never made an improper advance towards her or even given her a suggestive look. 'He's a homosexual?' she asked.

Larry nodded. 'That's why I've left you in his tender care.'

The Count picked Catherine up early, and they started driving south towards the broad plain of Thessaly. Peasant women dressed in black walked along the road bent over with heavy loads of wood strapped to their backs.

'Why don't the men do the heavy work?' Catherine asked.

The Count shot her an amused glance.

'The women don't want them to,' he replied. 'They want their men fresh at night for other things.'

There's a lesson there for all of us, Catherine thought wryly.

In the late afternoon they approached the forbidding-looking Pindus Mountains, their rocky crags towering high in the sky. The road was blocked by a flock of sheep being herded by a shepherd and a scrawny sheep dog. Count Pappas stopped the car as they waited for the sheep to clear the road. Catherine watched in wonder as the dog nipped at the heels of the stray sheep, keeping them in line and forcing them in the direction he wanted them to go.

'That dog is almost human,' Catherine exclaimed admiringly.

The Count gave her a brief look. There was something in it that she did not understand.

'What's the matter?' she asked.

The Count hesitated. 'It's a rather unpleasant story.'

'I'm a big girl.'

The Count said, 'This is a wild area. The land

is rocky and inhospitable. At best the crops are meagre, and when the weather turns bad, there are no crops at all and a good deal of hunger.' His voice trailed off.

'Go on,' Catherine prompted.

'A few years ago there was a bad storm here and the crops were ruined. There was little food for anyone. All the sheep dogs in this area revolted. They deserted the farms they worked on and gathered together in a large band.' As he continued, he tried to keep the horror out of his voice. 'They began attacking the farms.'

'And killed the sheep!' Catherine said.

There was a silence before he answered. 'No. They killed their masters. And ate them.'

Catherine stared at him, shocked.

'They had to send in federal troops from Athens to restore human government here. It took almost a month.'

'How horrible.'

'Hunger does terrible things,' Count Pappas said quietly.

The sheep had crossed the road now. Catherine looked at the sheep dog again and shuddered.

As the weeks went by, the things that had seemed so foreign and strange to Catherine began to become familiar to her. She found the people open and friendly. She learned where to do her marketing and where to shop for clothes on Voukourestiou Street. Greece was a marvel of organized inefficiency, and one had to relax and enjoy it. No one was in a hurry, and if you asked someone for directions he was likely to take you where you wanted to go. Or he might say, when you asked how far it was: '*Enos cigarou dromos*,' which Catherine learned meant 'one cigarette away.' She walked the streets and explored the city and drank the warm dark wine of the Greek summer.

Catherine and Larry visited Mykonos with its colourful windmills and Melos, where the Venus de Milo was discovered. But Catherine's favourite place was Paros, a graceful, verdant island capped by a flower-covered mountain. When their boat docked, a guide stood on the quay. He asked if they would like him to guide them to the top of the mountain on muleback, and they clambered aboard two bony mules.

Catherine was wearing a broad-brimmed straw hat to protect her from the hot sun. As she and Larry rode up the steep path leading towards the mountain top, black-clad women called out, '*Ke-lee meh-ra*,' and handed Catherine gifts of fresh herbs, oregano and basil to put in her hat band. After a two-hour ride, they reached a plateau, a beautiful tree-filled plain with millions of flowers in spectacular bloom. The guide stopped the mules and they gazed in wonder at the incredible profusion of colours.

'This named Valley of the Butterflies,' the guide said in halting English.

Catherine looked around for a butterfly but saw

none. 'Why do they call it that?' she asked.

The guide grinned as though he had been waiting for her question. 'I show you,' he said. He dismounted from his mule and picked up a large fallen limb. He walked over to a tree and hit the limb against it with all his might. In a split second the 'flowers' on hundreds of trees suddenly took to the air in a wild rainbow of flight, leaving the trees bare. The air was filled with hundreds of thousands of gaily coloured butterflies dancing in the sunlight.

Catherine and Larry gazed in awe. The guide stood watching them, his face filled with a deep pride, as though he felt responsible for the beautiful miracle they were seeing. It was one of the loveliest days of Catherine's life, and she thought that if she could choose one perfect day to relive, it would be the day she spent with Larry on Paros.

'Hey, we got a VIP this morning,' Paul Metaxas grinned cheerfully. 'Wait till you see her.'

'Who is it?'

'Noelle Page, the boss's lady. You can look, but you mustn't touch.'

Larry Douglas remembered the brief glimpse he had had of the woman in Demiris' home the morning Douglas had arrived in Athens. She was a beauty and she looked familiar, but that of course was because he had seen her on the screen, in a French picture that Catherine had once dragged him to. No one had to tell Larry the rules of self-preservation. Even if the world were not filled with eager females, he would not have gone anywhere near Constantin Demiris' girl friend. Larry liked his job too much to jeopardize it by doing anything so stupid. Well, maybe he would get her autograph for Catherine.

The limousine taking Noelle to the airport was slowed down several times by work gangs repairing the roads, but Noelle welcomed the delays. She was going to see Larry Douglas for the first time since the meeting at Demiris' house. Noelle had been deeply shaken by what had happened. Or, more accurately, what had not happened.

Over the past six years Noelle had imagined their encounter in a hundred different ways. She had played the scene over and over in her mind. The one thing that had never even occurred to her was that Larry would not remember her. The most important event in her life had meant nothing more to him than another little cheap affair, one of hundreds. Well, before she was through with him, he would remember her.

Larry was crossing the airfield, flight plan in hand, when a limousine pulled up in front of the big plane, and Noelle Page emerged. Larry walked over to the car and said pleasantly, 'Good morning, Miss Page, I'm Larry Douglas. I'll be flying you and your guests to Cannes.'

Noelle turned and walked past him as though

he had not spoken, as though he did not exist. Larry stood there, looking after her, bewildered.

Thirty minutes later the other passengers, a dozen of them, had boarded the plane, and Larry and Paul Metaxas took off. They were flying the group to the Côte d'Azur where they would be picked up and taken aboard Demiris' yacht. It was an easy flight except for the normal turbulence off the southern coast of France in summer, and Larry landed the plane smoothly and taxied over to where some limousines were waiting for his passengers. As Larry left the plane with his stubby little copilot, Noelle walked up to Metaxas, ignoring Larry, and said in a voice filled with contempt, 'The new pilot is an amateur, Paul. You should give him flying lessons.' And Noelle got into a car and was driven away, leaving Larry standing there, filled with a stunned, helpless anger.

He told himself that she was a bitch and he had probably happened to catch her on a bad day. But the next incident a week later convinced him that he was facing a serious problem.

On Demiris' orders Larry picked Noelle up in Oslo and flew her to London. Because of what had happened Larry had gone over the flight plan with particular care. There was a high pressure area to the north and some possible thunder-heads building up to the east. Larry worked out a route that skirted these areas, and the flight proved to be perfectly smooth. He brought the ship down in a flawless three-point landing, and he and Paul

Metaxas strolled back to the cabin. Noelle Page was putting on some lipstick. 'I hope you enjoyed your flight, Miss Page,' Larry said politely.

Noelle glanced up at him a moment, her face expressionless, then turned to Paul Metaxas. 'I'm always nervous when I'm flown by an incompetent.'

Larry felt his face redden. He started to speak, and Noelle said to Metaxas, 'Please ask him not to address me in the future unless I speak to him first.'

Metaxas swallowed and mumbled, 'Yes, ma'am.'

Larry stared at Noelle, his eyes filled with fury, as she rose and left the plane. His impulse had been to slap her, but he knew that would have been the end of him. He loved this job more than anything he had ever done, and he did not intend to let anything happen to it. He knew that if he were fired, it could be the last flying job he would ever get. No, he would have to be very careful in the future.

When Larry got home, he talked to Catherine about what had happened.

'She's out to get me,' Larry said.

'She sounds horrible,' Catherine replied. 'Could you have offended her in some way, Larry?'

'I haven't spoken a dozen words to her.'

Catherine took his hand. 'Don't worry,' she said, consolingly. 'Before you're through, you'll charm her. Wait and see.'

The next day when Larry flew Constantin Demiris on a brief business trip to Turkey, Demiris came into the cockpit and took Metaxas' seat. He dismissed the copilot with a wave of his hand, and Larry and Demiris were alone. They sat there in silence, watching the small stratus clouds slicing the plane into fluffy geometric patterns.

'Miss Page has taken a dislike to you,' Demiris said, finally.

Larry felt his hands tighten on the controls and deliberately forced them to relax. He fought to keep his voice calm. 'Did – did she say why?'

'She said you were rude to her.'

Larry opened his mouth to protest, then thought better of it. He would have to work this out in his own way.

'I'm sorry. I'll try to be more careful, Mr Demiris,' he said evenly.

Demiris got to his feet. 'Do that. I would suggest that you not offend Miss Page any further.' He left the cockpit.

Any further! Larry racked his brain, trying to think of what he might have done to offend her. Perhaps she just did not like his type. Or she could have been jealous of the fact that Demiris liked and trusted him, but that didn't make sense. Nothing Larry could think of made any sense. And yet Noelle Page was trying to get him fired.

Larry thought about what it was like being out of a job, the indignity of filling out applications like a damned schoolboy, the interviews, the waiting, the endless hours of trying to kill time with cheap bars and amateur whores. He remembered Catherine's patience and tolerance and how he had hated her for it. No, he could not go through all that again. He could not stand another failure.

On a layover in Beirut a few days later Larry passed a movie theatre and noticed that the picture playing there starred Noelle Page. On an impulse he went to see it, prepared to hate the picture and its star, but Noelle was so brilliant in it that he found himself completely carried away by her performance. Again he had the curious feeling of familiarity. The following Monday, Larry flew Noelle Page and some business associates of Demiris' to Zurich. Larry waited until Noelle Page was alone and then approached her. He had hesitated about talking to her, remembering her last warning to him, but he had decided that the only way he could break through her antagonism was to go out of his way to be pleasant to her. All actresses were egotistical and liked to be told they were good, and so now he came up to her and said, with careful courtesy, 'Excuse me, Miss Page, I just wanted to tell you that I saw you in a movie the other night. *The Third Face*. I think you're one of the greatest actresses I've ever seen.'

Noelle stared at him a moment and then replied, 'I would like to believe that you are a better critic than you are a pilot, but I doubt very much that you have either the intelligence or the taste.' And she walked away.

Larry stood rooted there, feeling as though he had been struck. The goddamned cunt! For an instant he was tempted to follow her and tell her what he thought of her, but he knew it would be playing into her hands. No. From now on he would simply do his job and keep as far away from her as possible.

During the next few weeks Noelle was his passenger on several flights. Larry did not speak to her at all, and he tried desperately hard to arrange it so that she did not see him. He kept out of the cabin and had Metaxas handle any necessary communications with the passengers. There were no further comments from Noelle Page, and Larry congratulated himself on having solved the problem.

As it turned out, he congratulated himself too soon.

One morning Demiris sent for Larry at the villa. 'Miss Page is flying to Paris for me on some confidential business. I want you to stay at her side.'

'Yes, Mr Demiris.'

Demiris studied him for a moment, started to add something else, then changed his mind. 'That's all.'

Noelle was the only passenger on the flight to Paris and Larry decided to fly the Piper. He arranged for Paul Metaxas to make Noelle comfortable and stayed in the cockpit, out of sight during the entire flight. When they landed, Larry walked back to her seat and said, 'Excuse me, Miss Page. Mr Demiris asked me to stay with you while you're in Paris.'

She looked up at him with contempt and said,

'Very well. Just don't let me know that you're around.'

He nodded in icy silence.

They rode into the city from Orly in a private limousine. Larry sat up front with the driver and Noelle Page sat in back. She did not speak to him during the journey into the city. Their first stop was Paribas, the Banque de Paris et des Bas. Larry went into the lobby with Noelle and waited while she was ushered into the office of the president and then down to the basement where the safe-deposit boxes were kept. Noelle was gone about thirty minutes, and when she returned, she swept straight past Larry without a word. He stared after her a moment, then turned and followed her.

Their next stop was the rue du Faubourg-St-Honoré. Noelle dismissed the car. Larry followed her into a department store and stood nearby while she selected the items she wanted, then handed him the packages to carry. She shopped in half a dozen stores: Hermes for some purses and belts, Guerlain for perfume, Celine for shoes, until Larry was burdened down with packages. If she was aware of his discomfiture, Noelle gave no sign. Larry might have been some pet animal that she was leading around.

As they walked out of Celine's, it began to rain. Pedestrians were scurrying to take shelter. 'Wait here for me,' Noelle commanded.

Larry stood there and watched her disappear into a restaurant across the street. He waited in the driving rain for two hours, his arms full of packages, cursing her and cursing himself for putting up with her behaviour. He was trapped and he did not know how to get out of it.

And he had a terrible foreboding that it was going to get worse.

The first time Catherine met Constantin Demiris was at his villa. Larry had gone there to deliver a package he had flown in from Copenhagen, and Catherine had gone to the house with him. She was standing in the huge reception hall admiring a painting, when a door opened and Demiris came out. He watched her a moment, then said, 'Do you like Manet, Mrs Douglas?'

Catherine swung around and found herself face to face with the legend she had heard so much about. She had two immediate impressions: Constantin Demiris was taller than she had imagined, and there was an overpowering energy in him that was almost frightening. Catherine was amazed that he knew her name and who she was. He seemed to go out of his way to put her at ease. He asked Catherine how she liked Greece, whether her apartment was comfortable, and to let him know if he could do anything to help make her stay pleasant. He even knew – though God alone knew how! – that she collected miniature birds. 'I saw a lovely one,' he told her. 'I will send it to you.'

Larry appeared, and he and Catherine left.

'How did you like Demiris?' Larry asked.

'He's a charmer,' she said. 'No wonder you enjoy working for him.'

'And I'm going to keep working for him.' There was a grimness in his voice that Catherine did not understand.

The following day a beautiful porcelain bird was delivered to Catherine.

Catherine saw Constantin Demiris twice after that, once when she went to the races with Larry and once at a Christmas party Demiris gave at his villa. Each time he went out of his way to be charming to her. All in all, Catherine thought, Constantin Demiris was quite a remarkable person.

In August the Athens Festival began. For two months the city presented plays, ballets, operas, concerts – all given in the Herodes Atticus, the ancient open-air theatre at the foot of the Acropolis. Catherine saw several of the plays with Larry, and when he was away she went with Count Pappas. It was fascinating to watch ancient plays staged in their original settings by the race that had created them.

One night after Catherine and Count Pappas had gone to see a production of *Medea*, they were talking about Larry.

'He's an interesting man,' Count Pappas said. '*Polymechanos*.'

'What does that mean?'

'It is difficult to translate.' The Count thought for a moment. 'It means "fertile in devices."'

'You mean "resourceful"?'

'Yes, but more than that. Someone who is always very ready with a new idea, a new plan.'

'*Polymechanos*,' Catherine said. 'That's my boy.'

Above them there was a beautiful, waxing gibbous moon. The night was balmy and warm. They walked through the Plaka towards Omonia Square. As they started to cross the street, a car raced around the corner, headed straight towards them and the Count pulled Catherine to safety.

'Idiot!' he yelled after the disappearing driver.

'Everyone here seems to drive like that,' Catherine said.

Count Pappas smiled ruefully. 'Do you know the reason? The Greeks haven't made the transition to automobiles. In their hearts they're still driving donkeys.'

'You're joking.'

'Unfortunately no. If you want insight into the Greeks, Catherine, don't read the guidebooks; read the old Greek tragedies. The truth is, we still belong to other centuries. Emotionally we're very primitive. We're filled with grand passions, deep joys and great sorrows, and we haven't learned how to cover them up with a civilized veneer.'

'I'm not sure that's a bad thing,' Catherine replied.

'Perhaps not. But it distorts reality. When outsiders look at us, they are not seeing what they think they see. It is like looking at a distant star. You are not really seeing the star, you are looking at a reflection of light that was there perhaps a million years ago. That is the way it is with us Greeks. In us you are looking at a reflection of the past.'

They had reached the square. They passed a row of little stores with signs in the windows that said 'Fortune-Telling.'

'There are a lot of fortune-tellers here, aren't there?' Catherine asked.

'We are a very superstitious people.'

Catherine shook her head. 'I'm afraid I don't believe in it.'

They had reached a small taverna. A hand-lettered sign in the window read: 'MADAME PIRIS, FORTUNE-TELLING.'

'Do you believe in witches?' Count Pappas asked.

Catherine looked at him to see if he was teasing. His face was serious. 'Only on Halloween.'

'By a witch I do not mean broomsticks and black cats and boiling kettles.'

'What do you mean?'

He nodded towards the sign. 'Madame Piris is a witch. She can read the past and the future.'

He saw the scepticism on Catherine's face. 'I will tell you a story,' Count Pappas said. 'Many years ago, the Chief of Police in Athens was a man named Sophocles Vasilly. He was a friend of mine and I used my influence to help him get into office. Vasilly was a very honest man. There were people who wished to corrupt him and since he would not be corrupted, they decided that he would have to be eliminated.' He took Catherine's arm and they crossed the street towards the park.

'One day, Vasilly came to tell me of a threat that had been made on his life. He was a brave man, but this threat disturbed him because it came from a powerful and ruthless racketeer. Detectives were assigned to watch the racketeer and to protect Vasilly, but still he had an uneasy feeling that he did not have long to live. That was when he came to me.'

Catherine was listening, fascinated. 'What did you do?' she asked.

'I advised him to get a reading from Madame Piris.' He was silent, his thoughts prowling restlessly in some dark arena of the past.

'Did he go?' Catherine finally asked.

'What? Oh, yes. She told Vasilly that death was going to come to him unexpectedly and quickly and warned him to beware of a lion at noon. There are no lions in Greece, except for a few old mangy ones at the zoo and the stone ones you have seen on Delos.'

Catherine could feel the tension in Pappas' voice as he continued.

'Vasilly went to the zoo personally to check the cages to make sure that the animals were secure, and he made inquiries as to any wild animals that might have recently been brought into Athens. There were none.

'A week went by and nothing happened, and

Vasilly decided that the old witch had been wrong and that he had been a superstitious fool for paying any attention to her. On a Saturday morning I dropped by the police station to pick him up. It was his son's fourth birthday, and we were going to take a boat trip to Kyron to celebrate.

'I drove up in front of the station just as the clock in the Town Hall was striking twelve. As I reached the entrance, there was a tremendous explosion from inside the building. I hurried inside to Vasilly's office.' His voice sounded stiff and awkward. 'There was nothing left of the office or of Vasilly.'

'How horrible,' Catherine murmured.

They walked on for a moment in silence. 'But the witch was wrong, wasn't she?' Catherine asked. 'He wasn't killed by a lion.'

'Ah, but he was, you see. The police reconstructed what had happened. As I told you, it was the boy's birthday. Vasilly's desk was piled with gifts that he was going to bring to his son. Someone had brought in a birthday gift, a toy, and laid it on Vasilly's desk.'

Catherine felt the blood leaving her face. 'A toy lion.'

Count Pappas nodded. 'Yes. "Beware of a lion at noon."'

Catherine shuddered. 'That gives me the creeps.'

He looked down at her sympathetically. 'Madame Piris is not a "fun" fortune-teller to go to.'

They had crossed through the park and reached

Piraios Street. An empty taxi was passing by. The Count hailed it, and ten minutes later Catherine was back at her apartment.

As she prepared for bed, she told Larry the story, and as she told it, her flesh began to crawl again. Larry held her tightly and made love to her, but it was a long time before Catherine was able to fall asleep.

FIFTEEN

Noelle and Catherine

Athens: 1946

If it had not been for Noelle Page, Larry Douglas would have had no worries. He was where he wanted to be, doing what he wanted to do. He enjoyed his job, the people he met, and the man for whom he worked. On the ground his life was equally satisfactory. When he was not flying, he spent a good part of his time with Catherine; but because Larry's job was so mobile, Catherine was not always aware of where he was, and Larry found innumerable opportunities to go out on his own. He went to parties with Count Pappas and Paul Metaxas, his copilot, and a satisfying number of them turned into orgies. Greek women were filled with passion and fire. He had found a new one, Helena, a stewardess who worked for Demiris, and when they had a stopover away from Athens, she and Larry shared a hotel room. Helena was a beautiful, slim, dark-eyed girl, and insatiable. Yes, everything considered, Larry Douglas decided that his life was perfect.

Except for Demiris' blond bitch mistress.

Larry had not the slightest clue as to what made Noelle Page despise him, but whatever it was, it was endangering his way of life. Larry had tried being polite, aloof, friendly, and each time Noelle Page succeeded in making him look like a fool. Larry knew that he could go to Demiris, but he had no illusions about what would happen if it came to a choice between him and Noelle. Twice, he had arranged for Paul Metaxas to take over Noelle's flight but shortly before each flight Demiris' secretary had telephoned to tell him that Mr Demiris would like to have Larry pilot her himself.

On an early morning in late November Larry received a call that he was to fly Noelle Page to Amsterdam that afternoon. Larry checked with the airport and received a negative report on the weather in Amsterdam. A fog was beginning to roll in and by afternoon they expected zero visibility. Larry phoned Demiris' secretary to tell her that it would be impossible to fly to Amsterdam that day. The secretary said she would get back to him. Fifteen minutes later she phoned to say that Miss Page would be at the airport at two o'clock, ready to take off. Larry checked with the airport again, thinking that perhaps there had been a break in the weather, but the report was the same.

'Jesus Christ,' Paul Metaxas exclaimed. 'She must be in one hell of a hurry to get to Amsterdam.'

But Larry had the feeling that Amsterdam was not the issue. This was a contest of wills between the two of them. For all he cared Noelle Page could crash into a mountain peak and good riddance, but Larry was damned if he was going to risk his own neck for the stupid bitch. He tried to phone Demiris to discuss it with him, but he was in a meeting and unavailable. Larry slammed down the phone, seething. He had no choice now but to go to the airport and try to talk his passenger out of making the flight. He arrived at the airport at 1:30. By three o'clock Noelle Page had not appeared. 'She probably changed her mind,' Metaxas said.

But Larry knew better. As the time wore on, he became more and more furious, until he realized that that was her intention. She was trying to drive him into a rash action that would cost him his job. Larry was in the terminal building talking to the airport manager when Demiris' familiar grey Rolls drove up and Noelle Page emerged. Larry walked outside to meet her.

'I'm afraid the flight's off, Miss Page,' he said, making his voice flat. 'The airport at Amsterdam is fogged in.'

Noelle looked past Larry as though he did not exist and said to Paul Metaxas, 'The plane carries automatic landing equipment, does it not?'

'Yes, it does,' Metaxas said, awkwardly.

'I'm really surprised,' she replied, 'that Mr Demiris would hire a pilot who's a coward. I'll speak to him about it.'

Noelle turned and walked towards the plane. Metaxas looked after her and said, 'Jesus Christ! I don't know what's gotten into her. She never used to act like this. I'm sorry, Larry.'

Larry watched Noelle walk across the field, her blond hair blowing in the wind. He had never hated anyone so much in his life.

Metaxas was watching him. 'Are we going?' he asked.

'We're going.'

The copilot gave a deep, expressive sigh, and the two men slowly walked towards the plane.

Noelle Page was sitting in the cabin, leisurely thumbing through a fashion magazine when they entered the plane. Larry stared at her a moment, so filled with anger that he was afraid to speak. He went up into the cockpit and began his preflight check.

Ten minutes later he had received clearance from the tower and they were airborne for Amsterdam.

The first half of the flight was uneventful. Switzerland lay below in a mantle of snow. By the time they were over Germany, it was dusk. Larry radioed ahead to Amsterdam for a weather check. They reported that fog was blowing in from the North Sea and getting thicker. He cursed his bad luck. If the winds had changed and the fog had cleared, his problem would have been solved, but now he had to decide whether to risk an instrument landing at Amsterdam or fly to an alternate airport. He was tempted to go back and discuss it with his passenger, but he could visualize the contemptuous look on her face.

'Special Flight one-oh-nine, would you give us your flight plan, please?' It was the tower at Munich. Larry had to make a decision swiftly. He could still land at Brussels, Cologne or Luxembourg.

Or Amsterdam.

The voice crackled over the speaker again. 'Special Flight one-oh-nine, would you give us your flight plan, please?'

Larry snapped down the transmitting key. 'Special Flight one-oh-nine to Munich Tower. We're going to Amsterdam.' He flicked the switch up and was aware of Metaxas watching him.

'Jesus, maybe I should have doubled my life insurance,' Metaxas said. 'You really think we're going to make it?'

'Do you want to know the truth?' Larry said, bitterly. 'I don't give a shit.'

'Fantastic! I'm up in a plane with two fucking maniacs!' Metaxas moaned.

For the next hour Larry was wholly absorbed in flying the aircraft, listening to the frequent weather reports without comment. He was still hoping for a wind change, but thirty minutes out of Amsterdam the report was still the same. Heavy fog. The field was closed to all air traffic except for emergencies. Larry made contact with the control tower at Amsterdam. 'Special Flight one-oh-nine to Amsterdam Tower. Approaching airport from 75 miles east of Cologne, ETA nineteen hundred hours.'

Almost instantly a voice on the radio crackled back, 'Amsterdam Tower to Special Flight one-oh-nine. Our field is closed down. We suggest you return to Cologne or land at Brussels.'

Larry spoke into the handmike. 'Special Flight one-oh-nine to Amsterdam Tower. Negative. We have an emergency.'

Metaxas turned to stare at him in surprise.

A new voice came over the speaker. 'Special Flight one-oh-nine, this is Chief of Operations at Amsterdam Airport. We are completely fogged in here. Visibility zero. Repeat: visibility zero. What is the nature of your emergency?'

'We're running out of fuel,' Larry said. 'I have barely enough to reach you.'

Metaxas' eyes went to the fuel gauges, which registered half full. 'For Christ's sakes,' Metaxas exploded. 'We could fly to China!'

The radio was silent. Suddenly it exploded into life again.

'Amsterdam Tower to Special Flight one-oh-nine. You have an emergency clearance. We'll bring you in.'

'Roger.' Larry flicked off the switch and turned to Metaxas. 'Jettison the fuel,' he ordered.

Metaxas swallowed and said in a choked voice, '*J – jettison the fuel*?'

'You heard me, Paul. Leave just enough to bring us in.'

'But, Larry . . .'

'Damn it, don't argue. If we roll in there with

a tank half full of gas, they'll jerk our licences away so fast you won't know what hit you.'

Metaxas nodded glumly and reached for the fuel-ejection handle. He began to pump, keeping a close eye on the gauge. Five minutes later they were in the fog, wrapped in a soft white cotton that wiped out everything but the dimly lit cockpit they sat in. It was an eerie sensation, cut off from time and space and the rest of the world. The last time Larry had been through this was in the Link Trainer. But that was a game where there were no risks. Here the stakes were life and death. He wondered what it was doing to his passenger. He hoped it gave her a heart attack. The Amsterdam control tower came on again.

'Amsterdam control tower to Special Flight one-oh-nine. I am going to bring you in on A.L.S. You will please follow my instructions exactly. We have you on our radar. Turn three degrees west and maintain present altitude until further instructions. At your present airspeed, you should be landing in eighteen minutes.'

The voice coming over the radio sounded tense. With good reason, thought Larry grimly. One slight mistake and the plane would plough into the sea. Larry made the correction and shut out everything from his mind but the disembodied voice that was his sole link to survival. He flew the plane as though it were a part of himself, flying it with his heart, his soul and his mind. He was dimly aware of Paul Metaxas sweating beside him, calling out a constant instrument check in a low, strained voice, but if they came out of this alive, it would be Larry Douglas who did it. Larry had never seen fog like this. It was a ghostly enemy, charging at him from every side, blinding him, seducing him, trying to lure him into making one fatal mistake. He was hurtling through the sky at two hundred and fifty miles an hour, unable to see beyond the windshield of the cockpit. Pilots hated fog, and the first rule was: Climb over it or dive under it, but get out of it! Now there was no way, because he was locked into an impossible destination by the whim of a spoiled tart. He was helpless, at the mercy of instruments that could go wrong and men on the ground who could make mistakes. The disembodied voice came over the speaker again, and it seemed to Larry that it had a new, nervous quality.

'Amsterdam Tower to Special Flight one-oh-nine. You are coming into the first leg of your landing pattern: Lower your flaps and begin your descent. Descend to two thousand feet . . . fifteen hundred feet . . . one thousand feet . . .'

Still no sign of the airport below. They could have been in the middle of nowhere. He could feel the ground rushing up to meet the plane.

'Decrease your airspeed to one hundred twenty . . . lower your wheels . . . you're at six hundred feet . . . airspeed one hundred . . . you're at four hundred feet . . .' And still no sign of the goddamn airport! The blanket of smothering cotton seemed thicker now.

Metaxas' forehead gleamed with perspiration. 'Where in the hell is it?' he whispered.

Larry stole a swift glance at the altimetre. The needle was edging down towards three hundred feet. Then it was below three hundred feet. The ground was rushing up to meet them at one hundred miles per hour. The altimetre showed only one hundred fifty feet. Something was wrong. He should have been able to see the airport lights by now. He strained to see ahead of the plane, but there was only the treacherous, blinding fog whipping across the windshield.

Larry heard Metaxas' voice, tense and hoarse. 'We're down to sixty feet.' And still nothing.

'Forty feet.'

And the ground racing up to meet them in the darkness.

'Twenty feet.'

It was no good. In another two seconds, the margin of safety would be gone and they would crash. He had to make an instant decision.

'I'm going to take it back up,' Larry said. His hand tightened on the wheel and started to pull back and at that instant, a row of electric arrows blazed out on the ground ahead of them, lighting up the runway below. Ten seconds later, they were on the ground, taxiing towards the Schiphol terminal.

When they had come to a stop, Larry switched off the engines with numb fingers and sat motionless for a long time. Finally he pushed himself to his feet and was surprised to find that his knees were trembling. He noticed a strange odour in the air and turned to Metaxas. Metaxas grinned sheepishly.

'Sorry,' he said. 'I shat.'

Larry looked down at him and nodded. 'For both of us,' he said. He turned and walked back into the cabin. The bitch was in there, calmly thumbing through a magazine. Larry stood there studying her, aching to tell her off, wishing desperately that he could find the key to what made her tick. Noelle Page must have known how close she had come to death in the past few minutes, and yet she sat there looking serene and undisturbed, not a hair out of place.

'Amsterdam,' Larry announced.

They drove into Amsterdam in a heavy silence, Noelle in the back seat of the Mercedes 300 and Larry in front with the chauffeur. Metaxas had stayed at the airport to have the plane serviced. The fog was still thick and they drove slowly until suddenly, when they reached the Lindenplatz, it began to lift.

They rode through the City Square, crossed the Eider Bridge over the Amstel River and stopped in front of the Amstel Hotel. When they reached the lobby, Noelle said to Larry, 'You will pick me up at ten sharp tonight,' then turned away and walked towards the elevator, the manager of the hotel bowing and scraping at her heels. A bellboy led

Larry to a small, uncomfortable single room at the back of the hotel on the first floor. The room was next to the kitchen, and through the wall Larry could hear the clatter of dishes and smell the mixed aromas from the steaming kettles.

Larry took one look at the tiny room and snapped, 'I wouldn't put my dog in here.'

'I'm sorry,' the bellboy said apologetically. 'Miss Page requested the cheapest room we had for you.'

Okay, Larry thought, *I'll find a way to beat her. Constantin Demiris isn't the only man in the world who uses a private pilot. I'll start checking around tomorrow. I've met a lot of his rich friends. There are half a dozen of them who would be damned glad to hire me*. But then, he thought: *Not if Demiris fires me. If that happens, none of them will touch me. I have to hang in there*. The bathroom was down the hall, and Larry unpacked and took out a robe so that he could go take a bath, then thought: *To hell with it, why should I bathe for her? I hope I smell like a pig*. He went to the hotel bar to have a badly needed drink. He was on his third martini when he looked up at the clock over the bar and saw that it was 10:15. *Ten o'clock sharp*, she had said. Larry was filled with a sudden panic. He hastily slapped some bills on the bar and headed towards the elevator. Noelle was in the Emperor Suite on the fifth floor. He found himself running down the long corridor and cursing himself for letting her do this to him. He knocked at the door to her suite, his mind forming excuses for his tardiness. No one answered his knock and when Larry turned the knob, it was off the latch. He walked into the large, luxuriously furnished living room and stood there a moment, uncertainly, then called out, 'Miss Page.' There was no answer. So *that* was her plan.

I'm sorry, Costa darling, but I warned you that he was unreliable. I asked him to pick me up at ten o'clock, but he was down in the bar getting drunk. I had to leave without him.

Larry heard a sound from the bathroom and went towards it. The bathroom door was open. He walked inside just as Noelle Page stepped out of the shower. She wore nothing but a turkish towel turbanned around her head.

Noelle turned and saw him standing there. An apology sprang to Larry's lips, trying to head off her indignation, but before he could speak, Noelle said indifferently, 'Hand me that towel,' as though he were a maid. Or a eunuch. Larry could have coped with her indignation or anger, but her arrogant indifference made something explode inside him.

He moved towards her and grabbed her, knowing as he did it that he was throwing away everything he wanted for the cheap satisfaction of a petty revenge, but there was no way he could have stopped himself. The rage inside him had been building up for months, fed by the indignities he had received from her, the gratuitous insults, the humiliation, the risking of his life. All these things were burning in him as he reached for her naked body. If Noelle had screamed, Larry would have knocked her senseless. But she saw the wild look on his face and made no sound as he picked her up and carried her into the bedroom.

Somewhere in Larry's mind a voice was shouting to him to stop, to apologize, to say that he was drunk, to get out before it was too late to save himself, but he knew it was already too late. There was no going back. He threw her savagely down on the bed and moved towards her.

He concentrated on her body, refusing to let his mind think of what his punishment was going to be for what he was doing. He had no illusions as to what Demiris would do to him for this, for the Greek's honour would not be satisfied with merely firing him. Larry knew enough about the tycoon to know that his vengeance would be far more terrible, and yet knowing this Larry could not stop himself. She lay on the bed looking up at him, her eyes blazing. He moved down on top of her and was entering her, never realizing until that instant how much he had been wanting to do this all along, and somehow the need was all mixed up with the hate, and he felt her arms wrap around his neck, holding him close, as though she would never let him go, and she said, 'Welcome back,' and it flashed through Larry's mind that she was crazy or she was confusing him with someone else, but he didn't care because her body was twisting and writhing beneath him, and he forgot everything else in the sensation of what was happening to him, and the sudden blinding wonderful knowledge that now everything was going to be all right.

SIXTEEN

Noelle and Catherine

Athens: 1946

Inexplicably, Time had become Catherine's enemy. She was unaware of it at first, and looking back she could not have told the exact moment that Time began to work against her. She was not aware when Larry's love had gone or why or how, but one day it had simply disappeared somewhere down the endless corridor of time and all that was left was a cold hollow echo. She sat in the apartment alone day after day, trying to figure out what had happened, what had gone wrong. There was nothing specific Catherine could think of, no single moment of revelation that she could point to and say, *That was it, that was when Larry stopped loving me*. Possibly it had started when Larry came back after three weeks in Africa where he had flown Constantin Demiris on a safari. Catherine had missed Larry more than she had thought possible. *He's away all the time*, she thought. *It's like during the war, only this time there's no enemy.*

But she was wrong. There was an enemy.

'I haven't told you the good news,' Larry said. 'I got a raise. Seven hundred a month. How about that?'

'That's wonderful,' she replied. 'We can go back home that much sooner.' She saw his face tighten. 'What's the matter?'

'*This* is home,' Larry said, curtly.

She stared at him uncomprehendingly. 'Well, for now,' she agreed weakly, 'but I mean – you wouldn't want to live here forever.'

'You've never had it so good,' Larry retorted. 'It's like living at a vacation resort.'

'But it's not like living in America, is it?'

'Fuck America,' Larry said. 'I risked my ass for it for four years and what did it get me? A handful of two-bit medals. They wouldn't even give me a job after the war.'

'That's not true,' she said. 'You . . .'

'I what?'

Catherine did not want to provoke an argument, particularly on his first night back. 'Nothing, darling,' she said. 'You're tired. Let's go to bed early.'

'Let's not.' He went to the bar to pour himself a drink. 'A new act's opening at the Argentina Night Club. I told Paul Metaxas that we'd join him and a few friends.'

Catherine looked at him. 'Larry –' She had to fight to keep her voice steady. 'Larry, we haven't seen each other for almost a month. We never get a chance to – to just sit and talk.'

'I can't help it if my work takes me away,' he replied. 'Don't you think I'd like to be with you?'

She shook her head and said, 'I don't know. I'll have to ask the Ouija board.'

He put his arms around her then and grinned that innocent, boyish grin. 'To hell with Metaxas and the whole crowd. We'll stay in tonight, just the two of us. Okay?'

Catherine looked into his face and knew that she was being unreasonable. Of course he couldn't help it if his job took him away from her. And when he got home, it was natural that he would want to see other people. 'We'll go out if you like,' she decided.

'Uhn-uhn.' He held her close. 'Just the two of us.'

They did not leave the apartment all weekend. Catherine cooked and they made love and sat in front of the fire and talked and played gin rummy and read, and it was everything that Catherine could have asked.

Sunday night after a delicious dinner that Catherine prepared, they went to bed and made love again. She lay in bed watching Larry as he walked towards the bathroom, naked, and she thought what a beautiful man he is and how lucky I am that he belongs to me, and the smile was still on her face when Larry turned at the bathroom door and said casually, 'Make a lot of dates next week, will you, so we won't have to be stuck with each other like this again with nothing to do.' And he went into the bathroom leaving Catherine with the smile still frozen on her face.

Or perhaps the trouble had started with Helena, the beautiful Greek stewardess. One hot summer afternoon, Catherine had been out shopping. Larry was out of town. She was expecting him home the following day and had decided to surprise him with his favourite dishes. As Catherine was leaving the market with her arms full of groceries, a taxi passed her. In the back seat was Larry, his arms around a girl in a stewardess' uniform. Catherine had one brief glimpse of their faces laughing together, and then the taxi turned a corner and was out of sight.

Catherine stood there numb, and it was not until some small boys came running up to her that she realized the grocery bags had slipped from her nerveless fingers. They had helped Catherine pick up everything and she had stumbled home, her mind refusing to think. She had tried to tell herself that it had not been Larry she had seen in the taxi, it had been someone who resembled him. But the truth was that no one in the world resembled Larry. He was unique, an original work of God, a priceless creation of nature. And he was all hers. Hers and the brunette's in the taxi, and how many others?

Catherine sat up all that night waiting for Larry to walk in, and when he did not come home, she knew that there was no excuse that he could give her that could hold their marriage together, and no excuse that she could give herself. He was a liar and a cheat, and she could not stay married to him any longer.

Larry did not return home until late the following afternoon.

'Hi,' he said, cheerfully, as he walked into the apartment. He put down his flight bag and saw her face. 'What's wrong?'

'When did you get back to town?' Catherine asked stiffly.

Larry looked at her, puzzled. 'About an hour ago. Why?'

'I saw you in a taxi yesterday with a girl.' *It was as simple as that*, Catherine thought. *Those are the words that ended my marriage. He's going to deny it, and I'm going to call him a liar and leave him and never see him again.*

Larry was standing there staring at her.

'Go ahead,' she said. 'Tell me it wasn't you.'

Larry looked at her, nodding. 'Of course it was me.' The sudden sharp pain Catherine felt at the pit of her stomach made her realize how much she had wanted him to deny it.

'Christ,' he said, 'what have you been thinking?'

She started to speak and her voice trembled with anger. 'I –'

Larry held up a hand. 'Don't say anything you'll be sorry for.'

Catherine looked at him incredulously. '*I'll* be sorry for?'

'I flew back to Athens yesterday for fifteen minutes to pick up a girl named Helena Merelis to fly her to Crete for Demiris. Helena works for him as a stewardess.'

'But . . .' It was possible. Larry could have been telling the truth; or was it *polymechanos*, fertile in devices? 'Why didn't you telephone me?' Catherine asked.

'I did,' Larry said curtly. 'There was no answer. You were out, weren't you?'

Catherine swallowed. 'I – I went out shopping for your dinner.'

'I'm not hungry,' Larry snapped. 'Nagging always makes me lose my appetite.' He turned and walked out the door, leaving Catherine standing there, her right hand still raised, as though it was silently beseeching him to come back.

It was shortly after that that Catherine began to drink. It started in a small, harmless way. She would be expecting Larry home for dinner at seven o'clock, and when nine o'clock came and he had not called, Catherine would have a brandy to help kill the time. By ten o'clock, she would have had several brandies, and by the time he came home, if he did, the dinner would have been long since ruined, and she would be a little tight. It made it much easier to face what was happening to her life.

Catherine could no longer hide from herself the fact that Larry was cheating on her and had probably been cheating from the time they were married. Going through his uniform trousers one day before sending them to the cleaners, she found a lace handkerchief stiff with dried semen. There was lipstick on his shorts.

She thought of Larry in the arms of some other woman.

And she wanted to kill him.

SEVENTEEN

Noelle and Catherine

Athens: 1946

As Time had become Catherine's enemy, so it had become Larry's friend. The night in Amsterdam had been nothing less than a miracle. Larry had courted disaster and in so doing had, incredibly, found the solution to all his problems. *It's the Douglas luck*, he thought with satisfaction.

But he knew that it was more than luck. It was some obscure, perverse instinct in him that needed to challenge the Fates, to brush against the parameters of death and destruction, a testing, a pitting of himself against Fortune for life-and-death stakes.

Larry remembered a morning over the Truk Islands when a squadron of Zeros had zoomed out of a cloud cover. He had been flying point, and they had concentrated their attack on him. Three Zeros had manoeuvred him away from the rest of the squadron and opened fire on him. In a kind of supra-clarity that came to him in moments of danger, he was blindingly aware of the island below, the dozens of ships bobbing on the rolling seas, the roaring planes slashing at each other in the bright blue sky. It was one of the happiest moments of Larry's life, the fulfilment of Life and the mocking of Death.

He had put the plane into a spin and had pulled out of it on the tail of one of the Zeros. He had watched it explode as he opened up with his machine guns. The other two planes had closed in on either side. Larry watched them as they raced down to him, and at the last instant he pulled the plane into an Immelmann, and the two Japanese planes collided in mid-air. It was a moment Larry savoured in his mind often.

For some reason it had come back to him that night in Amsterdam. He had made wild, violent love to Noelle, and afterwards she had lain in his arms, talking of the two of them in Paris together before the war, and it suddenly brought back a dim memory of an eager young girl, but good God, there had been hundreds of eager young girls since then, and Noelle was no more than an elusive, half-recalled wisp of memory in his past.

How lucky it was, Larry thought, that their paths had crossed again accidentally, after all these years.

'You belong to me,' Noelle said. 'You're mine now.'

Something in her tone made Larry uneasy. *And yet*, he asked himself, *what do I have to lose?*

With Noelle under his control, he could stay on with Demiris forever, if he wanted to.

She was studying him as though reading his mind, and there was an odd expression in her eyes that Larry did not understand.

It was just as well.

On a return trip from Morocco Larry took Helena out to dinner and spent the night at her apartment.

In the morning he drove to the airport to check out his plane. He had lunch with Paul Metaxas.

'You look like you hit the jackpot,' Metaxas said. 'Can you spare a piece for me?'

'My boy,' Larry grinned, 'you couldn't handle them. It takes a master.'

They had a pleasant lunch and then Larry drove back into town to pick up Helena, who was to be on his flight.

He knocked at the door of her apartment and after a long while, Helena slowly opened it. She was naked. Larry stared at her, not recognizing her. Her face and body were a mass of ugly bruises and puffy swellings. Her eyes were slits of pain. She had been beaten up by a professional.

'Christ!' Larry exclaimed. 'What happened?'

Helena opened her mouth and Larry saw that three of her upper front teeth had been knocked out. 'T – two men,' she chattered. 'They came in as soon as you l – left.'

'Didn't you call the police?' Larry demanded, horrified.

'Th – they said they would kill me if I told anyone. They meant it, L – Larry.' She stood there in shock, holding onto the door for support.

'Did they rob you?'

'N – no. They f – forced their way in and raped me and then they – they beat me up.'

'Get some clothes on,' he ordered. 'I'm taking you to the hospital.'

'I can't g – go out with my face like this,' she said.

And of course she was right. Larry telephoned a doctor who was a friend of his and arranged for him to come over.

'I'm sorry I can't stay,' Larry told Helena. 'I have to fly Demiris out in half an hour. I'll see you as soon as I return.'

But he never saw her again. When Larry returned two days later, the apartment was empty, and the landlady told him that the young lady had moved and had left no forwarding address. Even then Larry had no suspicion of the truth. It was not until several nights later when he was making love to Noelle that he had an inkling of what had happened. 'You're so goddamn fantastic,' he said. 'I've never known anybody like you.'

'Do I give you everything you want?' she asked.

'Yes,' he moaned, 'Oh, Christ, yes.'

Noelle stopped what she was doing. 'Then don't ever sleep with another woman,' she said softly. 'Next time, I'll kill her.'

Larry remembered her words: You belong to me.

And they suddenly took on a new and ominous meaning. For the first time he had the premonition that this was not some fly-by-night affair that he could get out of anytime he felt like it. He sensed the cold, deadly, untouchable centre that was in Noelle Page, and he was chilled and a little frightened by it. Half a dozen times during the night he started to bring up the subject of Helena, and each time he stopped because he was afraid to know, afraid to have it put into words, as though the words had more power than the deed itself. If Noelle were capable of that . . .

At breakfast the next morning Larry studied Noelle when she was unaware of it, looking for signs of cruelty, of sadism, but all he saw was a loving, beautiful woman, telling him amusing anecdotes, anticipating and catering to his every want. *I have to be wrong about her,* he thought. But after that he was careful not to date any other girls, and in a few short weeks he had lost all desire to do so because Noelle had become a complete obsession with him.

From the beginning Noelle warned Larry that it was essential that they keep their affair from Constantin Demiris.

'There must never be the slightest whisper of suspicion about us,' Noelle cautioned.

'Why don't I rent an apartment?' Larry suggested. 'A place where we . . .'

Noelle shook her head. 'Not in Athens. Someone would recognize me. Let me think about it.'

Two days later Demiris sent for Larry. At first Larry was apprehensive, wondering whether the Greek tycoon could have heard about Noelle and him, but Demiris greeted him pleasantly and led him into a discussion of a new plane he was considering buying.

'It's a converted Mitchell Bomber,' Demiris told him. 'I want you to have a look at it.'

Larry's face lit up. 'It's a great plane,' he said. 'For its weight and size, it will give you the best ride you can buy.'

'How many passengers will it carry?'

Larry thought a moment. 'Nine in luxury, plus a pilot, navigator and flight engineer. It flies at four hundred eighty miles an hour.'

'It sounds interesting. Will you check it out for me and give me a report?'

'I can't wait,' Larry grinned.

Demiris rose to his feet. 'By the way Douglas, Miss Page is going to Berlin in the morning. I want you to fly her there.'

'Yes, sir,' Larry said. And then added, innocently, 'Did Miss Page tell you that we're getting along better?'

Demiris looked up at him. 'No,' he said puzzled. 'As a matter of fact this morning she complained to me about your insolence.'

Larry stared at him in surprise, and then as realization flooded through him, he quickly tried to cover up his blunder. 'I'm trying, Mr Demiris,' he said, earnestly. 'I'll try harder.'

Demiris nodded. 'Do that. You're the best pilot I've ever had, Douglas. It would be a shame to . . .' He let his voice trail off, but the message was clear.

On the drive home Larry cursed himself for a fool. He had better remember he was playing in the big leagues now. Noelle had been bright enough to realize that any sudden change in her attitude towards Larry would make Demiris suspicious. The old relationship between them was a perfect cover for what they were doing. Demiris was trying to bring them together. The thought made Larry laugh aloud. It was a good feeling to know that he had something that one of the most powerful men in the world thought belonged to him.

On the flight to Berlin Larry turned the wheel over to Paul Metaxas and told him that he was going back to talk to Noelle Page.

'Aren't you afraid of getting your head bitten off?' Metaxas asked.

Larry hesitated, tempted to brag. But he conquered the impulse. 'She's a bitch on wheels,' Larry shrugged, 'but if I don't find some way to soften her up, I could find myself out on my ass.'

'Good luck,' Metaxas said soberly.

'Thanks.'

Larry carefully closed the cockpit door and went back to the lounge where Noelle was seated. The two stewardesses were at the rear of the plane. Larry started to sit down across from Noelle.

'Be careful,' she warned softly. 'Everyone who works for Constantin reports back to him.'

Larry glanced towards the stewardesses and thought of Helena.

'I've found a place for us,' Noelle said. There was pleasure and excitement in her voice.

'An apartment?'

'A house. Do you know where Rafina is?'

Larry shook his head. 'No.'

'It's a little village on the sea, a hundred kilometres north of Athens. We have a secluded villa there.'

He nodded. 'Whose name did you rent it in?'

'I bought it,' Noelle said, 'in someone else's name.'

Larry wondered what it must feel like to be able to afford to buy a villa just to get in the hay with someone once in a while. 'Great,' he said. 'I can't wait to see it.'

She studied him a moment. 'Will you have any trouble getting away from Catherine?'

Larry looked at Noelle in surprise. It was the first time she had ever mentioned his wife. He had certainly made no secret of his marriage, but it was a strange feeling to hear Noelle use Catherine's name. Obviously she had done some checking, and knowing her as well as he was beginning to, it was probably very thorough. She was waiting for an answer. 'No,' Larry replied. 'I come and go as I please.'

Noelle nodded, satisfied. 'Good. Constantin is going on a business cruise to Dubrovnik. I've told him I can't go with him. We'll have ten lovely days together. You'd better go now.'

Larry turned and walked back to the cockpit.

'How did it go?' Metaxas asked. 'Loosen her up any?'

'Not much,' Larry replied, carefully. 'It's going to take time.'

Larry owned a car, a Citroen convertible, but at Noelle's insistence, he went to a small rent-a-car agency in Athens and hired an automobile. Noelle had driven up to Rafina alone and Larry was to join her there. The drive was a pleasant one on a winding ribbon of dusty road high above the sea. Two and a half hours out of Athens Larry came to a tiny, charming village nestled along the coastline. Noelle had given him careful directions so that he would not have to stop and inquire at the village. As he reached the outskirts of the village, he turned to the left and drove down a small dirt road that led to the sea. There were several villas, each one secluded behind high stone walls. At the end of the road built on an outcropping of rock on a promontory that jutted out over the water was a large, luxurious-looking villa.

Larry drove up to the gate and rang the bell. A moment later the electric gate swung open. He drove inside and the gate closed behind him. He found himself in a large courtyard with a fountain in the centre. The sides of the courtyard were filled with a profusion of flowers. The house itself was a typical Mediterranean villa, as impregnable as a fortress.

The front door opened and Noelle appeared, wearing a white cotton dress. They stood there smiling at each other, and then she was in his arms.

'Come and see your new house,' she said eagerly, and she took him inside.

The interior of the house was cavernous, large spacious rooms with high domed ceilings. There was an enormous living room downstairs, a library, a formal dining room and an old-fashioned kitchen with a circular cooking range in the centre. The bedrooms were upstairs.

'What about the servants?' Larry asked.

'You're looking at them.'

Larry regarded her in surprise. '*You're* going to do the cooking and cleaning?'

She nodded. 'There will be a couple coming in to clean after we leave here, but they will never see us. I arranged it through an agency.'

Larry grinned sardonically.

There was a warning note in Noelle's voice. 'Don't ever make the mistake of underestimating Constantin Demiris. If he finds out about us, he will kill both of us.'

Larry smiled. 'You're exaggerating,' he said. 'The old man may not like it, but . . .'

Her violet eyes locked on his. 'He will kill us both.' There was something in her voice that sent a feeling of apprehension through him.

'You're serious, aren't you?'

'I was never more serious in my life. He's ruthless.'

'But when you say he'll *kill* us,' Larry protested, 'he wouldn't . . .'

'He won't use bullets,' Noelle said flatly. 'He'll find a complicated, ingenious way to do it, and he'll never be punished for it.' Her tone lightened. 'But he won't find out, darling. Come, let me show you our bedroom.' She took his hand and they went up the sweeping stairway. 'We have four guest bedrooms,' she said and added with a smile, 'we can try them all.' She took him into the master bedroom, a huge corner suite that overlooked the sea. From the window Larry could see a large terrace and the short path that wound down to the water. There was a dock with a large sailboat and a motor boat moored to it.

'Who do the boats belong to?'

'You,' she said. 'It's your welcome-home present.'

He turned to her and found that she had slipped out of her cotton dress. She was naked. They spent the rest of the afternoon in bed.

The next ten days flew by. Noelle was quicksilver, a nymph, a genie, a dozen beautiful servants catering to Larry's every wish before he even knew what he wanted. He found the library in the villa stocked with his favourite books and records. Noelle cooked all his favourite dishes to perfection, sailed with him, swam in the warm blue sea with him, made love to him, gave him massages at night until he fell asleep. In a sense they were prisoners there together, for they dared not see anyone else. Every day Larry found new facets in Noelle. She entertained him with fascinating anecdotes about famous people she knew. She tried to discuss business and politics with him until she found that he was interested in neither.

They played poker and gin rummy, and Larry was furious because he could never win. Noelle taught him chess and backgammon and he could never beat her at either. On their first Sunday at the villa she fixed a delicious picnic lunch, and they sat on the beach in the sun and enjoyed it. While they were eating, Noelle looked up and saw two men in the distance. They were strolling towards them along the beach.

'Let's go inside,' Noelle said.

Larry looked up and saw the men. 'Jesus, don't be so jumpy. They're just a couple of villagers out for a walk.'

'Now,' she commanded.

'OK,' he said ungraciously, irritated by the incident and by her tone.

'Help me pack up the things.'

'Why don't we just leave them?' he asked.

'Because it would look suspicious.'

Quickly they stuffed everything into the picnic hamper and started towards the house. Larry was silent for the rest of the afternoon. He sat in the library, his mind preoccupied, while Noelle worked in the kitchen.

Late in the afternoon she came into the library

and sat at his feet. With her uncanny knack of reading his mind, she said. 'Stop thinking about them.'

'They were just a couple of goddamn villagers,' Larry snapped. 'I hate sneaking around like some kind of criminal.' He looked at her and his voice changed. 'I don't want to have to hide from anybody. I love you.'

And Noelle knew that this time it was true. She thought of the years during which she had planned to destroy Larry and of the fierce pleasure she had taken in imagining his destruction: And yet the moment Noelle had seen Larry again she had known instantly that there was something deeper than hate still alive in her. When she had pushed him to the brink of death, forcing him to risk both their lives on that terrible flight to Amsterdam, it was as though she were testing his love for her in a wild defiance of fate. She had been with Larry in that cockpit, flying the plane with him, suffering with him, knowing that if he died they would die together, and he had saved them both. And when he had come to her room in Amsterdam and made love to her, her hatred and her love had become intermingled with their two bodies, and somehow time had expanded and contracted and they were back in their little hotel room in Paris and Larry was saying to her, 'Let's get married; we'll find some little *maire* in the country,' and the present and the past had exploded dazzlingly into one and Noelle knew then that they were timeless, had always been timeless, that nothing had really changed and that the depths of her hatred for Larry had come from the heights of her love. If she destroyed him she would be destroying herself, for she had given herself completely to him long ago and nothing could ever change that.

It seemed to Noelle that everything she had achieved in her life had been through her hatred. Her father's betrayal had moulded and shaped her, annealed and hardened her, filled her with a hunger for vengeance that could be satisfied with nothing less than a kingdom of her own in which she was all-powerful, in which she could never be betrayed again, never be hurt. She had finally achieved that. And now she was ready to give it up for this man. Because she knew now that what she had always wanted was for Larry to need her, to love her. And, at last, he did. And that, finally, was her real kingdom.

EIGHTEEN

Noelle and Catherine

Athens: 1946

For Larry and Noelle the next three months was one of those rare, idyllic periods when everything went right, a magic time of floating from one wonderful day to the next, with not the faintest cloud on the horizon. Larry spent his working hours doing what he loved to do, flying, and whenever he had time off he went to the villa in Rafina and spent a day or a weekend or a week with Noelle. In the beginning Larry had been afraid that the arrangement would become a millstone that would drag him down into the kind of domesticity that he loathed; but each time he saw Noelle, he became more enchanted and he began to look eagerly forward to the hours he would spend with her. When she had to cancel one weekend because of an unexpected trip with Demiris, Larry stayed alone at the villa, and he found himself angry and jealous, thinking about Noelle and Demiris together. When he saw Noelle the following week, she was surprised and pleased by his eagerness.

'You missed me,' she said.

He nodded. 'A lot.'

'Good.'

'How's Demiris?'

She hesitated a moment. 'All right.'

Larry noticed her hesitation. 'What is it?'

'I was thinking of something you said.'

'What?'

'You said you hated the feeling of sneaking around like a criminal. I hate it too. Every moment I was with Constantin, I wanted to be with you. I once told you, Larry, I want all of you. I meant it. I don't want to share you with anyone. I want you to marry me.'

He stared at her in surprise, caught off guard.

Noelle was watching him. 'Do you want to marry me?'

'You know I do. But how? You keep telling me what Demiris will do if he finds out about us.'

She shook her head. 'He won't find out. Not if we're clever and plan it properly. He doesn't own me, Larry. I'll leave him. There's nothing he can do about that. He has too much pride to try to stop me. A month or two later, you'll quit your job. We'll go away somewhere, separately, perhaps to the United States. We can be married there. I have more money than we'll ever need. I'll buy you a charter airline, or a flying school or whatever you like.'

He stood there listening to what she was saying,

weighing what he would be giving up against what he would be gaining. And what would he be giving up? A lousy job as a pilot. The thought of owning his own planes sent a small thrill coursing through him. He'd have his own converted Mitchell. Or maybe the new DC-6 that had just come out. Four radial engines, eighty-five passengers. And Noelle, yes, he wanted Noelle. Jesus, what was he even hesitating about?

'What about my wife?' he asked.

'Tell her you want a divorce.'

'I don't know if she'll give me one.'

'Don't ask her,' Noelle replied. 'Tell her.' There was a final implacable note in her voice.

Larry nodded. 'All right.'

'You won't be sorry, darling. I promise,' Noelle said.

For Catherine time had lost its circadian rhythm; she had fallen into a tesseract of time, and day and night blended into one. Larry was almost never home, and she had long since stopped seeing any of their friends, because she did not have the energy to make any more excuses or to face people. Count Pappas had made half a dozen attempts to see her, and had finally given up. She found herself only able to cope with people secondhand: by telephone or letter or cable. But face to face, she turned to stone, and conversations flinted off her in hopeless, futile sparks. Time brought pain and people brought pain, and the only surcease Catherine found was in the wonderful forgetfulness of liquor. Oh how it eased the suffering, softened the sharp edge of rebuffs and gentled down the pitiless sun of reality that beat down on everyone else.

When Catherine had first come to Athens, she and William Fraser had written to each other frequently, swapping news and keeping each other up-to-date on the activities of their mutual friends and foes. Since Catherine's problems with Larry had begun, however, she had not had the heart to write to Fraser. His last three letters had gone unanswered, and his last letter had gone unopened. She simply did not have the energy to cope with anything outside the microcosm of self-pity in which she was trapped.

One day a cable arrived for Catherine, and it was still lying on the table unopened a week later, when the doorbell rang and William Fraser appeared. Catherine stared at him, unbelievingly. 'Bill!' she said, thickly. 'Bill Fraser!'

He started to speak and she saw the excited look in his eyes turn to something else, something startled and shocked.

'Bill, darling,' she said. 'What are you doing here?'

'I had to come to Athens on business,' Fraser explained. 'Didn't you get my cable?'

Catherine looked at him, trying to remember. 'I don't know,' she said finally. She led him into the living room, strewn with old newspapers, filled ashtrays and plates of half-eaten food. 'Sorry the place is such a mess,' she said, waving a vague hand. 'I've been busy.'

Fraser was studying her worriedly. 'Are you all right, Catherine?'

'Me? Fantastic. How about a little drink?'

'It's only eleven o'clock in the morning.'

She nodded. 'You're right. You're absolutely right, Bill. It's too early to have a drink, and to tell you the truth I wouldn't have one except to celebrate your coming here. You're the only one in the whole world who could make me have a drink at eleven o'clock in the morning.'

Fraser watched with dismay as Catherine staggered to the liquor cabinet and poured a large drink for herself and a smaller one for him.

'Do you like Greek brandy?' she asked as she carried his drink to him. 'I used to hate it, but you get used to it.'

Fraser took his drink and set it down. 'Where's Larry?' he asked quietly.

'Larry? Oh, good old Larry's flying around somewhere. He works for the richest man in the world, you know. Demiris owns everything, even Larry.'

He studied her a moment. 'Does Larry know you drink?'

Catherine slammed down her glass and stood swaying in front of him. 'What do you mean, does Larry know I drink?' she demanded indignantly. 'Who says I drink? Just because I want to celebrate seeing an old friend, don't you start attacking me!'

'Catherine,' he began, 'I'm . . .'

'You think you can come in here and accuse me of being some kind of a drunk?'

'I'm sorry, Catherine,' Fraser said painfully, 'I think you need help.'

'Well you're wrong,' she retorted. 'I don't need any help. Do you know why? Because I'm – I'm self – I'm self . . .' she groped for the word and finally gave it up. 'I don't need any help.'

Fraser watched her for a moment. 'I have to go to a conference now,' he said 'Have dinner with me tonight.'

'OK.' She nodded.

'Good. I'll pick you up at eight.'

Catherine watched Bill Fraser as he walked out the door. Then with unsteady steps, she walked into her bedroom and slowly opened the closet door, staring into the mirror hanging on the back of the door. She stood there frozen, unable to believe what she was seeing, sure that the mirror was playing some dreadful trick on her. Inside she was still the pretty little girl adored by her father, still the young college girl standing in a motel room with Ron Peterson and hearing him say, 'My God, Cathy, you're the most beautiful thing I've ever seen,' and Bill Fraser holding her in his arms and saying, 'You're so beautiful, Catherine,' and Larry saying, 'Stay this beautiful, Cathy, you're gorgeous,' and she looked at the figure in the mirror and croaked aloud, 'Who are you?' and the sad, shapeless woman in the mirror began to cry, hopeless, empty tears that coursed down the obscene bloated face. Hours later the doorbell rang. She heard Bill Fraser's voice calling, 'Catherine! Catherine, are you there?' And then the bell rang some more, and finally the voice stopped and the ringing stopped and Catherine was left alone with the stranger in the mirror.

At nine o'clock the following morning. Catherine took a taxi to Patission Street. The doctor's name was Nikodes and he was a large, burly man with a white shaggy mane, a wise face with kind eyes, and an easy, informal manner.

A nurse ushered Catherine in to his private office and Doctor Nikodes indicated a chair. 'Sit down, Mrs Douglas.'

Catherine took a seat, nervous and tense, trying to stop her body from trembling.

'What seems to be your problem?'

She started to answer and then stopped, helplessly. *Oh, God*, she thought, *where can I begin*? 'I need help,' she said, finally. Her voice was dry and scratchy, and she ached for a drink.

The doctor was leaning back in his chair watching her. 'How old are you?'

'Twenty-eight.' She watched his face as she said it. He tried to conceal the look of shock, but she caught it and in some perverse way was pleased by it.

'You're an American?'

'Yes.'

'Are you living in Athens?'

She nodded.

'How long have you lived here?'

'A thousand years. We moved here before the Peloponnesian Wars.'

The doctor smiled. 'I feel that way sometimes too.' He offered Catherine a cigarette. She reached for it, trying to control the trembling of her fingers. If Doctor Nikodes noticed, he said nothing. He lit it for her. 'What kind of help do you need, Mrs Douglas?'

Catherine looked at him helplessly. 'I don't know,' she whispered. 'I don't know.'

'Do you feel ill?'

'I am ill. I think I must be very ill. I've become so ugly.' She knew she was not crying and yet she felt tears running down her cheeks.

'Do you drink, Mrs Douglas?' the doctor asked gently.

Catherine stared at him in panic, feeling cornered, attacked. 'Sometimes.'

'How much?'

She took a deep breath. 'Not much. It – it depends.'

'Have you had a drink today?' he asked.

'No.'

He sat there studying her. 'You're not really ugly, you know,' he said gently. 'You're overweight, your body is bloated and you haven't been taking care of your skin or your hair. Underneath that facade there's a very attractive young woman.'

She burst into tears, and he sat there letting her cry herself out. Dimly over her racking sobs

Catherine heard the buzzer on his desk ring several times, but the doctor ignored it. The spasm of sobbing finally subsided. Catherine pulled out a handkerchief and blew her nose. 'I'm sorry,' she apologized. 'C – can you help me?'

'That depends entirely on you,' Doctor Nikodes replied. 'We don't really know what your problem is yet.'

'Take a look at me,' Catherine responded.

He shook his head. 'That's not a problem, Mrs Douglas, that's a symptom. Forgive me for being blunt, but if I am to help you, we must be totally honest with each other. When an attractive young woman lets herself go as you have, there must be a very strong reason. Is your husband alive?'

'Holidays and weekends.'

He studied her. 'Do you live with him?'

'When he's home.'

'What is his work?'

'He's Constantin Demiris' personal pilot.' She saw the reaction on the doctor's face, but whether he was reacting to the name of Demiris or whether he knew something about Larry, she could not tell. 'Have you heard of my husband?' she asked.

'No.' But he could have been lying. 'Do you love your husband, Mrs Douglas?'

Catherine opened her mouth to answer and then stopped. She knew that what she was going to say was very important, not only to the doctor, but to herself. Yes, she loved her husband and yes, she hated him, and yes, at times she felt such a rage towards him that she knew she was capable of killing him, and yes, at times she was so overwhelmed by a tenderness for him that she knew she would gladly die for him and what was the word that could say all that? Perhaps it was love. 'Yes,' she said.

'Does he love you?'

Catherine thought of the other women in Larry's life and his unfaithfulness and she thought of the awful stranger in the mirror last night and she could not blame Larry for not wanting her. But who was to say which came first? Was the woman in the mirror created by his infidelity, or did his infidelity create the woman in the mirror? She became aware that her cheeks were wet with tears again.

Catherine shook her head helplessly. 'I – I don't know.'

'Have you ever had a nervous breakdown?'

She was watching him now, her eyes wary. 'No. Do you think I need one?'

He did not smile. He spoke slowly, choosing his words with care. 'The human psyche is a delicate thing, Mrs Douglas. It can take only so much pain and when the pain becomes unbearable, it escapes into hidden recesses of the mind that we are just beginning to explore. Your emotions are stretched very tight.' He looked at her a moment. 'I think it is a good thing you came to someone for help.'

'I know I'm a little nervous,' Catherine said defensively. 'That's why I drink. To relax me.'

'No,' he said bluntly. 'You drink to escape.' Nikodes got up and walked over to her. 'I think there's probably a good deal we can do for you. By "we," I mean you and I. It will not be simple.'

'Tell me what to do.'

'To begin with I am going to send you to a clinic for a thorough physical examination. My feeling is that they will find nothing basically wrong with you. Next, you are going to stop drinking. Then I am going to put you on a diet. All right so far?'

Catherine hesitated, then nodded.

'You are going to enrol in a gymnasium, where you will work out regularly to get your body back in shape. I have an excellent physiotherapist who will give you massages. You will go to a beauty parlour once a week. All this will take time, Mrs Douglas. You did not get in this condition overnight, and it will not be changed overnight.' He smiled at her reassuringly. 'But I can promise you that in a few months – even a few weeks – you will begin to look and feel like a different woman. When you look in your mirror, you will feel proud – and when your husband looks at you, he will find you attractive.'

Catherine stared at him, her heart lifting. It was as though some unbearable burden had been removed from deep inside her, as though she had suddenly been given a new chance to live.

'You must clearly understand that I can only suggest this programme for you,' the doctor was saying. 'It is you who must do it.'

'I will,' Catherine said fervently. 'I promise.'

'To stop drinking will be the most difficult part.'

'No, it won't,' Catherine said. And as she said it, she knew it was true. The doctor had been right: She had been drinking in order to escape. Now she had a goal, she knew where she was going. She was going to win back Larry. 'I won't touch another drop,' she said firmly.

The doctor saw the look on her face and nodded, satisfied. 'I believe you, Mrs Douglas.'

Catherine rose to her feet. It amazed her how clumsy and awkward her body was, but all that would change now. 'I'd better go out and start buying some skinny clothes,' she smiled.

The doctor wrote something on a card. 'This is the address of the clinic. They will be expecting you. I will see you again after you have had your examination.'

On the street Catherine looked for a taxi, then she thought, *to hell with that. I might as well start getting used to exercise*. She began to walk. She passed a shop window and stopped to stare at her reflection.

She had been so quick to blame Larry for the disintegration of their marriage without ever questioning what share of the blame was hers. Why would he want to come home to someone who looked like she did? How slowly and subtly this stranger had crept in without her being aware of it. She wondered how many marriages had died in this same way, not with a bang – *and there certainly hasn't been much of that lately*, Catherine thought, wryly – but with a whimper, just like good old T.S. Eliot said. Well, that was all in the past. From now on she would not look back, she would only look ahead to the wonderful future.

Catherine had reached the fashionable Salonika district. She was walking past a beauty parlour and on a sudden impulse she turned and went inside. The reception room was white marble, large and elegant. A haughty receptionist looked at Catherine disapprovingly and said, 'Yes, may I help you?'

'I want to make an appointment for tomorrow morning,' Catherine said. 'I want everything. The works.' The name of their top hair stylist suddenly popped into her head. 'I want Aleko.'

The woman shook her head. 'I can give you an appointment, Madame, but you will have to take someone else.'

'Listen,' Catherine said firmly, 'you tell Aleko that he either takes me or I'll go around Athens telling everyone I'm one of his regular customers.'

The woman's eyes opened wide in shocked surprise. 'I – I will see what I can do,' she said hastily. 'Come in at ten in the morning.'

'Thanks,' Catherine grinned. 'I'll be here.' And she walked out.

Ahead of her she saw a small taverna with a sign in the window that read 'MADAME PIRIS – FORTUNE-TELLING.' It seemed vaguely familiar and she suddenly remembered the day that Count Pappas had told her a story about Madame Piris. It was something about a policeman and a lion – but she could not remember the details.

Catherine did not believe in fortune-tellers and yet the impulse to go in was irresistible. She needed reassurance, someone to confirm her feeling about her wonderful new future, to tell her that life was going to be beautiful again, worth living again. She opened the door and walked inside.

After the bright sunshine it took Catherine several moments to get used to the cavernous darkness of the room. She made out a bar in the corner and a dozen tables and chairs. A tired-looking waiter walked up to her and addressed her in Greek.

'Nothing to drink, thank you,' Catherine said. She enjoyed hearing herself say the words and she repeated them. 'Nothing to drink. I want to see Madame Piris. Is she here?'

The waiter gestured towards an empty table in the corner of the room and Catherine walked over and sat down. A few minutes later, she felt someone standing at her side, and looked up.

The woman was incredibly old and thin, dressed in black, with a face that had been washed by time into desiccated angles and planes.

'You asked to see me?' Her English was halting.

'Yes,' Catherine said. 'I would like a reading, please.'

The woman sat down and raised a hand, and the waiter came over to the table bearing a cup of thick black coffee on a small tray. He set it down in front of Catherine.

'Not for me,' Catherine said. 'I . . .'

'Drink it,' Madame Piris said.

Catherine looked at her in surprise, then picked up the cup and took a sip of the coffee. It was strong and bitter. She put down the cup.

'More,' the woman said.

Catherine started to protest, then thought, *What the hell. What they lose on the fortune-telling, they make up on the coffee.* She swallowed another mouthful. It was vile.

'Once more,' Madame Piris said.

Catherine shrugged and took a final sip. In the bottom of the cup were thick, viscous dregs. Madame Piris nodded, reached over and took the cup from Catherine. She stared into it for a long time, saying nothing. Catherine sat there feeling foolish. *What's a nice, intelligent girl like me doing in a place like this, watching an old Greek nut staring into an empty coffee cup*?

'You come from a faraway place,' the woman said suddenly.

'Bull's eye,' Catherine said flippantly.

Madame Piris looked up into her eyes and there was something in the look of the old woman that chilled Catherine.

'Go home.'

Catherine swallowed. 'I – I am home.'

'Go back where you came from.'

'You mean – America?'

'Anywhere. Get away from this place – quickly!'

'Why?' Catherine said, a sense of horror slowly filling her. 'What's wrong?'

The old woman shook her head. Her voice was

harsh and she was finding it difficult to get the words out. 'It is all around you.'

'*What* is?'

'Get out!' There was an urgency in the woman's voice, a high, shrill keening sound like an animal in pain. Catherine could feel the hair on her scalp begin to rise.

'You're frightening me,' she moaned. 'Please tell me what's wrong.'

The old woman shook her head from side to side, her eyes wild. 'Go away before it gets you.'

Catherine felt a panic rising in her. It was difficult for her to breathe. 'Before *what* gets me?'

The old woman's face was contorted with pain and terror. 'Death. It is coming for you.' And the woman rose and disappeared into the back room.

Catherine sat there, her heart pounding, her hands trembling, and she clasped them tightly together to stop them. She caught the waiter's eye and started to order a drink, but stopped herself. She was not going to let a crazy woman spoil her bright future. She sat there breathing deeply until she had gotten control of herself, and after a long time she rose, picked up her purse and gloves and walked out of the taverna.

Out in the dazzlingly bright sunlight Catherine felt better again. She had been foolish to let an old woman frighten her. A horror like that should be arrested instead of being allowed to terrify people. *From now on*, Catherine told herself, *you'll stick to fortune cookies*.

She stepped into her apartment and looked at the living room, and it was as though she were seeing it for the first time. It was a dismaying sight. Dust was thick everywhere, and articles of clothing were strewn around the room. It was incredible to Catherine that in her drunken haze she had not even been aware of it. Well, the first exercise she was going to get was making this place look spic and span. She was starting towards the kitchen when she heard a drawer close in the bedroom. Her heart leaped in sudden alarm, and she moved cautiously towards the bedroom door.

Larry was in the bedroom. A closed suitcase lay on his bed, and he was finishing packing a second suitcase. Catherine stood there a moment, watching him. 'If those are for the Red Cross,' she said, 'I already gave.'

Larry glanced up. 'I'm leaving.'

'Another trip for Demiris?'

'No,' he said without stopping, 'this one's for me. I'm getting out of here.'

'Larry . . .'

'There's nothing to discuss.'

She moved into the bedroom, fighting for self-control. 'But – but there is. There's a lot to discuss. I went to see a doctor today and he told me I'm going to be fine.' The words were coming out in a torrent. 'I'm going to stop drinking and . . .'

'Cathy, it's over. I want a divorce.'

The words hit her like a series of blows to the stomach. She stood there, clamping her jaw tight so that she would not retch, trying to fight down the bile that rose in her throat. 'Larry,' she said, speaking slowly to keep her voice from trembling, 'I don't blame you for the way you feel. A lot of it is my fault – maybe most of it – but it's going to be different. I'm going to change – I mean *really* change.' She held out her hand pleadingly. 'All I ask is a chance.'

Larry turned to face her and his dark eyes were cold and contemptuous. 'I'm in love with someone else. All I want from you is a divorce.'

Catherine stood there a long moment, then turned and walked back into the living room and sat on the couch, looking at a Greek fashion magazine while he finished packing. She heard Larry's voice saying, 'My attorney will be in touch with you' and then the slam of a door. Catherine sat there carefully turning the pages of the magazine, and when she had come to the end she set it down neatly in the centre of the table, went into the bathroom, opened the medicine chest, took out a razor blade and slashed her wrists.

NINETEEN

Noelle and Catherine

Athens: 1946

There were ghosts in white and they floated around her and then drifted away into space with soft whispers in a language that Catherine could not understand, but she understood that this was Hell and that she had to pay for her sins. They kept her strapped down on the bed, and she supposed that was part of her punishment, and she was glad of the straps because she could feel the earth spinning around through space and she was afraid she was going to fall off the planet. The most diabolical thing they had done was to put all her nerves on the outside of her body so that she felt everything a thousand-fold, and it was unbearable. Her body was alive with terrifying and unfamiliar noises. She could hear the blood as it ran through her veins, and it was like a roaring red river moving through her. She heard the strokes of her heart, and it sounded like an enormous drum being pounded by giants. She had no eyelids and the white light poured into her brain, dazzling her with its brightness. All the muscles of her body were alive, in constant, restless motion like a nest of snakes under her skin ready to strike.

Five days after Catherine had been admitted to Evangelismos Hospital, she opened her eyes and found herself in a small, white hospital room. A nurse in a starched white uniform was adjusting her bed, and Dr Nikodes had a stethoscope to her chest.

'Hey, that's cold,' she protested weakly.

He looked at her and said, 'Well, well, look who's awake.'

Catherine moved her eyes slowly around the room. The light seemed normal and she could no longer hear the roaring of her blood or the pounding of her heart or the dying of her body.

'I thought I was in Hell.' Her voice was a whisper.

'You have been.'

She looked at her wrists. For some reason, they were bandaged. 'How long have I been here?'

'Five days.'

She suddenly remembered the reason for the bandages. 'I guess I did a dumb thing,' she said.

'Yes.'

She squeezed her eyes shut and said, 'I'm sorry,' and opened them and it was night and Bill Fraser was sitting in a chair beside her bed, watching her. Flowers and candy were on her bedside table.

'Hi there,' he said cheerfully. 'You're looking much better.'

'Better than what?' she asked weakly.

He put his hand over hers. 'You really gave me a scare, Catherine.'

'I'm so sorry, Bill.' Her voice started to choke up, and she was afraid that she was going to cry.

'I brought you some flowers and candy. When you're feeling stronger, I'll bring you some books.'

She looked at him, at his kind strong face, and she thought: *Why don't I love him? Why am I in love with the man I hate? Why did God have to turn out to be Groucho Marx?* 'How did I get here?' Catherine asked.

'In an ambulance.'

'I mean – who found me?'

Fraser paused. 'I did. I tried phoning you several times and when you didn't answer, I got worried and broke in.'

'I suppose I should say thanks,' she said, 'but to tell you the truth, I'm not sure yet.'

'Do you want to talk about it?'

Catherine shook her head and the movement caused her head to begin throbbing. 'No,' she said in a small voice.

Fraser nodded. 'I have to fly home in the morning. I'll keep in touch.'

She felt a gentle kiss on her forehead and closed her eyes to shut out the world and when she opened them again, she was alone and it was the middle of the night.

Early the next morning Larry came to visit her. Catherine watched him as he walked into the room and sat down in a chair next to her bed. She had expected him to be drawn-looking and unhappy, but the truth was that he looked wonderful, lean and tan and relaxed. Catherine wished desperately that she had had a chance to comb her hair and put on some lipstick.

'How do you feel, Cathy?' he asked.

'Terrific. Suicide always stimulates me.'

'They didn't expect you to pull through.'

'I'm sorry to have disappointed you.'

'That's not a very nice thing to say.'

'It's true though, isn't it, Larry? You'd have been rid of me.'

'For Christ's sake, I don't want to be rid of you that way, Catherine. All I want is a divorce.'

She looked at him, this bronzed, handsome man she had married, his face a little more dissipated now, his mouth a little harder, his boyish charm worn a bit thin. What was she hanging onto? Seven years of dreams? She had given herself to him with such love and high hopes and she could not bear to let them go, could not bear to admit that she had made a mistake that had turned her life into a barren wasteland. She remembered Bill Fraser and their friends in Washington and the fun they had known. She could not remember the last time she had laughed aloud, or even smiled. But none of that really mattered. In the end the reason that she would not let Larry go was that she still loved him. He was standing there waiting for an answer. 'No,' Catherine said. 'I'll never give you a divorce.'

Larry met Noelle that night at the deserted monastery of Kaissariani in the mountains and reported his conversation with Catherine.

Noelle listened intently and asked, 'Do you think she will change her mind?'

Larry shook his head. 'Catherine can be as stubborn as hell.'

'You must speak to her again.'

And Larry did. For the next three weeks he exhausted every argument he could think of. He pleaded, cajoled, raged at her, offered her money, but nothing moved Catherine. She still loved him, and she was sure that if he gave himself a chance he could love her again.

'You're my husband,' she said stubbornly. 'You're going to be my husband until I die.'

He repeated what she had said to Noelle.

Noelle nodded. 'Yes,' she said.

Larry looked at her, puzzled. 'Yes, what?'

They were lying on the beach at the villa, fluffy white towels spread out beneath them, shielding their bodies from the hot sand. The sky was a deep, blazing blue, dotted with white patches of cirrus clouds.

'You must get rid of her.' She rose to her feet and strode back to the villa, her long graceful legs moving smoothly across the sand. Larry lay there, bewildered, thinking that he must have misunderstood her. Surely she had not meant that she wanted him to *kill* Catherine.

And then he remembered Helena.

They were having supper on the terrace. 'Don't you see? She doesn't deserve to live,' Noelle said. 'She's holding onto you to be vengeful. She's trying to ruin your life, our lives, darling.'

They lay in bed smoking, the glowing embers of the cigarette ends winking into the infinity of the mirrors covering the ceiling.

'You would be doing her a favour. She's already tried to kill herself. She wants to die.'

'I could never do it, Noelle.'

'Couldn't you?'

She stroked his naked leg, gently moving up towards his belly, making small circles with the tips of her fingernails.

'I'll help you.'

He started to open his mouth to protest, but Noelle's two hands had found him, and they began working on him, moving in opposite directions, one softly and slowly, the other one hard and quickly. And Larry moaned and reached for her and put Catherine out of his mind.

Sometime during the night Larry awakened in a cold sweat. He had dreamed that Noelle had run away and left him. She was lying in bed next to him, and he took her in his arms and held her close. He lay awake the rest of the night, thinking what it would do to him if he lost her. He was not aware that he had made any decision, but in the morning while Noelle was preparing breakfast, Larry said suddenly, 'What if we're caught?'

'If we're clever, we won't be.' If she was pleased by his capitulation, she gave no sign of it.

'Noelle,' he said earnestly, 'every busybody in Athens knows that Catherine and I don't get along. If anything happened to her, the police would be damned suspicious.'

'Of course they would be,' Noelle agreed calmly. 'That is why everything will be planned very carefully.'

She served them both and then sat down and began to eat. Larry pushed his plate away from him, his food untasted.

'Isn't it good?' Noelle asked, concerned.

He stared at her, wondering what kind of person she was, able to enjoy a meal while she was planning the murder of another woman.

Later, sailing on the boat, they talked about it further, and the more they talked about it, the more of a reality it became, so that what had begun as a casual idea had been fleshed out with words until it had become a fact.

'It must look like an accident,' Noelle said, 'so that there will be no police investigation. The police in Athens are very clever.'

'What if they *should* investigate?'

'They won't. The accident will not happen here.'

'Where, then?'

'Ioannina.' She leaned forwards and began to talk. He listened to her as she elaborated on her plan, meeting every objection that he raised, improvising brilliantly. At the end when Noelle finished, Larry had to admit that the plan was flawless. They could really get away with it.

Paul Metaxas was nervous. The Greek pilot's usually jovial face was drawn and tense and he could feel a nervous tic pulling at the corner of his mouth. He had had no appointment with Constantin Demiris, and one did not simply barge in on the great man, but Metaxas had told the butler it was urgent, and now Paul Metaxas found himself standing in the enormous hallway of Demiris' villa, staring at him and stammering clumsily, 'I – I am terribly sorry to bother you, Mr Demiris.' Metaxas surreptitiously wiped the sweaty palm of his hand against the leg of his flight uniform.

'Has something happened to one of the planes?'

'Oh, no, sir. I – It's – it's a personal matter.'

Demiris studied him without interest. He made it a policy never to get involved in the affairs of his underlings. He had secretaries to handle that kind of thing for him. He waited for Metaxas to go on.

Paul Metaxas was becoming more nervous by the second. He had spent a lot of sleepless nights before making the decision that had brought him here. What he was doing now was alien to his character and therefore distasteful, but he was a man of fierce loyalty, and his first allegiance was to Constantin Demiris.

'It's about Miss Page,' he said, finally.

There was a moment of silence.

'Come in here,' Demiris said. He led the pilot into the panelled library and closed the doors. Demiris took a flat Egyptian cigarette out of a platinum case and lit it. He looked up at the perspiring Metaxas. 'What about Miss Page?' he asked, almost absently.

Metaxas swallowed, wondering if he had made a mistake. If he had estimated the situation correctly, his information would be appreciated, but if he was mistaken . . .

He cursed himself for his rashness in having come here, but he had no choice now but to plunge ahead.

'It's – it's about her and Larry Douglas.' He watched Demiris' face, trying to read his expression. There was not even the faintest flicker of interest. Christ! Metaxas forced himself to stumble on. 'They – they're living in a beach house together in Rafina.'

Demiris flicked the ash of the cigarette into a gold, domeshaped ashtray. Metaxas had the feeling that he was about to be dismissed, that he had made a terrible blunder and that it was going to cost him his job. He had to convince Demiris that he was telling the truth. The words began spilling out of him. 'My – my sister is a housekeeper in one of the villas there. She sees the two of them on the beach together all the time. She recognized Miss Page from her pictures in the paper, but she didn't think anything about it until a couple of nights ago when she came down to the airport to have dinner with me. I introduced her to Larry Douglas and – well, she told me he was the man Miss Page is living with.'

Demiris' olive black eyes stared at him, completely devoid of expression.

'I – I just thought you would want to know,' Metaxas finished lamely.

When Demiris spoke, his voice was toneless. 'What Miss Page does with her private life is her own affair. I am sure she would not appreciate anyone's spying on her.'

Metaxas' forehead was beaded with sweat. Jesus Christ, he had gotten the whole situation wrong. And he had only wanted to be loyal. 'Believe me, Mr Demiris, I was only trying to . . .'

'I am sure you thought you were serving my best interests. You were mistaken. Is there anything else?'

'No – no, sir.' Metaxas turned and fled.

Constantin Demiris leaned back in his chair, his black eyes fixed on the ceiling, staring at nothing.

At nine o'clock the following morning Paul Metaxas received a call to report to Demiris' mining company in the Congo, where Metaxas was to spend ten days ferrying equipment from Brazzaville to the mine. On a Wednesday morning on the third flight his plane crashed into the dense, green jungle. No traces of Metaxas' body or the wreckage were ever found.

Two weeks after Catherine was released from the hospital, Larry came to visit her. It was a Saturday evening, and Catherine was in the kitchen preparing an omelette. The sounds of cooking had prevented her from hearing the front door open, and she was not aware of Larry's presence until she turned and saw him standing in the doorway. She jumped involuntarily, and he said, 'Sorry if I scared you. I just dropped in to see how you were getting along.'

Catherine felt her heart beating faster and despised herself because he could still affect her that way.

'I'm just fine,' she said. She turned and took the omelette out of the pan.

'Smells good,' Larry said. 'I haven't had time for dinner. If it isn't too much trouble, would you mind fixing me one of those?'

She looked at him a long moment, then shrugged.

She made him dinner but she was so unnerved by his presence that Catherine could not eat a bite. He talked to her, telling her about a flight he had just made and an amusing anecdote about one of Demiris' friends. He was the old Larry, warm and charming and irresistible as though nothing had gone wrong between them, as though he had not smashed their lives together.

When dinner was over, Larry helped Catherine wash and dry the dishes. He stood next to her at the sink, and his nearness gave her a physical ache. How long had it been? It did not bear thinking about.

'I've really enjoyed it,' Larry was saying, with that easy, boyish grin of his. 'Thanks, Cathy.'

And that, Catherine thought, was the end of that.

Three days later, the phone rang and it was Larry phoning from Madrid to say that he was on his way home and to ask whether she would go out to dinner with him that evening. Catherine clutched the phone, listening to his friendly, easy voice, determined not to go. 'I'm free for dinner tonight,' she said.

They dined at Tourkolimano at the harbour at Piraeus. Catherine was barely able to touch her food. Being with Larry was far too painful a reminder of other restaurants they had dined in, of too many exciting evenings together in the long-dead past, of the love that was going to last them both a lifetime.

'You're not eating, Cathy. Would you like me to order something else for you?' he asked, concerned.

'I had a late lunch,' she lied. *He probably won't ever ask me out again*, Catherine thought, *but if he does I will say no.*

A few days later Larry called and they had lunch at a lovely restaurant in a hidden maze off Syntagma Square. It was called Gerofinikas, the Old Palm Tree, and was reached through a long, cool passageway with a palm tree in front of it. They had an excellent meal, with Hymettus, the light, dry Greek wine. Larry was at his most entertaining.

The following Sunday he asked Catherine to fly to Vienna with him. They had dinner at the Sacher Hotel and flew back the same night. It had been a wonderful evening, filled with wine and music and candlelight, but Catherine had the eerie feeling that somehow it didn't belong to her. It belonged to that other Catherine Douglas who was long since dead and buried. When they got back to the apartment, she said, 'Thank you, Larry, it was a lovely day.'

He moved towards her and took her in his arms and started to kiss her. Catherine pulled away, her body rigid, her mind filled with a sudden, unexpected panic.

'No,' she said.

'Cathy . . .'

'No!'

He nodded. 'All right. I understand.'

Her body was trembling. 'Do you?' she asked.

'I know how badly I've behaved,' Larry said

softly. 'If you'll give me a chance, I'd like to make it up to you, Cathy.'

Good God, she thought. She pressed her lips together, willing herself not to cry and shook her head, her eyes bright with unshed tears. 'It's too late,' she whispered.

And she stood there watching him walk out the door.

Catherine heard from Larry again within the week. He sent flowers with a little note and, after that, miniature birds from the various countries to which he flew. He had obviously gone to a great deal of trouble, for there was an astonishing variety, one in porcelain, one in jade, one in teak, and she was touched that he had remembered.

When the phone rang one day and Catherine heard Larry's voice on the other end saying, 'Hey, I found a wonderful Greek restaurant that serves the best Chinese food this side of Peking,' she laughed and said, 'I can't wait.'

And that was when it really began again. Slowly, tentatively, hesitantly, but it was a beginning. Larry did not attempt to kiss her again, nor would she have let him, because Catherine knew that if she let go of her emotions, if she gave herself wholeheartedly to this man she loved, and he betrayed her again, it would destroy her. Finally and forever. And so she dined with him and laughed with him, but all the time the deep secret personal part of her lay back in reserve, carefully aloof, untouched and untouchable.

They were together almost every night. Some evenings Catherine cooked dinner at home, other nights Larry took her out. Once she mentioned the woman that he had said he was in love with, and he replied tersely, 'It's over,' and Catherine never brought it up again. She watched closely for signs that Larry was seeing other women, but there were none. He was totally attentive to her, never pressing, never demanding. It was as though he were doing penance for the past.

And yet Catherine admitted to herself that it was something more than that. He really seemed interested in her as a woman. At night she would stand in front of the mirror, naked, and examine her reflection and try to figure out why. Her face was not bad, the face of a once-pretty girl who had gone through pain, a sadness in the solemn grey eyes that stared back at her. Her skin was a little puffy and her chin was heavier than it should be, but there was really nothing wrong with the rest of her body that diet and massage could not take care of. She remembered the last time she had thought about this and had wound up with her wrists slashed. A shudder went through her. To hell with Larry, she thought defiantly. If he really wants me, he'll have to take me as I am.

They had been to a party and Larry had brought her home at four A.M. It had been a marvellous evening, and Catherine had worn a new dress and looked rather attractive and made people laugh and Larry had been proud of her. When they walked into the apartment, Catherine reached for the light switch and Larry put his hand over hers and said, 'Wait. I can say this easier in the dark.' His body was close to hers, not even touching her, yet she could feel the physical waves that pulled at her.

'I love you, Cathy,' he said. 'I've never really loved anyone else. I want another chance.'

He switched on the light then to look at her. She was standing there, rigid and frightened, on the brink of panic. 'I know you may not be ready yet, but we could start slowly.' He grinned. That darling, boyish grin. 'We could start out by holding hands.'

He reached out and took her hand. And she pulled him to her and they were kissing and his lips were gentle and tender and careful, and hers were demanding and wild with all the pent-up longing that had been stored in her body these long, lonely months. And they were in bed together, making love and it was as though no time had passed, and they were on their honeymoon. But it was more than that. The passion was still there, fresh and wonderful, but with it an appreciation for what they had together, the knowledge that this time it would be all right, this time they would not hurt each other.

'How would you like to go away on a second honeymoon?' Larry was asking.

'Oh, yes, darling. Can we?'

'Sure, I have a vacation coming. We'll leave on Saturday. I know a wonderful little place we can go. It's called Ioannina.'

TWENTY

Noelle and Catherine

Athens: 1946

The drive to Ioannina took nine hours. To Catherine, the scenery seemed almost Biblical, something out of another age. They drove along the Aegean Sea, past small whitewashed cottages with crosses on the roofs and endless fields of fruit trees, lemon and cherry and apple and orange. Every inch of the land was terraced and farmed and the windows and roofs of the farmhouses were painted with gay blue colours as though in defiance of the hard life being carved out of the rocky soil. Stands of tall, graceful cypress trees grew in wild profusion on the steep mountainsides.

'Look, Larry,' Catherine exclaimed, 'aren't they beautiful?'

'Not to the Greeks,' Larry said.

Catherine looked at him. 'What do you mean?'

'They consider them a bad omen. They use them to decorate cemeteries.'

They passed field after field of primitive scarecrows, with a scrap of cloth tied to each fence.

'They certainly must have gullible crows around here,' Catherine laughed.

They drove through a series of small villages with impossible names: Mesologian and Agelkastron and Etolikon and Amfilhoia.

Late in the afternoon they reached the village of Rion, sloping gently down to the Rio River, where they were to catch the ferryboat to Ioannina. Five minutes later they were sailing towards the island of Epirus where Ioannina lay.

Catherine and Larry sat on a bench outside on the ferry's upper deck where in the distance ahead of them they saw a large island begin to loom out of the afternoon mist. It seemed wild to Catherine and somehow a little ominous. It had a primitive look to it as though it had been created for the Greek gods, and mere mortals were unwelcome intruders. As the boat steamed closer, Catherine could see that the bottom of the island was ringed with sheer rock that dropped off to the sea below. The foreboding mountain had a scarred, gashed look where men had gouged a road out of it. Twenty-five minutes later the ferry was docking at the little harbour of Epirus, and a few moments later Catherine and Larry were driving up the mountain towards Ioannina.

Catherine was reading to Larry from the guidebook.

'Nestled high in the Pindus Mountains, in a steep

bowl surrounded by towering Alps, from a distance Ioannina takes on the shape of a double-headed eagle, and at the claw of the eagle is the bottomless Lake Pamvotis, where excursion boats carry passengers across its dark green water to the island in the centre of the lake and then on to the distant shores across the lake.'

'It sounds perfect,' Larry said.

They arrived in the late afternoon and drove directly to their hotel, an old beautifully kept one-storey building on a hill high above the town, with a series of guest bungalows scattered about the grounds. An old man in a uniform came out to greet them. He looked at their happy faces.

'Honeymooners,' he said.

Catherine glanced at Larry and smiled. 'How did you know?'

'You can always tell,' the old man declared. He led them into the lobby where they registered and then showed them to their bungalow. It consisted of a living room and bedroom, a bathroom and kitchen and a large terrazzo terrace. Over the tops of the cypresses they had a magnificent view of the village and the lake below, dark and brooding. It had the unreal beauty of a picture postcard.

'It's not much' – Larry smiled – 'but it's all yours.'

'I'll take it,' Catherine exclaimed.

'Happy?'

She nodded. 'I don't remember when I've been so happy.' She walked over to him and held him tightly. 'Don't ever let me go,' she whispered.

His strong arms were around her, holding her close. 'I won't,' he promised.

While Catherine was unpacking, Larry strolled back to the lobby to talk to the room clerk.

'What do people do around here?' Larry asked.

'Everything,' the clerk said proudly. 'In the hotel we have a health spa. Around the village there is hiking, fishing, swimming, boating.'

'How deep is the lake?' Larry inquired casually.

The clerk shrugged. 'No one knows, sir. It is a volcanic lake. It is bottomless.'

Larry nodded thoughtfully. 'What about the caves near here?' he asked.

'Ah! The Caves of Perama. They are only a few miles from here.'

'Have they been explored?'

'A few of them. Some are still closed.'

'I see,' said Larry.

The clerk continued. 'If you like mountain climbing, I suggest Mount Tzoumerka. If Mrs Douglas is not afraid of heights.'

'No,' smiled Larry. 'She's quite an expert climber.'

'Then she will enjoy it. You're lucky with the weather. We've been expecting the *meltemi*, but it hasn't come. Now it probably won't.'

'What's the *meltemi*?' Larry asked.

'It's a terrible wind that blows down from the north. I suppose it is like your hurricane. When it comes, everyone stays indoors. In Athens, even ocean liners are forbidden to leave the harbour.'

'I'm glad we missed it,' Larry said.

When Larry returned to the bungalow, he suggested to Catherine that they go down to the village for dinner. They took the steep, rocky footpath that led down the slope to the edge of the village. Ioannina consisted of a main street, King George Avenue, with two or three smaller streets on both sides of it. Off of those streets, a warren of tiny dirt roads radiated out to homes and apartments. The buildings were old and weatherbeaten, made of stone carried down by cart from the mountains.

The middle of King George Avenue was sectioned off by ropes, so that cars drove on the left side of the street and pedestrians were free to walk on the right side.

'They should try that on Pennsylvania Avenue,' Catherine said.

At the town square was a charming little park with a high tower with a large, lighted clock in it. A street lined with huge Platanus trees ran down to the lake. It appeared to Catherine that all the streets in the village led to the water. It seemed to her that there was something frightening about the lake. It had a strange, brooding quality. All along the shores grew clumps of tall reeds that reached out like greedy fingers, as though waiting for someone.

Catherine and Larry walked down the colourful little shopping centre, with shops crowded together on each side. There was a jewellery store and next to it a bakery shop, an open air butcher shop, a tavern, a shoe store. Children stood outside a barber shop, silently watching a customer getting shaved. Catherine thought they were the most beautiful children she had ever seen.

In the past, Catherine had talked to Larry about having a baby, but he had always dismissed the idea, saying that he was not ready to settle down. Now, however, he might feel differently. Catherine glanced at him as he walked at her side, taller than the other men, looking like a Greek god, and she resolved that she would discuss it with him before they left. After all, it was their honeymoon.

They passed a movie theatre, the Palladian. Two very old American pictures were playing. They stopped to look at the display posters.

'We're in luck,' Catherine joked. '*South of Panama* with Roger Pryor and Virginia Vale, and *Mr D.A. in The Carter Case*.'

'Never even heard of them,' Larry snorted. 'This theatre must be older than it looks.'

They ate *moussaka* in the square, seated outdoors under an unbelievable full moon and then went back to the hotel and made love. It had been a perfect day.

In the morning Catherine and Larry drove around the lovely countryside, exploring the narrow road that wound along the lake, running along the rocky coast for a few miles, then drunkenly weaving its way back up again into the hills. Stone houses were perched on the edge of the steep mountainsides. High above the shore set back in the woods they caught a glimpse of a huge white-washed building that looked like an ancient castle.

'What's that?' Catherine asked.

'I have no idea,' Larry said.

'Let's find out.'

'All right.'

Larry swung the car onto the dirt track that led to the building, through a meadow, past grazing goats and a shepherd who stared at them as they drove by. They pulled up in front of the deserted entrance to the building. Up close it looked like an old ruined fortress.

'It must be a leftover ogre's castle,' Catherine said. 'Probably out of the Brothers Grimm.'

'Do you really want to find out?' Larry asked.

'Sure. We may be just in time to rescue a maiden in distress.'

Larry gave Catherine a quick, strange look.

They got out of the car and walked up to the massive wooden door with a huge iron knocker fastened to the centre. Larry hit it several times and they waited. There were no sounds except the buzz of summer insects in the meadow and the whisper of the breeze through the grass.

'I guess no one's home,' Larry said.

'They're probably getting rid of the bodies,' Catherine whispered.

Suddenly the huge door began to creak open slowly. A nun dressed in black stood facing them.

It caught Catherine off guard. 'I – I'm sorry,'

she said. 'We didn't know what this place was. There's no sign or anything.'

The nun regarded the two of them for a moment, then gestured for them to enter. They stepped through the doorway and found themselves in a large courtyard that was the centre of a compound. There was a strangely still atmosphere, and Catherine suddenly realized what was missing: the sound of human voices.

She turned to the Sister and said. 'What place is this?'

The Sister silently shook her head and motioned for them to wait there. They watched as she turned and walked towards an old stone building at the end of the compound.

'She's gone to get Bela Lugosi,' Catherine whispered.

Beyond the building towards a promontory that rose above the sea, they could see a cemetery framed by rows of tall cyprus trees.

'This place gives me the creeps.' Larry said.

'It's as though we've stumbled into another century.' Catherine replied. Unconsciously they were whispering, as though afraid to disturb the heavy silence. Through the window of the main building they could see inquisitive faces staring out at them, all women, all of them dressed in black.

'It's some kind of religious nuthouse,' Larry decided.

A tall, thin woman emerged from the building and started walking briskly towards them. She wore a nun's habit and had a pleasant, friendly face.

'I am Sister Theresa,' she said. 'May I help you?'

'We were just passing by,' Catherine said, 'and we were curious about this place.' She looked at the faces peering from the windows. 'We didn't mean to disturb you.'

'We are not honoured with many visitors,' Sister Theresa said. 'We have almost no contact with the outside world. We are an Order of Carmelite nuns. We have taken a vow of silence.'

'For how long?' Larry asked.

'*Gia panta* – for the rest of our lives. I am the only one here permitted to speak and then only when necessary.'

Catherine gazed around at the large, silent courtyard and repressed a shudder. 'Does no one ever leave here?'

Sister Theresa smiled. 'No. There is no reason to. Our life is within these walls.'

'Forgive us for troubling you,' Catherine said.

The Sister nodded. 'Not at all. Go with God.'

As Catherine and Larry walked out, the huge gate slowly swung closed behind them. Catherine turned to look back at it. It was like a prison. But somehow this seemed worse. Perhaps because it was a voluntary penance, a waste, and Catherine thought of the young women she had seen from the window, walled up here, shut away from the world for the rest of their lives, living in the deep permanent silence of the grave. She knew she would never forget this place.

TWENTY-ONE

Noelle and Catherine

Athens: 1946

Early the following morning Larry went down to the village. He asked Catherine to join him, but she demurred, telling him that she was going to sleep late. The moment he left, Catherine got out of bed, hurriedly dressed and went over to the hotel gymnasium which she had investigated the day before. The instructress, a Greek Amazon, told her to strip, then examined her body critically.

'You have been lazy, lazy,' she scolded Catherine. 'That was a good body. If you are willing to work hard, *Theou thellondos* – God willing – it can be good again.'

'I'm willing,' said Catherine. 'Let's see how God shapes up.'

Under the tutelage of the Amazon Catherine worked out every day, going through the agonies of body-contouring massage, a Spartan diet and gruelling exercises. She kept all this from Larry, but by the end of the fourth day the change in her was noticeable enough for him to comment on it.

'This place really agrees with you,' he said. 'You look like a different girl.'

'I am a different girl,' Catherine replied, suddenly shy.

On Sunday morning Catherine went to church. She had never seen a Greek Orthodox mass. In a village as small as Ioannina she had expected to find a little country church, but to her surprise she walked into a large, richly decorated church with beautiful elaborate carvings on the walls and ceiling and a marble floor. In front of the altar were a dozen enormous silver candelabras, and around the room were frescoes of Biblical paintings. The priest was thin and swarthy with a black beard. He wore an elaborate gold and red robe and a tall black hat, and he stood on what looked to Catherine like a sedan chair on a raised platform.

Along the wall were individual wooden benches and next to them a row of wooden chairs. The men sat in the front of the church and the women in the rear. *I guess the men get to Heaven first*, Catherine thought.

A chanting began in Greek, and the priest stepped down from the platform and moved to the altar. A red curtain parted and behind it was a lavishly robed, white-bearded patriarch. On a table in front of him stood a symbolical jewelled hat and a gold cross. The old man lit three candles tied together, representing, Catherine supposed, the

Holy Trinity, and handed them to the priest.

The mass lasted for one hour, and Catherine sat there savouring the sights and sounds and thinking about how lucky she was and she bowed her head and gave a prayer of gratitude.

The next morning Catherine and Larry were having breakfast on their bungalow terrace that overlooked the lake. It was a perfect day. The sun was shining down, and a lazy breeze was coming off the water. A pleasant young waiter had brought the food. Catherine was wearing a negligee and when the waiter came in, Larry had put his arms around Catherine and kissed her on the neck. 'What a great night,' Larry murmured.

The waiter had stifled a smile and discreetly retreated. Catherine had been a little embarrassed. It was unlike Larry to be affectionate in front of strangers. He really has changed, Catherine thought. It seemed that every time a maid or bellboy came into the room, Larry would put his arm around Catherine and show his affection, as though he wanted the whole world to know how much he loved her. Catherine found it very touching.

'I have a great morning planned for us,' Larry said. He pointed to the east, where they could see a giant peak towering into the sky. 'We're going to climb Mount Tzoumerka.'

'I have a rule,' Catherine declared. 'I never climb anything I can't spell.'

'Come on, they say there's a fantastic view from up there.'

Catherine saw that Larry was serious. She looked up at the mountain again. It looked as though it went straight up. 'Climbing's not what I do best, darling,' she said.

'It's an easy hike. Paths all the way up.' He hesitated. 'If you don't want to go with me, I can go alone.' There was sharp disappointment in his voice.

It would be so simple to say no, so simple to just sit here and enjoy the day. The temptation was almost overpowering. But Larry wanted her with him. That was enough for Catherine.

'OK. I'll see if I can find an alpine hat,' she said.

A look of such relief came over Larry's face that Catherine was glad she had decided to go. Besides it might be interesting.

She had never climbed a mountain before.

They drove to a meadow at the edge of the village where the mountain trail began and parked the car. There was a small food stand at the side of the road, and Larry bought some sandwiches, fruit, candy bars and a large thermos of coffee.

'If it's nice up there,' he told the proprietor, 'My bride and I may want to spend the night.' He gave Catherine a hug, and the proprietor grinned.

Catherine and Larry walked up to the beginning of the trail. There were really two trails, branching off in opposite directions. Catherine admitted to herself that it looked like an easy climb. The paths seemed wide and not too steep. When she turned her head to gaze at the top of the mountain, it seemed grim and forbidding, but then they would not be going that high. They would climb a little way up and have a picnic.

'This way,' Larry said, and he led Catherine towards the path going to the left. As they started to climb, the Greek proprietor watched them with concern. Should he run after them and tell them they had taken the wrong path? The one they were on was dangerous, for expert climbers only. At that moment some customers came up to the stand and the proprietor put the two Americans out of his mind.

The sun was hot, but as they climbed higher, the breezes grew cooler, and Catherine thought that the combination of the two was delicious. It was a beautiful day and she was with the man she loved. From time to time Catherine glanced down and was amazed at how high they had already climbed. The air seemed to be getting thinner, and breathing was becoming more difficult. She had been walking behind Larry, for the path was now too narrow to permit them to walk side by side. She wondered when they were going to stop and have their picnic.

Larry became aware that Catherine was straggling behind and he stopped to wait for her.

'Sorry,' Catherine gasped. 'The altitude is beginning to get to me a little.' She looked down. 'It's going to take a long time to get down.'

'No, it won't,' Larry replied. He turned and

started up the narrow path again. Catherine looked after him, sighed and doggedly started up the trail.

'I should have married a chess player,' she called after him. Larry made no response.

He had come to a sudden, sharp turn in thc path, and in front of him was a small wooden bridge with a single rope for a handhold that had been built across a deep gorge. The bridge was swaying in the wind and did not look secure enough to carry the weight of a man. Larry put one foot on a rotting wooden plank of the bridge and it started to sink with his weight, then held. He looked down. The gorge was about one thousand feet below. Larry started across, carefully testing each step, and heard Catherine's voice, 'Larry!'

He turned. She had reached the foot of the bridge.

'We're not going to cross on *that*, are we?' Catherine asked. 'That wouldn't hold a *cat*!'

'We are unless you can fly.'

'But it doesn't look safe.'

'People cross it every day.' Larry turned and started moving across it again, leaving Catherine standing at the foot of the bridge.

Catherine stepped on the bridge, and it began to vibrate. She looked down at the deep gorge, and fear began to fill her. This was no longer fun; it was dangerous. Catherine looked ahead and saw that Larry had almost reached the other side. She gritted her teeth, grabbed the rope and started walking across, the bridge swaying with every step. On the other side Larry had turned to watch her.

Catherine was moving slowly, keeping one hand tightly on the rope, trying not to look down at the abyss below. Larry could see the fear written on her face. When Catherine reached Larry's side, she was shivering, either from terror or from the chill wind that was beginning to sweep across the snow-capped mountain tops.

Catherine said, 'I don't think I'm cut out to be a mountain climber. Could we go back now, darling?'

Larry looked at her in surprise. 'We haven't even seen the view yet, Cathy.'

'I've seen enough to last me a lifetime.'

He put his arms on hers. 'Tell you what,' he smiled, 'up ahead is a nice quiet place for our picnic. We'll stop there. How's that?'

Catherine nodded reluctantly. 'All right.'

'That's my girl.'

Larry gave her a brief smile, then turned and started up the path again, Catherine following behind him. Catherine had to admit that the view of the village and the valley far below was breathtaking, a peaceful idyllic scene out of a Currier & Ives postcard. She was really glad that she had come. It had been a long time since she had seen Larry so exuberant. He seemed to be possessed by a sense of excitement that kept growing as they climbed higher. His face was flushed, and he chattered on about trivia as though he had to keep talking to release some of his nervous energy. Everything seemed to excite him: the climb, the view, the flowers along the path. Each thing seemed to take on an extraordinary importance as though his senses had somehow been stimulated beyond normal. He was climbing effortlessly, not even out of breath, while the increasingly rarefied air was making Catherine pant.

Her legs were beginning to feel like lead. Her breath was coming in laboured gasps now. She had no idea how long they had been climbing, but when she looked down, the village was a tiny miniature far below. It seemed to Catherine that the path was getting steeper and narrower. It wound along the edge of a precipice and Catherine hugged the side of the mountain as closely as she could. Larry had said that it was an easy climb. *For a mountain goat*, Catherine thought. The trail was almost nonexistent, and there was no sign that anyone else had used it. The flowers had thinned out and the only vegetation was moss and a strange-looking, brownish weed that seemed to be growing out of the stones. Catherine was not sure how much longer she could keep climbing. As they rounded a sharp turn, the path suddenly dropped away and a dizzying abyss appeared below her feet.

'Larry!' It was a scream.

He was at Catherine's side instantly. He grabbed her arm and pulled her back, guiding her over the rocks to where the path resumed. Catherine's heart was pounding wildly. *I must be crazy*, she thought. *I'm too old to go on safari*. The altitude and the exertion had made her dizzy and her head was swimming. She turned to speak to Larry, and above him around the next turn, she saw the top of the mountain. They had arrived.

Catherine lay there on the flat ground getting her strength back, feeling the cool breeze teasing at her hair. The terror had subsided. There was nothing more to fear now. Larry had said the way down was easy. Larry sat down beside her.

'Feeling better?' he asked.

She nodded. 'Yes.' Her heart had stopped pounding and she was beginning to breathe normally again. She took a deep breath and smiled up at him.

'The hard part's finished, isn't it?' Catherine asked.

Larry looked at her a long moment. Then he said, 'Yes. It's finished, Cathy.'

Catherine raised herself up on one elbow. A wooden observation platform had been set up on the small plateau. There was an old railing around the edge, from which there was a spectacular view of the dizzying panorama below. A dozen feet away Catherine could see the path leading down the other side of the mountain.

'Oh, Larry, it *is* beautiful,' Catherine said. 'I feel like Magellan.' She smiled at him, but Larry was looking away and Catherine realized that he wasn't listening to her. He seemed preoccupied – *tense*, as though he were worried about something. Catherine glanced up and said. 'Look!' A fluffy white cloud was drifting towards them, pushed along by the brisk mountain breezes. 'It's coming this way. I've never stood in the clouds before. It must be like being in Heaven.'

Larry watched as Catherine scrambled to her feet and moved towards the edge of the cliff to the rickety wooden railing. Larry leaned forwards on his elbows, suddenly thoughtful, watching the cloud as it moved towards Catherine. It had almost reached her, was starting to envelope her.

'I'm going to stand in it,' she called, 'and let it go right through me!'

An instant later Catherine was lost in the swirling grey mist.

Quietly, Larry rose to his feet. He stood there a moment, stock still, then began to move silently towards her. In seconds he was immersed in the fog. He stopped, not sure exactly where she was. Then ahead of him he heard her voice, calling, 'Oh, Larry, this is wonderful! Come and join me.' He started moving slowly forwards towards the sound of her voice, muffled by the cloud. 'It's like a soft rain,' she cried. 'Can you feel it?' Her voice was closer now, only a few feet ahead of him. He took another step forwards, his hands outstretched, groping for her.

'Larry! Where are you?'

He could make out her figure now, wraithlike in the mist, just in front of him at the very edge of the cliff. His hands reached out towards her and at that moment the cloud blew past them, and she turned and they were facing each other, no more than three feet apart.

She took a step back in surprise, so that her

right foot was at the very edge of the cliff. 'Oh! You startled me,' she exclaimed.

Larry took another step towards her, smiling reassuringly, and he reached out for her with his two hands, and at that moment a loud voice said, 'For Chrissakes, we got bigger mountains than this in Denver!'

Larry swung around in shock, his face white. A group of tourists led by a Greek guide emerged from the far path around the other face of the mountain. The guide stopped as he saw Catherine and Larry.

'Good morning,' he said in surprise. 'You must have climbed the east slope.'

'Yes,' Larry said tightly.

The guide shook his head. 'They're crazy. They should have told you that that is the dangerous way. The other slope is much easier.'

'I'll remember next time,' Larry said. His voice was hoarse.

The excitement that Catherine had noticed seemed to have gone out of him, as though a switch had been suddenly turned off.

'Let's get the hell out of here,' Larry said.

'But – we just got here. Is anything wrong?'

'No,' he snapped. 'I just hate mob scenes.'

They took the easy path back, and on the way down Larry did not speak at all. It was as though he were filled with an icy rage and Catherine could not imagine why. She was sure she had not said or done anything to offend him. It had been when the other people appeared that his manner had changed so abruptly. Suddenly Catherine thought she guessed the reason for his mood, and smiled. He had wanted to make love to her in the cloud! That was why he had started moving towards her with his arms outstretched. And his plans had been spoiled by the group of tourists. She almost laughed aloud with joy. She watched Larry as he strode down the trail ahead of her, and she was infused with a feeling of warmth. *I'll make it up to him when we get back to the hotel*, she promised herself.

But when they returned to their bungalow, and Catherine put her arms around him and started to kiss him, Larry told her that he was tired.

At three o'clock in the morning Catherine lay in bed, too excited to sleep. It had been a long day and a frightening one. She thought of the mountain path and the shaky bridge and the climb up the face of the rock. And finally she fell asleep.

The following morning Larry went to talk to the reception clerk.

'Those caves you mentioned the other day,' Larry began.

'Ah, yes,' the clerk replied. 'The Caves of Perama. Very colourful. Very interesting. You must not miss them.'

'I guess I'll have to see them,' Larry said lightly. 'I don't care for caves much, but my wife heard about them and she's been after me to take her there. She loves that kind of thing.'

'I am certain you will both enjoy it, Mr Douglas. Just be sure to hire a guide.'

'Do I need one?' Larry asked.

The clerk nodded. 'It is advisable. There have been several tragedies there, people getting lost.' He lowered his voice. 'One young couple has not been found to this day.'

'If it's so dangerous,' Larry asked, 'why do they allow people in?'

'It is only the new section that is dangerous,' the clerk explained. 'It has not been explored yet and there are no lights. But with a guide you will not have to worry.'

'What time do they close the caves?'

'At six o'clock.'

Larry found Catherine outside, reclining under a giant oxya tree, the beautiful Greek oak, reading.

'How's the book?' he asked.

'Put-downable.'

He hunched beside her. 'The hotel clerk told me about some caves near here.'

Catherine looked up, faintly apprehensive. 'Caves?'

'He said it's a must. All the honeymooners go there. You make a wish inside, and it comes true.' His voice was boyish and eager. 'How about it?'

Catherine hesitated a moment, thinking how like a little boy Larry really was. 'If you would like it,' she said.

He smiled. 'Great. We'll go after lunch. You go ahead and read. I have to drive into town and pick up a few things.'

'Would you like me to come with you?'

'No,' he said easily, 'I'll be right back. You take it easy.'

She nodded. 'All right.'

He turned and left.

In town Larry found a small general store that was able to supply him with a pocket flashlight, some fresh batteries and a ball of twine.

'Are you staying up at the hotel?' the shopkeeper asked as he counted out Larry's change.

'No,' Larry said. 'Just passing through on my way to Athens.'

'I'd be careful if I was you,' the man advised.

Larry looked up at him sharply. 'Of what?'

'There's a storm coming up. You can hear the sheep crying.'

Larry returned to the hotel at three o'clock. At four o'clock, Larry and Catherine left for the caves. A troubled wind had sprung up, and to the north large thunderheads were starting to form, erasing the sun from the sky.

The Caves of Perama lie thirty kilometres east of Ioannina. Over the centuries tremendous stalagmites and stalactites have formed into the shapes of animals and palaces and jewels, and the caves have become an important tourist attraction.

When Catherine and Larry arrived at the caves, it was five o'clock, one hour before closing. Larry bought two tickets and a pamphlet at the ticket booth. A shabbily dressed guide came up and offered his services.

'Only fifty drachmas,' he intoned, 'and I will give you the best guided tour.'

'We don't need a guide,' Larry said, curtly.

Catherine looked at him, surprised by his sharp tone.

He took Catherine's arm. 'Come on.'

'Are you sure we shouldn't have a guide?'

'What for? It's a racket. All we do is go inside and look at the cave. The pamphlet will tell us anything we need to know.'

'All right,' Catherine said agreeably.

The entrance to the cave was larger than she had expected, brightly lit with flood lamps and filled with milling tourists. The walls and roof of the cave seemed to be crammed with heroic figures sculpted out of the rocks: birds and giants and flowers and crowns.

'It's fantastic,' Catherine exclaimed. She studied the pamphlet. 'No one knows how old it is.'

Her voice sounded hollow, reverberating against the rock ceiling. Over their heads, stalactites hung down. A tunnel carved into the rock led to a second smaller room that was lit by naked bulbs wired near the ceiling of the cave. There were more fanciful figures in here, a wild profligate display of nature's art. At the far end of the cave was a printed sign that read: *Danger: Keep Away*.

Beyond the sign was the entrance to a yawning black cavern. Casually Larry walked over to it and looked around. Catherine was studying a carving near the entrance. Larry took the sign and tossed it to one side. He walked back to Catherine.

'It's damp in here,' she said. 'Shall we leave?'

'No.' Larry's tone was firm.

She looked at him in surprise.

'There's more to see,' Larry explained. 'The hotel clerk told me that the most interesting part is the new section. He said we mustn't miss it.'

'Where is it?' Catherine asked.

'Over there.' Larry took her arm and they walked towards the rear of the cave and stood in front of the gaping black chasm.

'We can't go in there,' Catherine said. 'It's dark.'

Larry patted her arm. 'Not to worry. He told me to bring a flashlight.' He produced it from his pocket. 'And – *voilà* – see?' He turned it on, and its narrow beam lit up a long dark corridor of ancient rock.

Catherine stood there, staring at the tunnel. 'It looks so big,' she said uncertainly. 'Are you sure it's safe?'

'Of course,' Larry replied. 'They bring schoolchildren here.'

Catherine still hesitated, wishing they could stay with the other tourists. Somehow this seemed dangerous to her.

'All right,' she said.

They started into the passage. They had travelled only a few feet when the circle of light from the main cave behind them was swallowed up in the blackness. The passage made an abrupt turn to the left and then curved to the right. They were alone in a cold, timeless primeval world. In the beam of Larry's flashlight Catherine caught a glimpse of his face in the reflection of light and she saw that look of animation again. It was the same way he had looked on the mountain. Catherine tightened her grip on his arm.

Ahead of them the tunnel forked. Catherine could see the rough stone on the low ceiling as it split off in separate directions. She thought of Theseus and the Minotaur in the cave, and she wondered whether they were going to bump into them. She opened her mouth to suggest that they turn back, but before she could speak, Larry said, 'We go to the left.'

She looked at him and said in what she hoped was a casual voice, 'Darling, don't you think we should start back? It's getting late. The caves will be closing.'

'They're open until nine,' Larry replied. 'There's one particular cave I want to find. They just excavated it. It's supposed to be really fantastic.' He started to move forwards.

Catherine hesitated, casting about for an excuse not to go further. After all why *shouldn't* they go exploring? Larry was enjoying it. If that was what it took to make him happy, she would become the world's greatest – what was the word? – spelunker.

Larry had stopped and was waiting for her. 'Coming?' he asked impatiently.

She tried to sound enthusiastic. 'Yes. Just don't lose me,' she said.

Larry did not reply. They took the fork that branched to the left and began walking, careful of the small stones that slipped under their feet. Larry reached into his pocket, and a moment later Catherine heard something fall to the ground. Larry kept walking.

'Did you drop something?' Catherine asked. 'I thought I heard –'

'I kicked a stone,' he said. 'Let's walk faster.' And they moved ahead, Catherine unaware that behind them a ball of twine was unwinding.

The ceiling of the cave seemed to be lower here and the walls damper and – Catherine laughed at herself for thinking it – ominous. It was as though the tunnel was beginning to close in on them, threatening and maleficent. 'I don't think this place likes us,' Catherine said.

'Don't be ridiculous, Cathy; it's just a cave.'

'Why do you suppose we're the only ones here?'

Larry hesitated. 'Not many people know about this section.'

They walked on and on until Catherine began to lose all sense of time and place.

The passage was narrowing again, and the rocks on the sides tore at them with sharp, unexpected protuberances.

'How much further do you think it is?' Catherine asked. 'We must be getting near China.'

'It's not far now.'

When they spoke, their voices sounded muffled and hollow, like a series of continuous dying echoes.

It was getting cold now, but it was a damp, clammy cold. Catherine shivered. Ahead the beam of the flashlight caught another bifurcation of the passage. They walked up to it and stopped. The tunnel running to the right seemed smaller than the one to the left.

'They should put up neon road signs,' Catherine said. 'We've probably gone too far.'

'No,' Larry said. 'I'm sure it's the one on the right.'

'I'm really getting chilly, darling,' she said. 'Let's go back now.'

He turned to look at her. 'We're almost there, Cathy.' He squeezed her arm. 'I'll warm you up when we get back to our bungalow.' He saw the reluctance on her face. 'I'll tell you what – if we haven't found the place in the next two minutes, we'll turn around and go home. OK?'

Catherine felt her heart lighten. 'OK,' she said thankfully.

'Come on.'

They turned down the tunnel to the right, the beam of the flashlight making an eerie, wavering pattern on the grey rock ahead. Catherine glanced back over her shoulder and behind her was complete blackness. It was as though the little flashlight was carving brightness out of the Stygian gloom, moving it forwards a few feet at a time, encapsulating them in its tiny womb of light. Larry stopped suddenly.

'Damn!' he said.

'What's the matter?'

'I think we took the wrong turn back there.'

Catherine nodded. 'All right. Let's go back.'

'Let me make sure. You stay here.'

She looked at him in surprise. 'Where are you going?'

'Just a few feet. Back to that entrance.' His voice sounded strained and unnatural.

'I'll come with you.'

'I can do it faster alone, Catherine. I just want to check the fork where we made the last turn.' He sounded impatient. 'I'll be back in ten seconds.'

'All right,' she said, uneasily.

Catherine stood there watching as Larry turned away from her and walked back into the dark from which they had come, enclosed in a halo of light like a moving angel in the bowels of the earth. A moment later the light disappeared, and she was plunged into the deepest blackness she had ever known. She stood there, shivering, counting off the seconds in her mind. And then the minutes.

Larry did not return.

Catherine waited, feeling the blackness lapping around her like malicious invisible waves. She called out, 'Larry?' and her voice was hoarse and uncertain, and she cleared her throat and tried again louder. 'Larry?' She could hear the sound dying a few feet away from her, murdered by the darkness. It was as though nothing could live in this place, and Catherine began to feel the first tendrils of terror. *Of course Larry will be right back*, she told herself. *All I have to do is stay where I am and remain calm.*

The black minutes dragged by, and she began to face the fact that something had gone terribly wrong. Larry could have had an accident, he could have slipped on the loose stones and hit his head on the sharp sides of the cave. Perhaps at this moment he was lying just a few feet away from her, bleeding to death. Or perhaps he was lost. His flashlight could have gone out and he might be somewhere in the bowels of this cave trapped, as she was trapped.

A feeling of suffocation began to close in on Catherine, choking her, filling her with a mindless panic. She turned and began to walk slowly in the direction from which she had come. The tunnel was narrow, and if Larry was lying on the ground, helpless and hurt, she had a good chance of finding him. Soon she would come to the place where the passage had divided. She moved cautiously, the loose stones rolling beneath her feet. She thought she heard a distant sound and stopped to listen. Larry? It was gone, and she began to move again, and then she heard it once more. It was a whirring sound, as though someone were running a tape recorder. There *was* someone down here!

Catherine yelled aloud and then listened as the sound of her voice drowned in the silence. There it was again! The whirring noise. It was coming this way. It grew louder, racing towards her in a great screaming rush of wind. It was getting closer and closer. Suddenly it leaped on her in the dark; cold and clammy skin brushed against her cheeks and kissed her lips and she felt something crawling on her head and sharp claws in her hair and her face was smothered by the mad beating of wings of some nameless horror attacking her in the blackness.

She fainted.

She was lying on a sharp spike of stone and the discomfort of it brought her back to consciousness. Her cheek was warm and sticky, and it was a minute before Catherine realized that it was her blood. She remembered the wings and the claws that had attacked her in the dark and she began to shiver.

There were bats in the cave.

She tried to recall what she knew about bats. She had read somewhere that they were flying rats and that they congregated by the thousands. The only other information she could conjure up from her memory was that there were vampire bats, and she quickly dropped that thought. Reluctantly Catherine sat up, the palms of her hands stinging from being scraped on the sharp stones.

You can't just sit here, she told herself. *You've got to get up and do something.* Painfully she dragged herself to her feet. She had lost a shoe somehow and her dress was torn, but Larry would buy her a new one tomorrow. She pictured the two of them going into a little shop in the village, laughing and happy and buying a white summer dress for her, but somehow the dress became a shroud and her mind began to fill with panic again. She must keep thinking about tomorrow, not the nightmare she was engulfed in now. She must keep walking. But which way? She was turned around. If she walked the wrong way, she would be going deeper into the cave, and yet she knew she could not stay here. Catherine tried to estimate how much time had elapsed since they had entered the cave. It must have been an hour, possibly two. There was no way of knowing how long she had been unconscious. Surely they would be looking for Larry and her. But what if no one missed them? There was no check on who went in or out of the caves. She could be down here forever.

She took off her other shoe and began to walk, taking slow, careful steps, holding her burning hands out to avoid bumping into the rough sides of the tunnel. *The longest journey begins with but a single step*, Catherine told herself. *The Chinese said that and look how smart they are. They invented firecrackers and chop suey, and they were too clever to get caught in some dark hole in the ground where no one could find them. If I keep walking, I'm going to bump into Larry or some tourists and we'll go back to the hotel and have a drink and laugh about all this. All I have to do is keep walking.*

She stopped suddenly. In the distance she could hear the whirring sound again, moving towards her like some ghostly, phantom express train, and her body began to tremble uncontrollably, and she began to scream. An instant later, they were on her, hundreds of them, swarming over her, beating at her with their cold, clammy wings and smothering her with their furry rodent bodies in a nightmare of unspeakable horror.

The last thing she remembered before losing consciousness was calling Larry's name.

She was lying on the cold, damp floor of the cave. Her eyes were closed, but her mind had suddenly awakened, and she thought, *Larry wants to kill me*. It was as though her subconscious had put the idea there intact. In a series of kaleidoscopic flashes she heard Larry saying, *I'm in love with someone else . . . I want a divorce* . . . and Larry moving towards her through the cloud on the mountaintop, his hands reaching for her . . . She remembered looking down the steep mountain and saying, *It will take a long time to get down*, and Larry saying, *No, it won't* . . . and Larry saying, *We don't need a guide . . . I think we took the wrong turn. Wait here . . . I'll be back in ten seconds* . . . And then the terrifying blackness.

Larry had never intended to return for her. The reconciliation, the honeymoon . . . it was all pretence, part of a plan to murder her. All the time she had been smugly thanking God for giving her a second chance, Larry was plotting to kill her. And he had succeeded, for Catherine knew she would never get out of here. She was buried alive in a black tomb of horror. The bats had gone, but she could feel and smell the filthy slime they had left all over her face and body, and she knew that they would be back for her. She did not know if she could keep her sanity through another attack. The thought of them made her begin to tremble again, and she forced herself to take slow, deep breaths.

And then Catherine heard it again and knew she could not stand it another time. It started as a low humming, and then a louder wave of sound, moving towards her. There was a sudden, anguished scream, and it rang out into the darkness over and over, and the other sound kept coming louder and louder, and out of the black tunnel a light appeared, and she heard voices calling out and hands began to reach for her and lift her and she wanted to warn them about the bats, but she was unable to stop screaming.

TWENTY-TWO

Noelle and Catherine

Athens: 1946

She lay still and rigid so that the bats could not find her, and she listened for the whirr of their wings, her eyes tightly shut.

A man's voice said, 'It is a miracle that we found her.'

'Is she going to be all right?'

It was Larry's voice.

Terror suddenly flooded through Catherine again. It was as though her body were filled with screaming nerves that warned her to flee. Her killer had come for her. She moaned, 'No . . .' and opened her eyes. She was in her bed in the bungalow. Larry stood at the foot of the bed, and next to him was a man she had never seen before. Larry moved towards her. 'Catherine . . .'

She flinched as he started towards her. 'Don't touch me!' Her voice was weak and hoarse.

'Catherine!' Larry's face was filled with distress.

'Get him away from me,' Catherine begged.

'She is still in shock,' the stranger said. 'Perhaps it would be better if you waited in the other room.'

Larry studied Catherine a moment, his face expressionless. 'Of course. I want whatever is best for her.' He turned and walked out.

The stranger came closer. He was a short, fat man with a pleasant face and a nice smile. He spoke English with a heavy accent. 'I am Doctor Kazomides. You have had a most unpleasant time, Mrs Douglas, but I assure you you are going to be fine. A mild concussion and a severe shock, but in a few days you will be good as new.' He sighed. 'They should close those damned caves. This is the third accident this year.'

Catherine started to shake her head, then stopped, as it began to throb violently. 'It was no accident,' she said thickly. 'He tried to kill me.'

He looked down at her. 'Who tried to kill you?'

Her mouth was dry and her tongue was thick. It was difficult to get the words out. 'M – my husband.'

'No,' he said.

He did not believe her. Catherine swallowed and tried again. 'He l – left me in the cave to die.'

He shook his head. 'It was an accident. I am going to give you a sedative and when you wake up, you will feel much better.'

A surge of fear flowed through her. 'No!' she pleaded. 'Don't you understand? I'll never wake up. Take me out of here. Please!'

The doctor was smiling reassuringly. 'I told you you are going to be fine, Mrs Douglas. All you need is a nice, long sleep.' He reached into a black medical bag and began searching for a hypodermic.

Catherine tried to sit up, but a searing pain shot through her head and she was instantly bathed in perspiration. She fell back on the bed, her head pounding unbearably.

'You must not try to move yet,' Dr Kazomides warned. 'You have been through a terrible ordeal.' He took out the hypodermic, filled the needle from a vial of amber fluid and turned to her. 'Turn over, please. When you waken, you will feel like a new person.'

'I won't waken,' Catherine whispered. 'He'll murder me while I'm asleep.'

There was a look of concern on the doctor's face. He walked over to her. 'Please turn over, Mrs Douglas.'

She stared at him, her eyes stubborn.

Gently he turned Catherine on her side, pulled up her nightgown and she felt a sharp sting in her hip. 'There you are.'

She rolled on her back and whispered. 'You've just killed me.' Her eyes filled with helpless tears.

'Mrs Douglas,' the doctor said, quietly, 'do you know how we found you?'

She started to shake her head, then remembered the pain. His voice was gentle. 'Your husband led us to you.'

She stared at him, not comprehending what he was saying.

'He took the wrong turn and got lost in the cave,' he explained. 'When he could not find you, he became frantic. He summoned the police and we immediately organized a search party.'

She looked at him, still not understanding. 'Larry . . . sent for help?'

'He was in a terrible state. He blamed himself for what happened.'

She lay there trying to take it in, trying to adjust to this new information. If Larry had tried to kill her, he would not have organized a search party to find her, he would not have been frantic about her safety. She was filled with a terrible confusion. The doctor was watching her sympathetically.

'You will sleep now,' he told her. 'I will come back to see you in the morning.'

She had believed that the man she loved was a murderer. She knew she had to tell Larry and ask his forgiveness, but her head was getting heavy and her eyes kept closing. *I'll tell him later*, she thought, *when I wake up. He'll understand and he'll forgive me. And everything will be wonderful again, just the way it was. . . .*

She was awakened by a sudden, sharp cracking sound, and her eyes flew open, her pulse racing. A torrent of rain was savagely drumming against the bedroom window, and a flash of lightning lit everything in a pale blue light that made the room look like an overexposed photograph. The wind was clawing at the house, trying to scream its way in and the rain beating on the roof and windows sounded like a thousand tiny drums. Every few seconds there was an ominous roll of thunder followed by a flash of lightning.

It was the sound of thunder that had awakened Catherine. She dragged herself up to a sitting position and looked at the small bedside clock. She was groggy from the sedative that the doctor had given her, and she had to squint to make out the figures on the dial. It was three A.M. She was alone. Larry must be in the other room keeping vigil, worried about her. She had to see him, to apologize. Carefully Catherine swung her feet off the edge of the bed and tried to stand up. A wave of dizziness swept over her. She started to fall and held herself against the bedpost until it passed. She walked unsteadily to the door, her muscles feeling stiff and unused, and the pounding in her head a painful, aching throb. She stood there a moment, clinging to the door knob for support, then opened the door and stepped into the living room.

Larry was not there. There was a light on in the kitchen, and she stumbled towards it. Larry was standing in the kitchen, his back to her, and she called out, 'Larry!' but her voice was washed away by the loud clap of thunder. Before she could call again, a woman moved into view. Larry said, 'It's dangerous for you to –' The screaming wind carried the rest of his words away.

'– had to come. I had to make sure you –'

'– see us together. No one will ever –'

'– I told you I'd take care of –'

'– went wrong. There's nothing they can –'

'– now, while she's asleep.'

Catherine stood there paralysed, unable to move. It was like listening to stroboscopic sounds, quick pulsating phrases of words. The rest of the sentences were lost in the howling wind and crack of thunder.

'– we have to move quickly before she –'

All the old terrors returned, shuddering through her body, engulfing her in a nameless, sickening panic. Her nightmare had been real. He was trying to kill her. She had to get out of here before they found her, before they murdered her. Slowly, her whole body trembling, she started backing away. She brushed against a lamp, and it started to fall, but she caught it before it could hit the floor. The pounding of her heart was so loud that she was afraid they would be able to hear it over the sound of the thunder and the rain. She reached the front door and opened it and the wind almost tore it out of her hands.

Catherine stepped outside into the night and quickly closed the door behind her. She was instantly drenched by the cold, driving rain, and for the first time she became aware that she was wearing nothing but a thin nightgown. It did not matter. All that mattered was that she escape. Through the torrents of rain she could see the lights of the hotel lobby in the distance. She could go there and ask for help. But would they believe her? She remembered the doctor's face when she had told him Larry was trying to kill her. No, they would think she was hysterical, they would turn her over to Larry. She must get away from this place. She headed for the steep rocky path that led down to the village.

The torrential storm had turned the path into a muddy, slippery mire that sucked at her bare feet and slowed her down so that she had the feeling that she was running in a nightmare, vainly trying to escape in slow motion while her pursuers raced after her. She kept slipping and falling to the ground and her feet were bleeding from the sharp stones on the path, but she was not even aware of it. She was in a state of shock, moving like an automaton, falling when a gust of wind hurled her down and picking herself up and moving down the path towards the village again, unaware of where she was running. She was no longer conscious of the rain.

The path suddenly opened out onto a dark, deserted street on the edge of the village. She kept stumbling ahead like a hunted animal, mindlessly putting one foot in front of the other, terrified by the awful sounds that rent the night and the flashes of lightning that turned the sky into an inferno.

She reached the lake and stood there staring at it, the wind whipping the thin nightgown around her body. The calm water had turned into a seething, churning ocean driven by demonic winds that built up high waves that brutally smashed against one another.

Catherine stood there, trying to remember what she was doing here. And suddenly it came to her. She was on her way to meet Bill Fraser. He was waiting for her at his beautiful mansion so they could be married. Across the water Catherine caught a glimpse of a yellow light through the driving rain. Bill was there, waiting. But how was she going to get to him? She looked down and below her she saw the rowboats tied to their moorings, spinning around in the turbulent water, straining to break free.

She knew then what she had to do. She scrambled down to a boat and jumped in. Fighting to keep her balance she untied the rope holding it to the dock. Instantly the boat leaped away from the dock, soaring in its sudden freedom. Catherine was knocked off her feet. She pulled herself onto a seat and picked up the oars, trying to remember how Larry had used them. But there was no Larry. It must have been Bill. Yes, she could remember Bill rowing with her. They were going to meet his mother and father. Now she tried to use the oars, but the giant waves kept pitching the boat from side to side and spinning it around, and the oars were pulled out of her hands and sucked into the water. She sat there watching them disappear from sight. The boat was hurtling towards the centre of the lake. Catherine's teeth began to chatter from the cold, and she began to shiver in an uncontrollable spasm. She felt something lap at her feet and she looked down and saw that the boat was filling with water. She started to cry, because her wedding dress was going to get wet. Bill Fraser had bought it for her and now he was going to be angry with her.

She wore a wedding gown because she and Bill were in a church and the minister who looked like Bill's father said *if anyone objects to this marrige speak up now or . . .* and then a woman's voice said, *now, while she's asleep*, and the lights went out and Catherine was back in the cave and Larry was holding her down and the woman was throwing water on her, drowning her. She looked around for the yellow light in Bill's house, but it was gone. He did not want to marry her any more, and now she had no one.

The shore was very far away now, hidden somewhere beyond the beating, driving rain, and Catherine was alone in the stormy night, with the screaming, banshee wind of the *meltemi* in her ears. The boat began to rock treacherously as the huge waves smashed against it. But Catherine was no longer afraid. Her body was slowly filling with a delicious warmth, and the rain felt like soft velvet on her skin. She clasped her hands in front of her like a small child and began to recite the prayer that she had learned as a little girl.

'Now I lay me down to sleep . . . I pray the Lord my soul to keep . . . If I should die before I wake . . . I pray the Lord my soul to take.' And she was filled with a wonderful happiness because she knew at last that everything was all right. She was on her way home.

At that moment a large wave caught the stern of the boat, and it slowly began to overturn in the black bottomless lake.

BOOK THREE

TWENTY-THREE

The Trial

Athens: 1947

Five hours before the murder trial of Noelle Page and Larry Douglas was to begin, Room 33 in the Arsakion Courthouse in Athens was overflowing with spectators. The courthouse is an enormous grey building that takes up an entire square block on University Street and Stada. Of the thirty courtrooms in the building, only three rooms are reserved for criminal trials: Rooms 21, 30 and 33. Number 33 had been chosen for this trial because it was the largest. The corridors outside Room 33 were jammed and police in grey uniforms and grey shirts were stationed at the two entrances to control the crowd. The sandwich stand in the corridor was sold out in the first five minutes, and there was a long line in front of the telephone booth.

Georgios Skouri, the Chief of Police, was personally supervising the security arrangements. Newspaper photographers were everywhere and

Skouri managed to have his photograph taken with pleasing frequency. Passes to the courtroom were at a premium. For weeks members of the Greek judiciary had been besieged with requests from friends and relatives. Insiders who were able to secure them bartered them in exchange for other favours or sold them to the jackals who were scalping them for as high as five hundred drachmas apiece.

The actual setting of the murder trial was commonplace. Courtroom 33 on the second floor of the courthouse was musty and old, the arena of thousands of legal battles that had taken place over the years. The room was about forty feet wide and three hundred feet long. The seats were divided into three rows, six feet apart, with nine wooden benches to each row.

At the front of the courtroom was a raised dais behind a six-foot polished mahogany partition with high-backed leather chairs for the three presiding judges. The centre chair was for the President of the Court and above it hung a square, dirty mirror reflecting a section of the courtroom.

In front of the dais was the witness stand, a small raised platform on which was fixed a reading lectern with a wooden tray to hold papers. On the lectern in gold leaf was the crucifix, Jesus on the cross with two of his disciples by his side. Against the far wall was the jury box, filled now with its ten jurors. On the far left was the box where the accused sat. In front of the defendants' box was the lawyers' table.

The walls of the room were of stucco, and there was linoleum on the floor in contrast to the worn wooden floors in the courtrooms on the first floor. A dozen electric light bulbs hung from the ceiling, covered with glass globes. In a far corner of the room, the airduct of an old-fashioned heater ascended into the ceiling. A section of the room had been reserved for the press, and representatives were there from Reuters, United Press, International News Service, Shsin Hau Agency, French Press Agency and Tass, among others.

The circumstances of the murder trial itself would have been sensational enough, but the personae were so famous that the excited spectators did not know where to look first. It was like a three-ring circus. In the first row of benches was Philippe Sorel, the star, who, it was rumoured, was a former lover of Noelle Page. Sorel had smashed a camera on the way into the courtroom and had adamantly refused to speak to the press. He sat in his seat now, withdrawn and silent, an invisible wall around him. One row in back of Sorel sat Armand Gautier. The tall, saturnine director was constantly scanning the courtroom as though mentally making notes for his next picture. Near Gautier sat Israel Katz, the famous French surgeon and resistance hero.

Two seats away from him sat William Fraser, special assistant to the President of the United States. Next to Fraser a seat had been reserved and a rumour swept through the courtroom like wildfire that Constantin Demiris was going to appear.

Everywhere the spectators turned was a familiar face: a politician, a singer, a well-known sculptor, an internationally famous author. But though the audience in the judicial circus was filled with celebrities, the main focus of attention was in the centre ring.

At one end of the defendant's box sat Noelle Page, exquisitely beautiful, her honey skin a bit paler than usual, and dressed as though she had just stepped out of Madame Chanel's. There was a regal quality about Noelle, a noble presence that heightened the drama of what was happening to her. It whetted the excitement of the spectators and sharpened their blood-lust.

As an American newsweekly expressed it: *The emotion that flowed towards Noelle Page from the crowd that had come to witness her trial was so strong that it became an almost physical presence in the courtroom. It was not a feeling of sympathy or of enmity, it was simply a feeling of expectation. The woman being tried for murder by the state was a superwoman, a goddess on a golden pedestal, who was high above them, and they were there to watch their idol being brought down to their level and destroyed. The feeling in the courtroom must have been the same feelings that were in the hearts of the peasants who watched Marie Antoinette riding to her doom in the tumbrel.*

Noelle Page was not the only act in the legal circus. At the other end of the defendant's box sat Larry Douglas, filled with a smouldering anger. His handsome face was pale, and he had lost weight, but those things only served to accentuate his sculptured features, and many of the women in the courtroom had an urge to take him in their arms and console him in one way or another. Since Larry had been arrested, he had received hundreds of letters from women all over the world, dozens of gifts and proposals of marriage.

The third star of the circus was Napoleon Chotas, a man who was as well known in Greece as Noelle Page. Napoleon Chotas was acknowledged to be one of the greatest criminal lawyers in the world. He had defended clients ranging from heads of government who had been found with their fingers in the public coffers, to murderers who had been caught red-handed by the police, and he had never lost a major case. Chotas was thin and emaciated-looking and he sat in the court-room watching the spectators with large, sad bloodhound eyes in a ruined face. When Chotas addressed a jury, his speech was slow and hesitant, and he had great difficulty expressing himself. Sometimes he was in such an agony of embarrassment that a juror would helpfully blurt out the word that Napoleon Chotas was fumbling for, and when this happened the lawyer's face would fill with such relief and inexpressible gratitude that the entire panel of jurors would feel a wave of affection for the man. Outside the courtroom Chotas was a crisp, incisive speaker with a consummate mastery of language and syntax. He spoke seven languages fluently and when his busy schedule permitted, he gave lectures to jurists all over the world.

Seated on the lawyer's bench a few feet away from Chotas, was Frederick Stavros, the defence attorney for Larry Douglas. The experts agreed that while Stavros might be competent enough to handle routine cases, he was hopelessly out of his depth in this one.

Noelle Page and Larry Douglas had already been tried in the newspapers and in the minds of the populace and had been found guilty. No one doubted their guilt for a moment. Professional gamblers were offering thirty to one that the defendants would be convicted. To the trial, then, was lent the added excitement of watching the greatest criminal lawyer in Europe work his magic against enormous odds.

When it had been announced that Chotas was going to defend Noelle Page, the woman who had betrayed Constantin Demiris and held him up to public ridicule, the news had created a furore. As powerful as Chotas was, Constantin Demiris was a hundred times more powerful and no one could imagine what had possessed Chotas to go against Constantin Demiris. The truth was even more interesting than the bizarre rumours that were flying around.

The lawyer had taken on Noelle Page's defence at the personal request of Demiris.

Three months before the trial was scheduled to begin, the warden himself had come to Noelle's cell at the Saint Nikodemous Street Prison to tell her that Constantin Demiris had asked permission to visit her. Noelle had wondered when she would hear from Demiris. There had been no word from him since her arrest, only a deep, foreboding silence.

Noelle had lived with Demiris long enough to know how deep was his sense of *amour-propre* and to what lengths he would go to avenge even the smallest slight. Noelle had humiliated him as no other person ever had before, and he was powerful enough to exact a terrible retribution. The only question was: How would he go about it? Noelle was certain Demiris would disdain anything as simple as the bribing of a jury or judges. He would be satisfied with no less than some complex Machiavellian plot to exact his revenge, and Noelle had lain awake on her cell cot night after night putting herself in Demiris' mind, discarding strategy after strategy, just as he must have done, searching for a perfect plan. It was like playing mental chess with Demiris, except that she and Larry were the pawns, and the stakes were life and death.

It was probable that Demiris would want to destroy her and Larry, but Noelle knew better than anyone the subtlety of Demiris' mind, so it was also possible that he might plan to destroy only one of them and let the other one live and suffer. If Demiris arranged for them both to be executed, he would have his vengeance, but it would be over with too quickly – there would be nothing left for him to savour. Noelle had carefully examined every possibility, each possible variation of the game, and it seemed to her that Constantin Demiris might arrange to let Larry die and let her live, either in prison or under Demiris' control, because that would be the surest way to prolong his vengeance indefinitely. First Noelle would suffer the pain of losing the man she loved, and then she would have to endure whatever exquisite agonies Demiris had planned for her future. Part of the pleasure Demiris would derive from his vengeance would be in telling Noelle in advance, so she could taste the full measure of despair.

It had therefore come as no surprise to Noelle when the warden had appeared at her cell to tell her that Constantin Demiris wished to see her.

Noelle had been the first to arrive. She had been ushered into the warden's private office where she had been discreetly left alone with a makeup case brought by her maid, to prepare herself for Demiris' visit.

Noelle ignored the cosmetics and the combs and brushes that lay on the desk and walked over to the window and looked out. It was the first sight she had had of the outside world in three months, other than the quick glimpses when she had been taken from the Saint Nikodemous Street Prison to the Arsakion, the courthouse, on the day of her arraignment. She had been transported to the courthouse in a prison van with bars and escorted to the basement, where a narrow cage elevator had carried her and her warders to the second-floor corridor. The hearing had been held there and she had been remanded for trial and returned to the prison.

Now Noelle stared out the window and watched the traffic below on University Street, men and women and children hurrying home to be united with their families. For the first time in her life Noelle felt frightened. She had no illusions about her chances of acquittal. She had read the newspapers and she knew that this was going to be more than a trial. This was going to be a blood bath in which she and Larry were to be served up as victims to satisfy the conscience of an outraged society. The Greeks hated her because she had mocked the sanctity of marriage, envied her because she was young and beautiful and rich and despised her because they sensed that she was indifferent to their feelings.

In the past Noelle had been careless of life, recklessly squandering time as though it were eternal: but now something in her had changed. The imminent prospect of death had made Noelle realize for the first time how much she wanted to live. There was a fear in her that was like a growing cancer, and if she could, she was ready to make a deal for her life, even though she knew that Demiris would find ways to make it a hell on earth. She would face that when it happened. When the time came, she would find a way to outwit him.

Meanwhile she needed his help to stay alive. She had one advantage. She had always taken the idea of death lightly, so Demiris had no idea how much life meant to her now. If he had, he would surely let her die. Noelle wondered again what webs he had been weaving for her over the past few months, and even as she wondered, she heard the office door open and she turned around and saw Constantin Demiris standing in the doorway and after one shocked look at him, Noelle knew that she had nothing more to fear.

Constantin Demiris had aged ten years in the few months since Noelle had seen him. He looked gaunt and haggard, and his clothes hung loosely on his frame. But it was his eyes that held her attention. They were the eyes of a soul that had been through hell. The essence of power that had been within Demiris, the dynamic, overpowering core of vitality was gone. It was as though a light switch had been turned off, and all that was left was the pale afterglow of a faded, once remembered brilliance. He stood there, staring at her, his eyes filled with pain.

For a split second Noelle wondered whether this could be some kind of trick, part of a plan, but no man on earth could be that good an actor. It was Noelle who broke the long silence. 'I'm sorry, Costa,' she said.

Demiris nodded slowly, as though the movement cost him an effort.

'I wanted to kill you,' he said wearily, and it

was an old man's voice. 'I had everything all worked out.'

'Why didn't you?'

He replied quietly, 'Because you killed me first. I've never needed anyone beforc. I suppose I've never really been in pain before.'

'Costa –'

'No. Let me finish. I'm not a forgiving man. If I could do without you, believe me I would. But I can't. I can't go through any more. I want you back, Noelle.'

She fought to show nothing of what she was feeling inside. 'That's really not up to me anymore, is it?'

'If I could have you freed, would you come back to me? To stay?'

To stay. A thousand images flashed through Noelle's mind. She would never see Larry again, never touch him, hold him. Noelle had no choice, but even if she had, life was sweeter. And as long as she was alive, there was always a chance. She looked up at Demiris.

'Yes, Costa.'

Demiris stared at her, his face filling with emotion. When he spoke, his voice was husky. 'Thank you,' he said. 'We're going to forget the past. It's gone and nothing will change it.' His voice brightened. 'It's the future I'm interested in. I'm going to engage an attorney for you.'

'Who?'

'Napoleon Chotas.'

And that was the moment that Noelle really knew she had won the chess match. Check. Checkmate.

Now Napoleon Chotas sat at the long wooden lawyer's table thinking about the battle that was about to take place. Chotas would have much preferred that the trial be held in Ioannina rather than in Athens, but that was impossible, since by Greek law a trial could not take place in the district where the crime had been committed. Chotas had not the slightest doubt about the guilt of Noelle Page, but that was unimportant to him, for like all criminal lawyers he felt that the guilt or innocence of a client was immaterial. Everyone was entitled to a fair trial.

The trial that was about to begin, however, was something different. For the first time in his professional life Napoleon Chotas had allowed himself to become emotionally involved with a client: He was in love with Noelle Page. He had gone to see her at Constantin Demiris' request and though Chotas had been familiar with the public image of Noelle Page, he had been totally unprepared for the reality. She had received him as though he were a guest paying a social call. Noelle had showed neither nervousness nor fear, and at first Chotas had attributed it to her lack of understanding of the desperateness of her situation. The opposite had proved to be true. Noelle was the most intelligent and fascinating woman he had ever encountered and certainly the most beautiful. Chotas, though his appearance belied it, was a connoisseur of women, and he recognized the special qualities that Noelle possessed. It was a joy for Chotas merely to sit and talk with her. They discussed law and art and crime and history, and she was a constant amazement to him. He could fully appreciate Noelle's liaison with a man like Constantin Demiris, but her involvement with Larry Douglas puzzled him. He felt that she was far above Douglas, and yet Chotas supposed that there was some unexplainable chemistry that made people fall in love with the most unlikely partners. Brilliant scientists married empty-headed blondes, great writers married stupid actresses, intelligent statesmen married trollops.

Chotas remembered the meeting with Demiris. They had known each other socially over the years, but Chotas' law firm had never done any work for him. Demiris had asked Chotas to his home at Varkiza. Demiris had plunged into the conversation without preamble. 'As you may know,' he had said, 'I have a deep interest in this trial. Miss Page is the only woman in my life I have ever truly loved.' The two men had talked for six hours, discussing every aspect of the case, every possible strategy. It was decided that Noelle's plea would be Not Guilty. When Chotas rose to leave, a deal had been agreed upon. For undertaking Noelle's defence Napoleon Chotas would be given double his usual fee, and his firm would become the major legal counsel to Constantin Demiris' far-flung empire, a plum worth untold millions.

'I don't care how you do it,' Demiris had concluded, fiercely. 'Just see to it that nothing goes wrong.'

Chotas had accepted the bargain. And then, ironically, he had fallen in love with Noelle Page. Chotas had remained a bachelor, though he kept a string of mistresses, and now when he had found the one woman he wanted to marry, she was out of his reach. He looked at Noelle now, sitting in the defendant's box, beautiful and serene. She wore a simple black wool suit with a plain, high-necked white blouse, and she looked like a Princess from a fairy tale.

Noelle turned and saw Chotas staring at her and gave him a warm smile. He smiled back, but his mind was already turning to the difficult task that lay ahead of him. The clerk was calling the Court to order.

The spectators rose as two judges in business suits entered and took their seats on the bench. The third judge, the President of the Court, followed and took the centre seat. He intoned, '*I synethriassis archetai.*'

The trial had begun.

Peter Demonides, Special Prosecutor for the State, nervously rose to make his opening address to the jury. Demonides was a skilled and able prosecutor, but he had been up against Napoleon Chotas before – many times, in fact – and the results were invariably the same. The old bastard was unbeatable. Almost all trial lawyers browbeat hostile witnesses, but Chotas coddled them. He nurtured them and loved them and before he was through, they were contradicting themselves all over the place, trying to be helpful to him. He had a knack of turning hard evidence into speculation and speculation into fantasy. Chotas had the most brilliant legal mind Demonides had ever encountered and the greatest knowledge of jurisprudence, but that was not his strength. His strength was his knowledge of people. A reporter had once asked Chotas how he had learned so much about human nature.

'I don't know a damned thing about human nature,' Chotas had answered. 'I only know about *people*,' and the remark had been widely quoted.

In addition to everything else this was the kind of trial that was tailor-made for Chotas to take before a jury, filled as it was with glamour, passion and murder. Of one thing Demonides was certain: Napoleon Chotas would let nothing stop him from winning this case. But neither would Demonides. He knew that he had a strong evidential case against the defendants, and while Chotas might be able to spellbind the jury into overlooking the evidence, he would not be able to sway the three judges on the bench. So it was with a feeling of determination mixed with apprehension that the Special Prosecutor for the State began his opening address.

In skilful, broad strokes Demonides outlined the State's case against the two defendants. By law the foreman of the ten-man jury was an attorney, so

Demonides directed his legal points to him and his general points to the rest of the jury.

'Before this trial has ended,' Demonides said, 'the State will prove that these two people conspired together to cold-bloodedly murder Catherine Douglas because she stood in the way of their plans. Her only crime was in loving her husband, and for this she was killed. The two defendants have been placed at the scene of the murder. They are the only ones who had the motive and the opportunity. We shall prove beyond a shadow of a doubt . . .'

Demonides kept his address short and to the point, and it was the turn of the Attorney for the Defence.

The spectators in the courtroom watched Napoleon Chotas as he clumsily gathered his papers together and prepared to make his opening speech. Slowly he approached the jury box, his manner hesitant and difficult as though awed by his surroundings.

Watching him William Fraser could not but marvel at his skill. If he had not once spent an evening with Chotas at a party in the British Embassy, Fraser too would have been deceived by the man's manner. He could see the jurors helpfully straining forwards to catch the words that fell softly from Napoleon Chotas' lips.

'This woman on trial,' Chotas was saying to the jurors, 'is not being tried for murder. There has been no murder. If there *had* been a murder, I am sure that my brilliant colleague for the State would have been good enough to have shown us the body of the victim. He has not done so, so we must assume that there is no body. And therefore no murder.' He stopped to scratch the crown of his head and looked down at the floor as though trying to remember where he had left off. He nodded to himself, then looked up at the jury. 'No, gentlemen, that is not what this trial is about. My client is being tried because she broke *another* law, an unwritten law that says you must not fornicate with another woman's husband. The press has already found her guilty of that charge, and the public has found her guilty, and now they are demanding that she be punished.'

Chotas stopped to pull out a large white handkerchief, stared at it a moment as if wondering how it had gotten there, blew his nose and replaced the handkerchief in his pocket. 'Very well. If she has broken a law, let us punish her. But not for murder, gentlemen. Not for a murder that was never committed. Noelle Page was guilty of being the mistress of –' he paused delicately '– a most important man. His name is a secret, but if you must know it, you can find it on the front page of any newspaper.'

There was appreciative laughter from the spectators.

Auguste Lanchon swung around in his seat and glared at the spectators, his little piggy eyes blazing with rage. How dare they laugh at his Noelle!

Demiris meant nothing to her, nothing. It was the man to whom a woman gave up her virginity that she always cherished. The fat little shopkeeper from Marseille had not been able to communicate with Noelle yet, but he had paid four hundred precious drachmas for a courtroom pass, and he would be able to watch his beloved Noelle every day. When she was acquitted, Lanchon would step forwards and take over her life. He turned his attention to the lawyer.

'It has been said by the prosecution that the two defendants, Miss Page and Mr Lawrence Douglas, murdered Mr Douglas' wife so that the defendants could marry each other. Look at them.'

Chotas turned to look at Noelle Page and Larry Douglas and every eye in the courtroom did the same.

'Are they in love with each other? Possibly. But does that make them plotters and schemers and murderers? No. If there are any victims in this trial, you are looking at them now. I have gone into all the evidence very carefully and I have convinced myself, as I will convince you, that these two people are innocent. Please let me make it clear to the jury that I am not representing Lawrence Douglas. He has his own counsel and a very able fellow he is. But it has been alleged by the state that the two people sitting there are fellow conspirators, that they have plotted and committed murder together. So if one is guilty, both are guilty. I tell you now that both are innocent. And nothing less than the corpus delicti will make me change my mind. And there is none.'

Chotas' voice was growing angrier. 'It is a fiction. My client has no more idea than you do whether Catherine Douglas is dead or alive? How would she know? She has never even met her, let alone harmed her. Imagine the enormity of being accused of killing someone you have never laid eyes on. There are many theories as to what could have happened to Mrs Douglas. That she was murdered is one of them. But *only* one. The most probable theory is that somehow she discovered that her husband and Miss Page were in love, and out of a feeling of hurt – not fear, gentlemen – *hurt*, she ran away. It is as simple as that, and for that you do not execute an innocent woman and an innocent man.'

Frederick Stavros, Larry Douglas' attorney, gave a surreptitious sigh of relief. His constant nightmare had been that Noelle Page would be acquitted, while his client would be convicted. If that happened he would become the laughing-stock of the legal profession. Stavros had been looking for a way to hitch onto Napoleon Chotas' star and now Chotas had done it for him. By linking the two defendants together as he had just done, Noelle's defence had become his own client's defence. Winning this trial was going to change Frederick Stavros' entire future, give him everything he had ever wanted. He was filled with a feeling of warm gratitude for the old master.

Stavros noted with satisfaction that the jury was hanging on Chotas' every word.

'This was not a woman who was interested in material things,' Chotas was saying with admiration. 'She was willing to give everything up without hesitation for the man she loved. Surely, my good friends, that is not the character of a scheming, conniving murderess.'

As Chotas went on, the emotions of the jurors shifted like a visible tide, reaching out towards Noelle Page with growing empathy and understanding. Slowly and skilfully the attorney built up a portrait of a beautiful woman who was the mistress of one of the most powerful and richest men in the world, who had every luxury and privilege lavished upon her, but who in the end had succumbed to her love for a penniless young pilot she had only known a short time.

Chotas played on the emotions of the jurors like a master musician, making them laugh, bringing tears to their eyes and always holding their rapt attention. When his opening address was over, Chotas clumsily shuffled back to the long table and awkwardly sat down, and it was all that the spectators could do to keep from applauding.

Larry Douglas sat in the witness box listening to Chotas' defence of him, and Larry was furious. He did not need anyone to defend him. He had done nothing wrong, this whole trial was a stupid mistake, and if there was any blame it was Noelle's. It had all been her idea. Larry looked at her now, beautiful and serene. But he felt no stirring of desire, only the memory of a passion, a faint emotional shadow, and he marvelled that he had put his life in jeopardy for this woman. Larry's eyes swung towards the press box. An attractive girl reporter in her twenties was staring at him. He gave her a little smile and watched her face light up.

Peter Demonides was examining a witness.

'Would you please tell the Court your name?'

'Alexis Minos.'

'And your occupation?'

'I am an attorney.'

'Would you look at the two defendants seated in the defendant's box, Mr Minos, and tell the Court if you have ever seen either of them before?'

'Yes, sir. One of them.'

'Which one?'

'The man.'

'Mr Lawrence Douglas?'

'That's correct.'

'Would you tell us, please, under what circumstances you saw Mr Douglas?'

'He came to my office six months ago.'

'Did he come to consult you in your professional capacity?'

'Yes.'

'In other words he required some legal service of you?'

'Yes.'

'And would you please tell us what it was that he wanted you to do for him?'

'He asked me to get him a divorce.'

'And did he retain you for this purpose?'

'No. When he explained the circumstances to me, I told him it would be impossible for him to get a divorce in Greece.'

'And what were the circumstances?'

'First of all he said there must not be any publicity, and secondly he said that his wife refused to give him a divorce.'

'In other words he had asked his wife for a divorce and she had refused?'

'That is what he told me.'

'And you explained to him that you couldn't help him? That unless his wife was willing to give him a divorce, it would be difficult or impossible for him to obtain one, and that there very well might be publicity?'

'That is correct.'

'So, short of taking desperate measures, there was nothing the defendant could –'

'Objection!'

'Sustained.'

'Your witness.'

Napoleon Chotas lifted himself out of his chair with a sigh and slowly walked over to the witness. Peter Demonides was not worried. Minos was a lawyer and too experienced to be deceived by Chotas' forensic bag of tricks.

'You're an attorney, Mr Minos.'

'I am.'

'And an excellent one, I'm sure. I'm surprised that our professional paths have not crossed sooner. The firm I'm with deals in many branches of law. Perhaps you've run across one of my partners in some corporate litigation?'

'No. I don't do corporate work.'

'I beg your pardon. Perhaps in some tax case, then?'

'I am not a tax lawyer.'

'Oh.' Chotas was beginning to look puzzled and ill-at-ease, as though he was making a fool of himself. 'Securities?'

'No.' Minos was beginning to enjoy the lawyer's humiliation. His face took on a smug look and Peter Demonides began to worry. How many times had he seen that look on the faces of witnesses that Napoleon Chotas was preparing for the slaughter?

Chotas was scratching his head in bafflement. 'I give up,' he said ingenuously. 'What kind of law do you specialize in?'

'Divorce cases.' The answer was a barbed shaft, perfectly delivered.

A rueful look appeared on Chotas' face and he shook his head. 'I should have known my good friend Mr Demonides would have an expert up here.'

'Thank you, sir.' Alexis Minos made no attempt to conceal his smugness now. Not every witness got a chance to score off Chotas and in Minos' mind he was already embellishing the story to tell at the club that evening.

'I've never even handled a divorce case,' Chotas was confiding in an embarrassed voice, 'so I'll have to defer to your expertise.'

The old lawyer was caving in completely. It would make an even better story than Minos had anticipated.

'I'll bet you keep very busy,' Chotas said.

'I have as many cases as I can handle.'

'As many as you can handle!' There was open admiration in Napoleon Chotas' voice.

'Sometimes more.'

Peter Demonides looked down at the floor, unable to watch what was happening.

Chotas' voice took on an awed tone. 'I don't want to pry into your personal business, Mr Minos, but as a matter of professional curiosity, how many clients would you say walk through your door in a year?'

'Well, that's pretty difficult to say.'

'Come on now, Mr Minos. Don't be modest. Make a guess.'

'Oh, I suppose two hundred. That's an approximation, you understand.'

'Two hundred divorces a year! The paper work alone must be staggering.'

'Well, there aren't actually two hundred divorces.'

Chotas rubbed his chin, perplexed. 'What?'

'They're not *all* divorces.'

A puzzled look came over Chotas' face. 'Didn't you say that you only handled divorce cases?'

'Yes, but –' Minos' voice wavered.

'But what?' Chotas asked in bewilderment.

'Well, what I mean is, they don't all get divorced.'

'But isn't that why they come to see you?'

'Yes, but some of them – well – change their minds for one reason or another.'

Chotas nodded in sudden understanding. 'Ah! You mean there's a reconciliation or something of the sort?'

'Exactly,' Minos said.

'So that what you're saying is that – what? – ten percent don't bother to go through with the divorce action?'

Minos shifted in his chair uneasily. 'The percentage is a bit higher.'

'How much higher? Fifteen percent? Twenty?'

'Closer to forty.'

Napoleon Chotas stared at him in amazement. 'Mr Minos, are you telling us that almost half the people who come to see you decide not to get a divorce?'

'Yes.'

Tiny beads of sweat were popping out on Minos' forehead. He turned to look at Peter Demonides, but Demonides was studiously concentrating on a crack in the floor.

'Well I'm sure it's not a lack of confidence in your ability,' said Chotas.

'Certainly not,' Minos said defensively. 'They very often come to me on a stupid impulse. A husband or wife will have a fight and feel they hate each other and think they want a divorce, but when you come right down to it, in most cases they change their minds.'

He stopped abruptly as he realized the full import of his words.

'Thank you,' Chotas said gently. 'You've been most helpful.'

Peter Demonides was examining the witness.

'Your name, please?'

'Kasta. Irene Kasta.'

'Miss or Mrs?'

'Mrs. I'm a widow.'

'What is your occupation, Mrs Kasta?'

'I'm a housekeeper.'

'Where do you work?'

'For a rich family in Rafina.'

'That's a village near the sea, is it not? A hundred kilometres north of Athens?'

'Yes.'

'Would you please take a look at the two defendants seated at the table? Have you ever seen them before?'

'Sure. Lots of times.'

'Would you tell us under what circumstances?'

'They live in the house next to the villa where I work. I seen them on the beach a lot. They was naked.'

There was a gasp from the spectators and then a quick buzz of conversation. Peter Demonides glanced over at Chotas to see if he was going to object, but the old lawyer sat at the table, a dreamy smile on his face. The smile made Demonides more nervous than ever. He turned back to the witness.

'You are certain that these are the two people you saw? You are under oath, you know.'

'Them's the two, all right.'

'When they were together on the beach, did they seem friendly?'

'Well, they didn't act like brother and sister.'

A laugh from the spectators.

'Thank you, Mrs Kasta.' Demonides turned to Chotas. 'Your witness.'

Napoleon Chotas nodded amiably and rose and ambled over to the formidable-looking woman in the witness box.

'How long have you worked at this villa, Mrs Kasta?'

'Seven years.'

'Seven years! You must be very good at your job.'

'You bet I am.'

'Perhaps you could recommend a good housekeeper for me. I've been thinking about buying a place on the beach at Rafina. My problem is, I need privacy so I can work. As I remember those villas, they're all bunched together.'

'Oh, no, sir. Each villa is separated by a big wall.'

'Oh, good. And they're not crowded next to one another?'

'No, sir, not at all. Those villas are at least a

hundred yards away from each other. I know one that's up for sale. You'd have all the privacy you need and I can recommend my sister to do the housekeeping for you. She's good and she's tidy and she cooks a bit.'

'Well, thank you, Mrs Kasta, that sounds wonderful. Perhaps I could call her this afternoon.'

'She does a bit of day work. She'll be home at six.'

'What time is it now?'

'I don't carry a watch.'

'Ah. There's a large clock on the wall over there. What does it say?'

'Well, it's hard to make out. It's clear across the room.'

'How far away would you say that clock was?'

'About – er – fifty feet.'

'Twenty-three feet, Mrs Kasta. No more questions.'

It was the fifth day of the trial. Doctor Israel Katz's missing leg was paining him again. While he was performing an operation, he could stand on his artificial leg for hours on end, and it never bothered him. But sitting here without the intense concentration to divert his attention, the nerve ends kept sending memory messages to a limb that was no longer there. Katz shifted restlessly in his seat, trying to ease the pressure on his hip. He had tried to see Noelle every day since he had arrived in Athens but with no success. He had spoken to

Napoleon Chotas, and the lawyer had explained that Noelle was too upset to see old friends and that it would be best to wait until the trial was over. Israel Katz had asked him to tell Noelle that he was here to help her in every way he could, but he could not be certain that she ever received the message. He had sat in court day after day, hoping Noelle would look his way, but she never even glanced at the spectators.

Israel Katz owed his life to her, and he felt frustrated because there was no way he could help repay that debt. He had no idea how the trial was going or whether Noelle would be convicted or acquitted. He had learned from Chotas that by law there were only two possible verdicts: Innocent or Guilty. If Noelle was found innocent, she would be freed. If she was found guilty, she would be executed.

A witness for the prosecution was being sworn in.

'Your name?'

'Christian Barbet.'

'You are a French national, Mr Barbet?'

'Yes.'

'And where is your residence?'

'In Paris.'

'Would you tell the Court your occupation?'

'I am the owner of a private detective agency.'

'And where is that agency located?'

'The main office is in Paris.'

'What kind of cases do you handle?'

'Many kinds . . . commercial pilfering, missing

persons, surveillance for jealous husbands or wives. . . .'

'Monsieur Barbet, would you be good enough to look around this courtroom and tell us whether anyone in this room has ever been a client of yours?'

A long, slow look around the room. 'Yes, sir.'

'Would you tell the Court who this person is, please?'

'The lady sitting over there. Miss Noelle Page.'

A murmur of interest from the spectators.

'Are you telling us that Miss Page hired you to do some detective work for her?'

'I am, monsieur.'

'And would you tell us exactly what that work consisted of?'

'Yes, sir. She was interested in a man named Larry Douglas. She wanted me to find out everything I could about him.'

'That is the same Larry Douglas who is on trial in this courtroom?'

'Yes, sir.'

'And Miss Page paid you for this?'

'Yes, sir.'

'Would you please look at these exhibits in my hand. Are these the records of the payments that were made to you?'

'That is correct.'

'Tell us, Monsieur Barbet, how did you go about obtaining this information on Mr Douglas?'

'It was very difficult, monsieur. You see I was

in France, and Mr Douglas was in England and later the United States, and with France occupied by the Germans –'

'I beg your pardon?'

'I said, with France occupied –'

'Just a moment. I want to be sure that I understand what you are saying, Monsieur Barbet. We have been told by Miss Page's attorney that she and Larry Douglas met a few short months ago and fell madly in love. Now you are telling this Court that their love affair started – how long ago?'

'At least six years ago.'

Pandemonium.

Demonides flashed Chotas a triumphant look. 'Your witness.'

Napoleon Chotas rubbed his eyes, rose from the long table at which he was sitting and walked over to the witness box.

'I won't detain you long, Mr Barbet. I know you must be anxious to get back to your family in France.'

'You may take your time, monsieur.' Smugly.

'Thank you. Forgive me for being personal, but that's certainly a fine-looking suit you're wearing, Mr Barbet.'

'Thank you, monsieur.'

'Made in Paris, was it?'

'Yes, sir.'

'It fits beautifully. I don't seem to have any luck with my suits. Have you ever tried the English tailors? They're supposed to be excellent, also.'

'No, monsieur.'

'I'm sure you've been to England many times?'

'Well – no.'

'Never?'

'No, sir.'

'Have you been to the United States of America?'

'No.'

'Never?'

'No, sir.'

'Have you ever visited the South Pacific?'

'No, sir.'

'Then you must truly be a fantastic detective, Mr Barbet. My hat is off to you. These reports of yours cover the activities of Larry Douglas in England and the United States and the South Pacific – and yet you tell us that you have never even been to any of these places. I can only assume that you are psychic.'

'Permit me to correct you, monsieur. It was not necessary for me to have been in any of those places. I employ what we call correspondent agencies in England and in America.'

'Ah, forgive my stupidity. Of course! So it was actually *those* people who covered the activities of Mr Douglas?'

'Exactement.'

'And so the fact is that you yourself have no personal knowledge of Larry Douglas' movements.'

'Well . . . no, sir.'

'So in reality all your information is second-hand.'

'I suppose . . . in a sense, yes.'

Chotas turned to the judges. 'I move to strike the entire testimony of this witness, Your Honours, on the grounds that it is hearsay.'

Peter Demonides leaped to his feet. 'Objection, Your Honours! Noelle Page hired Mr Barbet to get information on Larry Douglas. That is not hearsay –'

'My learned colleague has submitted the records as evidence,' Chotas said gently. 'I am perfectly willing to accept it – if he wishes to bring the men here who actually conducted the surveillance of Mr Douglas. Otherwise I must ask the Court to assume that there was no such surveillance and ask that the testimony of this witness be held inadmissible.'

The President of the Court turned to Demonides. 'Are you prepared to bring your witnesses here?' he asked.

'That's impossible,' Peter Demoinides spluttered. 'Mr Chotas knows that it would take weeks to locate them!'

The President turned to Chotas. 'Motion granted.'

Peter Demonides was examining.

'Would you state your name, please?'

'George Mousson.'

'What is your occupation?'

'I am a reception clerk at the Palace Hotel at Ioannina.'

'Would you please take a look at the two

defendants sitting at the table. Have you ever seen them before?'

'The man. He was a guest at the hotel last August.'

'That would be Mr Lawrence Douglas?'

'Yes, sir.'

'Was he alone when he checked into the hotel?'

'No, sir.'

'Would you tell us who he was with?'

'His wife.'

'Catherine Douglas?'

'Yes, sir.'

'They registered as Mr and Mrs Douglas?'

'Yes, sir.'

'Did you and Mr Douglas ever discuss the Caves of Perama?'

'Yes, sir, we did.'

'Did you bring up the subject or did Mr Douglas?'

'As I recall, he did. He asked me about them and said his wife was anxious for him to take her there. That she loved caves. I thought that was unusual.'

'Oh? Why was that?'

'Well, women aren't interested in exploring and things like that.'

'You didn't happen to discuss the caves with Mrs Douglas at any time, did you?'

'No, sir. Only with Mr Douglas.'

'And what did you tell him?'

'Well, I remember telling him that the caves could be dangerous.'

'Was anything said about a guide?'

The clerk nodded. 'Yes, I'm sure I suggested that he use a guide. I recommend one to all our guests.'

'No more questions. Your witness, Mr Chotas.'

'How long have you been in the hotel business, Mr Mousson?'

'Over twenty years.'

'And before that you were a psychiatrist?'

'Me? No, sir.'

'A psychologist perhaps?'

'No, sir.'

'Oh. Then you're *not* an expert on the behaviour of women?'

'Well, I may not be a psychiatrist, but in the hotel business you learn a lot about women.'

'Do you know who Osa Johnson is?'

'Osa –? No.'

'She's a world famous explorer. Have you ever heard of Amelia Earhart?'

'No, sir.'

'Margaret Mead?'

'No, sir.'

'Are you married, Mr Mousson?'

'Not now. But I've been married three times, so I *am* something of an expert on women.'

'On the contrary, Mr Mousson. I suggest that if you were really an expert on women, you would have been able to handle *one* marriage. No further questions.'

* * *

'Your name, please?'

'Christopher Cocyannis.'

'Would you tell us your occupation?'

'I am a guide at the Caves of Perama.'

'How long have you been a guide there?'

'Ten years.'

'Is business good?'

'Very good. Thousands of tourists come to see the caves every year.'

'Would you please look at the man sitting over in that box. Have you ever seen Mr Douglas before?'

'Yes, sir. He came to the caves in August.'

'Are you sure?'

'Positive.'

'Well now, I'm sure that puzzles all of us, Mr Cocyannis. Out of all the thousands of people who come to the caves, you can remember one individual?'

'I'm not likely to forget him.'

'Why is that, Mr Cocyannis?'

'First of all he wouldn't take a guide.'

'Do all of your visitors take guides?'

'The Germans and the French are too stingy, but all the Americans do.'

Laughter.

'I see. Was there any other reason you remembered Mr Douglas?'

'You bet there was. I wouldn't have noticed him especially except for the guide thing, and the woman with him seemed kind of embarrassed when he said no. Then about an hour later, I saw him hurry out of the entrance, and he was alone and he seemed awfully upset, and I thought maybe the woman had had an accident or something. I went up to him and asked if the lady was all right, and he stared at me kind of funny and said, "What lady?" and I said, "The lady you took in the caves with you." And he turned kind of white and I thought he was going to hit me. Then he started yelling. "I've lost her. I need help," and he began carrying on like a crazy man.'

'But he didn't call for help until you asked where the missing woman was?'

'That's right.'

'What happened next?'

'Well, I organized the other guides and we began a search. Some damned fool had moved the Danger sign from the new section. That's not open to the public. That's where we finally found her about three hours later. She was in pretty bad shape.'

'One last question. And answer this very carefully. When Mr Douglas first came out of the cave, was he looking around for someone to help him, or did you get the impression that he was leaving?'

'He was leaving.'

'Your witness.'

Napoleon Chotas' voice was very gentle.

'Mr Cocyannis, are you a psychiatrist?'

'No, sir. I'm a guide.'

'And you're not psychic?'

'No, sir.'

'I ask this because over the past week, we've had hotel clerks who are experts on human psychology, eyewitnesses who are nearsighted, and now you tell us that you can look at a man who attracted your attention because he seemed agitated, and you can read his mind. How did you *know* he wasn't looking for help when you went up and spoke to him?'

'He didn't look like it.'

'And you can remember his behaviour that well?'

'That's right.'

'You obviously have a remarkable memory. I want you to look around the courtroom. Have you ever seen anyone in this room before today?'

'The defendant.'

'Yes. Aside from him? Take your time.'

'No.'

'If you had, you would have remembered?'

'Absolutely.'

'Have you ever seen me before today?'

'No, sir.'

'Would you look at this piece of paper, please. Can you tell me what it is?'

'It's a ticket.'

'To what?'

'The Caves of Perama.'

'And the date on it?'

'Monday. Three weeks ago.'

'Yes. That ticket was purchased and used by me,

Mr Cocyannis. There were five others in my party. You were our guide. No further questions.'

'What is your occupation?'

'I'm a bellboy at the Palace Hotel in Ioannina.'

'Would you please look at the defendant seated in the defendant's box. Have you ever seen her before?'

'Yes, sir. In movies.'

'Did you ever see her in person before today?'

'Yes, sir. She came into the hotel and asked me what room Mr Douglas was staying in. I told her she'd have to inquire at the desk and she said she preferred not to bother them, so I gave her the number of his bungalow.'

'And this was when?'

'The first day of August. The day of the *meltemi*.'

'And are you sure that this is the same woman?'

'How could I forget her? She tipped me two hundred drachmas.'

The trial was going into its fourth week. Everyone agreed that Napoleon Chotas was conducting the best defence they had ever witnessed. But in spite of this the web of guilt was being woven tighter and tighter.

Peter Demonides was building up a picture of two lovers, desperate to be together, to be married, with only Catherine Douglas standing in their way. Slowly day by day, Demonides elaborated on the plot to murder her.

Larry Douglas' attorney, Frederick Stavros, had gladly abdicated his position and relied on Napoleon Chotas. But now even Stavros began to feel that it would take a miracle to get an acquittal. Stavros stared at the empty chair in the packed courtroom and wondered if Constantin Demiris was really going to make an appearance. If Noelle Page was convicted, the Greek tycoon would probably not come, for it would mean that he had been defeated. On the other hand, if the tycoon knew there would be an acquittal, he would probably show up. The empty chair was becoming a symbol of which way the trial would go.

The seat remained empty.

It was on a Friday afternoon that the case finally exploded.

'Would you state your name, please?'

'Doctor Kazomides. John Kazomides.'

'Did you ever meet Mr or Mrs Douglas, Doctor?'

'Yes, sir. Both of them.'

'What was the occasion?'

'I got a call to come to the Caves of Perama. A woman had been lost in there, and when the search party finally found her, she was in a state of shock.'

'Had she been hurt physically?'

'Yes. There were multiple contusions. Her hands and arms and cheeks had been badly scraped on the rocks. She had fallen down and hit her head, and I diagnosed a probable concussion. I immediately gave her a shot of morphine for the pain and ordered them to take her to the local hospital.'

'And is that where she went?'

'No, sir.'

'Would you tell the jury why not?'

'At her husband's insistence she was taken back to their bungalow at the Palace Hotel.'

'Did that strike you as peculiar, Doctor?'

'He said he wanted to look after her himself.'

'So Mrs Douglas was taken back to her hotel. Did you accompany her there?'

'Yes. I insisted on going back to her bungalow with her. I wanted to be at her bedside when she awakened.'

'And were you there when she awakened?'

'Yes, sir.'

'Did Mrs Douglas say anything to you?'

'She did.'

'Would you tell the Court what she said.'

'She told me that her husband had tried to murder her.'

It was a full five minutes before they could quiet the uproar in the courtroom, and it was not until the President threatened to clear the room that the hubbub finally subsided. Napoleon Chotas had walked over to the defendant's box and was holding a hurried conference with Noelle Page. For the first time she seemed upset. Demonides was going on with the questioning.

'Doctor, you said in your testimony that Mrs Douglas was in shock. In your professional opinion was she lucid when she told you that her husband tried to murder her?'

'Yes, sir. I had already given her one sedative at the caves, and she was relatively calm. However when I told her I was going to give her another sedative, she became extremely agitated and begged me not to.'

The President of the Court leaned down and asked, 'Did she explain why?'

'Yes, Your Honour. She said that her husband would kill her while she was asleep.'

The President leaned back in his chair thoughtfully and said to Peter Demonides, 'You may continue.'

'Dr Kazomides, did you in fact administer a second sedative to Mrs Douglas?'

'Yes.'

'While she was in her bed at the bungalow?'

'Yes.'

'How did you administer it?'

'By hypodermic. In the hip.'

'And she was asleep when you left?'

'Yes.'

'Was there any chance Mrs Douglas could have awakened any time in the next few hours, gotten out of bed without assistance, dressed herself and walked out of that house unaided?'

'In her condition? No. It would be most unlikely. She was very heavily sedated.'

'That is all, thank you, Doctor.'

The jurors were staring at Noelle Page and Larry

Douglas and their faces had turned cold and unfriendly. A stranger could have walked into the courtroom and known instantly how the case was going.

Bill Fraser's eyes were bright with satisfaction. After Dr Kazomides' testimony there could no longer be the slightest doubt that Catherine had been murdered by Larry Douglas and Noelle Page. There was nothing Napoleon Chotas would be able to do to eradicate from the minds of the jurors the image of a terrified woman, drugged and defenceless, begging not to be left in the hands of her murderer.

Frederick Stavros was in a panic. He had gladly let Napoleon Chotas run the show, following his lead in blind faith, confident that Chotas would be able to secure an acquittal for his client and therefore for Stavros' client. Now he felt betrayed. Everything was falling apart. The doctor's testimony had been irreparably damaging, both for its evidential and its emotional impact. Stavros looked around the room. Except for the one mysteriously reserved seat the room was filled. The world press was here, waiting to report what happened next.

Stavros had a momentary vision of himself leaping to his feet, confronting the doctor and brilliantly tearing his testimony to shreds. His client would be acquitted and he, Stavros, would be a hero. He knew this would be his last chance. The outcome of this case would mean the difference between fame and obscurity. Stavros could actually feel his thigh muscles bunching up, urging him to get to his feet. But he could not move. He sat there, paralysed by the overpowering spectre of failure. He turned to look at Chotas. The deep, sad eyes in the bloodhound face were studying the doctor on the witness stand, as though trying to come to some decision.

Slowly Napoleon Chotas rose to his feet. But instead of walking over to the witness, he moved towards the bench and quietly addressed the judges.

'Mr President, Your Honours, I do not wish to cross-examine the witness. With the Court's permission, I would like to ask for a recess in order to confer *in camera* with the Court and the Prosecuting Attorney.'

The President of the Court turned to the Prosecutor. 'Mr Demonides?'

'No objection,' Demonides said, his voice wary.

The Court was recessed. Not one person moved from his chair.

Thirty minutes later Napoleon Chotas returned to the courtroom alone. The instant he walked through the chamber door, everyone in the courtroom sensed that something important had taken place. There was an air of secret self-satisfaction in the lawyer's face, his walk was faster and springier, as though some charade had ended and it was no longer necessary to play games. Chotas walked over to the defendant's box and stared down at Noelle. She looked up into his face, her violet eyes probing, anxious. And suddenly a smile touched the lawyer's lips, and from the light in his eyes Noelle knew that somehow he had done it, he had performed the miracle in spite of all the evidence, in spite of all the odds. Justice had triumphed, but it was the Justice of Constantin Demiris. Larry Douglas was staring at Chotas, too, filled with fear and with hope. Whatever Chotas had done would have been for Noelle. But what about him?

Chotas addressed Noelle in a carefully neutral voice. 'The President of the Court has given me permission to speak with you in his chambers.' He turned to Frederick Stavros, who was sitting in an agony of uncertainty, not knowing what was going on. 'You and your client have permission to join us if you wish.'

Stavros nodded. 'Of course.' He scrambled to his feet, almost knocking over his chair in his eagerness.

Two bailiffs accompanied them to the empty chambers of the President. When the bailiffs had left and they were alone, Chotas turned to Frederick Stavros. 'What I am about to say,' he said quietly, 'is for the benefit of my client. However, because they are co-defendants, I have been able to arrange for your client to be accorded the same privilege as mine.'

'Tell me!' Noelle demanded.

Chotas turned to her. He spoke slowly, choosing his words with great care. 'I have just had a conference with the judges,' he said. 'They were impressed with the case the prosecution has made against you. However –' he paused, delicately, 'I was able to – er – persuade them that the interests of justice would not be served by punishing you.'

'What's going to happen?' Stavros demanded in a fever of impatience.

There was a note of deep satisfaction in Chotas' voice as he continued, 'If the defendants are willing to change their pleas to guilty, the judges have agreed to give each of them a five-year sentence.' He smiled and added, 'Four years of which will be suspended. In reality they will not have to serve more than six months.' He turned to Larry. 'Because you are an American, Mr Douglas, you will be deported. You will never be permitted to return to Greece.'

Larry nodded, his body flooding with relief.

Chotas turned back to Noelle. 'This was not an easy thing to accomplish. I must tell you in all honesty that the primary reason for the leniency of the Court is the interest of your – er – patron. They feel he has already suffered unduly because of all this publicity, and they are anxious to see it ended.'

'I understand,' Noelle said.

Napoleon Chotas hesitated in embarrassment. 'There is one more condition.'

She looked at him. 'Yes?'

'Your passport will be taken away. You will never be permitted to leave Greece. You will remain here under the protection of your friend.'

So it had been done.

Constantin Demiris had kept his bargain. Noelle did not for a moment believe that the judges were being lenient because they were concerned about Demiris' being subjected to unpleasant publicity. No, he had had to pay a price for her freedom, and Noelle knew that it must have been a heavy one. But in return Demiris was getting her back and arranging it so that she could never leave him. Or see Larry again. She turned to Larry and read the relief in his face. He was going to be set free, and that was all he cared about. There was no regret about losing her and about what had happened. But Noelle understood it because she understood Larry, for he was her alter ego, her *Doppelgänger*, and they both had the same reckless zest for life, the same insatiable appetites. They were kindred spirits beyond mortality, beyond laws they had never made and never lived by. In her way Noelle would miss Larry very much, and when he left, a part of her would go with him. But she knew now how precious her life was to her and how terrified she had been of losing it. And so on balance it was a very good bargain, and she accepted it gratefully. She turned to Chotas and said, 'That is satisfactory.'

Chotas looked at her, and there was a sadness in his eyes as well as the satisfaction. Noelle understood that, too. He was in love with her and had had to use all his skill to save her for another man. Noelle had deliberately encouraged Chotas to fall in love with her because she needed him, needed to make sure that he would stop at nothing to save her. And everything had worked out.

'I think it's absolutely marvellous,' Frederick Stavros was babbling. 'Absolutely marvellous.'

In truth Stavros felt that it was a miracle, nearly as good as an acquittal, and while it was true that Napoleon Chotas would reap most of the benefit from it, the peripheral fallout would still be tremendous. From this moment on Stavros would have his choice of clients, and each time he told the story of the trial, his role in it would get bigger and bigger.

'It sounds like a good deal,' Larry was saying. 'The only thing is, we're not guilty. We didn't kill Catherine.'

Frederick Stavros turned on him in a fury. 'Who gives a damn whether you're guilty or not?' he shouted. 'We're making you a present of your life.' He shot a quick glance at Chotas to see if he had reacted to the 'we' but the lawyer was listening, his attitude one of aloof neutrality.

'I want you to understand,' Chotas said to Stavros, 'that I am only advising *my* client. Your client is free to make his own decision.'

'What would have happened to us without this deal?' Larry asked.

'The jury would have –' Frederick Stavros began.

'I want to hear it from *him*,' Larry interrupted, curtly. He turned to Chotas.

'In a trial, Mr Douglas,' Chotas replied, 'the most important factor is not innocence or guilt, but the *impression* of innocence or guilt. There is no absolute truth, there is only the interpretation of truth. In this case it does not matter whether you are innocent of murder, the jury has the *impression* of guilt. That is what you would have been convicted for, and in the end you would have been just as dead.'

Larry looked at him for a long moment, then nodded. 'OK,' he said. 'Let's get it over with.'

Fifteen minutes later the two defendants stood before the judges' bench. The President of the Court was seated in the centre, flanked by the two justices. Napoleon Chotas stood next to Noelle Page and Frederick Stavros stood at the side of Larry Douglas. The courtroom was charged with an electric tension, for word had flashed about the room that a dramatic development was about to take place. But when it came. it caught everyone completely off guard. In a formal, pedantic voice, as though he had not just made a secret bargain with the three jurists on the bench, Napoleon Chotas said, 'Mr President, Your Honours, my client wishes to change her plea from *not guilty* to *guilty*.'

The President of the Court leaned back in his chair and stared at Chotas in surprise, as though he were hearing the news for the first time.

He's playing it to the hilt, Noelle thought. *He wants to earn his money, or whatever it is Demiris is paying him off with.*

The President leaned forwards and consulted with the other justices in a flurry of whispers. They nodded and the President looked down at Noelle and said, 'Do you wish to change your plea to guilty?'

Noelle nodded and said firmly, 'I do.'

Frederick Stavros spoke up quickly, as though afraid of being left out of the procedure. 'Your Honours, my client wishes to change his plea from not guilty to guilty.'

The President turned to regard Larry. 'Do you wish to change your plea to guilty?'

Larry glanced at Chotas and then nodded. 'Yes.'

The President studied the two prisoners, his face grave. 'Have your attorneys advised you that under Greek law the penalty for the crime of premeditated murder is execution?'

'Yes, Your Honour.' Noelle's voice was strong and clear.

The President turned to look at Larry.

'Yes, sir,' he said.

There was another whispered consultation among the judges. The President of the Court turned to Demonides. 'Does the Prosecutor for the State have any objections to the change of plea?'

Demonides looked at Chotas a long moment, then said, 'None.'

Noelle wondered if he were in on the payoff also, or whether he was simply being used as a pawn.

'Very well,' the President said. 'This Court has no choice but to accept the change of plea.' He turned to the jury. 'Gentlemen, in view of this new development, you are herewith released from your duties as jurymen. In affect the trial has come to an end. The Court will pass sentence. Thank you for your services and for your cooperation. The Court will recess for two hours.'

In the next moment the reporters began to tumble out of the room, racing to their telephones and teletype machines to report the latest sensational development in the murder trial of Noelle Page and Larry Douglas.

Two hours later the courtroom was packed to overflowing as the Court was reconvened. Noelle glanced around the courtroom at the faces of the spectators. They were watching her with expressions of eager expectation, and it was all Noelle could do to keep from laughing aloud at their naïveté. These were the common people, the masses, and they really believed that justice was meted out fairly, that under a democracy all men were created equal, that a poor man had the same rights and privileges as a rich man.

'Will the defendants now rise and approach the bench?'

Gracefully Noelle rose to her feet and moved towards the bench, Chotas at her side. Out of the corner of her eye she saw Larry and Stavros stepping forwards.

The President of the Court spoke. 'This has been a long and difficult trial,' he began. 'In capital cases where there is a reasonable doubt of guilt, the Court is always inclined to let the accused have the benefit of the doubt. I must admit that in this case we felt that there existed such a doubt. The fact that the State was unable to produce a *corpus delicti* was a very strong point in favour of the defendants.' He turned to look at Napoleon Chotas. 'I am sure that the able counsel for the defence is well aware that the Greek Courts have never given the death penalty in a case where a murder has not been definitely proven to have been committed.'

A faint sense of unease was beginning to brush Noelle, nothing alarming yet, just the merest whisper, the slightest hint. The President was going on.

'My colleagues and I were, for that reason, frankly surprised when the defendants decided to change their pleas to guilty, in mid-trial.'

The feeling was in the pit of Noelle's stomach now, growing, moving upward, beginning to constrict her throat, so that she was suddenly finding it difficult to breathe. Larry was staring at the judge, not fully comprehending yet what was happening.

'We appreciate the agonizing soul-searching that must have taken place before the defendants decided to confess their guilt before this Court and before the world. However, the easing of their consciences cannot be accepted as atonement for the terrible crime they have admitted committing, the cold-blooded murder of a helpless, defenceless woman.'

It was at that moment that Noelle knew, with a sudden, mind-smashing certainty that she had been tricked. Demiris had set up a charade to lull her into a feeling of false security so that he could do this to her. This was his game, this was the trap he had baited. He *had* known how terrified she was of dying, so he had held out the hope of life to her and she had accepted it, had believed him, and he had outwitted her. Demiris had wanted his vengeance *now*, not later. Her life could have been saved. Of course Chotas had known that she would not get the death penalty unless a corpse was produced. He had made no deal with the judges. Chotas had rigged this whole defence to lure Noelle to her death. She turned to look at him. He looked up to meet her gaze, and his eyes were filled with a genuine sadness. He loved her and he had murdered her, and if he had it to do over again, he would do the same thing, for in the end he was Demiris' man, just as she was Demiris' woman, and neither of them could fight his power.

The President was speaking. '. . . and so under the powers invested in me by the State, and in accord with its laws, I pronounce that the sentence on the two defendants, Noelle Page and Lawrence Douglas shall be execution by a firing squad. . . . the sentence to be carried out within ninety days from this date.'

The Court was in pandemonium, but Noelle neither heard nor saw it. Something had made her turn around. The vacant seat was no longer empty. Constantin Demiris sat in it. He was freshly shaved and barbered. He was dressed in a blue raw-silk suit, flawlessly tailored, a light blue shirt, and a foulard tie. His olive black eyes were bright and alive. There was no sign of the defeated, crumbling man who had come to visit her in prison, because that man had never existed.

Constantin Demiris had come to watch Noelle in the moment of her defeat, savouring the terror in her. His black eyes were locked on hers and for one split instant she saw in them a deep, malevolent satisfaction. And there was something else. Regret, perhaps, but it was gone before she could capture it, and it was all too late now anyway.

The chess game was finally over.

Larry had listened to the President's last words in shocked disbelief, and when a bailiff stepped forward and took him by the arm, Larry shook loose and turned back to the bench.

'Wait a minute!' he yelled. 'I didn't kill her! They framed me!'

Another bailiff hurried forwards and the two men held Larry. One of them pulled out a pair of handcuffs.

'No!' Larry was screaming. 'Listen to me! I didn't kill her!'

He tried to jerk away from the bailiffs, but the

handcuffs snapped on his wrists and he was yanked away, out of the room.

Noelle felt a pressure on her arm. A matron was waiting there to escort her out of the courtroom.

'They're waiting for you, Miss Page.'

It was like a theatre call. *They're waiting for you, Miss Page*. Only this time when the curtain went down, it would never rise again. The realization hit Noelle that this was the last time in her life that she would ever be in public, the last time that she would be around other people, uncaged. This was her farewell appearance, this dirty, dreary Greek courtroom, her final theatre. *Well*, she thought defiantly, *at least I have a good house*. She looked around the packed courtroom for the last time. She saw Armand Gautier staring at her in stunned silence, shaken for once out of his cynicism.

There was Philippe Sorel, his rugged face trying hard for an encouraging smile and not quite managing it.

Across the room was Israel Katz, his eyes closed and his lips moving as though in silent prayer. Noelle remembered the night she had smuggled him into the trunk of the General's car, under the nose of the albino Gestapo officer, and the fear that had been in her then. But it was nothing to the terror that was possessing her now.

Noelle's eyes moved across the room and rested on the face of Auguste Lanchon, the shopkeeper.

She could not recall his name, but she remembered his porcine face and his gross squat body and the dreary hotel room in Vienne. When he saw her looking at him, he blinked and lowered his eyes.

A tall, attractive, grey-haired American-looking man was standing up staring at her as though wanting to tell her something. Noelle had no idea who he was.

The matron was tugging at her arm now, saying, 'Come along, Miss Page. . . .'

Frederick Stavros was in a state of shock. He had not only been a witness to a cold-blooded frame-up; he had been a party to it. He could go to the President of the Court and tell him what had happened: what Chotas had promised. But would they believe him? Would they take his word against the word of Napoleon Chotas? It really didn't matter, Stavros thought bitterly. After this he would be finished as a lawyer. No one would ever hire him again. Someone spoke his name and he turned and Chotas was standing there saying, 'If you're free tomorrow, why don't you come and have lunch with me, Frederick? I'd like you to meet my partners. I think you have a very promising future.'

Over Chotas' shoulder, Frederick Stavros could see the President of the Court exiting through the door that led to his private chambers. Now would be the time to talk to him, to explain what had happened. Stavros turned back to Napoleon Chotas, his mind still filled with the horror of what this man had done, and he heard himself saying, 'That's very kind of you, sir. What would be a convenient time . . . ?'

By Greek law executions take place on the little island of Ageana, an hour out of the port of Piraeus. A special government boat transports condemned prisoners to the island. A series of small grey cliffs leads to the harbour itself and high on a hill is a lighthouse built on an outcropping of rock. The prison on Ageana is on the north side of the island, out of sight of the little harbour where excursion boats regularly disgorge excited tourists for an hour or two of shopping and sightseeing before sailing on to the next island. The prison is not on the sightseeing schedule, and no one approaches it except on official business.

It was 4:00 A.M. on a Saturday morning. Noelle's execution was scheduled to take place at 6:00 A.M.

They had brought Noelle her favourite dress to wear, a wine-red, brushed-wool Dior, and matching red suede shoes. She had all new silk handstitched lingerie and a white jabot of Venetian lace for her throat. Constantin Demiris had sent Noelle's regular hairdresser to do her hair. It was as though Noelle were preparing to go to a party.

Intellectually Noelle knew that there would be no last-minute reprieve, that in a little while her body was going to be brutally violated and her blood spilled upon the ground. And yet emotionally she could not keep from hoping that Constantin Demiris would make a miracle and spare her life. It would not even have to be a miracle – it only needed a phone call, a word, a wave of his golden hand. If he spared her now, she would make it up to him. She would do anything. If she could only see him, she would tell him she would never look at another man, that she would devote herself to making him happy for the rest of his life. But she knew that it would do no good to beg. If Demiris came to her, yes. If she had to go to him, no.

There were still two hours.

Larry Douglas was in another part of the prison. Since his conviction, his mail had increased tenfold. Letters poured in from women in all parts of the world, and the warden, who considered himself a sophisticated man, was shocked by some of them.

Larry Douglas would probably have enjoyed them if he had known of them. But he was in a drugged world of half-twilight where nothing touched him. During his first few days on the island, he had been in a state of violence, screaming day and night that he was innocent and demanding a new trial. The prison doctor had finally ordered that he be kept on tranquillizers.

At ten minutes before five A.M., when the prison warden and four guards came to Larry Douglas' cell, he was seated on his bunk, quiet and withdrawn. The warden had to speak his name twice before Larry was aware that they had come for him. He rose to his feet, his movements dreamlike and lethargic.

The warden led him out to the corridor, and they walked in a slow procession towards a guarded door at the far end of the corridor. As they reached the door, the guard opened it and they were outside in a walled courtyard. The predawn air was chilly and Larry shivered as he stepped through the door. There was a full moon in the sky and bright stars. It reminded him of the mornings in the South Pacific islands when the pilots left their warm bunks and gathered under the chilly stars for a last minute briefing before takeoff. He could hear the sound of the sea in the distance, and he tried to remember which island he was on and what his mission was. Some men led him to a post in front of a wall and tied his arms behind his back.

There was no anger in him now, only a kind of drowsy wonder about the way the briefing was being handled. He was filled with a deep lassitude but he knew he must not fall asleep because he had to lead the mission. He raised his head and saw men in uniform lined up. They were aiming guns at him. Old, buried instincts began to take over. They would attack from different directions and try to separate him from the rest of his squadron, because they were afraid of him. He saw a movement at three o'clock low and knew they were coming for him. They would expect him to bank out of range, but instead he shoved the stick all the way forwards and went into an outside loop that nearly tore the wings off his plane. He pulled out at the bottom of the dive and executed a snap roll to the left. There was no sign of them. He had outmanoeuvred them. He began to climb, and below him he saw a Zero. He laughed aloud and gave his plane right stick and rudder until the Zero was centred in his gunsights. Then he swooped down like an avenging angel, closing the distance with dizzying speed. His finger began to tighten on the trigger button when a sudden excruciating pain smashed through his body. And another. And another. He could feel his flesh tearing and his guts spilling out, and he thought, *Oh, my God, where did he come from? . . . There's a better pilot than me . . . I wonder who he is . . .*

And then he began spinning abruptly into space and everything grew dark and silent.

In her cell Noelle's hair was being coifed when she heard a volley of thunder outside.

'Is it going to rain?' she asked.

The hairdresser looked at her strangely for a moment and saw that she really did not know what the sound was. 'No,' she said quietly, 'it is going to be a beautiful day.'

And then Noelle knew.

And she was next.

At five-thirty A.M., thirty minutes before her execution was scheduled, Noelle heard footsteps approaching her cell. Her heart gave an involuntary leap. She had been sure that Constantin Demiris would want to see her. She knew that she had never looked more beautiful, and perhaps when he saw her . . . perhaps . . . The prison warden appeared, accompanied by a guard and a nurse carrying a black medical bag. Noelle looked behind them for Demiris. The corridor was empty. The guard opened the cell door, and the warden and nurse entered. Noelle found that her heart was pounding, the wave of fear beginning to lap at her again, drowning out the faint hope that had been stirring.

'It isn't time yet, is it?' Noelle asked.

The warden looked uncomfortable. 'No, Miss Page. The nurse is here to give you an enema.'

She looked at him, not understanding. 'I don't want an enema.'

He looked even more uncomfortable. 'It will save you being – embarrassed.'

And then Noelle understood. And her fear turned into a roaring agony, tearing at her stomach. She nodded her head and the warden turned and left the cell. The guard locked the door and tactfully walked down the corridor out of sight.

'We don't want to spoil that pretty dress,' the nurse was cooing. 'Why don't we just slip it off and you lie down right there? This will only take a minute.'

The nurse began to work on her, but Noelle felt nothing.

She was with her father and he was saying, *Look at her, a stranger could tell she was of royal blood*, and people were fighting to pick her up in their arms and hold her. A priest was in the room and he said, 'Would you like to make your confession to God, my child?' but she shook her head impatiently because her father was talking and she wanted to hear what he was saying. *You were born a princess and this is your kingdom. When you grow up, you're going to marry a handsome prince and live in a grand palace.*

She was walking down a long corridor with some men and someone opened a door and she was outside in a cold courtyard. Her father was holding her up to a window and she could see the tall masts of ships bobbing on the water.

The men led her to a post in front of a wall and fastened her hands behind her and tied her waist to the post and her father said, *Do you see those ships, Princess? That's your fleet. One day they'll carry you to all the magic places in the world.* And he held her close and she felt safe. She could not remember why, but he had been angry with her, but now everything was all right, and he loved her again, and she turned to him but his face was a blur, and she could not recall what he looked like. She could not remember her father's face.

She was filled with an overwhelming sadness, as though she had lost something precious, and she knew that she had to remember him or she would die, and she began to concentrate very hard, but before she could see it, there was a sudden roaring sound and a thousand knives of agony tore into her flesh and her mind screamed, *No! Not yet! Let me see my father's face!*

But it was lost forever in the darkness.

EPILOGUE

The man and woman moved through the cemetery, their faces dappled by the shadows of the tall, graceful cypresses that lined the path. They walked slowly in the shimmering heat of the noonday sun.

Sister Theresa said, 'I wish to tell you again how grateful we are for your generosity. I do not know what we would have done without you.'

Constantin Demiris waved a deprecating hand. '*Arkayto*,' he said. 'It is nothing, Sister.'

But Sister Theresa knew that without this saviour the nunnery would have had to close down years ago. And surely it was a sign from Heaven that now she had been able to repay him in some measure. It was a *thriamvos*, a triumph. She thanked Saint Dionysius again that the Sisters had been permitted to rescue the American friend of Demiris' from the waters of the lake on that terrible night of the storm. True, something had happened to the woman's mind and she was like a child, but she would be cared for. Mr Demiris had asked Sister Theresa to keep the woman here within these walls, sheltered and protected from the outside world for the rest of her life. He was such a good and kind man.

They had reached the end of the cemetery. A path wound down to a promontory where the woman stood, staring out at the calm, emerald lake below.

'There she is,' Sister Theresa said. 'I will leave you now. *Hayretay*.'

Demiris watched Sister Theresa start back towards the nunnery, then he walked down the path to where the woman stood.

'Good morning,' he said, gently.

She turned around slowly and looked at him. Her eyes were dull and vacant and there was no recognition on her face.

'I brought you something,' Constantin Demiris said.

He pulled a small jewellery box out of his pocket and held it out to her. She stared at it like a small child.

'Go on, take it.'

Slowly she reached out and took the box. She lifted the lid, and inside, nested in cotton, was a miniature, exquisitely made gold bird with ruby eyes and outstretched wings poised for flight. Demiris watched as the child-woman removed it from the box and held it up. The bright sun caught the gleam of its gold and the sparkle of its ruby eyes and sent tiny rainbows flashing through the air. She turned it from side to side, watching the lights dancing around her head.

'I will not be seeing you again,' Demiris said, 'but you won't have to worry. No one will harm you now. The wicked people are dead.'

As he spoke, her face happened to be turned towards him, and for one frozen instant in time it seemed to him that a gleam of intelligence, a look of joy came into her eyes, but a moment later it was gone and there was only the vacant, mindless stare. It could have been an illusion, a trick of the sunlight reflecting the sparkle of the golden bird across her eyes.

He thought about it as he walked slowly up the hill and out the huge stone gate of the nunnery to where his limousine was waiting to drive him back to Athens.

Chicago
London
Paris
Athens
Ioannina
Los Angeles

The Sands of Time

To Frances Gordon,
with love.

My special thanks go to Alice Fisher,
whose assistance in helping me research this novel
was invaluable.

Lives of great men all remind us
We can make our lives sublime,
And, departing, leave behind us
Footprints on the Sands of Time.

HENRY WADSWORTH
LONGFELLOW

The dead do not need to rise.

They are a part of the earth now and the earth can never be conquered for the earth endures forever, it will outlive all systems of tyranny. Those who have entered it honourably, and no men entered earth more honourably than those who died in Spain, have already achieved immortality.

ERNEST HEMINGWAY

AUTHOR'S NOTE

This is a work of fiction. And yet . . .

The romantic land of flamenco and Don Quixote and exotic-looking señoritas with tortoise-shell combs in their hair is also the land of Torquemada, the Spanish Inquisition and one of the bloodiest civil wars in history. More than half a million people lost their lives in the battles for power between the Republicans and the rebel Nationalists in Spain. In 1936, between February and June, 269 political murders were committed, and the Nationalists executed Republicans at the rate of a thousand a month, with no mourning permitted. One hundred and sixty churches were burned to the ground, and nuns were removed forcibly from convents, 'as though,' wrote the Duc de Saint-Simon, of an earlier conflict between the Spanish government and the church, 'they were whores in a bawdy house'. Newspaper offices were sacked and strikes and riots were endemic throughout the land. The Civil War ended in a victory for the Nationalists under Franco and, following his death, Spain became a monarchy.

The Civil War, which lasted from 1936 to 1939, may be officially over, but the two Spains that fought it have never been reconciled. Today another war continues to rage in Spain, the guerrilla war fought by the Basques to regain the autonomy they had won under the Republic and lost under the Franco regime. The war is being fought with bombs, bank robberies to finance the bombs, assassinations and riots.

When a member of ETA, a Basque guerrilla underground group, died in a Madrid hospital after being tortured by the police, the nationwide riots that followed led to the resignation of the Director General of Spain's police force, five security chiefs and two hundred senior police officers.

In 1986, in Barcelona, the Basques publicly burned the Spanish flag, and in Pamplona thousands fled in fear when Basque nationalists clashed with police in a series of mutinies that eventually spread across Spain and threatened the stability of the government. The para-military police retaliated by going on a rampage, firing at random at Basques' homes and shops. The terrorism that goes on is more violent than ever.

Dealing with two turbulent weeks in 1976, this is a work of fiction. And yet . . .

Chapter 1

Pamplona, Spain 1976

If the plan goes wrong, we will all die. He went over it again in his mind for the last time, probing, testing, searching for flaws. He could find none. The plan was daring, and it called for careful, split-second timing. If it worked, it would be a spectacular feat, worthy of the great El Cid. If it failed . . .

Well, the time for worrying is past, Jaime Miró thought philosophically. *It's time for action.*

Jaime Miró was a legend, a hero to the Basque people and anathema to the Spanish government. He was six feet tall, with a strong, intelligent face, a muscular body, and brooding dark eyes. Witnesses tended to describe him as taller than he was, darker than he was, fiercer than he was. He was a complex man, a realist who understood the enormous odds against him, a romantic ready to die for what he believed.

Pamplona was a town gone mad. It was the final morning of the running of the bulls, the Fiesta de San Fermin, the annual celebration held from 7 July to the 14th. Thirty thousand visitors had swarmed into the city from all over the world. Some had come merely to watch the dangerous bull-running spectacle, others to prove their manhood by taking part in it, running in front of the charging beasts. All the hotel rooms had long since been taken, and university students from Navarra had bedded down in doorways, bank entrances, cars, the public square, and even the streets and pavements of the town.

The tourists packed the cafés and hotels, watching the noisy, colourful parades of *papier mâché gigantes*, and listening to the music of the marching bands. Members of the parade wore violet cloaks, some with hoods of green, others garnet, and still others wearing golden hoods. Flowing through the streets, the processions looked like rivers of rainbows. Exploding firecrackers running along poles and wires of the tramways added to the noise and general confusion.

The crowd had come to attend the evening bullfights, but the most spectacular event was the *Encierro* – the early morning running of the bulls that would fight later in the day.

Ten minutes before midnight in the darkened streets of the lower part of town, the bulls had been driven from the *corrales de gas*, the reception pens, to run across the river on a bridge to the corral at the bottom of Calle Santo Domingo, where they would be kept for the night. In the morning they would be turned loose to run along the narrow Calle Santo Domingo, penned in the street by wooden barricades at each corner until at the end they would run into the corrals at the Plaza de Hemingway, where they would be held until the afternoon bullfight.

From midnight until 6.00 a.m., the visitors stayed awake, drinking and singing and making love, too excited to sleep. Those who would participate in the running of the bulls wore the red scarves of San Fermin around their throats.

At a quarter to six in the morning, bands started circulating through the streets, playing the stirring music of Navarre. At seven o'clock sharp, a rocket flew into the air to signal that the gates of the corral had been opened. The crowd was filled with feverish anticipation. Moments later a second rocket went up to warn the town that the bulls were running.

What followed was an unforgettable spectacle. First came the sound. It started as a faint, distant ripple on the wind, almost imperceptible, and then it grew louder and louder until it became an explosion of pounding hoofs, and suddenly bursting into view appeared six oxen and six enormous bulls.

Each weighing 1,500 pounds, they charged down the Calle Santo Domingo like deadly express trains. Inside the wooden barricades that had been placed at each intersecting street corner to keep the bulls confined to the one street, were hundreds of eager, nervous young men who intended to prove their bravery by facing the maddened animals.

The bulls raced down from the far end of the street, past the Calle Estafeta and the Calle de Javier, past *farmacias* and clothing stores and fruit markets, towards the Plaza de Hemingway, and there were cries of '*¡Olé!*' from the frenzied crowd. As the animals charged nearer, a mad scramble began to escape the sharp horns and lethal hoofs. The sudden reality of approaching death made some of the participants run for the safety of doorways and fire escapes. They were followed by taunts of '*cobardón*' – coward. A few in the path of the bulls stumbled and fell and were quickly hauled to safety.

A small boy and his grandfather were standing behind the barricades, both breathless with the excitement of the spectacle taking place only a few feet from them.

'Look at them!' the old man exclaimed. '*¡Magnífico!*'

The little boy shuddered. '*Tengo miedo, abuelo.* I'm afraid.'

The old man put his arm around him. '*Sí*, Manuel. It is frightening. But wonderful, too. I once ran with the bulls. There's nothing like it. You test yourself against death, and it makes you feel like a man.'

As a rule, it took two minutes for the animals to gallop the 900 yards along the Calle Santo Domingo to the arena, and the moment the bulls were safely in the corral, a third rocket would be sent into the air. On this day, the third rocket did not go off, for an incident occurred that had never happened in Pamplona's 400-year history of the running of the bulls.

As the animals raced down the narrow street, half a dozen men dressed in the colourful costumes of the *feria* shifted the wooden barricades and the bulls found themselves forced off the restricted street and turned loose into the heart of the city. What had a moment before been a happy celebration instantly turned into a nightmare. The frenzied beasts charged into the stunned onlookers. The young boy and his grandfather were among the first to die, knocked down and trampled by the charging bulls. Vicious horns sliced into a baby's pram, killing an infant and sending its mother down to the ground to be crushed. Death was in the air everywhere. The animals crashed into helpless bystanders, knocking down women and children, plunging their long, deadly horns into pedestrians, food stands, statues, sweeping aside everything unlucky enough to be in their path. People were screaming in terror, desperately fighting to get out of the way of the lethal behemoths.

A bright red truck suddenly appeared in the path of the bulls and they turned and charged towards it, down the Calle de Estrella, the street that led to the *cárcel*, Pamplona's prison.

The *cárcel* is a forbidding-looking two-storey stone building with heavily barred windows. There are turrets at each of its four corners, and the red and yellow Spanish flag flies over the door. A stone gate leads to a small courtyard. The second floor of the building consists of a row of cells that holds prisoners condemned to die.

Inside the prison, a heavyset guard in the uniform of the *policía armada* was leading a priest garbed in plain black robes along the second floor corridor. The policeman carried a sub-machine-gun.

Noting the questioning look in the priest's eye at the sight of the weapon, the guard said, 'One can't be too careful here, Father. We have the scum of the earth on this floor.'

The guard directed the priest to walk through a metal detector very much like those used at airports.

'I'm sorry, Father, but the rules –'

'Of course, my son.'

As the priest passed through the security portal, a

shrieking siren cut through the corridor. The guard instinctively tightened his grip on his weapon.

The priest turned and smiled back at the guard.

'My mistake,' he said as he removed a heavy metal cross that hung from his neck on a silver chain and handed it to the guard. This time as he passed through, the machine was silent. The guard handed the cross back to the priest and the two continued their journey deeper into the bowels of the prison.

The stench in the corridor near the cells was overpowering.

The guard was in a philosophical mood. 'You know, you're wasting your time here, Father. These animals have no souls to save.'

'Still, we must try, my son.'

The guard shook his head. 'I tell you the gates of hell are waiting to welcome both of them.'

The priest looked at the guard in surprise. 'Both of them? I was told there were three who needed confession.'

The guard shrugged. 'We saved you some time. Zamora died in the infirmary this morning. Heart attack.'

The men had reached the two farthest cells.

'Here we are, Father.'

The guard unlocked a cell door, then stepped cautiously back as the priest entered the cell. The guard locked the door again, and stood in the corridor, alert for any sign of trouble.

The priest went to the figure lying on the dirty prison cot. 'Your name, my son?'

'Ricardo Mellado.'

The priest stared down at him. It was difficult to tell what the man looked like. His face was swollen and raw. His eyes were almost shut. Through thick lips, he said, 'I'm glad you were able to come, Father.'

The priest replied, 'Your salvation is the church's duty, my son.'

'They are going to hang me this morning?'

The priest patted his shoulder gently. 'You have been sentenced to die by the garrotte.'

Ricardo Mellado stared up at him. 'No!'

'I'm sorry. The orders were given by the Prime Minister himself.'

The priest placed his hand on the prisoner's head and intoned: '*Dime tus pecados . . .*'

Ricardo Mellado said, 'I have sinned greatly in thought, word and deed, and I repent all my sins with all my heart.'

'*Ruego a nuestro Padre celestial por la salvación de tu alma. En el nombre del Padre, del Hijo y del Espíritu Santo . . .*'

The guard listening outside the cell thought to himself: *What a stupid waste of time. God will spit in that one's eye.*

The priest was finished. '*Adiós*, my son. May God receive your soul in peace.'

The priest moved to the cell door and the guard unlocked it, then stepped back, keeping his gun aimed at the prisoner. When the door was locked again, the guard moved to the adjoining cell and opened the door.

'He's all yours, Father.'

The priest stepped into the second cell. The man inside had also been badly beaten. The priest looked at him a long moment. 'What is your name, my son?'

'Felix Carpio.' He was a husky, bearded man with a fresh, livid scar on his cheek that the beard failed to conceal. 'I'm not afraid to die, Father.'

'That is well, my son. In the end none of us is spared.'

As the priest began to hear Carpio's confession, waves of distant sound, at first muffled, then growing louder, began to reverberate through the building. It was the thunder of pounding hoofs and the screams of the running mob. The guard listened, startled. The sounds were rapidly moving closer.

'You'd better hurry, Father. Something peculiar is happening outside.'

'I'm finished.'

The guard quickly unlocked the cell door. The priest stepped out into the corridor and the guard locked the door behind him. There was the sound of a loud crash from the front of the prison. The guard turned to peer out the narrow, barred window.

'What the hell was that noise?'

The priest said, 'It sounded as though someone wishes an audience with us. May I borrow that?'

'Borrow what?'

'Your weapon, *por favor*.'

As the priest spoke, he stepped close to the guard. He silently removed the top of the large cross that hung around his neck, revealing a long, wicked-looking stiletto. In one lightning move he plunged the knife into the guard's chest.

'You see, my son,' Jaime Miró said, as he pulled the sub-machine-gun from the dying guard's hands, 'God and I decided that you no longer have need of this weapon.'

The guard slumped to the cement floor. Jaime Miró took the keys from the body and swiftly opened the two cell doors. The sounds from the street were getting louder.

'Let's move,' Jaime commanded.

Ricardo Mellado picked up the machine gun. 'You make a damned good priest. You almost convinced me.' He tried to smile with his swollen mouth.

'They really worked you two over, didn't they? Don't worry. They'll pay for it.'

Jaime Miró put his arms around the two men and helped them down the corridor.

'What happened to Zamora?'

'The guards beat him to death. We could hear his screams. They took him off to the infirmary and said he died of a heart attack.'

Ahead of them was a locked iron door.

'Wait here,' Jaime Miró said.

He approached the door and said to the guard on the other side, 'I'm finished here.'

The guard unlocked the door. 'You'd better hurry, Father. There's some kind of disturbance going on out –' He never finished his sentence. As Jaime's knife went into him, blood welled out of the guard's mouth.

Jaime motioned to the two men. 'Come on.'

Felix Carpio picked up the guard's gun, and they started downstairs. The scene outside was chaos. The police were running around frantically trying to see what was happening and to deal with the crowds of screaming people in the courtyard who were scrambling to escape the maddened bulls. One of the bulls had charged into the front of the building, smashing the stone entrance. Another was tearing into the body of a uniformed guard on the ground. The red truck was in the courtyard, its motor running. In the confusion, the three men went almost unnoticed. Those who did see them were too busy saving themselves to do anything about them.

Without a word, Jaime and his men jumped into the back of the truck and it sped off, scattering frantic pedestrians through the crowded streets. The *guardia civil*, the paramilitary rural police decked out in green uniforms and black patent leather hats, were trying in vain to control the hysterical mob. The *policía armada*, stationed in provincial capitals, were also helpless in the face of the mad spectacle. People were struggling to flee in every direction, desperately trying to avoid the enraged bulls. The danger lay less with the bulls and more with the people themselves as they trampled one another in their eagerness to escape, and old men and women were pushed aside under the feet of the running mob.

Jaime stared in dismay at the stunning spectacle. 'It wasn't planned for it to happen this way!' he exclaimed. He stared helplessly at the carnage that was being wreaked, but there was nothing he could do to stop it. He closed his eyes to shut out the sight.

The truck reached the outskirts of Pamplona and headed south, leaving behind the noise and confusion of the rioting.

'Where are we going, Jaime?' Ricardo Mellado asked.

'There's a safe house outside Torré. We'll stay there until dark and then move on.'

Felix Carpio was wincing with pain.

Jaime Miró watched him, his face filled with compassion. 'We'll be there soon, my friend,' he said gently.

He was unable to get the terrible scene at Pamplona out of his mind.

Thirty minutes later they approached the little village of Torré, and skirted it to drive to an isolated house in the mountains above the village. Jaime Miró helped the two men out of the back of the red truck.

'You'll be picked up at midnight,' the driver said.

'Have them bring a doctor,' Jaime replied. 'And get rid of the truck.'

The three of them entered the house. It was a farmhouse, simple and comfortable, with a fireplace in the living room and a beamed ceiling. There was a note on the table. Jaime Miró read it and smiled at the welcoming phrase: *Mi casa es su casa.* On the bar were bottles of wine. Jaime Miró poured drinks.

Ricardo Mellado said, 'There are no words to thank you, my friend. Here's to you.'

Jaime raised his glass. 'Here's to freedom.'

There was the sudden chirp of a canary in a cage. Jaime Miró walked over to it, and he watched its wild fluttering for a moment. Then he opened the cage, gently lifted the bird out and carried it to an open window.

'Fly away, *pajarito*,' he said softly. 'All living creatures should be free.'

Chapter 2

Madrid

Prime Minister Leopoldo Martinez was in a rage. He was a small, bespectacled man, and his whole body shook as he talked. 'Jaime Miró must be stopped,' he cried. His voice was high and shrill. 'Do you understand me?' He glared at the half dozen men gathered in the room. 'We're looking for one terrorist, and the whole army and police force are unable to find him.'

The meeting was taking place at Moncloa Palace, where the Prime Minister lived and worked, five kilometres from the centre of Madrid, on the Carretera de Galicia, a highway with no identifying signs. The building itself was green brick, with wrought iron balconies, green window shades, and guard towers at each corner.

It was a hot, dry day, and through the windows, as far as the eye could see, columns of heat waves rose like battalions of ghostly soldiers.

'Yesterday Miró turned Pamplona into a battleground.' Martinez slammed a fist down on his desk. 'He murdered two prison guards and smuggled two of his terrorists out of prison. Many innocent people were killed by the bulls he let loose.'

For a moment no one said anything.

When the Prime Minister had taken office, he had declared, smugly, 'My first act will be to put a stop to these separatist groups. Madrid is the great unifier. It transforms Andalusians, Basques, Catalans and Galicians into Spaniards.'

He had been unduly optimistic. The fiercely independent Basques had other ideas, and the wave of bombings, bank robberies and demonstrations by terrorists of the ETA organization, Euzkadi ta Azkatasuna, had continued unabated.

The man at Martinez's right said quietly, 'I'll find him.'

The speaker was Colonel Ramón Acoca, head of the GOE, the *Grupo de Operaciones Especiales*, formed to pursue Basque terrorists. Acoca was a giant, in his middle sixties, with a scarred face and cold, obsidian eyes. He had been a young officer under Francisco Franco during the Civil War, and he was still fanatically devoted to Franco's philosophy, 'We are responsible only to God and to history.'

Acoca was a brilliant officer, and he had been one of Franco's must trusted aides. The Colonel missed the iron-fisted discipline, the swift punishment of those who questioned or disobeyed the law. He had gone through the turmoil of the Civil War, with its Nationalist alliance of Monarchists, rebel generals, landowners, church hierarchy and the fascist Falangists on one side, and the Republican government forces, including Socialists, Communists, liberals and Basque and Catalan separatists on the other. It had been a terrible time of destruction and killing in a madness that pulled in men and war matériel from a dozen countries and left a horrifying death toll. And now the Basques were fighting and killing again.

Colonel Acoca headed an efficient, ruthless cadre of anti-terrorists. His men worked underground, wore disguises and were neither publicized nor photographed for fear of retaliation.

If anyone can stop Jaime Miró, Colonel Acoca can, the Prime Minister thought. But there was a catch: *Who's going to be the one to stop Colonel Acoca?*

Putting the Colonel in charge had not been the Prime Minister's idea. He had received a phone call in the middle of the night on his private line. He recognized the voice immediately.

'We are greatly disturbed by the activities of Jaime Miró and his terrorists. We suggest that you put Colonel Ramón Acoca in charge of the GOE. Is that clear?'

'Yes, sir. It will be taken care of immediately.'

The line went dead.

The voice belonged to a member of the OPUS MUNDO. The organization was a secret cabal that included bankers, lawyers, heads of powerful corporations and government ministers. It was rumoured to have enormous funds at its disposal, but where the money came from or how it was used or manipulated was a mystery. It was not considered healthy to ask too many questions about it.

The Prime Minister had placed Colonel Acoca in charge, as he had been instructed to, but the giant had turned out to be an uncontrollable fanatic. His GOE had created a reign of terror. The Prime Minister thought of the Basque rebels Acoca's men had caught near Pamplona. They had been convicted and sentenced to hang. It was Colonel Acoca who had insisted that they be executed by the barbaric *garrote vil*, the iron collar fitted with a spike which gradually tightened, eventually cracked the vertebra and severed the victim's spinal cord.

Jaime Miró had become an obsession with Colonel Acoca.

'I want his head,' Colonel Acoca said. 'Cut off his head and the Basque movement dies.'

An exaggeration, the Prime Minister felt, although he had to admit that there was a core of truth in it. Jaime Miró was a charismatic leader, fanatical about his cause, and therefore dangerous.

But in his own way, the Prime Minister thought, *Colonel Acoca is just as dangerous.*

Primo Casado, the Director General de Seguridad, was speaking. 'Your Excellency, no one could have foreseen what happened in Pamplona. Jaime Miró is –'

'I *know* what he is,' the Prime Minister snapped. 'I want to know *where* he is.' He turned to Colonel Acoca.

'I'm on his trail,' the Colonel said. His voice chilled the

room. 'I would like to remind Your Excellency that we are not fighting just one man. We are fighting the Basque people. They give Jaime Miró and his terrorists food and weapons and shelter. The man is a hero to them. But do not worry. Soon he will be a hanging hero. After I give him a fair trial, of course.'

Not we. I. The Prime Minister wondered whether the others had noticed. *Yes*, he thought nervously. *Something will have to be done about the Colonel soon.*

The Prime Minister got to his feet. 'That will be all for now, gentlemen.'

The men rose to leave. All except Colonel Acoca. He stayed.

Leopoldo Martinez began to pace. 'Damn the Basques. Why can't they be satisfied just to be Spaniards? What more do they want?'

'They're greedy for power,' Acoca said. 'They want autonomy, their own language and their flag –'

'No. Not as long as I hold this office. I'm not going to permit them to tear pieces out of Spain. The government will tell them what they can have and what they can't have. They're nothing but rabble who . . .'

An aide came into the room. 'Excuse me, Your Excellency,' he said apologetically. 'Bishop Ibanez has arrived.'

'Send him in.'

The Colonel's eyes narrowed. 'You can be sure the church is behind all this. It's time we taught them a lesson.'

The Church is one of the great ironies of our history, Colonel Acoca thought bitterly.

In the beginning of the Civil War, the Catholic Church had been on the side of the Nationalist forces. The Pope backed Generalissimo Franco, and in so doing allowed him to proclaim that he was fighting on the side of God. But when the Basque churches and monasteries and priests were attacked, the Church withdrew its support.

'You must give the Basques and the Catalans more freedom,' the Church had demanded. 'And you must stop executing Basque priests.'

Generalissimo Franco had been furious. How dare the Church try to dictate to the government?

A war of attrition began. More churches and monasteries were attacked by Franco's forces. Nuns and priests were murdered. Bishops were placed under house arrest, and priests all over Spain were fined for giving sermons that the government considered seditious. It was only when the Church threatened Franco with excommunication that he stopped his attacks.

The goddamned Church! Acoca thought. With Franco dead it was interfering again.

He turned to the Prime Minister. 'It's time the bishop is told who's running Spain.'

Bishop Calvo Ibanez was a thin, frail-looking man with a cloud of white hair swirling around his head. He peered at the two men through his pince-nez spectacles.

'*Buenas tardes*.'

Colonel Acoca felt the bile rise in his throat. The very sight of clergymen made him ill. They were Judas goats leading their stupid lambs to slaughter.

The bishop stood there, waiting for an invitation to sit down. It did not come. Nor was he introduced to the Colonel. It was a deliberate slight.

The Prime Minister looked to Acoca for direction.

Acoca said curtly, 'Some disturbing news has been brought to our attention. Basque rebels are reported to be holding meetings in Catholic monasteries. It has also been reported that the Church is allowing monasteries and convents to store arms for the rebels.' There was steel in his voice. 'When you help the enemies of Spain, you *become* an enemy of Spain.'

Bishop Ibanez stared at him for a moment, then turned to Leopoldo Martinez. 'Your Excellency, with due respect, we are all children of Spain. The Basques are not your enemy. All they ask is the freedom to –'

'They don't ask,' Acoca roared. 'They demand! They go around the country pillaging, robbing banks and killing policemen, and you dare to say they are not our enemies?'

'I admit that there have been inexcusable excesses. But sometimes in fighting for what one believes –'

'They don't believe in anything but themselves. They care nothing about Spain. It is as one of our great writers said, "No one in Spain is concerned about the common good. Each group is concerned only with itself. The Church, the Basques, the Catalans. Each one says fuck the others."'

The bishop was aware that Colonel Acoca had misquoted Ortega y Gasset. The full quote had included the army and the government; but he wisely said nothing. He turned to the Prime Minister again, hoping for a more rational discussion.

'Your Excellency, the Catholic Church –'

The Prime Minister felt that Acoca had pushed far enough. 'Don't misunderstand us, Bishop. In principle, of course, this government is behind the Catholic Church one hundred per cent.'

Colonel Acoca spoke up again. 'But we cannot permit your churches and monasteries and convents to be used against us. If you continue to allow the Basques to store arms in them and to hold meetings, you will have to take the consequences.'

'I am sure that the reports that you have received are erroneous,' the bishop said smoothly. 'However, I shall certainly investigate at once.'

The Prime Minister murmured, 'Thank you, Bishop. That will be all.'

Prime Minister Martinez and Colonel Acoca watched him depart.

'What do you think?' Martinez asked.

'He knows what's going on.'

The Prime Minister sighed. *I have enough problems right now without stirring up trouble with the Church.*

'If the Church is for the Basques, then it is against us.' Colonel Acoca's voice hardened. 'I would like your permission to teach the bishop a lesson.'

The Prime Minister was stopped by the look of fanaticism

in the man's eyes. He became cautious. 'Have you really had reports that the churches are aiding the rebels?'

'Of course, Excellency.'

There was no way of determining if the man was telling the truth. The Prime Minister knew how much Acoca hated the Church. But it might be good to let the Church have a taste of the whip, providing Colonel Acoca did not go too far. Prime Minister Martinez stood there thoughtfully.

It was Acoca who broke the silence. 'If the churches are sheltering terrorists, then the churches must be punished.'

Reluctantly, the Prime Minister nodded. 'Where will you start?'

'Jaime Miró and his men were seen in Ávila yesterday. They are probably hiding at the convent there.'

The Prime Minister made up his mind. 'Search it,' he said.

That decision set off a chain of events that was to rock all of Spain and shock the world.

Chapter 3

Ávila

The silence was like a gentle snowfall, soft and hushed, as soothing as the whisper of a summer wind, as quiet as the passage of stars. The Cistercian Convent of the Strict Observance lay outside the walled town of Ávila, the highest city in Spain, 112 kilometres north-west of Madrid. The convent had been built for silence. The rules had been adopted in 1601 and remained unchanged through the centuries: liturgy, spiritual exercise, strict enclosure, penance and silence. Always the silence.

The convent was a simple, four-sided group of rough stone buildings around a cloister dominated by the church. Around the central court the open arches allowed the light to pour in on the broad flagstones of the floor where the nuns glided noiselessly by. There were forty nuns at the convent, praying in the church and living in the cloister. The convent at Ávila was one of seven left in Spain, a survivor out of hundreds that had been destroyed by the Civil War in one of the periodic anti-Church movements that took place in Spain over the centuries.

The Cistercian Convent of the Strict Observance was devoted solely to a life of prayer. It was a place without seasons or time and those who entered were forever removed from the outside world. The Cistercian life was contemplative and penitential; the divine office was recited daily and enclosure was complete and permanent.

All the sisters dressed identically, and their clothing, like everything else in the convent, was touched by the symbolism of centuries. The *capucha*, the cloak and hood, symbolized innocence and simplicity, the linen tunic the renouncement of the works of the world, and mortification, the scapular, the small squares of woollen cloth worn over the shoulders, the willingness to labour. A wimple, a covering of linen laid in plaits over the head and around the chin, sides of the face and neck, completed the habit.

Inside the walls of the convent was a system of internal passageways and staircases linking the dining room, community room, the cells and the chapel, and everywhere there was an atmosphere of cold, clean spaciousness. Thick-paned latticed windows overlooked a high-walled garden. Every window was covered with iron bars and was above the line of vision, so that there would be no outside distractions. The refectory, the dining hall, was long and austere, its windows shuttered and curtained. The candles in the ancient candlesticks cast evocative shadows on the ceilings and walls.

In four hundred years nothing inside the walls of the convent had changed, except the faces. The sisters had no personal possessions, for they desired to be poor, emulating the poverty of Christ. The church itself was bare of ornaments, save for a priceless solid gold cross that had been a long-ago gift from a wealthy postulant. Because it was so out of keeping with the austerity of the order, it was kept hidden away in a cabinet in the refectory. A plain, wooden cross hung at the altar of the church.

The women who shared their lives with the Lord lived together, worked together, ate together and prayed together, yet they never touched and never spoke. The only exception permitted was when they heard mass or when the Reverend Mother Prioress Betina addressed them in the privacy of her office. Even then, an ancient sign language was used as much as possible.

The Reverend Mother was a *religieuse* in her seventies, a bright-faced robin of a woman, cheerful and energetic, who gloried in the peace and joy of convent life, and of a life devoted to God. Fiercely protective of her nuns, she felt more pain when it was necessary to enforce discipline, than did the one being punished.

The nuns walked through the cloisters and corridors with downcast eyes, hands folded in their sleeves at breast level, passing and re-passing their sisters without a word or sign of recognition. The only voice of the convent was its bells – the bells that Victor Hugo called 'the Opera of the Steeples'.

The sisters came from disparate backgrounds and from many different countries. Their families were aristocrats, farmers, soldiers . . . They had come to the convent as rich and poor, educated and ignorant, miserable and exalted, but now they were one in the eyes of God, united in their desire for eternal marriage to Jesus.

The living conditions in the convent were spartan. In winter the cold was knifing, and a chill, pale light filtered in through leaded windows. The nuns slept fully dressed on pallets of straw, covered with rough woollen sheets, each in her tiny cell, furnished only with a straight-backed wooden chair. There was no washstand. A small earthenware jug and basin stood in a corner on the floor. No nun was ever permitted to enter the cell of another, except for the Reverend Mother Betina. There was no recreation of any kind, only work and prayers. There were work areas for knitting, book binding, weaving and making bread. There were eight hours of prayer each day: Matins, Lauds, Prime, Terce, Sext, None, Vespers and Compline. Besides these there were other devotions: benedictions, hymns and litanies.

Matins were said when half the world was asleep and the other half was absorbed in sin.

Lauds, the office of daybreak, followed Matins, and the

rising sun was hailed as the figure of Christ triumphant and glorified.

Prime was the church's morning prayer, asking for the blessings on the work of the day.

Terce was at nine o'clock in the morning, consecrated by St Augustine to the Holy Spirit.

Sext was at 11.30 a.m., evoked to quench the heat of human passions.

None was silently recited at three in the afternoon, the hour of Christ's death.

Vespers was the evening service of the church, as Lauds was her daybreak prayer.

Compline was the completion of the Little Hours of the day. A form of night prayers, a preparation for death as well as sleep, ending the day on a note of loving submission: *Manus tuas, domine, commendo spiritum meum. Redemisti nos, domine, deus, veritatis.*

In some of the other orders, flagellation had been stopped, but in the cloistered Cistercian convents and monasteries it survived. At least once a week, and sometimes every day, the nuns punished their bodies with the Discipline, a twelve-inch long whip of thin waxed cord with six knotted tails that brought agonizing pain, and was used to lash the back, legs and buttocks. Bernard of Clairvaux, the ascetic abbot of the Cistercians, had admonished: 'The body of Christ is crushed . . . our bodies must be conformed to the likeness of our Lord's wounded body.'

It was a life more austere than in any prison, yet the inmates lived in an ecstasy such as they had never known in the outside world. They had renounced physical love, possessions and freedom of choice, but in giving up those things they had also renounced greed and competition, hatred and envy, and all the pressures and temptations that the outside world imposed. Inside the convent reigned an all-pervading peace and the ineffable sense of joy at being one with God. There was an indescribable serenity within the walls of the convent and in the hearts of those who lived there. If the convent was a prison, it was a prison in God's

Eden, with the knowledge of a happy eternity for those who had freely chosen to be there and to remain there.

Sister Lucia was awakened by the tolling of the convent bell. She opened her eyes, startled and disoriented for an instant. The little cell she slept in was dismally black. The sound of the bell told her that it was 3.00 a.m., when the office of vigils began, while the world was still in darkness.

Shit! This routine is going to kill me, Sister Lucia thought.

She lay back on her tiny, uncomfortable cot, desperate for a cigarette. Reluctantly, she dragged herself out of bed. The heavy habit she wore and slept in rubbed against her sensitive skin like sandpaper. She thought of all the beautiful designer gowns hanging in her apartment in Rome and at her chalet in Gstaad. The Valentinos and Armanis and Giannis.

From outside her cell Sister Lucia could hear the soft, swishing movement of the nuns as they gathered in the passage. Carelessly, she made up her bed and stepped out into the long corridor, where the nuns were lining up, eyes downcast. Slowly, they all began to move towards the chapel.

They look like a bunch of penguins, Sister Lucia thought. It was beyond her comprehension why these women had deliberately thrown away their lives, giving up sex, pretty clothes and gourmet food. *Without those things, what reason is there to go on living? And the goddamned rules!*

When Sister Lucia had first entered the convent, the Reverend Mother had said to her, 'You must walk with your head bowed. Keep your hands folded under your habit. Take short steps. Walk slowly. You must never make eye contact with any of the other sisters, or even glance at them. You may not speak. Your ears are to hear only God's words.'

'Yes, Reverend Mother.'

For the next month Lucia took instruction.

'Those who come here come not to join others, but to dwell alone with God, *solitariamente*. Solitude of spirit is essential to a union with God. It is safeguarded by the rules of silence.'

'Yes, Reverend Mother.'

'You must always obey the silence of the eyes. Looking into the eyes of others would distract you with useless images.'

'Yes, Reverend Mother.'

'The first lesson you will learn here will be to rectify the past, to purge out old habits and worldly inclinations, to blot out every image of the past. You will do purifying penance and mortification to strip yourself of self-will and self-love. It is not enough for us to be sorry for our past offences. Once we discover the infinite beauty and holiness of God, we want to make up not only for our own sins, but for every sin that has ever been committed.

'Yes, Reverend Mother.'

'You must struggle with sensuality, what John of the Cross called, "the night of the senses".'

'Yes, Reverend Mother.'

'Each nun lives in silence and in solitude, as though she were already in heaven. In this pure, precious silence for which she hungers, she is able to listen to the infinite silence and possess God.'

At the end of the first month, Lucia took her initial vows. On the day of the ceremony she had her hair shorn. It was a traumatic experience. The Reverend Mother Prioress performed the act herself. She summoned Lucia into her office and motioned for her to sit down. She stepped behind her, and before Lucia knew what was happening, she heard the snip of scissors and felt something tugging at her hair. She started to protest, but she suddenly realized that what was happening could only improve her disguise. *I can always let it grow back later*, Lucia thought. *Meanwhile, I'm going to look like a plucked chicken.*

When Lucia returned to the grim cubicle she had been assigned, she thought: *This place is a snake pit.* The floor consisted of bare boards. The pallet and the hard-backed chair took up most of the room. She was desperate to get hold of a newspaper. *Fat chance*, she thought. In this place they had never heard of newspapers, let alone radio or television. There were no links to the outside world at all.

But what got on Lucia's nerves most of all was the unnatural silence. The only communication was through hand signals, and learning those drove her crazy. When she needed a broom, she was taught to move her outstretched right hand from right to left, as though sweeping. When the Reverend Mother was displeased, she brought together the tips of her little fingers three times in front of her body, the other fingers pressing into her palm. When Lucia was slow in doing her work, the Reverend Mother pressed the palm of her right hand against her left shoulder. To reprimand Lucia, she scratched her own cheek near her right ear with all the fingers of her right hand in a downward motion.

For Christ's sake, Lucia thought, *it looks like she's scratching a flea bite.*

They had reached the chapel. The nuns said a silent mass, the sequence from the age-old Sanctus to the Pater Noster, but Sister Lucia's thoughts were on more important things than God.

In another month or two, when the police stop looking for me, I'll be out of this madhouse.

After morning prayers, Sister Lucia marched with the others to the dining room, surreptitiously breaking the rule, as she did every day, by studying their faces. It was her only entertainment. It was incredible to think that none of them knew what the other sisters looked like.

She was fascinated by the faces of the nuns. Some were old, some were young, some pretty, some ugly. She could not understand why they all seemed so happy. There were three faces that Lucia found particularly interesting. One was Sister Teresa, a woman who appeared to be in her sixties. She was far from beautiful, and yet there was a spirituality about her that gave her an almost unearthly loveliness. She seemed always to be smiling inwardly, as though she carried some wonderful secret within herself.

Another nun that Lucia found fascinating was Sister Graciela. She was a stunningly beautiful woman in her early thirties. She had olive skin, exquisite features, and eyes that were luminous black pools.

She could have been a film star, Lucia thought. *What's her story? Why would she bury herself in a place like this?*

The third nun who captured Lucia's interest was Sister Megan. Blue-eyed, blonde eyebrows and lashes. She was in her late twenties and had a fresh, open faced look.

What is she doing here? What are any of these women doing here? They're locked up behind these walls, given a tiny cell to sleep in, rotten food, eight hours of prayers, hard work and too little sleep. They must be pazzo – all of them.

She was better off than they were, because they were stuck here for the rest of their lives, while she would be out of here in a month or two. *Maybe three*, Lucia thought. *This is a perfect hiding place. I'd be a fool to rush away. In a few months, the police will decide that I'm dead. When I leave here and get my money out of Switzerland, maybe I'll write a book about this crazy place.*

A few days earlier Sister Lucia had been sent by the Reverend Mother to the office to retrieve a paper and while there she had taken the opportunity to start looking through the files. Unfortunately she had been caught in the act of snooping.

'You will do penance by using the Discipline,' the Mother Prioress Betina signalled her.

Sister Lucia bowed her head meekly and signalled, 'Yes, Reverend Mother.'

Lucia returned to her cell, and minutes later the nuns walking through the corridor heard the awful sound of the whip as it whistled through the air and fell again and again.

What they could not know was that Sister Lucia was whipping the bed.

These freaks may be into S & M, but not yours truly.

Now they were seated in the refectory, forty nuns at two long tables. The Cistercian diet was strictly vegetarian. Because the body craved meat, it was forbidden. Long before dawn, a cup of tea or coffee and a few ounces of dry bread were served. The principal meal was taken at 11.00 a.m., and consisted of a thin soup, a few vegetables and occasionally a piece of fruit.

We are not here to please our bodies, but to please God.

I wouldn't feed this breakfast to my cat, Sister Lucia thought. *I've been here two months, and I'll bet I've lost ten pounds. It's God's version of a health farm.*

When breakfast was ended, two nuns brought washing-up bowls to each end of the table and set them down. The sisters seated about the table sent their plates to the sister who had the bowl. She washed each plate, dried it on a towel and returned it to its owner. The water got darker and greasier.

And they're going to live like this for the rest of their lives, Sister Lucia thought disgustedly. *Oh, well. I can't complain. At least it's better than a life sentence in prison . . .*

She would have given her immortal soul for a cigarette.

Five hundred yards down the road, Colonel Ramón Acoca and two dozen carefully selected men from the GOE, the *Grupo de Operaciones Especiales*, were preparing to attack the convent.

Chapter Four

Colonel Ramón Acoca had the instincts of a hunter. He loved the chase, but it was the kill that gave him a deep visceral satisfaction. He had once confided to a friend, 'I have an orgasm when I kill. It doesn't matter whether it's a deer or a rabbit or a man – there's something about taking a life that makes you feel like God.'

Acoca had been in military intelligence, and he had quickly achieved a reputation for being brilliant. He was fearless, ruthless and intelligent, and the combination brought him to the attention of one of General Franco's aides.

Acoca had joined Franco's staff as a lieutenant, and in less than three years he had risen to the rank of colonel, an almost unheard-of feat. He was put in charge of the Falangists, the special group used to terrorize those who opposed Franco.

It was during the war that Acoca had been sent for by a member of the OPUS MUNDO.

'I want you to understand that we're speaking to you with the permission of General Franco.'

'Yes, sir.'

'We've been watching you, Colonel. We are pleased with what we see.'

'Thank you, sir.'

'From time to time we have certain assignments that are – shall we say – very confidential. And very dangerous.'

'I understand, sir.'

'We have many enemies. People who don't understand the importance of the work we're doing.'

'Yes, sir.'

'Sometimes they interfere with us. We can't permit that to happen.'

'No, sir.'

'I believe we could use a man like you, Colonel. I think we understand each other.'

'Yes, sir. I'd be honoured to be of service.'

'We would like you to remain in the army. That will be valuable to us. But from time to time, we will have you assigned to these special projects.'

'Thank you, sir.'

'You are never to speak of this.'

'No, sir.'

The man behind the desk had made Acoca nervous. There was something overpoweringly frightening about him.

In time, Colonel Acoca was called upon to handle half a dozen assignments for the OPUS MUNDO. As he had been told, they were all dangerous. And very confidential.

On one of the missions Acoca had met a lovely young girl from a fine family. Up to then, all of his women had been whores or camp followers, and Acoca had treated them with savage contempt. Some of the women had genuinely fallen in love with him, attracted by his strength. He reserved the worst treatment for them.

But Susana Cerredilla belonged to a different world. Her father was a professor at Madrid University, and Susana's mother was a lawyer. Susana was seventeen years old, and she had the body of a woman and the angelic face of a Madonna. Ramón Acoca had never met anyone like this woman-child. Her gentle vulnerability brought out in him a tenderness he had not known he was capable of. He fell madly in love with her, and for reasons which neither her parents nor Acoca understood, she fell in love with him.

On their honeymoon, it was as though Acoca had never known another woman. He had known lust, but the combination of love and passion was something he had never previously experienced.

Three months after they were married, Susana informed him that she was pregnant. Acoca was wildly excited. To add to their joy, he was assigned to the beautiful little village of Castilbanca, in the Basque country. It was in the autumn of 1936 when the fighting between the Republicans and Nationalists was at its fiercest.

On a peaceful Sunday morning, Ramón Acoca and his bride were having coffee in the village plaza when the square suddenly filled with Basque demonstrators.

'I want you to go home,' Acoca said. 'There's going to be trouble.'

'But you –?'

'Please. I'll be all right.'

The demonstrators were beginning to get out of hand.

With relief, Ramón Acoca watched his bride walk away from the crowd towards a convent at the far end of the square. And as she reached it, the door to the convent suddenly swung open and armed Basques who had been hiding inside, swarmed out with blazing guns. Acoca had watched helplessly as his wife went down in a hail of bullets, and it was on that day that he had sworn vengeance on the Basques. The Church had also been responsible.

And now he was in Ávila, outside another convent. *This time they'll die.*

Inside the convent, in the dark before dawn, Sister Teresa held the Discipline tightly in her right hand and whipped it hard across her body, feeling the knotted tails slashing into her as she silently recited the *Miserere*. She almost screamed aloud, but noise was not permitted, and she kept the screams inside her. *Forgive me, Jesus, for my sins. Bear witness that I punish myself, as you were punished, and I inflict wounds upon myself, as wounds were inflicted upon you. Let me suffer, as you suffered.*

She was near fainting from the pain. Three more times she flagellated herself and then sank, agonized, upon her cot. She had not drawn blood. That was forbidden. Wincing against the agony that each movement brought, Sister Teresa returned the whip to its black case and rested it in a corner. It was always there, a constant reminder that the slightest sin had to be paid for with pain.

Sister Teresa's transgression had happened that morning as she was rounding the corner of a corridor, eyes down, and bumped into Sister Graciela. Startled, Sister Teresa had looked into Sister Graciela's face. Sister Teresa had immediately reported her infraction and the Reverend Mother Betina had frowned disapprovingly and made the sign of discipline, moving her right hand three times from shoulder to shoulder, her hand closed as though holding a whip, the tip of her thumb held against the inside of her forefinger.

Lying on her cot that night, Sister Teresa had been unable to get out of her mind the extraordinarily beautiful face of the young girl she had gazed at. Sister Teresa knew that as long as she lived she would never speak to her and would never even look at her again, for the slightest sign of intimacy between nuns was severely punished. In an atmosphere of rigid moral and physical austerity, no relationships of any kind were allowed to develop. If two sisters worked side by side and seemed to enjoy each other's silent company, the Reverend Mother would immediately have them separated. Nor were the sisters permitted to sit next to the same person at table twice in a row. The church delicately called the attraction of one nun to another 'a particular friendship', and the penalty was swift and severe. Sister Teresa had served her punishment for breaking the rule.

Now the tolling bell came to Sister Teresa as though from a great distance. It was the voice of God, reproving her.

In the next cell, the sound of the bell rang through the corridors of Sister Graciela's dreams, and the pealing of the bell was mingled with the lubricious creak of bedsprings. The Moor was moving towards her, naked, his manhood tumescent, his hands reaching out to grab her. Sister Graciela opened her eyes, instantly awake, her heart pounding frantically. She looked around, terrified, but she was alone in her tiny cell and the only sound was the reassuring tolling of the bell.

Sister Graciela knelt at the side of her cot. *Jesus, thank You for delivering me from the past. Thank You for the joy I have in being here in Your light. Let me glory only in the happiness of Your being. Help me, my Beloved, to be true to the call You have given me. Help me to ease the sorrow of Your sacred heart.*

Sister Graciela rose and carefully made her bed, then joined the procession of her sisters as they moved silently towards the chapel for Matins. She could smell the familiar scent of burning candles and feel the worn stones beneath her sandalled feet.

In the beginning when Sister Graciela had first entered the convent, she had not understood it when the Mother Prioress had told her that a nun was a woman who gave up everything in order to possess everything. Sister Graciela had been fourteen years old then. Now, seventeen years later, it was clear to her. In contemplation she possessed everything, for contemplation was the mind replying to the soul, the waters of Siloh that flowed in silence. Her days were filled with a wonderful peace.

Thank You for letting me forget the terrible past, Father. Thank You for standing beside me. I couldn't face my terrible past without you . . . Thank You . . . Thank You . . .

When Matins were over, the nuns returned to their cells to sleep until Lauds, the rising of the sun.

Outside, Colonel Ramón Acoca and his men moved swiftly in the darkness. When they reached the convent, Colonel Acoca said, 'Jaime Miró and his men will be armed. Take no chances.'

He looked at the front of the convent, and for an instant,

he saw that other convent with Basque partisans rushing out of it, and Susana going down in a hail of bullets.

'Don't bother taking Jaime Miró alive,' he said.

Sister Megan was awakened by the silence. It was a different silence, a moving silence, a hurried rush of air, a whisper of bodies. There were sounds she had never heard in her fifteen years in the convent. She was suddenly filled with a premonition that something was terribly wrong.

She rose quietly in the darkness and opened the door to her cell. Unbelievably, the long stone corridor was filled with men. A giant with a scarred face was coming out of the Reverend Mother's cell, pulling her by the arm. Megan stared in shock. *I'm having a nightmare*, Megan thought. *These men can't be here.*

'Where are you hiding him?' Colonel Acoca demanded.

The Reverend Mother Betina had a look of stunned horror on her face. 'Ssh! This is God's temple. You are desecrating it.' Her voice was trembling. 'You must leave at once.'

The Colonel's grip tightened on her arm and he shook her. 'I want Miró, Sister.'

The nightmare was real.

Other cell doors were beginning to open, and nuns were appearing, looks of total confusion on their faces. There had never been anything in their experience to prepare them for this extraordinary happening.

Colonel Acoca pushed Sister Betina away and turned to Patricio Arrieta, one of his lieutenants. 'Search the place. Top to bottom.'

Acoca's men began to spread out, invading the chapel, the refectory and the cells, waking those nuns who were still asleep, and forcing them roughly to their feet through the corridors and into the chapel. The nuns obeyed wordlessly, keeping even now their vows of silence. To Megan the scene was like a film with the sound turned off.

Acoca's men were filled with a sense of vengeance. They were all Falangists, and they remembered only too well how the Church had turned against them during the Civil War and supported the Loyalists against their beloved leader, Generalissimo Franco. This was their chance to get their own back. The nuns' strength and silence made the men more furious than ever.

As Acoca passed one of the cells, a scream echoed from it. Acoca looked in and saw one of his men ripping the habit from a nun. Acoca moved on.

Sister Lucia was awakened by the sounds of men's voices yelling. She sat up in a panic. *The police have found me*, was her first thought. *I've got to get out of here.* There was no way out of the convent except through the front door.

She hurriedly rose and peered out into the corridor. The sight that met her eyes was astonishing. The corridor was filled not with policemen, but with men in civilian clothes, carrying weapons, smashing lamps and tables. There was confusion everywhere as they raced around.

The Reverend Mother Betina was standing in the centre of the chaos, praying silently, watching them desecrate her beloved convent. Sister Megan moved to her side, and Lucia joined them.

'What the h – what's happening? Who are they?' Lucia asked. They were the first words she had spoken aloud since entering the convent.

The Reverend Mother put her right hand under her left armpit three times, the sign for *hide*.

Lucia stared at her unbelievingly. 'You can talk now. Let's get out of here, for Christ's sake. And I mean for Christ's sake.'

Patricio Arrieta, the Colonel's key aide, hurried up to Acoca. 'We've searched everywhere, Colonel. There's no sign of Jaime Miró or his men.'

'Search again,' Acoca said stubbornly.

It was then that the Reverend Mother remembered the one treasure that the convent had. She hurried over to Sister Teresa and whispered, 'I have a task for you. Remove the gold cross from the chapel and take it to the convent at Mendavia. You must get it away from here. Hurry!'

Sister Teresa was shaking so hard that her wimple fluttered in waves. She stared at the Reverend Mother, paralyzed. Sister Teresa had spent the last thirty years of her life in the convent. The thought of leaving it was beyond imagining. She raised her hand and signed, *I can't.*

The Reverend Mother was frantic. 'The cross must not fall into the hands of these men of Satan. Now do this for Jesus.'

A light came into Sister Teresa's eyes. She stood very tall. She signed, *for Jesus*. She turned and hurried towards the chapel.

Sister Graciela approached the group, staring in wonder at the wild confusion around her.

The men were getting more and more violent, smashing everything in sight. Colonal Acoca watched them, approvingly.

Lucia turned to Megan and Graciela. 'I don't know about you two, but I'm getting out of here. Are you coming?'

They stared at her, too dazed to respond.

Sister Teresa was hurrying towards them, carrying something wrapped in a piece of canvas. Some of the men were herding more nuns into the refectory.

'Come on,' Lucia said.

Sisters Teresa, Megan and Graciela hesitated for a moment, then followed Lucia towards the front door. As they turned at the end of the long corridor, they could see that the huge door had been smashed in.

A man suddenly appeared in front of them. 'Going somewhere, ladies? Get back. My friends have plans for you.'

Lucia said, 'We have a gift for you.' She picked up one of the heavy metal candlesticks that lined the hallway tables and smiled.

The man was looking at it, puzzled. 'What can you do with that?'

'This.' Lucia swung the candelabra against his head, and he fell to the ground, unconscious.

The three nuns stared in horror.

'Move!' Lucia said.

A moment later Lucia, Megan, Graciela and Teresa were outside in the front courtyard, hurrying through the gate into the starry night.

Lucia stopped. 'I'm leaving you. They're going to be searching for you, so you'd better get away from here.'

She turned and started towards the mountains that rose in the distance, high above the convent. *I'll hide out up there until the search cools off and then I'll head for Switzerland. Of all the rotten luck. Those bastards blew a perfect cover.*

As Lucia made her way towards higher ground, she glanced down. From her vantage point she could see the three sisters. Incredibly, they were still standing in front of the convent gate, like three black-clad statues. *For God's sake*, she thought. *Get going before they catch you. Move!*

They could not move. It was as though all their senses had been paralyzed for so long that they were unable to take in what was happening to them. The nuns stared down at their feet. They were so dazed they could not think. They had been cloistered for so long behind the gates of God, secluded from the world, that now that they were outside the protective gates, they were filled with feelings of confusion and panic. They had no idea where to go or what to do. Inside, their lives had been organized for them. They had been fed, clothed, told what to do and when to do it. They had lived by the Rule. Suddenly there was no Rule. What did God want from them? What was His plan? They stood huddled together, afraid to speak, afraid to look at one another.

Hesitantly, Sister Teresa pointed to the lights of Ávila in the distance and signed, *that way*. Uncertainly, they began to move towards the town.

Watching them from the hills above, Lucia thought: *No, you idiots! That's the first place they'll look for you. Well, that's your problem. I have my own problems.* She stood there for a moment, watching them walk towards their doom, going to their slaughter. *Shit.*

Lucia scrambled down the hill, stumbling over the loose scree, and ran after them, her cumbersome habit slowing her down.

'Wait a minute,' she called. 'Stop!'

The sisters stopped and turned.

Lucia hurried up to them, out of breath. 'You're going the wrong way. The first place they'll search for you is in town. You've got to hide out somewhere.'

The three sisters stared at her in silence.

Lucia said impatiently, 'The mountains. Get up to the mountains. Follow me.'

She turned and started back towards the mountains. The others watched, and after a moment, they began to trail after her, one by one.

From time to time Lucia looked back to make sure they were following. *Why can't I mind my own business?* she thought. *They're not my responsibility. It's more dangerous if we're all together.* She kept climbing, making sure they stayed in sight.

The others were having a difficult time of it, and every time they slowed down, Lucia stopped to let them catch up with her. *I'll get rid of them in the morning.*

'Let's move faster,' Lucia called.

At the Abbey, the raid had come to an end. The dazed nuns, their habits wrinkled and bloodstained, were being rounded up and put into unmarked, closed trucks.

'Take them back to my headquarters in Madrid,' Colonel Acoca ordered. 'Keep them in isolation.'

'What charge –?'

'Harbouring terrorists.'

'Yes, Colonel,' Patricio Arrieta said. He hesitated. 'Four of the nuns are missing.'

Colonel Acoca's eyes turned cold. 'Find them.'

Colonel Acoca flew back to Madrid to report to the Prime Minister. 'Jaime Miró escaped before we reached the convent.'

Prime Minister Martinez nodded. 'Yes, I heard.' And he wondered whether Jaime Miró had ever been in the convent to begin with. There was no doubt about it. Colonel Acoca was getting dangerously out of control. There had been angry protests about the brutal attack on the convent. The Prime Minister chose his words carefully, 'The newspapers have been hounding me about what happened.'

'The newspapers are making a hero of this terrorist,' Acoca said, stone faced. 'We must not let them pressure us.'

'He's causing the government a great deal of embarrassment, Colonel. And those four nuns – if they talk –'

'Don't worry. They can't get far. I'll catch them and I'll find Miró.'

The Prime Minister had already decided that he could not afford to take any more chances. 'Colonel, I want you to be sure the thirty-six nuns you have are well-treated, and I'm ordering the army to join the search for Miró and the others. You'll work with Colonel Sostelo.'

There was a long, dangerous pause. 'Which one of us will be in charge of the operation?' Acoca's eyes were icy.

The Prime Minister swallowed. 'You will be, of course.'

Lucia and the three sisters travelled through the early dawn, moving north-east into the mountains, heading away from Ávila and the convent. The nuns, used to moving in silence, made little noise. The only sounds were the rustle of their robes, the clicking of their rosaries, an occasional snapping twig, and their gasps for breath as they climbed higher and higher.

They reached a plateau of the Guadarrama mountains and walked along a rutted road bordered by stone walls. They passed fields with sheep and goats. By sunrise they had covered several miles and found themselves in a wooded area outside the small village of Villacastin.

I'll leave them here, Lucia decided. *Their God can take care of them now. He certainly took great care of me*, she thought bitterly. *Switzerland is farther away than ever. I have no money and no passport, and I'm dressed like an undertaker. By now those men know we've escaped. They'll keep looking until they find us. The sooner I get away by myself, the better.*

But at that instant, something happened that made her change her plans.

Sister Teresa was moving through the trees when she stumbled and the package she had been so carefully guarding fell to the ground. It spilled out of its canvas wrapping and Lucia found herself staring at a large, exquisitely wrought gold cross glowing in the rays of the rising sun.

That's real gold, Lucia thought. *Someone up there is looking after me. That cross is manna. Sheer manna. It's my ticket to Switzerland.*

Lucia watched as Sister Teresa picked up the cross and carefully put it back in its wrapping. Lucia smiled to herself. It was going to be easy to take it. These nuns would do anything she told them.

The town of Ávila was in an uproar. News of the attack on the convent had spread quickly, and Father Berrendo was elected to confront Colonel Acoca. The priest was in his seventies, with an outward frailty that belied his inner strength. He was a warm and understanding shepherd to his parishioners. But at the moment he was filled with a cold fury.

Colonel Acoca kept him waiting for an hour, then allowed the priest to be shown into his office.

Father Berrendo said without preamble, 'You and your men attacked a convent without provocation. It was an act of madness.'

'We were simply doing our duty,' the Colonel said curtly. 'The Abbey was sheltering Jaime Miró and his band of murderers, so the sisters brought this on themselves. We're holding them for questioning.'

'Did you find Jaime Miró in the Abbey?' the priest demanded angrily.

Colonel Acoca said smoothly, 'No. He and his men escaped before we got there. But we'll find them, and justice will be done.'

My justice, Colonel Acoca thought savagely.

Chapter 5

The nuns travelled slowly. Their garb was ill-designed for the rugged terrain. Their sandals were too thin to protect their feet against the stony ground, and their habits caught on everything. Sister Teresa found she could not even say her rosary. She needed both hands to keep the branches from snapping in her face.

In the light of day, freedom seemed even more terrifying than before. God had cast the sisters out of Eden into a strange, frightening world, and His guidance that they had leaned on for so long was gone. They found themselves in an uncharted country with no map and no compass. The walls that had protected them from harm for so long had vanished and they felt naked and exposed. Danger was everywhere, and they no longer had a place of refuge. They were aliens. The unaccustomed sights and sounds of the country were dazzling. There were insects and bird songs and hot, blue skies assaulting the senses. And there was something else that was disturbing.

When they first fled the convent, Teresa, Graciela and Megan had carefully avoided looking at one another, instinctively keeping to the rules. But now, each found herself avidly studying the faces of the others. Also, after all the years of silence, they found it difficult to speak, and when they did speak, their words were halting, as though they were learning a strange new skill. Their voices sounded strange in their ears. Only Lucia seemed uninhibited and sure of herself, and the others automatically turned to her for leadership.

'We might as well introduce ourselves,' Lucia said. 'I'm Sister Lucia.'

There was an awkward pause, and Graciela said shyly, 'I'm Sister Graciela.'

The dark-haired, arrestingly beautiful one.

'I'm Sister Megan.'

The young blonde with the striking blue eyes.

'I'm Sister Teresa.'

The eldest of the group. Fifty? Sixty?

As they lay in the woods resting outside of the village, Lucia thought: *They're like newborn birds fallen out of their nests. They won't last five minutes on their own. Well, too bad for them. I'll be on my way to Switzerland with the cross.*

Lucia walked to the edge of the clearing they were in and peered through the trees towards the little village below. A few people were walking along the street, but there was no sign of the men who had raided the convent. *Now*, Lucia thought. *Here's my chance.*

She turned to the others. 'I'm going down to the village to try to get us some food. You wait here.' She nodded towards Sister Teresa. 'You come with me.'

Sister Teresa was confused. For thirty years she had obeyed only the orders of Reverend Mother Betina and now suddenly this sister had taken charge. *But what is happening is God's will*, Sister Teresa thought. *He has appointed her to help us, so she speaks with His voice.* 'I must get this cross to the convent at Mendavia as soon as possible.'

'Right. When we get down there, we'll ask for directions.'

The two of them started down the hill towards the town, Lucia keeping a careful lookout for trouble. There was none.

This is going to be easy, Lucia thought.

They reached the outskirts of the little town. A sign said, 'Villacastin'. Ahead of them was the main street. To the left was a small, deserted street.

Good, Lucia thought. There would be no one to witness what was about to happen.

Lucia turned into the side street. 'Let's go this way. There's less chance of being seen.'

Sister Teresa nodded and obediently followed Lucia. The question now was how to get the cross away from her.

I could grab it and run, Lucia thought, *but she'd probably scream and attract a lot of attention. No, I'll have to make sure she stays quiet.*

The small limb of a tree had fallen to the ground in front of her, and Lucia paused, then stooped to pick it up. It was heavy. *Perfect.* She waited for Sister Teresa to catch up to her.

'Sister Teresa . . .'

The nun turned to look at her, and as Lucia started to raise the club, a male voice from out of nowhere said, 'God be with you, Sisters.'

Lucia spun around, ready to run. A man was standing there, dressed in the long brown robe and cowl of a friar. He was tall and thin, with an aquiline face and the saintliest expression Lucia had ever seen. His eyes seemed to glow with a warm inner light, and his voice was soft and gentle.

'I'm Friar Miguel Carrillo.'

Lucia's mind was racing. Her first plan had been interrupted. But now, suddenly, she had a better one. 'Thank God you found us,' Lucia said.

This man was going to be her escape. He would know the easiest way for her to get out of Spain.

'We come from the Cistercian convent near Ávila,' Lucia explained. 'Last night some men raided it. All the nuns were taken. Four of us managed to escape.'

When the friar replied, his voice was filled with anger. 'I come from the monastery at Saint Generro, where I have been for the past twenty years. We were attacked the night before last.' He sighed. 'I know that God has some plan for all His children, but I must confess that at this moment I don't understand what it might be.'

'These men are searching for us,' Lucia said. 'It is important that we get out of Spain as fast as possible. Do you know how that can be done?'

Friar Carrillo smiled gently. 'I think I can help you, Sister. God has brought us together. Take me to the others.'

Lucia brought the friar to the group.

'This is Friar Carrillo,' she said. 'He's been in a monastery for the last twenty years. He's come to help us.'

Their reactions to the friar were mixed. Graciela dared not look directly at him. Megan studied him with quick, interested glances, and Sister Teresa regarded him as a messenger sent by God, who would lead them to the convent at Mendavia.

Friar Carrillo said, 'The men who attacked the convent will undoubtedly keep searching for you. But they will be looking for four nuns. The first thing we must do is get you a change of clothing.'

Megan reminded him, 'We have no clothes to change into.'

Friar Carrillo gave her a beatific smile. 'Our Lord has a very large wardrobe. Do not worry, my child. He will provide. Let us go into town.'

It was two o'clock in the afternoon, siesta time, and Friar Carrillo and the four sisters walked down the main street of the village, alert for any signs of their pursuers. The shops were closed, but the restaurants and bars were open and from them they could hear strange music issuing, hard, dissonant and raucous sounding.

Friar Carrillo saw the look on Sister Teresa's face. 'That's rock and roll,' he said. 'Very popular with the young these days.'

A pair of young women standing in front of one of the bars stared at the nuns as they passed. The nuns stared back, wide-eyed, at the strange clothing the pair wore. One wore a skirt so short it barely covered her thighs, the other wore a longer skirt that was split up to the sides of her thighs. Both wore tight knitted bodices with no sleeves.

They might as well be naked, Sister Teresa thought, horrified.

In the doorway stood a man who wore a turtleneck sweater, a strange-looking jacket without a collar, and a jewelled pendant.

Unfamiliar odours greeted the nuns as they passed a bodega. Nicotine and whisky.

Megan was staring at something across the street. She stopped.

Friar Carrillo said, 'What is it? What's the matter?' He turned to look.

Megan was watching a woman carrying a baby. How many years had it been since she had seen a baby, or even a small child? Not since the orphanage, fourteen years ago. The sudden shock made Megan realize how far her life had been removed from the outside world.

Sister Teresa was staring at the baby, too, but she was thinking of something else. *It's Monique's baby.* The baby across the street was screaming. *It's screaming because I deserted it. But no, that's impossible. That was thirty years ago.* Sister Teresa turned away, the baby's cries ringing in her ears. They moved on.

They passed a cinema. The poster read, *Three Lovers*, and the photographs displayed showed skimpily-clad women embracing a bare-chested man.

'Why, they're – they're almost naked!' Sister Teresa exclaimed.

Friar Carrillo frowned. 'Yes. It's disgraceful what the cinema is permitted to show these days. That film is pure pornography. The most personal and private acts are there for everyone to see. They turn God's children into animals.'

They passed a hardware store, a hairdressing salon, a flower shop, a sweet shop, all closed for the siesta, and at each shop the sisters stopped and stared at the windows, filled with once familiar, faintly remembered goods.

When they came to a women's dress shop, Friar Carrillo said, 'Stop.'

The blinds were pulled down over the front windows and a sign on the front door said, 'Closed'.

'Wait here for me, please.'

The four women watched as he walked to the corner and turned out of sight. They looked at one another blankly. Where was he going, and what if he did not return?

A few minutes later, they heard the sound of the front

door of the shop opening, and Friar Carrillo stood in the doorway, beaming. He motioned them inside. 'Hurry.'

When they were all in the shop and the friar had locked the door, Lucia asked, 'How did you –?'

'God provides a back door as well as a front door,' the friar said gravely. But there was an impish edge to his voice that made Megan smile.

The sisters looked around the shop in awe. The store was a multi-coloured cornucopia of dresses and sweaters and bras and stockings, high-heeled shoes and boleros. Objects they had not seen in years. And the styles seemed so strange. There were handbags and scarves and compacts and blouses. It was all too much to absorb. The women stood there, gaping.

'We must move quickly,' Friar Carrillo warned them, 'and leave before siesta is over and the shop reopens. Help yourselves. Choose whatever fits you.'

Lucia thought: *Thank God I can finally dress like a woman again.* She walked over to a rack of dresses and began to sort through them. She found a beige skirt and tan silk blouse to go with it. *It's not Balenciaga, but it will do for now.* She picked out panties and a bra and a pair of soft boots. She stepped behind a clothes rack, stripped and in a matter of minutes was dressed and ready to go.

The others were slowly selecting their outfits.

Graciela chose a white cotton dress that set off her black hair and dark complexion, and a pair of sandals.

Megan chose a patterned blue cotton dress that fell below the knees and low-heeled shoes.

Sister Teresa had the most difficult time choosing something to wear. The array of choices was too dazzling. There were silks and flannels and tweeds and leather. There were cottons and twills and corduroys, and there were plaids and checks and stripes of every colour. And they all seemed – *skimpy*, was the word that came to Sister Teresa's mind. For the past thirty years she had been decently covered by the heavy robes of her calling. And now she was being asked to shed them and put on these indecent creations. She finally selected the longest skirt she could find, and a long-sleeved, high-collared cotton blouse.

Friar Carrillo urged, 'Hurry, Sisters. Get undressed and change.'

They looked at one another in embarrassment.

He smiled. 'I'll wait in thc office, of course.'

He walked to the back of the shop and entered the office.

The sisters began to undress, painfully self-conscious in front of one another.

In the office, Friar Carrillo had pulled a chair up to the transom and was looking out through it, watching the sisters strip. He was thinking: *Which one am I going to screw first?*

Miguel Carrillo had begun his career as a thief when he was only ten years old. He was born with curly blond hair and an angelic face, and they had proved to be of inestimable value in his chosen profession. He started at the bottom, snatching handbags and shoplifting, and as he got older, his career expanded and he began robbing drunks and preying on wealthy women. Because of his enormous appeal, he was very successful. He devised several original swindles, each more ingenious than the last. Unfortunately, his latest swindle had proved to be his undoing.

Posing as a friar from a distant monastery, Carrillo travelled from church to church begging sanctuary for the night. It was always granted, and in the morning when the priest came to open the church doors, all the valuable artefacts would be missing, along with the good friar. Unfortunately, fate had double-crossed him and two nights earlier in Benjar, a small town near Ávila, the priest had returned unexpectedly and Miguel Carrillo had been caught in the act of pilfering the church treasury. The priest was a beefy, heavy-set man, and he had wrestled Carrillo to the floor and announced that he was going to turn him over to the police. A heavy silver chalice had fallen to the floor, and Carrillo had picked it up and hit the priest with it. Either the chalice was too heavy, or the priest's skull was too thin, but in any case the priest lay dead on the floor. Miguel Carrillo had fled, panicky, anxious to put himself as far away from the scene of the crime as possible. He had passed through Ávila and heard the story of the attack on the convent by Colonel Acoca and the secret GOE. It was fate that Carrillo had chanced upon the four escaped nuns.

Now, eager with anticipation, he studied their naked bodies, and thought: *There's another interesting possibility. Since Colonel Acoca and his men are looking for the sisters, there is probably a nice, fat reward on their heads. I'll lay them first, and then turn them over to Acoca.*

The women, except for Lucia, who was already dressed, were totally naked. Carrillo watched as they awkwardly put on the new underclothes. Then they finished dressing, clumsily buttoning unaccustomed buttons and fastening zips, hurrying to get away before they were caught.

Time to get to work, Carrillo thought happily. He got down from the chair and walked out into the shop. He approached the women, studied them approvingly, and said, 'Excellent. No one in the world would ever take you for nuns. I might suggest scarves for your heads.' He selected one for each of them and watched them put them on.

Miguel Carrillo had made his decision. Graciela was going to be the first. She was undoubtedly one of the most beautiful women he had ever seen. And that body! *How could she have wasted it on God? I'll show her what to do with it.*

He said to Lucia, Teresa and Megan, 'You must all be hungry. I want you to go to the café we passed and wait for us there. I'll go to the church and borrow some money from the priest so we can eat.' He turned to Graciela. 'I want you to come with me, Sister, to explain to the priest what happened at the convent.'

'I – very well.'

Carrillo said to the others, 'We'll be along in a little while. I would suggest you use the back door.'

He watched as Lucia, Teresa and Megan left. When he heard the door close behind them, he turned to Graciela.

She's fantastic, he thought. *Maybe I'll keep her with me, break her in to some cons. She could be a big help.*

Graciela was watching him. 'I'm ready.'

'Not yet.' Carrillo pretended to study her for a moment. 'No, I'm afraid it won't do. That dress is all wrong for you. Take it off.'

'But – why?'

'It doesn't fit properly,' Carrillo said glibly. 'People will notice, and you don't want to attract attention.'

She hesitated, then moved behind a rack.

'Hurry, now. We have very little time.'

Awkwardly, Graciela slipped the dress over her head. She was in her panties and brassiere when Carrillo suddenly appeared.

'Take everything off.' His voice was husky.

Graciela stared at him. 'What? No!' she cried. 'I – I can't. Please – I –'

Carrillo moved closer to her. 'I'll help you, Sister.'

His hands reached out and he ripped off her brassiere and tore at her panties.

'No!' she screamed. 'You mustn't! Stop it!'

Carrillo grinned. '*Carita*, we're just getting started. You're going to love this.'

His strong arms were around her. He forced her to the floor and lifted his robe.

It was as though a curtain in Graciela's mind suddenly descended. It was the Moor trying to thrust himself inside her, tearing into the depths of her, and her mother's shrill voice was screaming.

And Graciela thought, terrified, *No, not again. No, please – not again . . .*

She was struggling fiercely now, fighting Carrillo off, trying to get up.

'Goddamn you,' he cried.

He slammed his fist into her face, and Graciela fell back, stunned and dizzy.

She found herself spinning back in time.

Back . . . Back . . .

Chapter 6

Las Navas del Marqués, Spain 1950

She was five years old. Her earliest memories were of a procession of naked strangers climbing in and out of her mother's bed.

Her mother explained, 'They are your uncles. You must show them respect.'

The men were gross and crude and lacked affection. They stayed for a night, a week, a month, and then vanished. When they left, Dolores Pinero would immediately look for a new man.

In her youth, Dolores Pinero had been a beauty, and Graciela had inherited her mother's looks. Even as a child, Graciela was stunning to look at, with high cheekbones, an olive complexion, shiny black hair and thick, long eyelashes. Her young body was nubile with promise. With the passage of years, Dolores Pinero's body had turned to fat and her wonderfully boned face had become bruised with the bitter blows of time.

Although Dolores Pinero was no longer beautiful, she was accessible, and she had the reputation of being a passionate bed partner. Making love was her one talent, and she employed it to try to please men into bondage, hoping to keep them by buying their love with her body. She made a meagre living as a seamstress because she was an indifferent one, and was hired only by the women of the village who could not afford the better ones.

Graciela's mother despised her daughter, for she was a constant reminder of the one man whom Dolores Pinero had ever loved. Graciela's father was a handsome young mechanic who had proposed to the beautiful young Dolores, and she had eagerly let him seduce her. When she had broken the news that she was pregnant, he had disappeared, leaving Dolores with the curse of his seed.

Dolores Pinero had a vicious temper, and she took her vengeance out on the child. Any time Graciela did something to displease her, her mother would hit her and scream, 'You're as stupid as your father!'

There was no way for the child to escape the rain of blows or the constant screaming. Graciela would wake up every morning and pray: 'Please, God, don't let Mama beat me today.

'Please, God, make Mama happy today.

'Please, God, let Mama say she loves me today.'

When she was not attacking Graciela, her mother ignored her. Graciela prepared her own meals and took care of her clothes. She made her lunch to take to school, and she would say to her teacher, 'My mother made me *empanadas* today. She knows how much I like *empanadas*.'

Or: 'I tore my dress, but my mother sewed it up for me. She loves doing things for me.'

Or: 'My mother and I are going to the pictures tomorrow.'

And it would break her teacher's heart. Las Navas del Marqués is a small village an hour from Ávila, and like all villages everywhere, everyone knew everyone else's business. The lifestyle of Dolores Pinero was a disgrace, and it reflected on Graciela. Mothers refused to let their children play with the little girl, lest their morals be contaminated. Graciela went to the school on Plazoleta del Cristo, but she had no friends and no playmates. She was one of the brightest students in the school, but her exam results were poor. It was difficult for her to concentrate, for she was always tired.

Her teacher would admonish her, 'You must get to bed

earlier, Graciela, so that you are rested enough to do your work properly.'

But her exhaustion had nothing to do with getting to bed late. Graciela and her mother shared a small, two-room *casa*. The girl slept on a couch in the tiny room, with only a thin, worn curtain separating it from the bedroom. How could Graciela tell her teacher about the obscene sounds in the night that awakened her and kept her awake, as she listened to her mother making love to whichever stranger happened to be in her bed?

When Graciela brought home her report card, her mother would scream, 'These are the cursed marks I expected you to get, and do you know why you got these terrible marks? Because you're stupid. Stupid!'

And Graciela would believe it and try hard not to cry.

In the afternoons when school was over, Graciela would wander around by herself, walking through the narrow, winding streets lined with acacia and sycamore trees, past the whitewashed stone houses, where loving fathers lived with their families. Graciela had many playmates, but they were all in her mind. There were beautiful girls and handsome boys, and they invited her to all their parties, where they served wonderful cakes and ice cream. Her imaginary friends were kind and loving, and they all thought she was very smart. When her mother was not around, Graciela would carry on long conversations with them.

Would you help me with my homework, Graciela? I don't know how to do sums, and you're so good at them.

What shall we do tonight, Graciela? We could go to the pictures, or walk into town and have a lemonade.

Will your mother let you come to dinner tonight, Graciela? We're having paella.

No, I'm afraid not. Mother gets lonely if I'm not with her. I'm all she has, you know.

On Sundays, Graciela rose early and dressed quietly, careful not to awaken her mother and whichever uncle was in her bed, and walked to the San Juan Bautista Church, where Father Perez talked of the joys of life after death, a fairytale life with Jesus; and Graciela could not wait to die and meet Jesus.

Father Perez was an attractive priest in his early forties. He had ministered to the rich and the poor, and the sick and the vital, since he had come to Las Navas del Marqués several years earlier, and there were no secrets in the little village to which he was not privy. Father Perez knew Graciela as a regular church-goer, and he, too, was aware of the stories of the constant stream of strangers who shared Dolores Pinero's bed. It was not a fit home for a young girl, but there was nothing anyone could do about it. It amazed the priest that Graciela had turned out as well as she had. She was kind and gentle and never complained or talked about her home life.

Graciela would appear at church every Sunday morning wearing a clean, neat outfit that he was sure she had washed herself. Father Perez knew she was shunned by the other children in town, and his heart went out to her. He made it a point to spend a few moments with her after mass each Sunday, and when he had time, he would take her to a little café for a treat of *helado*.

In the winter Graciela's life was a dreary landscape, monotonous and gloomy. Las Navas del Marqués was in a valley surrounded by the Cruz Verde mountains and, because of that, the winters were six months long. The summers were easier to bear, for then the tourists arrived and filled the town with laughter and dancing and the streets came alive. The tourists would gather at the Plaza de Manuel Delgado Barredo, with its little bandstand built on stone, and listen to the orchestra and watch the natives dance the Sardana, the centuries-old traditional folk dance, barefoot, their hands linked, as they moved gracefully around in a colourful circle. Graciela watched the visitors as they sat at the pavement cafés drinking *aperitivos* or shopping at the *pescadería* – the fish market, or the *farmacia*. At one o'clock in the afternoon the *bodega* was always filled with tourists drinking *chateo* and picking at *tapas*, seafood and olives and chips.

The most exciting thing for Graciela was to watch the *paseo* each evening. Boys and girls would walk up and down the Plaza Mayor in segregated groups, the boys eyeing the girls, while parents and grandparents and friends watched, hawk-eyed, from sidewalk cafés. It was the traditional mating ritual, observed for centuries. Graciela longed to join in it, but her mother forbade her.

'Do you want to be a *puta*?' she would scream at Graciela. 'Stay away from boys. They want only one thing from you. I know from experience,' she added bitterly.

If the days were bearable, the nights were an agony. Through the thin curtain that separated their beds, Graciela could hear the sounds of savage moaning and writhings and heavy breathing, and always the obscenities.

'Faster . . . harder!'

'*¡Cógeme!*'

'*¡Mámame la verga!*'

'*¡Métela en el culo!*'

Before she was ten years old, Graciela had heard every obscene word in the Spanish vocabulary. They were whispered and shouted and shuddered and moaned. The cries of passion repelled Graciela, and at the same time awakened strange longings in her.

When Graciela was fourteen years old, the Moor moved in. He was the biggest man Graciela had ever seen. His skin was shiny black, and his head was shaved. He had enormous shoulders, a barrel chest and huge arms. The Moor had arrived in the middle of the night when Graciela was asleep, and she got her first sight of him in the morning when he pushed the curtain aside and walked stark naked past Graciela's bed to go outside to the outhouse in the yard.

Graciela looked at him and almost gasped aloud. He was enormous, in every part. *That will kill my mother*, Graciela thought.

The Moor was staring at her. 'Well, well. And who do we have here?'

Dolores Pinero hurried out of her bed and moved to his side. 'My daughter,' she said curtly.

A wave of embarrassment swept over Graciela, as she saw her mother's naked body next to the man.

The Moor smiled, showing beautiful white, even teeth. 'What's your name, *guapa*?'

Graciela was too shamed by his nakedness to speak.

'Her name's Graciela. She's retarded.'

'She's beautiful. I'll bet you looked like that when you were young.'

'I'm still young,' Dolores Pinero snapped. She turned to her daughter. 'Get dressed. You'll be late for school.'

'Yes, Mama.'

The Moor stood there, eyeing her.

The older woman took his arm and said cajolingly, 'Come back to bed, *querido*. We're not finished yet.'

'Later,' the Moor said. He was still looking at Graciela.

The Moor stayed. Every day when Graciela came home from school she prayed that he would be gone. For reasons she did not understand, he terrified her. He was always polite to her and never made any advances, yet the mere thought of him sent shivers through her body.

His treatment of her mother was something different. The Moor stayed in the small house most of the day, drinking heavily. He took whatever money Dolores Pinero earned. Sometimes at night in the middle of lovemaking, Graciela would hear him beating her mother, and in the morning Dolores Pinero would appear with a blackened eye or split lip.

'Mama, why do you put up with him?' Graciela asked.

'You wouldn't understand,' she said sullenly. 'He's a real

man, not a midget like the others. He knows how to satisfy a woman.' She ran her hand through her hair coquettishly. 'Besides, he's madly in love with me.'

Graciela did not believe it. She knew that the Moor was using her mother, but she did not dare protest again. She was too terrified of her mother's temper, for when Dolores Pinero was really angry, a kind of insanity took possession of her. She had once chased Graciela with a kitchen knife because she had dared make a pot of tea for one of the 'uncles'.

Early one Sunday morning Graciela rose to get ready for church. Her mother had left early to deliver some dresses. As Graciela pulled off her nightgown, the curtain was pushed aside and the Moor appeared. He was naked.

'Where's your mother, *guapa*?'

'Mama went out early. She had some errands to do.'

The Moor was studying Graciela's nude body. 'You really are a beauty,' he said softly.

Graciela felt her face flush. She knew what she should do. She should cover her nakedness, put on her skirt and blouse and leave. Instead, she stood there, unable to move. She watched his manhood begin to swell and grow before her eyes. She could hear the voices ringing in her ears:

'Faster . . . Harder!'

She felt faint.

The Moor said huskily, 'You're a child. Get your clothes on and get out of here.'

And Graciela found herself moving. Moving towards him. She reached up and slid her arms around his waist and felt his male hardness against her body.

'No,' she moaned. 'I'm not a child.'

The pain that followed was like nothing Graciela had ever known. It was excruciating, unbearable. It was wonderful, exhilarating, beautiful. She held the Moor tightly in her arms, screaming with ecstasy. He brought her to orgasm after orgasm, and Graciela thought: *So this is what the mystery is all about.* And it was so wonderful to finally know the secret of all creation, to be a part of life at last, to know what joy was for now and for ever.

'*What the fuck are you doing?*'

It was Dolores Pinero's voice screaming, and for an instant everything stopped, frozen in time. Dolores Pinero was standing at the side of the bed, staring down at her daughter and the Moor.

Graciela looked up at her mother, too terrified to speak. Dolores Pinero's eyes were filled with an insane rage.

'You bitch!' she yelled. 'You rotten bitch.'

'Mamá – please –'

Dolores Pinero picked up a heavy iron ashtray at the bedside and slammed it against her daughter's head.

That was the last thing Graciela remembered.

She awoke in a large, white hospital ward with two dozen beds in it, all of them occupied. Harried nurses scurried back and forth, trying to attend to the needs of the patients.

Graciela's head was racked with excruciating pain. Each time she moved, rivers of fire flowed through her. She lay there, listening to the cries and moans of the other patients.

Late in the afternoon, a young doctor stopped by the side of her bed. He was in his early thirties, but he looked old and tired.

'Well,' he said. 'You're finally awake.'

'Where am I?' It hurt her to speak.

'You're in the charity ward of the Hospital Provincial in Ávila. You were brought in yesterday. You were in terrible shape. We had to stitch up your forehead.' The doctor went on: 'Our chief surgeon decided to sew you up himself. He said you were too beautiful to have scars.'

He's wrong, Graciela thought. *I'll be scarred for the rest of my life.*

On the second day Father Perez came to see Graciela. A nurse moved a chair to the bedside. The priest looked at the beautiful, pale young girl lying there and his heart melted. The terrible thing that had happened to her was the scandal of Las Navas del Marqués, but there was nothing anyone could do about it. Dolores Pinero had told the *policía* that her daughter had injured her head in a fall.

Now, Father Perez asked, 'Are you feeling better, child?'

Graciela nodded, and the movement made her head pound.

'The *policía* have been asking questions. Is there anything you would like me to tell them?'

There was a long silence. Finally she said, 'It was an accident.'

He could not bear the look in her eyes. 'I see.'

What he had to say was painful beyond words. 'Graciela, I spoke with your mother . . .'

And Graciela knew. 'I – I can't go home again, can I?'

'No, I'm afraid not. We'll talk about it.' Father Perez took Graciela's hand. 'I'll come back to see you tomorrow.'

'Thank you, Father.'

When he left, Graciela lay there, and she prayed: *Dear God, please let me die. I don't want to live.*

She had nowhere to go and no one to go to. Never again would she see her home. She would never see her school again, or the familiar faces of her teachers. There was nothing in the world left for her.

A nurse stopped at her bedside. 'You need anything?'

Graciela looked up at her in despair. What was there to say?

The following day the doctor appeared again.

'I have good news,' he said awkwardly. 'You're well enough to leave now.' That was a lie, but the rest of his speech was true. 'We need the bed.'

She was free to go – but go where?

When Father Perez arrived an hour later, he was accompanied by another priest.

'This is Father Berrendo, an old friend of mine.'

Graciela glanced up at the frail-looking priest. 'Father.'

He was right, Father Berrendo thought. *She is beautiful.*

Father Perez had told him the story of what had happened to Graciela. The priest had expected to see some visible signs of the kind of environment the child had lived in, a hardness, a defiance, or self-pity. There were none of those things in the young girl's face.

'I'm sorry you've had such a bad time,' Father Berrendo told her. The sentence carried a deeper meaning.

Father Perez said, 'Graciela, I must return to Las Navas del Marqués. I am leaving you in Father Berrendo's hands.'

Graciela was filled with a sudden sense of panic. She felt as though her last link with home was being cut. 'Don't go,' she pleaded.

Father Perez took her hand in his. 'I know you feel alone,' he said warmly, 'but you're not. Believe me, child, you're not.'

A nurse approached the bed carrying a bundle. She handed it to Graciela. 'Here are your clothes. I'm afraid you're going to have to leave now.'

An even greater panic seized her. '*Now?*'

The two priests exchanged a look.

'Why don't you get dressed and come with me?' Father Berrendo suggested. 'We can talk.'

Fifteen minutes later Father Berrendo was helping Graciela out of the hospital door into the warm sunlight. There was a garden in front of the hospital with brightly coloured flowers, but Graciela was too dazed even to notice them.

When they were seated in his office, Father Berrendo said, 'Father Perez told me that you have no place to go.'

Graciela nodded.

'No relatives?'

'Only –' It was difficult to say it. 'Only – my mother.'

'Father Perez said that you were a regular churchgoer in your village.'

A village she would never see again. 'Yes.'

Graciela thought of those Sunday mornings, and the beauty of the church services and how she had longed to be with Jesus and escape from the pain of the life she lived.

'Graciela, have you ever thought of entering a convent?'

'No.' She was startled by the idea.

'There is a convent here in Ávila – the Cistercian convent. They would take care of you there.'

'I – I don't know.' The idea was frightening.

'It is not for everyone,' Father Berrendo told her. 'And I must warn you, it is the strictest order of them all. Once you walk through the gates and take the vows, you have made a promise to God never to leave.'

Graciela sat there, her mind filled with conflicting thoughts, staring out the window. The idea of shutting herself away from the world was terrifying. *It would be like going to prison.* But on the other hand, what did the world have to offer her? Pain and despair beyond bearing. She had often thought of suicide. This might offer a way out of her misery.

Father Berrendo said, 'It's up to you, my child. If you like, I will take you to meet the Reverend Mother Prioress.'

Graciela nodded. 'All right.'

The Reverend Mother studied the face of the young girl before her. Last night for the first time in many, many years she had heard the voice. *A young child will come to you. Protect her.* 'How old are you, my dear?'

'Fourteen.'

She's old enough. In the fourth century the Pope decreed that girls could be permitted to become nuns at the age of twelve.

'I'm afraid,' Graciela said to the Reverend Mother Betina.

I'm afraid. The words rang in Betina's mind: *I'm afraid* . . .

That had been so many long years ago. She was speaking

to her priest. 'I don't know if I have a calling for this, Father. I'm afraid.'

'Betina, the first contact with God can be very disturbing, and the decision to dedicate your life to Him is a difficult one.'

How did I find my calling? Betina had wondered.

She had never been even faintly interested in religion. As a young girl she had avoided church and Sunday school. In her teens she was more interested in parties and clothes and boys. If her friends in Madrid had been asked to select possible candidates to become a nun, Betina would have been at the bottom of the list. More accurately, she would not even have been on their list. But when she was nineteen, events started to happen that changed her life.

She was in her bed, asleep, when a voice said, 'Betina, get up and go outside.'

She opened her eyes and sat up, frightened. She turned on the bedside lamp. She was alone. *What a strange dream.*

But the voice had been so real. She lay down again, but it was impossible to go back to sleep.

Betina, get up and go outside.

It's my subconscious, she thought. *Why would I want to go outside in the middle of the night?*

She turned out the light and a moment later turned it on again. *This is crazy.*

But she put on a dressing-gown and slippers and went downstairs. The household was asleep.

She opened the kitchen door, and as she did a wave of fear swept over her, because somehow she knew that she was supposed to go out the back into the yard. She looked around in the darkness, and her eye caught a glint of moonlight shining on an old refrigerator that had been abandoned and was used to store tools.

Betina suddenly knew why she was there. She walked over to the refrigerator as though hypnotized, and opened it. Her three-year-old brother was inside, unconscious.

That was the first incident. In time, Betina rationalized it as a perfectly normal experience. *I must have heard my brother get up and go out into the yard, and I knew the refrigerator was there, and I was worried about him so I went outside to check.*

The next experience was not so easy to explain. It happened a month later.

In her sleep, Betina heard a voice say, 'You must put out the fire.'

She sat up, wide awake, her pulse racing. Again, it was impossible to go back to sleep. She put on a dressing-gown and slippers and went into the landing. No smoke. No fire. She opened her parents' bedroom door. Everything was normal there. There was no fire in her brother's bedroom. She went downstairs and looked through every room. There was no sign of a fire.

I'm an idiot, Betina thought. *It was only a dream.*

She went back to bed, just as the house was rocked by an explosion. She and her family escaped, and the firemen managed to put out the fire.

'It started in the basement,' a fireman explained. 'And a boiler exploded.'

The next incident happened three weeks later. This time it was no dream.

Betina was on the patio, reading, when she saw a stranger walking across the yard. He looked at her and in that instant she felt a malevolence coming from him that was almost palpable. He turned away and was gone.

Betina was unable to get him out of her mind.

Three days later, she was in an office building, waiting for the lift. The lift door opened, and she was about to step into it when she looked at the lift operator. It was the man she had seen in her garden. Betina backed away, frightened. The lift door closed and the lift went up. Moments later, it crashed, killing everyone in it.

The following Sunday, Betina went to church.

Dear Lord, I don't know what's happening to me, and I'm scared. Please guide me and tell me what you want me to do.

The answer came that night as Betina slept. The voice said one word. *Devotion.*

She thought about it all night, and in the morning she went to talk to the priest.

He listened intently to what she had to say.

'Ah. You are one of the fortunate ones. You have been chosen.'

'Chosen for what?'

'Are you willing to devote your life to God, my child?'

'I – I don't know. I'm afraid.'

But in the end, she had joined the convent.

I chose the right path, the Reverend Mother Betina thought, *because I have never known so much happiness . . .*

And now there was this battered child saying, 'I'm afraid.'

The Reverend Mother took Graciela's hand. 'Take your time, Graciela. God won't go away. Think about it and come back and we can discuss it.'

But what was there to think about? *I've got nowhere else in the world to go*, Graciela thought. And the silence would be welcome. *I have heard too many terrible sounds.* She looked at the Reverend Mother and said, 'I will welcome the silence.'

That had been seventeen years earlier, and in that time Graciela had found peace for the first time in her life. Her life was dedicated to God. The past no longer belonged to her. She was forgiven the horrors she had grown up with. She was Christ's bride, and at the end of her life, she would join Him.

As the years passed in deep silence, despite the occasional nightmares, the terrible sounds in her mind gradually faded away.

Sister Graciela was assigned to work in the garden, tending the tiny rainbows of God's miracle, never tiring of their splendour. The walls of the convent rose high above her on all sides like a stone mountain, but Graciela never felt that they were shutting her in; they were shutting the terrible world out, a world she never wanted to see again.

Life in the convent was serene and peaceful. But now, suddenly her terrible nightmares had turned into a reality. Her world had been invaded by barbarians. They had forced her out of her sanctuary, into the world she had renounced for ever. And her sins came flooding back, filling her with horror. The Moor had returned. She could feel his hot breath on her face. As she fought him, Graciela opened her eyes, and it was the friar on top of her trying to penetrate her. He was saying, 'Stop fighting me, Sister. You're going to enjoy this!'

'Mama,' Graciela cried aloud. 'Mama! Help me!'

Chapter 7

Lucia Carmine felt wonderful as she walked down the street with Megan and Teresa. It was marvellous to wear feminine clothes again and hear the whisper of silk against her skin. She glanced at the others. They were walking nervously, unaccustomed to their new clothes, looking self-conscious and embarrassed in their skirts and stockings. *They look as though they've been dropped from another planet. They certainly don't belong on this one*, Lucia thought. *They might as well be wearing signs that say: 'Catch Me.'*

Sister Teresa was the most uncomfortable of the women. Thirty years in the convent had deeply ingrained a sense of modesty in her, and it was being violated by the events that had been thrust upon her. This world to which she had once belonged now seemed unreal. It was the convent that was real, and she longed to hurry back to the sanctuary of its protective walls.

Megan was aware that men were eyeing her as she walked down the street, and she blushed. She had lived in a world of women for so long that she had forgotten what it was like to see a man, let alone have one smile at her. It was embarrassing, indecent . . . exciting. The men aroused feelings in Megan that had been long since buried. For the first time in years, she was conscious of her femaleness.

They were passing the bar they had gone by before and the music was blaring out into the street. What had Friar Carrillo called it? *Rock and roll. Very popular with the young.* Something bothered her. And suddenly Megan realized what it was. When they had passed the cinema, the friar had said:

It's disgraceful what the cinema is permitted to show these days. That film is pure pornography. The most personal and private acts are there for everyone to see.

Megan's heart began to beat faster. If Friar Carrillo had been locked up in a monastery for the past twenty years, how could he possibly have known about rock music or what was in the film? Something was terribly wrong.

She turned to Lucia and Teresa and said urgently, 'We've got to return to the shop.'

They watched as Megan turned and ran back, and they quickly began to follow her.

Graciela was on the floor, desperately fighting to get free, scratching and clawing at Carrillo.

'God damn you! Hold still!' He was getting winded.

He heard a sound and glanced up. He saw the heel of a shoe swinging towards his head, and that was the last thing he remembered.

Megan picked up the trembling Graciela and held her in her arms. 'Shh. It's all right. He won't bother you any more.'

It was several minutes before Graciela could speak. 'He – he – it wasn't my fault this time,' she said pleadingly.

Lucia and Teresa had come into the shop. Lucia sized up the situation at a glance.

'The bastard!'

She looked down at the unconscious, half-naked figure on the floor. As the others watched, Lucia grabbed some belts from a counter and tied Miguel Carrillo's hands tightly behind his back. 'Tie his feet,' she told Megan.

Megan went to work.

Finally, Lucia stood up, satisfied. 'There. When they open up the shop this afternoon, he can explain to them what he was doing here.' She looked at Graciela closely. 'Are you all right?'

'I – I – yes.' She tried to smile.

'We'd better get out of here,' Megan said. 'Get dressed. Quickly.'

When they were ready to leave, Lucia said, 'Wait a minute.'

She went over to the cash register and pressed a key. There were a few hundred peseta notes inside. She scooped them up, picked up a purse from a counter and put the money inside. She saw the disapproving expression on Teresa's face.

Lucia said, 'Look at it this way, Sister. If God didn't want us to have this money, He wouldn't have put it there for us.'

They were seated in the café, having a conference. Sister Teresa was speaking. 'We must get the cross to the convent at Mendavia as quickly as possible. There will be safety there for all of us.'

Not for me, Lucia thought. *My safety is that Swiss bank. But first things first. I've got to get hold of that cross.*

'The convent at Mendavia is north of here, isn't it?'

'Yes.'

'The men will be looking for us in every town. So we'll sleep in the hills tonight.'

Nobody will hear her even if she does scream.

A waitress brought menus to the table and handed them out. The sisters examined them, their expressions confused. Suddenly Lucia understood. It had been so many years since they had been given choices of any kind. At the convent they had automatically eaten the simple food placed before them. Now they were confronted with a cornucopia of unfamiliar delicacies.

Sister Teresa was the first to speak. 'I – I will have some coffee and bread, please.'

Sister Graciela said, 'I, too.'

Megan said, 'We have a long, hard journey ahead of us. I suggest that we order something more nourishing, like eggs.'

Lucia looked at her with new eyes. *She's the one to keep an eye on*, Lucia thought. Aloud she said, 'Sister Megan is right. Let me order for you, Sisters.'

She ordered sliced oranges, *tortillas de patatas*, bacon, hot rolls, jam and coffee.

'We're in a hurry,' she told the waitress.

Siesta ended at 4.30, and the town would be waking up. She wanted to be out of there before that happened, before they discovered Miguel Carrillo in the dress shop.

When the food arrived, the sisters sat there staring at it.

'Help yourselves,' Lucia urged them.

They began to eat, hesitatingly at first, and then with gusto, overcoming their feelings of guilt.

Sister Teresa was the only one having a problem. She took one bite of food and said, 'I – I can't. It's – it's surrendering.'

Megan said, 'Sister, you want to get to the convent, don't you? Then you must eat to keep up your strength.'

Sister Teresa said primly, 'Very well. I'll eat. But I promise you, I won't enjoy it.'

It was all Lucia could do to keep a straight face. 'Good, Sister. Eat.'

When they had finished, Lucia paid the bill with some of the money she had taken from the cash register and they walked out into the hot sunshine. The streets were beginning to come alive, and the shops were starting to open. *By now they have probably caught Miguel Carrillo*, Lucia thought.

Lucia and Teresa were impatient to get out of town, but Graciela and Megan were walking slowly, fascinated by the sights and sounds and the smells of the town.

Not until they had reached the outskirts and headed towards the mountains did Lucia begin to relax. They moved steadily north, climbing upwards, making slow progress in the hilly terrain. Lucia was tempted to ask Sister Teresa if she would like her to carry the package, but she did not want to say anything that might make the older woman suspicious.

When they reached a small glade in the highland, surrounded by trees, Lucia said, 'We can spend the night here. In the morning we'll head for the convent at Mendavia.'

The others nodded, believing her.

*

The sun moved slowly across the blue sky, and the glade was silent, except for the soothing sounds of summer. Finally, night fell.

One by one the women stretched out on the green grass.

Lucia lay there, breathing lightly, listening for a deeper silence, waiting for them to fall asleep so that she could make her move.

Sister Teresa was finding it difficult to sleep. It was a strange experience sleeping out under the stars, surrounded by her sisters. They had names now, and faces and voices, and she was afraid that God was going to punish her for this forbidden knowledge. She felt terribly lost.

Sister Megan, too, was having difficulty getting to sleep. She was filled with the excitement of the day's events. *How did I know that the friar was a fraud?* she wondered. *And where did I get the courage to save Sister Graciela?* She smiled, unable to keep from being a tiny bit pleased with herself, even though she knew such a feeling was a sin.

Graciela was asleep, emotionally drained by what she had gone through. She tossed and turned in her sleep, haunted by dreams of being chased down dark, long, endless corridors.

Lucia Carmine lay still, waiting. She lay there for almost two hours and then quietly sat up and moved through the darkness towards Sister Teresa. She would take the package and disappear.

As she neared Sister Teresa, Lucia saw that the nun was awake on her knees, praying. Damn! Lucia hurriedly retreated.

Lucia lay down again, forcing herself to be patient. Sister Teresa could not pray all night. She had to get some sleep.

Lucia planned. The money taken from the cash register would be enough for her to take a bus or a train to Madrid. Once there, it would be simple to find a pawnbroker. She saw herself walking in and handing him the golden cross. The pawnbroker would suspect that it was stolen, but that would not matter. He would have plenty of customers eager to buy it.

I will give you one hundred thousand pesetas for it.

She would pick it up from the counter. *I would rather sell my body first.*

One hundred and fifty thousand pesetas.

I would prefer to melt it down and let the gold run in the gutter.

Two hundred thousand pesetas. That is my last offer.

You are robbing me blind, but I will accept it.

The pawnbroker would eagerly reach for it.

On one condition.

A condition?

Yes. I misplaced my passport. Do you know someone who can arrange a passport for me? Her hands would still be on the golden cross.

He would hesitate, then say, *I happen to have a friend who does things like that.*

And the deal would be done. She would be on her way to Switzerland and freedom. She remembered her father's words: *There is more money there than you could spend in ten lifetimes.*

Her eyes began to close. It had been a long day.

In her half-sleep, Lucia heard the sound of a church bell from the distant village. It sent memories flooding through her, of another place, another time . . .

Chapter 8

Taormina, Sicily 1968

She was awakened every morning by the distant sound of the bells of the Church of San Domenico, high in the Peloritani mountains surrounding Taormina. She enjoyed waking up slowly, languorously stretching like a cat. She kept her eyes closed, knowing that there was something wonderful to remember. *What was it?* The question teased at her mind, and she pushed it back, not wanting to know just yet, wanting to savour the surprise. And suddenly her mind was joyously flooded with it. She was Lucia Maria Carmine, the daughter of Angelo Carmine, and that was enough to make anyone in the world happy.

They lived in a large, storybook villa filled with more servants than the fifteen-year-old Lucia could count. A bodyguard drove her to school each morning in an armoured limousine. She grew up with the prettiest dresses and the most expensive toys in all of Sicily, and was the envy of her schoolmates.

But it was her father around whom Lucia's life centred. In her eyes, he was the most handsome man in the world. He was short and heavyset, with a strong face and stormy brown eyes that radiated power. He had two sons, Arnaldo and Victor, but it was his daughter whom Angelo Carmine adored. And Lucia worshipped him. In church when the priest spoke of God, Lucia always thought of her father.

He would come to her bedside in the morning and say, 'Time to get up for school, *faccia del angelo*.' Angel face.

It was not true, of course. Lucia knew she was not really beautiful. *I'm attractive*, she thought, studying herself objectively in the mirror. Yes. Striking, rather than beautiful. Her reflection showed a young girl with an oval face, creamy skin, even, white teeth, a strong chin – too strong? – voluptuous, full lips – too full? – and dark, knowing eyes. But if her face fell just short of being beautiful, her body more than made up for it. At fifteen, Lucia had the body of a woman, with round, firm breasts, a narrow waist and hips that moved with sensuous promise.

'We're going to have to marry you off early,' her father would tease her. 'Soon you will drive the young men *pazzi*, my little virgin.'

'I want to marry someone like you, Papa, but there is no one like you.'

He laughed. 'Never mind. We'll find you a prince. You were born under a lucky star, and one day you will know what it is like to have a man hold you in his arms and make love to you.'

Lucia blushed. 'Yes, Papa.'

It was true that no one had made love to her – not for the past twelve hours. Benito Patas, one of her bodyguards, always came to her bed when her father was out of town. Having Benito make love to her in her house added to the thrill because Lucia knew that her father would kill them both if he ever discovered what was going on.

Benito was in his thirties, and it flattered him that the beautiful young virgin daughter of the great Angelo Carmine had chosen him to deflower her.

'Was it as you expected?' he asked the first time he bedded her.

'Oh, yes,' Lucia breathed. 'Better.'

She thought: *While he's not as good as Mario, Tony or Enrico, he's certainly better than Roberto and Leo.* She could not remember the names of all the others.

At thirteen, Lucia had felt that she had been a virgin long

enough. She had looked around and decided that the lucky boy would be Paolo Costello, the son of Angelo Carmine's doctor. Paolo was seventeen, tall and husky, and the star soccer player at his school. Lucia had fallen madly in love with Paolo the first time she had seen him. She managed to run into him as often as possible. It never occurred to Paolo that their constant meetings had been carefully contrived. He regarded the attractive young daughter of Angelo Carmine as a child. But on a hot summer day in August, Lucia decided she could wait no longer. She telephone Paolo.

'Paolo – this is Lucia Carmine. My father has something he would like to discuss with you, and he wondered whether you could meet him this afternoon at our pool house?'

Paolo was both surprised and flattered. He was in awe of Angelo Carmine, but he had not known that the powerful Mafioso was even aware of his existence. 'I would be delighted,' Paolo said. 'What time would he like me to be there?'

'Three o'clock.'

Siesta time, when the world would be asleep. The pool house was isolated, at the far end of their widespread property, and her father was out of town. There would be no chance of their being interrupted.

Paolo arrived promptly at the appointed hour. The gate leading to the garden was open, and he walked directly to the pool house. He stopped at the closed door and knocked. 'Signore Carmine? *Pronto* . . .?'

There was no response. Paolo checked his watch. Cautiously, he opened the door and stepped inside. The room was dark.

'Signore Carmine?'

A figure moved towards him. 'Paolo . . .'

He recognized Lucia's voice. 'Lucia, I'm looking for your father. Is he here?'

She was closer to him now, close enough for Paolo to see that she was stark naked.

'My God!' Paolo gasped. 'What –?'

'I want you to make love to me.'

'You're *pazza*! You're only a child. I'm getting out of here.' He started towards the door.

'Go ahead. I'll tell my father you raped me.'

'No, you wouldn't.'

'Leave, and you'll find out.'

He stopped. If Lucia carried out her threat, there was not the slightest doubt in Paolo's mind as to what his fate would be. Castration would be only the beginning.

He walked back to Lucia to reason with her. 'Lucia, dear –'

'I like it when you call me dear.'

'No – listen to me, Lucia. This is very serious. Your father will kill me if you tell him I raped you.'

'I know.'

He made another stab at it. 'My father would be disgraced. My whole family would be disgraced.'

'I know.'

It was hopeless. 'What do you want from me?'

'I want you to do it to me.'

'No. It is impossible. If your father found out, he would kill me.'

'And if you leave here, he will kill you. You haven't got much choice, have you?'

He stared at her, panicky. 'Why me, Lucia?'

'Because I'm in love with you, Paolo!' She took his hands and pressed them gently between her legs. 'I'm a woman. Make me feel like one.'

In the dim light Paolo could see the twin mounds of her breasts, her hard nipples, and the soft, dark hair between her legs.

Jesus, Paolo thought. *What can a man do?*

She was leading him to a couch, helping him out of his trousers and his shorts. She knelt and put his male hardness in her mouth, sucking it gently, and Paolo thought: *She's done this before*. And when he was on top of her, plunging deep inside her, and she had her hands tightly wrapped around his backside, her hips thrusting hungrily against his, Paolo thought: *My God, she's marvellous.*

Lucia was in heaven. It was as though she had been born for this. Instinctively she knew exactly what to do to please him and to please herself. Her whole body was on fire. She felt herself building to a climax, higher and higher, and when it finally happened, she screamed aloud in sheer joy. They both lay there, spent, breathing hard.

Lucia finally spoke. She said, 'Same time tomorrow.'

When Lucia was sixteen, Angelo Carmine decided that it was time for his daughter to see something of the world. With an elderly Aunt Rosa as chaperone, Lucia spent her school holidays in Capri and Ischia, Venice and Rome, and a dozen other places.

'You must be cultured – not a peasant, like your Papa. Travel will round out your education. In Capri Aunt Rosa will take you to see the Carthusian Monastery of St James and the Chapel of San Michele and the Palazzo a Mare . . .'

'Yes, Papa.'

'In Venice there is St Mark's Basilica, the Doges' Palace, the church of San Gregorio, and the Accademia Museum.'

'Yes, Papa.'

'Rome is the treasure house of the world. There you must visit the Citta Vaticano, and the Basilica of Santa Maria Maggiore, and the Galleria Borghese, of course.'

'Of course.'

'And Milano! You must go to the Conservatorio for a concert recital. I will arrange tickets for La Scala for you and Aunt Rosa. You will see the Municipal Museum of Art, and there are dozens of churches and museums.'

'Yes, Papa.'

With very careful planning, Lucia managed to see none of those places. Aunt Rosa insisted on taking a siesta every afternoon and retiring early each evening.

'You must get your rest too, child.'

'Certainly, Aunt Rosa.'

And so while Aunt Rosa slept, Lucia danced at the Quisisana in Capri, rode in a *carrozza* with a beplumed and behatted horse pulling it, joined a group of college boys at the Marina Piccola, went on picnics at Bagni di Tiberio, and took the *Funicolare* up to Anacapri, where she joined a group of French students for drinks at the Piazza Umertol.

In Venice a handsome gondolier took her to a disco, and a fisherman took her fishing at Chioggia. And Aunt Rosa slept.

In Rome Lucia drank wine from Apulia and discovered all the off-beat fun restaurants like Marte and Ranieri and Giggi Fazi.

Wherever she went, Lucia found hidden little bars and nightclubs and romantic, good-looking men, and she thought: *Dear Papa was so right. Travel has rounded out my education.*

In bed, she learned to speak several different languages, and she thought: *This is so much more fun than my language classes at school.*

When Lucia returned home to Taormina, she confided to her closest girl-friends: 'I was naked in Naples, stoned in Salermo, felt up in Florence, and laid in Lucca.'

Sicily itself was a wonder to explore, an island of Grecian temples, Roman Byzantine amphitheatres, chapels, Arab baths and Swabian castles.

Lucia found Palermo raucous and lively, and she enjoyed wandering around the Kalsa, the old Arab quarter, and visiting the Opera dei Pupi, the puppet theatre. But Taormina, where she was born, was her favourite. It was a picture postcard of a city on the Ionian Sea on a mountain overlooking the world. It was a city of dress shops and jewellery stores, bars and beautiful old squares, *trattorie* and colourful hotels like the Excelsior Palace and the San Domenico.

The winding road leading up from the seaport of Nachos is steep and narrow and dangerous, and when Lucia Carmine was given a car on her fifteenth birthday, she broke every traffic law in the book but was never once stopped by the *Carabiniere*. After all, she was the daughter of Angelo Carmine.

To those who were brave enough or stupid enough to inquire, Angelo Carmine was in the property business. And it was partially true, for the Carmine family owned the villa at Taormina, a house on Lake Como at Cernobbio, a lodge at Gstaad, an apartment in Rome, and a large farm outside Rome. But it happened that Angelo Carmine was also in more colourful businesses. He owned a dozen whorehouses, two gambling casinos, six ships that brought in cocaine from his plantations in Colombia, and an assortment of other very lucrative enterprises, including loan sharking. Angelo Carmine was the Capo of the Sicilian Mafiosi, so it was only appropriate that he lived well. His life was an inspiration to others, heartwarming proof that a poor Sicilian peasant who was ambitious and worked hard could become rich and successful.

Angelo Carmine had started out as an errand boy for the Mafiosi when he was twelve. By fifteen he had become an enforcer for the loan sharks, and at sixteen he had killed his first man and made his bones. Shortly after that, he married Lucia's mother, Anna. In the years that followed, Angelo Carmine had climbed the treacherous corporate ladder to the top, leaving a string of dead enemies behind him. He had grown, but Anna had remained the simple peasant girl he married. She bore him three fine children, but after that her contribution to Angelo's life came to a halt. As though knowing she no longer had a place in her family's life, she obligingly died and was considerate enough to manage it with a minimum of fuss.

Arnaldo and Victor were in business with their father, and from the time Lucia was a small girl, she eavesdropped on the exciting conversations between her father and her brothers, and listened to the tales of how they had outwitted or overpowered their enemies. To Lucia, her father was a knight in shining armour. She saw nothing wrong in what her father and brothers were doing. On the contrary, they were helping people. If people wanted to gamble, why let stupid laws stand in their way? If men took pleasure in buying sex, why not assist them? And how generous of her father and brothers to loan money to people who were turned away by the hard-hearted bankers. To Lucia, her father and brothers were model citizens. The proof of it lay in her father's friends. Once a week Angelo Carmine gave an enormous dinner party at the villa, and oh, the people who would be seated at the Carmine table! The mayor would be there, and a few aldermen, and judges, and seated next to them were film stars and opera singers and often the chief of police and a monsignor. Several times a year the governor himself would appear.

Lucia lived an idyllic life, filled with parties and beautiful clothes and jewels, cars and servants, and powerful friends. And then one February, on her twenty-third birthday, it all came to an abrupt end.

It began innocuously enough. Two men came to the villa to see her father. One of the men was their friend, the chief of police, and the other was his lieutenant.

'Forgive me, *Padrone*,' the police chief apologized, 'but this is a stupid formality which the Commissioner is forcing me to go through with. A thousand pardons, *Padrone*, but if you will be kind enough to accompany me to the police station, I will see to it that you are home in time to enjoy your daughter's birthday party.'

'No problem,' Angelo Carmine said genially. 'A man must do his duty.' He grinned. 'This new Commissioner who's been appointed by the President is – in the American phrase – "an eager beaver", eh?'

'I'm afraid that is so,' the police chief sighed. 'But don't worry. You and I have seen these pains-in-the-asses come and go very quickly, eh, *Padrone*?'

They laughed and left.

*

Angelo Carmine was not home for the party that day, nor the next. In fact, he never saw any of his homes again. The State entered a one-hundred-count indictment against him that included murder, drug trafficking, prostitution, arson, and scores of other crimes. Bail was denied. A police dragnet went out that swept up Carmine's crime organization. He had counted on his powerful connections in Sicily to have the charges against him dismissed, but instead he was taken to Rome in the middle of the night and held at the Regina Coeli, the notorious Queen of Heaven prison. He was put in a small cell that contained barred windows, a radiator, a narrow bed and a toilet with no seat. It was outrageous! It was an indignity beyond imagining.

In the beginning Angelo Carmine was sure that Tommaso Contorno, his lawyer, would have him released immediately.

When Contorno came to the visiting room of the prison, Carmine stormed at him, 'They've closed down my whorehouses and drug operation and they know everything about my money laundering operation. Somebody is talking. Find out who it is and bring me his tongue.'

'Do not worry, *Padrone*,' Contorno assured him. 'We will find him.'

His optimism turned out to be unfounded. In order to protect their witnesses, the State adamantly refused to reveal their names until the trial began.

Two days before the trial, Angelo Carmine and the other members of the Mafia were transferred to Rebibbia Prigione, a top-security prison twelve miles outside of Rome. A nearby courtroom had been fortified like a bunker. A hundred and sixty accused Mafia members were brought in through an underground tunnel wearing handcuffs and chains and put in thirty cages made of steel and bullet-proof glass. Armed guards surrounded the inside and outside of the courtroom and spectators were searched before they were allowed to enter.

When Angelo Carmine was marched into the courtroom, his heart leaped for joy, for the judge on the bench was Giovanni Buscetta, a man who had been on the Carmine payroll for the last fifteen years and who was a frequent guest at the Carmine house. Angelo Carmine knew at last that justice was going to be served.

The trial began. Angelo Carmine looked to *Omerta*, the Sicilian code of silence, to protect him. But to his astonishment, the chief witness for the State turned out to be none other than Benito Patas, the bodyguard. Benito Patas had been with the Carmine family so long and had been so trusted that he had been allowed to be in the room at meetings where confidential matters of business were discussed, and since that business consisted of every illegal activity on the police statutes, Patas was privy to a great deal of information. When the police had apprehended Patas minutes after he had cold-bloodedly murdered and mutilated the new boyfriend of his mistress, they had threatened him with life imprisonment, and Patas had reluctantly agreed to help the police build their case against Carmine in exchange for a lighter sentence. Now, to Angelo Carmine's horrified disbelief, he sat in the courtroom and listened to Patas reveal the innermost secrets of the Carmine fiefdom.

Lucia was also in the courtroom every day listening to the man who had been her lover destroying her father and her brothers.

Benito Patas' testimony opened the floodgates. Once the Commissioner's investigation began, dozens of victims came forward to tell their stories of what Angelo Carmine and his hoodlums had done to them. The Mafia had muscled into their businesses, blackmailed them, forced them into prostitution, murdered or crippled their loved ones, sold drugs to their children. The list of horrors was endless.

Even more damaging was the testimony of the *Pentiti*, the repentant members of the Mafia who decided to talk.

Lucia was allowed to visit her father in prison.

He greeted her cheerfully. He hugged her and whispered,

'Do not worry, *faccia del angelo*. Judge Giovanni Buscetta is my secret ace in the hole. He knows all the tricks of the law. He will use them to see that your brothers and I are acquitted.'

Angelo Carmine proved to be a poor prophet.

The public had been outraged by the excesses of the Mafia, and when the trial finally ended, Judge Giovanni Buscetta, an astute political animal, sentenced the Mafia members to long prison terms and sentenced Angelo Carmine and his two sons to the maximum permitted by Italian law, life imprisonment, a mandatory sentence of twenty-eight years.

For Angelo Carmine it was a death sentence.

All of Italy cheered. Justice had finally triumphed. But to Lucia, it was a nightmare beyond imagining. The three men she loved most in the world were being sent to hell.

Once again, Lucia was allowed to visit her father in his cell. The overnight change in him was heartbreaking. In the space of a few days, he had become an old man. His figure had shrunk and his healthy, ruddy complexion had turned sallow.

'They have betrayed me,' he moaned. 'They have all betrayed me. Judge Giovanni Buscetta – I owned him, Lucia! I made him a wealthy man, and he did this terrible thing to me. And Patas. I was like a father to him. What has the world come to? Whatever happened to honour? They are Sicilians, like me.'

Lucia took her father's hand in hers and said in a low voice, 'I am Sicilian, too, Papa. You shall have your vengeance. I swear it to you, on my life.'

'My life is over,' her father told her. 'But yours is still ahead of you. I have a numbered account in Zurich. The Bank Leu. There is more money there than you could spend in ten lifetimes.' He whispered a number in her ear. 'Leave cursed Italy. Take the money and enjoy yourself.'

Lucia held him close. 'Papa –'

'If you ever need a friend, you can trust Dominic Durell. We are like brothers. He has a home in France at Béziers, near the Spanish border.'

'I'll remember.'

'Promise me you'll leave Italy.'

'Yes, Papa. But there is something I have to do first.'

Having a burning desire for revenge was one thing. Figuring out a way to get it was another. She was alone, and it was not going to be easy. Lucia thought of the Italian expression, '*Rubare il mestiere.*' *You steal their profession. I must think the way they do.*

A few weeks after her father and brothers had started serving their prison sentences, Lucia Carmine appeared at the home of Judge Giovanni Buscetta. The judge himself opened the door.

He stared at Lucia in surprise. He had seen her often when he was a guest at the Carmine home, but they had never had much to say to each other.

'Lucia Carmine? What are you doing here? You shouldn't have –'

'I have come to thank you, Your Honour.'

He studied her suspiciously. 'Thank me for what?'

Lucia looked deep into his eyes. 'For exposing my father and brothers for what they were. I was an innocent, living in that house of horrors. I had no idea what monsters –' She broke down and began to sob.

The judge stood there uncertainly, then patted her shoulder. 'There, there. Come in and have some tea.'

'Th – thank you.'

When they were seated in the living room, Judge Buscetta said, 'I had no idea that you felt that way about your father. I had the impression that you were very close.'

'Only because I had no idea what he and my brothers were really like. When I found out –' She shuddered. 'You don't know what it was like,' Lucia said. 'I wanted to get away, but there was no escape for me.'

'I didn't understand.' He patted her hand. 'I'm afraid I misjudged you, my dear.'

'I was terrified of him.' Her voice was filled with passion.

Judge Buscetta noticed, not for the first time, what a beautiful young girl Lucia was. She was wearing a simple black dress that revealed the outlines of her lush body. He looked at her rounded breasts and could not help observing how grown up she had become.

It would be amusing, Buscetta thought, *to sleep with the daughter of Angelo Carmine. He's powerless to hurt me now. The old bastard thought he owned me, but I was too smart for him. Lucia is probably a virgin. I could teach her a few things in bed.*

An elderly housekeeper brought in a tray of tea and a plate of biscuits. She put them on a table. 'Shall I pour?'

'Let me,' Lucia said. Her voice was warm and filled with promise.

Judge Buscetta smiled at Lucia. 'You can go,' he told the housekeeper.

'Yes, sir.'

The judge watched as Lucia walked over to the small table where the tray had been set down and carefully poured out tea for the judge and herself.

'I have a feeling you and I could become very good friends, Lucia,' Giovanni Buscetta said, probing.

Lucia gave him a seductive smile. 'I would like that very much, Your Honour.'

'Please – Giovanni.'

'Giovanni.' Lucia handed him his cup. She raised her cup in a toast. 'To the death of villains.'

Smiling, Buscetta lifted his cup. 'To the death of villains.' He took a swallow and grimaced. The tea tasted bitter.

'Is it too –?'

'No, no. It is fine, my dear.'

Lucia raised her cup again. 'To our friendship.'

She took another sip, and he joined her.

'To –'

Buscetta never finished his toast. He was seized by a sudden spasm, and he felt a red-hot poker stabbing at his heart. He grabbed his chest. 'Oh, my God! Call a doctor . . .'

Lucia sat there, calmly sipping her tea, watching him stumble to his feet and fall to the floor. He lay there, his body twitching, and then he was still.

'That's one, Papa,' Lucia said.

Benito Patas was in his cell playing solitaire when the jailer announced, 'You have a conjugal visitor.'

Benito beamed. He had been given special status as an informer, with many privileges, and conjugal visits was one of them. Patas had half a dozen girl-friends, and they alternated their visits. He wondered which one had come today.

He studied himself in the little mirror hanging on the wall of his cell, put some pomade on his hair, slicked it back, then followed the guard through the prison corridor to the section where there were private rooms.

The guard motioned him inside. Patas strutted into the room, filled with anticipation. He stopped and stared in surprise.

'Lucia! My God, what the hell are you doing here? How did you get in?'

Lucia said softly, 'I told them we were engaged, Benito.'

She was wearing a stunning red, low-cut silk dress that clung to the curves of her body.

Benito Patas backed away from her. 'Get out.'

'If you wish. But there is something you should hear first. When I saw you get up on the stand and testify against my father and brothers, I hated you. I wanted to kill you.' She moved closer to him. 'But then I realized that what you were doing was an act of bravery. You dared to stand up and tell the truth. My father and my brothers were not evil men, but they did evil things, and you were the only one strong enough to stand up against them.'

'Believe me, Lucia,' he said, 'the police forced me to –'

'You don't have to explain,' she said softly. 'Not to me. Remember the first time we made love? I knew then that I was in love with you and that I always would be.'

'Lucia, I would never have done what I –'

'*Caro*, I want us to forget what happened. It's done. What's important now is you and me.'

She was close to him now, and he could smell her heady perfume. His mind was in a state of confusion. 'Do – do you mean that?'

'More than I've ever meant anything in my life. That's why I came here today, to prove it to you. To show you that I'm yours. And not with just words.'

Her fingers went to her shoulder straps, and an instant later her dress shimmered to the floor. She was naked. 'Do you believe me now?'

By God, she was beautiful. 'Yes, I believe you.' His voice was husky.

Lucia moved close to him, and her body brushed against his. 'Get undressed,' she whispered. 'Hurry!'

She watched Patas as he undressed. When he was naked, he took her hand and led her to the little bed in the corner of the room. He did not bother with foreplay. In a moment he was on top of her, spreading her legs, plunging deep inside her, an arrogant smile on his face.

'It's like old times,' he said smugly. 'You couldn't forget me, could you?'

'No,' Lucia whispered in his ear. 'And do you know why I couldn't forget you?'

'No, *mi amore*. Tell me.'

'Because I'm Sicilian, like my father.'

She reached behind her head and removed the long, ornate pin that held her hair in place.

Benito Patas felt something stab him under his rib cage, and the sudden pain made him open his mouth to scream, but Lucia's mouth was on his, kissing him, and as Benito's body bucked and writhed on top of her, Lucia had an orgasm.

A few minutes later she was clothed again, and the pin had been replaced in her hair. Benito was under the blanket, his eyes closed. Lucia knocked at the cell door and smiled at the guard who opened it to let her out. 'He's asleep,' she whispered.

The guard looked at the beautiful young woman and smiled. 'You probably wore him out.'

'I hope so,' Lucia said.

The sheer daring of the two murders took Italy by storm. The beautiful young daughter of a Mafioso had avenged her father and brothers, and the excitable Italian public cheered her, rooting for her to escape. The police, quite naturally, took a rather different point of view. Lucia Carmine had murdered a respected judge and had then committed a second murder within the very walls of a prison. In their eyes, equal to her crimes was the fact that she had made fools of them. The newspapers were having a wonderful time at their expense.

'I want her neck,' the police commissioner roared to the deputy commissioner. 'And I want it *today*.'

The manhunt intensified. The object of all this attention was hiding in the home of Salvatore Giuseppe, one of her father's men who had managed to escape the firestorm.

In the beginning, Lucia's only thought had been to avenge the honour of her father and brothers. She had fully expected to be caught and was prepared to sacrifice herself. When she had managed to walk out of the prison and make her escape, however, her thoughts changed from vengeance to survival. Now that she had accomplished what she had set out to do, life suddenly became precious again. *I'm not going to let them capture me*, she vowed to herself. *Never*.

Salvatore Giuseppe and his wife had done what they could to disguise Lucia. They had lightened her hair, stained her teeth, and bought her glasses and some ill-fitting clothes. Salvatore examined their handiwork critically.

'It is not bad,' he said. 'But it is not enough. We must get you out of Italy. You have to go somewhere where your picture is not on the front page of every newspaper. Somewhere you can hide out for a few months.'

And Lucia remembered:

If you ever need a friend, you can trust Dominic Durell. We are like brothers. He has a home in France at Béziers, near the Spanish border.

'I know where I can go,' Lucia said. 'I'll need a passport.'

'I will arrange it.'

Twenty-four hours later Lucia was looking at a passport in the name of Lucia Roma, with a photograph taken in her new persona.

'Where will you go?'

'My father has a friend in France who will help me.'

Salvatore said, 'If you wish me to accompany you to the border –?'

Both of them knew how dangerous that could be.

'No, Salvatore,' Lucia said. 'You have done enough for me. I must do this alone.'

The following morning Salvatore Giuseppe rented a Fiat in the name of Lucia Roma and handed her the keys.

'Be careful,' he pleaded.

'Don't worry. I was born under a lucky star.'

Had not her father told her so?

At the Italian–French border the cars waiting to get into France were advancing slowly in a long line. As Lucia moved closer to the immigration booth, she became more and more nervous. They would be looking for her at all exit points. If they caught her, she knew she would be sentenced to prison for life. *I'll kill myself first*, Lucia thought.

She had reached the immigration officer.

'Passport, signorina.'

Lucia handed him her black passport through the car window. As the officer took it, he glanced at Lucia, and she saw a puzzled look come into his eyes. He looked from the passport to her face and back again, this time more carefully. Lucia felt her body tense.

'You're Lucia Carmine,' he said.

Chapter 9

'Lucia Carmine.'

'No!' Lucia cried. The blood drained from her face. She looked around for a way to escape. There was none. And suddenly, to her disbelief, the guard was smiling. He leaned towards her and whispered, 'Your father was good to my family, signorina. You may pass through. Good luck.'

Lucia felt dizzy with relief. '*Grazie.*'

She stepped on the accelerator and drove the twenty-five yards towards the French border. The French immigration officer prided himself on being a connoisseur of beautiful women, and the woman who pulled up before him was certainly no beauty. She had mousy hair, thick glasses, stained teeth and was dowdily dressed.

Why can't Italian women look as beautiful as French women? he thought disgustedly. He stamped Lucia's passport and waved her through.

She arrived in Béziers many hours later.

The phone was answered on the first ring, and a smooth male voice said, 'Hello.'

'Dominic Durell, please.'

'This is Dominic Durell. Who is this speaking?'

'Lucia Carmine. My father told me –'

'Lucia!' His voice was warm with welcome. 'I was hoping to hear from you.'

'I need help.'

'You can count on me.'

Lucia's heart lightened. It was the first good news she had heard in a long time. She suddenly realized how drained she was.

'I need a place where I can hide out from the police.'

'No problem. My wife and I have a perfect place for you to use for as long as you like.'

It was almost too good to be true.

'Thank you.'

'Where are you, Lucia?'

'I'm –'

At that moment the blare of a police shortwave radio crackled over the phone. It was instantly shut off.

'Lucia –'

A loud alarm rang in her head.

'Lucia – where are you? I'll come and get you.'

Why would he have a police radio in his house? And he had answered the telephone on the first ring. Almost as though he had been expecting her call.

'Lucia – can you hear me?'

She knew, with an absolute certainty, that the man on the other end of the line was a policeman. So the dragnet was out for her. This call was being traced.

'Lucia –'

She replaced the receiver and walked quickly away from the telephone booth.

I've got to get out of France, she thought.

She returned to her car and took a map from the glove compartment. The Spanish border was only a short distance away. She replaced the map and started off. She turned a corner and headed south towards San Sebastian.

It was at the Spanish border that things started to go wrong.

'Passport, please.'

Lucia handed the Spanish immigration officer her passport. He gave it a cursory glance and started to hand it back, but something made him hesitate. He took a closer look at Lucia, and his expression changed.

'Just a moment, please. I will have to have this stamped inside.'

He recognized me, Lucia thought desperately. She watched him walk into the little office kiosk and show the passport to another officer. The two of them were talking excitedly. She had to escape. She opened the door on the driver's side and stepped out. A group of German tourists who had just cleared customs was noisily boarding an excursion coach next to Lucia's car. The sign on the front of the coach read 'Madrid'.

'*Achtung!*' their guide was calling out. '*Schnell.*'

Lucia glanced towards the hut. The guard who had taken her passport was yelling into the telephone.

'All aboard, *bitte*.'

Without a second thought, Lucia moved towards the laughing, chattering tour group and stepped on to the coach, averting her face from the guide. She took a seat in the rear of the coach, keeping her head down. *Move!* she prayed. *Now.*

Through the window Lucia saw that another guard had joined the first two and the three of them were examining her passport. As though in answer to Lucia's prayer, the coach door closed and the engine sprang into life. A short time later the coach was rolling out of San Sebastian towards Madrid. What would happen when the border guards found that she had left her car? Their first thought would be that she had gone to the ladies' room. They would wait and finally send someone in to get her. Their next step would be to search the area to see if she had hidden somewhere. By then dozens of cars and buses would have passed through. The police would have no idea where she had gone, nor in which direction she was travelling.

The tour group on the coach was obviously having a happy holiday. *Why not?* Lucia thought bitterly. *They haven't got the police snapping at their heels. Was it worth risking the rest of my life for?* She thought about it, reliving the scenes with Judge Buscetta and Benito in her mind.

I have a feeling you and I could become very good friends, Lucia . . . To the death of villains.

And Benito Patas: *It's like old times. You couldn't forget me, could you?*

And she had made the two traitors pay for their sins against her family. *Was it worth it?* They were dead, but her father and brothers would suffer for the rest of their lives. *Oh, yes*, Lucia thought. *It was worth it.*

Someone on the coach started a German song, and the others joined in:

'*In München ist ein Hofbrau Haus, ein, zwei, drei . . .*'

I'll be safe with this group for a while, Lucia thought. *I'll decide what to do next when I get to Madrid.*

She never reached Madrid.

At the walled city of Ávila, the tour coach made a scheduled stop for refreshments and what the guide delicately referred to as a 'comfort station'.

'*Alle raus aus dem Bus*,' he called.

Lucia stayed in her seat, watching the passengers rise and scramble for the front door of the coach. *I'll be safer if I stay here.* But the guide noticed her.

'Out, *Fräulein*,' he said. 'We have only fifteen minutes.'

Lucia hesitated, then reluctantly rose and moved towards the door.

As she passed the guide, he said, '*Warten Sie, bitte!* You are not of this tour.'

Lucia gave him a warm smile. 'No,' she said. 'You see, my car broke down in San Sebastian and it is very important that I get to Madrid, so I –'

'*Nein!*' the guide bellowed. 'This is not possible. This is a private tour.'

'I know,' Lucia told him, 'but you see, I need –'

'You must arrange this with the company headquarters in Munich.'

'I can't. I'm in a terrible hurry and –'

'*Nein, nein.* You will get me in trouble. Go away or I will call the police.'

'But –'

Nothing she said could sway him. Twenty minutes later Lucia watched the coach pull away and roar down the highway towards Madrid. She was stranded with no passport and almost no money, and by now the police of half a dozen countries would be looking for her to arrest her for murder.

She turned to examine her surroundings. The coach had stopped in front of a circular building with a sign in front that read '*Estación de Autobuses*'.

I can get another bus here, Lucia thought.

She walked into the station. It was a large building with marble walls, and scattered around the room were a dozen ticket windows with a sign over each one: *Segovia . . . Muñogalindo . . . Valladolid . . . Salamanca . . . Madrid.* Stairs and an escalator led to the downstairs level where the buses departed. There was a *pastelería* where they sold doughnuts and sweets and sandwiches wrapped in wax paper, and Lucia suddenly realized that she was starved.

I'd better not buy anything, she thought, *until I find out how much a bus ticket costs.*

As she started towards the window marked Madrid, two uniformed policemen hurried into the station. One of them was carrying a photograph. They moved from window to window showing the picture to the clerks.

They're looking for me. That damned bus driver reported me.

A family of newly arrived passengers was coming up the escalator. As they moved towards the door, Lucia stepped up beside them, mingling with them, and went outside.

She walked down the cobblestoned streets of Ávila, trying not to rush, afraid of drawing attention to herself. She turned into the Calle de la Madre Soledad, with its granite buildings and black wrought-iron balconies, and when she reached the

Plaza de la Santa, she sat down on a park bench to try to figure out her next move. A hundred yards away, several women and some couples were seated in the park, enjoying the afternoon sunshine.

As Lucia sat there, a police car appeared. It pulled up at the far end of the square and two policemen got out. They moved over to one of the women seated alone and began questioning her. Lucia's heart began to beat faster.

She forced herself to get to her feet slowly, her heart pounding, and turned away from the policemen and kept walking. The next street was called, unbelievably, 'The Street of Life and Death'. *I wonder if it's an omen.*

There were realistic-looking stone lions in the plaza, their tongues out, and in Lucia's fevered imagination, they seemed to be snapping at her. Ahead of her was a large cathedral, and on its façade was a carved medallion of a young girl and a grinning skull. The very air seemed to be filled with death.

Lucia heard the sound of a church bell and looked up through the open city gate. In the distance, high on a hill, rose the walls of an abbey. She stood there, staring at it.

'Why have you come to us, my daughter?' the Reverend Mother Betina asked softly.

'I need a place of refuge.'

'And you have decided to seek the refuge of God?'

Exactly. 'Yes.' Lucia began to improvise. 'This is what I have always wanted – to devote myself to the life of the spirit.'

'In our souls it is what we all wish for, is it not, daughter?'

Jesus, she's really falling for it, Lucia thought happily.

The Reverend Mother went on: 'You must understand that the Cistercian Order is the strictest of all the orders, my child. We are completely isolated from the outside world.'

Her words were music to Lucia's ears.

'Those who enter these walls have vowed never to leave.'

'I never want to leave,' Lucia assured her. *Not for the next few months, anyway.*

The Reverend Mother rose. 'It is an important decision. I suggest that you go and think about it carefully before you make up your mind.'

Lucia felt the situation slipping away from her and she began to panic. She had nowhere to go. Her only hope was to stay behind these walls.

'I have thought about it,' Lucia said quickly. 'Believe me, Reverend Mother, I've thought about nothing else. I want to renounce the world.' She looked the Mother Prioress in the eye. 'I want to be here more than I want to be anywhere else in the world.' Lucia's voice rang with truth.

The Reverend Mother was puzzled. There was something unsettled and frantic about this woman that was disturbing. And yet what better reason for anyone to come to this place where their spirit would be calmed by meditation and prayer?

'Are you Catholic?'

'Yes.'

The Reverend Mother picked up an old-fashioned quill pen. 'Tell me your name, child.'

'My name is Lucia Car – *Roma*.'

'Are your parents alive?'

'My father is.'

'What does he do?'

'He was a businessman. He's retired.' She thought of how pale and wasted he looked the last time she had seen him, and a pang went through her.

'Do you have any brothers or sisters?'

'Two brothers.'

'And what do they do?'

Lucia decided she needed all the help she could get. 'They're priests.'

'Lovely.'

The catechism went on for three hours. At the end of that time, the Reverend Mother Betina said, 'I will find you a bed for the night. In the morning you will begin instructions and when they are finished, if you still feel the same, you may join the order. But I warn you, it is a very difficult path you have chosen.'

'Believe me,' Lucia said earnestly. 'I have no choice.'

The night wind was soft and warm, whispering its way across the wooded glade, and Lucia slept. She was at a party in a beautiful villa, and her father and brothers were there, and everyone was having a wonderful time, and a stranger walked into the room and said, 'Who the hell are these people?' And the lights went out and a bright flashlight shone in her face and she came awake and sat up, the light blinding her.

There were half a dozen men surrounding the nuns in the clearing. With the light in her eyes, Lucia could only dimly make out their shapes.

'Who are you?' the man demanded again. His voice was deep and rough.

Lucia was instantly awake, her mind alert. She was trapped. But if these men were from the police, they would have known who the nuns were. And what were they doing in the woods at night?

Lucia took a chance. 'We are sisters from the convent at Ávila,' she said. 'Some government men came and –'

'We heard about it,' the man interrupted.

The other sisters were all sitting up now, awake and terrified.

'Who – who are you?' Megan asked.

'My name is Jaime Miró.'

There were six of them, dressed in rough trousers, leather jackets, turtleneck sweaters and canvas rope-soled shoes, and the traditional Basque berets. They were heavily armed, and in the dim moonlight they had a demonic look. Two of the men looked as though they had been badly beaten.

The man who called himself Jaime Miró was tall and lean, with fierce black eyes. 'They could have been followed here.'

He turned to one of the members of his band. 'Have a look around.'

'*Sí.*'

Lucia realized that it was a woman who answered. Lucia watched her move silently into the trees.

'What are we going to do with them?' Ricardo Mellado asked.

Jaime Miró said, '*Nada*. We leave them and move on.'

One of the men protested, 'Jaime – these are little sisters of Jesus.'

'Then let Jesus take care of them,' Jaime Miró said curtly. 'We have work to do.'

The nuns were all standing now, waiting. The men were gathered around Jaime, arguing with him.

'We can't let them get caught. Acoca and his men are searching for them.'

'They're searching for us, too, *amigo*.'

'The sisters will never make it without our help.'

Jaime Miró said firmly, 'No. We're not risking our lives for them. We have problems of our own.'

Felix Carpio, one of his lieutenants, said, 'We could escort them part of the way, Jaime. Just until they get away from here.' He turned to the nuns. 'Where are you sisters headed?'

Teresa spoke up, the light of God in her eyes. 'I have a holy mission. There is a convent at Mendavia that will shelter us.'

Felix Carpio said to Jaime Miró, 'We could escort them there. Mendavia's on our way to San Sebastian.'

Jaime Miró turned on him, furious. 'You damned fool! Why don't you put up a signpost telling everyone where we're going?'

'I only meant –'

'*Mierda!*' His voice was filled with disgust. 'Now we have no choice. We'll have to take them with us. If Acoca finds them, he'll make them talk. They're going to slow us down and make it that much easier for Acoca and his butchers to track us.'

Lucia was only half listening. The gold cross lay within

tempting reach. *But these damned men! You have lousy timing, God, and a weird sense of humour.*

'All right,' Jaime Miró was saying. 'We'll have to make the best of it. We'll take them as far as the convent and drop them, but we can't all travel together like some bloody circus.' He turned to the nuns. He could not keep the anger out of his voice. 'Do any of you even know where Mendavia is?'

The sisters looked at one another.

Graciela said, 'Not exactly.'

'Then how the hell did you ever expect to get there?'

'God will lead us,' Sister Teresa said firmly.

Another one of the men, Rubio Arzano, grinned. 'You're in luck.' He nodded towards Jaime. 'He came down to guide you in person, sister.'

Jaime silenced him with a look. 'We'll split up. We'll take three different routes.'

He pulled a map out of a backpack and the men squatted down on the ground, shining flashlights on the map.

'The convent at Mendavia is here, south-east of Logroño. I'll head north through Valladolid, then up to Burgos.' He ran his fingers along the map and turned to Rubio, a tall, pleasant-looking man. 'You take the route to Olmedo up to Peñafiel and Aranda de Duero.'

'Right, *amigo*.'

Jaime Miró was concentrating on the map again. He looked up at Ricardo Mellado, one of the men whose face was bruised. 'Ricardo, head for Segovia, then take the mountain route to Cerezo de Abajo, then to Soria. We'll all meet at Logroño.' He put the map away. 'Logroño is two hundred and ten kilometres from here.' He calculated silently. 'We'll meet there in seven days. Keep away from the main roads.'

Felix asked, 'Where in Logroño shall we meet?'

Ricardo said, 'The Cirque Japon will be playing in Logroño next week.'

'Good. We'll meet there. The matinee performance.'

Felix Carpio, the bearded one, spoke up. 'Who are the nuns going to travel with?'

'We'll split them up.'

It was time to put a stop to this, Lucia decided. 'If the soldiers are searching for you, signore, then we'd be safer travelling on our own.'

'But *we* wouldn't be, Sister,' Jaime said. 'You know too much about our plans now.'

'Besides,' the man called Rubio added, 'you wouldn't have a chance. We know the country. We're Basques, and the people up north are our friends. They'll help us and hide us from the nationalist soldiers. You'd never get to Mendavia by yourselves.'

I don't want to get to Mendavia, you idiot.

Jaime Miró was saying, grudgingly, 'All right, then, let's get moving. I want us far away from here by dawn.'

Sister Megan stood quietly listening to the man who was giving orders. He was rude and arrogant, but somehow he seemed to radiate a reassuring sense of power.

Jaime Miró looked over at Teresa and pointed to Tomas Sanjuro and Rubio Arzano. 'They will be responsible for you.'

Sister Teresa said, 'God is responsible for me.'

'Sure,' Jaime replied drily. 'I suppose that's how you got here in the first place.'

Rubio walked over to Teresa. 'Rubio Arzano at your service, Sister. How are you called?'

'I am Sister Teresa.'

Lucia spoke up quickly. 'I will travel with Sister Teresa.' There was no way she was going to let them separate her from the gold cross.

Jaime Miró nodded. 'All right.' He pointed to Graciela. 'Ricardo, you'll take this one.'

Ricardo Mellado nodded. '*Bueno.*'

The woman, whom Jaime had sent to reconnoitre, had returned to the group. 'It's all clear,' she said.

'Good.' Jaime Miró looked at Megan. 'You come with us, Sister.'

Megan nodded. Jaime Miró fascinated her. And there was something intriguing about the woman. She was dark and fierce-looking, with the hawk-like features of a predator. Her mouth was a red wound. There was something intensely sexual about her.

The woman walked up to Megan. 'I'm Amparo Jiron. Keep your mouth shut, Sister, and there will be no trouble.'

Jaime said to the others, 'Let's get moving. We'll meet in Logroño in seven days. Don't let the sisters out of your sight.'

Sister Teresa and the man called Rubio Arzano had already started to move down the path. Lucia hurried after them. She had seen the map that Rubio Arzano had put in his backpack. *I'll take it*, Lucia decided, *when he's asleep*.

Their flight across Spain began.

Chapter 10

Miguel Carrillo was nervous. In fact, Miguel Carrillo was *very* nervous. It had not been a wonderful day for him. What had started so well in the morning when he had encountered the four nuns and convinced them that he was a friar, had ended up with him being knocked unconscious and tied hand and foot and left on the floor of the dress shop.

It was the owner's wife who had discovered him. She was a heavyset, elderly woman with a moustache and a foul temper. She had looked down at him, trussed up on the floor and said, '*¡Madre de Dios!* Who are you? What are you doing here?'

Carrillo had turned on all his charm. 'Thank heavens you've come, *señorita*.' He had never met anyone who was more obviously a *señora*. 'I've been trying to get out of these straps so I could use your phone to call the police.'

'You haven't answered my question.'

He tried to struggle into a more comfortable position. 'The explanation is simple, *señorita*. I am Friar Gonzales. I come from a monastery near Madrid. I was passing by your beautiful shop when I saw two young men breaking into it. I felt it was my duty as a man of God to stop them. I followed them inside hoping to persuade them of the errors of their ways, but they overpowered me and tied me up. Now, if you would be good enough to untie me –'

'*¡Mierda!*'

He stared at her. 'I beg your pardon?'

'Who are you?'

'I told you, I'm –'

'What you are is the worst liar I've ever heard.'

She walked over to the robes that the nuns had discarded.

'What are those?'

'Ah. Those, yes. The two young men were wearing them as disguises, you see, and –'

'There are four outfits here. You said there were two men.'

'Right. The other two joined them later, and –'

She walked over to the phone.

'What are you doing?'

'Calling the police.'

'That's not necessary, I assure you. As soon as you release me, I'm going right to the police station to make a full report.'

The woman looked down at him.

'Your robe is open, Friar.'

The police were even less sympathetic than the woman had been. Carrillo was being questioned by four members of the *guardia civil*. Their green uniforms and eighteenth-century black patent leather hats were enough to inspire fear throughout Spain, and they certainly worked their magic on Carrillo.

'Are you aware that you answer to the exact description of a man who murdered a priest up north?'

Carrillo sighed. 'I am not surprised. I have a twin brother, may heaven punish him. It is because of him that I joined the monastery. Our poor mother –'

'Spare us.'

A giant with a scarred face walked into the room.

'Good afternoon, Colonel Acoca.'

'Is this the man?'

'Yes, Colonel. Because of the nuns' robes that we found with him in the shop, we thought you might be interested in questioning him yourself.'

Colonel Ramón Acoca walked up to the hapless Carrillo. 'Yes. I'm very interested.'

Carrillo gave the Colonel his most ingratiating smile. 'I'm glad you're here, Colonel. I'm on a mission for my church, and it's very important that I get to Barcelona as quickly as possible. As I tried to explain to these nice gentlemen, I am a victim of circumstances simply because I tried to be a good samaritan.'

Colonel Acoca nodded pleasantly. 'Since you are in a hurry, I will try not to waste your time.'

Carrillo beamed at him. 'Thank you, Colonel.'

'I'm going to ask you a few simple questions. If you answer truthfully, everything will be fine. If you lie to me, it will be very painful for you.' He slipped something into his hand.

Carrillo said righteously, 'Men of God do not lie.'

'I'm very happy to hear that. Tell me about the four nuns.'

'I don't know anything about four nuns, Col –'

The fist that hit him in the mouth had brass knuckles on it, and blood spurted across the room.

'My God! What are you doing?' Carrillo gasped.

Colonel Acoca repeated his question. 'Tell me about the four nuns.'

'I don't –'

The fist slammed into Carrillo's mouth again, breaking teeth.

Carrillo was choking on his blood. 'Don't. I –'

'Tell me about the four nuns.' Acoca's voice was soft and reasonable.

'I –' He saw the fist being raised. 'Yes! I – I –'

The words came tumbling out. 'They were in Villacastin, running away from their convent. Please don't hit me again.'

'Go on.'

'I – I told them I would help them. They needed to change clothes.'

'So you broke into the shop . . .'

'No. I – yes. I – they stole some clothes and then they knocked me out and left me.'

'Did they say where they were headed?'

A peculiar sense of dignity suddenly took possession of Carrillo. 'No.' His not mentioning Mendavia had nothing to do with protecting the nuns. Carrillo did not give a damn about them. It was because the Colonel had ruined his face. It was going to be very difficult to make a living after he was released from prison.

Colonel Acoca turned to the members of the *guardia civil*. 'See what a little friendly persuasion can do? Send him to Madrid and hold him for murder.'

•

Lucia, Sister Teresa, Rubio Arzano and Tomas Sanjuro walked north-east, heading towards Olmeda, staying away from the main roads and walking through fields of grain. They passed flocks of sheep and goats, and the innocence of the pastoral countryside was in ironic contrast to the grave danger they were all in. They walked through the night, and at dawn they headed for a secluded spot in the hills.

Rubio Arzano said, 'The town of Olmeda is just ahead. We'll stop here until nightfall. You both look as though you could do with some sleep.'

Sister Teresa was physically exhausted. But something was happening to her emotionally that was far more disturbing. She felt she was losing touch with reality. It had begun with the disappearance of her precious rosary. Had she lost it – or had someone stolen it? She was not sure. It had been her solace for more years than she could remember. How many thousands of Hail Marys and how many Our Fathers and how many Hail, Holy Queens? It had become a part of her, her security, and now it was missing.

Had she lost it in the convent during the attack? And had there really been an attack? It seemed so unreal now. She was no longer sure what was real and what was imaginary. The baby she had seen. Was it Monique's baby? Or was God playing tricks on her? It was all so confusing. When she was young, everything had been so simple. When she was young . . .

Chapter 11

Èze, France 1924

When she was only eight years old, most of the happiness in Teresa DeFosse's life came from the church. It was like a sacred flame drawing her to its warmth. She visited the Chapelle des Penitents Blancs, and prayed at the cathedral in Monaco and Notre Dame Bon Voyage in Cannes, but most frequently she attended services at the church in Èze.

Teresa lived in a château on a mountain above the medieval village of Èze, near Monte Carlo, overlooking the Côte d'Azur. The village was perched high on a rock and it seemed to Teresa that she could look down upon the whole world. There was a monastery at the top, with rows of houses cascading down the side of the mountain to the blue Mediterranean below.

Monique, a year younger than Teresa, was the beauty in the family. Even when she was a child, one could see that she would grow up to be an exquisite woman. She had fine-boned features, sparkling blue eyes, and an easy self-assurance that suited her looks.

Teresa was the ugly duckling. The truth was that the DeFosses were embarrassed by their elder daughter. If Teresa had been conventionally ugly, they might have sent her to a plastic surgeon and had her nose shortened, or her chin brought forward, or her eyes fixed. But the problem was that all Teresa's features were just slightly askew. Everything seemed out of place, as though she were a comedienne who had donned her face for laughter.

But if God had cheated her in the matter of looks, He had compensated for it by blessing her with a remarkable gift. Teresa had the voice of an angel. It had been noticed the first time she sang in the church choir. The parishioners listened in astonishment to the pure, clear tones that came from the young child. And as Teresa grew older, her voice grew even more beautiful. She was given all the solos to sing in church. There, she felt as though she belonged. But away from church, Teresa was inordinately shy, painfully aware of her appearance.

At school it was Monique who had all the friends. Boys and girls alike flocked to her side. They wanted to play with her, be seen with her. Monique was invited to all the parties. Teresa was invited also, but it was an after-thought, the fulfilling of a social obligation, and Teresa was painfully aware of it.

'Now, Renée. You can't invite one of the DeFosse children without the other. It would be bad manners.'

Monique was ashamed to have an ugly sister. She felt that it was somehow a reflection on her.

Teresa's parents behaved properly towards their elder daughter. They fulfilled their parental duty punctiliously, but it was obvious that it was Monique they adored. The one ingredient that Teresa longed for was missing: love.

She was an obedient child, willing and eager to please, a good student who loved music, history and foreign languages and worked hard in school. Her teachers and the servants and the townspeople felt sorry for her. As a tradesman said one day when Teresa left his shop, 'God wasn't paying attention when he made her.'

Where Teresa found love was in the church. The priest loved her, and Jesus loved her. She went to mass every morning and made the fourteen stations of the cross. Kneeling in the cool, vaulted church, she felt God's presence. When she sang there, Teresa was filled with a sense of hope, of expectation. She felt as though something wonderful were about to happen to her. It was the only thing that made her life bearable.

Teresa never confided her unhappiness to her parents or to her sister, for she did not want to burden them, and she hugged to herself the secret of how much God loved her and how much she loved God.

Teresa adored her sister. They played together in the estate grounds surrounding their château, and she let Monique win the games they played. They went exploring together, down the steep stone steps cut into the mountain to Èze Village below, and wandered down the narrow streets of artists' shops to watch the artists in front selling their wares.

As the girls grew into their teens, the predictions of the villagers came true. Monique grew more beautiful. The boys came flocking around Monique, while Teresa stayed in her room sewing or reading or went shopping in the village.

As Teresa passed the drawing room one day, she heard her mother and father in a discussion.

'She's going to be an old maid. We're going to have her on our hands all our lives.'

'Teresa will find someone. She has a very sweet disposition.'

'That's not what the young men of today are after. They want someone they can enjoy having in their bed.'

Teresa fled.

Teresa still sang in church on Sundays, and because of that an event occurred that almost changed her life. In the congregation was a Madame Neff, the aunt of a radio station director in Nice.

She stopped to speak to Teresa one Sunday morning. 'You're wasting your life here, my dear. You have an extraordinary voice. You should be using it.'

'I am using it. I –'

'I'm not talking about –' She looked around the church. '– *this*. I'm talking about your using your voice professionally. I pride myself on knowing talent when I hear it. I want you to sing for my nephew. He can put you on the radio. Are you interested?'

'I – I don't know.' The very thought of it terrified Teresa.

'Talk it over with your family.'

'I think it's a wonderful idea,' Teresa's mother said.

'It could be a good thing for you,' her father agreed.

It was Monique who had reservations about it. 'You're not a professional,' she said. 'You could make a fool of yourself.' Which had nothing to do with Monique's reasons for trying to discourage her sister. What Monique was afraid of was that Teresa would *succeed*. Monique was the one who had always been in the limelight. *It's not fair*, she thought, *that God should have given Teresa a voice like that. What if she should become famous? I would be left out, ignored.*

And so Monique tried to persuade her sister not to audition.

But the following Sunday at church, Madame Neff stopped Teresa and said, 'I've talked to my nephew. He is willing to give you an audition. He's expecting you on Wednesday at three o'clock.'

And so it was that the following Wednesday a very nervous Teresa appeared at the radio station in Nice and met the director.

'I'm Louis Bonnet,' he said curtly. 'I can give you five minutes.'

Teresa's physical appearance only confirmed his worst fears. His aunt had sent him talent before.

I should tell her to stick to her kitchen. But he knew that he would not. The problem was that his aunt was very rich, and he was her only heir.

Teresa followed Louis Bonnet down a narrow corridor into a small broadcasting studio.

'Have you ever sung professionally?'

'No, sir.' Her blouse was soaked with perspiration. *Why did I ever let myself get talked into this?* Teresa wondered. She was in a panic, ready to flee.

Bonnet placed her in front of a microphone. 'I don't have a piano player around today, so you're going to have to sing *a capella*. Do you know what *a capella* means?'

'Yes, sir.'

'Wonderful.' He wondered, not for the first time, if his aunt was rich enough to make all these stupid auditions worthwhile.

'I'll be in the control booth. You'll have time for one song.'

'Sir – what shall I –?'

He was gone. Teresa was alone in the room staring at the microphone in front of her. She had no idea what she was going to sing. 'Just go and meet him,' his aunt had said. 'The station has a musical programme every Saturday evening, and . . .'

I've got to get out of here.

Louis' voice came out of nowhere. 'I haven't got all day.'

'I'm sorry. I can't –'

But the director was determined to punish her for wasting his time.

'Just a few notes,' he insisted. Enough so he could report to his aunt what a fool the girl had made of herself. Perhaps that would persuade her to stop sending him her protégées.

'I'm waiting,' he said.

He leaned back in his chair and lit a Gitane. Four more hours to go. Yvette would be waiting for him. He would have time to call at her apartment before he went home to his wife. Maybe there would even be time to –

He heard it then, and he could not believe it. It was a voice so pure and so sweet that it sent chills down his spine. It was a voice filled with longing and desire, a voice that sang of loneliness and despair, of lost loves and dead dreams, and it brought tears to his eyes. It stirred emotions in him that he had thought long since dead. All he could say to himself was, 'Jesus Christ! Where has she been?'

An engineer had wandered into the control booth, and he stood there listening, mesmerized. The door was open and others began to come in, drawn by the voice. They stood there silently listening to the poignant sound of a heart desperately crying out for love, and there was not another sound in the room.

When the song ended, there was a long silence, and one of the women said, 'Whoever she is, don't let her get away.'

Louis Bonnet hurried out of the room into the broadcasting studio. Teresa was getting ready to leave.

'I'm sorry I took too long. You see, I've never –'

'Sit down, Maria.'

'Teresa.'

'Sorry.' He took a deep breath. 'We do a musical radio broadcast every Saturday night.'

'I know. I listen to it.'

'How would you like to be on it?'

She stared at him, unable to believe what she was hearing. 'You mean – you want to *employ* me?'

'Beginning this week. We'll start you at the minimum. It will be a great showcase for you.'

It was almost too good to be true. *They're* going to pay me to sing.

'Pay you? How much?' Monique asked.

'I don't know. I don't care.' *The important thing is that somebody wants me*, she almost said, but she stopped herself.

'That's wonderful news. So you're going to be on the radio!' her father said.

Her mother was already making plans.

'We'll see that all our friends listen, and we'll have them send in letters saying how good you are.'

Teresa looked at Monique, waiting for her to say, *You don't have to do that. Teresa is good.*

But Monique said nothing. *It will blow over quickly*, she thought.

She was wrong.

That Saturday night at the broadcasting station, Teresa was in a panic.

'Believe me,' Louis Bonnet assured her, 'it's perfectly natural. All artists go through this.'

They were seated in the small green-room used by performers.

'You're going to be a sensation.'

'I'm going to be sick.'

'There's no time. You're on in two minutes.'

Teresa had rehearsed that afternoon with the small orchestra that was going to accompany her. The rehearsal had been extraordinary. The stage from which they broadcast was crowded with station personnel who had heard about the young girl with the incredible voice. They listened in awed silence as Teresa rehearsed the songs she was going to sing. There was no question in any of their minds but that they were witnessing the birth of an important star.

'It's too bad she's not better looking,' a stage manager commented, 'but in radio who can tell the difference?'

Teresa's performance that evening was superb. She was aware that she had never sung better. And who knew where this could lead? She might become famous and have men at her feet, begging her to marry them. As they begged Monique.

As though reading her thoughts, Monique said, 'I'm really happy for you, Sis, but don't let yourself get carried away by all this. These things never last.'

This will, Teresa thought happily. *I'm finally a person. I'm somebody.*

On Monday morning, there was a long-distance telephone call for Teresa.

'It's probably somebody's idea of a joke,' her father warned her. 'He says he's Jacques Raimu.' *The most important stage director in France.*

Teresa picked up the telephone, wary. 'Hello?'

'Miss DeFosse?'

'Yes.'

'Teresa DeFosse?'

'Yes.'

'This is Jacques Raimu. I heard your radio programme on Saturday night. You're exactly what I'm looking for.'

'I – I don't understand.'

'I'm staging a play at the Comédie Française, a musical. I start rehearsals next week. I've been searching for someone with a voice like yours. To tell you the truth, there *is* no one with a voice like yours. Who is your agent?'

'Agent? I – I have no agent.'

'Then I'll come up there and we'll work out a deal between us.'

'Monsieur Raimu – I – I'm not very pretty.' It was painful for her to say the words, but she knew that it was necessary. *He mustn't have any false expectations.*

He laughed. 'You will be when I get through with you. Theatre is make-believe. Stage makeup can do all kinds of incredible magic.'

'But –'

'I'll drive up to see you tomorrow.'

It was a dream on top of a fantasy. To be starring in a play by Raimu!

'I'll work out the contract with him,' Teresa's father said. 'You must be careful when you deal with theatre people.'

'We must get you a new dress,' her mother said. 'And I'll invite him to dinner.'

Monique said nothing. What was happening was unbearable. It was unthinkable that her sister was going to become a star. Perhaps there was a way . . .

Monique saw to it that she was the first one downstairs when Jacques Raimu arrived at the DeFosse château that afternoon. He was greeted by a young girl so beautiful that his heart jumped. She was dressed in a simple white afternoon frock that set off her figure to perfection.

My God, he thought. *Those looks and that voice! She's perfect. She's going to be an enormous star.*

'I can't tell you how happy I am to meet you,' Raimu said.

Monique smiled warmly. 'I'm very happy to meet you. I'm a big admirer of yours, Monsieur Raimu.'

'Good. Then we'll work well together. I brought a script with me. It's a beautiful love story, and I think –'

Teresa came into the room. She was wearing a new dress, but she looked awkward in it. She stopped as she saw Jacques Raimu.

'Oh – hello. I didn't know you were here. I mean – you're early.'

He looked at Monique inquiringly.

'This is my sister,' Monique said. 'Teresa.'

They both watched the expression on his face change. It went from shock to disappointment to disgust.

'You're the singer?'

'Yes.'

He turned to Monique. 'And you're –'

Monique smiled innocently. 'I'm Teresa's sister.'

Raimu turned to examine Teresa again, then shook his head. 'I'm sorry,' he said to Teresa. 'You're too –' he fumbled for a word. '– You're too young. If you'll excuse me, I must get back to Paris.'

And they stood there watching him walk out the door.

It worked, Monique thought jubilantly. *It worked.*

That was the last broadcast Teresa ever made. Louis Bonnet pleaded with her to come back, but the hurt was too deep.

After looking at my sister, Teresa thought, *how could anyone want me? I'm so ugly.*

As long as she lived, she would never forget the look on Jacques Raimu's face.

It's my fault for having silly dreams, Teresa told herself. *It's God's way of punishing me.*

After that, Teresa would only sing in church, and she became more of a recluse than ever.

During the next ten years the beautiful Monique turned down more than a dozen marriage proposals. She was proposed to by the sons of the mayor, the banker, the doctor, the merchants in the village. Her suitors ranged from young men fresh out of school to established and successful men in their forties and fifties. They were rich and poor, handsome and ugly, educated and uneducated. And to all of the Monique said *non*.

'What are you looking for?' her father asked, baffled.

'Papa, everyone here is boring. Èze is such an unsophisticated place. My dream prince is in Paris.'

And so her father dutifully sent her to Paris. As an afterthought, he sent Teresa with her. The two girls stayed at a small hotel near the Bois de Boulogne.

Each sister saw a different Paris. Monique attended charity balls and glamorous dinner parties and had tea with titled young men. Teresa visited Les Invalides and the Louvre. Monique went to the races at Longchamps and to galas at Malmaison. Teresa went to the Cathedral of Notre Dame to pray, and walked along the tree-shaded path of the Canal St Martin. Monique went to Maxim's and the Moulin Rouge, while Teresa strolled along the Quays, browsing at the book stalls and the flower vendors and stopping at the Basilica St Denis. Teresa enjoyed Paris, but as far as Monique was concerned, the trip was a failure.

When she returned home, she said, 'I can't find any man I want to marry.'

'You met no one who interested you?' her father asked.

'Not really. There was a young man who took me to dinner at Maxim's. His father owns coal mines.'

'What was he like?' her mother asked eagerly.

'Oh, he was rich, handsome, polite, and he adored me.'

'Did he ask you to marry him?'

'Every ten minutes. Finally I simply refused to see him again.'

Her mother stared at Monique in amazement. 'Why?'

'Because all he could talk about was coal: bituminous coal, lump coal, black coal, grey coal. Boring, boring, boring.'

The following year Monique decided she wanted to return to Paris again.

'I'll pack my things,' Teresa said.

Monique shook her head. 'No. This time I think I'll go alone.'

So while Monique went to Paris, Teresa stayed at home and went to church every morning and prayed that her sister would find a handsome prince. And one day the miracle occurred. A miracle because it was to Teresa that it happened. His name was Raoul Giradot.

He had gone to church on Sunday and heard Teresa sing. He had never heard anything like it. *I must meet her*, he vowed.

Early on Monday morning, Teresa called at the village general store to buy fabric for a dress she was making. Raoul Giradot was working behind the counter.

He looked up as Teresa walked in, and his face lit up. 'The voice!'

She stared at him, flustered. 'I – I beg your pardon?'

'I heard you sing in church yesterday. You are magnificent.'

He was handsome and tall, with intelligent, flashing dark eyes and lovely, sensual lips. He was in his early thirties, a year or two older than Teresa.

Teresa was so taken aback by his appearance that she could only stammer. She stared at him, her heart pounding. 'T – thank you,' Teresa said. 'I – I – I would like three yards of muslin, please.'

Raoul smiled. 'It will be my pleasure. This way.'

It was suddenly difficult for Teresa to concentrate on her errand. She was overpoweringly aware of the young man's presence, his good looks and charm, the masculine aura surrounding him.

When Teresa had decided on her purchase and Raoul was wrapping it for her, she dared to say, 'You're – you're new here, aren't you?'

He looked at her and smiled, and it sent shivers through Teresa.

'*Oui*. I arrived in Èze a few days ago. My aunt owns this shop and she needed help, so I thought I would work here for a while.'

How long is a while? Teresa found herself wondering.

'You should be singing professionally,' Raoul told her.

She remembered the expression on Raimu's face when he had seen her. No, she would never risk exposing herself publicly again. 'Thank you,' Teresa mumbled.

He was touched by her embarrassment and shyness. He tried to draw her into conversation.

'I haven't been to Èze before. It's a beautiful little town.'

'Yes,' Teresa mumbled.

'Were you born here?'

'Yes.'

'Do you like it?'

'Yes.'

Teresa picked up her parcel and fled.

The following day Teresa found an excuse to go back to the shop again. She had stayed up half the night preparing what she was going to say to Raoul.

I'm glad you like Èze . . .

The monastery was built in the fourteenth century, you know . . .

Have you ever visited Saint-Paul-de-Vence? There's a lovely chapel there . . .

I enjoy Monte Carlo, don't you? It's wonderful to have it so close to here. Sometimes my sister and I drive down the Grand Corniche and go to the Fort Antoine Theatre. Do you know it? It's the big, open-air theatre . . .

Did you know that Nice was once called Nkaia? Oh, you

didn't? Yes, it was. The Greeks were there a long time ago. There's a museum in Nice with the remains of cavemen who lived there thousands of years ago. Isn't that interesting?

Teresa was prepared with dozens of such verbal gambits. Unfortunately, the moment she walked into the shop and saw Raoul everything flew out of her head. She simply stared at him, unable to speak.

'*Bonjour*,' Raoul said cheerfully. 'It's nice to see you again, Mademoiselle DeFosse.'

'*M – merci*.' She felt like an idiot. *I'm thirty years old*, she told herself, *and I'm acting like a silly schoolgirl. Stop it.*

But she could not stop it.

'And what may I do for you today?'

'I – I need more muslin.'

Which was the last thing she needed.

Teresa watched Raoul as he went to get the bolt of fabric. He set it on the counter and started to measure it out.

'How many yards would you like?'

She started to say two, but what came out was, 'Are you married?'

He looked up at her with a warm smile on his face. 'No,' he said. 'I haven't been that fortunate yet.'

You are going to be, Teresa thought. *As soon as Monique returns from Paris.*

Monique was going to adore this man. They were perfect for each other. The thought of Monique's reaction when she met Raoul filled Teresa with happiness. It would be lovely to have Raoul Giradot as her brother-in-law.

The following day as Teresa was passing the shop, Raoul caught sight of her and hurried outside.

'Good afternoon, Mademoiselle. I was about to take a break. If you're free, would you care to join me for tea?'

'I – I – yes, thank you.'

She was tongue-tied in his presence, and yet Raoul could not have been more pleasant. He did everything he could to put her at ease, and soon Teresa found herself telling this stranger things she had never told anyone before. They talked of loneliness.

'Crowds can make one lonely,' Teresa said. 'I always feel like an island in a sea of people.'

He smiled. 'I understand.'

'Oh, but you must have so many friends.'

'Acquaintances. In the end, does anyone really have many friends?'

It was as though she were speaking to a mirror image. The hour melted away so quickly, and soon it was time for him to go back to work.

As they rose, Raoul asked, 'Will you join me for lunch tomorrow?'

He was being kind, of course. Teresa knew that no man could ever be attracted to her. Especially someone as wonderful as Raoul Giradot. She was sure that he was kind to everyone.

'I would enjoy that,' Teresa said.

When she went to meet Raoul the following day, he said boyishly, 'I've been given the afternoon off. If you're not too busy, why don't we drive down to Nice?'

They drove along the Moyen Corniche, with his car top down, and the city was spread out like a magic carpet below. Teresa leaned back in her seat and thought: *I've never been so happy.* And then, filled with guilt: *I'm being happy for Monique.*

Monique was returning from Paris the following day. Raoul would be Teresa's gift to her sister. Teresa was realistic enough to know that the Raouls of the world were not for her. She had had enough pain in her life. She had long since learned what was real and what was impossible. The handsome man seated beside her driving the car was an impossible dream she dared not even let herself think about.

They had lunch at Le Chantecler in the Negrecso Hotel in Nice. It was a superb meal, but afterwards Teresa had no recollection of what she had eaten. It seemed to her that she and Raoul had not stopped talking. They had so much to say to each other. He was witty and charming, and he appeared to find Teresa interesting – really interesting. He asked her opinion about many things and listened attentively to her answers. They agreed on almost everything. It was as though they were soul mates. If Teresa had any regrets about what was about to happen, she resolutely forced them out of her mind.

'Would you like to come to dinner at the château tomorrow night? My sister is returning from Paris. I would like you to meet her.'

'I'd be delighted, Teresa.'

When Monique returned home the following day, Teresa hurried to greet her at the door.

In spite of her resolve, Teresa could not help asking, 'Did you meet anyone interesting in Paris?' And she held her breath, waiting for her sister's answer.

'The same boring men,' Monique replied.

So God had made the final decision.

'I've invited someone to dinner tonight,' Teresa said. 'I think you're going to like him.'

I must never let anyone know how much I care for him, Teresa thought.

That evening at half seven promptly, the butler ushered Raoul Giradot into the drawing room where Teresa, Monique and their parents were waiting.

'This is my mother and father. Monsieur Raoul Giradot.'

'How do you do?'

Teresa took a deep breath. 'And my sister, Monique.'

'How do you do?' Monique's expression was polite, nothing more.

Teresa looked at Raoul, expecting him to be stunned by Monique's beauty.

'Enchanted.' Merely courteous.

Teresa stood there, holding her breath, waiting for the sparks that she knew would start flying between them. But Raoul was looking at Teresa.

'You look lovely tonight, Teresa.'

She blushed and stammered, 'Th – thank you.'

Everything about that evening was topsy-turvy. Teresa's plan to bring Monique and Raoul together, to watch them get married, to have Raoul as a brother-in-law – none of it even began to happen. Incredibly, Raoul's attention was focused entirely on Teresa. It was like some impossible dream come true. She felt like Cinderella, only she was the ugly sister and the prince had chosen her. It was unreal, but it was happening, and Teresa found herself struggling to resist Raoul and his charm because she knew that it was too good to be true, and she dreaded being hurt again. All these years she had hidden her emotions, guarding against the pain that came with rejection. Now, instinctively, she tried to do the same. But Raoul was irresistible.

'I heard your daughter sing,' Raoul said. 'She is a miracle!'

Teresa found herself blushing.

'Everyone loves Teresa's voice,' Monique said sweetly.

It was a heady evening. But the best was yet to come.

When dinner was finished, Raoul said, 'Your grounds look lovely.' He turned to Teresa. 'Would you show me the gardens?'

Teresa looked over at Monique, trying to read her sister's emotions, but Monique seemed completely indifferent.

She must be deaf, dumb and blind, Teresa thought.

And then she recalled all the times Monique had gone to Paris and Cannes and St Tropez looking for her perfect prince but had never found him.

So it's not the fault of the men. It's the fault of my sister. She has no idea what she wants.

Teresa turned to Raoul. 'I would love to.'

Outside, Teresa could not let the subject drop.

'How did you like Monique?'

'She seems very nice,' Raoul replied. 'Ask me how I like her sister.'

And he took Teresa in his arms and kissed her.

It was like nothing Teresa had ever experienced before.

She trembled in his arms, and she thought: *Thank you, God. Oh, thank you.*

'Will you have dinner with me tomorrow night?' Raoul asked.

'Yes,' Teresa breathed. 'Oh, yes.'

When the two sisters were alone, Monique said, 'He really seems to like you.'

'I think so,' Teresa said shyly.

'Do you like him?'

'Yes.'

'Well, be careful, big sister,' Monique laughed. 'Don't get in over your head.'

Too late, Teresa thought helplessly. *Too late.*

Teresa and Raoul were together every day after that. Monique usually chaperoned them. The three of them walked along the promenades and beaches at Nice and laughed at the wedding-cake hotels. They lunched at a charming bistro at Cap d'Antibes, and visited the Matisse Chapel in Vence. They dined at the Château de la Chèvre d'Or, and at the fabulous La Ferme St Michel. One morning at 5.00 a.m. the three of them went to the open farmers' market that filled the streets of Monte Carlo and bought fresh breads and vegetables and fruit.

On Sundays, when Teresa sang in church, Raoul and Monique were there to listen, and afterwards Raoul would hug Teresa and say, 'You really are a miracle. I could listen to you sing for the rest of my life.'

Four weeks after Teresa met him, Raoul proposed.

'I'm sure you could have any man you want, Teresa,' Raoul said, 'but I would be honoured if you chose me.'

For one terrible moment Teresa thought he was ridiculing her, but before she could speak, he went on.

'My darling, I must tell you that I have known many

women, but you are the most sensitive, the most talented, the warmest –'

Each word was music to Teresa's ears. She wanted to laugh; she wanted to cry. *How blessed I am*, she thought, *to love and be loved.*

'Will you marry me?'

And her look was answer enough.

When Raoul left, Teresa went flying into the library where her sister, mother and father were having coffee.

'Raoul asked me to marry him.' Her face was glowing, and there was almost a beauty about her.

Her parents stared at her, stunned. It was Monique who spoke.

'Teresa, are you sure he's not after the family money?'

It was like a slap in the face.

'I don't mean that unkindly,' Monique went on, 'but it all seems to be happening so fast.'

Teresa was determined not to let anything spoil her happiness. 'I know you want to protect me,' she told her sister, 'but Raoul has money. His father left him a small inheritance, and he's not afraid to work for a living.' She took her sister's hand in hers and begged, 'Please be glad for me, Monique. I never thought I'd know this feeling. I'm so happy I could die.'

And then the three of them embraced her and told her how pleased they were for her and they began to talk excitedly about plans for the wedding.

Very early the next morning Teresa went to church and knelt to pray.

'Thank you, Father. Thank You for giving me such happiness. I will do everything to make myself worthy of your love and of Raoul's. Amen.'

Teresa walked into the general store, her feet above the ground, and said, 'If you please, sir, I would like to order some material for a wedding gown.'

Raoul laughed and took her in his arms. 'You're going to make a beautiful bride.'

And Teresa knew he meant it. That was the miracle.

The wedding was set to take place a month later in the village church. Monique, of course, was to be the maid of honour.

At five o'clock on Friday afternoon, Teresa spoke to Raoul for the last time. At 12.30 on Saturday, standing in the church vestry waiting for Raoul, who was thirty minutes late, Teresa was approached by the priest. He took her arm and led her aside, and she wondered at his agitation. Her heart began to pound.

'What is it? Is something wrong? Has anything happened to Raoul?'

'Oh, my dear,' her father said. 'My poor, dear Teresa.'

She was beginning to panic. 'What is it, Father? Tell me!'

'We – we just received word a moment ago. Raoul –'

'Is it an accident? Was he hurt?'

'Giradot left town a half an hour ago.'

'*He what?* Then some emergency must have come up to make him –'

'He left with your sister. They were seen taking the train to Paris.'

The room began to whirl. *No*, Teresa thought. *I mustn't faint. I mustn't embarrass God.*

She had only a hazy memory of the events that followed. Teresa's mother put her arms around her daughter and said, 'My poor Teresa. That your own sister could be so cruel. I'm so sorry.'

But Teresa was suddenly calm. She knew how to make everything all right.

'Don't worry, Mama. I don't blame Raoul for falling in love with Monique. Any man would. I should have known that no man could ever love me.'

'You're wrong,' her father cried. 'You're worth ten of Monique.'

But his compassion came years too late.

'I would like to go home now, please.'

They made their way through the crowd. The guests at the church moved aside to let them pass, staring silently after them.

When they returned to the château, Teresa said again, 'Please don't worry about me. I promise you that everything is going to be fine.'

Then she went up to her father's room, took out his razor and slashed her wrists.

Chapter 12

When Teresa opened her eyes, the family doctor and the village priest were standing beside her bed.

'No!' she screamed. 'I don't want to come back. Let me die. Let me die!'

The priest said, 'Suicide is a mortal sin. God gave you life, Teresa. Only He may decide when it is finished. You are young. You have a whole lifetime ahead of you.'

'To do what?' Teresa sobbed. 'Suffer more? I can't stand the pain I'm in. I can't stand it!'

He said gently, 'Jesus stood the pain and died for the rest of us. Don't turn your back on Him.'

The doctor finished examining Teresa. 'You need to rest. I've told your mother to put you on a light diet for a while.' He wagged a finger at her. 'That does not include razor blades.'

The following morning Teresa dragged herself out of bed. When she walked into the drawing room, her mother said in alarm, 'What are you doing up? The doctor told you –'

Teresa said hoarsely, 'I have to go to church. I have to talk to God.'

Her mother hesitated. 'I'll go with you.'

'No. I must go alone.'

'But –'

Her father nodded. 'Let her go.'

They watched the dispirited figure walk out of the house.

'What's going to happen to her?' Teresa's mother moaned.

'God only knows.'

*

She entered the familiar church, walked up to the altar and knelt.

'I've come to Your house to tell You something, God. I despise You. I despise You for letting me be born ugly. I despise You for letting my sister be born beautiful. I despise You for letting her take away the only man I ever loved. I spit on You.'

Her last words were so loud that the people inside turned to stare at her as she rose and stumbled out of the church.

Teresa had never believed there could be such pain. It was unbearable. It was impossible to think of anything else. She was unable to eat or sleep. The world seemed muffled and far away. Memories kept flashing into her mind, like scenes from a film.

She remembered the day she and Raoul and Monique had walked along the beach at Nice.

'It's a beautiful day for a swim,' Raoul said.

'I'd love to go, but we can't. Teresa doesn't swim.'

'I don't mind if you two go ahead. I'll wait for you at the hotel.'

And she had been so pleased that Raoul and Monique were getting along so well together.

They were lunching at a small inn near Cagnes. The maître d' said, 'The lobster is particularly good today.'

'I'll have it,' Monique said. 'Poor Teresa can't. Shellfish makes her break out in hives.'

St Tropez. 'I miss horseback riding. I used to ride every morning at home. Do you want to ride with me, Teresa?'

'I – I'm afraid I don't ride, Raoul.'

'I wouldn't mind going with you,' Monique said. 'I love to ride.'

And they had been gone all morning.

There were a hundred clues, and she had missed all of them. She had been blind because she wanted to be blind. The looks that Raoul and Monique had exchanged, the innocent touching of hands, the whispers and the laughter.

How could I have been so stupid?

At night when Teresa finally managed to doze off, she had dreams. It was always a different dream. It was always the same dream.

Raoul and Monique were on a train, naked, making love and the train was crossing a trestle high over a canyon, and the trestle collapsed and everyone on the train plunged to their deaths.

Raoul and Monique were in a hotel room, naked in bed, and Raoul laid down a cigarette and the room exploded in flames and the two of them were burned to death, and their screams awakened Teresa.

Raoul and Monique fell from a mountain, drowned in a river, died in an airplane crash.

It was always a different dream.

It was always the same dream.

Teresa's mother and father were frantic. They watched their daughter wasting away, and there was nothing they could do to help her. And then suddenly Teresa began to eat. She ate constantly. She could not seem to get enough food. She gained her weight back, and then kept gaining and gaining until her body was gross.

When her mother and father tried to talk to her about her pain, Teresa said, 'I'm fine now. Don't worry about me.'

Teresa carried on her life as though nothing were wrong. She continued to go into town and shop and do all the errands she had always done. She joined her mother and father for dinner each evening and read or sewed. She had built an emotional fortress around herself, and she was determined that no one would ever breach it. *No man will ever want to look at me. Never again.*

Outwardly, Teresa seemed fine. Inside, she was sunk in an abyss of deep, desperate loneliness. Even when she was surrounded by people, she sat in a lonely chair in a lonely room, in a lonely house, in a lonely world.

A little over a year after Raoul had left Teresa, her father was packing to leave for Ávila.

'I have some business to transact there,' he told Teresa. 'But after that, I'll be free. Why don't you come with me? Ávila is a fascinating town. It will do you good to get away from here for a while.'

'No, thank you, Father.'

He looked at his wife and sighed. 'Very well.'

The butler walked into the drawing room.

'Excuse me, Miss DeFosse. This letter just arrived for you.'

Even before Teresa opened it, she was filled with a prescience of something terrible looming before her.

The letter read:

> Teresa, my darling Teresa:
>
> God knows I do not have a right to call you darling, after the terrible thing I have done, but I promise to make it up to you if it takes me a lifetime. I don't know where to begin.
>
> Monique has run off and left me with our two-month-old daughter. Frankly, I am relieved. I must confess that I have been in hell ever since the day I left you. I will never understand why I did what I did. I seem to have been caught up in some kind of magic spell of Monique's, but I knew from the beginning that my marriage to her was a terrible mistake. It was you I always loved. I know now that the only place I can find my happiness is at your side. By the time you receive this letter, I will be on my way back to you.
>
> I love you, and I have always loved you, Teresa.

For the sake of the rest of our lives together, I beg your forgiveness. I want . . .

She could not finish reading the letter. The thought of seeing Raoul again and his and Monique's baby was unthinkable, obscene.

She threw the letter down, hysterical.

'I must get out of here,' Teresa screamed. 'Tonight. Now. Please . . . please!'

It was impossible for them to calm her.

'If Raoul is coming here,' her father said, 'you should at least talk to him.'

'No! If I see him, I'll kill him.' She grabbed her father's arms, tears streaming down her face. 'Take me with you,' Teresa pleaded.

She would go anywhere, as long as she escaped from this place.

And so that evening Teresa and her father set out for Ávila.

Teresa's father was distraught over his daughter's unhappiness. He was not by nature a compassionate man, but in the last year Teresa had won his admiration by her courageous behaviour. She had faced the townspeople with her head held high and had never complained. He felt helpless, unable to console her.

He remembered how much solace she had once found in the church, and when they arrived in Ávila he said to Teresa, 'Father Berrendo, the priest here, is an old friend of mine. Perhaps he can help you. Will you speak to him?'

'No.' She would have nothing to do with God.

Teresa stayed in the hotel room alone while her father conducted his business. When he returned, Teresa was seated in the same chair, staring at the walls.

'Teresa, please see Father Berrendo.'

'No.'

He was at a loss. Teresa refused to leave the hotel room and she refused to return to Èze.

In the end, the priest came to see Teresa.

'Your father tells me that you once attended church regularly.'

Teresa looked into the eyes of the frail-looking priest and said coldly, 'I'm no longer interested. The Church has nothing to offer me.'

Father Berrendo smiled. 'The Church has something to offer everyone, my child. The Church gives us hope and dreams . . .'

'I've had my fill of dreams. Never again.'

He took her hands in his thin hands and saw the white scars of razor slashes on her wrists, as faint as a long ago memory.

'God doesn't believe that. Talk to Him and He will tell you.'

Teresa sat there, staring at the wall, and when the priest finally made his way out, she was not even aware of it.

The following morning Teresa walked into the cool, vaulted church, and almost immediately the old, familiar feeling of peace stole over her. The last time she had been in a church was to curse God. A feeling of deep shame filled her. It was her own weakness that had betrayed her, not God.

'Forgive me,' she whispered. 'I have sinned. I have lived in hate. Help me. Please help me.'

She looked up, and Father Berrendo was standing there. When she finished, he led her into his office behind the vestry.

'I don't know what to do, Father. I don't believe in anything any more. I've lost faith.' Her voice was filled with despair.

'Did you have faith when you were a young girl?'

'Yes. Very much.'

'Then you still have it, my child. Faith is real and permanent. It is everything else that is transient.'

They talked that day for hours.

When Teresa returned to the hotel late in the afternoon,

her father said, 'I must get back to Èze. Are you ready to leave?'

'No, Papa. Let me stay here for a while.'

He hesitated. 'Will you be all right?'

'Yes, Father. I promise.'

Teresa and Father Berrendo met every day after that. Father Berrendo's heart went out to Teresa. He saw in her not a fat, unattractive woman, but a beautiful, unhappy spirit. They spoke of God and creation and the meaning of life, and slowly, almost in spite of herself, Teresa began to find comfort again. Something that Father Berrendo said one day triggered a deep response.

'My child, if you do not believe in this world, then believe in the next world. Believe in the world where Jesus is waiting to receive you.'

And for the first time since the terrible thing that had happened to her, Teresa began to feel at peace again. The church had become her haven, just as it had once been. But there was her future to think about.

'I have no place to go.'

'You could return home.'

'No. I could never go back there. I could never face Raoul again. I don't know what to do. I want to hide, and there is no place to hide.'

Father Berrendo was silent for a long time. Finally he spoke. 'You could stay here.'

She looked around the office, puzzled. 'Here?'

'The Cistercian convent is nearby.' He leaned forward. 'Let me tell you about it. It is a world inside a world, where everyone is dedicated to God. It is a place of peace and serenity.'

And Teresa's heart began to lift. 'It sounds wonderful.'

'I must caution you. It is one of the strictest orders in the world. Those who are admitted take a vow of chastity, silence and obedience. No one who enters there ever leaves.'

The words sent a thrill through Teresa. 'I will never want

to leave. It is what I have been searching for, Father. I despise the world I live in.'

But Father Berrendo was still concerned. He knew that Teresa would be facing a life totally different from anything she had ever experienced.

'There can be no turning back.'

'I won't turn back.'

Early the next day, Father Berrendo took Teresa to the convent to meet the Reverend Mother Betina. He left the two of them there to talk.

The moment Teresa entered the convent, she knew. *At last*, she thought exultantly. *At last.*

Teresa telephoned her mother and father.

'I've been so worried,' her mother said. 'When are you coming home?'

'I am home.'

The Bishop of Ávila performed the rite:

'Creator, Lord, send thy benediction upon thy handmaid that she shall be fortified with celestial virtue, that she may maintain complete faith and unbroken fidelity.'

Teresa responded, 'The kingdom of this world and all secular adornings, I have despised for the love of our Lord, Jesus Christ.'

The bishop made the sign of the cross over her.

'*De largitatis tuae fonte defluxit ut cum honorem nupiarum nulla interdicta minuissent ac super sanctum conjugium nuptialis benedictio permaneret existerent connubium, concupiscerent sacramentum, nec imitarentur quod nuptiis agitur, sed diligerent quod nuptiis prae notatur.* Amen.'

'Amen.'

'I espouse thee to Jesus Christ, the son of the Supreme Father. Therefore receive the seal of the Holy Ghost, so that thou be called the spouse of God, and if thou serve him faithfully, be crowned everlastingly.' The bishop rose. 'God, the Father Almighty, Creator of heaven and earth, who hath vouchsafed to choose you to an espousalship like that of the blessed Mary, mother of our Lord, Jesus Christ – *ad beatae Mariae matris Domini nostri* Jesus Christ consortium – hallow you, that in the presence of God and of His angels, you may persevere, untouched and undefiled, and hold to your purpose, love, chastity, and keep patience that you may merit to receive the crown of His blessing, through the same Christ our Lord. God make you strong when frail, strengthen you when weak, relieve and govern your mind with piety and direct your ways. Amen.'

Now, thirty years later, lying in the woods watching the sun come up over the horizon, Sister Teresa thought: *I came to the convent for all the wrong reasons. I was not running to God. I was running away from the world. But God read my heart.*

She was sixty years old, and the last thirty years of her life had been the happiest she had ever known. And now she had suddenly been flung back into the world she had run away from. And her mind was playing strange tricks on her.

She was no longer sure what was real and what was unreal. The past and the present seemed to be blending together in a strange dizzying blur. *Why is this happening to me? What does God have planned for me?*

Chapter 13

For Sister Megan, the journey was an adventure. She had become used to the new sights and sounds that surrounded her, and the speed with which she had adapted surprised her.

She found her companions fascinating. Amparo Jiron was a powerful woman, easily able to keep up with the two men, and yet at the same time she was very feminine.

Felix Carpio, the husky man with a reddish beard and a scar, seemed amiable and pleasant.

But to Megan, the most compelling of the group was Jaime Miró. There was a relentless strength about him, an unshakable faith in his beliefs that reminded Megan of the nuns in the convent.

When they began the journey, Jaime and Amparo and Felix were carrying sleeping-bags and rifles on their shoulders.

'Let me carry one of the sleeping-bags,' Megan suggested.

Jaime Miró had looked at her in surprise, then shrugged. 'All right, Sister.'

He handed her the bag. It was heavier than Megan had expected, but she did not complain. *As long as I'm with them, I'm going to do my share.*

It seemed to Megan that they had been walking for ever, stumbling through the darkness, hit by branches, scratched by underbrush, attacked by insects, guided only by the light of the moon.

Who are these people? Megan wondered. *And why are they being hunted?* Because Megan and the other nuns were also being pursued, Megan felt a strong rapport with her new companions.

There was little talking, but from time to time they held cryptic conversations.

'Is everything set at Valladolid?'

'Right, Jaime. Rubio and Tomas will meet us at the bank during the bullfight.'

'Good. Send word to Largo Cortez to expect us. But don't give him a date.'

'*Comprendo.*'

Who are Largo Cortez and Rubio and Tomas? Megan wondered. And what was going to happen at the bullfight and the bank? She almost started to ask, but thought better of it. *I have the feeling they wouldn't welcome a lot of questions.*

Near dawn they smelled smoke from the valley below them.

'Wait here,' Jaime whispered. 'Be quiet.'

They watched as Jaime made his way towards the edge of the forest and disappeared from sight.

Megan said, 'What is it –?'

'Shut up!' Amparo Jiron hissed.

Fifteen minutes later Jaime Miró returned.

'Soldiers. We'll circle around them.'

They back-tracked for half a mile, then moved cautiously through the woods until they reached a side road. The countryside stretched out ahead of them, redolent with the odours of mown hay and ripe fruit.

Megan's curiosity got the better of her. 'Why are the soldiers looking for you?' she asked.

Jaime Miró said, 'Let's say we don't see eye to eye.'

And she had to be satisfied with that. *For now*, she thought. She was determined to know more about this man.

Half an hour later when they reached a sheltered clearing, Jaime said, 'The sun's up. We'll stay here until nightfall.' He looked at Megan. 'Tonight we're going to have to travel faster.'

She nodded. 'Very well.'

Jaime took the sleeping-bags and rolled them out.

Felix Carpio said to Megan, 'You take mine, Sister. I'm used to sleeping on the ground.'

'It's yours,' Megan said. 'I couldn't –'

'For Christ's sake,' Amparo snapped. 'Get into the bag. We don't want you to keep us awake screaming about god-damned spiders.' There was an animosity in her tone that Megan did not understand.

Without another word, Megan climbed into the sleeping-bag. *What's bothering her?* Megan wondered.

Megan watched as Jaime unrolled his sleeping-bag a few feet away from where she lay. He crawled into the bag. Amparo Jiron crawled in beside him. *I see*, Megan thought.

Jaime looked over at Megan. 'You'd better get some sleep,' he said. 'We have a long way ahead of us.'

Megan was awakened by a moaning. It sounded as though someone were in terrible pain. Megan sat up, concerned. The sounds were coming from Jaime's sleeping-bag. *He must be terribly ill*, was her first thought.

The moaning was getting louder, and then Megan heard Amparo Jiron's voice saying, 'Oh, yes, yes. Give it to me, *querido*. Harder! Yes! Now! Now!'

And Megan's face flushed. She tried to close her ears to the sounds she was hearing, but it was impossible. And she wondered what it would be like to have Jaime Miró make love to her.

Instantly Megan crossed herself and began to pray: *Forgive me, Father. Let my thoughts be filled only with You. Let my spirit seek You that it may find its source and good in You.*

And the sounds went on. Finally, when Megan thought she would be unable to bear it an instant longer, they stopped. But there were other noises to keep her awake. The sounds of the forest ricocheted around her. There was a cacophony of mating birds and crickets and the chattering of small animals and the guttural growlings of larger ones.

Megan had forgotten how noisy the outside world could be. She missed the wonderful silence of the convent. To her own astonishment, she even missed the orphanage. The terrible, wonderful orphanage . . .

Chapter 14

Ávila 1957

They called her 'Megan the Terror'.
They called her 'Megan the Blue-eyed Devil'.
They called her 'Megan the Impossible'.
She was ten years old.

She had been brought to the orphanage when she was an infant, left on the doorstep of a farmer and his wife who were unable to care for her.

The orphanage was an austere, two-storey, white-washed building on the outskirts of Ávila, in the poorer section of the city, off the Plaza de San Vicente, run by Mercedes Angeles, an Amazon of a woman with a fierce manner that belied the warmth she felt for her wards.

Megan was different from the other children, an alien with blonde hair and bright blue eyes, standing out in stark contrast to the dark-eyed, dark-haired children. But from the beginning, Megan was different in other ways. She was a fiercely independent child, a leader, a mischief-maker. Whenever there was trouble at the orphanage, Mercedes Angeles could be certain that Megan was at the bottom of it.

Over the years, Megan led riots protesting about the food, she tried to form the children into a union, and she found inventive ways of tormenting the supervisors, including half a dozen escape attempts. Needless to say, Megan was immensely popular with the other children. She was younger than many of them, but they all turned to her for guidance.

She was a natural leader. And the younger children loved to have Megan tell them stories. She had a wild imagination.

'Who were my parents, Megan?'

'Ah. Your father was a clever jewel thief. He climbed over the roof of a hotel in the middle of the night to steal a diamond belonging to a famous actress. Well, just as he was putting the diamond in his pocket, the actress woke up. She turned on the light and saw him.'

'Did she have him arrested?'

'No. He was very handsome.'

'What happened then?'

'They fell in love and got married. Then you were born.'

'But why did they send me to an orphanage? Didn't they love me?'

That was always the difficult part. 'Of course they loved you. But – well – they were skiing in Switzerland and they were killed in a terrible avalanche –'

'What's a terrible avalanche?'

'That's when a bunch of snow comes down all at once and buries you.'

'And my mother and father both died?'

'Yes. And their last words were that they loved you. But there was no one to take care of you, so you were sent here.'

Megan was as anxious as the others to know who her parents were, and at night she would put herself to sleep by making up stories to herself: 'My father was a soldier in the Civil War,' she would think. 'He was a captain and very brave. He was wounded in battle, and my mother was the nurse who took care of him. They married, and he went back to the front and was killed. My mother was too poor to keep me, so she had to leave me at the farmhouse, and it broke her heart.' And she would weep with pity for her courageous, dead father and her bereaved mother.

Or: 'My father was a bullfighter. He was one of the great Matadors. He was the toast of Spain. Everyone adored him. My mother was a beautiful flamenco dancer. They were married, but he was killed one day by a huge, dangerous bull. My mother was forced to give me up.'

Or: 'My father was a clever spy from another country . . .'
The fantasies were endless.

There were thirty children in the orphanage, ranging from abandoned newborn infants to fourteen-year-olds. Most of them were Spanish, but there were children there from half a dozen countries, and Megan became fluent in several languages. She slept in a dormitory with a dozen other girls. There were late-night whispered conversations about dolls and clothes, and as the girls grew older, about sex. It soon became the primary topic of conversation.

'I hear it hurts a lot.'

'I don't care. I can't wait to do it.'

'I'm going to get married, but I'm never going to let my husband do it to me. I think it's dirty.'

One night, when everyone was asleep, Primo Conde, one of the young boys at the orphanage, crept into the girls' dormitory. He moved to the side of Megan's bed.

'Megan . . .' His voice was a whisper.

She was instantly awake. 'Primo? What's the matter?'

He was sobbing, frightened. 'Can I get into bed with you?'

'Yes. Be quiet.'

Primo was thirteen, the same age as Megan, but he was small for his age, and had been an abused child. He suffered from terrible nightmares and would wake up in the middle of the night screaming. The other children tormented him, and Megan was the one who always protected him.

Primo climbed into bed beside her, and Megan felt the tears running down his cheeks. She held him close in her arms.

'It's all right,' Megan whispered. 'It's all right.'

She rocked him gently and his sobs subsided. His body was pressed against hers, and she could feel his growing excitement.

'Primo . . .'

'I'm sorry. I – I can't help it.'

His erection was pressing into her.

'I love you, Megan. You're the only one I care about in the whole world.'

'You haven't been out in the world yet.'

'Please don't laugh at me.'

'I'm not.'

'I have no one but you.'

'I know.'

'I love you.'

'I love you, too, Primo.'

'Megan – would you – let me make love to you? Please.'

'No.'

There was silence. 'I'm sorry I bothered you. I'll go back to my bed.' His voice was filled with pain. He started to move away.

'Wait.' Megan held him close to her, wanting to ease his suffering, feeling aroused herself. 'Primo, I – I can't let you make love to me, but I can do something to make you feel better. Will that be all right?'

'Yes.' His voice was a murmur.

He was wearing pyjamas. Megan pulled the cord that held his pyjama bottom up and reached inside. *He's a man*, Megan thought. She held him gently in her hand and began to stroke him. Primo groaned and said, 'Oh, that feels wonderful,' and a moment later, 'God, I love you, Megan.'

Her body was on fire, and if at that moment he had said, 'I want to make love to you,' she would have said yes.

But he lay there, silent, and in a few minutes he returned to his own bed.

There was no sleep for Megan that night. And she had never allowed him to come into her bed again.

The temptation was too great.

From time to time the children would be called into the supervisor's office to meet a prospective foster parent. It was always a moment of great excitement for the children, for it would mean a chance to escape from the dreary routine of the orphanage, a chance to have a real home, to belong to someone.

Over the years Megan watched as other orphans were chosen. They went to the homes of merchants, farmers, bankers, shopkeepers. But it was always the other children, never Megan. Her reputation proceeded her. She would hear the prospective parents talk among themselves.

'She's a very pretty child, but I hear she's difficult.'

'Isn't she the one who smuggled twelve dogs into the orphanage last month?'

'They say she's a ringleader. I'm afraid she wouldn't get along with our children.'

They had no idea how much the other children adored Megan.

Father Berrendo came to the orphanage once a week to visit the wards, and Megan looked forward to his visits. Megan was an omnivorous reader, and the priest and Mercedes Angeles saw to it that she was well supplied with books. She could discuss things with the priest that she dared not talk about with anyone else. It was Father Berrendo to whom the farm couple had turned over the infant Megan.

'Why didn't they want to keep me?' Megan asked.

The old priest said gently, 'They wanted to very much, Megan, but they were old and ill.'

'Why do you suppose my real parents left me at that farm?'

'I'm sure it was because they were poor and couldn't afford to keep you.'

As Megan grew up, she became more and more devout. She was stirred by the intellectual aspects of the Catholic Church. She read St Augustine's Confessions, the writings of St Francis of Assisi, Thomas Merton, Thomas More, and a dozen others. Megan went to church regularly, and she enjoyed the solemn rituals, the Gloria Patri, receiving the Eucharist, the doxology, the benediction. Perhaps most of all, she loved the wonderful feeling of serenity that always stole over her in church.

'I want to become a Catholic,' Megan told Father Berrendo one day.

He took her hand in his and said with a twinkle, 'Perhaps you are already, Megan, but we'll hedge our bets.' He gave her the Catholic cathechism:

'Quid petis ab Ecclesia dei?'

'Fidem!'

'Fides quid tibi praestat?'

'Vitam Aeternam.'

'Abrenuntias Satanae?'

'Sic.'

'Dost thou believe in God the Father Almighty, creator of heaven and earth?'

'Credo!'

'Dost thou believe in Jesus Christ, His only son, who was born and suffered?'

'Credo!'

'Dost thou believe in the Holy Spirit in the Holy Catholic Church, the communion of saints, the remission of sins, the resurrection of the body and eternal life?'

'Credo!'

The priest blew gently into her face. '*Exi ab eo spiritus immunde.* Depart from her, thou impure spirit and give place to the Holy Spirit, the paraclete.' He breathed again into her face. 'Megan, receive the good Spirit through this breathing and receive the blessing of God. Peace be with thee.'

At fifteen Megan had become a beautiful young woman, with long blonde hair and a milky complexion that set her off even more from most of her companions.

One day she was summoned to the office of Mercedes Angeles. Father Berrendo was there.

'Hello, Father.'

'Hello, my dear Megan.'

Mercedes Angeles said, 'I'm afraid we have a problem, Megan.'

'Oh?' She wracked her brain, trying to remember her latest misdeed.

The head mistress went on: 'There is an age limit here of fifteen, and you've reached your fifteenth birthday.'

Megan had long known of the rule, of course. But she had put it in the back of her mind, because she did not want to face the fact that she had nowhere in the world to go, that no one wanted her, and that she was going to be abandoned once again.

'Do I – do I have to leave?'

The kindly Amazon was upset, but she had no choice. 'I'm afraid we must abide by the rules. We can find a position for you as a maid.'

Megan had no words.

Father Berrendo spoke. 'Where would you like to go?'

As she thought about it, an idea came to Megan. There *was* somewhere for her to go.

From the time Megan was twelve years old, she had helped earn her keep at the orphanage by making outside deliveries in town, and many of them were made to the Cistercian convent. They were always delivered to the Reverend Mother Betina. Megan had sneaked glimpses of the nuns praying, or walking through the corridors, and she had sensed an almost overpowering feeling of serenity. She envied the joy that the nuns seemed to radiate. To Megan, the convent seemed a house of love.

The Reverend Mother had taken a liking to the bright young girl, and they had had long talks over the years.

'Why do people join convents?' Megan had asked.

'People come to us for many reasons. Most come to dedicate themselves to God. But some come because they have no hope. We give them hope. Some come because they feel they have no reason to live. We show them that God is the reason. Some come because they are running away. Others come here because they are alienated and they want to belong.'

That was what had struck a responsive chord in the young girl. *I've never really belonged to anyone*, Megan thought. *This is my chance.*

'I think I would like to join the convent.'

Six weeks later, Megan took her vows.

And finally Megan had found what she had been searching for so long. She belonged. These were her sisters, the family she had never had, and they were all one under their Father.

Megan worked in the convent as a bookkeeper, keeping the records. She was fascinated by the ancient sign language that the sisters used when they needed to communicate with the Reverend Mother. There were 472 signs, enough to convey among themselves everything they needed to express.

When it was a sister's turn to dust the long corridors, Prioress Betina held out her right hand with the heel forward and blew on the back of it. If a nun had a fever, she went to the Reverend Mother and pressed the tip of her right forefinger and middle finger on the outside of her left wrist. If a request was to be delayed, Prioress Betina held her right fist before her right shoulder and pushed it slightly forward and down. *Tomorrow.*

One November morning Megan was introduced to the rites of death. A nun was dying, and a wooden rattle was rung in the cloister, the signal for the beginning of a ritual unchanged since the year 1030. All those who could answer the call hurried to kneel in the infirmary for the anointing and the psalms. They silently prayed for the saints to intercede for the departing sister's soul. To signify that it was time for the last sacraments to be given, the Mother Prioress held out her left hand with the palm up and drew a cross on it with the tip of her right thumb.

And finally, there was the sign of death itself, a sister placing the tip of her right thumb under her chin and raising it slightly.

When the last prayers had been said, the body was left alone for an hour so that the soul could go in peace. At the foot of the bed the great Paschal candle, the Christian symbol of eternal light, burned in its wooden holder.

The infirmarian washed the body and clothed the dead

nun in her habit, black scapular over white cowl, rough stockings and handmade sandals. From the garden one of the nuns brought fresh flowers, woven into a crown. When the dead woman was dressed, six of the nuns in a procession carried her to the church and placed her on the white-sheeted bier facing the altar. She would not be left alone before her God, and in their stalls by her side, two nuns stayed through the rest of the day and on through the night praying, while the Paschal candle flickered at her side.

The next afternoon, after the requiem mass, she was carried through the cloister by the nuns to the private, walled cemetery where even in death the nuns kept their enclosure. The sisters, three and three, lowered her carefully into the grave, supported on white bands of linen. It was the Cistercian custom for their dead to lie uncovered in the earth, buried without a coffin. And the last service they performed for their sister was for two nuns to start to drop soil softly on to her still body before they all returned to the church to say the psalms of penance. Three times they begged that God have mercy on her soul:

Domine miserere super peccatrice
Domine miserere super peccatrice
Domine miserere super peccatrice

There were often times when young Megan was filled with melancholy. The convent gave her serenity, and yet she was not completely at peace. It was as though a part of her was missing. She felt longings that she should have long ago forgotten. She found herself thinking about the friends she had left behind in the orphanage, and wondering what had happened to them. And she wondered what was happening in the outside world, the world that she had renounced, a world where there was music and dancing and laughter.

Megan went to Reverend Mother Betina.

'It happens to all of us from time to time,' she assured Megan. 'The church calls it "acedia". It is a spiritual malaise, an instrument of Satan. Do not worry about it, child. It will pass.'

And it did.

But what did not pass was the bone-deep longing to know who her parents were. *I'll never know*, Megan thought despairingly. *Not as long as I live.*

Chapter 15

New York City 1976

The reporters gathered outside the grey façade of New York's Waldorf Astoria Hotel watched the parade of celebrities in evening dress alight from their limousines, enter the revolving doors and head for the Grand Ballroom on the third floor. The guests had come from around the world.

Cameras flashed as reporters called out, 'Mr Vice President, would you look this way, please?'

'Governor Adams, could I have one more picture, please?'

There were senators and representatives from several foreign countries, business tycoons and celebrities. And they were all there to celebrate Ellen Scott's sixtieth birthday. In truth, it was not so much Ellen Scott that they were honouring as the philanthropy of Scott Industries, one of the most powerful conglomerates in the world. The huge, sprawling empire included oil companies and steel mills, communications systems and banks. All the money raised this evening would go to international charities.

Scott Industries had interests in every part of the world. Twenty-five years earlier, its President, Milo Scott, had died unexpectedly of a heart attack, and his wife, Ellen, had taken over the management of the huge conglomerate and in the ensuing years had proved to be a brilliant executive, more than tripling the assets of the company.

The Grand Ballroom of the Waldorf Astoria is an enormous room, decorated in beige and gold, with a red-carpeted stage at one end and a balcony curving around the entire room, holding thirty-three boxes with a chandelier over each one. In the centre balcony sat the guest of honour. There were at least 600 men and women present, dining at tables gleaming with silver.

When dinner was finished, the Governor of New York strode on to the stage.

'Mr Vice President, ladies and gentlemen, honoured guests, we are all here tonight for one purpose: to pay tribute to a remarkable woman and to her unselfish generosity over the years. Ellen Scott is the kind of person who could have made a success in any field. She would have been a great scientist or doctor. She would also have made a great politician, and I must tell you that if Ellen Scott decides to run for President of the United States, I'll be the first one to vote for her. Not in the next election, of course, but the one after that.'

There was laughter and applause.

'But Ellen Scott is much more than just a brilliant woman. She is a charitable, compassionate human being who never hesitates to get involved in the problems that face the world today –'

The speech went on for ten more minutes, but Ellen Scott was no longer listening. *How wrong he is*, she thought wryly. *How wrong they all are. Scott Industries isn't even my company. Milo and I stole it. And I'm guilty of a far greater crime than that. It doesn't matter any longer. Not now. Because I'll be dead soon.*

She remembered the doctor's exact words as he read the lab report that was her death sentence.

'I'm dreadfully sorry, Mrs Scott, but I'm afraid there's no way to break this to you gently. The cancer has spread throughout your lymphatic system. It's inoperable.'

She had felt the sudden leaden weight in her stomach.

'How . . . how long do I have?'

He hesitated. 'A year – maybe.'

Not enough time. Not with so much still to do. 'You will say nothing of this, of course.' Her voice was steady.

'Certainly not.'

'Thank you, doctor.'

She had no recollection of leaving the Presbyterian Medical Center or of the drive downtown. Her only thought was: *I must find her before I die.*

Now the Governor's speech was over.

'Ladies and gentlemen, it is my honour and privilege to introduce Mrs Ellen Scott.'

Ellen Scott rose to a standing ovation. She walked towards the stage, a thin, grey-haired, straight-backed woman, smartly dressed and projecting a vitality she no longer felt.

Looking at me is like seeing the distant light of a long dead star, she thought bitterly. *I'm not really here any more.*

On the stage she waited for the applause to die down. *They're applauding a monster. What would they do if they knew?* When she spoke, her voice was firm.

'Mr Vice President, Senators, Governor Adams . . .'

A year, she was thinking. *I wonder where she is and if she is still alive. I must find out.*

She talked on, automatically saying all the things her audience expected to hear. 'I gladly accept this tribute not for myself, but for all those who have worked so hard to lighten the burden of those who are less fortunate than we are . . .'

Her mind was drifting back forty-two years to Gary, Indiana . . .

At eighteen, Ellen Dudash was employed at the Scott Industries automotive parts plant in Gary, Indiana. She was an attractive, outgoing girl, popular with her fellow workers. On the day Milo Scott came to inspect the plant, Ellen was selected to escort him around.

'Hey! How about you, Ellie? Maybe you'll marry the boss's brother and we'll all be working for you.'

Ellen Dudash laughed. 'Right. And that's when pigs will grow wings.'

Milo Scott was not at all what Ellen had expected. He was

in his early thirties, tall and slim. *Not bad looking*, Ellen thought. He was shy and almost deferential.

'It's very kind of you to take the time to show me around, Miss Dudash. I hope I'm not taking you away from your work.'

She grinned. 'I hope you are.'

He was so easy to talk to.

I can't believe I'm kidding around with the big boss's brother. Wait till I tell Mom and Pop about this.

Milo Scott seemed genuinely interested in the workers and their problems. Ellen took him through the department where the round drive gears and the long driven gears were made. She showed him through the annealing room, where the soft gears were put through a hardening process, and the packing section and the shipping department, and he seemed properly impressed.

'It's certainly a large operation, isn't it, Miss Dudash?'

He owns all of this, and he acts like an awed kid. I guess it takes all kinds.

It was in the assembly section where the accident happened. An overhead cable car carrying metal bars to the machine shop snapped and a load of iron came tumbling down. Milo Scott was directly beneath it. Ellen saw it coming a fraction of a second before it hit, and without thinking, shoved Milo Scott out of harm's way. Two of the heavy iron bars hit her before she could escape, and she was knocked unconscious.

She awakened in a private suite in a hospital. The room was literally filled with flowers. When Ellen opened her eyes and looked around, she thought: *I've died and gone to heaven.*

There were orchids and roses and lilies and chrysanthemums and rare blooms she could not even begin to identify.

Her right arm was in a cast and her ribs were taped and felt bruised.

A nurse came in. 'Ah, you're awake, Miss Dudash. I'll inform the doctor.'

'Where – where am I?'

'Blake Center – it's a private hospital.'

Ellen looked around the large suite. *I can never afford to pay for all this.*

'We've been screening your calls.'

'What calls?'

'The press has been trying to get in to interview you. Your friends have been calling. Mr Scott has telephoned several times . . .'

Milo Scott! 'Is he all right?'

'I beg your pardon?'

'Was he hurt in the accident?'

'No. He was here again early this morning, but you were asleep.'

'He came to see *me*?'

'Yes.' She looked around the room. 'Most of these flowers are from him.'

Unbelievable.

'Your mother and father are in the waiting room. Do you feel up to seeing them now?'

'Of course.'

'Thank you. I'll send them in.'

Boy, I've never been treated like this in a hospital before, Ellen thought.

Her mother and father walked in and came up to the bed. Ellen's parents had been born in Poland and their English was tentative. Ellen's father was a mechanic, a burly, rough-hewn man in his fifties, and Ellen's mother was a bluff, northern European peasant.

'I brought you some soup, Ellen.'

'Mom – they feed people in hospitals.'

'Not my soup, they don't feed you in the hospital. Eat it and you'll get well faster.'

Her father said, 'Have you see the papers? I brung you copy.'

He handed the newspaper to her. The headline read:

FACTORY WORKER RISKS LIFE TO SAVE BOSS.

She read the story twice.

'That was brave thing you done to save him.'

Brave? It was stupid. If I had had time to think, I would have saved myself. That was the dumbest thing I ever did. Why, I could have been killed!

Milo Scott came to see Ellen later that morning. He was carrying another bouquet of flowers.

'These are for you,' he said awkwardly. 'The doctor tells me you're going to be fine. I – I can't tell you how grateful I am to you.'

'It was nothing.'

'It was the most courageous act I've ever seen. You saved my life.'

She tried to move, but it sent a sharp pain through her arm.

'Are you all right?'

'Sure.' Her side was beginning to throb. 'What did the doc say was wrong with me?'

'You have a broken arm and three broken ribs.'

He couldn't have given her worse news. Her eyes filled with tears.

'What's the matter?'

How could she tell him? He would only laugh at her. She had been saving up for a long-awaited vacation to New York, on a tour with some of the girls from the factory. It had been her dream. *Now I'll be out of work for a month or more. There goes Manhattan.*

Ellen had worked since she was fifteen. She had always been fiercely independent and self-sufficient, but now she thought: *Maybe if he's so grateful he'll pay part of my hospital bills. But I'll be damned if I'll ask him.* She was beginning to feel drowsy. *It must be the medication.*

She said sleepily, 'Thank you for all the flowers, Mr Scott. And it was nice meeting you.' *I'll worry about the hospital bills later.*

Ellen Dudash slept.

*

The following morning, a tall, distinguished-looking man came into Ellen's suite.

'Good morning, Miss Dudash. How are you feeling this morning?'

'Better, thank you.'

'I'm Sam Norton. I'm chief public relations officer for Scott Industries.'

'Oh.' She had never seen him before. 'Do you live here?'

'No. I flew in from Washington.'

'To see me?'

'To assist you.'

'To assist me *what*?'

'The press is outside, Miss Dudash. Since I don't believe you've ever held a press conference, I thought perhaps you could use some help.'

'What do they want?'

'Mainly, they're going to ask you to tell them about how and why you saved Mr Scott.'

'Oh. That's easy. If I had stopped to think, I'd have run like hell.'

Norton stared at her. 'Miss Dudash – I don't think I would say that, if I were you.'

'Why not? It's the truth.'

This was not at all what he had expected. The girl seemed to have no idea of her situation.

There was something worrying Ellen, and she decided to get it out in the open. 'Are you going to see Mr Scott?'

'Yes.'

'Would you do me a favour?'

'If I can, certainly.'

'I know the accident's not his fault, and he didn't ask me to push him out of the way, but –' The strong, independent streak in her made her hesitate. 'Oh, never mind.'

Ah, here it comes, Norton thought. How much reward was she going to try to extort? Would it be cash? A better job? What? 'Please, go on, Miss Dudash.'

She blurted it out. 'The truth is, I don't have a lot of money, and I'm going to lose some pay because of this, and

I don't think I can afford all these hospital bills. I don't want to bother Mr Scott, but if he could arrange a loan for me, I'd pay it back.' She saw the expression on Norton's face, and misread it. 'I'm sorry. I guess I sound mercenary. It's just that I've been saving up for a trip, and – well, this screws everything up.' She took a deep breath. 'It's not his problem. I'll manage.'

He almost kissed her. *How long has it been since I've come across real innocence? It's enough to restore my faith in womankind.*

He sat down at the side of her bed, and his professional manner disappeared. He took her hand. 'Ellen, I have a feeling you and I are going to be great friends. I promise you, you're not going to have to worry about money. The first thing we have to do is get you through this press conference. We want you to come out of this looking good, so that –' He stopped himself. 'I'm going to be honest. My job is to see that Scott Industries comes out of this looking good. Do you understand?'

'I guess so. You mean it wouldn't sound so good if I said I wasn't really interested in saving Milo Scott? It would sound better if I said something like, "I like working for Scott Industries so much that when I saw Milo Scott was in danger, I knew I had to try to save him, even at the risk of my own life?"'

'Yes.'

She laughed. 'Okay. If it'll help you. But I don't want to kid you, Mr Norton. I don't know what made me do it.'

He smiled. 'That will be our secret. I'll let the lions in.'

There were more than two dozen reporters and photographers from radio, newspapers and magazines. It was a man-bites-dog story, and the press intended to make the most of it. It was not every day that a pretty young employee risked her life to save her boss. And the fact that her employer happened to be Milo Scott did not hurt the story one bit.

'Miss Dudash – when you saw all that iron hurtling down at you, what was your first thought?'

Ellen looked over at Sam Norton with a straight face and

said, 'I thought, "I must save Mr Scott. I'd never forgive myself if I let him be killed."'

The press conference proceeded smoothly, and when Sam Norton saw that Ellen was beginning to tire, he said, 'That's it, ladies and gentlemen. Thank you very much.'

'Did I do all right?'

'You were great. Now get some sleep.'

She slept fitfully. She dreamed that she was in the lobby of the Empire State Building, and they would not let her in because she did not have enough money to buy a ticket.

Milo Scott came to visit Ellen Dudash that afternoon. She was surprised to see him. She had heard that his home was in New York.

'I heard the press conference went very well. You're quite a heroine.'

'Mr Scott – I have to tell you something. I'm not a heroine. I didn't stop to think about saving you. I – I just did it.'

'I know. Sam Norton told me.'

'Well, then –'

'Ellen, there are all kinds of heroism. You didn't think about saving me, but you did it instinctively, instead of saving yourself.'

'I – I just wanted you to know.'

'Sam also told me that you're worried about the hospital bills.'

'Well –'

'They're all taken care of. And as for your losing some wages –' He smiled. 'Miss Dudash, I – I don't think you know how much I owe you.'

'You don't owe me anything.'

'The doctor told me that you'll be leaving the hospital tomorrow. Will you let me buy you dinner?'

He doesn't understand, Ellen thought. *I don't want his charity. Or his pity.* 'I meant it when I said you don't owe me anything. Thanks for taking care of the hospital bills. We're even.'

'Good. Now may I buy you dinner?'

That was how it began. Milo Scott stayed in Gary for a week, and he saw Ellen every night.

Ellen's mother and father warned, 'Be careful. Big bosses don't go out with factory girls unless they want something.'

That had been Ellen Dudash's attitude at the beginning. Milo Scott changed her mind. He was a perfect gentleman at all times, and the truth finally dawned on Ellen: *He really enjoys being with me.* Where Milo was shy and reserved, Ellen was forthright and open. All his life, Milo had been surrounded by women whose burning ambition was to become a part of the powerful Scott dynasty. They had played their calculating games. Ellen Dudash was the first totally honest woman Milo had ever met. She said exactly what was on her mind. She was bright, she was attractive, and most of all, she was fun to be with. By the end of the week, they were both falling in love.

'I want to marry you,' Milo Scott said. 'I can't think about anything else. Will you marry me?'

'No.'

Nor had Ellen been able to think about anything else. The truth was that she was terrified. The Scotts were as close as America could come to royalty. They were famous, rich and powerful. *I don't belong in their circle. I would only make a fool of myself. And of Milo.* But she knew she was fighting a losing battle.

They were married by a justice of the peace in Greenwich, and returned to Manhattan so that Ellen Dudash could meet her in-laws.

Byron Scott greeted his brother with, 'What the fuck have you done – marry a Polish hooker? Are you out of your mind?'

Susan Scott was just as ungiving. 'Of course she married Milo for his money. When she finds out he doesn't have any, we'll arrange an annulment. This marriage will never last.'

They badly underestimated Ellen Dudash.

'Your brother and sister-in-law hate me, but I didn't marry them. I married you. I don't want to come between you and Byron. If this is making you too unhappy, Milo, say so, and I'll leave.'

He took his bride in his arms and whispered, 'I adore you, and when Byron and Susan really get to know you, they'll adore you.'

She held him closely and thought: *How naïve he is. And how I love him.*

Byron and Susan were not unpleasant to their new sister-in-law. They were patronizing. To them, she would always be the little Polish girl who worked in one of the Scott factories.

Ellen studied, and read, and learned. She watched how the wives of Milo's friends dressed and copied them. She was determined to become a fit wife to Milo Scott, and in time she succeeded. But not in the eyes of her in-laws. And slowly her naïveté turned to cynicism. *The rich and powerful aren't all that wonderful*, she thought. *All they want is to be richer and more powerful.*

Ellen was fiercely protective of Milo, but there was little she could do to help him. Scott Industries was one of the few privately held conglomerates in the world, and all the stock belonged to Byron. Byron's younger brother was a salaried employee, and he never let him forget it. Byron treated his brother shabbily. Milo was given all the dirty jobs to do, and never given credit.

'Why do you put up with it, Milo? You don't need him. We could move away from here. You could start your own business.'

'I couldn't leave Scott Industries. Byron needs me.'

But in time, Ellen came to understand the real reason. Milo was weak. He needed someone strong to lean on. Ellen knew then that he would never have the courage to leave the company.

All right, she thought fiercely. *One day the company will be his. Byron can't live for ever. Milo is his only heir.*

When Susan Scott announced that she was pregnant, it was a blow to Ellen. *The baby's going to inherit everything.*

When the baby was born, Byron Scott said, 'It's a girl, but I'll teach her how to run the company.'

The bastard, Ellen Scott thought. Her heart ached for Milo.

All Milo said was, 'Isn't she a beautiful baby?'

Chapter 16

The pilot of the Lockheed Lodestar was worried.

'A front is closing in. I don't like the look of it.' He nodded to the co-pilot. 'Take over.' He left the cockpit to go back to the cabin.

There were five passengers on board besides the pilot and co-pilot: Byron Scott, the brilliant, dynamic founder and chief executive officer of Scott Industries, his attractive wife, Susan; their year-old daughter, Patricia; Milo Scott, Byron Scott's younger brother; and Milo's wife, Ellen Scott. They were flying in one of the company planes from Paris to Madrid. Bringing the baby had been a last-minute impulse on Susan Scott's part.

'I hate to be away from her for so long,' she told her husband.

'Afraid she'll forget us?' he teased. 'All right. We'll take her with us.'

Now that World War II was over, Scott Industries was rapidly expanding into the European market. In Madrid, Byron Scott would investigate the possibilities of opening a new steel mill.

The pilot approached him.

'Excuse me, sir. We're heading into some thunder clouds. It doesn't look very good ahead. Do you want to turn back?'

Byron Scott looked out of the small window. They were flying through a grey mass of cumulus clouds, and every few seconds distant lightning illuminated them. 'I have a meeting in Madrid tonight. Can you go around the storm?'

'I'll try. If I can't, then I'm going to have to turn us around.'

Byron Scott nodded. 'All right.'

'Would you all fasten your seat belts, please?'

The pilot hurried back to the cockpit.

Susan Scott had heard the conversation. She picked up the baby and held her in her arms, suddenly wishing she had not brought her along. *I've got to tell Byron to have the pilot turn back*, she thought.

'Byron –'

They were suddenly caught in the eye of the storm, and the plane began bucking up and down, caught in the gusting winds. The motion began to grow more violent. Rain was smashing against the windows. The storm had closed off all visibility. The passengers felt as though they were riding on a rolling cotton sea.

Byron Scott flicked down the intercom switch. 'Where are we, Blake?'

'We're a hundred kilometres northwest of Madrid, over the town of Ávila.'

Byron Scott looked out of the window again. 'We'll forget Madrid tonight. Let's turn around and get the hell out of here.'

'Roger.'

He was a fraction too late. As the pilot started to bank the plane, a mountain peak looked suddenly in front of him. There was no time to avoid the crash. There was a rending tear, and the sky exploded as the plane tore into the side of the mountain, ripping apart, scattering chunks of fuselage and wings along a high plateau.

There was an unnatural silence that lasted for what seemed an eternity. It was broken by the crackle of flames starting to lick at the undercarriage.

'Ellen –'

Ellen Scott opened her eyes. She was lying under a tree. Her husband was bending over her, lightly slapping her face.

When he saw that she was alive, he said, 'Thank God.'

Ellen Scott sat up, dizzy, her head throbbing, every muscle in her body aching. She looked around at the obscene pieces of wreckage that had once been an airplane filled with human bodies, and shuddered.

'The others?' she asked hoarsely.

'They're dead.'

She stared at her husband. 'Oh, my God! No!'

He nodded, his face tight with grief. 'Byron, Susan, the baby, the pilots, everyone.'

Ellen Scott closed her eyes again and said a silent prayer. *Why were Milo and I spared?* she wondered. It was hard to think clearly. *We have to go down and get help. But it's too late. They're all dead.* It was impossible to believe. They had been so full of life just a few minutes before.

'Can you stand up?'

'I – I think so.'

Milo Scott helped his wife to her feet. There was a surge of sickening dizziness, and she stood there, waiting for it to pass.

Milo turned to look at the plane. Flames were beginning to get higher. 'Let's get out of here,' he said. 'The damned thing is going to blow up any second.'

They quietly moved away and watched it burn. A moment later, there was an explosion as the gas tanks blew apart and the plane was engulfed in flames.

'It's a miracle we're alive,' Milo Scott said.

It was a miracle. But not for the others.

Ellen Scott looked at the burning plane. Something was nagging at the edges of her mind, but she was having trouble thinking clearly. Something about Scott Industries. And then suddenly she knew.

'Milo?'

'Yes?' He was not really listening.

'It's fate.'

The fervour in her voice made him turn. 'What?'

'Scott Industries – it belongs to you, now.'

'I don't –'

'Milo, God left it to you.' Her voice was filled with a burning intensity. 'All your life you've lived in the shadow of your big brother.' She was thinking clearly now, coherently, and she forgot her headache and the pain. The words came tumbling out now in a spate that shook her whole body. 'You worked for Byron for twenty years building up the company. You're as responsible for its success as he is, but did he – did he ever give you credit for it? No. It was always *his* company, his success, his profits. Well now you – you finally have a chance to come into your own.'

He looked at her, horrified. 'Ellen – their bodies are – how can you even think about –?'

'I know. But we didn't kill them. It's our turn, Milo. We've finally come into our own. There's no one alive to claim the company but us. It's ours! Yours!'

And at that moment they heard the cry of a baby. Ellen and Milo Scott stared at each other unbelievingly.

'It's Patricia! She's *alive*. Oh, my God!'

They found the baby near a clump of bushes. By some miracle she was unhurt.

Milo Scott picked her up gently and held her close. 'Ssh! It's all right, darling,' he whispered. 'Everything's going to be all right.'

Ellen was standing at his side, a look of shock on her face. 'You – you said she was dead.'

'She must have been knocked unconscious.'

Ellen Scott stared at the baby for a long time. 'She should have been killed with the others,' she said in a strangled voice.

He looked up at her, shocked. 'What are you saying?'

'Byron's will leaves everything to Patricia. You can look forward to spending the next twenty years being her guardian so that when she grows up she can treat you as shabbily as her father did. Is that what you want?'

He was silent.

'We'll never have a chance like this again.' She was staring at the baby, and there was a wild look in her eyes that Milo had never seen before. It was almost as though she wanted to –

She's not herself. She's suffering from a concussion. 'For God's sake, Ellen, what are you thinking?'

She looked at her husband for a long moment, and the wild light faded from her eyes. 'I don't know,' she said calmly. After a pause she said, 'There's something we can do. We can leave her somewhere, Milo. The pilot said we were near Ávila. There should be plenty of tourists there. There's no reason for anyone to connect the baby with the plane crash.'

He shook his head. 'Their friends know that Byron and Susan took Patricia with them.'

Ellen Scott looked at the burning plane. 'That's no problem. They all burned up in the crash. We'll have a private memorial service here.'

'Ellen,' he protested. 'We can't do this. We'd never get away with it.'

'God did it for us. We *have* gotten away with it.'

Milo Scott looked at the baby. 'But she's so –'

'She'll be fine,' Ellen said soothingly. 'We'll drop her off at a nice farmhouse outside of town. They'll adopt her and she'll grow up to have a lovely life here.'

He shook his head. 'I can't do it. No.'

'If you love me you'll do this for us. You have to choose, Milo. You can either have me, or you can spend the rest of your life working for your brother's child.'

'Please, I –'

'Do you love me?'

'More than my life,' he said simply.

'Then prove it.'

They made their way carefully down the mountainside in the dark, whipped by the wind. Because the plane had crashed in a high wooded area, the sound was muffled, so the townspeople would be unaware of what had happened.

Three hours later, on the outskirts of Ávila, Ellen and

Milo reached a small farmhouse. It was not yet dawn.

'We'll leave her here,' Ellen whispered.

He made one last try. 'Ellen, couldn't we –?'

'Do it!' she said fiercely.

Without another word, he turned and carried the baby to the door of the farmhouse. She was wearing only a torn pink nightgown and had a blanket wrapped around her.

Milo Scott looked at Patricia for a long moment, his eyes filled with tears, then laid her gently down.

He whispered, 'Have a good life, darling.'

The crying awakened Anunción Moras. For a sleepy moment, she thought it was the bleating of a goat or a lamb. How had it got out of its pen?

Grumbling, she rose from her warm bed, put on an old faded dressing-gown, and walked to the door.

When she saw the infant lying on the ground screaming and kicking, she said, '*¡Madre de Dios!*' and yelled for her husband.

They brought the child inside and stared at it. It would not stop crying, and it seemed to be turning blue.

'We've got to get her to the hospital.'

They hurriedly wrapped another blanket around the baby, carried her to their pick-up truck and drove her to the hospital. They sat on a bench in the long corridor waiting for someone to attend to them, and thirty minutes later a doctor came and took the baby away to examine her.

When he returned, he said, 'She's got pneumonia.'

'Is she going to live?'

The doctor shrugged.

Milo and Ellen Scott stumbled into the police station at Ávila.

The desk sergeant looked up at the two bedraggled tourists. '*Buenos días*. Can I help you?'

'There's been a terrible accident,' Milo Scott said. 'Our plane crashed up in the mountains and . . .'

One hour later a rescue party was on its way to the mountainside. When they arrived, there was nothing to see but the smouldering, charred remains of an aircraft and its passengers.

The investigation of the airplane accident conducted by the Spanish authorities was cursory.

'The pilot should not have attempted to fly into such a bad storm. We must attribute the accident to pilot error.'

There was no reason for anyone in Ávila to associate the airplane crash with a small child left on the doorstep of a farmhouse.

It was over.

It was just beginning.

Milo and Ellen Scott held a private memorial service for Byron Scott, his wife Susan, and their daughter, Patricia. When they returned to New York, they held a second memorial service, attended by the shocked friends of the Scotts.

'What a terrible tragedy. And poor little Patricia.'

'Yes,' Ellen Scott said sadly. 'The only blessing is that it happened so quickly that none of them suffered.'

The financial community was shaken by the news. It was almost unanimously agreed that with Byron Scott's death, Scott Industries had suffered an irreparable loss.

'Don't listen to what any of them say,' Ellen Scott told her husband, 'you're better than Byron ever was. The company is going to be bigger than ever.'

Milo took her in his arms. 'I don't know what I would do without you.'

She smiled. 'You'll never have to. From now on we're

going to have everything in the world we've ever dreamed of.'

She held him close and thought: *Who would have believed that Ellen Dudash, from a poor Polish family in Gary, Indiana, would have one day said, 'From now on, we're going to have everything in the world we ever dreamed of?'*

And meant it.

For ten days the baby remained in the hospital, fighting for her life, and when the crisis was past, Father Berrendo went to see the farmer and his wife.

'I have joyous news for you,' he said happily. 'The child is going to be all right.'

The Morases exchanged an uncomfortable look.

'I'm glad for her sake,' the farmer said evasively.

Father Berrendo beamed. 'She is a gift from God.'

'Certainly, Father. But my wife and I have talked it over and decided that God is too generous to us. His gift requires feeding. We can't afford to keep it.'

'But she's such a beautiful baby,' Father Berrendo pointed out. 'And –'

'Agreed. But my wife and I are old and sick, and we can't take on the responsibility of bringing up a baby. God will have to take back his gift.'

And so it was that with nowhere else to go the baby was sent to the orphanage in Ávila.

They were seated in the law offices of Byron Scott's attorney for the reading of the will. Besides the lawyer, only Milo and Ellen Scott were present. Ellen Scott was filled with a sense of almost unbearable excitement. A few words on a piece of paper were going to make her and Milo rich beyond imagining.

We'll buy old masters and a place in Southampton, and a castle in France. And that's only the beginning.

The lawyer started to speak, and Ellen turned her attention

to him. Months before she had seen a copy of Byron Scott's will and knew exactly what it said:

In the event that my wife and I should both be deceased, I bequeath all my stock in Scott Industries to my only child, Patricia, and I appoint my brother, Milo, as executor of my estate until she reaches the legal age and is able to take over, etc., etc.

Well, all that is changed now, Ellen thought excitedly.

The lawyer, Lawrence Gray, said solemnly, 'This has been a terrible shock to all of us. I know how much you loved your brother, Milo, and as for that darling little baby . . .' He shook his head. 'Well, life must go on. You may not be aware that your brother had changed his will. I won't bother you with the legalese. I will just read you the gist of it.' He thumbed through the will and came to the paragraph he was looking for. 'I amend this will so that my daughter, Patricia, will receive the sum of five million dollars plus a distribution of one million dollars a year for the rest of her life. All the stock in Scott Industries held in my name will go to my brother, Milo, as a reward for the faithful and valuable services he has provided the company through the years.'

Milo Scott felt the room begin to sway.

Mr Gray looked up. 'Are you all right?'

Milo was finding it difficult to breathe. *Good God, what have we done? We've taken away her birthright, and it wasn't necessary at all. Now we can give it back to her.*

He turned to say something to Ellen, but the look in her eyes stopped him.

'There has to be *something* we can do, Ellen. We can't just leave Patricia there. Not now.'

They were in their Fifth Avenue apartment getting dressed to go to a charity dinner.

'That's exactly what we're going to do,' Ellen told him. 'Unless you'd like to bring her back here and try to explain why we said she was burned to death in the airplane crash.'

He had no answer to that. He thought for a moment. 'All

right, then. We'll send her money every month so she –'

'Don't be a fool, Milo.' Her voice was curt. 'Send her money? And have the police start checking on why someone is sending her money and trace it back to us? No. If your conscience bothers you, we'll have the company give money to charity. Forget about the child, Milo. She's dead. Remember?'

Remember . . . remember . . . remember . . .

The words echoed in Ellen Scott's mind as she looked out at the audience in the Waldorf Astoria ballroom and finished her speech. There was another standing ovation.

You're standing up for a dead woman, she thought.

That night the ghosts came again. She had thought she had exorcised them long ago. In the beginning, after the memorial services for her brother-in-law and sister-in-law, and Patricia, the night visitors had come frequently. Pale mists had hovered over her bed and voices had whispered in her ear. She would awaken, her pulse racing, but there was nothing to see. She told none of this to Milo. He was weak, and it might have terrified him into doing something foolish, something that would jeopardize the company. If the truth got out, the scandal would destroy Scott Industries, and Ellen Scott was determined that that must never happen. And so she suffered the ghosts in silence, until finally they went away and left her in peace.

Now, the night of the banquet, they returned. She awakened and sat up in her bed and looked around. The room was empty and quiet, but she knew they had been there. What were they trying to tell her? Did they know she would be joining them soon?

Ellen Scott rose and walked into the spacious, antique-filled drawing room of the beautiful townhouse she had bought after Milo had passed away. She looked around the lovely room and thought: *Poor Milo.* He had had so little time to enjoy any of the benefits of his brother's death. He had died of a heart attack a few years after the plane crash, and Ellen Scott had taken over the company, running it with an efficiency and expertise that had catapulted Scott Industries into greater international prominence.

The company belongs to the Scott family, she thought. *I'm not going to turn it over to faceless strangers.*

And that led her thoughts to Byron's and Susan's daughter. The rightful heiress to the throne that had been stolen from her. Was there fear in her thoughts? Was it a wish to make an atonement before her own death?

Ellen Scott sat in her drawing room all night staring into nothingness, thinking and planning. How long ago had it been? Twenty-eight years. Patricia would be a grown woman now, assuming that she was still alive. What had her life become? Had she married a farmer or a merchant in the village? Did she have children? Was she still living in Ávila, or had she gone away to some other place?

I must find her, Ellen Scott thought. *And quickly. If Patricia is still alive, I've got to see her, talk to her. I have to finally set the account straight. Money can turn lies into truth. I'll find a way to solve the situation without ever letting her know what really happened.*

The following morning Ellen Scott sent for Alan Tucker, chief of security for Scott Industries. He was a former detective, in his forties, a thin, balding, sallow-looking man, hard-working and brilliant.

'I want you to go on a mission for me.'

'Yes, Mrs Scott.'

She studied him for a moment, wondering how much she could tell him. *I can tell him nothing*, she decided. *As long as I am alive, I refuse to put myself or the company in jeopardy. Let him find Patricia first, and then I'll decide how to handle her.*

She leaned forward. 'Twenty-eight years ago, an orphan was left on the doorstep of a farmhouse outside of Ávila,

Spain. I want you to find out where she is today and bring her back here to me as quickly as possible.'

Alan Tucker's face remained impassive. Mrs Scott did not like her employees to show emotion.

'Yes, ma'am. I'll leave tomorrow.'

Chapter 17

Colonel Ramón Acoca was in an expansive mood. All the pieces were finally falling into place.

An orderly came into the office. 'Colonel Sostelo has arrived.'

'Show him in.'

I won't be needing him any more, Acoca thought. *He can go back to his tin soldiers.*

Colonel Fal Sostelo walked in. 'Colonel.'

'Colonel.'

It's ironic, Sostelo thought. *We hold the same rank, but the scarred giant has the power to break me. Because he's connected to the OPUS MUNDO.*

It was an indignity for Sostelo to have to answer Acoca's summons, as though he were some unimportant subordinate. But he managed to show none of his feelings. 'You wanted to see me?'

'Yes.' Acoca waved him to a chair. 'Sit down. I have some news for you. Jaime Miró has the nuns.'

'*What?*'

'Yes. They're travelling with Miró and his men. He's split them up into three groups.'

'How – how do you know that?'

Ramón Acoca leaned back in his chair. 'Do you play chess?'

'No.'

'Pity. It's a very educational game. In order to be a good player, it's necessary to get into the mind of your opponent. Jaime Miró and I play chess with each other.'

Fal Sostelo was staring at him. 'I don't understand how –'

'Not literally, Colonel. We don't use a chess board. We use our minds. I probably understand Jaime Miró better than anyone in the world. I know how his mind works. I knew that he would try to blow up the dam at Puente la Reina. We captured two of his lieutenants there, and it was only by luck that Miró himself got away. I knew that he would try to rescue them, and Miró knew that I knew it.' Ramón Acoca shrugged. 'I didn't anticipate that he would use the bulls to effect their escape.' There was a note of admiration in his voice.

'You sound as though you –'

'Admire him? I admire his mind. I despise the man.'

'Do you know where Miró is headed?'

'He is travelling north. I will catch him within the next three days.'

Colonel Sostelo was gaping at him, stunned.

'It will finally be checkmate.'

It was true that Colonel Acoca understood Jaime Miró, and the way his mind worked, but it was not enough for him. The Colonel wanted an edge, to ensure victory, and he had found it.

'How –?'

'One of Miró's terrorists,' Colonel Acoca said, 'is an informer.'

Rubio, Tomas and the two sisters avoided the large cities and took side roads, passing old stone villages with grazing sheep and goats, and shepherds listening to music and soccer games on their transistor radios. It was a colourful juxtaposition of the past and the present, but Lucia had other things on her mind.

She stayed close to Sister Teresa, watching for the first opportunity to get the cross and leave. The two men were always at their side. Rubio Arzano was the more considerate of the two, a tall, pleasant-looking, cheerful man. *A simple-minded peasant*, Lucia decided.

Tomas Sanjuro was slight and balding. *He looks more like a shop assistant than a terrorist. It will be easy to outwit them both.*

They walked across the plains north of Ávila by night, cooled by the winds blowing down from the Guadarrama Steppe. There was a haunting emptiness about the plains by moonlight. They passed *granjas* of wheat and olive trees and vines and maize, and they foraged for potatoes and lettuce, fruit from the trees and eggs and chickens from the hen coops.

'The whole countryside of Spain is a huge market,' said Rubio Arzano.

Tomas Sanjuro grinned. 'And it's all for free.'

Sister Teresa was totally oblivious to her surroundings. Her only thought was to reach the convent at Mendavia. The cross was getting heavy, but she was determined not to let it out of her hands. *Soon*, she thought. *We'll be there soon. We're fleeing from Gethsemane and our enemies to the new mansion He has prepared for us.*

Lucia said, 'What?'

Sister Teresa was unaware that she had spoken aloud.

'I – nothing,' she mumbled.

Lucia took a closer look at her. The older woman seemed distracted and vaguely disoriented, unaware of what was happening around her.

Lucia nodded towards the canvas package that Sister Teresa carried. 'That must be heavy,' Lucia said sympathetically. 'Wouldn't you like me to carry it for a while?'

Sister Teresa clutched it to her body more tightly. 'Jesus carried a heavier burden. I can carry this for Him.' Did it not say in Luke: *If any man would come after me, let him deny himself and take up his cross daily and follow me.*

'I'll carry it,' Teresa said stubbornly.

There was something odd in her tone.

'Are you all right, Sister?'

'Of course.'

*

Sister Teresa was far from all right. She had not been able to sleep. She felt dizzy and feverish. Her mind was playing tricks again. *I mustn't let myself become ill*, she thought. *Sister Betina will scold me.* But Sister Betina was not there. It was so confusing. And who were these men? *I don't trust them. What do they want with me?*

Rubio Arzano had attempted to strike up a conversation with Sister Teresa, trying to make her feel at ease.

'It must seem strange to you, being out in the world again, Sister. How long were you in the convent?'

Why did he want to know? 'Thirty years.'

'My, that's a long time. Where are you from?'

It was painful for her even to say the word. 'Èze.'

His face brightened. 'Èze? I spent a summer there once on holiday. It's a lovely town. I know it well. I remember –'

I know it well. How well? Did he know Raoul? Had Raoul sent him? And the truth hit her like a bolt of lightning. These strangers had been sent to bring her back to Èze, to Raoul Giradot. They were kidnapping her. God was punishing her for deserting Monique's baby. She was certain now that the baby she had seen in the village square in Villacastin was her sister Monique's. *But it couldn't have been, could it? That was thirty years ago*, Teresa muttered to herself. *They're lying to me.*

Rubio Arzano was watching her, listening to her mumbling. 'Is something wrong, Sister?'

Sister Teresa shrank away from him. 'No.'

She was on to them now. She was not going to let them take her back to Raoul and the baby. She had to get to the convent at Mendavia and hand over the gold crucifix, and then God would forgive her for the terrible sin she had committed. *I must be clever. I must not let them know I am on to their secret.*

She looked up at Rubio Arzano. 'I am fine,' Sister Teresa said.

They moved on across the dry, sunbaked plains. They came to a small village where peasant women dressed in black were doing their wash at a spring covered by a roof resting on four ancient beams. The water poured into a long wooden trough and out again, so that it was always fresh, and the women scrubbed their wash on stone slabs and rinsed it clean in the running water.

It's such a peaceful scene, Rubio thought. It reminded him of the farm he had left behind. *It's what Spain used to be like. No bombs, no killing. Will we ever know peace again?*

'*Buenos días*.'

'*Buenos días*.'

'I wonder if we might have a drink? Travelling is thirsty work.'

'Certainly. Please help yourselves.'

The water was cold and refreshing.

'*Gracias. Adiós.*'

'*Adiós.*'

Rubio hated to leave.

The two women and their escorts moved on, past cork and olive trees, the summer air filled with the smell of ripe grapes and oranges. They went by orchards of apples and cherry and plum trees, and farms noisy with the sound of chickens and pigs and goats.

Rubio and Tomas walked ahead, talking quietly together. *They are talking about me. They think I do not know their plan.* Sister Teresa moved nearer to them so she could hear what they were saying.

'. . . A reward of five hundred thousand pesetas on our heads. Of course Colonel Acoca would pay more for Jaime, but he doesn't want his head. He wants his *cojones*.'

The men laughed.

As Sister Teresa listened to them talk, her conviction grew stronger. *These men are killers doing Satan's work, messengers of the devil sent to damn me to everlasting hell. But God is stronger than they are. He will not let them take me back home.*

Raoul Giradot was at her side, smiling the smile that she knew so well.

The voice!

I beg your pardon?

I heard you sing yesterday. You are magnificent.

May I help you?

I would like three yards of muslin, please.

Certainly. This way . . . My aunt owns this shop and she needed help, so I thought I'd work for her for a while.

I'm sure you could have any man you want, Teresa, but I hope you will choose me.

He looked so handsome.

I have never known anyone like you, my darling.

Raoul was taking her in his arms and kissing her.

You're going to make a beautiful bride.

But now I'm Christ's bride. I can't return to Raoul.

Lucia was watching her closely. Sister Teresa was talking to herself, but Lucia could not make out the words.

She's cracking up, Lucia thought. *She's not going to make it. I've got to get hold of that cross soon.*

It was dusk when they saw the town of Olmedo in the distance.

Rubio stopped. 'There will be soldiers there. Let's move up to the hills and skirt the city.'

They moved off the road and left the plains, headed for the hills above Olmedo. The sun was skipping across the mountain tops and the sky was beginning to darken.

'We've only a few more miles to go,' Rubio Arzano said reassuringly. 'Then we can rest.'

They had reached the top of a high ridge when Tomas Sanjuro suddenly held up a hand. 'Hold it,' he whispered.

Rubio Arzano walked to his side and they moved to the edge of the ridge and looked down into the valley below. There was an encampment of soldiers there.

'*¡Mierda!*' Rubio whispered. 'There must be a whole platoon. We'll stay up here for the rest of the night. They'll probably pull out in the morning and we can move on.' He turned to Lucia and Sister Teresa, trying not to show how worried he was. 'We'll spend the night here, Sisters. We must be very quiet. There are soldiers down there and we don't want them to find us.'

It was the best news Lucia could have heard. *It's perfect*, she thought. *I'll disappear with the cross during the night. They won't dare try to follow me because of the soldiers.*

To Sister Teresa, the news had a different meaning. She had heard the men say that someone named Colonel Acoca was searching for them. *They called Colonel Acoca the enemy. But these men are the enemy, so Colonel Acoca must be my friend. Thank you, dear God, for sending me Colonel Acoca.*

The tall man called Rubio was speaking to her.

'Do you understand, Sister? We must all be very, very quiet.'

'Yes, I understand.' *I understand more than you think.* They had no idea that God permitted her to see into their evil hearts.

Tomas Sanjuro said kindly, 'I know how difficult this must be for both of you, but don't worry. We'll see that you get safely to the convent.'

To Èze, he means. Oh, but he is cunning. He speaks the honeyed words of the devil. But God is within me, and He is guiding me. She knew what she must do. But she had to be careful.

The two men arranged the sleeping-bags for the women, next to each other.

'Both of you get some sleep now.'

The women got into the unfamiliar sleeping-bags. The night was incredibly clear and the sky was spangled with glimmering stars. Lucia looked up at them and thought happily: *In just a few hours now, I'll be on my way to freedom. As soon as they're all asleep.*

She yawned. She had not realized how tired she was. The long, hard journey and the emotional strain had taken their toll. Her eyes felt heavy. *I'll just rest for a little while*, Lucia thought.

She slept.

Sister Teresa lay near Lucia, wide awake, fighting the

demons trying to possess her, trying to send her soul to hell. *I must be strong. The Lord is testing me. I have been exiled, so that I can find my way back to Him. And these men are trying to stop me. I must not let them.*

At four o'clock in the morning, Sister Teresa silently sat up and looked around. Tomas Sanjuro was asleep only a few feet from her. The tall, dark man called Rubio was keeping watch at the edge of the clearing, his back to her. She could see his silhouette against the trees.

Very quietly, Sister Teresa rose. She hesitated, thinking about the cross. *Should I carry it with me? But I'll be coming back here very soon. I must find a place where it will be safe until I return.* She looked over to where Sister Lucia lay sleeping. *Yes. It will be safe with my sister in God*, Sister Teresa decided.

Silently she moved over to the sleeping-bag and gently slipped the wrapped cross inside. Lucia did not stir. Sister Teresa turned and moved into the woods, out of Rubio Arzano's sight, and carefully began to make her way downhill towards the soldiers' camp. The hill was steep and slippery with dew, but God gave her wings and she sped downhill without stumbling or falling, hurrying towards her salvation.

In the darkness ahead the figure of a man suddenly materialized.

A voice called out, 'Who goes there?'

'Sister Teresa.'

She approached the sentry. He wore an army uniform and was carrying a rifle, pointed at her.

'Where did you come from, old woman?' he demanded.

She looked at him with golden eyes. 'God sent me.'

The sentry stared at her. 'Did He, now?'

'Yes. He sent me to see Colonel Acoca.'

The guard shook his head. 'You'd better tell Him you're not the Colonel's type. *Adiós, señora.*'

'You don't understand. I am Sister Teresa from the Abbey Cistercian. I have been taken prisoner by Jaime Miró and his men.' She watched the stunned expression that came over his face.

'You're – you're from the convent?'

'Yes.'

'The one at Ávila?'

'Yes,' Teresa said impatiently. What was the matter with the man? Didn't he realize how important it was that she be rescued from those evil men?

The soldier said carefully, 'The Colonel isn't here just now, Sister –'

It was an unexpected blow.

'– But Colonel Sostelo is in charge. I can take you to him.'

'Will he be able to help me?'

'Oh, I'm sure he will. Follow me, please.'

The sentry was scarcely able to believe his good fortune. Colonel Fal Sostelo had sent squadrons of soldiers scouring the entire countryside searching for the four nuns, and they had had no success. Now one of the sisters had stumbled into the camp and given herself up to him. The Colonel was going to be pleased. The Colonel was going to be very pleased.

They reached the tent where Colonel Fal Sostelo and his second in command were poring over a map. The men looked up as the sentry and a woman entered.

'Excuse me, Colonel. This is Sister Teresa from the Cistercian convent.'

Colonel Sostelo stared at her, unbelievingly. All of his energies for the last three days had been focused on finding Jaime Miró and the nuns, and now, here in front of him was one of them. There *was* a God.

'Sit down, Sister.'

There is no time for that, Sister Teresa thought. She had to make him realize how urgent this was. 'We must hurry. They are trying to take me back to Èze.'

The Colonel was puzzled. 'Who's trying to take you back to Èze?'

'The men of Jaime Miró.'

He got to his feet. 'Sister – do you by any chance happen to know where these men are?'

Sister Teresa said impatiently, 'Of course.' She turned and pointed. 'They're up in those hills hiding from you.'

Chapter 18

Alan Tucker arrived in Ávila the day after his conversation with Ellen Scott. It had been a long flight, and Tucker should have been exhausted, but he was exhilarated. Ellen Scott was not a woman given to whims. *There's something strange going on behind all this*, Alan Tucker thought, *and if I play my cards right, I have a hunch it could be very profitable for me.*

He checked into the Cuatro Postes Hotel and said to the clerk behind the desk, 'Is there a newspaper office around here?'

'Down the street, *señor*. To your left, two blocks. You can't miss it.'

'Thank you.'

'*De nada*.'

Walking down the main street, watching the town come alive after its afternoon siesta, Tucker thought about the mysterious girl he had been sent to bring back. This had to be something important. But important *why*? He could hear Ellen Scott's voice.

If she's alive, bring her back to me. You are not to discuss this with anyone.

No, ma'am. What shall I tell her?

Simply tell her that a friend of her father's wishes to meet her. She'll come.

Tucker found the newspaper office. Inside, he approached one of the half a dozen people working behind desks. '*Perdón*. I would like to see the managing editor.'

The man pointed to an office. 'In there, *señor*.'

'*Gracias*.'

Tucker walked over to the open door and looked inside. A man in his mid-thirties was seated behind a desk, busily editing copy.

'Excuse me,' Tucker said. 'Could I speak to you for a moment?'

The man looked up. 'What can I do for you?'

'I'm looking for a *señorita*.'

The editor smiled. 'Aren't we all, *señor*?'

'She was left at a farmhouse around here when she was an infant.'

The smile faded. 'Oh. She was abandoned?'

'Yes.'

'And you are trying to find her?'

'Yes.'

'How many years ago would that be, *señor*?'

'Twenty-eight.'

The young man shrugged. 'It was before my time.'

Perhaps it's not going to be so easy. 'Would you happen to know anything about the woman or could you suggest someone who might be able to help me?'

The editor leaned back in his chair, thinking. 'As a matter of fact, I can. I would suggest you speak with Father Berrendo.'

Father Berrendo sat in his study, a rug over his thin legs, listening to the stranger.

When Alan Tucker had finished talking, Father Berrendo said, 'Why do you wish to know about this matter, *señor*? It happened so long ago. What is your interest in it?'

Tucker hesitated, choosing his words carefully. 'I am not at liberty to say. I can only assure you that I mean the woman no harm. If you could just tell me where the farmhouse is where she was left –?'

The farmhouse. Memories came flooding back of the day the Morases had come to him after they had taken the little girl to hospital.

I think she's dying, Father. What shall we do?

Father Berrendo had talked to his friend, Don Morago, the chief of police.

'I think the baby was abandoned by tourists visiting Ávila. Could you check the hotels and inns and see if anyone arrived with a baby and left without one?'

The police had gone through the registration cards that all hotels were required to fill out, but they were of no help.

'It is as if the baby just dropped out of the sky,' Don Morago said.

And he had no idea of how close he had come to solving the mystery.

When Father Berrendo had taken the infant to the orphanage, Mercedes Angeles had asked, 'Has the baby got a name?'

'I don't know.'

'Wasn't there a blanket or something with the name on it?'

'No.'

Mercedes Angeles looked at the infant in the priest's arms. 'Well, we'll just have to give her a name, won't we?'

She had recently finished reading a romantic novel, and she liked the name of the heroine in it.

'Megan,' she said. 'We'll call her Megan.'

And fourteen years later, Father Berrendo had taken Megan to the Abbey Cistercian.

So many years after that, this stranger was looking for her. *Life always comes full circle*, Father Berrendo thought. *In some mysterious way, it has come full circle for Megan.* No, not Megan. That was the name given her by the orphanage.

'Sit down, *señor*,' Father Berrendo said. 'There is much to tell you.'

And he told him.

When the priest had finished, Alan Tucker sat there quietly, his mind racing. There had to be a strong reason for Ellen Scott's interest in a baby abandoned at a farmhouse in Spain twenty-eight years earlier. A woman now called Megan, according to the priest.

Tell her that a friend of her father's wishes to meet her.

If he remembered correctly, Byron Scott and his wife and daughter had died in an airplane crash many years ago somewhere in Spain. Could there be a connection? Alan Tucker felt a growing sense of excitement.

'Father – I'd like to get into the convent to see her. It's very important.'

The priest shook his head. 'I'm afraid you are too late. The convent was attacked two days ago by agents of the government.'

Alan Tucker stared at him. 'Attacked? What happened to the nuns?'

'They were arrested and taken to Madrid.'

Alan Tucker got to his feet. 'Thank you, Father.' He would catch the first plane to Madrid.

Father Berrendo went on: 'Four of the nuns escaped. Sister Megan was one of them.'

Things were becoming complicated. 'Where is she now?'

'No one knows. The police and the army are searching for her and the other sisters.'

'I see.' Under ordinary circumstances, Alan Tucker would have telephoned Ellen Scott and informed her that he had reached a dead end. But all his instincts as a detective told him that there was something here that warranted further investigation.

He placed a call to Ellen Scott.

'There's a complication, Mrs Scott.' He repeated his conversation with the priest.

There was a long silence. 'No one knows where she is?'

'She and the others are on the run, but they can't hide out

much longer. The police and half the Spanish army are looking for them. When they surface, I'll be there.'

Another silence. 'This is very important to me, Tucker.'

'Yes, Mrs Scott.'

Alan Tucker returned to the newspaper office. He was in luck. It was still open.

He said to the editor, 'I would like to look through your files, if I may.'

'Are you looking for something in particular?'

'Yes. There was an airplane crash here.'

'How long ago, *señor*?'

If I'm right – 'Twenty-eight years ago. Nineteen forty-eight.'

It took Alan Tucker fifteen minutes to find the item he was looking for. The headline leaped out at him.

> PLANE CRASH KILLS EXECUTIVE FAMILY
> 1 October 1948. Byron Scott, President of Scott Industries, his wife, Susan, and their one-year-old daughter, Patricia, were burned to death in an airplane crash . . .

I've hit the jackpot! He could feel his pulse begin to race. *If this is what I think it is, I'm going to be a rich man . . . a* very *rich man.*

Chapter 19

She was naked in her bed, and she could feel the male hardness of Benito Patas pressing into her groin. His body felt wonderful, and she moved closer to him, grinding her hips against him, feeling the heat growing in her loins. She started to stroke him, to excite him. But something was wrong. *I killed Patas*, she thought. *He's dead.*

Lucia opened her eyes and sat up, trembling, looking around wildly. Benito was not there. She was in the forest, in a sleeping-bag. Something was pressing against her thigh. Lucia reached down inside the sleeping-bag and pulled out the canvas-wrapped cross. She stared at it, unbelievingly. *God has just performed a miracle for me*, Lucia thought.

She had no idea how the cross had got there, nor did she care. She had it in her hands at last. All she had to do now was to slip away from the others.

She crept out of the sleeping-bag and looked over to where Sister Teresa had slept. She was gone. Lucia looked around in the darkness, and she could barely make out the figure of Tomas Sanjuro at the edge of the clearing, facing away from her. She was not sure where Rubio was. *It doesn't matter. It's time to get out of here*, Lucia thought.

She started to move to the edge of the clearing, away from Sanjuro, bending low so she would not be seen.

At that instant all hell broke loose.

Colonel Fal Sostelo had had a command decision to make. He had been given orders by the Prime Minister himself to work closely with Colonel Ramón Acoca to help capture Jaime Miró and the nuns. But fate had blessed him by delivering one of the nuns into his hands. Why share the credit with Colonel Acoca when he could catch the terrorists and keep all the glory? *Fuck Colonel Acoca*, Fal Sostelo thought. *This one is mine. Maybe the OPUS MUNDO will use me instead of Acoca, with all his bullshit about chess games and getting into the minds of people. No, it's time to teach the scarred giant a lesson.*

Colonel Sostelo gave specific orders to his men.

'Don't take any prisoners. You're dealing with terrorists. Shoot to kill.'

Major Ponte hesitated. 'Colonel, there are nuns up there with Miró's men. Shouldn't we –?'

'Let the terrorists hide behind the nuns? No. We'll take no chances.'

Fal Sostelo selected a dozen men to accompany him on the raid and he saw to it that they were heavily armed. They moved noiselessly in the dark, up the slope of the mountain. The moon had disappeared behind clouds. There was almost no visibility. *Good. They won't be able to see us coming.*

When his men were in position, Colonel Sostelo shouted, for the sake of the record, 'Put down your arms. You're surrounded.' And in the same breath he called out the command, 'Fire! Keep firing!'

A dozen automatic weapons began spraying the clearing.

Tomas Sanjuro never had a chance. A hail of machine gun bullets caught him in the chest and he was dead before he hit the ground. Rubio Arzano was at the far edge of the clearing when the firing started. He saw Sanjuro fall, and he whirled and started to raise his gun to return the fire but stopped. It was pitch black in the clearing and the soldiers were firing blindly. If he returned their fire, he would give his position away.

To his amazement, he saw Lucia crouched two feet away from him.

'Where's Sister Teresa?' he whispered.

'She's – she's gone.'

'Stay low,' Rubio told her.

He grabbed Lucia's hand and zigzagged towards the forest, away from the enemy fire. Shots whizzed dangerously close as they ran, but moments later, Lucia and Rubio were among the trees. They continued running.

'Hold on to me, Sister,' he said.

They heard the sound of their attackers behind them, but gradually it died away. It was impossible to pursue anyone through the inky blackness of the woods.

Rubio stopped to let Lucia catch her breath.

'We've lost them for now,' Rubio told her. 'But we have to keep moving.'

Lucia was breathing hard.

'If you want to rest for a minute –?'

'No,' she said. She was exhausted, but she had no intention of letting them catch her. Not now when she had the cross. 'I'm fine,' she said. 'Let's get out of here.'

Colonel Fal Sostelo was facing disaster. One terrorist dead, but God alone knew how many had escaped. He did not have Jaime Miró and he had only one of the nuns. He knew he would have to inform Colonel Acoca of what had happened. He was not looking forward to it.

The second call from Alan Tucker to Ellen Scott was even more disturbing than the previous call.

'I've come across some rather interesting information, Mrs Scott,' he said cautiously.

'Yes?'

'I went through some old newspaper files here, hoping to get more information on the girl.'

'And?' She braced herself for what she knew was coming.

Tucker kept his voice casual. 'It seems that the girl was abandoned about the time of your plane crash.'

Silence.

He went on: 'The one that killed your brother-in-law and his wife and their daughter, Patricia.'

Blackmail. There was no other explanation. So he had found out.

'That's right,' Ellen Scott said casually. 'I should have mentioned that. I'll explain everything when you get back. Have you any more news of the girl?'

'No, but she can't hide out for very long. The whole country's looking for her.'

'Let me hear from you as soon as she's found.'

The line went dead.

Alan Tucker sat there, staring at the dead telephone in his hand. *She's a cool lady*, he thought admiringly. *I wonder how she's going to feel about having a partner?*

I made a mistake in sending him, Ellen Scott thought. *Now I'll have to stop him.* And what was she going to do about the girl? *A nun! I won't judge her until I see her.*

Her secretary buzzed her on the intercom.

'They're ready for you in the board room, Mrs Scott.'

'I'm coming.'

Lucia and Rubio Arzano kept moving through the woods, stumbling and slipping, attacked by tree limbs and bushes and insects, but each step took them farther away from their pursuers.

Finally, Rubio Arzano said, 'We can stop here. They won't find us.'

They were high in the mountains in the middle of a dense forest.

Lucia lay down on the ground, fighting to catch her breath. In her mind, she replayed the terrible scene she had witnessed earlier. Tomas shot down without warning. *And the bastards intended to murder us all*, Lucia thought. The only reason she was still alive was because of the man sitting beside her.

Lucia watched Rubio as he got to his feet and scouted the area around them.

'We can spend the rest of the night here, Sister.'

'All right.' She was impatient to get moving, but she knew she needed to rest.

As though reading her mind, Rubio Arzano said, 'We'll move on again at dawn.'

Lucia felt a gnawing in her stomach. Even as she was thinking about it, Rubio Arzano said, 'You must be hungry. I'll go and find some food for us. Will you be all right here by yourself?'

'Yes. I'll be fine.'

The big man crouched down beside her.

'Please try not to be frightened. I know how difficult it must be for you to be out in the world again after all those years in the convent. Everything must seem very strange to you.'

Lucia looked up at him and said tonelessly, 'I'll try to get used to it.'

'You're very brave, Sister.' Rubio rose. 'I'll be back soon.'

She watched Rubio disappear into the trees. It was time to make a decision, and she had two choices: she could escape now, try to reach a nearby town and trade the gold cross for a passport and enough money to get to Switzerland, or she could stay with this man until they got farther away from the soldiers. *That will be safer*, Lucia decided.

Lucia heard a noise in the woods and swung around. It was Rubio Arzano. He moved towards her, smiling. In his hand he held his beret, bulging with tomatoes, grapes and apples.

He sat down on the ground next to her. 'Supper. A nice, plump poulet was available but the fire we would have needed to cook it would have given us away.'

Lucia stared at the contents of the beret. 'It looks like manna from heaven. I'm starving.'

*

They had finished eating and were sitting against a tree. Rubio Arzano was talking, but Lucia was paying no attention, absorbed in her own thoughts.

'Ten years, you said you were in the convent, Sister?'

Lucia was startled out of her reverie. 'What?'

'You've been in the convent for ten years?'

'Oh. Yes.'

He shook his head. 'Then you have no idea what's been happening in all that time.'

'Uh – no.'

'In the last ten years the world has changed a great deal, Sister.'

'Has it?'

'*Sí.*' Rubio said earnestly, 'Franco has died.'

'No!'

'Oh, yes. Last year.'

And named Don Juan Carlos, his heir.

'You may find this very hard to believe, but a man has walked on the moon. That is the truth.'

'Really?' *Actually, two men*, Lucia thought. *What were their names? Neil Armstrong and Buzz Something.*

'Oh, yes. North Americans. And there is now a plane for passengers that travels faster than sound.'

'Incredible.' *I can't wait to travel in Concorde*, Lucia thought.

Rubio was childlike, so pleased to be bringing her up to date on world events.

'There has been a revolution in Portugal, and in the United States of America, their President Nixon was involved in a big scandal and had to resign.'

Rubio is really sweet, Lucia decided.

He took out a pack of Ducados cigarettes, the heavy black tobacco of Spain. 'I hope it won't offend you if I smoke, Sister?'

'No,' Lucia said. 'Please go ahead.'

She watched him light up, and the moment the smoke reached her nostrils she was desperate to have a cigarette.

'Do you mind if I try one?'

He looked at her in surprise. 'You wish to try a cigarette?'

'Just to see what it's like,' Lucia said quickly.

'Oh. Of course.'

He held the pack towards her. She took out a cigarette, put it between her lips and he lit the end of it for her. Lucia inhaled deeply, and as the smoke filled her lungs, she felt wonderful.

Rubio was watching her, puzzled.

Lucia coughed. 'So that's what a cigarette tastes like.'

'Do you like it?'

'Not really, but –'

She took another deep, satisfying puff. God, how she had missed this. But she knew she had to be careful. She did not want to make him suspicious. She put out the cigarette she had held clumsily in her fingers. She had been in the convent for only a few months, and yet Rubio was right. It did seem strange to be out in the world again. She wondered how Megan and Graciela were doing. And what had happened to Sister Teresa? Had she been captured by the soldiers?

Lucia's eyes were beginning to sting. It had been a long, tension-filled night. 'I think I may take a little nap.'

'Don't worry. I will watch over you, Sister.'

'Thank you,' she smiled. Within moments, she was asleep.

Rubio Arzano looked down at her and thought: *I have never seen a woman like this one.* She was so spiritual that she had dedicated her life to God, and yet at the same time there was an earthiness about her. And she had behaved this night as bravely as any man. *You are a very special woman*, Rubio Arzano thought as he watched her sleep. *Little sister of Jesus.*

Chapter 20

Colonel Fal Sostelo was on his tenth cigarette. *I can't put it off any longer*, he decided. *Bad news is best got out of the way quickly.*

He took several deep breaths to calm himself and then he dialled a number. When he had Ramón Acoca on the telephone, he said, 'Colonel, we raided a terrorist camp last night, where I was informed Jaime Miró was, and I thought you should know about it.'

There was a dangerous silence.

'Did you catch him?'

'No.'

'You undertook this operation without consulting me?'

'There was no time to –'

'But there was time to let Miró escape.' Ramón Acoca's voice was filled with fury. 'What led you to undertake this magnificently executed operation?'

Colonel Sostelo swallowed. 'We caught one of the nuns from the convent. She led us to Miró and his men. We killed one of them in the attack.'

'But the others all escaped?'

'Yes, Colonel.'

'Where is the nun now? Or did you let her get away, too?' His tone was scathing.

'No, Colonel,' Sostelo said quickly. 'She is here at the camp. We have been questioning her and –'

'Don't. I'll question her myself. I'll be there in one hour.

See if you can manage to hang on to her until I get there.' He slammed down the receiver.

Exactly one hour later, Colonel Ramón Acoca arrived at the camp where they were holding Sister Teresa. With him were a dozen of his men from the GOE.

'Bring the nun to me,' Colonel Acoca ordered.

Sister Teresa was brought to the headquarters tent where Colonel Acoca was waiting for her. He stood up politely when she entered the tent and smiled.

'I am Colonel Acoca.'

At last! 'I knew you would come. God told me.'

He nodded pleasantly. 'Did he? Good. Please sit down, Sister.'

Sister Teresa was too nervous to sit. 'You must help me.'

'We're going to help each other,' the Colonel assured her. 'You escaped from the Abbey Cistercian at Ávila, is that correct?'

'Yes. It was terrible. All those men. They did godless things and –'

And stupid things. We let you and the others escape. 'How did you get here, Sister?'

'God brought me here. He's testing me as He once tested –'

Colonel Acoca said patiently, 'As well as God, did some men also bring you here, Sister?'

'Yes. They kidnapped me. I had to escape from them.'

'You told Colonel Sostelo where he could find those men?'

'Yes. The evil ones. Raoul is behind it all, you see. He sent me a letter and said –'

'Sister, the man we're looking for in particular is Jaime Miró. Have you seen him?'

She shivered. 'Yes. Oh, yes. He –'

The Colonel leaned forward. 'Excellent. Now you must tell me where I can find him.'

'He and the others are on their way to Èze.'

He frowned, puzzled. 'To Èze? To France?'

Her words were a wild babble. 'Yes. Monique deserted Raoul, and he sent the men to kidnap me because of the baby so –'

He tried to control his growing impatience. 'Miró and his men are headed north. Èze is to the east.'

'– You must not let them take me back to Raoul. I don't want to see him ever again. You can understand that. I couldn't face him –'

Colonel Acoca said curtly, 'I don't give a damn about this Raoul. I want to know where I can find Jaime Miró.'

'I told you. He is in Èze waiting for me. He wants to –'

'You're lying. I think you're trying to protect Miró. Now I don't want to hurt you, so I'm going to ask you once more. Where is Jaime Miró?'

Sister Teresa stared at him helplessly. 'I don't know,' she whispered. She looked around wildly. 'I don't know.'

'A moment ago you said he was in Èze.' His voice was like a whiplash.

'Yes. God told me.'

Colonel Acoca had had enough. The woman was either demented or a brilliant actress. Either way, she sickened him with all her talk of God.

He turned to Patricio Arrieta, his lieutenant. 'The sister's memory needs prodding. Take her to the quartermaster's tent. Perhaps you and your men can help her remember where Jaime Miró is.'

'Yes, Colonel.'

Patricio Arrieta and the men with him had been part of the group that had attacked the convent at Ávila. They felt responsible for letting the four nuns escape. *Well, we can make up for that now*, Arrieta thought.

Arrieta turned to Sister Teresa. 'Come along with me, Sister.'

'Yes.' *Dear blessed Jesus, thank You.* She babbled on. 'Are we leaving now? You won't let them take me to Èze, will you?'

'No,' Arrieta assured her. 'You're not going to Èze.'

The Colonel is right, he thought. *She is playing games with us. Well, we'll show her some new games. I wonder if she'll lie quietly, or if she'll scream?*

When they reached the quartermaster's tent, Arrieta said, 'Sister, we've going to give you one last chance. Where is Jaime Miró?'

Haven't they asked me that before? Or was that someone else? Was it here or – it's all terribly confusing. 'He kidnapped me for Raoul because Monique deserted him and he thought –'

'*Bueno.* If that's the way you want it,' Arrieta said, 'we'll see if we can't refresh your memory for you.'

'Yes. Please. Everything is so puzzling.'

Half a dozen of Acoca's men had entered the tent, along with some of Sostelo's uniformed soldiers.

Sister Teresa looked up. She blinked dazedly. 'Are these men going to take me to the convent now?'

'They're going to do better than that,' Patricio Arrieta grinned. 'They're going to take you to heaven, Sister.'

The men moved closer to her, surrounding her.

'That's a pretty dress you're wearing,' a soldier said. 'Are you sure you're a nun, darling?'

'Oh, yes,' she said. Raoul had called her darling. Was this Raoul? 'You see, we had to change clothes to escape from the soldiers.' But these were soldiers. Everything was muddled.

One of the men pushed Teresa down on the cot. 'You're no beauty, but let's see what you look like underneath all those clothes.'

'What are you doing?'

He reached down and ripped off the top of her dress while another man tore at her skirt.

'That's not a bad body for an old lady, is it, fellows?'

Teresa screamed.

She looked up at the circle of men surrounding her. *God will strike them all dead. He will not let them touch me, for I am His vessel. I am one with the Lord, drinking from His fountain of purity.*

One of the soldiers unfastened his belt. An instant later she felt rough hands pushing her legs apart, and as the soldier sprawled on top of her, she felt his hard flesh penetrate her and again she screamed.

'Now, God! Punish them now.'

She waited for the clap of thunder, the bright flash of lightning that would destroy them all.

Nothing happened.

Another soldier climbed on top of her. A red haze came over her eyes. Teresa lay there waiting for God to strike, almost unaware of the men who were ravaging her. She no longer felt the pain.

Lieutenant Arrieta was standing next to the cot. After each man finished with Teresa, he said, 'Have you had enough, Sister? You can stop this at any time. All you have to do is tell me where Jaime Miró is.'

Sister Teresa did not hear him. She screamed in her mind: *Smite them down with Your power, Lord. Wipe them out as You wiped out the other wicked ones at Sodom and Gomorrah.*

Incredibly, He did not answer. It was not possible, for God was everywhere. And then she knew. As the sixth man entered her body, the epiphany suddenly came to her.

God was not listening to her because there was no God. All these years she had deceived herself into worshipping a Supreme power and had served Him faithfully. But there was no Supreme Power. *If God exists, He would have saved me.*

The red haze lifted from Sister Teresa's eyes and she got a clear look at her surroundings for the first time. There were at least a dozen soldiers in the tent waiting their turn to rape her. Lieutenant Arrieta was standing at one side of the bed watching. The soldiers in line were in full uniform, not bothering to undress.

As one soldier lifted himself from Teresa, the next soldier opened his fly and took out his penis. He squatted down over her and a moment later penetrated her.

There is no God, but there is a Satan, and these are his helpers, Sister Teresa thought. *And they must die. All of them.*

As the soldier plunged into her, Sister Teresa grabbed the pistol from his holster and before anyone could react, she turned the pistol on Arrieta. The bullet hit him in the throat.

Sister Teresa pointed the gun at the other soldiers and kept firing. Four of them fell to the floor dead before the others came to their senses and began shooting at her. Because of the soldier on top of her, they had difficulty aiming.

Sister Teresa and her last ravisher died at the same moment.

Chapter 21

Jaime Miró came awake instantly, aroused by a movement at the edge of the clearing. He slipped out of the sleeping-bag and rose, gun in hand. He saw Megan on her knees, praying. He stood there, studying her. There was an unearthly beauty about the image of this lovely woman praying in the forest in the middle of the night, and Jaime found himself resenting it. *If Felix Carpio hadn't blurted out that we were headed for San Sebastian, I wouldn't have been burdened with the sister in the first place.*

It was imperative that he get to San Sebastian as quickly as possible. Colonel Acoca and his men and the army were all around them, and it would have been difficult enough slipping through their net alone. With the added burden of this woman to slow him down, the danger was increased tenfold.

He walked over to Megan, angry, and his voice was harsher than he had intended.

'I told you to get some sleep. I don't want you slowing us down tomorrow.'

Megan looked up and said quietly, 'I'm sorry if I've angered you.'

'Sister, I save my anger for more important things. Your kind just bore me. You spend your lives hiding behind stone walls waiting for a free trip to the next world. You make me sick, all of you.'

'Because we believe in the next world?'

'No, Sister. Because you don't believe in this one. You ran away from it.'

'To pray for you. We spend our lives praying for you.'

'And you think that will solve the problems of the world?'

'In time, yes.'

'There is no time. Your God can't hear your prayers because of the noise of the cannons and the screams of children being torn apart by bombs.'

'When you have faith –'

'Oh, I have lots of faith, Sister. I have faith in what I'm fighting for. I have faith in my men, and in my guns. What I don't have faith in are people who walk on water. If you think your God is listening now, tell him to get us to the convent at Mendavia so I can be rid of you.'

He was angry with himself for losing his temper. It wasn't her fault that the church had stood idly by while Franco's Falangists tortured and raped and murdered Basques and Catalans. *It wasn't her fault*, Jaime told himself, *that my family was among the victims.*

Jaime had been a young boy then, but it was a memory that would be etched for ever in his brain . . .

He had been awakened in the middle of the night by the noise of bombs falling. They fell from the sky like deadly flowers of sound planting their seeds of destruction everywhere.

'Get up, Jaime. Hurry!'

The fear in his father's voice was more frightening to the boy than the terrible roar of the aerial bombardment.

Guernica was a stronghold of the Basques and General Franco had decided to make it an object lesson.

'Destroy it.'

The dreaded Nazi Condor Legion and half a dozen Italian planes had mounted a concentrated attack, and they showed no mercy. The townspeople tried to flee from the rain of death pouring down from the skies, but there was no escape.

Jaime, his mother and father and two older sisters fled with the others.

'To the church,' Jaime's father said. 'They won't bomb the church.'

He was right. Everyone knew that the church was on the side of the Caudillo, turning a blind eye to the savage treatment of his enemies.

The Miró family headed for the church, fighting their way through the panicky crowds trying to flee.

The young boy held his father's hand in a fierce grip and tried not to hear the terrible noises around him. He remembered a time when his father was not frightened, was not running away.

'Are we going to have a war, Papa?'

'No, Jaime. That's just newspaper talk. All we're asking is that the government give us a reasonable amount of independence. The Basques and the Catalans are entitled to have their own language and flag and holidays. We're still one nation. And Spaniards will never fight against Spaniards.'

Jaime was too young then to understand it, but of course it was more than the issue of the Catalans and Basques that was at stake. It was a deep ideological conflict between the Republican government and the right-wing Nationalists, and what started out as a spark of dissension quickly became an uncontrollable conflagration that drew in a dozen foreign powers.

When Franco's superior forces had defeated the Republicans and the Nationalists were firmly in control of Spain, Franco turned his attention to the intransigent Basques.

'Punish them.'

And the blood continued to flow.

A hard core of Basque leaders had formed ETA, a movement for a Basque Free State, and Jaime's father was asked to join.

'No. It is wrong. We must gain what is rightfully ours by peaceful means. War accomplishes nothing.'

But the hawks proved stronger than the doves, and ETA quickly became a prime target.

Jaime had friends whose fathers were members of ETA, and he listened to the stories of their heroic exploits.

'My father and a group of his friends bombed the headquarters of the *guardia civil*,' they would say.

Or, 'Did you hear about the bank robbery in Barcelona? My father did that. Now they can buy weapons to fight the fascists.'

And Jaime's father was saying, 'Violence is wrong. We must negotiate.'

'We blew up one of their factories in Madrid. Why isn't your father on our side? Is he a coward?'

'Don't listen to your friends, Jaime,' his father told him. 'What they are doing is criminal.'

'Franco ordered a dozen Basques executed without even a trial. We're staging a nationwide strike. Is your father going to join us?'

'Papa –?'

'We are all Spaniards, Jaime. We must not let anyone divide us.'

And the boy was torn. *Are my friends right? Is my father a coward?* Jaime believed his father.

And now – armageddon. The world was collapsing around him. The streets of Guernica were crowded with a screaming mob trying to escape from the falling bombs. All around them buildings and statues and pavements were exploding in showers of concrete and blood.

Jaime and his mother and father and sisters had reached the large church, the only building in the square still standing. A dozen people were pounding at the door.

'Let us in! In the name of Jesus, open up!'

'What's going on?' cried Jaime's father.

'The priests have locked the church. They won't let us in.'

'Let's break the door in!'

'No!'

Jaime looked at his father in surprise.

'We don't break into God's house,' his father said. 'He will protect us wherever we are.'

Too late, they saw the squad of Falangists that appeared from around the corner and opened machine-gun fire on them, mowing down the unarmed crowd of men, women and children in the square. Even as Jaime's father felt the bullets tearing into him, he grabbed his son and pushed him down to safety, his own body shielding Jaime from the deadly hail of bullets.

An eerie silence seemed to blanket the world. The sounds of guns and running feet and screams vanished, a trick of magic. Jaime opened his eyes and lay there for a long time, feeling the weight of his father's body on him, like a loving blanket. His father and mother and sisters were dead, along with hundreds of others. And in front of their bodies were the locked doors of the church.

Late that night, Jaime made his way out of the city and two days later when he reached Bilbao, he joined ETA.

The recruiting officer had looked at him and said, 'You're too young to join, son. You should be in school.'

'You're going to be my school,' Jaime Miró said quietly. 'You're going to teach me how to fight to avenge the murder of my family.'

He never looked back. He was battling for himself and for his family, and his exploits became legendary. Jaime planned and executed daring raids against factories and banks and carried out the executions of the oppressors. When any of Jaime's men were captured, he conducted daredevil missions to rescue them.

When Jaime heard about the GOE being formed to pursue Basques, he smiled and said, 'Good. They've noticed.'

Jaime never asked himself if the risks he took had anything to do with the cries of, 'Your father is a coward,' or if he was trying to prove anything to himself and to others. It was enough that he proved his bravery again and again, that he was not afraid to risk his life for what he believed in.

Now, because one of his men had talked too freely, Jaime found himself saddled with a nun.

It's ironic that her Church is on our side now. But it's much too late, unless they can arrange a Second Coming and include my mother and father and sisters, he thought bitterly.

They walked through the woods at night, the white moonlight dappling the forest around them. They avoided the towns and main roads, alert for any sign of danger. Jaime ignored Megan. He walked with Felix, talking about past adventures, and Megan found herself intrigued. She had never known anyone like Jaime Miró. He was filled with such self-assurance.

If anyone can get me to Mendavia, Megan thought, *this man can.*

There had been moments when Jaime had felt pity for the sister, and even a reluctant admiration for the way she coped on the arduous journey. He wondered how his other men were getting along with their charges from God.

At least he had Amparo Jiron. At night Jaime found her a great comfort.

She's as dedicated as I am, Jaime thought. *She has even more reason than I do to hate the government.*

Amparo's entire family had been wiped out by the Nationalist army. She was fiercely independent, and filled with a deep passion.

At dawn they were nearing Salamanca, on the banks of the Rio Tormes.

'Students come here from all over Spain,' Felix explained to Megan, 'to attend the university here. It's probably the best in all of Spain.'

Jaime was not listening. He was concentrating on his next move. *If I were the hunter, where would I set my trap?*

He turned to Felix. 'We'll skip Salamanca. There's a *parador* just outside town. We will stop there.'

*

The *parador* was a small inn away from the mainstream of tourist traffic. Stone steps led to the lobby, which was guarded by an ancient knight in armour.

As the group approached the entrance, Jaime said to the two women, 'Wait here.'

He nodded to Felix Carpio and the two men disappeared.

'Where are they going?' Megan asked.

Amparo Jiron gave her a contemptuous look. 'Maybe they went looking for your God.'

'I hope they find him,' Megan said evenly.

Ten minutes later the men were back.

'All clear,' Jaime told Amparo. 'You and the sister will share a room. Felix will stay with me.' He handed her a key.

Amparo said petulantly, '*Querido*, I want to stay with you, not –'

'Do as I say. Keep an eye on her.'

Amparo turned to Megan. '*Bueno*. Come along, Sister.'

Megan followed Amparo up the stairs.

The room was one of a dozen set in a row along the grey, bare corridor. Amparo unlocked the door and the two women entered. The room was small and drab and sparsely furnished, with wooden floors, stucco walls, a bed, a small cot, a battered dressing-table and two chairs.

Megan looked around the room and exclaimed, 'It's lovely.'

Amparo Jiron swung around in anger, thinking that Megan was being sarcastic. 'Who the hell are you to complain about –?'

'It's so large,' Megan went on.

Amparo looked at her for a moment, then laughed. Of course it would seem large compared to the cells that the sisters lived in.

Amparo started to get undressed.

Megan could not help staring at her. It was the first time she had really looked at Amparo Jiron in the daylight. The woman was beautiful, in an earthy way. She had red hair, white skin, and was full-breasted, with a small waist and hips that swayed as she moved.

Amparo saw her watching. 'Sister – would you tell me something? Why would anyone join a convent?'

It was a simple question to answer. 'What could be more wonderful than to devote oneself to the glory of God?'

'Offhand, I could think of a thousand things.' Amparo walked over to the bed and sat down. 'You can sleep on the cot. From what I've heard about convents, your God doesn't want you to be too comfortable.'

Megan smiled. 'It doesn't matter. I'm comfortable inside.'

In their room across the corridor, Jaime Miró was stretching out on the bed. Felix Carpio was trying to get settled on the small cot. Both men were fully dressed. Jaime's gun was under his pillow. Felix's gun was on the small, battered table next to him.

'What do you think makes them do it?' Felix wondered aloud.

'Do what, *amigo*?'

'Lock themselves up in a convent all their lives like prisoners.'

Jaime Miró shrugged. 'Ask the sister. I wish to hell we were travelling alone. I have a bad feeling about this.'

'Jaime, God will thank us for this good deed.'

'Do you really believe that? Don't make me laugh.'

Felix did not pursue the subject. It was not tactful to discuss the Catholic Church with Jaime. The two men were silent, each preoccupied with his own thoughts.

Felix Carpio was thinking: *God put the sisters in our hands. We must get them to a convent safely.*

Jaime was thinking about Amparo. He wanted her badly now. *That damned nun.* He started to pull up the covers when he realized there was something he still had to do.

In the small, dark lobby downstairs, the manager sat quietly, waiting until he was sure that the new guests were asleep.

His heart was pounding as he picked up the telephone and dialled a number.

A lazy voice answered, 'Police Headquarters.'

The manager whispered into the telephone to his nephew, 'Florian, I have Jaime Miró and three of his people here. How would you like the honour of capturing them?'

Chapter 22

Many miles to the east, in a wooded area along the way to Peñafiel, Lucia Carmine was asleep.

Rubio Arzano sat watching her, reluctant to awaken her. *She sleeps like an angel*, he thought.

But it was almost dawn, time to be moving on.

Rubio leaned over and whispered gently in her ear, 'Sister Lucia . . .'

Lucia opened her eyes.

'It is time for us to go.'

She yawned and stretched lazily. The blouse she was wearing had become unbuttoned and part of her breast was showing. Rubio hastily looked away.

I must guard my thoughts. She is the bride of Jesus.

'Sister . . .'

'Yes?'

'I – I wonder if I could ask a favour of you.' He was almost blushing.

'Yes?'

'I – it's been a long time since I prayed. But I was brought up a Catholic. Would you mind saying a prayer?'

That was the last thing Lucia had expected.

How long has it been since I said a prayer? she wondered.

The convent did not count. While the others were praying, her mind had been busy with plans to escape.

'I – I don't –'

'I'm sure it would make us both feel better.'

How could she explain that she did not remember any prayers? 'I – er –' *Yes.* There was one she remembered. She had been a little girl kneeling at her bedside and her father had stood beside her, ready to tuck her into bed. Slowly, the words of the twenty-third Psalm started coming.

'The Lord is my shepherd. I shall not want. He maketh me to lie down in green pastures. He leadeth me beside the still waters. He restoreth my soul. He leadeth me in the paths of righteousness, for His name's sake . . .'

Memories came flooding back.

She and her father had owned the world. And he had been so proud of her.

You were born under a lucky star, faccia del angelo.

And hearing that, Lucia had felt lucky and beautiful. Nothing could ever hurt her. Was she not the beautiful daughter of the great Angelo Carmine?

'. . . Yea, though I walk through the valley of the shadow of death, I will fear no evil . . .'

The evil ones were the enemies of her father and brothers. And she had made them pay.

'. . . For Thou art with me; Thy rod and Thy staff they comfort me . . .'

Where was God when I needed comforting?

'Thou preparest a table before me in the presence of mine enemies; Thou anointest my head with oil, my cup runneth over. . .'

She was speaking more slowly now, her voice a whisper. What had happened, she wondered, to the little girl in the white communion dress? The future had been so golden. Somehow it had all gone wrong. Everything. *I've lost my father and my brothers and myself.*

In the convent she had not thought about God. But now, out here with this simple peasant . . .

Would you mind saying a prayer for us?

Lucia went on. 'Surely goodness and mercy shall follow me all the days of my life; And I will dwell in the house of the Lord for ever.'

Rubio was watching her, moved.

'Thank you, Sister.'

Lucia nodded, unable to speak. *What's the matter with me?* Lucia asked herself.

'Are you ready, Sister?'

She looked at Rubio Arzano and said, 'Yes. I'm ready.'

Five minutes later they were on their way.

They were caught in a sudden downpour and took shelter in a deserted cabin. The rain beat against the roof and sides of the cabin like angry fists.

'Do you think the storm will ever let up?'

Rubio smiled. 'It's not a real storm, Sister. It's what we Basques call a *sirimiri*. It will stop as quickly as it started The earth is dry right now. It needs this rain.'

'Really?'

'Yes. I'm a farmer.'

It shows, Lucia thought.

'Forgive me for saying this, Sister, but you and I have a lot in common.'

Lucia looked over at the country bumpkin and thought: *That will be the day*. 'We do?'

'Yes. I truly believe that in many ways being on a farm must be much like being in a convent.'

The connection eluded her. 'I don't understand.'

'Well, Sister, in a convent you think a lot about God and His miracles. Is that not true?'

'Yes.'

'In a sense a farm is God. One is surrounded by creation – all the things that grow from God's earth, whether it's wheat or olives or grapes – everything comes from God, does it not? These are all miracles, and you watch them happen every day, and because you help them grow, you are part of the miracle.'

Lucia had to smile at the enthusiasm in his voice.

Suddenly the rain stopped.

'We can move on now, Sister.'

*

'We will be coming to Rio Duero soon,' Rubio said. 'The Peñafiel Falls is just ahead of us. We will go on to Aranda de Duero and then Logroño, where we will meet the others.'

You'll be going to those places, Lucia thought. *And good luck to you. I'll be in Switzerland, my friend.*

They heard the sound of the Falls half an hour before they reached them. The Peñafiel Falls was a beautiful sight cascading down into the swift-moving river. The roar of it was almost deafening.

'I want to bathe,' Lucia said. It seemed years since she had last had a bath.

Rubio Arzano stared at her. 'Here?'

No, you idiot, in Rome. 'Yes.'

'Be careful. The river is swollen because of the rain.'

'Don't worry.' She stood there, patiently waiting.

'Oh. I will go away while you undress.'

'Stay nearby,' Lucia said quickly. There were probably wild animals in the woods.

As Lucia started to undress, Rubio hastily walked a few yards away and turned his back.

'Don't go in too far, Sister,' he called. 'The river is treacherous.'

Lucia put down the wrapped cross where she could keep an eye on it. The cool morning air felt wonderful on her naked body. When she had stripped completely, she stepped into the water. It was cold and invigorating. She turned and saw that Rubio was steadfastly looking in the other direction, his back turned to her. She smiled to herself. All the other men she had known would be feasting their eyes.

She stepped in deeper, avoiding the rocks that were all around, and splashed the water over herself, feeling the rushing river tugging hard at her legs.

A few feet away a small tree was being swept downstream. As Lucia turned to watch it, she suddenly lost her balance and slipped, screaming. She fell hard, slamming her head against a boulder.

Rubio turned and watched in horror as Lucia disappeared downstream in the raging waters.

Chapter 23

At the police station in Salamanca, when Sergeant Florian Santiago replaced the receiver, his hands were trembling.

I have Jaime Miró and three of his people here. How would you like the honour of capturing them?

The government had offered a large reward for the head of Jaime Miró, and now the Basque outlaw was in his hands. The reward money would change his whole life. He could afford to send his children to a better school, he could buy a washing machine for his wife and jewellery for his mistress. Of course he would have to share some of the reward money with his uncle. *I'll give him twenty per cent*, Santiago thought. *Or maybe ten per cent.*

He was well aware of Jaime Miró's reputation, and he had no intention of risking his life trying to capture the terrorist. *Let others face the danger and give me the reward.*

He sat at his desk deciding the best way to handle the situation. Colonel Acoca's name immediately sprang to his mind. Everybody knew there was a blood vendetta between the Colonel and the outlaw. Besides, the Colonel had the whole GOE at his command. Yes, that was definitely the way to proceed.

He picked up a telephone, and ten minutes later he was speaking to the Colonel himself.

'This is Sergeant Florian Santiago calling from the police station at Salamanca. I have tracked down Jaime Miró.'

Colonel Ramón Acoca fought to keep his voice even. 'Are you certain of this?'

'Yes, Colonel. He is at the Parador Nacional Raimundo

de Borgon, just outside of town. He is spending the night. My uncle is the manager. He telephoned me himself. There is another man and two women with Miró.'

'Your uncle is positive it is Miró?'

'Yes, Colonel. He and the others are sleeping in the two back rooms on the second floor of the inn.'

Colonel Acoca said, 'Listen to me very carefully, Sergeant. I want you to go to the *parador* immediately and stand watch outside to make certain none of them leaves. I should be able to reach there in an hour. You are not to go inside. And stay out of sight. Is that clear?'

'Yes, sir. I will leave immediately.' He hesitated. 'Colonel, about the reward money –'

'When we catch Miró, it's yours.'

'Thank you, Colonel. I am most –'

'Go.'

'Yes, sir.'

Florian Santiago replaced the receiver. He was tempted to call his mistress to tell her the exciting news, but that could wait. He would surprise her later. Meanwhile, he had a job to do.

He summoned one of the policemen on duty upstairs.

'Take over the desk. I have an errand to do. I'll be back in a few hours.' *And I'll come back a rich man*, he thought. *The first thing I'll buy will be a new car – a Seat. A blue one. No, maybe it will be white.*

Colonel Ramón Acoca replaced the receiver and sat still, letting his brain go to work. This time there would be no slip-up. It was the final move in the chess game between them. He would have to proceed very carefully. Miró would have sentries alert for trouble.

Acoca called in his aide-de-camp.

'Yes, Colonel?'

'Pick out two dozen of your best marksmen. See that they're armed with automatic weapons. We're leaving for Salamanca in fifteen minutes.'

'Yes, sir.'

There would be no escape for Miró. The Colonel was already planning the raid in his mind. The *parador* would be completely surrounded by a cordon that would move in quickly and quietly. *A sneak attack before the butcher has a chance to murder any more of my men. We'll kill them all in their sleep.*

Fifteen minutes later, his aide returned.

'We're ready to move, Colonel.'

Sergeant Santiago lost no time in getting to the *parador*. Even without the Colonel's warning, he would have had no intention of going after the terrorists. But now, in obedience to Acoca's orders, he stood in the shadows, twenty yards away from the inn, where he had a good view of the front door. There was a chill in the night air, but the thought of the reward money kept Santiago warm. He wondered whether the two women inside were pretty and whether they were in bed with the men. Of one thing Santiago was certain: in a few hours, they would all be dead.

The army truck moved into town quietly and drove towards the *parador*.

Colonel Acoca flicked on a flashlight and looked at his map, and when they were a mile from the inn, he said, 'Stop here. We'll walk the rest of the way. Maintain silence.'

Florian Santiago was unaware of their approach until a voice in his ear startled him with, 'Who are you?'

He turned and found himself facing Colonel Ramón Acoca. *My God, he's frightening-looking*, Santiago thought.

'I am Sergeant Santiago, sir.'

'Has anyone left the inn?'

'No, sir. They're all inside, probably asleep by now.'

The Colonel turned to his aide. 'I want half our men to

form a perimeter around the hotel. If anyone tries to escape, they are to shoot to kill. The others will come with me. The fugitives are in the two back bedrooms upstairs. Let's go.'

Santiago watched as the Colonel and his men entered the front door of the *parador*, moving quietly. Santiago wondered if there would be a lot of shooting. And if there was, he wondered if his uncle might be killed in the cross-fire. That would be a pity. But on the other hand, there would be no one he would have to share the reward money with.

When Colonel Acoca and his men reached the top of the stairs, he whispered, 'Take no chances. Open fire as soon as you see them.'

His aide asked, 'Colonel, would you like me to go ahead of you?'

'No.' He intended to have the pleasure of killing Jaime Miró himself.

At the end of the corridor were the two rooms where Miró and his group were staying. Colonel Acoca silently motioned six of his men to cover one door and the other six to cover the other door.

'Now!' he screamed.

It was the moment he had been burning for. At his signal, the soldiers kicked in both doors simultaneously and rushed into the rooms, weapons ready. They stood there in the middle of the empty rooms staring at the rumpled beds.

'Spread out. Hurry! Downstairs!' Acoca shrieked.

The soldiers raced through every room in the hotel, smashing doors open, waking up startled guests. Jaime Miró and the others were nowhere to be found. The Colonel stormed downstairs to confront the hotel manager. There was no one in the lobby.

'Hello,' he called out. 'Hello.' There was no response. The coward was hiding.

One of the soldiers was staring at the floor behind the desk. 'Colonel . . .'

Acoca strode over to his side and stared down at the floor.

The bound and gagged body of the manager was slumped against the wall. A sign had been hung around his neck. It read:

PLEASE DO NOT DISTURB.

Chapter 24

Rubio Arzano watched in horror as Lucia disappeared under the rushing waters and was swept downstream. In a split second, he turned to race along the river bank, leaping over small logs and bushes. At the first bend of the river, he caught a glimpse of Lucia's body coming towards him. Diving in, he swam frantically to reach her, struggling against the powerful current. It was almost impossible. He felt himself being pulled away. Lucia was ten feet from him, but it seemed like miles. He made one last heroic effort and grabbed her arm, his fingers almost slipping away. He held her in a death grip, as he began grappling his way to the safety of the shore.

When Rubio finally reached the river bank, he pulled Lucia up on to the grass and he lay there, fighting for breath. Lucia was unconscious and not breathing. Rubio turned her over on her stomach, straddled her and began applying pressure against her lungs. A minute went by, then two, and just as he was beginning to despair, a stream of water gushed out of her mouth and she groaned. Rubio uttered a prayer of thanks.

He kept up the pressure, gentler now, until her heartbeat was steady. She began to shiver from the cold. Rubio hurried over to a clump of trees and pulled down handfuls of leaves. He carried them over to her and started to dry her body with them. He was wet and cold, and his clothes were soaked, but he paid no attention. He had been panicky with fear that Sister Lucia would die. Now, as he gently rubbed her naked body with the dry leaves, unworthy thoughts came into his mind.

She has the body of a goddess. Forgive me, Lord, she belongs to You, and I must not think these wicked thoughts . . .

Lucia was gradually awakened by the gentle stroking of her body. She was on the beach with Ivo, and his soft tongue was moving down her body. *Oh, yes,* she thought. *Oh, yes. Don't stop, caro.* She was aroused before she even opened her eyes.

When Lucia had fallen into the river, her last thought had been that she was going to die. But she was alive, and she found herself looking up at the man who had saved her. Without even thinking, Lucia reached up and pulled Rubio down to her. There was a look of shocked surprise on his face.

'Sister –' he protested. 'We can't –'

'Sh!'

Her lips were on his, fierce and hungry and demanding, and her tongue was exploring his mouth. It was too much for Rubio.

'Hurry,' Lucia whispered. 'Hurry.'

She watched as Rubio nervously stripped off his wet clothes. *He deserves a reward*, she thought. *So do I.*

As Rubio moved hesitantly towards her, he said, 'Sister, we shouldn't –'

Lucia was in no mood for conversation. She felt him joining his body to hers in a timeless, mindless ritual, and she gave herself up to the glorious sensations that flooded her. It was all the sweeter because of her close brush with death.

Rubio was a surprisingly good lover, both gentle and fierce at the same time. He had a vulnerability that took Lucia completely by surprise. And there was a look of such tenderness in his eyes that Lucia felt a sudden lump in her throat.

I hope the big oaf isn't falling in love with me. He's so eager to please me. When was the last time a man cared about pleasing me? Lucia wondered. And she thought of her father. And she wondered how he would have liked Rubio Arzano. And then she wondered why she wondered whether her father would have liked Rubio Arzano. *I must be crazy. This man is a farmer. I'm Lucia Carmine, the daughter of Angelo Carmine. Rubio's life has nothing to do with my life. We were thrown together by a stupid accident of fate.*

Rubio was holding her and saying over and over, 'Lucia. My Lucia.'

And the shining in his eyes told her everything he felt. *He's so dear*, she thought. And then: *What is the matter with me? Why am I even thinking about him like this? I'm running away from the police and* – She suddenly remembered the gold cross and gasped. *Oh, my God! How could I have forgotten it even for a moment?*

She sat up quickly. 'Rubio, I left a – a package on the bank of the river back there. Would you bring it to me, please? And my clothes?'

'Of course. I'll be right back.'

Lucia sat there waiting, frantic that something might have happened to the cross. What if it was gone? What if someone had come along and picked it up?

It was with an enormous feeling of relief that Lucia saw Rubio returning with the wrapped cross under his arm. *I mustn't let it out of my sight again*, she thought. 'Thank you.'

Rubio handed Lucia her clothes. She looked up at him and said softly, 'I won't need these right away.'

The sun on her naked skin made her feel lazy and warm, and there was a wonderful comfort in Rubio's arms. It was as though they had found a peaceful oasis and the dangers they had been running away from seemed light years away.

'Tell me about your farm,' Lucia said idly.

His face lit up, and there was pride in his voice. 'It was a small farm outside a little village near Bilbao. It was in my family for generations.'

'What happened to it?'

His expression darkened. 'Because I am Basque, the government in Madrid punished me with extra taxes. When I refused to pay, they confiscated the farm. That was when

I met Jaime Miró. I joined him to fight against the government for what is right. I have a mother and two sisters, and one day we will have our farm back, and I will run it again.'

Lucia thought of her father and two brothers locked away in a prison for ever. 'Are you close to your family?'

Rubio smiled warmly. 'Of course. Families are our first love, are they not?'

Yes, Lucia thought. *But I will never see mine again.*

'Tell me about your family, Lucia,' Rubio said. 'Before you joined the convent, were you close to them?'

The conversation was taking a dangerous turn. *What can I tell him? My father is a mafioso. He and my two brothers are in prison for murder.* 'Yes – we are very close.'

'What does your father do?'

'He – he's a businessman.'

'Have you got brothers and sisters?'

'I have two brothers. They work for him.'

'Lucia, why did you enter the convent?'

Because the police are looking for me for murdering two men. I've got to stop this conversation, Lucia thought. Aloud, she said, 'I needed to get away.' *That's close enough to the truth.*

'You felt the world was – was too much for you?'

'Something like that.'

'I have no right to say this, Lucia, but I am in love with you.'

'Rubio –'

'I want to marry you. In all my life, I have never said that to another woman.'

There was something so touching and earnest about him. *He doesn't know how to play games*, she thought. *I must be careful not to hurt him. But the idea of Angelo Carmine's daughter being a farmer's wife!* Lucia almost laughed aloud.

Rubio misunderstood the smile on Lucia's face. 'I will not live in hiding for ever. The government will have to make peace with us. Then I will return to my farm. *Querida* – I want to spend the rest of my life making you happy. We will have many children and the girls will all look like you . . .'

I can't let him go on like this, Lucia decided. *I should stop him now*. But somehow she could not bring herself to do it. She listened to Rubio paint romantic pictures of their life together, and she found herself almost wishing it could happen. She was so tired of running away. It would be wonderful to find a haven where she could be safe, taken care of by someone who loved her . . . *I must be losing my mind*.

'Let's not talk about it now,' Lucia said. 'We should be moving on.'

They travelled northeast, following the winding banks of the Duero River, with its hilly countryside and lush green trees. They stopped at the picturesque village of Villalba de Duero at the foot of the mountains, and stopped to buy bread and cheese and wine and had an idyllic picnic in a grassy meadow.

Lucia felt content at Rubio's side. There was a quiet strength about him that seemed to give her strength. *He's not for me, but he's going to make some lucky woman very happy*, she thought.

When they had finished eating, Rubio said, 'The next town is Aranda de Duero. It's a fairly large town. It would be best if we skirted around it to avoid the GOE and the soldiers.'

It was the moment of truth, time to leave him. She had been waiting for them to reach a large town. Rubio Arzano and his farm were a dream, escaping to Switzerland was the reality. Lucia knew how much she was going to hurt him, and she could not bear to look into his eyes when she said, 'Rubio – I'd like us to go into town.'

He frowned. 'That could be dangerous, *querida*. The soldiers –'

'They won't be looking for us there.' She thought quickly. 'Besides, I – I need a change of clothes. I can't keep going on in this.'

The idea of entering the town disturbed Rubio, but all he said was, 'If that is what you wish.'

In the distance the walls and buildings of Aranda de Duero

loomed before them, like a man-made mountain hewn out of the earth.

Rubio tried one more time. 'Lucia – you're sure you must go into the town?'

'Yes. I'm sure.'

The two of them crossed the long bridge that led to the main street, Avenida Castilla, and headed for the centre of town. They passed a sugar factory and churches and poultry shops, and the air was thick with their smells. Shops and blocks of flats lined the avenue. They walked slowly, careful not to draw attention to themselves. Finally, to her relief, Lucia saw what she had been looking for – a sign that read: '*Casa de Empeños*' – a pawnshop. She said nothing.

They reached the village square, with its shops and markets and bars, and they passed the *Taverna Cueva*, with its long bar and wooden tables. There was a juke box inside, and hanging from the oak beam ceiling were hams and strings of garlic.

Lucia saw her opportunity. 'I'm thirsty, Rubio,' she said. 'Can we go in there?'

'Of course.'

Rubio took Lucia's arm and led her inside.

There were half a dozen men crowded around the bar. Lucia and Rubio took a table in the corner.

'What would you like, *querida*?'

'Order a glass of wine for me, please. I'll be right back. There's something I have to do.'

She rose and walked out into the street, leaving Rubio staring after her, puzzled.

Outside, Lucia turned and hurried back to the *Casa de Empeños*, clutching her tightly wrapped package. Across the street she saw a door with a black sign in white lettering that read, '*Policía*'. She stared at it a moment, her heart skipping a beat, then skirted it and entered the pawnshop.

A shrunken man with a large head stood behind the counter, barely visible.

'*Buenos días, señorita.*'

'*Buenos días, señor.* I have something I would like to sell.' She was so nervous that she had to press her knees together to keep them from shaking.

'*Sí?*'

Lucia unwrapped the gold cross and held it out. 'Would – would you be interested in buying this?'

The pawnbroker took it in his hands, and Lucia watched the light that came into his eyes.

'May I ask where you acquired this?'

'It was left to me by an uncle who has just died.' Her throat was so dry she could hardly speak.

The man fingered the cross, turning it over in his hands slowly. 'How much are you asking for it?'

Her dream was coming to life. 'I want two hundred and fifty thousand pesetas.'

He frowned and shook his head. 'No. It is worth only a hundred thousand pesetas.'

'I would sell my body first.'

'Perhaps I could go as high as one hundred and fifty thousand pesetas.'

'I would rather melt it down and let the gold run in the streets.'

'Two hundred thousand pesetas. That is my last offer.'

Lucia took the gold cross from him. 'You are robbing me blind, but I will accept it.'

She could see the excitement in his face. '*Bueno, señorita.*' He reached for the cross.

Lucia pulled it back. 'There is a condition.'

'What condition would that be, *señorita*?'

'My passport was stolen. I need a new one in order to get out of the country to visit my stricken aunt.'

He was studying her now, his eyes wise. He nodded. 'I see.'

'If you can help me with my problem, then the cross is yours.'

He sighed. 'Passports are difficult to come by, *señorita*. The authorities are very strict.'

Lucia watched him, saying nothing.

'I don't see how I can help you.'

'Thank you, anyway, *señor*.' She started towards the door.

He let her reach it before he said, '*Momentito*.'

Lucia stopped.

'Something has just occurred to me. I have a cousin who is sometimes involved in delicate matters like this. He is a *distant* cousin, you understand.'

'I understand.'

'I could speak to him. When do you require this passport?'

'Today.'

The large head nodded slowly. 'And if I can do this thing, we have a deal?'

'When I get my passport.'

'Agreed. Come back after eight o'clock and my cousin will be here. He will arrange to take the necessary photograph and insert it in the passport.'

Lucia could feel her heart pounding. 'Thank you, *señor*.'

'Would you like to leave the cross here for safekeeping?'

'It will be safe with me.'

'Eight o'clock, then. *Hasta luego*.'

She left the shop. Outside she carefully avoided the police station and headed back to the *taverna*, where Rubio was waiting. Her footsteps slowed. She had finally succeeded. With the money from the cross, she would be able to get to Switzerland and freedom. She should have been happy. Instead she felt strangely depressed.

What's wrong with [illegible]? I'm on my way. Rubio will get over me soon enough. He'll find someone else.

She remembered the look in his eyes when he said, *I want to marry you. In all my life, I have never said that to another woman.*

Damn the man, she thought. *Well, he's not my problem.*

Outside the *taverna* she paused and took a deep breath. She forced a smile and walked inside to join him.

Chapter 25

The news media were in a feeding frenzy. The headlines tumbled over one another. There was the attack on the convent; the wholesale arrest of the nuns for sheltering terrorists; the escape of four nuns; the murder of half a dozen soldiers by one of the nuns before she was shot and killed. The international news wires were on fire.

Reporters had arrived in Madrid from all parts of the world and Prime Minister Martinez, in an effort to cool things down, had agreed to a press conference. They were gathered in his office, almost four dozen reporters, from all over the world. Colonel Ramón Acoca and Colonel Fal Sostelo were at the Prime Minister's side. The Prime Minister had seen that afternoon's headline in the London *Times*: TERRORISTS AND NUNS EVADE SPAIN'S ARMY AND POLICE.

A reporter from *Paris Match* was asking, 'Mr Prime Minister, do you have any idea where the missing nuns are now?'

Prime Minister Leopoldo Martinez replied, 'Colonel Acoca is in charge of the search operation. I will let him answer that.'

Colonel Acoca said, 'We have reason to believe that they are in the hands of the Basque terrorists. I'm also sorry to say there is evidence to indicate that the nuns are collaborating with the terrorists.'

The reporters were scribbling feverishly.

'What about the shooting of Sister Teresa and the soldiers?'

'We have information that Sister Teresa was working with

Jaime Miró. Under the pretext of helping us find Miró, she went into an army camp and murdered half a dozen soldiers before she could be stopped. I can assure you that the army and the GOE are bending every effort to bring the criminals to justice.'

'And the nuns who were arrested and taken to Madrid?'

'They are being interrogated,' Colonel Acoca said.

The Prime Minister was anxious to end the meeting. It was difficult for him to keep his temper in check. The failure to locate the nuns or capture the terrorists made his government – and himself – look inept and foolish, and the press was taking full advantage of the situation.

'Can you tell us anything about the backgrounds of the four nuns who escaped, Prime Minister?' asked a reporter from OGGI.

'I'm sorry. I can give you no further information. I repeat, ladies and gentlemen, the government is doing everything in its power to find the nuns.'

'Prime Minister, there have been reports about the brutality of the attack on the convent at Ávila. Would you respond to that?'

It was a sore point with Martinez because it was true. Colonel Acoca had grossly exceeded his authority. But he would deal with the Colonel later. This was the time for a show of unity.

He turned to the Colonel and said smoothly, 'Colonel Acoca can respond to that.'

Colonel Acoca said, 'I, too, have heard those unfounded reports. The facts are simple. We received reliable information that the terrorist Jaime Miró and a dozen of his men were hiding in the Abbey Cistercian and that they were heavily armed. By the time we raided the abbey, they had fled.'

'Colonel, we heard that some of your men molested –'

'That is an outrageous accusation.'

Prime Minister Martinez said, 'Thank you, ladies and gentlemen. That will be all. You will be informed of any further developments.'

The press conference was over. When the reporters left, the Prime Minister turned to Colonel Acoca and Colonel Sostelo. 'They're making us look like savages in the eyes of the world.'

Colonel Acoca had not the slightest interest in the Prime Minister's opinion. What concerned him was a telephone call he had received in the middle of the night.

'Colonel Acoca?'

It was a voice he was all too familiar with. He was instantly wide awake.

'Yes, sir.'

'We're disappointed in you. We had hoped to see some results before this.'

'Sir, I'm closing in on them.' He found that he was perspiring heavily. 'I ask that you be a little more patient. I won't disappoint you.'

He held his breath, waiting for a response.

'You're running out of time.'

The line went dead.

Colonel Acoca replaced the receiver and sat there, frustrated. *Where is that bastard Miró?*

Chapter 26

I'm going to kill her, Ricardo Mellado thought. *I could strangle her with my bare hands, throw her off the mountain, or simply shoot her. No, I think strangling her would give me the greatest pleasure.*

Sister Graciela was the most exasperating human being he had ever encountered. She was impossible. In the beginning when Jaime Miró had assigned him to escort her, Ricardo Mellado had been pleased. True, she was a nun, but she was also the most ravishing beauty he had ever laid eyes on. He was determined to get to know her, to find out why she had decided to lock up all that exquisite beauty behind convent walls for the rest of her life. Under the skirt and blouse she was wearing, he could discern the rich, nubile curves of a woman. *It's going to be a very interesting trip*, Ricardo decided.

But things had taken a totally unexpected turn. The problem was that Sister Graciela refused to speak to him. She had not said one word since their journey began, and what completely baffled Ricardo was that she did not appear to be angry or frightened or upset. Not at all. She simply retreated into some remote part of herself and appeared totally uninterested in him and in what was going on around her. They had travelled at a good pace, walking along hot, dusty side roads, past fields of wheat, rippling golden in the sunlight, and fields of barley, oats and grapevines. They skirted the little villages along the way and went by fields of sunflowers with their wide yellow faces following the sun.

When they crossed the Moros River, Ricardo asked, 'Would you like to rest awhile, Sister?'

Silence.

They were approaching Segovia before heading north-east to the snow-capped Guadarrama mountains. Ricardo kept trying to make polite conversation, but it was completely hopeless.

'We will be at Segovia soon, Sister.'

No reaction.

What could I have done to offend her? 'Are you hungry, Sister?'

Nothing.

It was as though he were not there. He had never felt so frustrated in his life. *Perhaps the woman is retarded*, he thought. *That must be the answer. God gave her an unearthly beauty and then cursed her with a feeble mind.* But he did not believe it.

When they reached the outskirts of Segovia, Ricardo noted that the town was crowded, which meant that the *guardia civil* would be even more alert than usual.

As they approached the Plaza del Conde de Cheste, Ricardo saw soldiers of the *guardia civil* strolling in their direction. He whispered, 'Hold my hand, Sister. We must look like two lovers out for a stroll.'

She ignored him.

Jesus, Ricardo thought. *Maybe she's deaf and dumb.*

He reached over and took her hand in his, and her sudden fierce resistance surprised him. She pulled away as if she had been stung.

The guards were getting closer.

Ricardo leaned towards Graciela. 'You mustn't be angry,' he said loudly. 'My sister feels the same way. After dinner last night when she put the children to bed she was saying that it would be much better if we men didn't sit around together smoking smelly cigars and telling stories while you women went off by yourselves. I'll bet –'

The guards had passed. Ricardo turned to look at Graciela. Her face was expressionless. Mentally, Ricardo began to curse Jaime, wishing he had given him one of the other nuns. This one was made of stone, with no chisel hard enough to penetrate that cold exterior.

In all modesty, Ricardo Mellado knew that he was attractive to women. Enough of them had told him so. He was light complexioned, tall and well-built, with a patrician nose, an intelligent face and perfect white teeth. He came from one of the most prominent Basque families. His father was a banker from the Basque country in the north and had seen to it that Ricardo was well educated. He had gone to the University of Salamanca, and his father had looked forward to his son joining him in the family business.

When Ricardo returned home, he dutifully went to work at the bank, but within a short period of time he became involved with the problems of his people. He began attending meetings and rallies and protests against the government and he soon became one of the leaders of ETA. His father learned about his son's activities and called him into his huge, panelled office and lectured him.

'I am a Basque, too, Ricardo, but I am also a businessman. We cannot foul our own nest by encouraging a revolution in the country where we make our living.'

'None of us is trying to overthrow the government, Father. All we're demanding is freedom. The government's oppression of the Basques and the Catalans is intolerable.'

The senior Mellado leaned back in his chair and studied his son. 'My good friend the Mayor had a quiet word with me yesterday. He suggested it would be to your benefit not to attend any more rallies. It would be better if you expended your energy on bank business.'

'Father –'

'Listen to me, Ricardo. When I was young, my blood ran hot, too. But there are other ways to cool it off. You're engaged to a lovely girl. I hope you will have many children.' He waved his hand at their surroundings. 'And you have much to look forward to in your future.'

'But don't you see –?'

'I see more clearly than you, my son. Your prospective father-in-law is also unhappy with your activities. I would not want anything to happen that would prevent the wedding. Do I make myself clear?'

'Yes, Father.'

The following Saturday Ricardo Mellado was arrested leading a Basque rally in an auditorium in Barcelona. He refused to let his father bail him out unless he would also bail out the other demonstrators who had been arrested. His father refused. Ricardo's career was ended and so was his engagement. That had been five years earlier. Five years of danger and narrow escapes. Five years filled with the excitement of fighting for a cause he passionately believed in. Now he was on the run, a fugitive from the police, escorting a retarded and mute nun across Spain.

'We'll go this way,' he said to Sister Graciela. He was careful not to touch her arm.

They turned off the main street on to St Valentin. On the corner was a shop that sold musical instruments.

Ricardo said, 'I have an idea. Wait here, Sister. I'll be right back.'

He entered the shop and walked up to a young clerk standing behind the counter.

'*Buenos días.* May I help you?'

'Yes. I would like to buy two guitars.'

The clerk smiled. 'Ah, you are in luck. We've just got in some Ramirezes. They are the best.'

'Perhaps something of not such a high quality. My friend and I are only amateurs.'

'As you wish, *señor*. What about these?' The clerk walked over to a section of the store where a dozen guitars were on display. 'I can let you have two Konos for five thousand pesetas apiece.'

'I think not.' Ricardo selected two inexpensive guitars. 'These will do nicely,' he said.

A few moments later Ricardo walked back out to the street, carrying the two guitars. He had half hoped Sister

Graciela would be gone. She was standing there, patiently waiting.

Ricardo opened the strap on one of the guitars and held out the instrument to her. 'Here, Sister. Put this over your shoulder.'

She stared at him.

'It isn't necessary for you to play it,' Ricardo said patiently. 'It is only for effect.'

He shoved the guitar at her, and she reluctantly took it. They walked along the winding streets of Segovia under the enormous viaduct built by the Romans centuries ago.

Ricardo decided to try again. 'You see this viaduct, Sister? There is no cement between the stones. Legend has it that it was built by the devil two thousand years ago, stone piled on stone, with nothing but the devil's magic to hold it together.' He looked at her for some reaction.

Nothing.

To hell with her, Ricardo Mellado thought. *I give up*.

The members of the *guardia civil* were everywhere, and whenever they passed them, Ricardo would pretend to be in earnest conversation with Graciela, always careful to avoid body contact.

The numbers of police and soldiers seemed to be increasing, but Ricardo felt reasonably safe. They would be looking for a nun in robes and a group of Jaime Miró's men, but they would have no reason to suspect two young tourists alone, carrying guitars.

Ricardo was feeling hungry, and even though Sister Graciela had said nothing, he was sure that she must be hungry also. They passed a small *bodega*.

'We'll stop in here and have a bite to eat, Sister.'

She stood there, watching him.

He sighed. 'Right. Suit yourself.'

He walked inside the small café. A moment later Graciela followed him.

When they were seated, Ricardo asked, 'What would you like to order, Sister?'

There was no response. She was infuriating.

Ricardo said to the waitress, 'Two *gazpachos* and two helpings of *chorizos*.'

When the soup and sausages came, Graciela ate what was put in front of her. He noticed that she ate automatically, without enjoyment, as though fulfilling some duty. The men seated at other tables were staring at her, and Ricardo could not blame them. *It would take the young Goya to capture her beauty*, he thought.

In spite of Graciela's sullen behaviour, Ricardo felt a lump in his throat every time he looked at her, and he cursed himself for a romantic fool. She was an enigma, buried behind some kind of impenetrable wall. Ricardo Mellado had known dozens of beautiful women, but none of them had ever affected him this way. There was something almost mystical about her beauty. The irony was that he had absolutely no idea what lay behind the breath-taking façade. Was she intelligent or stupid? Interesting or dull? Cold-blooded or passionate? *I hope she's stupid, dull, and cold-blooded*, Ricardo thought, *or I won't be able to stand losing her. As though I could ever have her. She belongs to God.* He looked away, afraid that she might sense what he was thinking.

When it was time to leave, Ricardo paid the bill and they rose. During the journey he had noticed that Sister Graciela was limping slightly. *I'll have to get us some kind of transportation*, he thought. *We still have a long way to go.*

They started down the street, and at the far end of town, in the Manzanares el Real, they came upon a gypsy caravan. There were four colourfully decorated wagons in the caravan, pulled by horses. In the back of the wagons were women and children, all dressed in gypsy costumes.

Ricardo said, 'Wait here, Sister. I'm going to try to get us a lift.'

He approached the driver of the front wagon, a burly man in full gypsy regalia, including wearing earrings.

'*Buenas tardes, señor*. I would consider it a great kindness if you could give my fiancée and me a lift.'

The gypsy looked over to where Graciela was standing. 'It is possible. Where are you headed?'

'To the Guadarrama mountains.'

'I can take you as far as Cerezo.'

'That would be of great value. Thank you.'

He shook the gypsy's hand and put money in it.

'Get in the last wagon.'

'*Gracias*.'

Ricardo returned to where Graciela was waiting. 'The gypsies are going to take us as far as Cerezo de Abajo,' he told her. 'We'll go in the last wagon.'

For an instant, he was sure she was going to refuse. She hesitated, then started towards the wagon.

There were half a dozen gypsies inside the wagon and they made room for Ricardo and Graciela. As they climbed aboard, Ricardo started to help the sister up, but the moment he touched her arm, she pushed him away with a fierceness that took him by surprise. *All right, to hell with you.* He caught a glimpse of Graciela's bare leg as she lifted herself on to the wagon, and he could not help thinking: *She has the most beautiful legs I've ever seen.*

They made themselves as comfortable as possible on the hard wooden floor of the wagon and the long journey began. Graciela sat in a corner, her eyes closed and her lips moving in prayer. Ricardo could not take his eyes off her.

As the day wore on, the sun became a hot furnace, beating down on them, baking the earth, and the sky was a deep, cloudless blue. From time to time as the wagon crossed the plains, huge birds soared overhead. *Buitre leonado*, Ricardo thought. The lion-coloured griffon vultures.

Late in the afternoon the gypsy caravan came to a stop. The leader approached their wagon.

'This is as far as we can take you. We're headed for Vinuelas.'

Wrong direction. 'This is fine,' Ricardo assured him. 'Thank you.'

He started to reach out a hand for Graciela and quickly thought better of it.

Ricardo turned to the leader of the gypsies. 'I would

consider it a kindness if you would sell some food to my fiancée and me.'

The chief turned to one of the women and said something in a foreign tongue, and a few moments later two packages of food were handed to Ricardo.

'*Muchas gracias*.' He pulled out some money.

The gypsy chief studied him for a moment. 'You and the sister have already paid for the food.'

You and the sister. So he knew. Yet Ricardo felt no sense of danger. The gypsies were as oppressed by the government as were the Basques and Catalans.

'*Vayan con Dios*.'

Ricardo stood there watching the caravan move out of sight. He turned to Graciela. She was watching him, silent, impassive.

'You won't have to put up with my company much longer,' Ricardo assured her. 'In two days we will be in Logroño. You'll meet your friends there and you'll be on your way to the convent at Mendavia.'

No reaction. He could have been talking to a stone wall. *I am talking to a stone wall.*

They had been dropped off in a peaceful valley rich with orchards of apple, pear and fig trees. A few feet away from them was the Tormes River, filled with fat trout. In the past, Ricardo had fished there often. It would have been an ideal place to stay and rest, but there was a long road to travel.

He turned to study the Guadarrama mountains, the range that lay ahead of them. Ricardo knew the area well. There were several trails that wound through the length of the mountains. *Cabras*, wild mountain goats, and wolves roamed the passes, and Ricardo would have chosen that if he had been travelling alone. But with Sister Graciela at his side, he decided on the safest.

'Well, we'd better get started,' Ricardo said. 'We have a long climb ahead of us.'

He had no intention of missing the rendezvous with the

others in Logroño. Let the silent sister become someone else's headache.

Sister Graciela stood there waiting for Ricardo to lead the way. He turned and began to climb. As they started up the steep mountain path, Graciela slipped on some loose pebbles and Ricardo instinctively reached out to help her. She jerked away from his hand and righted herself. *Fine*, he thought angrily. *Break your neck.*

They kept moving upwards, heading towards the majestic peak high above. The trail started to get steeper and narrower and the chilled air became thinner. They were heading east, passing through a forest of pine trees. Ahead of them lay a village that was a haven for skiers and mountain climbers. There would be hot food and warmth and rest there, Ricardo knew. It was tempting. *Too dangerous*, he decided. It would be a perfect place for Acoca to set a trap.

He turned to Sister Graciela. 'We'll skirt the village. Can you go on a little farther before we rest?'

She looked at him and, as her answer turned and began to walk.

The unnecessary rudeness offended him, and he thought: *Thank heavens at Logroño I will be rid of her. Why in the name of God do I have mixed feelings about that?*

They skirted the village, walking along the edge of the forest, and soon they were on the path again, climbing upwards. It was getting more difficult to breathe, and the path grew steeper. As they rounded a bend, they came upon an empty eagle's nest. They skirted another mountain village, quiet and peaceful in the afternoon sun, and rested outside it, stopping at a mountain stream where they drank the icy water.

By dusk they had reached a rugged area that was famous for its caves. After that the trail would start downwards.

From now on, Ricardo thought, *it will be easy. The worst is over.*

He heard a faint buzzing sound overhead. He looked up,

searching for the source of it. An army plane appeared suddenly over the top of the mountain, flying towards them.

'Down!' Ricardo shouted. 'Down!'

Graciela kept walking. The plane circled and began to swoop lower.

'Get down!' Ricardo yelled again.

He jumped on her and pushed her down to the ground, his body on top of hers. What happened next took him completely by surprise. Without any warning, Graciela began yelling hysterically, fighting him. She was kicking him in the groin, clawing at his face, trying to rip at his eyes. But the most astonishing thing was what she was saying. She was screaming out a string of obscenities that sent Ricardo into shock, a verbal torrent of filth that assailed him. He could not believe that these words were coming from that beautiful, innocent mouth.

He tried to grab her hands to protect himself from her raking nails. She was like a wildcat under him.

'Stop it!' he shouted. 'I'm not going to hurt you. It's an army scout plane. They've seen us. We've got to get out of here.'

He held her down until her frantic struggling finally ceased. Strange, strangled sounds were coming from her, and he realized that she was sobbing. Ricardo, with all his experience with women, was completely baffled. He was straddled atop a hysterical nun who had the vocabulary of a truck driver, and he had no notion of what to do next.

He made his voice as calm and as reasonable as possible. 'Sister, we have to find a place to hide quickly. The plane will have reported us and in a few hours there'll be soldiers swarming all over the place. If you ever want to reach the convent, you'll get up and come with me.'

He waited a moment, then carefully raised himself off her and sat alongside her until the sobs subsided. Finally Graciela sat up. Her face was smudged from the dirt, her hair was tousled, her eyes were red from crying, and yet her beauty made Ricardo ache.

He said quietly, 'I'm sorry I frightened you. I don't seem

to know how to behave with you. I promise to try to be more careful in the future.'

She looked up at him with her luminous black eyes filled with tears, and Ricardo had no idea what she was thinking. He sighed and rose. She followed suit.

'There are dozens of caves around here,' Ricardo told her. 'We'll hide in one of them for the night. By dawn we can be on our way again.'

His face was raw and bleeding where she had clawed at him, but in spite of what had happened, he felt a defencelessness about her, a fragility that touched him, that made him want to say something to reassure her. But now he was the one who was silent.

He could not think of a single thing to say.

The Cuevas del Águila have been carved out by aeons of winds and floods and earthquakes, and they come in an infinite variety. Some of the caves are mere indentations in the mountain rocks, others are endless tunnels never explored by man.

A mile from where they had spotted the plane, Ricardo found a cave that was to his satisfaction. The low entrance was almost covered by underbrush.

'Stay here,' he said.

He ducked into the entrance and walked into the cave. It was dark inside, with only faint light spilling through the opening. There was no telling what the length of the cave was, but it did not matter, for there was no reason to explore it.

He went back outside to Graciela.

'It looks safe,' Ricardo said. 'Wait inside, please. I'll gather some branches to cover up the mouth of the cave. I'll be back in a few minutes.'

He watched Graciela as she went silently into the cave, and Ricardo wondered whether she would be there when he returned. He realized that he desperately wanted her to be.

*

Inside the cave, Graciela watched him leave. She sank to the cold ground in despair.

I can't stand any more, she thought. *Where are you, Jesus? Please release me from this hell.*

And it had been hell. From the beginning Graciela had been fighting the attraction she felt towards Ricardo. She thought of the Moor. *I'm afraid of myself. Of the evil in me. I want this man, and I must not.*

And so she had built a barrier of silence between them, the silence she had lived with in the convent. But now, without the discipline of the convent, without the Instrument and prayers, without the crutch of the rigid routine, Graciela found herself unable to banish her inner darkness. She had spent years fighting the satanic urges of her body, fighting the remembered sounds, the moans and sighs that came from her mother's bed.

The Moor was looking at her naked body.

You're just a child. Get your clothes on and get out of here . . .

I'm a woman.

She had spent so many years trying to forget the feel of the Moor inside her, trying to push out of her mind the rhythm of their bodies moving together, filling her, giving her a feeling of being alive at last.

Her mother screaming, *You bitch!*

And the doctor saying: *Our chief surgeon decided to sew you up himself. He said you were too beautiful to have scars.*

All the years of praying had been to purge herself of guilt. And they had failed.

The first time Graciela looked at Ricardo Mellado, the past had come flooding back. He was handsome and gentle and kind. When Graciela was a little girl, she had dreamed of someone like Ricardo. And when he was near her, when he touched her, her body was instantly aflame and she was filled with a deep shame. *I am the bride of Christ, and my thoughts are a betrayal of God. I belong to You, Jesus. Please help me now. Cleanse my mind of impure thoughts.*

Graciela had tried desperately to keep the wall of silence

between them, a wall that no one but God could penetrate, a wall to keep out the devil. But did she want to keep the devil out? When Ricardo had jumped on her and pushed her to the ground, it was the Moor making love to her, and the friar trying to rape her, and in her surging panic, it was them she was fighting off. *No*, she admitted to herself, *that's not the truth.* It was her own deep desire she was fighting. She was torn between her spirit and the cravings of her flesh. *I must not give in. I must get back to the convent. He'll be back any minute. What should I do?*

Graciela heard a low mewing from the back of the cave and quickly turned. There were four green eyes staring at her in the dark, moving towards her. Graciela's heart began to beat faster.

Two baby wolf cubs trotted up to her on soft, padded feet, rubbing their heads against her. She smiled and began to stroke them gently. There was a sudden rustle from the entrance of the cave. *Ricardo is back*, she thought.

The next instant, an enormous grey wolf was flying at her throat.

Chapter 27

Lucia Carmine paused outside the *taverna* in Aranda de Duero and took a deep breath. Through the window she could see Rubio Arzano seated inside, waiting for her.

I must not let him suspect, she thought. *At eight o'clock I'll have a new passport and be on my way to Switzerland.*

She forced a smile and entered the *taverna*. Rubio grinned in relief when he saw her, and as he rose, the look in his eyes gave Lucia a pang.

'I was very worried, *querida*. When you were gone for so long, I was afraid something terrible had happened to you.'

Lucia put her hand over his. 'Nothing happened.' *Except that I've bought my way to freedom. I'll be out of the country tomorrow.*

Rubio sat there looking into her eyes, holding her hand, and there was such an intense feeling of love coming from him that Lucia felt uneasy. *Doesn't he know it could never work? No. Because I haven't the courage to tell him. He's not in love with me. He's in love with the woman he thinks I am. He'll be much better off without me.*

She turned away and looked around the room for the first time. It was filled with locals. Most of them seemed to be staring at the two strangers.

One of the young men in the café started to sing and others joined in. A man walked over to the table where Lucia and Rubio were sitting.

'You're not singing, *señor*. Join us.'

Rubio shook his head. 'No.'

'What's the problem, *amigo*?'

'It's your song.' Rubio saw the puzzled expression on Lucia's face, and explained. 'It is one of the old songs praising Franco.'

Other men began to gather around the table. It was obvious that they had been drinking.

'You were against Franco, *señor*?'

Lucia saw Rubio's fists clench. *Oh, God, not now. He mustn't start anything that will attract attention.*

She said to him warningly, 'Rubio . . .'

And, thank God, he understood.

He looked up at the young men and said pleasantly, 'I have nothing against Franco. I just don't know the words.'

'Ah. Then we'll all hum the song together.'

They stood there waiting for Rubio to refuse.

Rubio glanced at Lucia. '*Bueno.*'

The men began to sing again, and Rubio hummed loudly. Lucia could feel the tension in him as he held himself under control. *He's doing this for me.*

When the song ended, a man slapped Rubio on the back. 'Not bad, old man. Not bad at all.'

Rubio sat there silently willing them to go away.

One of the men saw the package in Lucia's lap.

'What are you hiding there, *querida*?'

His companion said, 'I'll bet she's got something better than that up her skirt.'

The men laughed.

'Why don't you pull your panties down and show us what you've got there?'

Rubio sprang to his feet and grabbed one of the men by the throat. He punched him so hard that he flew across the room, breaking a table.

'No!' Lucia screamed. 'Don't!'

But it was too late. In an instant it became a free-for-all, with everybody eagerly joining in. A wine bottle shattered the glass behind the bar. Chairs and tables were knocked over as men went flying through the air, screaming curses. Rubio knocked down two men and a third ran towards him and hit him in the stomach. He gave a grunt of pain.

'Rubio! Let's get out of here!' Lucia screamed.

He nodded. He was clutching his stomach. They pushed their way through the mêlée and found themselves outside on the street.

'We've got to get away,' Lucia said.

You will have your passport tonight. Come back after eight o'clock.

She had to find a place to hide until then. *Damn him! Why couldn't he have controlled himself?*

They turned down Calle Santa Maria, and the noises of the fight behind them gradually diminished. Two streets away they came to a large church, the Iglesia Santa Maria. Lucia ran up the steps, opened the door and peered inside. The church was deserted.

'We'll be safe in here,' she said.

They walked into the dimness of the church. Rubio was still holding his stomach.

'We can rest for a while.'

'Yes.'

Rubio let his hand fall away from his stomach, and blood came gushing out.

Lucia felt sick. 'My God! What happened?'

'A knife,' Rubio whispered. 'He used a knife.' He slumped to the floor.

Lucia knelt at his side, panicky. 'Don't move.'

She removed his shirt and pressed it against his stomach, trying to stem the flow of blood. Rubio's face was chalk white.

'You shouldn't have fought them, you idiot,' Lucia said angrily.

His voice was a slurred whisper. 'I could not let them speak to you that way.'

I could not let them speak to you that way.

Lucia was touched as she had never been touched before. She stood there staring at him and thought: *How many times has this man risked his life for me?*

'I won't let you die,' she said fiercely. 'I'm not going to let you die.' She stood up abruptly. 'I'll be right back.'

She found water and towels in the priest's changing room in the rear of the church and she bathed Rubio's wound. His face was hot to the touch, and his body was soaked in perspiration. Lucia put cold towels on his forehead. Rubio's eyes were closed and he seemed to be asleep. Lucia cradled his head in her arms and talked to him. It did not matter what she said. She was talking to keep him alive, forcing him to hold on to the thin thread of his existence. She babbled on, afraid to stop for even a second.

'We'll work your farm together, Rubio. I want to meet your mother and sisters. Do you think they'll like me? I want them to, so much. And I'm a good worker, *caro*. You'll see. I've never worked on a farm, but I'll learn. We'll make it the best farm in all of Spain.'

She spent the afternoon talking to him, bathing his fevered body, changing the dressing. The bleeding had almost stopped.

'You see, *caro*? You're getting better. You're going to be well. I told you. You and I will have such a wonderful life together, Rubio. Only please don't die. Please!'

She found that she was weeping.

She watched the afternoon shadows paint the church walls through the stained-glass windows and slowly fade away. The setting sun dimmed the sky and finally it was dark. Lucia changed Rubio's bandage again, and so close that it startled her, the church bell began to ring. She held her breath and counted. One . . . three . . . five . . . seven . . . eight. Eight o'clock. It was calling her, telling her it was time to return to the *Casa de Empeños*. Time to escape from this nightmare and save herself.

She knelt down beside Rubio and felt his forehead again. He was burning with fever. His body was soaked with perspiration and his breathing was shallow and rasping. She could see no sign of bleeding, but that could mean that he was bleeding internally. *God damn it. Save yourself, Lucia.*

'Rubio . . . darling . . .'

He opened his eyes, only half conscious.

'I have to leave for a little while,' Lucia said.

He gripped her hand. 'Please . . .'

'It's all right,' she whispered. 'I'll be back.'

She rose and took a long last look at him. *I can't help him*, she thought.

Lucia picked up the gold cross and turned and hurried out the church door, her eyes filled with tears. She stumbled out on to the street and began to walk rapidly, heading towards the pawnshop. The man and his cousin would be there waiting for her with her passport to freedom. *In the morning when church services begin, they'll find Rubio and get him to a doctor. They'll treat him and he'll get well. Except that he will not live through the night*, Lucia thought. *Well, that's not my problem.*

The *Casa de Empeños* was just ahead. She was only a few minutes late. She could see that the lights were on in the shop. The men were waiting for her.

She began walking faster, then running. She crossed the street and burst through the open door.

Inside the police station, a uniformed officer was behind the desk. He looked up as Lucia appeared.

'I need you,' Lucia cried. 'A man has been stabbed. He may be dying.'

The policeman did not ask questions. He picked up a telephone and spoke into it. When he put the phone down, he said, 'Someone will be with you in a moment.'

Two detectives appeared almost immediately.

'Someone has been stabbed, *señorita*?'

'Yes. Please follow me. Hurry!'

'We'll pick up the doctor on the way,' one of the detectives said. 'Then you can take us to your friend.'

They picked up the doctor at his home and Lucia hurried the group to the church.

When they entered the church the doctor walked over to the still figure on the floor and knelt beside him.

A moment later he looked up. 'He's alive, but barely. I'll call for an ambulance.'

Lucia sank to her knees and said silently, *Thank you, God. I've done all I can. Now let me get away safely and I'll never bother you again.*

One of the detectives had been staring at Lucia all the way to the church. She looked so familiar. And then he suddenly realized why. She bore an uncanny resemblance to the picture in the Red, Top Priority Circulation from Interpol.

The detective whispered something to his companion and now they both turned to study her. The two of them walked over to Lucia.

'Excuse me, *señorita*. Would you be good enough to come back to the station with us? We have a few questions we wish to ask you.'

Chapter 28

Ricardo Mellado was a short distance away from the mountain cave when suddenly he saw a large grey wolf trotting towards the entrance. He froze for a single instant, then moved as he had never moved in his life. He raced towards the mouth of the cave, and burst through the entrance.

'Sister!'

In the dim light he saw the huge, grey shape leaping towards Graciela. Instinctively, he reached for his pistol and fired. The wolf let out a yelp of pain and turned towards Ricardo. He felt the sharp fangs of the wounded beast tearing at his clothing and smelled the animal's fetid breath. The wolf was stronger than he had expected, heavily muscled and powerful. Ricardo tried to fight free, but it was impossible.

He felt himself beginning to lose consciousness. He was only dimly aware of Graciela coming towards him and he called, 'Get away!'

He saw Graciela's hand raised above his head, and as it started to descend towards him, he glimpsed a huge rock in it and he thought: *She's going to kill me.*

An instant later the rock swept past him and smashed into the wolf's skull. There was a last savage gasp and the animal lay still on the ground. Ricardo was huddled on the floor, fighting for breath. Graciela knelt at his side.

'Are you all right?' Her voice was trembling with concern.

He managed to nod. He heard a whimpering sound behind him and turned to see the cubs huddled in a corner.

He lay there, gathering his strength. Then he rose with difficulty.

They staggered out into the clean mountain air, shaken. Ricardo stood there, taking deep, lung-filling breaths until his head cleared. The physical and emotional shock of their close brush with death had taken a severe toll on both of them.

'Let's get away from this place. They may come looking for us here.'

Graciela shuddered at the reminder of how much danger they were still in.

They travelled along the steep mountain path for the next hour, and when they finally reached a small stream, Ricardo said, 'Let's stop here.'

With no bandages or antiseptic, they cleaned the scratches as best they could, bathing them in the clean, cold spring water. Ricardo's arm was so stiff that he had trouble moving it. To his surprise, Graciela said, 'Let me do it.'

He was even more surprised by the gentleness with which she did the task.

Without warning, Graciela began trembling violently in an aftermath of shock.

'It's all right,' Ricardo said. 'It's all over.'

She could not stop shaking.

Ricardo took her in his arms and said soothingly, 'Ssh. It's dead. There's nothing more to fear.'

He was holding her closely, and he could feel her thighs pressing against his body and her soft lips were on his and she was holding him close, whispering things he could not understand.

It was as though he had known Graciela always. And yet he knew nothing about her. *Except that she's God's miracle*, he thought.

Graciela was also thinking of God. *Thank you, God, for this joy. Thank you for finally letting me feel what love is.*

It had been an experience for which she had no words, beyond anything she had ever imagined.

Ricardo was watching her, and her beauty still took his breath away. *She belongs to me now*, Ricardo thought. *She doesn't have to go back to a convent. We'll get married and have beautiful children – strong sons.*

'I love you,' he said. 'I'll never let you go, Graciela.'

'Ricardo –'

'Darling, I want to marry you. Will you marry me?'

And without even thinking, Graciela said, 'Yes. Oh, yes.'

And she was in his arms again, and she thought: *This is what I wanted and thought I would never have.*

Ricardo was saying, 'We'll live in France for a while, where we'll be safe. This fight will be over soon, and we'll return to Spain.'

She knew that she would go anywhere with this man, and that if there was danger, she wanted to share it with him.

They talked of so many things. Ricardo told her how he had first become involved with Jaime Miró, and of the broken engagement and of his father's displeasure. But when Ricardo waited for Graciela to speak about her past, she was silent.

She looked at him and thought: *I can't tell him. He'll hate me.* 'Hold me,' Graciela begged.

They slept and woke up at dawn to watch the sun creeping over the ridge of the mountain, bathing the hills in a warm red glow.

Ricardo said, 'We'll be safer hiding out here today. We'll start travelling when it gets dark.'

They ate from the sack of food that the gypsies had given them, and planned their future.

'There are wonderful opportunities here in Spain,' Ricardo said. 'Or there will be when we have peace. I have dozens of ideas. We'll own our own business. We'll buy a beautiful home and raise handsome sons.'

'And beautiful daughters.'

'And beautiful daughters.' He smiled. 'I never knew I could be so happy.'

'Nor I, Ricardo.'

'We'll be in Logroño in two days and meet the others,' Ricardo said. He took her hand. 'We'll tell them you won't be returning to the convent.'

'I wonder if they'll understand.' Then she laughed. 'I don't really care. God understands. I loved my life in the convent,' she said softly, 'but –' She leaned over and kissed him.

Ricardo said, 'I have so much to make up to you.'

She was puzzled. 'I don't understand.'

'Those years you were in the convent, shut away from the world. Tell me, darling – does it bother you that you've lost all those years?'

How could she make him see? 'Ricardo – I didn't lose anything. Have I really missed so much?'

He thought about it, not knowing where to begin. He realized that events he thought of as important would not really have mattered to the nuns in their isolation. Wars, like the Arab–Israeli War? Assassinations of political leaders such as the American President John Kennedy and his brother Robert Kennedy? And of Martin Luther King, Jr., the great black leader of the non-violence movement for black equality? The Berlin Wall? Famines? Floods? Earthquakes? Strikes and demonstrations protesting at man's inhumanity to man?

In the end, how deeply would any of these things have affected her personal life? Or the personal lives of the majority of people on this earth?

Finally, Ricardo said, 'In one sense, you haven't missed much. But in another sense, yes. Something important has been going on. Life. While you were shut away all those years, babies have been born and have grown up; lovers have married; people have suffered and been happy; people have died, and all of us out here were a part of that, a part of the living.'

'And you think I never was?' Graciela asked. And the words came tumbling out before she could stop them. 'I was once a part of that life you are talking about, and it was a living hell. My mother was a whore, and every night I had a different uncle. When I was fourteen years old I gave my body to a man because I was attracted to him and jealous of my mother and what she was doing.' The words were coming in a torrent now. 'I would have become a whore, too, if I had stayed there to be part of the life you think is so precious. No, I don't believe I ran away from anything. I ran *to* something. I found a safe world that is peaceful and good.'

Ricardo was staring at her, horrified. 'I – I'm sorry,' he said. 'I didn't mean to –'

She was sobbing now, and he took her in his arms and said, 'Sh! It's all right. That's over. You were a child. I love you.'

And it was as though Ricardo had given her absolution. She had told him about the awful things she had done in the past, and still he forgave her. And – wonder of wonders – loved her.

He held her very close. 'There is a poem by Federico García Lorca:

> The night does not wish to come
> so that you cannot come
> and I cannot go.
> But you will come
> with your tongue burned by the salt rain.
> The day does not wish to come
> so that you cannot come
> and I cannot come
> and I cannot go.
> But I will come
> through the muddy waters of darkness.
> Neither night nor day wishes to come
> so that I may die for you and you die
> for me.'

And suddenly she thought of the soldiers who were hunting them and she wondered if she and her beloved Ricardo were going to live long enough to have a future together.

Chapter 29

There was a link missing, a clue to the past, and Alan Tucker was determined to find it. There had been no mention in the newspaper of a baby being abandoned, but it should be easy enough to find out the date it was brought to the orphanage. If the date coincided with the time of the plane crash, Ellen Scott would have some interesting explaining to do. *She couldn't be that stupid*, Alan Tucker thought. *To risk pretending that the Scott heiress was dead, and then leave her on the doorstep of a farmhouse. Risky. Very risky. On the other hand, look at the reward: Scott Industries. Yes, she could have pulled it off. If it is a skeleton in her closet, it's a live one, and it's going to cost her plenty.*

Tucker knew that he had to be very careful. He had no illusion about whom he was dealing with. He was confronting raw power. He knew he had to have all the evidence in hand before he made his move.

His first stop was to return to Father Berrendo.

'Father – I would like to speak to the farmer and his wife, where Patricia – Megan was dropped off.'

The old priest smiled. 'I hope your conversation with them will not take place for a long time.'

Tucker stared at him. 'You mean –?'

'They died many years ago.'

Damn. But there had to be other avenues to explore. 'You said the baby was taken to a hospital with pneumonia?'

'Yes.'

There would be records there. 'Which hospital was it?'

'It burned down in nineteen sixty-one. There is a new

hospital now.' He saw the look of dismay on his visitor's face. 'You must remember, *señor*, that the information you are seeking goes back twenty-eight years. Many things have changed.'

Nothing's going to stop me, Alan Tucker thought. *Not when I've come this close. There must be a file on her somewhere.*

There was still one place left to investigate. The orphanage.

He was reporting daily now to Ellen Scott.

'Keep me informed of every development. I want to know the moment the girl is found.'

And Alan Tucker wondered about the urgency in her voice.

She seems in an awful big rush over something that happened all those years ago. Why? Well, that can wait. First I have to get the proof I'm looking for.

That morning Alan Tucker visited the orphanage. He looked around the dreary community room where a noisy, chattering group of children were playing, and he thought: *This is where the heiress to the Scott dynasty grew up, while that bitch in New York kept all the money and all the power. Well, she's going to share some of that with yours truly. Yes, sir, we'll make a great team, Ellen Scott and me.*

A young woman came up to him and said, 'May I help you, *señor*?'

He smiled. *Yeah. You can help me to about a billion dollars*. 'I'd like to talk to whoever's in charge here.'

'That would be Señora Angeles.'

'Is she here?'

'*Sí, señor*. I will take you to her.'

He followed the woman through the main hall to a small office at the rear of the building.

'Go in, please.'

Alan Tucker entered the office. The woman seated at the desk was in her eighties. She had once been a very large woman, but her frame had shrunk, so she looked as though her body had at one time belonged to someone else. Her hair was grey and thin, but her eyes were bright and clear.

'Good morning, *señor*. May I help you? You have come to adopt one of our lovely children? We have so many delightful ones to choose from.'

'No, *señora*. I have come to inquire about a child who was left here many years ago.'

Mercedes Angeles frowned. 'I do not understand.'

'A baby girl was brought in here –' He pretended to consult a piece of paper – 'in October of nineteen forty-eight.'

'That is so long ago. She would not be here now. You see, we have a rule, *señor*, that at the age of fifteen –'

'No, *señora*. I know she's not here. What I wish to know is the exact date she was brought here.'

'I'm afraid I cannot help you, *señor*.'

His heart sank.

'You see, so many children are brought in here. Unless you know her name –'

Patricia Scott, he thought. Aloud, he said, 'Megan. Her name is Megan.'

Mercedes Angeles' face lit up. 'No one could forget that child. She was a devil, and everyone adored her. Do you know that one day she –'

Alan Tucker had no time for anecdotes. His instincts told him how close he was to getting hold of a piece of the Scott fortune. And this gabby old woman was the key to it. *I must be patient with her.* 'Señora Angeles – I don't have much time. Would you have that date in your files?'

'Of course, *señor*. We are commanded by the state to keep very accurate records.'

Tucker's heart lifted. *I should have brought a camera to take a picture of the file. Never mind. I'll have it photocopied.* 'Could I see that file, *señora*?'

She frowned. 'I don't know. Our records are confidential and –'

'Of course,' Tucker said smoothly, 'and I certainly respect that. You said you were fond of little Megan, and I know you'd want to do anything you could to help her. Well, that's why I'm here. I have some good news for her.'

'And for this you need the date she was brought in here?'

He said glibly, 'That's just so I'll have the proof that she's the person I think she is. Her father died and left her a small inheritance, and I want to make sure she gets it.'

The woman nodded wisely. 'I see.'

Tucker pulled a roll of bills from his pocket. 'And to show my appreciation for the trouble I've put you to, I'd like to contribute a hundred dollars to your orphanage.'

She was looking at the roll of bills, an uncertain expression on her face.

He peeled off another bill. 'Two hundred.'

She frowned.

'All right. Five hundred.'

Mercedes Angeles beamed. 'That is very generous of you, *señor*. I will go and get the file.'

I've done it, he thought jubilantly. *Jesus Christ, I've done it! She stole Scott Industries for herself. If it hadn't been for me, she would have gotten away with it.*

When he confronted Ellen Scott with his evidence there was no way she could deny it. The plane crash happened on 1 October. Megan was in the hospital for ten days. So she would have been brought into the orphanage around 11 October.

Mercedes Angeles returned to the office, holding a file in her hands. 'I found it,' she said proudly.

It was all Alan Tucker could do to keep from grabbing it out of her hands. 'May I look at it?' he asked politely.

'Certainly. You have been so generous.' She frowned. 'I hope you will not mention this to anyone. I should not be doing this at all.'

'It will be our secret, *señora*.'

She handed him the file.

He took a deep breath and opened it. At the top it said: 'Megan. Baby Girl. Parents unknown.' And then the date. But there was some mistake.

'It says here that Megan was brought in here on 14 June 1948.'

'*Sí, señor.*'

'That's impossible!' He was almost screaming. *The plane crash happened on 1 October.*

There was a puzzled expression on her face. 'Impossible, *señor*? I do not understand.'

'Who – who keeps these records?'

'I do. When a child is left here, I put down the date and whatever information is given to me.'

His dream was collapsing. 'Couldn't you have made a mistake? About the date, I mean – couldn't it have been October the eleventh?'

'*Señor*,' she said indignantly. 'I know the difference between June the fourteenth and October the eleventh.'

It was over. He had built a dream on too flimsy a foundation. So Patricia Scott had really died in the plane crash. It was a coincidence that Ellen Scott was searching for a girl who had been born around the same time.

Alan Tucker rose heavily and said, 'Thank you, *señora*.'

'*De nada, señor.*'

She watched him leave. He was such a nice man. And so generous. His five hundred dollars would buy many things for the orphanage. So would the hundred thousand dollar cheque sent by the kind lady who had telephoned from New York. *October the eleventh was certainly a lucky day for our orphanage. Thank you, Lord.*

Alan Tucker was reporting.

'Still no hard news, Mrs Scott. They're rumoured to be heading north. As far as I know, the girl is safe.'

The tone of his voice has completely changed, Ellen Scott thought. *The threat is gone. So he's visited the orphanage.*

He's back to being an employee. Well, after he finds Patricia, that will change, too.

'Report in tomorrow.'

'Yes, Mrs Scott.'

Chapter 30

'Preserve me, Oh God, for in Thee I take refuge. Thou art my Lord; I have no good apart from Thee. I love Thee, O Lord, my strength. The Lord is my rock and my fortress and my deliverer . . .'

Sister Megan glanced up to see Felix Carpio watching her, a concerned expression on his face.

She's really frightened, he thought.

Ever since they had started on their journey, he had seen Sister Megan's deep anxiety. *Of course. It's only natural. She's been locked up in a convent for God only knows how many years, and now she's suddenly thrown out into a strange, terrifying world. We'll have to be very gentle with the poor girl.*

Sister Megan was indeed frightened. She had been praying hard ever since leaving the convent.

Forgive me, Lord, for I love the excitement of what is happening to me, and I know that is wicked of me.

But no matter how hard Sister Megan prayed, she could not help thinking. *I don't remember when I've had such a good time.* It was the most amazing adventure she had ever had. In the orphanage she had often planned daring escapes, but that was child's play. This was the real thing. She was in the hands of terrorists, and they were being pursued by the police and the army. But instead of being terrified, Sister Megan felt strangely exhilarated.

After travelling all night they stopped at dawn. Megan and Amparo Jiron stood by as Jaime Miró and Felix Carpio huddled over a map.

'It's four miles to Medina del Campo,' Jaime said. 'Let's avoid it. There's a permanent army garrison stationed there. We'll keep heading north-east to Valladolid. We should reach it by early afternoon.'

Easily, Sister Megan thought happily.

It had been a long and gruelling night without rest, but Megan felt wonderful. Jaime was deliberately pushing the group, but Megan understood what he was doing. He was testing her, waiting for her to crack. *Well, he's in for a surprise*, she thought.

As a matter of fact, Jaime Miró found himself intrigued by Sister Megan. Her behaviour was not at all what he would have expected of a nun. She was miles away from her convent, travelling through strange territory, being hunted, and she seemed to be actually enjoying it. *What kind of nun is she?* Jaime Miró wondered.

Amparo Jiron was less impressed. *I'll be glad to be rid of her*, she thought. She stayed close to Jaime, letting the nun walk with Felix Carpio.

The countryside was wild and beautiful, caressed by the soft fragrance of the summer wind. They passed old villages, some of them deserted and forlorn, and saw an ancient abandoned castle high on a hill.

Amparo seemed to Megan like a wild animal – gliding effortlessly over hills and valleys, never seeming to tire.

When finally hours later Valladolid loomed up in the distance, Jaime called a halt.

Jaime turned to Felix. 'Everything is arranged?'

'Yes.'

Megan wondered exactly what had been arranged. She found out very quickly.

'Tomas is instructed to contact us at the bullring.'

'What time does the bank close?'

'Five o'clock. There will be plenty of time.'

Jaime nodded. 'And today there should be a fat payroll.'

Good Lord, they're going to rob a bank, Megan thought.

It was a little more excitement than she had bargained for.

'What about a car?' Amparo was asking.

'No problem,' Jaime assured her.

They're going to steal one, Megan thought. *God isn't going to like this.*

When the group reached the outskirts of Valladolid, Jaime warned, 'Stay with the crowds. Today is bullfight day and there will be thousands of people. Let's not get separated.'

Jaime Miró had been right about the crowds. Megan had never seen so many people. The streets were swarming with pedestrians and cars and motorcycles, for the bullfight had drawn not only tourists, but citizens from all the neighbouring towns. Even the children on the street were playing at bullfighting.

Megan was fascinated by the crowds and the noise and the bustle around her. She looked into the faces of passers-by and wondered what their lives were like. *Soon enough I'll be back in the convent where I won't be allowed to look at anyone's face again. I might as well take advantage of this while I can.*

The pavements were filled with vendors displaying trinkets, religious medals and crosses, and everywhere was the pungent smell of fritters frying in boiling oil.

Megan suddenly realized how hungry she was.

It was Felix who said, 'Jaime, we're all hungry. Let's try some of those fritters.'

Felix bought four of them and handed one to Megan. 'Try this, Sister. You'll like it.'

It was delicious. For so many of her years, food was not meant to be enjoyed, but to sustain the body for the glory of the Lord. *This one's for me*, Megan thought irreverently.

'The arena is this way,' Jaime said.

They followed the crowds past the park in the middle of town to the Plaza Poinente, which flowed into the Plaza de Toros. The arena itself was inside an enormous adobe structure, three storeys high. There were four ticket windows at the entrance. Signs on the left said, '*Sol*', and on the right,

'*Sombra*'. Sun or shade. There were hundreds of people standing in queues waiting to purchase tickets.

'Wait here,' Jaime ordered.

They watched him as he walked over to where half a dozen touts were hawking tickets.

Megan turned to Felix. 'Are we going to watch a bullfight?'

'Yes, but don't worry, Sister,' Felix reassured her. 'You will find it exciting.'

Worry? Megan was thrilled by the idea. At the orphanage, one of her fantasies had been that her father had been a great torero, and Megan had read every book on bullfighting that she could get her hands on.

Felix was saying, 'The real bullfights are held in Madrid and Barcelona. The bullfight here will be by *novilleros*, instead of professionals. They are amateurs. They have not been granted the *alternativa*.

Megan knew that the *alternativa* was the accolade given only to the top-ranked matadors.

'The ones we will see today fight in rented costumes instead of the gold-encrusted suit of lights, against bulls with filed, dangerous horns that the professionals refuse to fight.'

'Why do they do it?'

Felix Carpio shrugged. '*Mas cornadas da el hambre*. Hunger is more painful than horns.'

Jaime returned, holding four tickets. 'We're all set,' Jaime said. 'Let's go in.'

Megan felt a growing sense of excitement.

As they approached the entrance to the huge arena, they passed a poster plastered to the wall. Megan stopped and stared at it.

'Look!'

There was a picture of Jaime Miró, and under it:

WANTED FOR MURDER
JAIME MIRÓ
ONE MILLION PESETAS REWARD
FOR HIS CAPTURE
DEAD OR ALIVE

And suddenly it brought back to Megan the sober realization of the kind of man she was travelling with, the terrorist who held her life in his hands.

Jaime was studying the picture. 'Not a bad likeness.' He ripped off the poster, folded it and put it in his pocket.

What good will that do? Amparo wondered. *They must have posted hundreds of them.*

Jaime grinned. 'This particular one is going to bring us a fortune, *querida*.'

What a strange remark, Megan thought. She could not help admiring his coolness. There was an air of solid competence about Jaime Miró that Megan found reassuring. *The soldiers will never catch him*, she thought.

'Let's go inside.'

There were twelve widely spaced entrances to the building. The red iron doors had been flung open, each one numbered. Inside the entrance there were *puestos* selling cola and beer, and next to them small toilet cubicles. In the stands, each section and seat were numbered. The tiers of stone benches made a complete circle, and in the centre was the large arena covered with sand. There were commercial signs everywhere: BANCO CENTRAL . . . BOUTIQUE CALZADOS . . . SCHWEPPES . . . RADIO POPULAR . . .

Jaime had purchased tickets on the shady side and as they sat down on the stone benches, Megan looked around in wonder. It was not at all as she had imagined it. When she was a young girl, she had seen romantic colour photographs of the bullring in Madrid, huge and elaborate. This was a makeshift ring. The *tribunas* were rapidly filling up with spectators.

A trumpet sounded. The bullfight began.

Megan leaned forward in her seat, her eyes wide. A huge bull charged into the ring and a matador stepped out from behind a small wooden barrier at the side of the ring and began teasing the animal.

'The picadors will be next,' Megan said excitedly.

Jaime Miró looked at her in wonder. He had been concerned that the bullfight would make her ill and that she would attract attention to them. Instead, she seemed to be having a wonderful time. *Strange*.

A picador was approaching the bull, riding a horse covered with a heavy blanket. The bull lowered its head and charged at the horse, and as it buried its horns in the blanket, the picador drove an eight foot *pica* into the bull's shoulder.

Megan was watching, fascinated. 'He's doing that to weaken the bull's neck muscles,' she explained, remembering the well-loved books she had read all those years ago.

Felix Carpio blinked in surprise. 'That's right, Sister.'

Megan watched as the pairs of colourfully decorated *banderillas* were slammed into the bull's shoulders.

Now it was the matador's turn. He stepped into the ring holding at his side a red cape with a sword inside it. The bull turned and began to charge.

Megan was getting more excited. 'He will make his passes now,' she said. 'First the *pase verónica*, then the *media verónica*, and last the *rebolera*.'

Jaime could contain his curiosity no longer. 'Sister – where did you learn all this?'

Without thinking, Megan said, 'My father was a bullfighter. Watch!'

The action was so swift that Megan could barely follow it. The maddened bull kept charging at the matador, and each time he neared him, the matador swung his red cape to the side and the bull followed the cape. Megan was concerned.

'What happens if the bullfighter gets hurt?'

Jaime shrugged. 'In a place like this, the town barber will take him over to the barn and sew him up.'

The bull charged again, and this time the matador leapt out of the way. The crowd booed.

Felix Carpio said apologetically, 'I am sorry this is not a better fight, Sister. You should see the great ones. I have seen Manolete and el Cordobés and Ordonez. They made bullfighting a spectacle never to be forgotten.'

'I have read about them,' Megan said.

Felix asked, 'Have you ever heard the wonderful story about Manolete?'

'Which story?'

'At one time, the story goes, Manolete was just another bullfighter, no better and no worse than a hundred others. He was engaged to a beautiful young girl, but one day when Manolete was in the ring a bull gored him in the groin and the doctor patched him up and told him that he would no longer be able to have children. Manolete loved his fiancée so much that he didn't tell her, because he was afraid she wouldn't marry him. They married and a few months later she proudly told Manolete that she was going to have a baby. Well, of course he knew that it wasn't his baby, and he left her. The heartbroken girl killed herself. Manolete reacted like a madman. He had no more desire to live, so he went into the bullring and did things that no matador had ever done before. He kept risking his life, hoping to be killed, and he became the greatest matador in the world. Two years later he fell in love again and married the young lady. A few months after the wedding she came to him and proudly announced that she was going to have his baby. And that's when Manolete discovered that the doctor had been wrong.'

Megan said, 'How awful.'

Jaime laughed aloud. 'That's an interesting story. I wonder if there is any truth to it.'

'I would like to think so,' Felix said.

Amparo was listening, her face impassive. She had watched Jaime's growing interest in the nun with resentment. *The sister had better watch her step.*

Aproned food vendors were moving up and down the aisles calling out their wares. One of them approached the row where Jaime and the others were seated.

'*Empanadas*,' he called out. '*Empanadas calientes*.'

Jaime raised a hand. '*Aquí*.'

The vendor skilfully tossed a wrapped package across the crowd into Jaime's hands. Jaime handed ten pesetas to the man next to him to be passed to the vendor. Megan watched as Jaime lowered the wrapped *empanada* to his lap and carefully opened it. Inside the wrapping was a piece of paper. Jaime read it, then read it again, and Megan saw his jaw tighten.

Jaime slipped the paper into his pocket. 'We're leaving,' he said curtly. 'One at a time.' He turned to Amparo. 'You first. We'll meet at the gate.'

Wordlessly, Amparo got up and made her way across to the aisle.

Jaime nodded to Felix, and Felix rose and followed Amparo.

'What is happening?' Megan asked. 'Is something wrong?'

'We're leaving for Logroño.' He rose. 'Watch me, Sister. If I'm not stopped, go to the gate.'

Megan watched, tense, as Jaime made his way to the aisle and started towards the exit. No one seemed to pay any attention to him. When Jaime had disappeared from sight, Megan rose and started to leave. There was a roar from the crowd and she turned to look back at the bullring. A young matador was lying on the ground being gored by the savage bull. Blood was pouring on to the sand. Megan closed her eyes and offered up a silent prayer: *Oh, blessed Jesus, have mercy on this man. He shall not die, but he shall live. The Lord has chastened him sorely, but he has not given him over to death. Amen.* She opened her eyes, turned and hurried out.

Jaime, Amparo and Felix were waiting for her at the entrance.

'Let's move,' Jaime said.

They started walking.

'What's wrong?' Felix asked Jaime.

'The soldiers shot Tomas,' Jaime said tersely. 'He's dead. And the police have Rubio. He was stabbed in a bar fight.'

Megan crossed herself. 'What's happened to Sister Teresa and Sister Lucia?' she asked anxiously.

'I don't know.' Jaime turned to the others. 'We must hurry.' He looked at his watch. 'The bank should be busy.'

'Jaime, maybe we should wait,' Felix suggested. 'It's going to be dangerous for just the two of us to hold up the bank now.'

Megan listened to what he was saying and thought: *That won't stop him.* She was right.

The three of them were headed for the huge car-park behind the arena. When Megan caught up with them, Felix was examining a blue Seat sedan.

'This should do,' Felix said.

He fumbled with the lock on the door for a moment, opened it and put his head inside. He crouched down under the wheel, and a moment later the engine started.

'Get in,' Jaime told them.

Megan stood there, uncertainly. 'You're stealing a car?'

'For Christ's sake,' Amparo hissed. 'Stop acting like a nun and get into the car.'

The two men were in the front seat, with Jaime at the wheel. Amparo scrambled into the back.

'Are you coming or not?' Jaime demanded.

Megan took a deep breath and got into the car next to Amparo. They started off. Megan closed her eyes. *Dear Lord, where are You leading me?*

'If it makes you feel any better, Sister,' Jaime said, 'we're not stealing this car. We're confiscating it in the name of the Basque army.'

Megan started to say something, then stopped. There was nothing she could say that would make him change his mind. She sat there in silence as Jaime drove towards the centre of town.

He's going to rob a bank, Megan thought, *and in the eyes of God, I'll be as guilty as he is.* She crossed herself and began silently to pray.

The Banco de Bilbao is on the ground floor of a nine-storey apartment building on the Calle de Cervantes at the Plaza de Circular.

When the car pulled up in front of the building, Jaime said

to Felix, 'Keep the engine running. If there's any trouble, take off and meet the others in Logroño.'

Felix stared at him in surprise. 'What are you talking about? You're not going in there *alone*? You can't. The odds are too great, Jaime. It's too dangerous.'

Jaime slapped him on the shoulder. 'If they get hurt, they get hurt,' he said with a grin. He stepped out of the car.

They watched as Jaime walked into a leather goods shop next door to the bank. A few minutes later he emerged carrying an attache case. He nodded to the group in the car and entered the bank.

Megan could hardly breathe. She began to pray:

Prayer is a calling.
Prayer is a listening.
Prayer is a dwelling.
Prayer is a presence.
Prayer is a lamp
aflame with Jesus.
I am calm and filled with peace.

She was not calm and filled with peace.

Jaime Miró walked through two sets of doors that led to the marble lobby of the bank. Inside the entrance, mounted high on the wall, he noted a security camera. He gave it a casual glance, then looked the room over. Behind the counters a staircase led to a second floor, where bank officers were working at desks. It was near closing time and the bank was filled with customers eager to finish transacting their business. There were queues of people in front of the three tellers' cages, and Jaime noticed that several of the customers were carrying packages.

Jaime stepped into a queue and patiently waited his turn.

When he reached the teller's cage, he smiled pleasantly and said, '*Buenas tardes*.'

'*Buenas tardes, señor*. What can we do for you today?'

Jaime leaned against the window and pulled out the folded

wanted poster. He handed it to the teller. 'Would you take a look at this, please?'

The teller smiled. 'Certainly, *señor*.'

He unfolded it, and as he saw what it was, his eyes widened. He looked up at Jaime, and panic was in his eyes.

'It's a nice likeness, isn't it?' Jaime said softly. 'As you can tell from that, I have killed many people, so one more really won't make a difference to me. Do I make myself understood?'

'P-perfectly, *señor*. P-perfectly. I have a family. I beg of you –'

'I respect families, so I will tell you what I want you to do to save your children's father.' Jaime pushed the attaché case towards the teller. 'I want you to fill this for me. I want you to do it quickly and quietly. If you truly believe that the money is more important than your life, then go ahead and raise the alarm.'

The teller shook his head. 'No, no, no.'

He began to pull money out of the cash drawer and stuff it into the attaché case. His hands were trembling.

When the attaché case was full, the cashier said, 'There you are, *señor*. I – I promise you I won't raise any alarm.'

'That's very wise of you,' Jaime said. 'I'll tell you why, *amigo*.' He turned around and pointed to a middle-aged woman standing near the end of the line, carrying a package wrapped in brown paper. 'Do you see that woman? She is one of us. There is a bomb in that package. If the alarm should sound, she will set off the bomb instantly.'

The cashier turned even paler. 'No, please!'

'You will wait until ten minutes after she leaves the bank before you make a move,' Jaime warned.

'On my children's life,' the teller whispered.

'*Buenas tardes*.'

Jaime took the attaché case and moved towards the door. He felt the cashier's eyes riveted on him.

Jaime stopped at the side of the woman with the package.

'I must compliment you,' Jaime said. 'That is a most becoming dress you are wearing.'

She blushed. 'Why thank you, *señor – gracias.*'

'*De nada.*'

Jaime turned to nod to the cashier, then strolled out of the bank. It would be at least fifteen minutes before the woman finished her business and left. By that time, he and the others would be long gone.

As Jaime came out of the bank and walked towards the car, Megan almost fainted with relief.

Felix Carpio grinned. 'The bastard got away with it.' He turned to Megan. 'I beg your pardon, Sister.'

Megan had never been so glad to see anyone in her life. *He did it*, she thought. *And all by himself. Wait until I tell the sisters what happened.* And then she remembered. She could never tell this to anyone. When she went back to the convent, there would be only silence for the rest of her life. It gave her an odd feeling.

Jaime said to Felix, 'Move over, *amigo*. I'll drive.' He tossed the briefcase into the back seat.

'Everything went well?' Amparo asked.

Jaime laughed. 'Couldn't have gone better. I must remember to thank Colonel Acoca for his calling card.'

The car started down the street. At the first corner, Calle de Tudela, Jaime made a left turn. Suddenly, appearing out of nowhere, a policeman moved in front of the car and held out a hand signalling him to stop. Jaime stepped on the brake. Megan's heart began to pound.

The policeman walked over to the car.

Jaime asked calmly, 'What's the problem, officer?'

'The problem, *señor*, is that you are driving the wrong way down a one-way street. Unless you can prove you are legally blind, you are in trouble.' He pointed to the sign at the entrance. 'The street is clearly marked. Motorists are expected to respect a sign like that. That is the reason it has been placed there.'

Jaime said apologetically, 'A thousand pardons. My friends and I were in such a serious discussion that I did not see the sign.'

The policeman was leaning into the driver's window. He was studying Jaime, a puzzled expression on his face.

'You will be so good as to let me see your registration, please.'

'Of course,' Jaime said.

He reached down for the revolver which was under his jacket. Felix was ready to spring into action. Megan held her breath.

Jaime pretended to be searching his pockets. 'I know I have it here somewhere.'

At that moment from across the Plaza came a loud scream and the policeman turned to look. A man on the street corner was beating a woman, hitting her about the head and shoulders with his fists.

'Help!' she cried. 'Help me! He's killing me!'

The policeman hesitated for only an instant. 'Wait here,' he commanded.

He raced back down the street towards the man and woman.

Jaime put the car into gear and slammed down on the accelerator. The car shot down the one-way street, scattering traffic headed towards them, horns angrily blaring at them. When they reached the corner, Jaime made another turn towards the bridge that led out of town on the Avenida Sanchez Arjona.

Megan looked at Jaime and crossed herself. She could hardly breathe.

'Would you – would you have killed the policeman if that man had not attacked the woman?'

Jaime did not bother to answer.

'The woman wasn't being attacked, Sister,' Felix explained. 'Those were our people. We are not alone. We have many friends.'

Jaime's face was grim. 'We're going to have to get rid of this car.'

They were leaving the outskirts of Valladolid. Jaime turned on to N620, the highway to Burgos, on the way to Logroño. He was careful to stay within the speed limit.

'We'll get rid of the car as soon as we get past Burgos,' he announced.

I can't believe this is happening to me, Megan thought. *I escaped from the convent, I'm running away from the army, and I'm travelling in a stolen car with terrorists who have just robbed a bank. Lord, what else do You have in mind for me?*

Chapter 31

Colonel Ramón Acoca and half a dozen members of the GOE were in the middle of a strategy meeting. They were studying a large map of the countryside.

The scarred giant said, 'It's obvious that Miró is heading north towards Basque country.'

'That could mean Burgos, Vitoria, Logroño, Pamplona or San Sebastian.'

San Sebastian, Acoca thought. *But I've got to catch him before he reaches there.*

He could hear the voice on the phone: *You're running out of time.*

He could not afford to fail.

They were driving through the rolling hills that heralded the approach to Burgos.

Jaime was quiet behind the wheel. When he finally spoke, he said, 'Felix, when we get to San Sebastian, I want to make arrangements to get Rubio away from the police.'

Felix nodded. 'It will be a pleasure. It will drive them crazy.'

Megan said, 'What about Sister Lucia?'

'What?'

'Didn't you say that she had been captured, too?'

Jaime said wryly, 'Yes, but your Sister Lucia turned out to be a criminal wanted by the police for murder.'

The news shook Megan. She remembered how Lucia had

taken charge and had persuaded them to hide in the hills. She liked Sister Lucia.

She said stubbornly, 'Since you're going to rescue Rubio, you should save them both.'

What the devil kind of nun is this? Jaime wondered.

But she was right. Smuggling Rubio and Lucia out from under the noses of the police would be wonderful propaganda and would make headlines.

Amparo had sunk into a sullen silence.

Suddenly, in the distance, on the road ahead of them were three army trucks filled with soldiers.

'We'd better get off this road,' Jaime decided.

At the next intersection he turned on to Highway N120 and headed east.

'Santo Domingo de la Calzada is up ahead. There's an old deserted castle there. We can spend the night in it.'

They could see its outline from the distance, high on a hill. Jaime took a side road, avoiding the town, and the castle loomed larger and larger as they approached it. A few hundred yards from it was a lake.

Jaime stopped the car. 'Everybody out, please.'

When they were all out of the car, Jaime pointed the steering wheel down the hill towards the lake, jammed the accelerator down, released the handbrake and jumped clear. They stood there watching as the car disappeared into the water.

Megan was about to ask him how they were going to get to Logroño. She stopped herself. *Foolish question. He will steal another car, of course.*

The group turned to examine the abandoned castle. There was a huge stone wall circling it, with crumbling turrets on each corner.

'In the old days,' Felix told Megan, 'princes used these castles as prisons for their enemies.'

And Jaime is an enemy of the state, and if he is caught, there will be no prison for him. Only death, Megan thought. *He has no fear.* She remembered his words:

I have faith in what I'm fighting for. I have faith in my men, and in my guns.

They walked up the stone steps that led to the front gate. The gates were iron and had rusted away so badly that they were able to push them open and squeeze through into a courtyard paved in stone.

The inside of the castle seemed enormous to Megan. There were narrow passageways and rooms everywhere, and facing the outside were gun ports, where the defenders of the castle could repel attackers.

Stone steps led to a second floor and there was another *claustro*, an inner patio. The stone steps narrowed as they walked up to a third floor, and then a fourth. The castle was deserted.

'Well at least there are plenty of places to sleep here,' Jaime said. 'Felix and I will go forage for food. Pick out your rooms.'

The two men started downstairs again.

Amparo turned to Megan. 'Come on, Sister.'

They walked down the corridor and the rooms all looked alike to Megan. They were empty stone cubicles, cold and austere, some larger than others.

Amparo picked out the largest. 'Jaime and I will sleep here.' She looked at Megan and asked slyly, 'Would you like to sleep with Felix?'

Megan looked at her and said nothing.

'Or perhaps you'd rather sleep with Jaime.' Amparo stepped closer to Megan. 'Don't get any ideas, Sister. He's much too much man for you.'

'You don't have to concern yourself. I'm not interested.' And even as she said it, Megan wondered whether Jaime Miró was much too much man for her.

When Jaime and Felix returned to the castle an hour later, Jaime was clutching two rabbits and Felix was carrying firewood. Felix bolted the front door behind them. Megan watched as the men made a fire in the large fireplace. Jaime skinned and cooked the rabbits on a spit over the fire.

'Sorry we can't offer you ladies a real feast,' Felix said, 'but we'll eat well in Logroño. Meanwhile – enjoy.'

When they had finished their meagre meal, Jaime said, 'Let's get to sleep. I want to make an early start in the morning.'

Amparo said to Jaime, 'Come, *querido*. I have our bedroom picked out.'

'*Bueno*. Let's go.'

Megan watched them go upstairs, hand in hand.

Felix turned to Megan. 'Have you chosen your bedroom, Sister?'

'Yes, thank you.'

'All right, then.'

Megan and Felix walked up the stairs together.

'Good night,' Megan said.

He handed Megan a sleeping-bag. 'Good night, Sister.'

Megan wanted to ask Felix about Jaime, but she hesitated. Jaime might think she was prying, and for some reason, Megan wanted very much for Jaime to have a good opinion of her. *That's really odd*, Megan thought. *He's a terrorist, a murderer, a bank robber, and heaven only knows what else, and I'm worried about whether the man thinks well of me.*

But even as Megan thought it, she knew that there was another side to it. *He's a freedom fighter. He robs banks to finance his cause. He risks his life for what he believes in. He's a brave man.*

As Megan passed their bedroom, she heard Jaime and Amparo inside laughing. She walked into the small, bare room where she was to sleep and knelt on the cold stone floor. 'Dear God, forgive me for –' *Forgive me for what? What have I done?*

For the first time in her life, Megan was unable to pray. Was God up there listening?

Megan crawled into the sleeping-bag Felix had given her, but sleep was as remote as the cold stars she could see through the narrow window.

What am I doing here? Megan wondered. Her thoughts drifted back to the convent . . . the orphanage. And before the orphanage? *Why was I left there? I don't really believe that my father was a brave soldier or a great bullfighter. But wouldn't it be wonderful to know?*

It was almost dawn before Megan drifted off to sleep.

At the prison in Aranda de Duero, Lucia Carmine was a celebrity.

'You're a big fish in our little pond,' the guard told her. 'The Italian government is sending someone to escort you home. I'd like to escort you to my house, *bonita puta*. What bad thing did you do?'

'I cut off a man's balls for calling me *bonita puta*. Tell me – how is my friend?'

'He's going to live.'

Lucia said a silent prayer of gratitude. She looked around the stone walls of her grim, grey cell and thought: *How the hell do I get out of here?*

Chapter 32

The report of the bank robbery was handled through regular police channels, and it was not until two hours after the robbery occurred that a police lieutenant notified Colonel Acoca about it.

An hour later, Colonel Acoca was in Valladolid. He was furious at the delay.

'Why wasn't I informed immediately?'

'I'm sorry, Colonel, but it never occurred to us that –'

'You had him in your hands and you let him get away!'

'It wasn't our –'

'Send in the bank teller.'

The bank teller was filled with a sense of self-importance. 'It was my window he came to. I could tell he was a killer by the look in his eye. He –'

'There is no doubt in your mind that the man who held you up was Jaime Miró?'

'None. He even showed me a wanted poster of himself. It was –'

'Did he come into the bank alone?'

'Yes. He pointed to a woman in the queue and he said she was a member of his gang, but after Miró left I recognized her. She's a secretary who's a regular customer and –'

Colonel Acoca said impatiently, 'When Miró left, did you see in which direction he went?'

'Out the front door.'

The interview with the traffic policeman was no more helpful.

'There were four of them in the car, Colonel. Jaime Miró and another man and two women in the back.'

'In what direction were they headed?'

The policeman hesitated. 'They could have gone in any direction, sir, once they got off the one-way street.' His face brightened. 'I can describe the car, though.'

Colonel Acoca shook his head in disgust. 'Don't bother.'

She was dreaming, and in her dream there were the voices of a mob and they were coming for her to burn her at the stake for robbing a bank. *It wasn't for me. It was for the cause.* The voices grew louder.

Megan opened her eyes and sat up, staring at the unfamiliar castle walls. The sound of voices was real. They were coming from outside.

Megan rose and hurried over to the narrow window. Directly below, in front of the castle, was an encampment of soldiers. Megan was filled with a sudden panic. *They've caught us. I've got to find Jaime.*

She hurried to the room where he and Amparo had slept and looked inside. It was empty. She ran down the steps to the reception hall on the main floor. Jaime and Amparo were standing near the bolted front door, whispering.

Felix ran up to them. 'I checked the back. There's no other way out of here.'

'What about the back windows?'

'Too small. The only way out is through the front door.'

Where the soldiers are, Megan thought. *We're trapped.*

Jaime was saying, 'It's just our damned bad luck that they picked this place to camp.'

'What are we going to do?' Amparo whispered.

'There's nothing we can do. We'll have to stay here until they leave. If –'

And at that moment there was a loud knock at the front door. An authoritative voice called out, 'Open up in there.'

Jaime and Felix exchanged a quick look, and without a word drew their guns.

The voice called out again, 'We know there's someone in there. Open up.'

Jaime said to Amparo and Megan, 'Get out of the way.'

It's hopeless, Megan thought, as Amparo moved behind Jaime and Felix. *There must be two dozen armed soldiers out there. We haven't got a chance.*

Before the others could stop her, Megan moved swiftly to the front door and opened it.

'Thank the Lord you've come!' Megan exclaimed. 'You must help me.'

Chapter 33

The army officer stared at Megan. 'Who are you? What are you doing in there? I'm Captain Rodriguez, and we're looking for –'

'You're just in time, Captain.' She grabbed his arm. 'My two little sons have typhoid fever, and I've got to get them to a doctor. You must come in and help me with them.'

'Typhoid fever?'

'Yes.' Megan was pulling on his arm. 'It is terrible. They are burning up. They are covered with sores and are very sick. Bring your men in and help me carry them out to –'

'*Señora*! You must be mad. That is highly contagious.'

'Never mind that. They need your help. They may be dying.' She was pulling on his arm.

'Let go of me.'

'You can't leave me. What will I do?'

'Get back inside and stay there until we can notify the police to send an ambulance or a doctor.'

'But –'

'That's an order, *señora*. Get inside.'

He called out, 'Sergeant, we're moving out of here.'

Megan closed the front door, leaning against it, drained.

Jaime was staring at her in stunned amazement. 'My God, that was brilliant. Where did you learn to lie like that?'

Megan turned to him and sighed. 'When I was in the orphanage, we had to learn to defend ourselves. I hope God will forgive me.'

'I wish I could have seen the look on that Captain's face.' Jaime burst into laughter. 'Typhoid fever! Jesus Christ!' He saw the look on Megan's face. 'I beg your pardon, Sister.'

From outside they could hear the sounds of the soldiers packing their tents and moving out.

When the troops had departed, Jaime said, 'The police will be here soon. Anyway, we have an appointment in Logroño.'

Fifteen minutes after the soldiers had departed, Jaime said, 'It should be safe to leave now.' He turned to Felix. 'See what you can pick up in town. Preferably a sedan.'

Felix grinned. 'No problem.'

Half an hour later they were in a beat-up grey sedan heading east.

To Megan's surprise, she was seated next to Jaime. Felix and Amparo were in the back seat. Jaime glanced at Megan, a grin on his face.

'Typhoid fever,' he said. And burst out laughing.

Megan smiled. 'He *did* seem eager to get away, didn't he?'

'Did you say you were in an orphanage, Sister?'

'Yes.'

'Where?'

'In Ávila.'

'You don't look Spanish.'

'So I've been told.'

'It must have been hell for you in the orphanage.'

She was startled by the unexpected concern. 'It could have been,' she said. 'But it wasn't.' *I wouldn't let it be*, she thought.

'Have you any idea who your parents were?'

Megan recalled her fantasies. 'Oh, yes. My father was a brave Englishman who drove an ambulance for the loyalists in the Spanish Civil War. My mother was killed in the fighting and I was left on the doorstep of a farmhouse.' Megan shrugged. 'Or my father was a foreign prince who had an affair with a peasant girl and abandoned me to avoid a scandal.'

Jaime glanced at her, saying nothing.

'I –' she stopped abruptly. 'I don't know who my parents were.'

They drove on in silence for a while.

'How long were you behind the walls of the convent?'

'About fifteen years.'

Jaime was astonished. 'Jesus!' Hastily, he added, 'I beg your pardon, Sister. But it's like talking to someone from another planet. You have no idea what's happened in the world in the past fifteen years.'

'I'm sure that whatever changed is only temporary. It will change again.'

'Do you still want to go back to a convent?'

The question took Megan by surprise.

'Of course.'

'*Why?*' Jaime made a sweeping gesture. 'I mean – there is so much that you must miss behind the walls. Here we have music and poetry. Spain gave the world Cervantes and Picasso, Lorca, Pizarro, DeSoto, Cortez. This is a magical country.'

There was a surprising mellowness about this man, a soft fire.

Unexpectedly Jaime said, 'I'm sorry for wanting to desert you earlier, Sister. It was nothing personal. I have had bad experiences with your Church.'

'That is difficult to believe.'

'Believe it.' His voice was bitter.

In his mind's eye he could see the buildings and statues and streets of Guernica exploding in showers of death. He could still hear the screams of the bombs mingling with the screams of the helpless victims being torn apart. The only place of sanctuary was the church.

The priests have locked the church. They won't let us in.

And the deadly hail of bullets that had murdered his mother and father and sisters. *No. Not the bullets*, Jaime thought. *The Church.*

'Your Church stood behind Franco and allowed unspeakable things to be done to innocent civilians.'

'I'm sure the Church protested,' Megan said.

'No. It wasn't until nuns were being raped by his Falangists and priests were being murdered and churches were being burned that finally the Pope broke with Franco. But that didn't bring my mother or father or sisters back to life.'

The passion in his voice was frightening.

'I'm sorry. But that was long ago. The war is over.'

'No. Not for us it isn't. The government will still not permit us to fly the Basque flag or celebrate our national holidays or speak our own language. No, Sister. We're still being oppressed. We'll keep on fighting until we gain our independence. There are half a million Basques in Spain and a hundred and fifty thousand more in France. We want our independence – but your God is too busy to help us.'

Megan said earnestly, 'God cannot take sides, for He is in all of us. We are all a part of Him, and when we try to destroy Him, we destroy ourselves.'

To Megan's surprise, Jaime smiled. 'We are a lot alike, you and I, Sister.'

'We are?'

'We may believe in different things, but we believe with a passion. Most people go through life without caring deeply about anything. You devote your life to God; I devote my life to a cause. We care.'

And Megan thought: *Do I care enough? And if I do, why am I enjoying being with this man? I should be thinking only of returning to a convent.* There was a power in Jaime Miró that was like a magnet. *Is he like Manolete? Risking his life taking daring chances because he has nothing to lose?*

'What will they do to you if the soldiers catch you?' Megan asked.

'Execute me.' He said it so matter-of-factly that for a moment Megan thought she had misunderstood.

'Aren't you afraid?'

'Of course I'm afraid. We're all afraid. None of us wants to die, Sister. We'll meet your God soon enough. We don't want to rush it.'

'Have you done such terrible things?'

'That depends on your point of view. The difference between a patriot and a rebel depends on who is in power at the moment. The government calls us terrorists. We call ourselves freedom fighters. Jean Jacques Rousseau said that freedom is the power to choose our own chains. I want that freedom.' He studied her a moment. 'But you don't have to concern yourself with any of these things, do you? Once you're back in the convent, you'll no longer be interested in the world outside.'

Was that true? Being out in the world again had turned her life upside down. Had she given up her freedom? There was so much she wanted to know, so much she had to learn. She felt like an artist with a blank canvas about to start sketching a new life. *If I go back to a convent*, she thought, *I will be shut away from life again.* And even as she thought it, Megan was appalled by the word *if*. *When I go back*, she corrected herself hastily. *Of course I'm going back. I have nowhere else to go.*

They camped that night in the woods.

Jaime said, 'We're about thirty miles from Logroño and we aren't supposed to meet the others for two days. It will be safer for us to stay on the move until then. So tomorrow we will head toward Vitoria. The next day we'll go into Logroño and just a few hours after that, Sister, you'll be at the convent in Mendavia.'

For ever. 'Will you be all right?' Megan asked.

'Are you worried about my soul, Sister, or my body?'

Megan found herself blushing.

'Nothing will happen to me. I'll cross the border into France for a while.'

'I will pray for you,' Megan told him.

'Thank you,' he said gravely. 'I will think of you praying for me and it will make me feel safer. Get some sleep now. We'll make Leon tomorrow.'

As Megan turned to lie down, she saw Amparo staring at

her from the far end of the clearing. There was a look of naked hatred on Amparo's face.

No one takes my man from me. No one.

Chapter 34

Early the following morning, they reached the outskirts of Nanclares, a small village west of Vitoria. They came to a filling station with a garage, where a mechanic was working on a car. Jaime pulled into the garage.

'*Buenos días*,' the mechanic said. 'What is the problem?'

'If I knew,' Jaime replied, 'I would fix it myself and charge for it. This car is as useless as a mule. It sputters like an old woman and has no energy.'

'It sounds like my wife,' the mechanic grinned. 'I think you may have a carburettor problem, *señor*.'

Jaime shrugged. 'I know nothing about cars. All I know is that I have a very important appointment in Madrid tomorrow. Can you have it fixed by this afternoon?'

The mechanic said, 'I have two jobs ahead of you, *señor*, but –' He let the rest of the sentence hang in the air.

'I will be glad to pay you double.'

The mechanic's face brightened. 'Will two o'clock be all right?'

'Wonderful. We'll get something to eat and come back at two.'

Jaime turned to the others, who had been listening to the conversation in amazement. 'We're in luck,' Jaime said. 'This man is going to fix the car for us. Let's go eat.'

They got out of the car and followed Jaime down the street.

'Two o'clock,' the mechanic said.

'Two o'clock.'

When they were out of earshot, Felix said, 'What are you doing? There's nothing wrong with the car.'

Except that by now the police will be looking for it, Megan thought. *But they'll be looking on the road, not in a garage. It's a clever way to get rid of it.*

'By two o'clock we'll be gone, won't we?' Megan asked.

Jaime looked at her and grinned. 'I have to make a phone call. Wait here.'

Amparo took Jaime's arm. 'I'll go with you.'

Megan and Felix watched them walk off.

Felix looked at Megan and said, 'You and Jaime are getting along well, yes?'

'Yes.' She felt suddenly shy.

'He is not an easy man to know. But he is a man of great honour and great bravery. He is a very caring man. There is no one like him. Did I tell you how he saved my life, Sister?'

'No. I would like to hear.'

'A few months ago the government executed six freedom fighters. In revenge, Jaime decided to blow up the dam at Puente la Reina, south of Pamplona. The town below was headquarters for the army. We moved in at night, but someone tipped off the GOE, and Acoca's men caught three of us. We were sentenced to die. It would have taken an army to storm our prison, but Jaime figured out a way. He set the bulls loose in Pamplona, and in the confusion got two of us away. The third one was beaten to death by Acoca's men. Yes, Sister, Jaime Miró is very special.'

When Jaime and Amparo returned, Felix asked, 'What is happening?'

'Friends are picking us up. We'll have a lift into Vitoria.'

Half an hour later, a truck appeared. The back of it was covered by canvas.

'Welcome,' the driver said cheerfully. 'Hop in.'

'Thank you, *amigo*.'

'It's a pleasure to be of assistance to you, *señor*. It's good that you called. The damned soldiers are swarming around like fleas. It is not safe for you and your friends to be out in the open.'

They climbed into the back of the truck, and the huge vehicle headed northeast.

'Where will you be staying?' the driver asked.

'With friends,' Jaime said.

And Megan thought: *He doesn't trust anyone. Not even someone who is helping him. But how can he? His life is in danger.* And she thought of how terrible it must be for Jaime to be living under that shadow, running from the police and the army. And all because he believed in an ideal so much that he was willing to die for it. What was it he had said? *The difference between a patriot and a rebel depended on who was in power at the moment.*

The drive was a pleasant one. The thin canvas cover offered security, and Megan realized how much tension she had felt when they were out in the open fields, knowing that they were all being hunted. *And Jaime lives under that tension constantly. How strong he is.*

She and Jaime talked, and the conversation flowed easily as though they had known each other for ever. Amparo Jiron sat listening to them, saying nothing, her face impassive.

'When I was a boy,' Jaime told Megan, 'I wanted to be an astronomer.'

Megan was curious. 'What made you –?'

'I had seen my mother and father and sisters shot down, and friends murdered, and I couldn't face what was happening here on this bloody earth. The stars were an escape. They were millions of light years away, and I used to dream of going to them one day and getting away from this awful planet.'

She was watching him, silent.

'But there is no escape, is there? In the end, we all have to face up to our responsibilities. So I came back down to earth. I used to believe that one person could not make a difference. But I know now that that is not true. Jesus made a difference, Muhammad and Gandhi and Einstein and Churchill.' He smiled wryly. 'Don't misunderstand, Sister. I'm not comparing myself to any of them. But in my small way, I do what I can. I think we must all do what we can.'

And Megan wondered whether his words were meant to have a special meaning for her.

'When I got the stars out of my eyes, I studied to be an engineer. I learned to build buildings. Now I blow them up. And the irony is that some of the buildings I've blown up are ones that I've built.'

They reached Vitoria at dusk.

'Where shall I take you?' the truck driver asked.

'You can drop us off here, at the corner, *amigo*.'

The truck driver nodded. 'Right. Keep up the good fight.'

Jaime helped Megan down from the truck. Amparo watched, her eyes blazing. She allowed her man to touch no other woman. *She's a whore*, Amparo thought. *And Jaime is horny for that bitch of a nun. Well, that won't last. He will soon find that her milk is thin. He needs a real woman.*

The group took to the side streets, keeping a wary eye out for trouble. Twenty minutes later, they arrived at a one-storey stone house nestled in a narrow street and surrounded by a high fence.

'This is it,' Jaime said. 'We will stay here tonight and leave tomorrow when it is dark.'

They entered through the front gate and went to the door. It took Jaime but a moment to slip the lock and they all went inside.

'Whose house is this?' Megan asked.

'You ask too many questions,' Amparo said. 'Just be grateful we've kept you alive.'

Jaime looked at Amparo a moment. 'She's proved her right to ask questions.' He turned to Megan. 'It's the house of a friend. You're in Basque country now. From here on our journey will be easier. There will be comrades everywhere, watching and protecting us. You'll be at the convent the day after tomorrow.'

And Megan felt a small chill that was almost a sorrow.

What is the matter with me? she wondered. *Of course I want to go back. Forgive me, Lord. I asked that You bring me home to Your safety, and You are.*

'I'm starved,' Felix said. 'Let's see what's in the kitchen.'

It was completely stocked.

Jaime said, 'He left plenty of food for us. I will make us a wonderful dinner.' He smiled at Megan. 'I think we deserve it, don't you?'

Megan said, 'I didn't know men cooked.'

Felix laughed. 'Basque men take pride in their cooking. You are in for a treat. You will see.'

Handing Jaime the ingredients he asked for, they watched as he prepared a piperade of fresh roasted, peeled green peppers, sliced white onions, tomatoes, eggs and ham sautéed together. As it started to cook, Megan said, 'It smells delicious.'

'Ah, that's just the appetizer. I'm going to make a famous Basque dish for you, *pollo al chilindrón*.'

He didn't say 'for us', Amparo noted. *He said, 'for you'. For the bitch.*

Jaime cut up slices of chicken, sprinkled salt and pepper over them and browned the chicken in hot oil while in a separate pan he started cooking onions, garlic and tomatoes. 'We'll let it simmer for half an hour.'

Felix had found a bottle of red wine. He passed out glasses. 'The red wine of Rioja. You will like this.' He offered a glass to Megan. 'Sister?'

The last time Megan tasted wine had been at communion. 'Thank you,' she said.

Slowly Megan raised the glass to her lips and took a sip. It was delicious. She took another sip and she could feel a warmth moving down her body. It felt wonderful. *I must enjoy all this while I can*, Megan thought. *It will be over soon.*

During dinner, Jaime seemed unusually preoccupied.

'What's troubling you, *amigo*?' Felix asked.

Jaime hesitated. 'We have a traitor in the movement.'

There was a shocked silence.

'What – what makes you think that?' Felix demanded.

'Acoca. He keeps getting too close to us.'

Felix shrugged. 'He's the fox and we're the rabbits.'

'It's something more than that.'

'What do you mean?' Amparo asked.

'When we were going to blow up the dam at Puente la Reina, Acoca was tipped off.' He looked at Felix. 'He set a trap and caught you and Ricardo and Zamora. If I hadn't been delayed, I would have been captured with you. And look what happened at the *parador*.'

'You heard the manager telephoning the police,' Amparo pointed out.

Jaime nodded. 'Right. Because I had a feeling that something was wrong.'

Amparo's face was sombre. 'Who do you think it is?'

Jaime shook his head. 'I'm not sure. Someone who knows all our plans.'

'Then let's change our plans,' Amparo said. 'We'll meet the others at Logroño and skip Mendavia.'

Jaime glanced at Megan. 'We can't do that. We have to get the sisters to their convent.'

Megan looked at him and thought: *He's already done enough for me. I mustn't put him in greater danger than he's already in.*

'Jaime, I can –'

But he knew what she was going to say. 'Don't worry, Megan. We're all going to get there safely.'

He's changed, Amparo thought. *In the beginning he wanted nothing to do with any of them. Now he's willing to risk his life for her. And he calls her Megan. It's no longer Sister.*

Jaime was going on. 'There are at least fifteen people who know our plans.'

'We have to find out which one it is,' Amparo insisted.

'How do we do that?' Felix asked. He was nervously picking at the edges of the tablecloth.

Jaime said, 'Paco is in Madrid doing some checking for me. I've arranged for him to telephone me here.' He looked at Felix for a moment, then looked away.

What he had not said was that no more than half a dozen people knew the exact route that the three groups were taking. It was true that Felix Carpio had been imprisoned by Acoca. It was also true that that would have provided a perfect alibi for Felix. At the propitious moment, an escape could have been planned for him. *Except that I got him out first*, Jaime thought. *Paco is checking on him. I hope he calls soon.*

Amparo rose and turned to Megan. 'Help me with the dishes.'

The two women began clearing the table and the men went into the living room.

'The nun – she's holding up well,' Felix said.

'Yes.'

'You like her, don't you?'

Jaime found it difficult to look at Felix. 'Yes. I like her.' *And you would betray her along with the rest of us.*

'What about you and Amparo?'

'We're cut from the same cloth. She believes in the cause as much as I do. Her entire family was killed by Franco's Falangists.' Jaime rose and stretched. 'Time to turn in.'

'I don't think I'm going to be able to sleep tonight. Are you certain there's a spy?'

Jaime looked at him and said, 'I'm certain.'

When Jaime came downstairs for breakfast in the morning, Megan did not recognize him. His face had been darkened and he was wearing a wig and a moustache. He was dressed in scruffy clothes. He looked ten years older.

'Good morning,' he said. And his voice coming out of that body startled her.

'Where did you –?'

'This is a house I use from time to time. I keep an assortment of things here that I need.'

He said it casually, but it gave Megan a sudden insight into the kind of life he led. How many other houses and disguises did he need to stay alive? How many other close calls had he had that she knew nothing about? She remembered the ruthlessness of the men who had attacked the convent and she thought: *If they catch Jaime, they'll show him no mercy. I wish I knew how to protect him.*

And Megan's mind was filled with thoughts she had no right to be thinking.

Amparo prepared breakfast. *Bacalao* – steamed, salted codfish – goat's milk, cheese and thick, hot chocolate with *churros*.

As they were eating, Felix asked, 'How long are we going to stay here?'

Jaime replied casually, 'We'll leave when it gets dark.'

But he had no intention of letting Felix use that information.

'I have some errands to do,' he told Felix. 'I'll need your help.'

'Right.'

Jaime called Amparo aside. 'When Paco calls, tell him I'll be back shortly. Take a message.'

She nodded. 'Be careful.'

'Don't worry.' He turned to Megan. 'Your last day. Tomorrow you'll be at the convent. You must be eager to get there.'

She looked at him a long moment. 'Yes.' *Not eager*, Megan thought. *Anxious. I wish I weren't anxious. I'm going to shut myself away from this, but for the rest of my life, I'm going to wonder what happened to Jaime and Felix and the others.*

Megan stood there watching as Jaime and Felix left. She sensed a tension between the two men that she did not understand.

Amparo was studying her, and Megan remembered her words: *Jaime is too much man for you.*

Amparo said curtly, 'Make up the beds. I'll prepare lunch.'

'All right.'

Megan went into the bedroom. Amparo stood there watching her, then walked into the kitchen.

For the next hour, Megan worked, busily concentrating on cleaning and dusting and polishing, trying not to think, trying to keep her mind off what was bothering her.

I must put him out of my mind, she thought.

It was impossible. He was like a force of nature, taking over everything in his path.

She polished harder.

When Jaime and Felix returned, Amparo was waiting for them at the door. Felix looked pale.

'I'm not feeling too well. I think I'll lie down for a bit.'

They watched him disappear into a bedroom.

'Paco called,' Amparo said excitedly.

'What did he say?'

'He has some information for you, but he didn't want to discuss it on the phone. He's sending someone to meet you. This person will be at the town square at noon.'

Jaime frowned, thoughtful. 'He didn't say who it is?'

'No. Just that it was urgent.'

'Damn it. I – never mind. All right. I'll go and meet him. I want you to keep an eye on Felix.'

She looked at him, puzzled. 'I don't un–?'

'I don't want him using the telephone.'

A flash of understanding crossed her face. 'You think that Felix is –?'

'Please. Just do as I ask.' He looked at his watch. 'It's almost noon. I'll leave now. I should be back in an hour. Take care, *querida*.'

'Don't worry.'

Megan heard their voices.

I don't want him using the telephone.

You think that Felix is –?

Please. Just do as I ask.

So Felix is the traitor, Megan thought. She had seen him go into his bedroom and close the door. She heard Jaime leave.

Megan walked into the living room.

Amparo turned. 'Have you finished?'

'Not quite, I –' She wanted to ask where Jaime had gone,

what they were going to do with Felix, what was going to happen next, but she did not want to discuss that with this woman. *I'll wait until Jaime returns.*

'Finish up,' Amparo said.

Megan turned and went back into the bedroom. She thought about Felix. He had seemed so friendly, so warm. He had asked her many questions, but now that seeming act of friendliness took on a different meaning. The bearded man was looking for information that he could pass on to Colonel Acoca. All their lives were in danger.

Amparo may need help, Megan thought. She started towards the living room, then stopped.

A voice was saying, 'Jaime just left. He will be alone on a bench in the main plaza. Your men should have no trouble picking him up.'

Megan stood there, frozen.

'He's walking, so it should take him about fifteen minutes to get there.'

Megan listened with growing horror.

'Remember our deal, Colonel,' Amparo said into the telephone. 'You promised not to kill him.'

Megan backed into the hallway. Her mind was in a turmoil. So Amparo was the traitor. And she had sent Jaime into a trap.

Backing away quietly, so Amparo would not hear her, Megan turned and ran out the back door. She had no idea how she was going to help Jaime. She knew only that she had to do something. She stepped outside the gate and started down the street, moving as fast as she could without attracting attention, heading towards the centre of the town.

'Please, God. Let me be on time,' Megan prayed.

The walk to the town square was a pleasant one, with side streets shaded by towering trees, but Jaime was unaware of his surroundings. He was thinking about Felix. He had been like a brother to Felix, had given him his full trust. What had turned Felix into a traitor willing to put all their lives in jeopardy? Perhaps Paco's messenger would have the answer. *Why couldn't Paco have discussed it on the telephone?* Jaime wondered.

Jaime was approaching the town square. In the middle of the plaza was a fountain and shady trees with benches scattered around. Children were playing games. A couple of old men were playing *boule*. Half a dozen men were seated on park benches, enjoying the sunshine, reading, dozing, or feeding the pigeons. Jaime crossed the street, slowly moving along the path, and took a seat on one of the benches. He looked at his watch just as the tower clock began chiming noon. Paco's man should be coming.

Out of the corner of his eye, Jaime saw a police car pull up at the far end of the square. He looked in the other direction. A second police car arrived. Officers were getting out, moving towards the park. His heart began to beat faster. It was a trap. But who had set it? Was it Paco, who sent the message, or Amparo who delivered it? She had sent him to the park. But why? Why?

There was no time to worry about that now. He had to escape. But Jaime knew that the moment he tried to make a run for it, they would shoot him down. He could try to bluff it out, but they knew he was there.

Think of something. Fast!

A street away, Megan was hurrying towards the park. As it came into view, she took in the scene at a glance. She saw Jaime seated on a bench, and the policemen closing in on the park from both sides.

Megan's mind was racing. There was no way for Jaime to escape.

Megan was walking past a *tienda*. Ahead of her, blocking her path, a mother was pushing a pram. The woman stopped, set the pram against the wall of the shop and went inside to make a purchase. Without a moment's hesitation, Megan grabbed the handle of the pram and moved across the street into the park.

The police were walking along the benches now, questioning the men seated there. Megan elbowed her way past a policeman and went up to Jaime, pushing the pram ahead of her.

She yelled, '*¡Madre de Dios!* There you are, Manuel! I've been looking everywhere for you. I've had enough! You promised to paint the house this morning, and here you are sitting in the park like some millionaire. Mother was right. You're a good-for-nothing bum. I never should have married you in the first place!'

It took Jaime less than a fraction of a second. He got to his feet. 'Your mother is an expert on bums. She married one. If she –'

'Who are you to talk? If it wasn't for my mother, our baby would starve to death. You certainly don't bring any bread into the house . . .'

The policemen had stopped, taking in the argument.

'If that one was my wife,' one of them muttered, 'I'd send her back to her mother.'

'I'm damned tired of your nagging, woman,' Jaime roared. 'I've warned you before. When we get home, I'm going to teach you a lesson.'

'Good for him,' one of the policemen said.

Jaime and Megan noisily quarrelled their way out of the park, pushing the pram before them. The policemen turned their attention back to the men seated on the benches.

'Identification, please?'

'What's the problem, officer?'

'Never mind. Just show me your papers.'

All over the park, men were pulling out wallets and extracting bits of paper to prove who they were. In the midst of this, a baby began to cry. One of the policemen looked up. The pram had been abandoned at the corner. The quarrelling couple had vanished.

Thirty minutes later, Megan walked in at the front door of the house. Amparo was nervously pacing up and down.

'Where have you been?' Amparo demanded. 'You shouldn't have left the house without telling me.'

'I had to go out to take care of something.'

'What?' Amparo asked suspiciously. 'You don't know anyone here. If you –'

Jaime walked in through the door. The blood drained from her face. She quickly regained her composure.

'What – what happened?' Amparo asked. 'Didn't you go to the park?'

Jaime said quietly, 'Why, Amparo?'

And she looked into his eyes and she knew it was over.

'What made you change?'

She shook her head. 'I haven't changed. You have. I've lost everyone I loved in this stupid war you're fighting. I'm sick of all the bloodshed. Can you stand hearing the truth about yourself, Jaime? You're as bad as the government you're fighting. Worse, because they're willing to make peace, and you're not. You think you're helping our country? You're destroying it. You rob banks and blow up cars and murder innocent people, and you think you're a hero. I loved you, and I believed in you once, but –' Her voice broke. 'This bloodshed has to end.'

Jaime walked up to her, and his eyes were ice. 'I should kill you.'

'No,' Megan gasped. 'Please! You can't.'

Felix had come into the room and was listening to the conversation. 'Jesus Christ! So she's the one. What do we do with the bitch?'

Jaime said, 'We'll have to take her with us and keep an eye on her.' He took Amparo by the shoulders and said softly, 'If you try one more trick, I promise you you'll die.' He shoved her away and turned to Megan and Felix. 'Let's get out of here before her friends arrive.'

Chapter 35

'You had Miró in your hands and you let him escape?'

'Colonel – with all due respect – my men –'

'Your men are assholes. You call yourselves policemen? You're a disgrace to your uniforms.'

The chief of police stood there, cringing under the withering scorn of Colonel Acoca. There was nothing else he could do, for the Colonel was powerful enough to have his head. And Acoca was not yet through with him.

'I hold you personally responsible. I'll see that you're relieved from duty.'

'Colonel –'

'Get out. You make me sick to my stomach.'

Colonel Acoca was boiling with frustration. There had not been enough time for him to reach Vitoria and catch Jaime Miró. He had had to entrust that to the local police. And they had bungled it. God alone knew where Miró had gone to now.

Colonel Acoca went to the map spread out on a table in front of him. *They will be staying in Basque country, of course. That could be Burgos or Logroño or Bilbao or San Sebastian. I'll concentrate on the north-east. They'll have to surface somewhere.*

He recalled his conversation with the Prime Minister that morning.

'Your time is running out, Colonel. Have you read the morning papers? The world press is making us look like clowns. Miró and those nuns have made us a laughingstock.'

'Prime Minister, you have my assurance –'

'King Juan Carlos has ordered me to set up an official inquiry board into the whole matter. I can't hold it off any longer.'

'Delay the inquiry for just a few more days. I'll have Miró and the nuns by then.'

There was a pause. 'Forty-eight hours.'

It was not the Prime Minister whom Colonel Acoca was afraid of disappointing, nor was it the King. It was the OPUS MUNDO. When he had been summoned to the panelled office of one of Spain's leading industrialists, his orders had been explicit: 'Jaime Miró is creating an atmosphere harmful to our organization. Stop him. You will be well rewarded.'

And Colonel Acoca knew what the unspoken part of the conversation was: *Fail and you will be punished.* Now his career was in jeopardy. And all because some stupid policemen had let Miró walk away under their noses. Jaime Miró might hide anywhere. But the nuns . . . A wave of excitement coursed through Colonel Acoca. The nuns! They were the key. Jaime Miró might hide anywhere, but the sisters could find sanctuary only in another convent. And it would almost certainly be in a convent of the same order.

Colonel Acoca turned to study the map again. And there it was: *Mendavia.* There was a convent of the Cistercian order at Mendavia. *That's where they're headed*, Acoca thought triumphantly. *Well, so am I.*

Only I'll be there first, waiting for them.

The journey for Ricardo and Graciela was coming to an end.

The last few days had been the happiest that Ricardo had ever known. He was being hunted by the military and the police, his capture meant certain death, and yet none of that seemed to matter. It was as though he and Graciela had carved out an island in time, a paradise where nothing could touch them. They had turned their desperate journey into a wonderful adventure that they shared together.

They talked endlessly, exploring and explaining, and their words were tendrils that drew them even closer together.

They spoke of the past, the present, and the future. Particularly the future.

'We'll be married in church,' Ricardo said. 'You'll be the most beautiful bride in the world . . .'

And Graciela could visualize the scene and was thrilled by it.

'And we'll live in the most beautiful house . . .'

And she thought: *I've never had a house of my own, or a real room of my own.*

There was the little casa she shared with her mother and all the uncles, and then the convent cell, living with the sisters.

'And we'll have handsome sons and beautiful daughters . . .'

And I will give them all the things I never had. They will be so loved.

And Graciela's heart soared.

There was one thing troubling her. Ricardo was a soldier fighting for a cause he passionately believed in. Would he be contented living in France, withdrawing from the battle? She knew she had to discuss it with him.

Ricardo – how much longer do you think this revolution is going to go on?

It was a question she had not asked.

It's already gone on too long, Ricardo thought. The government had made peace overtures, but ETA had rejected them. It had done worse than reject them. It had responded to the offers with a series of increased terrorist attacks. Ricardo had tried to discuss it with Jaime.

'They're willing to compromise, Jaime. Shouldn't we meet them half way?'

'Their offer is a trick – they want to destroy us. They're forcing us to go on fighting.'

And because Ricardo loved Jaime and believed in him, he continued to support him. But the doubts refused to die. And as the bloodshed increased, so did his uncertainty. And now Graciela was asking, *How much longer do you think this revolution is going to go on?*

'I don't know,' Ricardo told her. 'I wish it were over. But I will tell you this, my darling. Nothing will ever come between us – not even a war. There will never be words enough to tell you how much I love you.'

And they went on dreaming.

They travelled during the night, making their way through the fertile, green countryside, past El Burgo and Soria. At dawn, from the top of a hill, they saw Logroño in the far distance. To the left of the road was a stand of pine trees and beyond that a forest of electric power lines. Graciela and Ricardo followed the winding road down to the outskirts of the bustling city.

'Where are we going to meet the others?' Graciela asked.

Ricardo pointed to a poster on a building they were passing. It read:

CIRQUE JAPON!
THE WORLD'S MOST SENSATIONAL CIRCUS FRESH FROM JAPAN!
24 JULY FOR ONE WEEK
AVENIDA CLUB DEPORTIVO

'There,' Ricardo told her. 'We'll meet them there this afternoon.'

In another part of the city, Megan, Jaime, Amparo and Felix were also looking at a circus poster. There was a feeling of enormous tension in the group. Amparo was never out of their sight. Ever since the incident at Vitoria, the men treated Amparo as an outcast, ignoring her most of the time and speaking to her only when necessary.

Jaime looked at his watch. 'The circus should be starting,' he said. 'Let's go.'

At police headquarters in Logroño, Colonel Ramón Acoca was finalizing his plans.

'Are the men deployed around the convent?'

'Yes, Colonel. Everything is in place.'

'Excellent.'

Acoca was in an expansive mood. The trap he had set was foolproof, and there would be no bungling policemen to spoil his plans this time. He was personally conducting the operation. The OPUS MUNDO was going to be proud of him. He went over the details with his officers once again.

'The nuns are travelling with Miró and his men. It's important that we catch them *before* they walk into the convent. We'll be spread out in the woods around it. Don't move until I give the signal to close in.'

'What are our orders if Jaime Miró resists?'

Acoca said softly, 'I hope he does try to resist.'

An orderly came into the room. 'Excuse me, Colonel. There is an American here who would like to speak to you.'

'I have no time now.'

'Yes, sir.' The orderly hesitated. 'He says it's about one of the nuns.'

'Oh? An American, did you say?'

'Yes, Colonel.'

'Send him in.'

A moment later, Alan Tucker was ushered in.

'I'm sorry to disturb you, Colonel. I'm Alan Tucker. I'm hoping you can help me.'

'Yes? How, Mr Tucker?'

'I understand that you're looking for one of the nuns from the Abbey Cistercian – a Sister Megan.'

The Colonel sat back in his chair, studying the American. 'How does that concern you?'

'I'm looking for her too. It's very important that I find her.'

Interesting, Colonel Acoca thought. *Why is it so important for this American to find a nun?* 'You have no idea where she is?'

'No. The newspapers –'

The goddamn press again. 'Perhaps you could tell me why you are looking for her.'

'I'm afraid I can't discuss that.'

'Then I'm afraid I can't help you.'

'Colonel – could you let me know if you find her?'

Acoca gave him a thin smile. 'You'll know.'

The whole country was following the hegira of the nuns. The press had reported the narrow escape of Jaime Miró and one of the nuns in Vitoria.

So they're heading north, Alan Tucker thought. *Their best bet to get out of the country is probably San Sebastian. I've got to get hold of her.* He sensed that he was in trouble with Ellen Scott. *I handled that badly*, he thought. *I can make up for it by bringing her Megan.*

He placed a call to Ellen Scott.

The Cirque Japon was held in Logroño's outlying district of Guanos, in a huge tent, and ten minutes before the circus was due to begin, the tent was filled to capacity. Megan, Jaime, Amparo and Felix made their way down the crowded aisle to their reserved seats. There were two empty seats next to Jaime.

He stared at them and said, 'Something's wrong. Ricardo and Sister Graciela were supposed to be here.' He turned to Amparo. 'Did you –?'

'No. I swear it. I know nothing about it.'

The lights dimmed and the show began. There was a roar from the crowd, and they turned to look at the arena. A bicycle rider was circling the ring, and as he pedalled an acrobat leaped onto his shoulder. Then, one by one, a swarm of other performers jumped on, clinging to the front and back and sides of the bicycle until it was invisible. The audience cheered.

A trained bear act was on next, and then a tightrope walker. The audience was enjoying the show tremendously, but Jaime and the others were too nervous to pay any attention. Time was running out.

'We'll wait another fifteen minutes,' Jaime decided. 'If they're not here by then –'

A voice said, 'Excuse me – are these seats taken?'

Jaime looked up to see Ricardo and Graciela, and grinned. 'No. Please sit down.' And then, in a relieved whisper, 'I'm damned glad to see you.'

Ricardo nodded at Megan and Amparo and Felix. He looked around. 'Where are the others?'

'Haven't you seen the newspapers?'

'Newspapers? No. We've been in the mountains.'

'I have bad news,' Jaime said. 'Rubio is in a prison hospital.'

Ricardo stared at him. 'How –?'

'He was stabbed in a bar fight. The police picked him up.'

'*Mierda!*' Ricardo was silent a moment, then sighed. 'We'll just have to get him out, won't we?'

'That's my plan,' Jaime agreed.

'Where's Sister Lucia?' Graciela asked. 'And Sister Teresa?'

It was Megan who answered. 'Sister Lucia has been arrested. She was – she was wanted for murder. Sister Teresa is dead.'

Graciela crossed herself. 'Oh, my Lord.'

In the arena a clown was walking a tightrope, carrying a poodle under each arm, and two Siamese cats in his capacious pockets. As the dogs tried to reach the cats, the wire swayed wildly and the clown pretended to be fighting to keep his balance. The audience was roaring. It was difficult to hear anything over the noise of the crowd. Megan and Graciela had so much to tell each other. Almost simultaneously, they began to talk in the sign language of the convent. The two men looked on in astonishment.

Ricardo and I are going to marry . . .

That's wonderful . . .

What has been happening to you?

Megan started to reply and realized there were no signs to convey the things she wanted to say. It would have to wait.

'Let's move,' Jaime said. 'There's a van outside waiting to take us to Mendavia. We'll drop the sisters off there and be on our way.'

They started up the aisle, Jaime holding Amparo's arm.

When they were outside in the car-park, Ricardo said, 'Jaime, Graciela and I are getting married.'

A grin lit up Jaime's face. 'That's wonderful! Congratulations.' He turned to Graciela. 'You couldn't have picked a better man.'

Megan put her arms around Graciela. 'I'm very happy for you both.'

And she thought: *Was it easy for her to make the decision to leave the convent? Am I wondering about Graciela? Or am I wondering about myself?*

Colonel Acoca was receiving an excited report from an aide.

'They were seen at the circus less than an hour ago. By the time we could bring up reinforcements, they had gone. They left in a blue and white van. You were right, Colonel. They are headed for Mendavia.'

So it's finally over, Colonel Acoca thought. The chase had been an exciting one, and he had to admit that Jaime Miró had been a worthy opponent. *The OPUS MUNDO will have even bigger plans for me now.*

Through a pair of high-powered Zeiss binoculars, Colonel Acoca watched the blue and white van appear over the crest of a hill and head for the convent below. Heavily armed troops were hidden among the trees along both sides of the road and around the convent itself. There was no way that anyone could escape.

As the van approached the entrance to the convent and braked to a stop, Colonel Acoca barked into his walkie-talkie, 'Close in! Now!'

The manoeuvre was executed perfectly. Two squads of soldiers armed with automatic weapons swung into position, blocking the road and surrounding the van. Colonel Acoca stood watching the scene for an instant, savouring his moment of glory. Then he slowly approached the van, gun in hand.

'You're surrounded,' he called out. 'You haven't got a chance. Come out with your hands up. One at a time. If you try to resist, you'll all die.'

There was a long moment of silence, and then the van door slowly opened and three men and three women emerged, trembling, their hands raised high above their heads.

They were strangers.

Chapter 36

High on a hill above the convent, Jaime and the others observed Acoca and his men move in on the van. They saw the terrified passengers get out, hands raised, and watched the scene played out in pantomime.

Jaime Miró could àlmost hear the dialogue:

Who are you?

We work at a hotel outside Logroño.

What are you doing here?

A man gave us five thousand pesetas to deliver this van to the convent.

What man?

I don't know. I never saw him before.

Is this his picture?

Yes. That's him.

'Let's get out of here,' Jaime said.

They were in a white station wagon, heading back to Logroño. Megan was looking at Jaime in wonder.

'How did you know?'

'That Colonel Acoca would be waiting for us at the convent? He told me.'

'*What?*'

'The fox has to think like the hunter, Megan. I put myself in Acoca's place. Where would he set a trap for me? He did exactly what I would have done.'

'And if he had not shown up?'

'Then it would have been safe to take you into the convent.'

'What happens now?' Felix asked.

It was the question uppermost in all their minds.

'Spain isn't safe for any of us for a while,' Jaime decided. 'We'll head directly for San Sebastian and into France.' He looked at Megan. 'There are Cistercian convents there.'

It was more than Amparo could bear.

'Why don't you give yourself up? If you keep on this way, there will be more blood spilled and more lives taken –'

'You've lost the right to speak,' Jaime said curtly. 'Just be grateful you're still alive.' He turned to Megan. 'There are ten mountain passes across the Pyrenees leading from San Sebastian to France. We'll cross there.'

'It's too dangerous,' Felix objected. 'Acoca's going to be looking for us in San Sebastian. He'll be expecting us to cross the border into France.'

'If it's that dangerous –' Graciela began.

'Don't worry,' Jaime assured her. 'San Sebastian is Basque country.'

The station wagon was approaching the outskirts of Logroño again.

'All the roads to San Sebastian will be watched,' Felix warned. 'How do you plan for us to get there?'

Jaime had already decided. 'We'll take the train.'

'The soldiers will be searching the trains,' Ricardo objected.

Jaime gave Amparo a thoughtful look. 'No. I don't think so. Our friend here is going to help us. Do you know how to reach Colonel Acoca?'

She hesitated. 'Yes.'

'Good. You're going to call him.'

They stopped at one of the telephone booths along the highway. Jaime followed Amparo into the booth and closed the door. He was holding a pistol to her side.

'You know what to say?'

'Yes.'

He watched her dial a number, and when a voice answered, she said, 'This is Amparo Jiron. Colonel Acoca is expecting my call . . . Thank you.' She looked up at Jaime. 'They're putting me through.' The gun was pressing against her. 'Do you have to –?'

'Just do as you were told.' His voice was ice.

A moment later, Jaime heard Acoca's voice come over the phone. 'Where are you?'

The gun pressed against her harder. 'I – I'm – we're just leaving Logroño.'

'Do you know where our friends are going?'

'Yes.'

Jaime's face was inches from her, his eyes hard.

'They've decided to reverse themselves to throw you off. They're on their way to Barcelona. He's driving a white Seat. He'll be taking the main highway.'

Jaime nodded at her.

'I – I have to go now. The car is here.'

Jaime pressed down the receiver. 'Very good. Let's go. We'll give him half an hour to call off his men here.'

Thirty minutes later they were at the railway station.

There were three classes of trains from Logroño to San Sebastian: the *Talgo* was the luxury train; the second class train was the *Ter;* and the worst and cheapest trains, uncomfortable and dirty, were misnamed the *expresos*, which stopped at every little station from Logroño to San Sebastian.

Jaime said, 'We'll take the *expreso*. By now all of Acoca's men will be busy stopping every white Seat on the road to Barcelona. We'll buy our tickets separately and meet in the last compartment of the train.' Jaime turned to Amparo. 'You go first. I'll be right behind you.'

And she knew why, and hated him for it. If Colonel Acoca had set a trap, she would be the bait. Well, she was Amparo Jiron. She would not flinch.

She walked into the station while Jaime and the others watched. There were no soldiers.

They're all out covering the highway to Barcelona. It's going to be a madhouse, Jaime thought wryly. *Every other car is a white Seat.*

One by one the group purchased their tickets and headed for the train. They boarded without incident. Jaime took the seat next to Megan. Amparo sat in front of them, next to Felix. Across the way Ricardo and Graciela sat together.

Jaime said to Megan, 'We'll reach San Sebastian in three hours. We'll spend the night there and in the early morning we'll cross over into France.'

'And after we get to France?'

She was thinking of what would happen to Jaime, but when he replied, he said, 'Don't worry. There's a Cistercian convent just a few hours across the border.' He hesitated. 'If that's what you still want.'

So he had understood her doubts. *Is that what I want?* They were coming to more than a border that divided two countries. This border would divide her old life from her future life . . . which would be . . . what? She had been desperate to return to a convent, but now she was filled with doubts. She had forgotten how exciting the world outside the walls could be. *I've never felt so alive.* Megan looked over at Jaime and admitted to herself: *And Jaime Miró is a part of it.*

He caught her glance and looked into her eyes, and Megan thought: *He knows it.*

The *expreso* stopped at every hamlet and village along the track. The train was packed with farmers and their wives, merchants and salesmen, and at each stop passengers noisily embarked and disembarked.

The *expreso* made its way slowly through the mountains, fighting the steep gradients.

When the train finally pulled into the station in San Sebastian, Jaime said to Megan, 'The danger is over. This is our city. I've arranged for a car to be here for us.'

A large sedan was waiting in front of the station. A driver wearing a large *boina vasca*, the wide-brimmed beret of the

Basques, greeted Jaime with warm hugs, and the group got into the car.

Megan noticed that Jaime stayed close to Amparo, ready to grab her if she tried to make a move. *What's he going to do with her?* Megan wondered.

'We were worried about you, Jaime,' the driver said. 'According to the press, Colonel Acoca is conducting a big hunt for you.'

Jaime laughed. 'Let him keep hunting, Gil. I am out of season.'

They drove down the Avenida Sancho el Sabio, towards the beach. It was a cloudless summer day and the streets were crowded with strolling couples bent on pleasure, and the harbour was alive with yachts and smaller craft. The distant mountains formed a picturesque backdrop for the city. Everything seemed so peaceful.

'What are the arrangements?' Jaime asked the driver.

'The Hotel Niza. Largo Cortez is waiting for you.'

'It will be good to see the old pirate again.'

The Niza was a medium class hotel in the Plaza Juan de Olezabal, off San Martin Street on the corner of a busy square. It was a white building with brown shutters and a big blue sign on the top of the roof. The rear of the hotel backed on to a beach.

When the car pulled up in front of the hotel, the group got out and followed Jaime into the lobby.

Largo Cortez, the hotel owner, ran up to greet them. He was a large man. He had only one arm as the result of a daring exploit, and he moved awkwardly, as though off-balance.

'Welcome,' he beamed. 'I have been expecting you for a week now.'

Jaime shrugged. 'We had a few delays, *amigo*.'

Largo Cortez grinned. 'I read about them. The papers are full of nothing else.' He turned to look at Megan and Graciela. 'Everyone is supporting you, Sisters. I have your rooms all prepared.'

'We'll be staying overnight,' Jaime told him. 'We'll leave first thing in the morning and cross into France. I want a good guide who knows all the passes – either Cabrera Infante or José Cebrian.'

'I will arrange it,' the hotel owner assured him. 'There will be six of you?'

Jaime glanced at Amparo. 'Five.'

Amparo looked away.

'I suggest that none of you registers,' Cortez said. 'What the police don't know won't hurt them. Why don't you let me take you to your rooms, where you can refresh yourselves? Then we'll have a magnificent supper.'

'Amparo and I are going to the bar to have a drink,' Jaime said. 'We'll join you later.'

Largo Cortez nodded. 'As you wish, Jaime.'

Megan was watching Jaime, puzzled. She wondered what he planned to do with Amparo. Was he going to cold-bloodedly –? She could not bear even to think about it.

Amparo was wondering, too, but she was too proud to ask.

Jaime led her into the bar at the far end of the lobby and took a table in the corner.

When the waiter approached them, Jaime said, 'A glass of wine, *por favor.*'

'One?'

'One.'

Amparo watched as Jaime took out a small packet and opened it. It contained a fine, powdery substance.

'Jaime –' There was desperation in Amparo's voice. 'Please listen to me! Try to understand why I did what I did. You're tearing the country apart. Your cause is hopeless. You must stop this insanity.'

The waiter reappeared and set a glass of wine on the table. When he walked away, Jaime carefully poured the contents of the packet into the glass and stirred it. He pushed the glass in front of Amparo.

'Drink it.'

'No!'

'Not many of us are privileged to choose the way we die,' Jaime said quietly. 'This way will be quick and painless. If I turn you over to my people, I can't make any such promise.'

'Jaime – I loved you once. You must believe me. Please –'

'Drink it.' His voice was implacable.

Amparo looked at him for a long moment, then picked up the glass. 'I'll drink to your death.'

He watched as Amparo put the glass to her lips and swallowed the wine in one gulp.

She shuddered. 'What happens now?'

'I'll help you upstairs. I'll put you to bed. You'll sleep.'

Amparo's eyes filled with tears. 'You're a fool,' she whispered. 'Jaime – I'm dying, and I tell you that I loved you so –' Her words were beginning to slur.

Jaime rose and helped Amparo to her feet. She stood up, unsteady. The room seemed to be rocking.

'Jaime –'

He guided her out of the door and into the lobby, holding her up. Largo Cortez was waiting for him with a key.

'I'll take her to her room,' Jaime said. 'See that she's not disturbed.'

'Right.'

Cortez watched as Jaime half-carried Amparo up the stairs.

In her room, Megan was thinking how strange it felt to be by herself in a hotel in a resort town. San Sebastian was filled with people on holiday, honeymooners, lovers enjoying themselves in a hundred other hotel rooms.

But what had Jaime done to Amparo? Could he possibly have . . . but no, he could never have done that. Or could he?

And suddenly Megan wished Jaime were there with her, and wondered what it would be like to have him making love to her. All the feelings that she had been suppressing for so long came flooding into her mind in a wild torrent of emotions. *I want him*, she thought. *Oh, Lord, what's happening to me? What can I do?*

Ricardo was whistling as he dressed. He was in a wonderful mood. *I'm the luckiest man in the world*, he thought. *We'll be married in France. There's a beautiful church across the border in Bayonne. Tomorrow . . .*

In her room, Graciela was taking a bath, luxuriating in the warm water, thinking of Ricardo. She smiled to herself and thought: *I'm going to make him so happy. Thank you, God.*

Felix Carpio was thinking about Jaime and Megan. *A blind man can see the electricity between them*, he thought. *It is going to bring bad luck. Nuns belong to God. It's bad enough that Ricardo has taken Sister Graciela from her calling.* But Jaime had always been reckless. What was he going to do about this one?

The five of them met for supper in the hotel dining room. No one mentioned Amparo.

Looking at Jaime, Megan felt suddenly embarrassed, as though he could read her mind. *It's better not to ask questions*, she decided. I know he could never do anything brutal.

They found that Largo Cortez had not exaggerated about the supper. The meal began with *gazpacho*, the thick, cold soup made from tomatoes, cucumbers and water-soaked bread, followed by a salad of fresh greens, a huge dish of *paella* – rice, shrimp, chicken and beef in a wonderful sauce, and ended with a delicious flan. It was the first hot meal Ricardo and Graciela had had in a long time.

When the meal was over, Megan rose. 'I should be getting to bed.'

'Wait,' Jaime said. 'I've got to talk to you.' He escorted her to a deserted corner of the lobby. 'About tomorrow . . .'

'Yes?'

And she knew what he was going to ask. What she did not know was what *she* was going to answer. *I've changed*, Megan thought. *I was so sure about my life before. I believed I had everything I wanted.*

And Jaime was saying, 'You don't really want to go back to a convent, do you?'

Do I?

He was waiting for an answer.

I have to be honest with him, Megan thought. She looked into his eyes and said, 'I don't know what I want, Jaime. I'm confused.'

Jaime smiled. He hesitated, choosing his words carefully. 'Megan – this fight will be over soon. We'll get what we want because the people are behind us. I can't ask you to share the danger with me now, but I would like you to wait for me. I have many Basque friends living in France. You would be safe with them.'

Megan looked at him a long time before she answered. 'Jaime – give me time to think about it.'

'Then you're not saying no?'

Megan said quietly, 'I'm not saying no.'

None of the group slept that night. They had too much to think about, too many conflicts to resolve. Megan stayed awake, reliving the past. The years in the orphanage, and the sanctuary of the convent . . . The sudden expulsion into a world she had given up for ever. Jaime Miró was risking his life fighting for what he believed in. *And what do I believe in?* Megan asked herself. *How do I want to spend the rest of my life?*

She had made a choice once. Now she was forced to choose again. She would have to have an answer by morning.

*

Graciela was thinking about the convent, too. *They were such happy, peaceful years. I felt so close to God. Will I miss that?*

Jaime was thinking about Megan. *She mustn't go back. I want her at my side. What will her answer be?*

Ricardo was too excited to sleep, busily making plans for the wedding. The church at Bayonne . . .

Felix was wondering how to dispose of Amparo's body. *Let Largo Cortez take care of it.*

Early the following morning, the group met in the lobby. Jaime approached Megan.

'Good morning.'

'Good morning.'

'Have you thought about our conversation?'

She had thought of nothing else all night. 'Yes, Jaime.'

He looked into her eyes, trying to read the answer there. 'Will you wait for me?'

'Jaime –'

At that moment Largo Cortez hurried up to them. With him was a leathery-looking man in his fifties.

'I'm afraid there won't be any time for breakfast,' Cortez said. 'You should be leaving. This is José Cebrian, your guide. He will take you across the mountains into France. He's the best guide in San Sebastian.'

'I'm glad to see you, José,' Jaime said. 'What's your plan?'

'We're going to take the first part of the journey by foot,' José Cebrian told the group. 'On the other side of the border, I've arranged for cars to be waiting for us. We should hurry. Come along, please.'

The group moved out into the street, painted yellow by the rays of the bright sun.

Largo Cortez came out of the hotel to see them off. 'Safe journey,' he said.

'Thank you for everything,' Jaime replied. 'We'll be back, *amigo*. Sooner than you think.'

'We go this way,' José Cebrian ordered.

The group started to turn towards the square. And at that moment, soldiers and members of the GOE suddenly materialized at both ends of the street, sealing it off. There were at least a dozen of them, all heavily armed. Colonel Ramón Acoca and Colonel Fal Sostelo were leading them.

Jaime glanced quickly towards the beach, looking for an escape route. Another dozen soldiers were approaching from there. There was no escape. They would have to fight. Jaime instinctively reached for his gun.

Colonel Acoca called out, 'Don't even think about it, Miró, or we'll shoot all of you down where you're standing.'

Jaime's mind was racing furiously, looking for a way out. How had Acoca known where to find him? Jaime turned and saw Amparo standing in the doorway, a look of profound sorrow on her face.

Felix said, 'What the bloody hell! I thought you –'

'I gave her sleeping pills. They should have knocked her out until we got across the border.'

'The bitch!'

Colonel Acoca walked towards Jaime. 'It's over.' He turned to one of his men. 'Disarm them.'

Felix and Ricardo were looking towards Jaime for guidance, ready to follow his lead. Jaime shook his head. Reluctantly, he handed over his gun, and Felix and Ricardo followed suit.

'What are you going to do with us?' Jaime asked.

Several passersby stopped to watch the proceedings.

Colonel Acoca's voice was curt. 'I'm taking you and your gang of murderers back to Madrid. We'll give you a fair military trial and then hang you. If I had my way, I'd hang you here, now.'

'Let the sisters go,' Jaime said. 'They had nothing to do with this.'

'They're accomplices. They're as guilty as you are.'

Colonel Acoca turned and gave a signal. The soldiers motioned to the onlookers to move aside to let three army trucks drive up.

'You and your assassins will travel in the middle truck,' the Colonel informed Jaime. 'My men will be in front of you and at the back of you. If any of you makes one false move, they have orders to kill all of you. Do you understand?'

Jaime nodded.

Colonel Acoca spat into Jaime's face. 'Good. Into the truck.'

There was an angry murmur from the growing crowd

Amparo watched impassively from the doorway as Jaime and Megan, Graciela and Ricardo and Felix climbed into the truck, surrounded by soldiers with automatic weapons.

Colonel Fal Sostelo walked up to the driver of the first truck. 'We'll head straight for Madrid. No stops along the way.'

'Yes, Colonel.'

By now, many people had gathered in the street to watch what was happening. Colonel Acoca started to climb into the first truck. He called out to those in front of the truck, 'Clear the way.'

From the side streets more people began to emerge.

'Move along,' Colonel Acoca called. 'Out of the way.'

And still they came, the men wearing the wide Basque *boinas*. It was as though they were responding to some invisible signal. *Jaime Miró is in trouble.* They came from shops and homes. Housewives dropped what they were doing and moved out into the street. Shopkeepers about to open for business heard the news and hurried on to the hotel. And still they came. Artists and plumbers and doctors, mechanics and salesmen and students, many carrying shotguns and rifles. They were Basques, and this was their homeland. It started with a few, and then a hundred, and within minutes it had swollen to more than a thousand, filling the pavements and streets, completely surrounding the army trucks. They were ominously silent.

Colonel Acoca observed the huge crowd in desperation. He screamed, 'Everybody get out of the way or we'll start shooting.'

Jaime called out, 'I wouldn't advise it. These people hate you for what you're trying to do to them. A word from me and they'll tear you and your men to pieces. There's one thing you forgot, Colonel. San Sebastian is a Basque town. It's my town.' He turned to his group. 'Let's get out of here.'

Jaime helped Megan down from the truck, and the others followed. Colonel Acoca watched helplessly, his face tight with fury.

The crowd was waiting, hostile and silent. Jaime walked up to the Colonel. 'Take your trucks and get back to Madrid.'

Acoca looked around at the still growing mob. 'I – you won't get away with this, Miró.'

'I have got away with it. Now get out of here.' He spat in Acoca's face.

The Colonel stared at him for a long, murderous moment. *It can't end this way*, he thought desperately. *I was so close. It was checkmate.* But he knew that it was worse than a defeat for him. It was a death sentence. The OPUS MUNDO would be waiting for him in Madrid. He looked at the sea of people surrounding him. He had no choice.

He turned to his driver, and his voice was choked with fury. 'We're moving out.'

The crowd stepped back, watching as the soldiers climbed into the trucks. A moment later, the trucks began rolling down the street, and the crowd began to cheer wildly. It started out as a cheer for Jaime Miró, and it grew louder and louder, and they were cheering for their freedom and their fight against tyranny, and their coming victory, and the streets reverberated with the noise of their celebration.

Two teenagers were screaming themselves hoarse. One turned to the other. 'Let's join ETA.'

An elderly couple held each other, and the woman said, 'Now maybe they'll give us back our farm.'

An old man stood alone in the crowd, silently watching the army trucks leave. When he spoke, he said, 'They'll be back one day.'

Jaime took Megan's hand and said, 'It's over. We're free. We'll be across the border in an hour. I'll take you to my aunt.'

She looked into his eyes. 'Jaime –'

A man pushed his way towards them through the crowd and hurried up to Megan.

'Excuse me,' he said breathlessly. 'Are you Sister Megan?'

She turned to him, puzzled. 'Yes.'

He breathed a sigh of relief. 'I've had quite a time finding you. My name is Alan Tucker. I wonder if I could speak to you for a moment?'

'Yes.'

'Alone.'

'I'm sorry. I'm just leaving for –'

'Please. This is very important. I've come all the way from New York to find you.'

She looked at him, puzzled. 'To find me? I don't understand. Why –?'

'I'll explain it to you, if you'll give me a moment.'

The stranger took her arm and walked her down the street, talking rapidly. Megan glanced back once at where Jaime Miró was standing, waiting for her.

Megan's conversation with Alan Tucker turned her world upside down.

'The woman I represent would like to see you.'

'I don't understand. What woman? What does she want with me?'

I wish I knew the answer to that, Alan Tucker thought. 'I'm not at liberty to discuss that. She's waiting for you in New York.'

It made no sense. There must be some mistake. 'Are you sure you have the right person – Sister Megan?'

'Yes. But your name isn't Megan. It's Patricia.'

And in a sudden, blinding flash, Megan knew. After all these years, her fantasy was about to come true. She was finally going to learn who she was. The very idea of it was thrilling . . . and terrifying.

'When – when would I have to leave?' Her throat was suddenly so dry that she could barely speak the words.

I want you to find out where she is and bring her back as quickly as possible.

'Right away. I'll arrange a passport for you.'

She turned and saw Jaime standing in front of the hotel, waiting.

'Excuse me a moment.'

Megan walked back to him in a daze, and she felt as though she were living a dream.

'Are you all right?' Jaime asked. 'Is that man bothering you?'

'No. He's – no.'

Jaime took Megan's hand. 'I want you to come with me now. We belong together, Megan.'

Your name isn't Megan. It's Patricia.

And she looked at Jaime's strong, handsome face, and she thought: *I want us to be together. But we'll have to wait. First I have to find out who I am.*

'Jaime – I want to be with you. But there is something I have to do first.'

He studied her, his face troubled. 'You're going to leave?'

'For a little while. But I'll be back.'

He looked at her for a long time, then slowly nodded. 'All right. You can reach me through Largo Cortez.'

'I'll come back to you. I promise.'

And she meant it. But that was before the meeting with Ellen Scott.

Chapter 37

'Deus Israel vos; et ipse sit vobiscum, qui, misertus est duobus unicis plenius benedis cere . . . The God of Israel joins you together, and He be with you and now, Lord, make them bless Thee more fully. Blessed are all they that love the Lord, that walk in His ways. Glory . . .'

Ricardo looked away from the priest and glanced at Graciela standing at his side. *I was right. She is the most beautiful bride in the world.*

Graciela was still, listening to the words of the priest echoing through the cavernous, vaulted church. There was such a sense of peace in the church. It seemed to Graciela to be filled with the ghosts of the past, all the thousands of people who had come here generation after generation, to find forgiveness and fulfilment and joy. It reminded her so much of the convent. *I feel as though I've come home again*, Graciela thought. *As though I belong.*

'Exaudi nos, omni potens et misericors deus; ut quod nostro ministratur officio tua benedictione potius impleatua per dominum . . . Hear us, Almighty and merciful God, that what is done by our ministry may be abundantly fulfilled with Thy blessing . . .'

He has blessed me, more than I deserve. Let me be worthy of Him.

'In te sperav, domine: Dixi: Tues deus meus: in manibus tuis tempora mea . . .'

'In Thee, O Lord, have I hoped; I said: Thou art my God; my times are in Thy hands . . .'

My times are in Thy hands. I took a solemn vow to devote the rest of my life to Him.

'Suscipe quaesumus domine, pro sacra connubii lege munus oblatum . . .'

'Receive, we beseech Thee, O Lord, the offering we make to Thee on behalf of the holy hands of wedlock . . .'

The words seemed to reverberate in Graciela's head. She felt as though time had stopped.

'Deus qui potestate virtutis tuae de nihilo cuneta fecisti . . .'

'Oh, God, who has hallowed wedlock to foreshadow the union of Christ with the church . . . look in Thy mercy upon this, Thy handmaid, who is to be joined in wedlock and entreats protection and strength from Thee . . .'

But how can He show me mercy when I am betraying Him?

Graciela was suddenly finding it difficult to breathe. The walls seemed to be closing in on her.

'Nihil in ea ex actibus suis ille auctor praevaricationis usurpet . . .'

'Let the father of sin work none of his evil deeds in her . . .'

That was the moment when Graciela knew. And she felt as though a great burden had been lifted from her. She was filled with an exalted, ineffable joy.

The priest was saying, 'May she win the peace of the kingdom of heaven. We ask Thee to bless this marriage, and –'

'I'm already married,' Graciela said aloud.

There was a moment of shocked silence. Ricardo and the priest were staring at her. Ricardo's face was pale.

'Graciela, what are you –?'

She took his arm and said gently, 'I'm sorry, Ricardo.'

'I – I don't understand. Have – have you stopped loving me?'

She shook her head. 'I love you more than my life. But my life doesn't belong to me any more. I gave it to God a long time ago.'

'No! I can't let you sacrifice your –'

'Darling Ricardo . . . It is not a sacrifice. It's a blessing.

In the convent I found the first peace I had ever known. You're a part of the world I gave up – the best part. But I did give it up. I must return to my world.'

The priest was standing there, listening, silent.

'Please forgive me for the pain I am causing you, but I can't go back on my vows. I would be betraying everything I believe in. I know that now. I could never make you happy, because I could never be happy. Please understand.'

Ricardo stared at her, shaken, and no words would come. It was as though something in him had died.

Graciela looked at his stricken face, and her heart went out to him. She kissed him on the cheek. 'I love you,' she said softly. Her eyes filled with tears. 'I will pray for you. I will pray for us both.'

Chapter 38

On a late Friday afternoon, a military ambulance drove up to the emergency entrance to the hospital at Aranda de Duero. An ambulance attendant accompanied by two uniformed policemen went through the swing doors and approached the supervisor behind the desk.

'We have an order here to pick up a Rubio Arzano,' one of the policemen said. He handed over the document.

The supervisor looked at it and frowned. 'I don't think I have the authority to release him. It should be handled by the administrator.'

'Fine. Get him.'

The supervisor hesitated. 'There's a problem. He's away for the weekend.'

'It's not our problem. There's our release order, signed by Colonel Acoca. Do you want to call him and tell him you won't honour it?'

'No,' he said hastily. 'That won't be necessary. I'll have them get the prisoner ready.'

Half a mile away, in front of the city jail, two detectives emerged from a police car and entered the building. They approached the desk sergeant.

One of the men showed his badge. 'We're here to pick up Lucia Carmine.'

The sergeant looked at the two detectives in front of him and said, 'No one told me anything about this.'

One of the detectives sighed. 'Goddamned bureaucracy.

The left hand never tells the right hand what it's doing.'

'Let me see that release order.'

The detectives handed it to him.

'Colonel Acoca signed it, huh?'

'That's right.'

'Where are you taking her?'

'Madrid. The Colonel is going to question her himself.'

'Is he? Well, I think I'd better check it out with him.'

'There's no need to do that,' the detective protested.

'Mister, we've got orders to keep a tight grip on this lady. The Italian government is having an orgasm over getting her back. If Colonel Acoca wants her, he's going to have to tell me himself.'

'You're wasting time, and –'

'I have a lot of time, *amigo*. What I don't have is another ass if I lose mine over this.' He picked up the phone and said, 'Get me Colonel Acoca in Madrid.'

'Jesus Christ!' the detective said. 'My wife is going to kill me if I'm late for dinner again. Besides, the Colonel's probably not even in, and –'

The phone on the desk rang. The sergeant reached for it.

'I have the Colonel's office on the line.'

The sergeant gave the detectives a triumphant look. 'Hello. This is the desk sergeant at the police station in Aranda de Duero. It is important that I speak to Colonel Acoca.'

One of the detectives looked at his watch impatiently. '*Mierda!* I have better things to do than stand around and –'

'Hello. Colonel Acoca?'

The voice boomed out over the phone. 'Yes. What is it?'

'I have two detectives here, Colonel, who want me to release a prisoner into your custody.'

'Lucia Carmine?'

'Yes, sir.'

'Did they show you an order signed by me?'

'Yes, sir. They –'

'Then what the fuck are you bothering me for? Release her.'

'I just thought –'
'Don't think. Follow orders.'
The line went dead.
The sergeant swallowed. 'He – er –'
'He has a short fuse, hasn't he?' the detective grinned.
The sergeant rose, trying to retain his dignity. 'I'll have her brought out.'
In the alley at the back of the police station, a small boy was watching a man on the telephone pole disconnect a clamp from a wire and climb down.
'What are you doing?' the boy asked.
The man ruffled his hand through the boy's hair. 'Helping out a friend, *muchacho*. Helping out a friend.'

Three hours later, at an isolated farmhouse to the north, Lucia and Rubio Arzano were reunited.

He was awakened by the telephone at 3.00 a.m. The familiar voice said, 'The Committee would like to meet with you.'
'Yes, sir. When?'
'Now, Colonel. A limousine will pick you up in one hour. Be ready, please.'
'Yes, sir.'
He replaced the receiver and sat on the edge of the bed. He lit a cigarette and let the smoke bite deep into his lungs.
A limousine will pick you up in one hour. Be ready, please.
He would be ready.
He went into the bathroom and examined his image in the mirror. He was looking into the eyes of a defeated man.
I was so close, he thought bitterly. *So close.*
Colonel Acoca began to shave, very carefully, and when he was finished, he took a long, hot shower, then selected the clothes he was going to wear.
Exactly one hour later, he walked to the front door and took a last look at the home he knew he would never see

again. There would be no meeting, of course. They would have nothing further to discuss with him.

There was a long, black limousine waiting in front of the house. A door opened as he approached the car. There were two men in the front and two in the back.

'Get in, Colonel.'

He took a deep breath and entered the car. A moment later, it sped away into the black night.

It's like a dream, Lucia thought. *I'm looking out the window at the Swiss Alps. I'm actually here.*

Jaime Miró had arranged for a guide to see that she reached Zurich safely. She had arrived late at night.

In the morning, I'll go to the Leu Bank.

The thought made her nervous. What if something had gone wrong? What if the money was no longer there? What if . . .?

As the first light of dawn inched over the mountains, Lucia was still awake.

A few minutes before nine, she left the Baur au Lac Hotel and stood in front of the bank, waiting for it to open.

A kindly-looking, middle-aged man unlocked the door. 'Come in, please. I hope you haven't been waiting long?'

Only a few months, Lucia thought. 'No. Not at all.'

He ushered her inside. 'What can we do for you?'

Make me rich. 'My father has an account here. He asked me to come in and – and take it over.'

'Is it a numbered account?'

'Yes.'

'May I have the number, please?'

'B2A149207.'

He nodded. 'One moment, please.'

She watched him disappear towards a vault at the back. The bank was beginning to fill with customers. *It must be there*, Lucia thought. *Nothing must go –*

The man was approaching her. She could read nothing in his face.

'This account – you say it was in your father's name?'

Her heart sank. 'Yes. Angelo Carmine.'

He studied her for a moment. 'The account carries two names.'

Did that mean she would not be able to touch it? 'What –' She could scarcely get the words out. '– What's the other name?'

'Lucia Carmine.'

And in that instant, she owned the world.

The account amounted to a little over thirteen million dollars.

'How would you like it handled?' the banker asked.

'Could you transfer it to a bank in Brazil? Rio?'

'Certainly. It will be there this afternoon.'

It was that simple.

Lucia's next stop was at a travel agency near the hotel. There was a large poster in the window advertising Brazil.

It's an omen, Lucia thought happily. She went inside.

'May I help you?'

'Yes. I would like two tickets to Brazil.'

There are no extradition laws there.

She could not wait to tell Rubio how well everything was going. He was in Biarritz waiting for her call. They would be going to Brazil together.

'We can live in peace there for the rest of our lives,' she had told him.

Now, everything was finally set. After all the adventure and the dangers . . . the arrest of her father and brothers and her vengeance against Benito Patas and Judge Buscetta . . . the police looking for her and her escape to the convent . . . Acoca's men and the phony friar . . . Jaime Miró and Teresa and the gold cross . . . and Rubio Arzano. Most of all, dear Rubio. How many times had he risked his life for her? He had saved her from the soldiers in the woods . . . from the raging waters at the waterfall . . . from the men in the bar at Aranda de Duero. The very thought of Rubio warmed Lucia.

She returned to her hotel room and picked up the telephone, waiting for the operator to answer.

There will be something for him to do in Rio. What? What can he do? He'll probably want to buy a farm somewhere out in the country. But then what would I do?

An operator's voice said, 'Number, please.'

Lucia sat there staring out of the window at the snow-covered Alps. *We have two different lives, Rubio and I. We live in different worlds. I'm the daughter of Angelo Carmine.*

'Number, please?'

He's a farmer. That's what he loves. How can I take him away from that? I can't do that to him.

The operator was getting impatient. 'Can I help you?'

Lucia said slowly, 'No. Thank you.' She replaced the receiver.

Early the following morning, she boarded a Swissair flight to Rio.

She was alone.

Chapter 39

The meeting had taken place in the luxurious drawing room of Ellen Scott's townhouse. She paced back and forth, waiting for Alan Tucker to arrive with the girl. No. Not a girl. A woman. A nun. What would she be like? What had life done to her? *What have I done to her?*

The butler walked into the room. 'Your guests have arrived, Madam.'

She took a deep breath. 'Show them in.'

A moment later, Megan and Alan Tucker entered.

She's beautiful, Ellen Scott thought.

Tucker smiled. 'Mrs Scott, this is Megan.'

Ellen Scott looked at him and said quietly, 'I won't need you any more.' And her words had a finality to them.

His smile faded.

'Goodbye, Tucker.'

He stood there a moment, uncertain, then nodded and left. He could not get over his feeling that he had missed something. Something important. *Too late*, he thought. *Too bloody late.*

Ellen Scott was studying Megan. 'Sit down, please.'

Megan took a chair, and the two women sat there inspecting each other.

She looks like her mother, Ellen Scott thought. *She's grown up to be a beautiful woman.* She recalled the terrible night of the accident, the storm and the burning plane.

You said she was dead . . . There's another way . . . The

pilot said we were near Ávila. There should be plenty of tourists there. There's no reason for anyone to connect the baby with the plane crash . . . We'll drop her off at a nice farmhouse outside of town. They'll adopt her and she'll grow up to have a lovely life here . . . You have to choose, Milo. You can either have me, or you can spend the rest of your life working for your brother's child.

And now here was the past confronting her. Where to begin?

'I'm Ellen Scott, President of Scott Industries. Have you heard of it?'

'No.'

Of course she would not have heard of it, Ellen Scott chided herself.

This was going to be more difficult than she had anticipated. She had concocted a story about an old friend of the family who had died, and a promise to take care of his daughter, and – but the moment she had looked at Megan, Ellen Scott knew that it would not work. She had no choice. She had to trust Patricia – Megan – not to destroy them all. Ellen Scott thought of what she had done to the woman seated before her, and her eyes filled with tears. *But it's too late for tears. It's time to make amends. It's time to tell the truth.*

Ellen Scott leaned across to Megan and took her hand. 'I have a story to tell you,' she said quietly.

That had been three years earlier. For the first year, until she became too ill to continue, Ellen Scott had taken Megan under her wing. Megan had gone to work for Scott Industries, and her aptitude and intelligence had delighted the older woman.

'You'll have to work hard,' Ellen Scott said. 'You'll learn, as I had to learn. In the beginning, it will be difficult, but in the end, it will become your life.'

And it had.

Megan worked hours that none of her employees could even begin to emulate.

'You get to your office at four o'clock in the morning and work all day. How do you do it?'

Megan smiled and thought: *If I slept until four o'clock in the morning at the convent, Sister Betina would scold me.*

Ellen Scott was gone, but Megan had kept learning, and kept watching the company grow. *Her* company. Ellen Scott had adopted her. 'So we won't have to explain why you're a Scott,' she said. But there was a note of pride in her voice.

It's ironic, Megan thought. *All those years at the orphanage when no one would adopt me. And now I'm being adopted by my own family.*

He has a wonderful sense of humour.

Chapter 40

A new man was behind the wheel of the getaway car, and it made Jaime Miró nervous.

'I'm not sure of him,' he told Felix Carpio. 'What if he drives off and leaves us?'

'Relax. He's my cousin's brother-in-law. He'll be fine. He's been begging for a chance to go out with us.'

'I have a bad feeling,' Jaime said.

They had arrived in Seville early that afternoon, and had examined half a dozen banks before choosing their target. The bank was on a side street, small, not too much traffic, close to a factory which would be making deposits there. Everything seemed perfect. Except for the man in the getaway car.

'Is he all that's worrying you?' Felix asked.

'No.'

'What, then?'

It was a difficult one to answer. 'Call it a premonition.' He tried to say it lightly, mocking himself.

Felix took it seriously. 'Do you want to call it off?'

'Because I have the nerves of an old washerman today? No, *amigo*. It will all go as smooth as silk.'

In the beginning, it had.

There were half a dozen customers in the bank, and Felix held them at bay with an automatic weapon while Jaime cleared out the cash drawers. Smooth as silk.

As the two men were leaving, heading for the getaway car, Jaime called out, 'Remember, *amigos*, the money is for a good cause.'

It was out in the street that it began to fall apart. There were police everywhere. The driver of the getaway car was on his knees on the pavement, a police pistol at his head.

As Jaime and Felix came into view, a detective called out, 'Drop your weapons.'

Jaime hesitated for one split second. Then he raised his gun.

Chapter 41

The converted 727 was flying at 35,000 feet, over the Grand Canyon. It had been a long, hard day. *And it's not over yet*, Megan thought.

She was on her way to California to sign the papers that would give Scott Industries one million acres of timberland north of San Francisco. She had struck a hard bargain.

It's their fault, Megan thought. *They shouldn't have tried to cheat me. I'll bet I'm the first bookkeeper they've ever come up against from a Cistercian convent.* She laughed aloud.

The steward approached her. 'Can I get you anything, Miss Scott?'

'No, thank you.'

She saw a stack of newspapers and magazines in the rack. She had been so busy with the deal that she had had no time to read anything. 'Let me see the *New York Times*, please.'

The story was on the front page and it leaped out at her. There was a photograph of Jaime Miró. Below it the communique read: 'Jaime Miró, leader of ETA, the radical Basque separatist movement in Spain, was wounded and captured by police during a bank hold-up yesterday afternoon in Seville. Killed in the attack was Felix Carpio, another of the alleged terrorists. The authorities had been conducting a search for Miró since . . .'

Megan read the rest of the article and sat there for a long time, frozen, remembering the past. It was like a distant dream, photographed through a gauze curtain, hazy and unreal.

This fight will be over soon. We'll get what we want because the people are behind us . . . I would like you to wait for me . . .

Long ago she had read of a civilization that believed if you saved a person's life, that you were responsible for him. Well, she had saved Jaime twice – once at the castle, and again at the park. *I'll be damned if I'm going to let them kill him now.*

She reached for the telephone next to her seat and said to the pilot, 'Turn the plane around. We're going back to New York.'

A limousine was there for her at La Guardia, and by the time she arrived in her office it was 2.00 a.m. Lawrence Gray Jr. was waiting for her. His father had been the company's attorney for years and had retired. The son was bright and ambitious.

Without preamble, Megan said, 'Jaime Miró. What do you know about him?'

The reply was immediate. 'He's a Basque terrorist, head of ETA. I think I just read that he was captured a day or so ago.'

'Right. The government is going to have to put him on trial. I want to have someone there. Who's the best trial lawyer in the country?'

'I'd say Curtis Hayman.'

'No. Too much of a gentleman. We need a killer.' She thought for a moment. 'Get Mike Rosen.'

'He's booked for the next hundred years, Megan.'

'Unbook him. I want him in Madrid for the trial.'

He frowned. 'We can't get involved in a public trial in Spain.'

'Sure we can. *Amicus curae.* We're friends of the defendant.'

He studied her a moment. 'Do you mind if I ask you a personal question?'

'Yes. Get on this.'

'I'll do my best.'

'Larry . . .'

'Yes?'

'And then some.' There was steel in her voice.

Twenty minutes later, Lawrence Gray walked into Megan's office. 'Mike Rosen is on the phone. I think I woke him up. He wants to talk to you.'

Megan picked up the telephone. 'Mr Rosen? What a pleasure this is. We've never met, but I have a feeling you and I are going to become very good friends. A lot of people sue Scott Industries just for the target practice, and I've been looking around for someone to take charge of all our litigation. Yours is the one name that keeps coming up. Naturally, I'm prepared to pay you a large retainer for –'

'Miss Scott –?'

'Yes.'

'I don't mind a little snow job, but you're giving me frostbite.'

'I don't understand.'

'Then let me put it in legal parlance for you. Cut out the bullshit. It's two o'clock in the morning. You don't hire people at two o'clock in the morning.'

'Mr Rosen –'

'Mike. We're going to be good friends, remember? But friends have to trust one another. Larry tells me you want me to go to Spain to try to save some Basque terrorist who's in the hands of the police.'

She started to say, 'He's not a terrorist –' but stopped herself. 'Yes.'

'What's your problem? Is he suing Scott Industries because his gun jammed?'

'He –'

'I'm sorry, friend. I can't help you. My schedule is so tight that I gave up going to the bathroom six months ago. I can recommend a few lawyers . . .'

No, Megan thought. *Jaime Miró needs you.* And she was suddenly seized by a sense of hopelessness. Spain was another world, another time. When she spoke, her voice sounded weary. 'Never mind,' she said. 'It's a personal matter. I'm sorry for coming on so strongly.'

'Hey! That's what CEOs are supposed to do. Personal is different, Megan. To tell you the truth, I'm dying to hear what interest the head of Scott Industries has in saving a Spanish terrorist. Are you free for lunch tomorrow?'

She was going to let nothing stand in her way. 'Yes.'

'Le Cirque at one o'clock?'

Megan felt her spirits lifting. 'Fine.'

'You make the reservation. But I have to warn you about something.'

'Yes?'

'I have a very nosy wife.'

They met at Le Cirque, and when Sirio had seated them, Mike Rosen said, 'You're better looking than your picture. I'll bet everybody tells you that.'

He was very short, and he dressed carelessly. But there was nothing careless about his mind. His eyes radiated a blazing intelligence.

'You've aroused my curiosity,' Mike Rosen said. 'What's your interest in Jaime Miró?'

There was so much to tell. Too much to tell. All Megan said was, 'He's a friend. I don't want him to die.'

Rosen leaned forward in his seat, his legs swinging in the air. 'I went through the newspaper files on him this morning. If Don Juan Carlos' government executes Miró only once, he'll be way ahead of the game. They're going to get hoarse just reading the charges against your friend.' He saw the expression on Megan's face. 'I'm sorry, but I have to be honest. Miró has been a very busy man. He holds up banks, blows up cars, murders people –'

'He's not a murderer. He's a patriot. He's fighting for his rights.'

'Okay, okay. He's my hero too. What do you want me to do?'

'Save him.'

'Megan, we're such good friends that I'm going to tell you the absolute truth. Jesus Christ himself couldn't save him. You're looking for a miracle that –'

'I believe in miracles. Will you help me?'

He studied her a moment. 'What the hell. What are friends for? Have you tried the paté? I hear they make it kosher.'

•

The Fax from Madrid read: 'Have spoken to half a dozen top European lawyers. They refuse to represent Miró. Tried to have myself admitted to trial as *amicus curae*. Court ruled against me. Wish I could pull off that miracle for you, friend, but Jesus hasn't risen yet. Am on my way home. You owe me a lunch. Mike.'

The trial was set to begin on 17 September.

'Cancel my appointments,' Megan told her assistant. 'I have some business to take care of in Madrid.'

'How long will you be gone?'

'I don't know.'

She planned her strategy on the plane flying over the Atlantic. *There has to be a way*, Megan thought. *I have money and I have power. The Prime Minister is the key. I have to get to him before the trial starts. After that, it will be too late.*

Megan had an appointment with Prime Minister Leopoldo Martinez twenty-four hours after she arrived in Madrid. He invited her to Moncloa Palace for lunch.

'Thank you for seeing me so promptly,' Megan said. 'I know what a busy man you are.'

He raised a hand in deprecation. 'My dear Miss Scott, when the head of an organization as important as Scott

Industries flies to my country to see me, I can only be honoured. Please tell me how I can assist you.'

'I really came here to assist you,' Megan said. 'It occurred to me that while we have a few factories in Spain, we're not using nearly enough of the potential that your country has to offer.'

He was listening closely now, his eyes shining. 'Yes?'

'Scott Industries is about to open a huge electronics plant. It should employ somewhere between a thousand and fifteen hundred people. If it is as successful as we think it will be, we'll open satellite factories.'

'And you have not decided in which country you wish to open this plant?'

'That's right. I'm personally in favour of Spain, but quite frankly, Your Excellency, some of my executives are not too happy with your civil rights record.'

'Really?'

'Yes. They felt that those who object to some of the policies of the state are treated too harshly.'

'Do you have anyone in particular in mind?'

'As a matter of fact, I do. Jaime Miró.'

He sat there staring at her. 'I see. And if we were to be lenient with Jaime Miró, we would get the electronics factory and –'

'And a lot more,' Megan assured him. 'Our factories will raise the standard of living in every community they're in.'

The Prime Minister frowned. 'I'm afraid there is one small problem.'

'What? We can negotiate further.'

'This is something that cannot be negotiated, Miss Scott. Spain's honour is not for sale. You cannot bribe us or buy us or threaten us.'

'Believe me, I'm not –'

'You came here with your handouts and expect us to run our courts to please you? Think again, Miss Scott. We don't need your factories.'

I've made it worse, Megan thought, despairingly.

*

The trial lasted six weeks in a heavily guarded courtroom that was closed to the public.

Megan remained in Madrid, following the news reports of the trial each day. From time to time, Mike Rosen telephoned her.

'I know what you're going through, friend. I think you should come home.'

'I can't, Mike.'

She tried to see Jaime.

'Absolutely no visitors.'

On the last day of the trial, Megan stood outside the courtroom, lost in a crowd of people. Reporters came streaming out of the building, and Megan stopped one of them.

'What happened?'

'They found him guilty on all counts. He's going to get the garrotte.'

Chapter 42

At five a.m. on the morning scheduled for the execution of Jaime Miró, crowds began to gather outside the central prison in Madrid. Barricades set up by the *guardia civil* kept the swelling mob of onlookers across the wide street, away from the front entrance to the prison. Armed troops and tanks blocked the iron prison gates.

Inside the prison, in the office of Warden Gomez de la Fuente, an extraordinary meeting was taking place. In the room were Prime Minister Leopoldo Martinez, Alonzo Sebastian, the new head of GOE, and the warden's executive deputies, Juanito Molinas and Pedros Arrango.

Warden de la Fuente was a heavyset, middle-aged, grim-faced man who had passionately devoted his life to disciplining the miscreants that the government had placed in his charge. Molinas and Arrango, his hard-bitten assistants, had served with de la Fuente for the past twenty years.

Prime Minister Martinez was speaking. 'I would like to know what arrangements you have made to ensure that there will be no trouble in carrying out Miró's execution.'

Warden de la Fuente replied, 'We have prepared for every possible contingency, Your Excellency. As Your Excellency observed when you arrived, a full company of armed soldiers is stationed around the prison. It would take an army to break in.'

'And inside the prison itself?'

'The precautions are even more stringent. Jaime Miró is locked in a double security cell on the second floor. The other prisoners on that floor have been temporarily transferred. Two guards are stationed at each end of the cell block. I have ordered a general lock-down, so that all prisoners will remain in their cells until after the execution.'

'What time will that take place?'

'At noon, Your Excellency. I have postponed mess hall until one o'clock. That will give us enough time to get Miró's body out of here.'

'What plans have you made for disposing of it?'

'I am following your suggestion, Excellency. His burial in Spain would cause the government embarrassment if the Basques should turn his grave into some kind of shrine. We have been in touch with his aunt in France. She lives in a small village outside Bayonne. She has agreed to bury him there.'

The Prime Minister rose. 'Excellent.' He sighed. 'I still think a hanging in the public square would have been more appropriate.'

'Yes, Your Excellency. But in that case, I could no longer have been responsible for controlling the mob outside.'

'I suppose you're right. There's no point in stirring up any more excitement than is necessary. The garrotte is more painful and slower. And if any man deserves the garrotte, it is Jaime Miró.'

Warden de la Fuente said, 'Excuse me, Your Excellency, but I understand that a commission of judges is meeting to consider a last minute appeal from Miró's attorneys. If it should come through, what should I –?'

The Prime Minister interrupted. 'It won't. The execution will proceed as scheduled.'

The meeting was over.

At 7.30 a.m., a bread truck arrived in front of the prison gate.

'Delivery.'

One of the prison guards stationed at the entrance looked in at the driver. 'You're new, aren't you?'

'Yeah.'

'Where's Julio?'

'He's sick in bed today.'

'Why don't you go join him, *amigo*?'

'What?'

'No deliveries this morning. Come back this afternoon.'

'But every morning –'

'Nothing goes in, and only one thing is going out. Now back up, turn around and get your ass out of here before my pals get nervous.'

The driver looked around at the armed soldiers staring at him. 'Sure. Okay.'

They watched as he turned the truck around and disappeared down the street. The commander of the post reported the incident to the warden. When the story was checked out, it was learned that the regular employee was in the hospital, a victim of a hit and run driver.

At eight a.m., a car bomb exploded across the street from the prison, wounding half a dozen bystanders. Under ordinary circumstances, the guards would have left their posts to investigate and assist the wounded. But they had strict orders. They remained at their stations and the *guardia civil* was summoned to take charge.

The incident was promptly reported to Warden de la Fuente.

'They're getting desperate,' he said. 'Be prepared for anything.'

At 9.15 a.m., a helicopter appeared over the prison grounds. Painted on its sides were the words: LA PRENSA, Spain's prominent daily newspaper.

Two anti-aircraft guns had been set up on the prison roof. The lieutenant in charge waved a flag to warn off the plane. It continued to hover. The officer picked up a field telephone.

'Warden, we have a copter overhead.'

'Any identification?'

'It says *La Prensa*, but the sign looks freshly painted.'

'Give it one warning shot. If it doesn't move, blow it out of the sky.'

'Yes, sir.' He nodded to his gunner. 'Put a close one in.'

The shot landed five yards to the side of the helicopter. They could see the pilot's startled face. The gunner loaded again. The helicopter swooped up and disappeared across the skies of Madrid.

What the hell is next? the lieutenant wondered.

At 11.00 a.m. Megan Scott appeared at the reception office of the prison. She looked drawn and pale. 'I want to see Warden de la Fuente.'

'Do you have an appointment?'

'No, but –'

'I'm sorry. The Warden isn't seeing anyone this morning. If you telephone this afternoon –'

'Tell him it's Megan Scott.'

He took a closer look at her. *So this is the rich American who's trying to get Jaime Miró released. I wouldn't mind having her work on me for a few nights.* 'I'll tell the Warden you're here.'

Five minutes later Megan was seated in Warden de la Fuente's office. With him were half a dozen members of the prison board.

'What can I do for you, Miss Scott?'

'I would like to see Jaime Miró.'

The warden sighed. 'I'm afraid that is not possible.'

'But I'm –'

'Miss Scott – we are all aware of who you are. If we could accommodate you, I assure you that we would be more than happy to do so,' he smiled. 'We Spaniards are really an understanding people. We are also sentimental, and from time to time we are not averse to turning a blind eye to certain rules and regulations.' His smile disappeared. 'But not today, Miss Scott. No. Today is a very special day. It has taken us years to catch the man you wish to see. So this is a day of rules and regulations. The next one to see Jaime Miró will be his God – if he has one.'

Megan stared at him, miserable. 'Could – could I just look at him for a moment?'

One of the members of the prison board, touched by the anguish in Megan's face, was tempted to intervene. He stopped himself.

'I'm sorry,' Warden de la Fuente said. 'No.'

'Could I send him a message?' Her voice was choked.

'You would be sending a message to a dead man.' He looked at his watch. 'He has less than an hour to live.'

'But he's appealing his sentence. Isn't a panel of judges meeting to decide if –?'

'They've voted against it. I received word from them fifteen minutes ago. Miró's appeal has been denied. The execution will take place. Now, if you'll excuse me –'

He rose, and the others followed suit. Megan looked around the room at their cold faces and shuddered.

'May God have mercy on all of you,' she said.

They watched, silent, as she fled from the room.

At ten minutes before the noon hour, the door to Jaime Miró's cell was opened. Warden Gomez de la Fuente was accompanied by his two assistants, Molinas and Arrango, and Dr Miguel Anunción. Four armed guards stood watch in the corridor.

The warden entered the cell. 'It's time.'

Jaime rose from his cot. He was handcuffed and shackled. 'I was hoping you'd be late.' There was an air of dignity about him that Warden de la Fuente could not help but admire.

At another time, under other circumstances, we might have been friends.

Jaime stepped out into the deserted corridor, his movements clumsy because of the shackles. He was flanked by the guards and Molinas and Arrango. 'The garrotte?' Jaime asked.

The warden nodded. 'The garrotte.' Excruciatingly painful, inhuman. It was a good thing, the warden thought, that the execution would take place in a private room, away from the eyes of the public and the press.

The procession made its way down the corridor. From outside, in the street, they could hear the chant of the crowd: 'Jaime . . . Jaime . . . Jaime . . .' It was a swelling, bursting from a thousand throats growing louder and louder.

'They're calling for you,' Pedros Arrango said.

'No. They're calling for themselves. They're calling for freedom. Tomorrow they'll have another name. I may die – but there will always be another name.'

They passed through two security gates to a small chamber at the end of the corridor, with an iron green door. From around the corner a black-robed priest appeared.

'Thank heavens I'm in time. I've come to give the condemned man the last rites.'

As he moved towards Miró, two guards blocked his way.

'Sorry, Father,' Warden de la Fuente said. 'Nobody goes near him.'

'But I'm –'

'If you want to give him his last rites, you'll have to do it through closed doors. Out of the way, please.'

A guard opened the green door. Standing inside, next to a chair bolted to the floor, with heavy armstraps, was a huge man wearing a half mask. In his hands he held the garrotte.

The warden nodded towards Molinas and Arrango and the doctor, and they entered the room after Jaime. The guards remained outside. The green door was locked and bolted.

Inside the room, assistants Molinas and Arrango led Jaime to the chair. They unlocked his handcuffs, then strapped him in, pulling the heavy straps against his arms, while Dr Anunción and Warden de la Fuente watched. Through the thick closed door, they could barely hear the chanting of the priest.

De la Fuente looked at Jaime and shrugged. 'It doesn't matter. God will understand what he is saying.'

The giant holding the garrotte moved to the back of Jaime. Warden Gomez de la Fuente asked, 'Do you want a cloth over your face?'

'No.'

The warden looked at the giant and nodded. The giant lifted the garrotte in his hand and reached forward.

Outside the guards at the door could hear the chanting of the mob in the street.

'You know something?' one of the guards grumbled. 'I wish I was out there with them.'

Five minutes later, the green door opened.

Dr Anunción said, 'Bring in the body bag.'

Following instructions, Jaime Miró's body was smuggled out through a back door of the prison. The body bag was thrown into the back of an unmarked van. But the moment the vehicle pulled out of the prison grounds, the crowd in the street pressed forward, as though drawn to it by some mystic magnet.

'Jaime . . . Jaime . . .'

But the cries were softer now. Men and women wept, and their children looked on in wonder, not understanding what was happening. The van made its way through the crowd and finally turned on to a highway.

'Jesus,' the driver said. 'That was spooky. The guy must have had something.'

'Yeah. And thousands of people knew it too!'

At two o'clock that afternoon, Warden Gomez de la Fuente and his two assistants, Juanito Molinas and Pedros Arrango appeared at the office of Prime Minister Martinez.

'I want to congratulate you,' the Prime Minister said. 'It was executed perfectly.'

The warden spoke. 'Mr Prime Minister, we're not here to receive your congratulations. We're here to resign.'

Martinez stared at them, baffled. 'I – I don't understand. What –?'

'It's a matter of humanity, Your Excellency. We just watched a man die. Perhaps he deserved to die. But not like that. It – it was barbaric. I want no more part of this or anything like it, and my colleagues feel the same way.'

'Perhaps you should give this more thought. Your pensions –'

'We have to live with our consciences.' Warden de la Fuente handed the Prime Minister three pieces of paper. 'Here are our resignations.'

Late that night, the van crossed the French border and headed for the village of Bidache, near Bayonne. They pulled up before a neat farmhouse.

'This is the place. Let's get rid of the body before it starts to smell.'

The door to the farmhouse was opened by a woman in her middle fifties. 'You brought him?'

'Yes, ma'am. Where would you like it – er – him?'

'In the parlour, please.'

'Yes, ma'am. I – I wouldn't wait too long to bury him. You know what I mean?'

She watched the two men carry in the body bag and set it on the floor.

'Thank you.'

'*De nada*.'

She stood there watching as they drove away.

Another woman walked in from the other room and ran towards the body bag. She hastily unzipped it.

Jaime Miró was lying there smiling up at them. 'Do you know something? That garrotte could be a real pain in the neck.'

'White wine or red?' Megan asked.

Chapter 43

At Barajas Airport in Madrid, former Warden Gomez de la Fuente and his former assistants, Molinas and Arrango, and Dr Anunción and the giant in the mask were in the departure lounge.

'I still think you're making a mistake not coming with me to Puerto Rico,' de la Fuente said. 'With your five million dollars, you can buy the whole fucking island.'

Molinas shook his head. 'Arrango and I are going to Switzerland. I'm tired of the sun. We're going to buy ourselves a few dozen snow bunnies.'

'Me, too,' the giant said.

They turned to Miguel Anunción.

'What about you, doctor?'

'I'm going to Bangladesh.'

'*What?*'

'That's right. I'm going to use the money to open a hospital there. You know, I thought about it a long time before I accepted Megan Scott's offer. But I figured that if I can save a lot of innocent lives by letting one terrorist live, it's a good trade-off. Besides, I must tell you, I liked Jaime Miró.'

Chapter 44

It had been a good season in the French countryside, with fine weather, showering farmers with an abundance of crops. *I wish that every year could be as wonderful as this*, Rubio Arzano thought. *It has been a good year in more ways than one.*

First his marriage and then, a year ago, the birth of the twins. *Whoever dreamed a man could be this happy?*

It was starting to rain. Rubio turned the tractor around and headed for the barn. He thought about the twins. The boy was going to be big and strapping. But his sister! She was going to be a handful. *She's going to give her man a lot of trouble*, Rubio grinned to himself. *She takes after her mother.*

He drove the tractor into the barn and headed for the house, feeling the cool rain against his face. He opened the door and stepped inside.

'You're just in time,' Lucia smiled. 'Dinner's ready.'

The Reverend Mother Prioress Betina awakened with a premonition that something wonderful was about to happen.

Of course, she thought, *enough good things have already happened.*

The Cistercian convent had long since been reopened, under the protection of King Don Juan Carlos. Sister Graciela and the nuns who had been taken to Madrid were safely returned to the convent, where they were allowed to retreat once again into the blessed solitude and silence.

Shortly after breakfast, the Mother Prioress walked into her office and stopped, staring. On her desk, shining with a dazzling brightness, lay the gold cross.

It was accepted as a miracle.

AFTERWORD

Madrid has tried to buy peace by offering the Basques limited autonomy, allowing them to have their own flag, their own language, and a Basque police department. ETA replied by assassinating Constantin Ortin Gil, Madrid's military governor, and later Luis Carrero Blanco, the man chosen by Franco to be his successor.

The violence keeps escalating.

In a three-year period, ETA terrorists have killed more than 600 victims. The slaughter continues and the retaliation by the police has been equally ruthless.

Not so many years ago, ETA had the sympathy of the two and a half million Basque people, but continued terrorism has eroded their support. In Bilbao, the very heart of the Basque homeland, 100,000 people took to the streets to demonstrate *against* ETA. The Spanish people feel it is time for peace, time to heal the wounds.

The OPUS MUNDO is more powerful than ever, but few people are willing to discuss it.

As for the Cistercian convents of the Strict Observance, there are in existence today fifty-four convents, worldwide, seven of them in Spain.

Their timeless ritual of eternal silence and seclusion remains unchanged.

Grateful acknowledgement is made to
Marcelle Bernstein for use of material from *Nuns*.

Grateful acknowledgement is made for use of 'Gacela of Desperate Love' by Frederico Garcia Lorca, from *Selected Poems of Frederico Garcia Lorca*, copyright © 1952 by New Directions Publishing Corporation. Translated by W.S. Merwin. Reprinted by permission of New Directions Publishing Corporation.

Grateful acknowledgement is made for use of the
Ernest Hemingway epigraph to the *New Masses Magazine*.

THE NEW INTERNATIONAL
NO.1 BESTSELLER

Nothing Lasts Forever

Sidney Sheldon

In the frenetic world of a big San Francisco hospital, events catapult three women doctors into a white-hot spotlight:

Dr Paige Taylor

She swore it was euthanasia, but when Paige inherited a million dollars from a patient, the District Attorney called it murder.

Dr Kat Hunter

She vowed never to let a man too close again - until she accepted the challenge of a deadly bet.

Dr Honey Taft

To make it in medicine, she knew she'd need something more than the brains God gave her.

Racing from the life and death decisions of the operating room to the tension-packed fireworks of a murder trial, *Nothing Lasts Forever* lays bare the ambitions and fears of healers and killers, lovers and betrayers in a heart-stopping story you wish would never end . . .

'Of all the popular novels I've read this summer this beats the lot for sheer storytelling mastery' *Today*

0 00 647658 9

Morning, Noon and Night

Sidney Sheldon

The Stanford family is one of the most respected in America - but behind the facade of fame and glamour lies a hidden web of blackmail, drugs and murder . . .

When Harry Stanford, one of the wealthiest men in the world, mysteriously drowns while cruising on his yacht, it sets off a chain of events that reverberates around the globe . . . At the family gathering following the funeral in Boston, a strikingly beautiful young woman appears. She claims to be Stanford's daughter and entitled to a share of the tycoon's estate. Is she genuine or is she an imposter?

Sweeping from the splendours of the Italian Riviera, to the fashion salons of Paris and New York, and the élite opulence of Boston and Florida, *Morning, Noon and Night* twists and turns its way through intrigue, smoke and mirrors to a surprise ending you'll never forget . . .

'Sheldon is a writer working at the height of his power . . . I hung on till the very end' *New York Times*

ISBN 0 00 649806 X